THE
WRATHBRINGER

THE HELLBORN KING SAGA, BOOK TWO

A fantasy novel by

CHRISTOPHER G. BRENNING

The Forlorn Sea
Rej Rhivoth
Teb River
Rit
The Hinterwood
Skaginlef
Siln River
Blackwolf Pass
Borjifa
Mot
The Bymist
Pelg
Khorrtal
Brimnora
Morden
Hok
Kepdon
The Plainhold
Dellhaven
The Great Sea
Mor Seveht
Aret
Greenwood Forest
Cardale
Naxonnos
Bentmont
Larssa
Vhos River
Willowsgrove
Corinope
Glimmergulf
Sothfort
Sommerwood River
The Everblue
CALDAKAS

ACKNOWLEDGMENTS

It's difficult for me to comprehend that this is my second book. Writing and releasing "The Hellborn King" was a tremendous challenge, one that I was uncertain if I could repeat. It was a passion project, a crazy idea, one that I spent countless hours crafting. I never could have imagined the response I would receive, and all the outpouring of support and praise. You've truly humbled me, and made me realize that this is what I'm meant to do.

I would like to thank all of the great friends and fans I've made since releasing "The Hellborn King". You've given me all the support in the world, and I cannot thank you enough. I hope I never let you down! I would also like to thank my beta readers, especially Christopher Jackson and Cheryl Timm. Your feedback helped this story reach its full potential.

I would also like to thank my best friend Tom Hunter for his support and encouragement. You've seen me through highs and lows, and this is about as high as it gets. I would like to thank my mother, Karen, for all of her steadfast support since the very beginning.

In conclusion, I truly hope you enjoy "The Wrathbringer," Book Two of "The Hellborn King Saga"! If you do, please remember to leave an awesome review on Amazon or Barnes & Noble, as well as Goodreads. Thank you so much!

CONTENTS

PROLOGUE

SOMETHING ABOUT THE RED SUNRISE FELT UNSETTLING. CRIMSON rays of light seeped into the morning sky in long, bloody streaks, heralding a new dawn. A wispy patchwork of gray clouds had formed to the south, and looked to be drifting closer to Pelg. It was a warm winter thus far, unusually warm, and more wet than anything. The village had been pounded so relentlessly by rain it was nearly washed away entirely.

Agla suspected more storms were on the way. She could smell it, even taste it in the air. Though the snow was beautiful, it was a mercy to be without the cold for once. Life in the small village was treacherous enough without the cruelty of winter, and its absence was hardly missed. As Agla rose from her hovel, she drew the scent of misty air into her lungs with a slow, deep breath.

The smell was intoxicating, the wind carrying all manner of intriguing aromas. She donned a cloak of thick animal skins over a simple linen gown, then secured her length of dark brown hair into a braid which hung across the front of her left shoulder. A quick glance over the breadth of the property told her the day would be long and laborious.

Her husband, Ontto, was already up and tending to their goats and chickens. He was a strong man, broad in the shoulders, wide in the chest, with thick, banded blonde hair hanging down his back. The stream which flowed through the heart of Pelg and into the Siln River was raging and dangerously close to spilling over its banks. Ontto was busy moving the animals to another pen further away from the stream, which had now become a raging river in its own right.

She saw their neighbor, Vigga, collecting several pails of water and bringing them back to their homestead. It was a reminder that the day's chores were waiting. Agla fetched a wooden bucket and walked down to the edge of the tributary, its waters restless and rampaging like a band of wild horses.

The soil squished with each step, nearly swallowing her feet up to her ankles. A few times, she had to stop and pull her leg up delicately, or else lose a boot to the grasp of the thick mud. When she reached the edge of the water, she nearly tumbled over and fell in, her hand sinking deep into the muck to break her fall.

Gods be good!

Agla shook the mud off her hand, then rinsed it clean in the river. The water was more of a dull, muddy brown as opposed to its typically bluish hue. It took several tries to get a bucket of water suitable enough to take back home. As she trudged back through the soupy slop, she spied Ontto overlooking the stream, hands resting on his hips. His face appeared just as distraught as her own.

"I don't know how much more of this she can take." He gestured to the tributary. "I remember walking across the ice this time last year. I've never seen anything like this before."

"Do you think our home is in danger?" she asked, clutching the bucket handle tightly.

"No, the ground is lower on the other side. It will flood there first."

"Linka and Sten will lose everything!" Agla replied in dismay, looking across the water at their friend's homestead, which was far more saturated than their own. "We've got to help them!"

"Aye. It would be wise for them to stay on this side for the time being. Once I'm finished, I'll head over there and see if they would like to stay with us until the waters calm themselves."

Since the days of her childhood, Agla had heard countless tales of ancient floods and other cataclysms, natural disasters which swept away entire civilizations. Her grandfather would tell such stories around the fire at night, filling her and the other children with wonderment and dread. He spoke of the gods, and how their anger could conjure such catastrophes if provoked. It was difficult to look around Pelg and not feel their anger, as if Kholdyr himself was pouring out his wrath.

The wooden bridge which spanned the tributary was swaying and flapping about like a banner in the wind, so violently that Agla grew anxious and concerned about her husband walking across it. One false step and it could send Ontto tumbling into the turbulent waters, likely never to be seen again. The thought made her shiver.

She set the bucket down just outside of their home and assisted with wrangling up the last of the animals, who themselves offered little protest. Even simpleminded beasts were able to sense the danger Pelg found itself in. After making sure their herd was secure, Agla slogged back to the edge of the stream. Ontto was already on the other side helping Linka move their modest belongings to safety. He held two large sacks, each slung over a shoulder.

He's so strong. And kind. The gods have truly blessed me.

Delicately, she took hold of the guide ropes and began walking across the wooden bridge. Ontto had told her on more than one occasion not to look down, but this time it was unavoidable. Mere inches away from her feet was a turbulent brown deluge that roared with the ferocity of a dragon. She swallowed hard, then willed herself across. When she stepped off the bridge, the soupy ground nearly swallowed her whole.

"Agla!" Ontto shouted, his voice barely audible. "Go back now, it's too dangerous."

"No, I want to help!"

Linka came toddling behind Ontto, her skirts lifted up to her knees. She was a dainty woman, with a face that looked ten years younger than the rest of her, and a head of the curliest brown hair Agla had ever seen. A simple wicker basket hung over her back, a newborn child secured snugly inside it.

"I cannot thank you and Ontto enough for the help," Linka shouted over the roar of the rushing current. "Gods be good, Agla, have you ever seen weather like this?"

"Perhaps in the spring, during the rainy season many years ago. But never at this time of year. And never this severe."

"Worry not Linka," Ontto said with his usual confidence, "this is good soil, and will dry quickly. If the gods are generous, we will have a warm and early spring."

Together, they traversed back across the treacherous bridge. Agla immediately set off to the barn to make it suitable for Linka and Sten to stay in. There was no room inside her hovel for them, so they would have to make do with a more modest accommodation. She spent the next hour preparing a sleeping area and cleaning off Ontto's woodworking table, so at least they would have a place to eat.

They'll need extra blankets. I should have a few more, somewhere.

Agla filled a small basket with some of Ontto's finely made tools to bring back to her hovel. Even though she never would have thought Linka and Sten to be thieves, it was nevertheless a sound idea to keep such valuable items inside their home. She took one final look around to see if anything else had been overlooked.

The horse stalls were properly cleaned, and fresh hay laid down. There was plenty of wood to build fires, and a bundle of candles as well. There were a few small openings in the roof where water had dripped in, but nothing Ontto could not fix. With everything appearing to be in order, Agla took up her basket and made her way toward the village square.

It was heartbreaking to see so many families huddled together near the market tents; children crying, mothers and fathers lost for hope. Many of the villagers were from upriver, most of whom Agla barely knew. But their suffering was tragic, and it made her feel selfishly blessed to be without such misfortune.

Poor souls. I pray the gods will show them mercy.

At the center of a crude square stood a large, bluish stone, its base sunk deep into the earth. It was the most sacred object in all of Pelg, considering such stones were nowhere to be found in the surrounding area. On its face was carved the effigy of Kholdyr, chieftain of the gods. Agla approached slowly and bowed her head.

"Kholdyr, I humbly ask you to have mercy on our village. Please, let the rains subside and the waters retreat. Let life and prosperity return to these lands, so we may continue to live in peace amongst all your creations."

She leaned forward and placed a gentle kiss on the feet of the carving, its markings said to have been made by the gods themselves before man walked the earth. Warm rays of light glistened off the stone, its surface wet with a light mist of rain. Perhaps they were actually Kholdyr's tears, a sign that he had seen enough suffering and would bestow his mercy in short order.

An unknown sound in the distance drew her attention. At first, she thought it could have been a distant peal of thunder, given the ever-growing field of gray clouds above. She shrugged, turned, and continued onward, but was given pause as the sound again met her ears. She spun around abruptly, scanning the fields to the south for signs of the disturbance.

Am I hearing things?

Apprehensively, she began walking home, but managed only a few steps before the sound grew steady and more noticeable. She turned again, and this time saw the faint outlines of a large group of riders in the distance. The shock was so great, Agla could not process what it was she was seeing, and stood dumbfounded as the horsemen rampaged closer.

Bright blue cloaks flapped behind them like the wings of eagles, their breastplates glinting with a few dull rays of morning sun. They rode toward the outskirts of Pelg like a swarm of locusts, spread so far apart they appeared to consume the entire horizon. Terror-stricken, Agla dropped her basket and ran, screaming her husband's name.

"Ontto! Ontto, come quickly!"

Her legs burned as she raced back home. Distant screams rang out as the thundering grew louder and louder, though the pounding of her heart was far more intense. Ontto came sprinting around the corner of their hovel, his face painted with a fear she had never seen before.

"Get inside, now!" He grabbed her by the arm and whisked her inside as if she were a ragdoll, the simple wooden door nearly flying off its hinges as he threw it open. Ontto dragged her over to a trunk near the far wall and slid it aside effortlessly. Underneath was a trap door where they kept their foodstuffs and what little treasure they owned.

"Get in, and stay quiet."

Tears were spilling down Agla's face. She was terrified beyond belief, and only the strong, comforting presence of her husband could quell her fear.

"Stay with me, please! Don't leave me alone!"

Screams and battle cries rang out all around their home. Ontto looked over his shoulder and out through the door, then scooped her up under the arms and set her down into the small, stone-walled cellar. "Stay here, and keep quiet! Don't let them hear you!"

He slammed the trap door shut before she could say anything, then slid the trunk back into place. No more than a second later, a dismounted soldier came storming inside, a shield in one hand and an arming sword in the other. He slammed into Ontto, the two colliding and falling onto the table at the center of the room.

Agla watched through the cracks in the floorboards, a hand clasped over her mouth. She saw her husband scuffling with the olive-skinned intruder, both men snarling and having at each other like wild beasts, punching and clawing and biting viciously. But Ontto's strength was too great. He shoved the soldier backward and sent him tumbling outside and landing in a heap on the wet ground.

He ran toward the fireplace and removed a great axe from the mantle. Roaring in anger, he stepped outside and began swinging the mighty weapon with both hands, the intruder dodging and parrying as best he could. Both men disappeared from view, and Agla felt a wave of panic wash over her. She could see nothing, and heard only terrified screams of the villagers and the pounding of horse hooves. Time seemed to drag on endlessly, with seemingly no end to the horror.

Suddenly, Ontto came stumbling back into the hovel, his tunic ripped across the chest, blood seeping freely into the fabric. His face was a gashed and ruined mess, one eye so swollen and bloodied it was nearly closed. He collapsed onto the floor, gasping like a fish out of water.

Agla tried frantically to open the trap door, but the trunk was too heavy. Again and again she threw herself against the wooden planks, but to no avail.

Gods, please! Give me strength!

Grunting and straining, she pushed with all of her might, until the trunk gave way and the door sprang open. She clawed her way out of the cellar and crawled to Ontto's side, sobbing and stammering, the words unable to form in her mouth.

"No… no… no…" She touched him on the cheeks, unsure of what to do.

"You… you need to get out of here," he croaked.

"No, I won't leave you." Agla tore a length of cloth from his tunic and placed it on his massive chest wound, applying pressure with both hands.

"Go… you must. They… are coming." He pushed her toward the door, but she stood reluctant, overwhelmed by despair. "They…"

The light faded from Ontto's eyes, his body turning limp and lifeless within a heartbeat. Were it not for a shrill scream that pierced the air, Agla might very well have collapsed in anguish. She turned and cautiously looked outside in the direction of the disturbance. Roughly a dozen soldiers stood around the barn, dragging Linka out by her hair. Sten was laying on the ground, his head separated from the rest of his body. She kicked and spat and shrieked when she saw the butchered corpse of her husband lying unceremoniously in the dirt.

The sight was more than Agla could bear. After making sure the coast was clear, she took off running to the river as Linka screamed one final time before going silent. The thought of what that meant was too terrifying to even imagine. As she slogged through the soupy mud, a voice called out in foreign sounding language, alerting the other marauders to her presence.

Gods please don't let me die! I don't want to die!

Wet, galloping horse hooves from behind her grew louder and louder. Agla's only hope was to reach the river in time, but even then, the waters were choppy and treacherous. She slipped and fell as an arrow whooshed by her head, but was able to continue on as another slapped the mud next to her. The river's edge was mere feet away, and though diving into its rushing current would mean certain death, she would likely be dead in minutes anyways.

"Gods, protect me!"

A horseman came swooping in like an eagle, nearly snatching her up with one arm. But she was too quick, diving headfirst into the foamy brown river before it was too late. The waters were undoubtedly powerful, and she fought with every ounce of strength to keep her head above the surface. Tumbling and gasping, and being dashed against the bottom, Agla was carried away by the powerful current while Pelg burned into nothingness.

MADELYN

S HE AWOKE IN THE MOONLIT DARKNESS, SHIVERING. A THIN CRUST of ice on Madelyn Everly's animal skin cloak crackled and turned to powder as she curled into a ball, her back pressed against the freezing bars of a cramped iron cage. She pulled the tattered furs tightly across her body, teeth clattering, hands trembling uncontrollably. The skins smelled horrid, but it was the one small mercy the barbarians had allowed. Without them, the icy grip of death would surely have claimed her.

Hazy clouds of hot breath met the frigid air, then faded away like ghosts before dawn. She was alive, and had survived horrors few could imagine. But her existence felt empty, empty like the inside of her heart, and as small and insignificant as snowflakes on the wind. Death would have been preferable to such suffering and humiliation, but the fates were not so kind.

A freezing gale came howling down from the north, rustling through the trees and kicking up whirlwinds of flurries. Madelyn's body shook violently, the last vestiges of her strength flickering like waning torchlight. Khorrtal was inhospitable, a place where the weather and the land itself seemed to take pleasure in her suffering. As her vision dimmed to black, she saw the faint outline of a figure in the distance. For half a heartbeat, the scent of Corbyn Scott was alive on the wind.

She thought of better days, in better places, and with far better company. Madelyn would have given anything to be back in Cardale and at the Seascape Inn. It was one of the most unforgettable days of her life: the trip down Auburn Row, the afternoon with the Droethien women, and the look on Corbyn's face when she returned to their room. As her shivering grew softer, she drifted off to a blissful slumber.

"You're beautiful," Corbyn said, his lips pressing against her forehead.

Madelyn felt the soft prickle of his chest hairs against her cheek, and the warmth radiating from his body. She stared at the gentle glow of a lantern on a nearby table and gave a deep, contented sigh. "Thank you for coming with me."

"I wouldn't have it any other way." He smiled, his fingers gently running across her scalp.

"I'm nervous about tomorrow. I've heard rumors about the King, and how unpredictable he's become…"

"Would you like me to come with you?"

She thought for a moment, pursing her lips. "I don't know. I just don't know. Gareth will likely be there, and Sir Edmund will certainly be around as well. I should be alright, but… it's the King! I never would have thought I'd be speaking to him personally."

"If anyone deserves the honor, it's you." Corbyn's hand ran down the length of her hair. The sensation was simply divine.

There were so many things she had wanted to say to him, and so many feelings she dared not to feel. Corbyn was the first man she had ever felt any measure of affection towards, and the only one to ever see her for who she truly was. It seemed out of place to open her heart to him, even an inch, but there was no better time than now.

We won't be young forever. And with what's happening in the west, who knows what tomorrow might bring.

Her mind was made up. Madelyn's pulse and breath quickened, her fingers trembling as she brushed a lock of hair behind one ear. Now was her moment, and there would be no turning back. She sat up to give him a kiss and profess her affections, but shrieked in terror at the sight of Corbyn's headless body laying on the bed, the sheets pooling with rivers of blood.

"No, please, no! Corbyn!"

Gasping, Madelyn awoke from her tormented slumber. Her body was shaking fiercely from the bitter cold, though it was difficult to feel much of anything. One eye was swollen shut from the beating she received two nights prior, and her skin was raked with lacerations and discolored from old bruises.

With a grunt, she muscled herself upright, her back cracking and popping. Madelyn's body had grown frail from weeks of endless sitting, though it could have been months. There was no real sense of time. Each torturous day seemed no different than the last. Not that it mattered, she was not going anywhere anytime soon, it seemed.

A small wooden plate sat nearby, just on the other side of the cage. On it was a moldy heel of bread, and a strip of what looked to be some sort of meat. She reached through the enclosure and took hold of the foul looking food, and retched as she bit into the hard bread. The meat was too disgusting to even contemplate eating. Madelyn washed her mouth out with a handful of muddy water from a puddle, coughing and gagging with each swallow.

"Ah, the bitch is awake I see." Sylvia Stormguard passed by the cage, a half-dozen Rhivothi warriors following closely behind. She was clad in a thick cloak of animal furs and held a lantern in one hand.

Fear of the shieldmaiden's wrath made Madelyn feel lightheaded. She slumped against the cage like a whipped dog, struggling to stay away, terror-stricken at the thought of what might happen next. Her vision grew blurry and dim, her stomach heaving and churning like a maelstrom.

"You look a little cold, lass. Perhaps I might warm you in my bed!" one of the warriors sneered, his kinsmen chuckling in kind.

"Bold of you to want to touch her after what those Zylmacians did," another said, drinking from a horn. "Nothing but animals, they are."

"Oh, I'm not picky," the first warrior said, grinning. "Not everyday you get to fuck a queen, you know!"

"I think the whore has had enough for now," Stormguard said. "She'll be leaving us soon, anyway."

Though Madelyn was barely conscious, she heard the words clearly enough. Could it be true? Would Damien Dreadfire finally be releasing her from this hell? She lifted her head and coughed, looking at her tormentors in disbelief.

"That's right, you're going home," Sylvia sneered, crouching down next to the cage. "Your High Marshal has agreed to our terms, and has sent your ransom to Hok. That's where you're going."

"H… how?" Madelyn asked, bewildered.

"We know there's Blackthorn all over Hok, so after we razed Morden, we sent a rider to negotiate terms. Took awhile to hear back, but an agreement was made. Needless to say, you're going to make us all very, very rich."

"I thought… I thought Damien would return me to Bentmont?"

"No," Sylvia chuckled. "You think we're stupid enough to travel all that way just to collect a ransom? Your people would ride us down immediately after the exchange. We're no fools, girl. I thought you would have learned after all this time."

It was impossible to hold back her tears. Wet streaks ran down Madelyn's icy-blue face and began hardening into crystals. Soon, thankfully, the nightmare would be over.

"When?" she asked, her voice thin and weak.

"Tomorrow." Sylvia stood. "Better get some rest, you're going to need it. It's a long way, and you're going to be walking."

Tomorrow. The word sounded too good to be true. Madelyn thought it might be another one of Stormguard's cruel japes, which she had come to know all too well, but the near disappointment in the shield-maiden's voice spoke volumes on its own. Still, it was a relief to hear that soon she would be free from this savage hellscape, and would be back among her kin in the Order.

She tried to stand and stretch her legs, but the pain was too intense. Madelyn landed with a thud, the soupy, half-frozen ground squishing beneath her. She tried to rub her aching knees, but it was too difficult to lean forward. Her belly had grown large and round, and was growing larger by the day. The child inside began to stir, each kick killing another small piece of her soul. It was not a source of joy, as any parent might feel, but a reminder of her violation, and everything which had been taken away.

It was a blessing to be without dreams that night, or at least none she could remember. Madelyn awoke the next morning, just as frozen as the day before, though thankfully the meal waiting for her was a bit more pleasant. The meat was fresh, as was the bread, and there was a cup of clean water as well. She would need the energy for such a grueling trek ahead.

"Eat. Hurry up and get on with it, I don't have all day." Sylvia Stormguard appeared alongside three score of her kinsmen. She wore riding leathers and an animal fur cloak. "Open the cage."

A burly Rhivothi warrior inserted a skeleton key into the rusted keyhole, the iron door opening with a shrill creak. Madelyn stuffed the remainder of her food into her mouth, struggling to chew and swallow it all before being hefted onto her feet. The pain was immense, like pure fire shooting throughout her body. She groaned something indiscernible, then steadied herself against the cage bars.

"I… I can't… walk…"

Sylvia chuckled. "Well, you're going to have to. Unless you'd like to stay awhile longer? Have you enjoyed your time here that much?"

The thought was incomprehensible. Another day in this living nightmare might very well be the end of her. Instinctively, Madelyn willed herself to walking, each step a stinging jolt of agony.

One step at a time. One foot in front of the other. Come on, Madelyn, you can do this. You have to do this. You must.

Some of the villagers emerged from their hovels as the procession began to form. Nearly a hundred warriors would be making the journey to Hok, along with a half-dozen wagons filled with provisions. It would take two weeks under ideal conditions, perhaps three if the weather chose not to cooperate.

"Bethard bitch!" someone shouted unceremoniously. Their jeers were echoed by some of the warriors, and some of the townsfolk alike. Northmen were easy to whip into a frenzy, and their ravenous appetite soon reared its ugly head once again. As Madelyn shambled through the muddy streets, she was met with a deluge of insults and debris, as if her suffering had not been severe enough.

The sackcloth gown she wore was caked in mud and splattered with refuse. Her long blonde hair was a knotted, gnarled mess that hung down to her upper thigh, and was discolored with dingy brown stains. It was the most humiliating experience of her life, aside from the night Damien Dreadfire's horde set upon her.

Stormguard, on the other hand, could not have looked more content. The shieldmaiden rode past Madelyn ahorse, splashing up showers of cold, dirty water onto her, and laughing.

What have I ever done to deserve this? Can they not leave me be?

But at least she was alive, or so she told herself. Alive, and going home. It was a small consolation, perhaps the smallest one of all. Her body was too ruined to be back in fighting shape, and leading men into battle would be next to an impossibility. It seemed Damien Dreadfire was right; Madelyn would never be capable of taking up the sword ever again.

She left the confines of Khorrtal and set off to the east, the Rhivothi prodding and antagonizing her all the way. There were no roads here, only well-trodden horse paths covered with a light glaze of snow, but more often than not were nothing more than cold, wet trenches filled with freezing water.

The pain was too intense, far too taxing on her frail body. Her baby had grown restless and was kicking her insides every which way, adding to a mountain of discomfort. Madelyn clutched at her belly and groaned, fighting the urge to vomit. Everything was beginning to spin and blur into a hazy mess of fuzzy colors. And then there was darkness, a long, black nothingness of exhausted sleep.

It was unclear how long she had been out. When Madelyn awoke, she was in the back of a wagon, covered in a heap of animal fur blankets. It was the warmest she had been in months, so warm that she was beginning to sweat underneath them. There was a large skin of water and a few small sacks of rations within reach.

"You're alive," a familiar voice said. It was Marvath Bonesplitter, mounted on a large warhorse. "Don't go dying now, you've made it this far."

Is it? Is it really him?

The barbarian was the only one Madelyn trusted, at least somewhat. It was agonizing to know he was powerless to stop Dreadfire's wolves from brutalizing her.

"Marvath?" Madelyn squinted, her vision still blurry.

"Yes, girl, I'm here."

A sudden rush of emotions broke her. This was a man who had risked death at the hands of the Zylmacians to keep her safe. He showed kindness and respect, and even, dare she think it, friendship.

"Why? Why did this happen to me?" she sobbed. "Why did you let them?"

The Rhivothi warchief averted his gaze in what could only be described as shame. He spoke not a word for what seemed like an eternity, a deep conflict playing out behind his eyes.

"I am truly sorry, Madelyn the Eveldanyr. What was done to you was…"

"Monstrous!" Her apoplectic rage cut through her sorrow, but only briefly.

"It was excessive, and dishonorable, to be certain. Know that if I had it in my power to spare you such cruelty, I would have."

"Why didn't you?" Her voice had fallen to a near whisper, the anguish choking off her words.

"Because it's not my place, girl. Though I am a warchief among my kin, I still serve under Damien's banner. I can no more disobey him than you can disobey your High Marshal. But you're here, and alive, and that is what truly matters."

Life seemed to mean so little now, even with it growing inside her. Everything she had trained and fought and struggled to achieve throughout the years had been taken away, and was likely never to return.

"I would rather be dead," she said, despondent. "Take my head, Marvath. At least give me an honorable death, you owe me that. And when you get to Hok, tell them I died well. Tell them I died with my men."

Bonesplitter shook his head. "I cannot do that, you know it. You're worth your weight in gold, and my people are expecting their coffers to be filled. Take heart, this will all be over soon. Think of home, Madelyn the Eveldanyr, think of it. Soon you will be there, and away from this place. And I pray you never return."

The Rhivothi nomad nudged his horse and rode on, his sandy-blonde hair and cloak fluttering behind him. The exchange left her feeling weak and lightheaded, and within a heartbeat her vision began to turn blurry. It was difficult to find sleep, however, as each rock and rut under the wagon's wheels jarred her back to consciousness. Frustrated and too exhausted to rest, she drank from a waterskin, nibbled at some bread, and focused on the eastern skyline.

Days came and went with little difference between them. Then, one day, the faint outline of stony walls around Hok came into view. Never had dreary gray stone looked more inviting in all of her life. She saw the King's colors flying high over the western gate, its eagle sigil appearing like a golden angel in the midday sun. The barbarians came to a halt a mile away from the city and formed themselves into a long line. Soon after, the gate opened and a band of Blackthorn Knights came riding out to meet them.

Madelyn's face tightened and quivered, but she was too weak to cry, even tears of joy. The black and gold banner of the Order was the sweetest thing she had ever seen. It flew at the head of two dozen men, their steel breastplates shimmering like polished gemstones. Behind them came a wagon with wooden chests on its bed.

"Do you speak our language?" the knight asked, coming to a halt. The insignia on his armor showed he was an Elite. He sat tall in the saddle, locks of dark-blonde hair dancing across a furrowed brow. His indigo eyes were distrusting of the barbarians, and flashed with a hint of hostility.

"As a matter of fact, you are speaking *our* language, but there's no need to get into that." Sylvia Stormguard gave an insidious grin.

"We brought your ransom, savage. Have you our Commander?"

"We have made good on our end of the bargain, Bethard scum." Stormguard gestured toward Madelyn. "Now give us our gold."

The riders atop each opposing wagon dismounted and took up their horse's bridles. Slowly, each man led their wagon to the other side, their eyes fixated on one another in apprehension. The exchange was made, and each driver returned to their respective side with their prize. A pair of knights trotted over to Madelyn's side to make certain it was truly her. The barbarians did likewise with their chests of gold and silver, examining their contents and searching for deception. Both parties appeared satisfied.

"A king's ransom for a broken whore." Sylvia snickered, some of her kinsmen echoing her amusement. "Perhaps we might do this again, since the High Marshal has proven himself so generous."

"Not a chance," the Elite shot back. "Go now, take your ransom, before we reclaim it from you brigands. Along with your heads."

His gaze was drawn to the west, where a large group of riders appeared. Sylvia turned and smiled, her confidence growing.

"What treachery is this?" the Elite asked, his knights stirring, the men on the walls equally as restless.

"Worry not, Betanthian. A little added assurance that you will remain true to your end of the bargain. And now that our business is concluded, we'll be safely on our way."

As the barbarians turned to leave with their ransom, one remained. Madelyn shifted wearily in the wagon and turned her head, and saw Marvath staring back at her. They shared a look which seemed to last an eternity, an unspoken understanding filled with sadness and regret.

"On your way now, savage," the Elite said sternly.

Marvath Bonesplitter gave the knight a distasteful glare and a grunt, then looked back at Madelyn one final time before putting a foot to his horse. She watched as he galloped in pursuit of his kinsmen, then slowly faded from sight. The knights stood firm until the barbarians were far away from Hok, on guard for any sort of treachery. Satisfied the danger had passed, the column turned and began riding back to the city walls.

"You're safe now, Commander. My name is Elite Deverell Avelio. I'll see to it personally that you're cleaned, fed, and given the softest bed in all of Betanthia." He smiled warmly. It was kind of him to speak so gently after being so gruff with the barbarians. "And once you're rested and able to travel, you'll be going home."

Home. It was a word which seemed difficult to comprehend. After everything she had seen and suffered through, home was the last place in the world she would have ever expected to be. The city gates opened hastily as they approached. This was the first time Madelyn had been in the northern mining community, and the sight was one she would never forget.

At the heart of Hok was a massive pit mine, so enormous it stretched nearly to the horizon. Here was where men toiled endlessly to pry fresh iron ore from the heart of the earth. Hundreds of small, crude shanties pimpled the barren landscape around the mine where the laborers dwelled. A blossoming city sat coiled around it, a city of gray stone and weathered wood, of dirt horse paths and cobblestone roads, of Betanthian architecture and barbarian squalor.

The population was thankfully more refined. Thousands had come from all corners of the kingdom to find a new life here. There were craftsmen from Cardale who could find no buyers, fishermen from Glimmergulf who could find no catch, and farmers from Willowsgrove who could grow no crop. While their old lives had proven fruitless, here there was opportunity to begin anew.

They rode through winding streets and narrow alleyways, and past a ramshackle marketplace. The layout was disheveled and disappointing. Dozens of weathered tents sat alongside wooden stalls, some newly constructed, though most were old and rotting. Trinket peddlers and swineherds alike hawked their wares to anyone with enough coin to buy. It was a far cry from the sprawling market district in Cardale, or even Bentmont, for that matter.

They passed by dreary hovels and beautiful estates carved of pure marble. Everything was changing in Hok, and for the better, but it was difficult to focus on such blooming splendor. There were hundreds of eyes watching from either side of the road, gazing, studying, and in all likelihood, judging. It made her cheeks flush with embarrassment.

Madelyn pulled the fur blankets tight, trying to hide her condition. It was only a matter of time before the knights would see her, however, and the thought was terrifying. How could she return to her post and resume her duties while heavy with child, or even after, given what the barbarians had done to her? What good was a Commander who was unable to lead from the front?

My life is over. Once the High Marshal finds out, he'll shuffle me off to some asylum for the destitute. I should have died that night, it would have been better if I did.

The Blackthorn arrived at their headquarters, a sprawling estate in its own right. Large black and gold banners ran nearly the height of the building, its heavy cloth rippled with a touch of western breeze. Its perimeter was lined with a row of stakes large enough to skewer an elephant, the walkway to the entrance obstructed by a wooden barricade.

"It's alright, Commander. I'll take you inside now." Deverell beckoned her forth.

She could not breathe. She could not think. The only thing Madelyn could do was pull the fur blankets even closer, until they were nearly up to her eyes.

"You're safe here, it's alright," he said again, slightly impatient this time.

You can't sit here forever. Might as well get this over with.

Slowly she pulled the blankets away and crawled to the edge of the wagon. The Elite extended a hand and delicately helped her down, though she was reluctant to take it. The knights bore somber expressions as they saw her in her fullness, some averting their eyes while others stared incredulously. Even Deverell appeared lost for words.

Step by painful step, Madelyn shuffled toward the ornate doors of the manor in shame. The stress was suffocating. She would have ran indoors to get away from them all, if it were possible. But her legs were frail and out of place from a countless number of beatings, and each step was its own separate torture.

Once inside and away from the gazes of her brethren, Madelyn was assisted to the infirmary, where a troop of sullen looking physicians awaited around a freshly made bed. She felt their eyes, and the eyes of everyone inside the room, fixated on her, studying every movement, every inch of her body. A tightening in her chest soon gave way to sweating and cold chills which grew exponentially in intensity.

The temperature in the room grew icy, and the infirmary began to melt and fade into a massive pool of blurry lights and dull colors. Suddenly, it appeared as though she was back at the barbarian camp on the night of her tribulation. Spectral visions of savage men, bare chested and splashed with war paint, filled the room. They danced and thrashed about like the beasts they were, taunting and laughing as they did on that fateful night.

She blinked hard, hoping the grim visions would fade, but found no such reprieve. The bed began to take on the form of the table inside Damien Dreadfire's command tent, the one on which she suffered an unspeakable number of violations. Perhaps this was no vision after all, she thought. Perhaps it was another cruel trick of Sylvia Stormguard's, and she had in fact been cleverly lured back to Khorrtal. The thought was too frightening to stomach.

Panicked, and with no ability to flee, Madelyn began to crumple to the ground, too terror-stricken to breathe. She clutched at the knights who attempted to keep her standing, but in her delirium they too appeared as barbarians, ready to satisfy their perversions.

"Deverell!" she sobbed, calling out the only name she knew. Men rushed forward to assist, but it only worsened her inconsolable panic.

The sound throughout the room quickly dampened, as if she were submerged underwater. Before even making it to the bed, the room turned intolerably hot, and spun wildly into a violent whirlwind. Her final thoughts before succumbing to the creeping blackness was of home, of those loved and lost, and hoping she would never wake.

TITAN

I *SHOULD HAVE STABBED THE MAN, FOR ALL THE TROUBLE THIS WAS.*

Tylar Bradshaw spat a mouthful of blood onto the dirt, his jaw throbbing and turning numb. The robbery went precisely as he hoped it would not, and it was only by some divine grace that no one was alerted. On any other day, pouncing on a man with his back turned would have been easy, but doing so without food for three days was more difficult than it appeared.

Either he was one tough old bastard, or I'm growing old myself. I can't believe he ate so many punches.

The encounter was nearly as disheartening as it was exhausting. After collecting his meagre prize, a nearly empty sack with a few dingy coins inside, he slunk away into the shadows, hoping to avoid detection. With each passing day, another wanted poster appeared around town, and after tonight, Mor Seveht was likely to be plastered with them. The pictures made him appear older than he really was, but it seemed by the day, more gray was creeping into his shaggy length of hair.

It was by far the most dangerous place to be, especially for a deserter and a thief. While Mor Seveht was claimed by no nation, it had seen an unprecedented swarm of Betanthian activity as of late. Titan thought he could have made a quick escape into Droethien lands after arriving here. However, he turned back a week into the journey after spotting an approaching detachment of Betanthian soldiers. They were headed east, likely recalled to prevent the northmen from spilling across the Plainhold, he supposed.

For months, Titan skulked about, stealing what he could and performing odd jobs when one was available. Each day was one spent teetering on the verge of starvation, but such misfortune was preferable to death at the end of a Blackthorn noose. One night while scavenging fresh meat from the local butcher, he was caught by a passing patrol, but was able to evade capture. Thankfully, such thieving was not uncommon in this part of the world, and Tylar was able to continue on without finding himself clapped in irons.

I can't go on like this, like some common street scum. If I'm going to change my fortunes, it's gold I'll need.

He remembered Silas, the man he robbed after fleeing Castle Morden. Traders were common in Mor Seveht, even more common than townsfolk, and one of them was bound to have a respectable amount of coin on their person. He knew attacking someone on the road was dangerous, but all he would need was one good score. For days, Tylar studied the comings and goings of the traveling merchants. Little was coming down from the north these days, and for good reason, but the Droethiens were still arriving from the south on a regular basis.

Those perfumed trinket peddlers are just the sort to have more gold than they know what to do with. Fuck them, I need it more.

And so, he decided to set an ambush. Tylar noticed on every fifth day, a caravan would arrive from the south, usually no more than five or six traders hauling two, maybe three wagons worth of goods. One morning, he stole a horse from outside the inn and made his way outside of town before daylight had broken.

No more than an hour passed before he saw them in the distance, lumbering slowly down a well-trodden path, right on schedule. There were four wagons, more than he was expecting, but nothing too insurmountable. Tylar took shelter behind a rocky formation on top of a small hill, an old, dead tree at its center. He sat patiently until the caravan drew closer, but could immediately tell something was amiss.

"Riders?" he said to himself in dismay. "What the… fuck… no, it couldn't be."

These were not the Droethien traders he was expecting. He saw a host of cavalry galloping toward the wagons, a familiar standard of black and gold flying high in the morning breeze. They formed ranks at the front and the rear of the wagons, and proceeded north as a unified column.

Cursing, Tylar raced down the hill and retrieved his horse, and began making a hasty retreat to Mor Seveht. Robbing peasants was one thing, tangling with a Blackthorn convoy was another, especially as a wanted man. He returned to town shortly before midday, and made certain to set the horse free before traversing the streets. Hunger was beginning to set in again, this time to the point of nausea. He drank some old water from a stolen skin, though it did nothing to quell the churning in his stomach.

Dinner was a scrawny rat he managed to catch inside an abandoned shack he had been squatting in. The meat tasted foul and unsatisfying, nearly as unsatisfying as his dreams. That night, he returned to Castle Morden as he often did, reliving the siege over and over again. Though his mind often crafted different scenarios of the battle, each one led to the same crushing defeat.

At the center of his nightmares was always Madelyn. Every night, Tylar fought and tried to save her, but it was always to no avail. It seemed the girl was destined to die, despite even the bravest of efforts. But these were little more than dreams, and even the most fantastical would do nothing to bring her back. He awoke the next morning, trembling, coated in sweat, and hungry to the point of vomiting.

He needed to eat, and soon. Thieving was producing pitiful results, but one last effort had to be made to find food and flee while there was still time. The best places to find sufficient coin would be the tavern, or one of the trading shanties near the town center. Both options were risky, even without the damned Blackthorn poking their noses around. But staying in town was simply not a possibility, not any longer.

One sack of gold, that's all I need. And then I'll never have to look over my shoulder ever again.

Tylar waited until dusk, when Mor Seveht began to clear. There were enough people moving about the dusty streets to avoid being singled out by a passing patrol, but at the same time, fewer eyes around that might recognize him. With a hooded cloak pulled over his head, he set off down the main avenue, hoping to find an aloof victim to rob, or perhaps a door left unattended. But pulling off a successful heist would prove difficult with a stomach rumbling like an earthquake.

If I don't get some food in me, and soon, I won't make it very far. Fuck...

His thoughts were soon interrupted by breastplates glinting in the dying light. About a half a score of knights were approaching from the east on patrol, and were quickly closing in on him. In his delirious and starved state, Tylar immediately suspected they were onto him, and were coming to take him into custody. Without thinking, he drew the hood of the cloak tightly to his face and entered the nearest building. To his fortune, or perhaps misfortune, he found himself inside the tavern.

The smell of beer and roasted pheasant was simply divine. Tylar stood in the doorway for a moment, breathing in the intoxicating aromas with eyes closed and mouth salivating. A large fire burned brightly inside a massive fire pit, and nearly two dozen patrons sat scattered about the tavern. Luckily, a fair number of them were at the bar, most of them standing. It would be easy enough to slip a coin out of a pocket or two, if he was careful enough.

The barkeep would undoubtedly recognize him, but thankfully his wife was on duty. She laughed and conversed with a group of patrons, men he had seen the first time he arrived at Mor Seveht. One particularly drunken oaf near the door made for the perfect target, and Tylar was able to lift a small purse of coins from his pocket.

Drunks… always easy pickings.

Raising a hand into the air, Tylar signaled for the barkeep's wife, and within a moment she came over to meet him.

"What can I get you for, sir?" she asked, still smiling from the previous conversation.

"An ale, and whatever you've got on the fire."

"Well, tonight's your lucky night. My husband is cooking up quite a feast. We've got potatoes and carrots, some fresh boar, grilled onions and leeks, and—"

"I'll take it," he interrupted.

"All of it?" the woman chuckled, slightly taken back. If the goal was to remain as anonymous as possible, he was already failing at it. But the rumbling in his stomach was too great, and it was only by some miracle the entire tavern had not taken notice.

"You heard me right. I have the coin. I'll be in the corner." Tylar slapped the coin purse into her hands before the drunkard at the bar could tell it was missing, and promptly made a retreat. With each step, he prayed no one would recognize him.

Pretty hard not to notice the biggest son of a bitch in the room…

There were a few awkward stares, but nothing out of the ordinary. Tylar Bradshaw sat with his back to the door, shoulders hunched and gaze lowered to the beer stained table surface. It seemed like an eternity had passed before he heard the gentle footfalls of a female, and smelled a delectable bounty she brought with her.

"Here you go, love. A proper feast for a proper man. You a soldier or something? I've seen a lot of your kind passing through here as of late."

She set a wooden plate and mug down onto the table, then wiped her hands on her apron.

"No. I'm just a trader, on my way through."

It took every ounce of restraint within him to not tell her to fuck right off, but Tylar reminded himself that discretion was the key to making it out of Mor Seveht alive. He bit into a large piece of boar meat, dripping wet with juices, and began to devour it with the appetite of a lion. The woman shrugged and returned to the bar, hopefully not suspecting anything unusual.

Tylar's stomach growled even worse with food in it. He even felt a few stabbing pains at first, but gradually the discomfort subsided. The house ale was particularly potent, and after a few sips he felt a warmth building in his face and chest. Could it really have been that long since he had a drink? The thought alone was astonishing.

Everything on the plate tasted absolutely divine, though if it had been at any other point in his life, he likely would have thrown it against the wall in disgust. The food was poorly prepared, to say the least. Both the potatoes and leeks were undercooked, and the boar had a swampy, nearly rancid taste to it, hastily covered up with an overuse of herbs and spices.

Perhaps the barkeep should have let his woman cook tonight. He obviously doesn't know his way around a kitchen. In fact I wonder if he could even find his cock with both hands?

Not that it mattered. Food was food, and in the span of a few minutes, Tylar had devoured every last trace of it. The ale was another matter, however. It was particularly tasty, and he made certain to nurse the mug instead of simply tossing it down his gullet. It smelled strongly of malt and hops, each in perfect balance, and while it was a bit thick for his taste, it was nevertheless delicious.

It was tempting to order another round, and likely the coin he had given the woman would have been enough to buy a few more. But as

Tylar turned in his chair, he noticed a detachment of Blackthorn had entered the tavern, and stood congregated near the door. He immediately turned back around, a sudden eruption of adrenaline kicking him out of his mild drunkenness.

They were saying something to the owners, but he was too far away to properly make it out. But judging by the way the knights were gripping their sword hilts, it obviously meant anything but good.

Shit... I better not have been discovered. But how could I? I've been more than careful...

About ten men fanned out into the tavern, steel and shields in hand. The merriment throughout the room died in a near instant. Tylar let out a long and heavy sigh, suspecting the worst was about to come. He heard the shifting and scuffling of chair legs as patrons began clearing out, though he remained perfectly still.

"You there," the commanding knight said, his voice booming. "Titan Bradshaw."

Shit... Fuck...

Tylar sat, mind racing, a hand on his mug and the other slowly shifting toward a dagger on his belt. Were it any other occasion, he would have been able to dispatch all ten men with relative ease. But in his current condition, the odds were much less in his favor. He could sense them drawing closer from behind, preparing to scrap.

"Remove your hood and slowly turn," an officer said, his agitation building.

This is it. They're either going to take you prisoner, or kill you right here and now. What are you going to do, Tylar? Let them parade you through the streets of Bentmont and hang you as a deserter? Fuck no. I'm going out on my terms, with steel in my hand.

Tylar stood and drew his dagger, ready for his final battle, but was immediately dissuaded by the sight of four crossbows pointed directly at his chest. It seemed that the western Blackthorn units either knew of him, or had received ample warning, and came well-prepared.

"Put your weapon down and come peacefully, Bradshaw, unless you're willing to die in this shithole. Although for you, it seems most fitting."

"Why don't you drop those crossbows and face me like real men?" he snarled. "I bet there isn't a set of balls among the lot of you."

The officer smiled, but refused to rise to such a taunt. "I *will* hurt you if I have to, don't think me to be some gullible greenhorn."

A good look at the man seemed to confirm as such. He was older, though not as old as Tylar, with only the faintest hints of gray in his close cropped beard. His eyes were as fiery as hot coals, and had not a single ounce of fear behind them.

"Bold little shit you are. Tell me, what's your name?"

"Stalling isn't going to get you anywhere, but if you must know, I'm Elite Conrak, back from rotation at Naxonnos."

"Can't say I've heard of you, but based on what I've seen, the Order is really scraping the barrel. If you were braver men, I would have been knee deep in blood from the second you walked in here." Tylar began sizing up the other nine men.

"We've heard all about you. The great Titan Bradshaw, an old drunkard that fled from battle and took to banditry. A real hero for the ages, you are."

Cocky son of a bitch. I'm almost starting to like him. Almost.

"Says the coward hiding behind crossbows," Tylar said, then spat. "We seem to be at an impasse here. Either you fight me like honest men, or you can go ahead and kill me. Either way, I'm not going anywhere."

The Elite shrugged, then took a step back. "Very well. As you wish."

Six of the knights lined up in a shield wall, sheathed their steel, and drew truncheons. Before Tylar could properly formulate a plan, a crossbow bolt sunk deep into the meat of his thigh, sending him reeling backwards, growling and cursing. The knights charged in tight formation and surrounded him with an impenetrable wall of shields.

The beating was merciless, and with his strength diminished, Tylar stood little chance. He was clubbed for what felt like an hour before Conrak ordered his knights to stand down. The room was spinning and beginning to turn black, but somehow he was able to remain awake.

"Had enough, Bradshaw?" asked Conrak. "Or would you rather us beat you unconscious instead? I can certainly make that happen."

Tylar laughed, spitting out a mouthful of blood, struggling to keep his eyes open. "I've fucked wenches that have hit me harder. Is that the best you can do?"

"Yes, yes, we're all terribly impressed," Conrak said, motioning for the knights to lift him to his feet. "Clap this traitor in irons and take him outside."

Well, I suppose this is it. At least I had a meal and some drink in me before the end.

Four knights hoisted Tylar onto his feet, and wasted little time in placing him in restraints. The pain in his leg was searing, but thankfully the crossbowman was skilled enough to miss the bone. Such an injury would prove to be more of an irritation, though he supposed it mattered little if Conrak intended on executing him on the spot.

A small crowd had gathered outside the tavern as the Blackthorn exited, dragging Tylar Bradshaw along with them. The wagons he had seen earlier were sitting in a column, one of them outfitted with steel bars. Two knights stood by its open gate, and assisted in unceremoniously dumping him inside it. The gate was shut and locked with a large, iron skeleton key.

"What's the matter, Conrak?" Tylar grumbled through the pain. "Not man enough to take my life with your own hands? Why don't you kill me now and save us all the trouble."

The Elite approached the gate of the wagon, a satisfied grin across his face. "Is that fear I'm sensing in you, Bradshaw? Perhaps the stories about you were wrong, because I have yet to see anything in you that resembles an ounce of courage." He motioned for his horse, then mounted it. "No, there won't be an easy way out for you. You're going back to Bentmont, to answer for your crimes."

It mattered little if the High Marshal took his head for desertion, he supposed. The most terrible thought about returning home was knowing that Madelyn Everly was not coming back with him. There was something supremely unfair about it all, but such was the life of a knight. If there was another world after death, perhaps the girl would be there, waiting. Hopefully such a thing was true, because in a few weeks time, Tylar Bradshaw would be joining her in the grave.

ZANDER

HE SAT BROODING AS WAGONS PARADED THROUGH KHORRTAL, cursing silently as the Rhivothi passed by. At the head of the caravan rode Marvath Bonesplitter, a man he could stomach as well rotten meat, and Sylvia Stormguard, a feast for any man's eyes. Zander the Zylmacian was uncertain which he preferred; her, or the Blackthorn bitch they were off to ransom.

He tasted the Eveldanyr's flesh on more than one occasion, though his appetite was far from satisfied. The spoils of their conquest were mere appetizers compared to the bounty that awaited in Cardale. But before it could be fully savored, preparations would have to be made.

Had I a few thousand more men, I'd kill those Rhivothi scum, take the Eveldanyr as my queen, and rule all of Caldakas without opposition. The Droethiens would fall to their knees after what I'd do to Betanthia.

It was an amusing thought, but the possibility of conquering the Kingdom without the northmen was low, far too low to try something so brazen. Dreadfire was another matter entirely, though for now, the Borjifan served his purpose.

Zander watched the wagons until they disappeared from sight, then strolled through the dirt streets of Khorrtal. He was greeted along the way with suspicious leers, a few men spitting their contempt in a not so subtle manner, and mothers corralling their children accordingly.

"A fine day, isn't it?" Zander grinned at a middle-aged man who was glaring at him, showing a mouth full of half-rotten teeth. There was no reply, but then again, there never was when speaking to the villagers. Not that it mattered, he told himself, soon the warband would march again and Khorrtal would be little more than a memory. He thought about returning to the western edge of the village, where the locals preferred his kinsmen to stay, but each sour look only enticed him to venture further.

The Zylmacian camp was a crude thing, itself a patchwork of tents and small huts which sat scattered throughout an open field like weeds. Constructed of sticks and whatever materials they could scavenge, the accommodations were as meagre as one could imagine. Thankfully, the gods had seen fit to bestow upon them a warm winter, making their unrefined dwellings far more tolerable.

Lurking nearby were the Zylmacians, thousands of them. By last count, they comprised nearly half of the warband. But if the rumors were to be believed, many more would soon be on their way. Zander found it encouraging, though a bit frustrating at the same time. He had journeyed east for glory and riches, and now others would be fighting for their share of it. *His* share.

It belongs to me, all of it. After everything I've done for this sorry lot, they owe it to me. Every single last coin. Not one of them was man enough to throw themselves against Morden's walls like I did.

He could only imagine which other chieftains might be arriving to join the fight, and their level of disagreeableness. If one thing could be said about life in the Bymist, it was that it was often brutish and short. Only the fierce and the merciless could survive in such barren and inhospitable lands, and resources were becoming more scarce with each passing year.

And now those vultures want to come and steal my glory. Well, we shall see about that. They'll learn that out east, Zander reigns supreme. But I suppose for now, one thing at a time…

The nearby Hinterwood provided all manner of game, both large and small. Procuring healthy portions of meat was never difficult, and Zander found himself eating better now than at any other point in his life. The Bymist was home to game hardly suited for any man's cooking pot, and nearly overrun with scavengers looking to pilfer their next meal.

One of the local butchers was cleaning half of a deer carcass, the other half prepared and ready for purchase. Zander strode over to the large market stall, slapped a few dingy silver coins on its old wooden surface, and selected a large portion of backstrap. The meat smelled so succulent, he nearly ate it raw on the spot. He made his way over to one of the many fire pits throughout Khorrtal, dug to accommodate the massive influx of warriors. There he built a small fire, roasted the delectable meat, and consumed it with a ravenous hunger.

Before he could finish, a sudden commotion erupted from among the villagers. They were looking to the west, pointing and fretting in increasing hysteria. He stood and draped an animal skin cloak over his shoulders, curious to see what the disturbance was. A horn blast rang out, long and loud, cutting through the chaos. In a near instant, hundreds of men were scrambling to gather their shields and spears.

Betanthians? No, it couldn't be. They wouldn't be coming from that direction.

It could only mean one thing. Excitedly, he ran to the western edge of the village, a few of his kinsmen following closely behind. The streets were buzzing with activity, with the Khorrtalli either gathering their children and fleeing to their hovels, or arming themselves and preparing to fight.

As he arrived at the outskirts, he saw a vast host approaching from the west like a swarm of ravens. Some of the villagers who had gathered out of curiosity suddenly panicked and fled, while others hastily formed a shield wall in defense.

"Could it be? Those… those are wildmen!" someone cried out in terror.

Zander smirked and turned to the small, dwindling crowd. "You're as skittish as cats. How quickly you northmen forget, you've had Zylmacians living among you for months now."

He stepped out from between a pair of Rhivothi and began walking out into the field, his arms spreading wide. These were his kin, likely ten thousand or more, who had come to seek their share of glory and spoils.

"Welcome my friends, welcome!" Zander shouted. He took notice of a black scorpion banner at the head of the army, the sigil of Jollkud and his marauders. It was only a matter of time before news of Castle Morden's plundering made its way through the Bymist, though it was surprising to see how so many had come so quickly.

Fortunately enough, Jollkud was one of the more agreeable wildmen, which said little in the first place. Even still, he was not a man to be trusted, few Zylmacian chieftains could be, and would likely prove to be a nuisance when the time came to divide the spoils of the coming year.

A lone rider broke from their ranks and came galloping toward him, and it was easy enough to see who it was. Jollkud was one of the few wildmen to ride a horse, as they were not native to the Bymist, and especially difficult to keep fed and watered in such unnaturally inhospitable conditions. Zander often quipped among his warriors that Jollkud was in fact wed to his horse, though Jollkud would likely skewer any man who dared to say such a thing to his face.

"About time you arrived. Here I was, thinking that Betanthia would be all my own by the time you—"

"Not today, Zander," Jollkud interrupted. "I ought to have your head for filling your coffers and not thinking to share any with your kin. You think yourself a rich and pretty man, eh?"

"Be mindful of your tone, mate. Remember, *you* were the one who refused to come with, even after Dreadfire kissed my ass for months to join his little army. You missed out, and you only have yourself to blame."

Jollkud spat, his horse rearing. "It's true, I would have thought you'd be dead in a field somewhere, but here you are."

"Here I am." Zander stretched his arms out arrogantly, his half-rotten teeth showing. "I didn't expect you to bring so many, unless your clansmen are fucking like rabbits."

"Word travels quickly, even through the Bymist. The Five Clans and the Sons of Solitude caught wind of what happened at Morden before we did, but they wouldn't dare march east and not tell me. That's real power, power not even Dreadfire himself could oppose."

Zander snorted. "You put too much stock in that bumbling oaf, mate. His real power lies with that witch he drags around."

It was amusing to see Jollkud squirm upon hearing mention of the crone, as most Zylmacians were superstitious by nature. He had begun to suspect Damien's success was less the product of supernatural forces, and more of precise timing and unrelenting momentum, things he planned to use to his own advantage.

"So what will it be then?" Jollkud asked, brow furrowed. "Honor dictates that this is your hunt, as you were the first of us to draw blood against Betanthia. What will you have us do?"

"Come, settle yourselves and we'll discuss the matter more," he replied. "I'm sure the Rhivothi are dying to meet you, heh!"

Jollkud wheeled about, arcing a hand wide through the air, signaling his clansmen to proceed into camp. Zander parted ways with him and ventured to the village outskirts, where a sizable number of Rhivothi and Khorrtalli warriors had gathered. Some gave dumbfounded stares, while others looked on with indignation.

"More of these western dogs?" Valerick the Red said, loud enough for Zander to hear.

"Scavengers always arrive after the kill has been made," a voice answered from the crowd.

Zander himself was amused and strode past the line of warriors, chest puffed out, snickering to himself softly. "For such proud people, you tree dwellers are quite the jealous ones. Where would any of you be if it weren't for me, hm?"

"Bold words for a man that shit himself trying to scale Morden's walls," Valerick taunted. "If my nostrils haven't betrayed me, I think I can still smell the stench of fear on you."

The nomad was growing increasingly more insufferable, as all Rhivothi were. However, Marvath Bonesplitter was still the most detestable by far.

"Says the man who washes himself in animal blood. I'm surprised you can speak with all those flies buzzing around you."

A poor retort, but Valerick's insult left him seething. The embarrassment of being sacrificed against the walls of Castle Morden on their first day was something he had yet to forget. And even after the stronghold was taken, there was neither praise nor congratulations from any of the other tribes, not even a tacit acknowledgement of his deeds.

They'll rue the day alright. For everything I did to topple that castle, they ought to have given me the lion's share of the loot. Bastards, every last one of them.

Zander sat around a fire further into the village, his presence causing the locals to scatter like birds. Not that he cared, as it meant less northmen to contend with. As the flames began to flicker and fade, he threw a pair of dry logs onto the fire, stoking it back into a raging inferno. He produced a small skin of mead and wrenched it open with his teeth, throwing back a few mighty swigs. The drink was the only northern thing he could stomach, and had come to prefer the taste over western swill.

Before long, Jollkud and his companions ventured over to the fire. They appeared to be impressed with what they saw along the way, but Khorrtal was anything but sophisticated. While the living conditions were greater than anything Zylmacia had to offer, it paled in comparison to what the Betanthians could build.

"There you are," Jollkud said, annoyed. "We thought you ran off with those pretty tree dwellers you surround yourself with." He took a seat by the fire, the other two wildmen chuckling. "Tell me, what does Dreadfire intend to do? When do we march?"

"The more important question you need to ask yourself is, what do *I* intend to do?" Zander's question seemed to produce more amusement than awe. "You may smile, you may even laugh, but before this year is out, none will be laughing, except for me."

"Quite a boast," one of the wildmen said, himself a retainer of Jollkud. "Come now, are you going to fill us in on your schemes, or is your greed going to get the better of you?"

"He's right," Jollkud interjected. "You keep enough secrets, Zander. Whatever it is you're planning, you had best make us aware. I didn't march all this way to be led around blindly."

"Very well," he conceded. "You'll come to realize soon enough how much these northmen hate us, just for being Zylmacian. Do not trust a single one of them. They see us as expendable, and will use us until our strength is spent. They've done it once before, and won't hesitate to do it again. They think us to be simpleminded beasts, and I plan to use that to my advantage."

"Our advantage." Jolljud shot Zander a distasteful glare, the light from the fire dancing in his gray eyes.

"You know what I meant, mate. If anyone is capable of getting close enough to the other warchiefs, and even Dreadfire himself, it's me, not you. But worry not, we'll play along and do what Damien bids us, for the time being. Here comes one of his Nothanek minions now. You need not fear these men, they're soft and pious."

Arik Akselson approached their fire at a determined pace. Zander snickered and shook his head, as the riverfolk had done their damndest to avoid the Zylmacians.

"I thought I smelled fish, and it appears my nostrils haven't betrayed me," Jollkud said, drawing a few chuckles. "You were right, Zander, they carry the stink of the river on them."

Arik's brows furrowed as he glared back in disapproval. "Damien has ordered us to assemble and prepare to move out at once. All men who wish to continue the conquest are to present themselves. We head east."

"East?" Zander asked, incredulous. "I'd have thought we'd be heading a bit more south. What's Dreadfire hope to find out east?"

"Our next conquest," Arik answered, then turned and started back to his warriors, who were already assembling.

"Is this what you've been reduced to, Zander?" Jollkud snorted. "Taking orders like an obedient dog from a whelp like this?"

The insult drew a few muffled chuckles, though most were eager to witness his response. Zander felt his rotten teeth beginning to grind. "Come now mate, I've spilled more blood in the last year than you have in the last decade. Have you still been raiding goat herders and putting old women to the sword?"

Laughter and a few surprised murmurs filled the air. Jollkud grinned, seemingly unphased by the slight. "Aye, the Bymist has come to learn my name well. Tell me, is it true what they say about Castle Morden, that you fled with your tail tucked?"

It appeared that the playful banter was becoming more dangerous by the second. In the interest of not jeopardizing his position, Zander forced a smile then turned, making his way to Damien's command tent. "The gods know what we sacrificed that day."

He was fuming, and wanted nothing more than to plant his axe into the skull of the first man he encountered. But now was neither the time nor the place.

Arrogant bastard. Perhaps I ought to task him with the first charge, see how he likes the taste of real steel, not pitchforks and sharpened stakes.

Memories from the first day at Morden still left a sour taste in his mouth, far more sour than his decaying teeth. His men fought bravely and did what no wildman had done before. It was an achievement for the ages, especially after the siege ended in such a decisive victory. *That was what mattered.*

He threw open the tent flap, expecting a full audience before Dreadfire. Instead, he saw Arik Akselson, Valerick the Red, and another Rhivothi, whose name he was unaware of. It was likely one of Sylvia Stormguard's shieldmaidens, judging by her ferocious yet beautiful appearance. He took notice of her long, golden hair, drawn back into a braid as thick as a rope, the sides of her head shaved.

"Well now," Zander exclaimed. "Isn't this a merry gathering! Only the finest company, it seems."

He moved toward the shieldmaiden with ravenous eyes, but Valerick stepped between them casually. Damien Dreadfire appeared a second later, his crimson cape flowing like a battle flag. Even Zander was wise enough to check his impulses, lest his hands find their way inside of the woman's jerkin. But there was a time and a place for everything, he supposed.

"My friends, the hour is upon us," Damien Dreadfire said, his attention immediately drawn to a map on a large table. "This is the moment we have waited for all winter, and gods be praised, it was a short one. Soon, we will strike at the heart of Betanthia."

He pointed at the mining community of Hok, well to the east of Khorrtal. The other warchiefs looked on curiously, though Zander could only wonder why they would be headed in such a direction.

"Why not march through the Plainhold and take them by surprise?" he asked. "We could sack Bentmont before they even knew what hit them. Why go that way?"

"This is where we shall make our next move," Damien continued, disregarding the interruption. "There is a Blackthorn garrison at Hok for certain, and likely a contingent of Betanthian soldiers. We must destroy these forces entirely if we are to keep our flanks secure. We cannot leave ourselves vulnerable so far from home."

"A sensible plan," Valerick the Red said. "Perhaps if we're swift enough, we can secure our ransom and recapture the Eveldanyr. The gods would prefer she stay in the north, treacherous though she may be."

"Perhaps." Dreadfire's face turned sour. "But the gods have no use for those who forsake them. My focus is on the gold the Blackthorn have promised. It will pay for our war effort several times over."

The conversation seemed to fade into the distant background as Zander's mind began to wander. His thoughts turned toward the next battle, and the battle after, and how such events might be maneuvered to his advantage. Many, if not most of his adversaries thought him to be simple, given his Zylmacian blood, though it might prove to be his greatest asset. A wry smile began to form in the corners of his mouth as Dreadfire's voice cut through his daydream.

"And now, we must leave Khorrtal and head east. We will make camp close to Hok, yet far enough away to not arouse suspicion. There, we will meet with Stormguard and discuss our plans further. For now, gather your forces and break camp. May the gods ride with you."

Zander was the first to leave the tent, eager to fight the next battle and acquire more spoils, and further etch his name into history. Jollkud and the others looked on curiously, but he paid them no attention. There were more important thoughts on his mind, far more important than a few chests of gold. Or even an entire kingdom, for that matter.

LUCETTA

A DENSE FOG LAY OVER THE LAND LIKE A BLANKET, COLD AND WET and smelling of death. It was nearly impossible to see more than a few feet in any direction, though Lucetta Eldon suspected they were not far away now. The skin on the back of her left hand was red and broken where she had scratched it raw, small flecks of blood collecting underneath her fingernails. This was what she had dreamt of, and suffered humiliation for, and only the stinging burn on her hand was enough to convince her the moment was even real at all.

Sneaking away from the family chateau was easy enough, though she was beginning to sense the suspicion of the servants, and her mother. But none of it mattered; this was a divine mission, after all, written long ago in the heavens. She would have the tongue of anyone at the chateau who would dare to question her movements, or inform the queen as to her whereabouts.

And the servants knew it, too. Keeping them in line would not be difficult with a man as capable as Pavlos. The Droethien was every bit as ruthless and resourceful as one could imagine, easily surpassing every rumor she had ever heard about such beastly people. There were even times when Lucetta feared what he might do should he turn disgruntled, but with the mountains of gold she had already paid out, such a possibility seemed remote.

Onward the carriage lumbered through the spongy field, rocking about in every direction like a ship on open waters. Nauseated, Lucetta opened the window to let in some fresh air, but the stench that wafted in was anything but pleasant.

"Relax," the woman in black said, sitting across from her. The entity wore its familiar dress of black silk, figure flattering and low cut. Its hair was as dark as the night, and danced across its collarbone. "Your queendom awaits you. It will not be long now."

It was almost too good to be true; a land of her own, created in her own image. It seemed like only yesterday when she was condemned to the life of a lesser child, doomed to live in the shadows of greater men. She thought of her husband and his near obsession with acting as the King's surrogate, and of Gareth, which was the most infuriating thought of all. He was someone who had squandered his birthright, bastardizing everything which had been given to him on a silver platter.

By what cruel twist of fate was I dealt this hand? Here I am, in the middle of nowhere, scraping together a future for myself, and yet he continues to defile the family name. Were I given everything in life, as he has, what a difference I could make in this world.

"Fret not, Lucetta Bethard," the woman in black consoled. "Your name and your deeds shall echo throughout eternity, never to be forgotten. Songs will be sung, and tales told, long after you have passed on. Your legacy shall never die."

She smiled, comforted by the entity's soothing words. Ages had passed since she felt frightened by the woman in black, who now seemed to be more of a guardian spirit than anything. Every moment of suffering she had been subjected to, up until now, had only served to forge her into something stronger, like steel emerging from a crucible.

The carriage soon came to a halt, the horses neighing and stirring from what lay ahead. It could only mean one thing; the journey was now over. Lucetta felt lightheaded with excitement as one of the Droethiens opened the door and extended a hand. When she stepped out, the most awful stench affronted her nostrils. The air stunk of burnt wood and burnt men, and wet, rotting vegetation. Black plumes of smoke still snaked into the air, though the battle had ended nearly three days prior. Lucetta covered her mouth with a handkerchief and coughed.

What have they done?

The Droethiens had proven to be far more ruthless than she had ever imagined. The speed and violence they employed to subdue the village was frightening, so much that she hesitated to move any closer.

"Come now," the woman in black said, pushing her forward gently by the small of her back. "You have not come all this way for nothing, have you?"

It was true. She had toiled diligently and suffered humiliation at the hands of Sir Bryce Whitewood to get this far, but did not expect the fruits of her labor to be dripping with blood and covered in ash. When Pavlos told her about a village near the banks of the Siln River, she was expecting it to be nothing more than a few shanties housing a handful of farmers, who could easily be relocated.

"Yes," Lucetta whispered, nervously stroking a lock of her long, auburn hair. "But... this isn't what I was expecting. This isn't what I wanted them to do!"

The woman in black chuckled, her voice low, unnaturally low, almost like a man's. "Do not be so naive, child. Empires are built on stone, but they are also built on blood. This is the site of your new realm, the place chosen by the fates. What was done here was necessary, and you should be grateful."

The ground was wet and treacherous, but not impassable. Lucetta lifted her skirts to her shins and trudged forward clumsily, like a child finding its legs for the first time. She glanced over her shoulder to speak to the woman, but instead she saw Pavlos riding toward her.

"Princess!" the Droethien exclaimed. "Why are you walking through this mud like some filthy commoner? Come." He extended a hand, though Lucetta was hesitant to take it. It seemed unnatural and dirty for her to sit on the back of such a beast.

"Most kind of you, but I would prefer to walk. My legs have grown sore from sitting."

"Very well." Pavlos shrugged. "As you can see, my princess, the White Spear have fought well and have brought these lands into your domain. I trust you are satisfied, yes?"

"Are they… all dead?" she asked, chewing her lip. "The people that dwelled here, have they…"

"We asked them to surrender, but they refused, and attacked us during negotiations. One of them tried to cut my throat, but Pavlos was too quick for him! We had no choice but to defend ourselves. They learned their new queen is not to be disrespected, yes?"

He gave a toothy smile, one she had come to know well, and still did not fully trust. But the mercenary had no reason to lie to her, not with such a generous wage and station which had been afforded to him.

"Worry not about your savage," the woman in black said, though she was nowhere to be seen. "He is simple and obedient, like all mercenaries are. Keep his purse full and you will have no reason to doubt him."

Lucetta swallowed hard. Every instinct inside of her was screaming to run away, but she could not. A morbid curiosity had taken hold like a poisonous weed, spreading its roots deep throughout her soul. While horrors were undoubtedly waiting just ahead, something inexplicable compelled her onward.

Each step was more frightening than the last, but she could not look away, much less flee. The first homesteads she passed were ravaged and burnt to cinders, with little evidence remaining of their existence. Small fires continued to burn here and there, filling the air with acrid smoke. All of the livestock were slain, and whole fields of crops put to the torch for reasons she could not understand.

Then she laid eyes upon them. A farmer and his wife were sprawled out on the dirt road, large pools of blackened blood staining the ground beneath them. Birds appeared to have feasted heartily on their remains, leaving behind only a ruined mess that only insects cared to touch. It was the first time she had seen a dead body since crossing the Camsby River in Cardale. But there was something the slain peasants were clutching, something which almost went unnoticed at first.

Lucetta peered forward, craning her head ever so slightly to avoid venturing too close. Upon further inspection, it appeared the farmer and his wife were more than just common laborers, they were also parents. Tucked tightly in their arms were the charred remains of two children, their bodies so incinerated it was impossible to determine if they were boys or girls.

Too terrified to speak, Lucetta averted her gaze and tried to flee, but was unable to control the movement of her legs. It was as if the woman in black had commandeered her flesh and forced her to continue on. Bodies lay strewn about as far as the eye could see, some appearing as if they were sleeping, others so burnt they were little more than effigies of ash. She covered her eyes with trembling hands, gasping and nearly in tears.

"Come now," the woman in black said kindly. "You must not dwell on what *is*, when what *will be* is so much sweeter. Do you see it? Come, look closely."

Lucetta was unsure what would be more terrifying; following the entity's command, or ignoring it. But an indescribable curiosity compelled her to part her fingers and peek once more at the grim landscape.

"Yes, yes. Go on," the woman said. "Look, and see with your own eyes. See your destiny."

Strangely, the air turned from a pungent cloud of smoke and death to a light breeze, smelling of fresh water and spring flowers. The sun emerged from behind a bed of clouds, caressing her face with soft rays of light. There was even the faint cooing of pigeons, as if she was back at her estate in Cardale.

When she opened her eyes, Lucetta gasped. The landscape was no longer a mass grave, but instead it was a city of cobbled roads and tall buildings, of alley and avenue, all teeming with activity. Thousands of peasants went casually about their business, ignoring her presence entirely as if she was a specter.

It was a sight more beautiful than anything she could have imagined. The streets were lined with small, finely pruned trees, and not a trace of refuse was to be found. There were shops and stalls and estates grander than her own, as difficult as it was to imagine. It was truly a paradise.

But perhaps the most awe inspiring sight was the palace. It was sleek and tall, taller than the Westwind Citadel, and shimmered like pure silver. Its peaks reached high into the heavens, so large they were nearly shrouded by thick, white clouds. The sight took Luceta's breath away. All she could do was gasp and place a hand to her heart, uncertain if it had stopped beating.

"There's the queen!" one of the commoners cried out.

A sudden excitement came over the people as word began to spread. At first, Lucetta thought they were referring to her mother, as if she had somehow found her way to this distant place. Panic began to take hold inside her chest, squeezing hard like a clenched fist. But as Lucetta scanned and studied the crowd, the truth became apparent.

Stepping out onto a large balcony came a figure in a flowing, golden dress. Jubilation swept over the masses as they showered their monarch with praise. Squinting and straining to get a better view, Lucetta muscled her way through the throngs of peasants. When she arrived nearest to the front, she could finally see who the people were so enamored with. It was *her.*

Lucetta nearly wept as she looked upon herself, looking more beautiful and happy than she could ever imagine. A golden crown sat atop her auburn tresses, a smile as warm as sunlight adorning her powdered face. She felt overwhelmed by the intense love emanating from the people, her heart nearly running away with excitement.

"Do you see it now?" the woman in black said, emerging from behind a tall, burly man. "This is the future that lies in store for you. This is what could be built on the ashes of this squalor."

But the sight of death was something she could never forget. It was enough to dash her happiness, turning it quickly into despair. Lucetta shook her head. "No. No future is worth building if it's done on the bodies of slain children. I cannot do it, and I will not."

"You ingrate!" The woman's voice sounded as if five or more people were speaking. "You would sacrifice this paradise to spare the lives of a few savages? Have you become simple? Should these children grow to adulthood, they will learn to wield the sword. And how long until those swords turn against you? You have an opportunity to be rid of your enemies before they are a threat. How many of your ancestors would sacrifice everything for such power?"

It was an interesting perspective, one Lucetta had not considered. The woman in black often had a way of speaking to her in a language she was only now beginning to understand. As disturbing as it was to stand at the feet of dead children, perhaps if she could build a new world, a better world, one in her image, no other children would need to suffer or die.

"You're right," she whispered, seeing Pavlos and a handful of his men approaching. The vision of her future paradise faded nearly as quickly as it arrived. "If father could have prevented this barbarian infestation in the west, I'm certain he would have. How many more innocents are going to die now before the war is over? Perhaps it's proper… just, even, to be proactive."

The Droethiens sauntered over, some chuckling and speaking in their native tongue. Pavlos grinned and nodded, the gold in his teeth glistening. "Princess, I trust you are satisfied, yes?"

She nodded in agreement, having grown weary of the sight of death. "Yes, I'm ready to return to Dellhaven. You have served me well, Pavlos. Your rewards will be plentiful."

"When would you like to begin construction of your new city, princess? We have several gifted architects in our ranks, capable of building great engines, or thick walls, should you command it."

"I will give it more thought, but for now I must rest. You may take your spoils, as you see fit."

Pavlos smiled. "You are as kind as you are generous, princess. My men will be most thankful to you."

It was a white lie, to be certain. It was easy to notice the Droethien's saddlebags, as they were already filled to bursting with treasures. It was curious how poor farmers could afford anything of value in the first place. Not that it mattered; they were dead and gone, and left among the charred ruin that used to be their simple life.

Feeling her stomach begin to churn, Lucetta started back to her carriage. As her feet sloshed in the mud, she could not help but see the brown water turn to a shade of deep red, though it was little more than her mind playing tricks.

"Be still now," the woman said, moving alongside her. "Everything that exists in this world grows from the ashes of something which came before it. Even Betanthia, if you know your history. Your ancestors took the barbarian settlements of their day and forged them into the mighty kingdom you see now. Let your mind not be troubled; this is merely the next phase of existence, of a divine plan of which you are now playing your part."

"I hate myself for ordering the death of children, even if the plan is divine," Lucetta lamented. "I don't know if I'll ever be able to forgive myself for such a thing."

"Hate?" the entity raised an eyebrow. "Why would you hate yourself? That emotion was never in the equation. There is no form of malice which made you do this, but instead it was love. In fact, it is the greatest form of love in the world, to use the generous sacrifice of these people to build a new paradise. They should be honored."

"I suppose you're right," she whispered, the driver of her carriage opening the door. She climbed inside, trying vainly to mask a look of despair.

There seemed little point in fretting over the turn of events, as nothing that was done here could be undone. She reminded herself of everything the woman in black had helped her to accomplish in the past year, and how far down the road to her destiny she had already traveled. The thoughts were reassuring. At least, somewhat.

Half of the mercenaries remained at the village in preparation for the next phase of her plan. The remaining half accompanied her carriage as it set off back to Dellhaven. The experience of the day, and even the grim excitement of it, was enough to make her drowsy. Leaning her head against the padded interior of the carriage, Lucetta Eldon drifted off to slumber, with visions of a silver palace shimmering in her mind.

CHARLOTTE

The bleak, brown landscape was the last thing Charlotte Bethard expected of a Dellhaven winter, much to her disappointment. She had long dreamed of snowy fields and trees covered in dusty white blankets, but all she experienced was rain, one downpour after another. Though discouraged, she reminded herself that of all the things one could control in life, the weather was the least of them.

Perhaps winter in Cardale wasn't such a bad thing after all, if it weren't for Marcellus. I think I'll always be a summer girl at heart.

Charlotte stood on the upper floor of the chateau, dressed in a heavy gown of deep blue linen, a thick fleece cloak draped across her shoulders. She stared out through an eastern window at the thrashing of the unfrozen sea, white, choppy waves pounding violently against the shoreline. The only solace to such unseasonably warm weather was the notion that it would be an early spring, and soon flowers would bloom and trees would bud once again.

She sighed, moving to a large fireplace across the room, a pair of logs crackling and glowing orange with flames. It was difficult to keep the chateau warm, despite the best efforts of Devin Brandybrook to maintain fires all throughout the day. But even though it was cold, this was still her home away from home, and she loved it here.

Not every day was pleasant and worry-free, however. Lucetta had been acting increasingly suspicious since her arrival, and while some days were better than others, it was still troubling to witness her steady decline. And to make matters worse, her daughter had been absent for some time, without so much as saying a word to anyone.

Devin had informed her that Lucetta claimed to be returning to her estate in Cardale, but one of Dellhaven's city watchmen claimed to have seen her turn west. Something was amiss, Charlotte could sense it. Nobody knew where her daughter was, or what she was doing. Perhaps it was simply paranoia on Charlotte's part, she told herself, and Lucetta was indeed heading back home.

With as dreary as the weather has been, I cannot blame her, if that truly is where she's heading.

And then there was Gareth. It felt like a lifetime had passed since he had left for Cardale to assume his place on the high council. Charlotte sometimes cried from missing him so much, and wondered constantly if he was well and what he was doing. Tears began to well in her eyes as she watched the fireplace, lonely and yearning to see her son again. After many months away from the Westwind Citadel, it had become easier to stave off despair, which had nearly driven her to take her life. But even the strongest sometimes faltered.

She also thought of Trace, and began missing his calm, reassuring presence. Forever the optimist, he was always there to help keep her grounded when panic or sad thoughts took hold. But there was a certain disconnection she felt when speaking to him, as if it were stony professionalism he was exhibiting and not genuine concern. Gareth's conversations, while more emotional, felt more genuine.

"My queen?" Emilee Harper said softly from the doorway, curtseying respectfully. "Breakfast has been prepared."

Charlotte dabbed water away from her eyes with an index finger, hoping Emilee would think it was irritation from smoke and not sorrow. "Thank you. Will you dine with me?"

"Absolutely, my queen." Emilee smiled.

Not that Charlotte needed to ask, as the two had grown accustomed to enjoying their meals together. But it was polite nevertheless. Devin and Brendan had become more comfortable with it as well, though they were always mindful of their true place. It was unprecedented for a monarch to interact with commoners in such a fashion, but Charlotte Bethard was no ordinary monarch.

She made her way down the hall with Emilee close behind. Servants gave pause and bowed, each one bidding the Queen a good morning as she passed by. The dining hall was bustling with activity as the table was set. Devin was overseeing every detail, as he did each morning, making sure fine silverware was expertly placed, and a bountiful breakfast made ready to serve. Fresh logs were hauled in from outside and placed on the fire, its dying embers stoked back into a warm, hearty blaze.

"Good morning, my queen. You look positively exquisite today. Blue is the most flattering color for you, I must say." He gave a warm smile and a bow of the head.

"Thank you Devin, I trust you slept well? Sometimes the sea is so restless I have to put a pillow over my head just to sleep."

"Indeed I did!" He chuckled. "When I first moved to Dellhaven, I could hardly sleep a minute when the sea was thrashing about. Now, I almost cannot sleep without it. There's a certain comfort to the noise, I've found. Give it time, my queen. You'll learn to love it, as I have."

Devin slid a chair at the end of the table out, and assisted Charlotte into her seat. Seconds later, a troupe of servants performed a well-choreographed routine as they served a portion of fried potatoes, eggs and beef, with fresh greens and onions onto her plate. While the meal was considered commoner food, Charlotte enjoyed it nevertheless. It was a reminder of her childhood at the family plantation in Glimmergulf.

Despite delicious food and enjoyable company, the Queen was nevertheless sad. Thoughts of Lucetta were never far from her mind, and she found herself glancing at a vacant chair at the table more than once. Emilee and the other servants appeared to take notice, however subtly, and seemed to shift the conversation just at the right moment. It was comforting to know those around her, however low-born, cared so deeply about her.

After she had finished eating, Charlotte dismissed herself hastily from the table, giving Devin a sharp glare which told him all he needed to know. He rose, clapped his hands together twice, and followed after the Queen as she exited the dining room. The other servants immediately sprang into action, clearing away the table until only cleanliness remained.

Together they stepped out into a brisk morning and began walking the estate's bleak grounds, its flowers and trees only beginning to awaken. A distant crashing of foamy waves provided enough background noise to muffle their conversation from unwelcome ears.

"Devin." Charlotte pursed her lips, then glanced back at the chateau. "There's something I need you to do for me."

"Absolutely, my queen. Is everything alright?" Somehow, he was able to sense an old, familiar apprehension in her voice.

"I need you to do this for me, and without reservation. Swear to me that you will."

The servant's brow furrowed. "Whatever you say, I will obey, Your Majesty. Please, tell me, what troubles you?"

"Something is wrong with Lucetta, Devin. In my bones, I know it. What in the world could she be doing out west? The nearest city is Kepdon, a week or more away! I simply cannot make sense of it!"

"Where did you come by that information, my queen?" he asked, running a hand down his face.

"The city watchmen have been reporting her whereabouts to me, and when last they saw her, she was traveling west. She isn't being truthful about where she's going and what she's doing. I'm scared for her safety."

Devin stood silent for a moment, deep in thought. "Worry not, Your Majesty. I know a reliable man who might be able to help. He's an expert hunter and trapper, and knows these lands better than anyone. His catches are served on your table regularly, as a matter of fact. I'll make contact with him immediately, and task him with tracking down your daughter. If there's anyone who can do it, he can."

"Thank you," she said, sighing deeply. "If there's any danger, he must send word to the Guardsmen immediately and have her brought back. I cannot risk my only daughter, Devin. She's so precious to me."

"I understand, my queen. I'll send word to him right away. He has a small homestead in the woods near the northern wall, so it shouldn't be difficult to locate him. Come now, allow me to show you back in. The wind is blowing off the sea, and you'll catch a cold if you stay out here much longer."

Together they made their way back to the chateau, and once Charlotte was safe inside, Devin dismissed himself. He was every bit as capable as he was thorough, and with any luck, his associate would be as well.

I pray it is so, for Lucetta's sake. Devin has yet to disappoint me, I have to remember that.

After returning to her chamber, Charlotte spent the next several hours flipping through the pages of long neglected books. She indulged in beautiful poetry and heartwarming love stories from one of Cardale's most famous playwrights. There was even a chalice or two of wine to go along with it. Around midday, there was a soft knocking at her door.

"Your lunch is served, my queen. Brendon said I'd find you here," Emilee said with a smile. "Is everything alright?"

The question was becoming tiresome to answer, largely because of how unsure she was in answering it. "Yes, and no. I'm worried about my daughter, but I trust Devin to find her and bring her back. I miss Gareth, and I wonder if he's well and what he's doing. I even miss Cardale, believe it or not. I never would have thought I would be saying that. It's just, the weather here is difficult to tolerate, and all I've ever known for ages is the Citadel. As much as I enjoy it here, it still feels a bit foreign to me."

"Yes, my queen, it is a bit gloomy. What if we went back for a brief visit? You could see your son, and perhaps enjoy some warmth for a few days."

A tempting suggestion, even though fear of King Marcellus still lurked in the deepest corners of her heart. Charlotte had to remind herself that Marcellus had not sent his men to Dellhaven to apprehend her, and likely her absence had gone completely unnoticed.

"I'm not so certain…"

"Do you trust me, my queen?" Emilee asked. It was an unusual question, but Charlotte nodded nevertheless. "Then I beseech you, go to Cardale. We have spent a great deal of time together, and I can sense when your mind begins to panic and run wild. I'm positive Lucetta will be brought home safely. Perhaps she'll even be at home, waiting."

There was something about the servant girl's calm and confident demeanor that seemed to soothe her anxiety. Perhaps she was right, and Lucetta had returned to Cardale after all. Perhaps the guard was wrong and mistook her carriage for that of a wealthy noble or merchant. It was a real possibility, one which Charlotte could have slapped herself senseless for not considering.

You mustn't always assume the worst. You know better than to do this to yourself, especially after how far you've come. You cannot overthink every single matter, you'll drive yourself as mad as Marcellus.

"You're right," Charlotte admitted. "There are times when I think you know me better than I know myself, Emilee. I'll go. I have to learn to have faith, and not paralyze myself with fear and indecision."

"It's quite alright, my queen, you've suffered a great deal over the years. You have to give yourself credit for coming this far. Would you ever have imagined a year ago being where you are now?"

It was a fair point, one which Charlotte had not taken into consideration. It was only a short time ago when living inside the Citadel seemed too terrible to tolerate, and the cold embrace of death was the only comfort she sought.

There were times in recent months when she could hardly recognize herself in the mirror. Her body had recovered much of the weight it had lost, and a warm, rosy hue returned to her skin. Even her hazel eyes began to sparkle once again with an inner light she thought was lost forever.

"No, I never would have thought life would have changed so dramatically for me. And I have Gareth to thank for all of it. If he had not come to my chamber that night, drunk and despondent… well, I cannot imagine what would have happened to me. As much as it pained me to see him in such despair, perhaps it was meant to be. Look at how his life has changed since that day!"

"That's precisely why I think you should see him. He's probably missing you as much as you're missing him. I'm sure Sir Edmund will make certain the King remains oblivious to your presence, so there's really nothing stopping you."

"Very well, Emilee." Charlotte gave a warm, confident smile. "I'll go, but the only thing Sir Edmund will be doing is standing by my side, because I intend to give Marcellus a piece of my mind before I leave for good. It's only right that he should know what he had, and what he's going to lose. If you would be so kind, please prepare my carriage, and bring only a small chest with. I can make do."

Not that she had many possessions in Dellhaven anyways. Most of her wardrobe and treasured belongings were still at the Citadel, all of which would have to be brought back with her. The maidservant curtsied and departed, herself looking just as excited. Charlotte was too anxious to wait for Emilee to pack for her, and began filling a trunk with clothing and a few necessities for a two day journey, then made her way to the foyer.

The smell of her lunch was too tempting to ignore. A fresh pheasant and roasted vegetables sat waiting on a silver plate, with thin wisps of steam snaking out from it. Charlotte stole a moment to sit and eat, and devoured most of the meal while the carriage made its way to the courtyard.

Brendon of Theeds rushed inside and hurried to her chamber, eager to fetch her items. She smiled in admiration at the servant boy for his diligence, and his ability to follow directions from Emilee without question. Outside in the courtyard, Devin was preparing the carriage and summoning the Guardsmen for an escort back to Cardale.

"Your presence will be missed, my queen," he said. "Even if it's only for a few days. But worry not, everything will be well taken care of until you return."

"Devin, I have something I need you to do," the queen said softly as she climbed into the carriage and smoothed out the length of her skirts.

"For you, my queen, anything. How may I be of service?"

"If Lucetta returns, please keep a close eye on her. If she inquires as to my whereabouts, tell her I'm off in the countryside, or somewhere close to Dellhaven, and that I might return at any moment. I want to know how she will react, as well as that man she keeps around. I must know the truth of what they're conspiring."

Devin Brandybrook closed the door to the carriage, and tugged gently on the handle to make certain it was secured. "Absolutely, Your Majesty. Your daughter shall be my highest priority. I'll instruct your bodyguard to send word to the city watch in Cardale, as well as the Guardsmen at her estate. If she turns up, we'll know about it. But if I may ask, where will you be heading, in actuality?"

With an uncertain sigh, Charlotte gave the estate a long glance before motioning for the Guardsmen to depart. "As a matter of fact, I'm off to Cardale, one final time."

SYLVIA

T HE CAMP WAS A MASSIVE, SPRAWLING BEAST THAT STRETCHED NEARLY to the horizon. Sylvia Stormguard brought her horse to a halt, surveying the expanse of the warband with wonderment. Before winter they were but twelve thousand, a collection of the last prominent northern tribes, and the wildmen who could be swayed to join. Now, their ranks had swollen to nearly sixty thousand strong.

As she sat idle, the wagon train proceeded past her and down a shallow hill to the encampment below. Soon, she and her kin would bask in the fruits of their conquest from the year prior. But something in the distance seemed amiss, something which set her stomach to a flutter.

There were many banners throughout their camp; flags bearing runic sigils for the Rhivothi and Nothanek clans, as well as Damien Dreadfire's personal standard near the command tent. His banner flying higher than all others, its black and crimson colors unmistakable. But there were many more, both strange and foreign. Peering, she saw a banner emblazoned with a black scorpion, among others. Some were little more than simple, tattered canvas splashed with what appeared to be old blood.

"Zylmacians…" Marvath Bonesplitter grunted. Sylvia was so lost in disbelief, his approach went unnoticed.

"Thousands of them, tens of thousands more," she said, dismayed.

"They must have arrived after we set out from Khorrtal. Now we're utterly infested with Bymist rats."

It appeared the Rhivothi were not the only ones expanding their ranks during the winter respite. Though several thousand nomads and natives of Rej Rhivoth ventured south to join the war effort, the wildmen had arrived nearly ten fold in numbers.

"They're scavengers. Opportunists," Stormguard said dismissively. "Easily satisfied by a few trinkets."

"A scavenger's appetite is never sated," Bonesplitter cautioned. "Who do you think they'll strike once Betanthia is in ruins? They'll cut our throats the second King Bethard is dead, believe that."

"The only thing a dog understands is strength. As long as Damien remains strong, they'll remain at heel. They had every opportunity to betray us after Morden fell, yet they remain true. Besides, they're content to throw themselves against any obstacle, no matter how many of them die. If it means more of our people can return home, then so be it."

The giant Rhivothi spat his disdain, then turned in the saddle as a wagon laden with spoils rode past. A chasm of a frown formed across his bearded face, as if the sight offended him more than the Zylmacians. Sylvia cocked her head curiously.

"What's the matter, Marvath? For a rich man you sure look grim."

Bonesplitter grunted, his gaze turning toward the distant sky. "Should have killed her clean and been done with it. Are a few coins worth staining your soul?"

"Don't tell me you're sour over that Blackthorn bitch? Have you gone soft?" she asked with a hint of hostility. "She's our enemy! Her Order is every bit as responsible for Borjifa as the Bethards, or did you forget while you two were galavanting through the trees together?"

There was never a time in her life when Sylvia thought Marvath would strike her, not until that moment. She saw a fierceness building within him, like the churning of magma, something typically reserved for an enemy on the battlefield.

"You are kin, Stormguard. But kin or not, I will not suffer such disrespect. We're Rhivothi, not dishonorable vermin like those Zylmacians down there. Lower yourself to their level, and the gods will never forgive it. Kill a man clean or free him, that's our way. Chains are for dogs."

"How can you say such things when our enemies have done far worse? If you ask me, they deserve everything they get."

"They may have forsaken the gods, but we have not. If we lose their favor, is there any hope of keeping Betanthia at bay? Do you really think the Hinterwood will deter them after Caldakas has been swallowed by the Bethards?"

"The gods demand justice for generations of conquest and bloodshed," she said, frowning. "Would we have won three battles, three seemingly hopeless battles, if we didn't have the gods on our side?"

"Be careful what you sow, Stormguard. Azldyr's thirst is like drinking seawater. You cannot quench it, and the more you try, the more your fate is sealed. Kill our enemies quick, and clean, and be done with it."

"You're beginning to sound like a Nothanek," she muttered, giving Marvath a quick and unsettled glance. "Perhaps you've been spending too much time around them."

The thought of Einarr crept into her mind, and how the war had changed him. There were times she cursed him for a fool, perhaps even a weakling, though such a label would be unfair. He fought just as bravely as any other warrior.

"Perhaps the Nothanek have the right idea," Bonesplitter said, jerking the reins of his horse and trotting off toward the camp.

Sylvia shook her head and sighed. *Am I one of the few that remembers why we're here? Every Betanthian that survives is a threat to our people and our way of life. Defeating them in battle isn't enough. We have to ensure they can never harm us again. Why can't he see it?*

It would be most unfortunate if Marvath were to lose heart as Einarr did, but perhaps it was simply boredom weighing heavy on him. Nothing could rejuvenate a Rhivothi's spirits quite like a battle, and there would certainly be plenty of them to come. Sylvia did her best to brush off the conversation, and rode into camp and off to her kinsmen.

The natives of Rej Rhivoth had congregated on the northern edge of the camp, their distinctive animal hide tents standing out from all others. Some of the warriors were tending to their equipment, making appropriate repairs to their armor and sharpening their weapons. Others trained, eager for their muscles to remember the feel of swinging an axe. Few took notice of Sylvia as she rode by, but those who did offered their respects.

She dismounted and tied her horse off to a hitching post, then walked briskly to the heart of the main encampment. The Nothanek were not far away, going about whatever business fisher folk usually went about. Sylvia half expected their entire clan to be at prayer, for as pious as they all seemed to be. Some of them, however, were making preparations of their own, fletching arrows and practicing their aim.

Thankfully, from here the Zylmacians were out of sight and out of mind. The thought of turning over hard-won treasure to unwashed scavengers seemed wrong, even insulting, in a way. But their numbers had grown alarmingly, and cheating them out of their share of the spoils would only invite trouble, she reminded herself.

A small band of camp followers were ahead, planting large wooden torches into the ground near her tent. They bestowed their courtesies as she threw open the flap and entered, hastily discarding her equipment onto the ground before stepping back outside. Damien Dreadfire was undoubtedly expecting her report about the exchange, and what she saw outside of Hok.

"Where is he?" she asked, the sour feelings from her conversation with Marvath subsiding. A young camp follower motioned to the north, where some of the wagons had congregated. Around them was a growing sea of warriors, pressed shoulder to shoulder, staring intently at something. Curiously, Sylvia approached, muscling her way past one man after another.

After coming into a clearing, she saw Damien standing by one of the chests, silver coins slipping through his fingers. For half a heartbeat, there appeared to be a smile forming in the corners of his mouth, though it faded as quickly as a shooting star. The warriors, however, were not so reserved. Their roars of satisfaction seemed to grow louder with each coin that fell back into the chest.

I wonder what Damien is thinking right now. I know he would trade every coin for everything he's lost, but he must be proud. He has to be! He's done something no one has dared to do in four hundred years, something that will be remembered for all time.

It seemed inappropriate to interrupt Damien as he basked in his well-earned glory. She watched as the riches were distributed to one warrior after another, a long and tedious process to be certain. Sylvia smiled as she watched for a few minutes, savoring the sweet fruits of their victory, her mind harkening back to their struggles and triumphs over the last year.

Later that evening, she made her way to the command tent, a fresh meal in her stomach and a horn of mead in hand. The warriors around her were sitting around small fires, feasting and drinking and boasting, each man eager to strike out on the next leg of the campaign. She raised a toast and smiled, continuing on until arriving at a perimeter of sharpened stakes surrounding a large tent.

A flickering light slipped out from the tent flap, along with the faint haze of smoked herbs and burning incense. She took a long drink, her hands unsteady, and sighed. There was no logical reason for her sudden nervousness, but perhaps it was simply anticipation to be on the march again.

Damien Dreadfire stood over a table at the center of the tent, towering over the warchiefs around him. Marvath Bonesplitter stood to his right, clad in furs and leather, both hands resting on the edge of the table. Arik Akselson was to his left, rhythmically puffing on a long wooden pipe, appearing near child-like in stature.

Zander stood opposite of Damien, with two other men she did not recognize. They were Zylmacians without a doubt, their heads bald and covered with tapestries of tattoos and tribal scars. Sylvia felt an immediate rush of anger at the sight, and even a slight feeling of uneasiness.

"Welcome, Stormguard," Dreadfire said, looking up from a large animal hide stretched across the table's surface. On it were scratchings in black ink, undoubtedly the well-laid plans he intended to execute. "Please, join us."

The other warchiefs turned and took notice, Arik nodding and the Zylmacians eyeing her like a side of fresh meat. Bonesplitter, however, failed to acknowledge her presence. It was disconcerting, but not entirely unexpected. While he was a large and savage man, he harbored many deep and complex emotions which sometimes seeped to the surface.

"We were just discussing Damien's plans for the next campaign," Arik said.

"Good. Have I missed anything?" she asked, moving to the table.

"No," Dreadfire answered. "We were just beginning. Welcome to all, on this, the first full war council of the new year. I am heartened to see faces both familiar and new. I trust the gods have kept you well this winter."

The warlord's attention turned back to the animal hide map. "Those of you who have wintered at Khorrtal know what has transpired over recent weeks. The traitor, Madelyn the Eveldanyr, has been ransomed at Hok, and the spoils distributed to those who fought throughout the last year. Each man has been paid in full for their services."

Zander appeared quite pleased at the mention of his loot, though his Zylmacian companions looked as if they were slighted. Perhaps they were expecting some sort of tribute for joining the ranks of the warband, but only a westerner could be so bold, and so stupid.

"Now," Damien continued. "Our scouts have kept a watchful eye on Hok for some time. Stormguard has seen it up close. Do you have any information that may be of use?"

"Aye," she said, glancing quickly to the wildmen at her side. "Hok is a mining community. At its center lies a large, open pit, where the Betanthians mine for iron ore. We know there's a detachment of the Blackthorn stationed there. But from the looks of things, if we strike hard and fast, we should be able to take it with ease. The perimeter is protected by a stone wall, but it's far smaller than what we encountered at Morden. Quite crude, if I may say. The mine is to the north and will prevent their escape, so we'll only need to attack on three sides instead of four. There shouldn't be more than a few thousand soldiers there."

"I was hoping for a palisade," Arik Akselson said, dismayed.

"Come now mate, a little wall shouldn't frighten you," Zander the Zylmacian taunted. "Besides, you'll be hiding in the back while we're storming over the top, I'm sure. Just like last time."

Marvath stepped forward, fists clenched as hard as boulders. "Mind your tongue, rat. This is a serious matter."

"Ah yes," Zander chuckled to his kin. "This here is the mighty Marvath Bonesplitter. He's quite taken with me, it seems. Ever since the day he laid eyes on me, he's—"

"Enough," Dreadfire interrupted, his voice booming. "Time is of the essence. The Blackthorn will be taking the Eveldanyr to Bentmont for safekeeping. We must make our move while their forces are split."

"Are you certain they're on the move?" Arik asked.

"Yes," Damien replied. "They will not risk keeping her so close to our grasp. She has seen the way we fight and how we set our defenses.

The knowledge she carries with her will be invaluable. However, the Betanthians have yet to realize her true power, as I have. Lazilyth is certain they are unaware of her blood strength."

The mere mention of the crone's name was enough to command a brief silence, even among the newly arrived Zylmacians. It was quite possible even they had heard whisperings of the old woman's other-worldly ways, even as far as the Bymist.

"By your will, Damien," Sylvia said, swallowing hard. "When do you wish to proceed?"

"At first light. We will arrive at the outskirts of Hok in the evening, then wait for the cover of darkness. From there, our forces will be divided into three parts, and we will surround them, so there is no escape. We must take care not to alert anyone to our presence. This means no banners, no fires, no drums, no singing or music of any kind. The element of surprise will be our greatest weapon."

"Perhaps they should fling themselves into the mine and spare us the trouble," she quipped.

"That's an awful lot of effort for so few men," Zander chimed in. "Is it even worth our time? It's not like there's anything worth pillaging."

"Those are Blackthorn in there, you idiot," Marvath said, scowling. "Not something to be ignored."

"Come now!" The wildman looked to his companions, who them-selves had visions of gold glistening in their eyes. "We've faced those pretty horsemen once already and made quick work of them. We should head south instead, where the real action is."

"They were defeated inside of a castle, with nowhere to run," Damien cautioned. "The Blackthorn are far deadlier on open ground. You have never seen them fight in their element. None of you have. Ignore them, and we place ourselves in great peril. Our supply lines and reinforce-ments will be left vulnerable to attack. Should they choose, they may ride north and sack our villages with impunity, or strike us unawares should we face King Bethard on the Plainhold. No, Hok must fall, and we must be swift about it."

Sylvia could sense disagreement in the tent, but the Zylmacians appeared reluctant enough to concede. They had far greater ambitions in mind than putting a few miners to the sword. "Agreed, Damien," she said, after a quick glance around. "The Rhivothi will be assembled at dawn and ready to ride at your command."

Not to be outdone, the other warchiefs answered in kind, each speaking or grunting their approval. A peculiar excitement began building in the air, like the moments before a thunderstorm, for they all longed for further glory and spoils and had grown bored throughout the winter.

Damien pursed his lips and dismissed them with a nod. "Gather your warriors, and may the blood of our enemies stain the ground red. May the gods quench their thirst on Bethard blood."

Word traveled quickly throughout the night, and before daylight had broken, the entire warband had come to life. The warriors began hastily taking down their tents and gathering their possessions. Camp followers swarmed about like flies over a fresh kill, snapping up everything they could get their hands on and loading it onto horses or wagons.

Sylvia stepped outside of her tent, closed her eyes, and took in a deep breath of morning air. It smelled fresh and was thick with moisture. Nearby were the remains of a fire, its flames low and barely clinging to life. On a spit was a freshly roasted rabbit, and some bread on a plate sitting next to it. Sylvia knelt down and helped herself to a quick meal, as there was no sense in letting perfectly good food go to waste.

She barely managed a swallow before one of her shieldmaidens came running over. From the corner of her eye, she saw it was Hilde, as her fair skin and pitch black hair made her appear like an otherworldly entity.

"Is it true, do we ride?" Hilde asked, her cyan eyes shimmering like the sea. It was the most excited Sylvia had ever seen her.

"Was everyone listening outside the tent?" she chuckled. "Yes, it's true. As soon as we're ready, we ride. I don't know who's more excited for battle; Azldyr, or you."

"I thought I was going to die of boredom after being stuck in Khorrtal all winter. I'm ready for adventure, and glory!" Hilde brushed her close-cropped hair behind one ear, a tapestry of tattoos on the side of her face accenting her anxious grin.

"Adventure, for certain. Glory, well, we might have to wait a bit longer for that. At least, where we're going." Sylvia approached her horse, fully saddled and readied by a waiting camp follower, who offered up the reins and a respectful bow.

"Where are we headed? Did Damien say?"

"We're going to Hok, to destroy the Blackthorn holdings there. Then it's off to the heart of Betanthia."

The news seemed to be of little disappointment to Hilde. "As long as I get to wet my sword and get my share of the loot, then I'll be satisfied." The shieldmaiden broke from Sylvia's company and raced off to gather her effects. The Rhivothi were howling like wild dogs and screaming like banshees, eager to take to the road.

In no time, her people were assembled and beginning their march eastward. After making certain the Rhivothi had broken camp and fallen into formation, she rode to the head of the warband. There seemed to be no end to the masses of warriors she passed by, a dense forest of spears and axes filling her with an indomitable confidence.

Seeing Dreadfire's large black and crimson banner at the head of the warband made her beam, and drive her horse even harder. There was an energy building inside her, as if Azldyr himself was charging her muscles with thunderbolts. She wanted to ride, and fight, and roar at the top of her lungs. And soon enough, Sylvia Stormguard would have the opportunity to do all three in plenty, much to the doom of Betanthia.

TITAN II

By the end of the second week, Titan was unsure of which he craved most; a skin of water, or a headsman's axe. The pain in his leg was beginning to grow worse, and if something was not done in short order, corruption would likely claim him. Tylar's complaints had fallen on deaf ears thus far, until one of the knights mistook him for dead.

"Conrak!" the man called out. The caravan was brought to a sudden halt. Elite Conrak wheeled his horse about and rode over to see what the disturbance was about.

"Yes, what is it?"

"I think he's dead, sir. I haven't seen him moving in hours."

The Elite ran his tongue across his teeth and scowled. "Well, we can't let him get off that easily, now can we?" Conrak stuck his riding stick through the steel bars and prodded the end into Titan's leg wound, a pool of fluid oozing out from his broken flesh. The pain was enough to jolt him awake, groaning and convulsing in agony.

"Fuck! What the fuck are you doing that for?" he snarled. "Can't you let a man die in peace, you vicious cunt? Fuck!"

The knights chuckled, Conrak most of all. "Come now, Bradshaw, we all know you're too stupid to know when to die. You seem to enjoy suffering, so why complain about a little more?"

"And you're too much of a pussy to unlock that cage. Even now, I could tear your head off and kill the rest of you cunts with it. Go on, give it a try."

"Enough, you're not intimidating anyone. Perhaps you are indeed too stupid to know when you've been bested. But I suppose you'll realize it soon enough when you're swinging from a rope."

"That leg *is* looking pretty rough, sir," one of the knights said. "If it festers, he'll never make it to Bentmont. Smells like it's already there."

Conrak sneered. "Very well. Might as well make camp anyway, this looks like the only place we might find water for a while. Bring him down from there, and get a fire going. I could use a meal anyways"

Even though Tylar was wounded and frail from sitting for weeks on end, the knights were nevertheless cautious when they opened the cage. He thought about pouncing on them and trying to seize a weapon as quickly as possible, but as they dragged him out, he realized just how weak he truly was.

Cowards. Each and every last fucking one of them. That's why they've left me like this, because they know that even now, I could still kill a few of them before they managed to take me down.

He spotted one of the knights drinking from a wineskin, and passing another to Conrak. The mere sight of it made his parched mouth even drier, if such a thing was possible. To make matters worse, the knights were preparing a fire, and with it, their evening meal.

"I'd kill any one of you for a drink," he croaked.

"All you get is water," the Elite said. "Can't have you dying on us, after all."

All Tylar received was a mouthful of warm, nearly stagnant water from an old skin. While the taste was disgusting, he swallowed it down, grimacing all the way. The wretched taste was soon forgotten as he spied Conrak stoking the fire with the end of a large knife. The flames were small at first, but with proper care, they soon grew into a mighty blaze.

Conrak placed the end of his blade into the fire, leaving it sit until the metal began to glow.

"Do refresh my memory." Conrak took a drink of wine from a skin, then poured the contents into a small kettle over the fire. "Are you supposed to douse the wound before, or after you cauterize it?" The question hung in the air for a moment, answered only by a few muffled chuckles. "Very well then."

The Elite nodded, and one of the knights lifted the kettle, his hand protected by a thick leather glove. The man poured its boiling contents onto Titan's leg with a smirk. The pain was unimaginable, so searing and intense that he nearly lost consciousness. All he could muster was a grunt, the sort of painful groan only a wounded animal could make.

"I bet you're not so fond of wine now, are you?" Conrak laughed. "What's the matter, has a little pain unmanned the great Titan Bradshaw?"

"Aren't you a sadistic bastard?" Tylar growled. "You sure you aren't a northman?"

"Come now, is that the best insult you can muster? I was told your wit was the strongest thing about you, but I can see now the stories were embellishments. And as a matter of fact, no, I don't enjoy doing this to another man. But the truth is, you are a coward and a deserter, and deserve neither pity nor respect. Were I a less gracious host, I would simply let your leg fester until it claimed your life."

Tylar's eyes began drifting from Conrak over to the knife, the steel turning red and orange, then slowly white. He knew what was coming, without the Elite having to say so much as a word.

"At least give me a swallow of wine, if you're as courteous as you say," he said, desperately trying to mask his nervousness.

Conrak grinned, then nodded at another knight, who produced a wineskin and held it in front of Titan's mouth. He took several desperate gulps, wine spilling down his chin and splattering onto the parched earth. For all of his villainy, at least Conrak allowed this small mercy, pompous prick though he was. With the skin nearly depleted, the knight pulled it away, Titan inching forward to try and steal another drop.

A rush of drunkenness was sudden and all too pleasant, a familiar warm tingle embracing his entire body like a long lost friend. The pain in his leg began to throb a bit less, though he knew well-enough the agony that was soon to follow. Titan stiffened his back, tightened his jaw, and gave Conrak a sour look.

"Get on with it. Go on, you piece of shit, and fuck yourself with it after you're done."

Conrak removed the knife from the fire, its steel hissing from the intense heat. He inspected the blade, eyeing it and nodding in approval. "Give him something to bite down on. Don't need him gnawing off his tongue before he has a chance to explain himself to the Marshal."

Another knight placed a wooden shim in Tylar's mouth. He bit down on it, panting and growling like a beaten dog, knowing the pain was mere moments away. Before he knew it, Conrak pressed the white hot knife onto his wound, the flesh sizzling and steaming as it was cooked and cleansed of corruption. The stench was nauseating, the pain so ferocious that all he could do was roar in agony before losing consciousness.

When he awoke, night had fallen. It was quiet, save for a soft humming of crickets and crackling of a fire near the other wagons. Tylar was drunk, refreshingly drunk, and felt no discomfort. Immediately he looked down at the wound on his leg, a fresh linen bandage protecting the cauterized flesh from further corruption. He supposed the nerves had been seared badly enough to mask the pain, which was fine enough by him.

He sat, staring at countless billions of stars in the sky, wishing he was somewhere among them. Thoughts of Madelyn came creeping back, and the times they shared riding through the Plainhold and at Castle Morden. There were nights when they sat beneath these very same stars, conversating for hours on end over some of Lord Valens' wine stock.

Tylar wondered what he ever did to deserve such a cruel life. When he was little, he was often hazed by other children, and the beatings his father would serve up afterward were especially traumatic. It was difficult to grow up small and weak, and to be punished for it, but Tylar never let such adversity conquer him. As a young man, he had grown larger and stronger than his peers, and with his coming of age, the cruel hazing came to an end.

It would have been easy to allow years of torment to turn into bitterness. But instead, Tylar found solace in helping others. He would often take his fists to the local bullies, cowards who hunted the weak in packs. He could still remember the first time he broke a man's skull, and the sickening crunching sound it made. But the villain had it coming, and his victim was eternally grateful for Tylar's selflessness.

It was his reason for joining the Order; to protect and safeguard the weak, and keep the wolves at bay. His father was righteously angry when the news was delivered, but there was nothing that could be done. Tylar dwarfed his father, and nearly used his newfound strength to seek righteous vengeance for decades of torment. Instead, he said nothing and left for Bentmont, never to return.

Such thoughts were comforting, given the situation. For all his years of safeguarding the innocent, it seemed unnaturally cruel for anyone to haul him away in chains, much less claim him a coward. He sighed, gazing at the twinkling of a distant star, its light brighter than those around it. Perhaps death was not such a terrible thing after all, he thought, and soon his spirit would be among all the stars in all the heavens.

A noise suddenly drew his attention. It was faint, barely noticeable over the snoring of the knights. Titan turned his head, pointing an ear toward the disturbance, which again presented itself. Something, or someone, was close.

"Hey," he whispered as loud as he dared. "Wake the fuck up. We have company."

One of the knights sleeping against the wagon's wheel opened an eye halfway, then shifted into a more comfortable position. He paid little attention to Tylar's warning.

"Wake up you mindless cunt! I'm telling you, there's someone here."

"Why don't you shut up and—" the knight fell silent as he heard the sounds of footsteps breaking stalks of tall grass. He gave the man next to him a stiff jab with an elbow, then held a finger to his mouth as he awoke in sudden agitation. The understanding between them was clear. Luckily, Conrak was nearby, and was the next to be prodded from his slumber.

"Shit," the Elite whispered. He nudged several other men nearby, looking at those who were awake and giving them a slow yet commanding nod of his head. The knights drew their weapons as silently as they could. Barely a third of the unit was awake, but it would be enough to defend against a surprise attack, Titan hoped. And likely, the ensuing carnage would be enough to rouse the others from their sleep before it was too late.

Moonlight glistened off the knight's swords as they scanned the darkness, ready to meet the unseen threat with steel. Tylar fidgeted with his shackles, eager to be free of his restraints and join the others in fending off whatever brigands might be lurking in the tall grass. Even though he was wounded and far from recovered, the adrenaline saturating his veins was enough to dull out the pain.

"Get these fucking chains off me if you want to live," he whispered to Conrak.

The Elite gave a low, sharp wave of his hand, glaring at Tylar with fiery hostility. No more than a second later, the camp erupted with screams and war cries in every direction, the grass rustling and swaying as the attackers charged in. Titan made himself as small as he could within the confines of the wagon, hoping to remain unseen in the shadows.

Steel leapt up to meet steel, and the knights that remained asleep were roused into action unceremoniously. Tylar could see the attackers, most of them bald and bare-chested, and slathered in a layer of dirt and filth. They flailed about without the discipline of a trained warrior, and several were cut down before they could penetrate the circle of wagons.

Conrak's skill at arms was impressive to behold. He handled his blade like a warrior poet, effortlessly crafting a masterpiece of swordplay which gave Tylar pause. His sword cleaved through the darkness with expert precision, finding its mark on one brigand after another. A jet of blood caught the light of the full moon as Conrak struck the neck of one foe, then wheeled about and ducked the frantic axe swing of another.

He suddenly reversed his grip on his sword, the steel singing as it sliced through air, then the soft belly of his attacker. The savage screamed woefully before Conrak removed his head, the corpse slumping to the ground amidst an eruption of blood.

Desperately, Titan tried to free himself of his bonds, jerking and pulling the shackles with all his might. He placed the chain against the bars and pressed with his good leg until the cuffs dug into his wrists, but it was to no avail. The steel was too strong, and his body too weak to break loose. He watched helplessly as more savages charged into the camp, axes and spears in hand. One of the knights fell, a wooden club smashing into the side of his face. The sound of bone shattering into fragments seemed to drown out the war cries for half a heartbeat.

"If it's steel you want, come and get it then!" Conrak shouted defiantly as four savages closed in around him. Titan watched as the Elite stood his ground, moving about in a slow circle with the nimbleness of a cat. He picked up a one-handed axe with his left hand, twirling it seamlessly before assuming a fighting stance.

One of the attackers charged in, his wild swing blocked with ease. Conrak gave him a stiff elbow to the head then parried a thrust from another, immediately shifting the man's momentum and sending his crude sword into the belly of another. With sword and axe, Conrak decapitated the first two attackers, then threw his axe with deadly precision. Titan heard a deep thump as it landed, and saw the shadow of its handle protruding from the savage's skull.

The chaos of combat soon subsided, and the field grew quiet once more, save for a few pitiful groans of dying men. Their suffering would not last long, as the knights dispatched the remainder of them with little mercy or hesitation. Conrak strode over to Titan, moonlight twinkling off splashes of blood across his torso.

"Do you still think of me as some greenhorn, Bradshaw?"

There was little Titan could say. The display of swordsmanship was nothing less than legendary, each blow delivered with expert precision. It was the sort of fighting he was unaccustomed to, as brawling and brute force was the style he preferred. It was easy enough to pound a man into pulp if you could lift twice his body weight with ease. But perhaps there was a place for Conrak's skill at arms after all. It certainly won the hour, despite overwhelming odds.

"You're a fighter, I'll give you that," Tylar conceded. "But an utter fool if you ask me. You needed me in that fight. I could have even saved a few lives. Those men of yours didn't need to die."

"You wouldn't have been any good to anyone, Bradshaw. You haven't held a sword in weeks, and even if you did, you're too weak to be of much use to anyone. Besides, I would rather watch you swing from the end of a Blackthorn rope than be butchered by a wildman's axe."

Tylar paused, cocking his head curiously. For a moment, he thought Conrak had said the word wildman, though his ears were suspicious. "You don't mean Zylmacians, do you? No fucking way they would come this far east, not across the Plainhold. Maybe you need to spend a little more time out west before you—"

The Elite stepped forward and tossed something at the base of the wagon. Titan leaned forward, though his shackles would only allow him the slightest bit of movement. In the pale moonlight, he saw the edge of a Zylmacian axe, the meat of its blade carved with crude symbols. It was a dull weapon, but retained enough of an edge to slice any man it encountered to death.

What the fuck would those filthy beasts be doing out here? It doesn't make any sense. Not at all. Were they following us this entire time?

"Don't look so surprised, Bradshaw," Conrak said. "We've been seeing more of these dogs venturing out of their kennels over the last few months. If I were a betting man, and I just so happen to be, I would say they're probing. I suspect we'll be seeing more of them in the near future."

Tylar stared at the axe, his mind harkening back to the siege of Castle Morden. He had seen wildmen there in large numbers, though it was not his first encounter with them. If they were daring enough to make such a treacherous journey across the barren Plainhold, it could only mean one thing; the horde which sacked Morden was on the move, and searching for its next target.

"Well then, we've got to warn the High Marshal as soon as possible. Fuck man, don't you see? Those animals are coming, and if they can find us all the way out here, what's to stop them from showing up on Bentmont's doorstep?"

"For as simple-minded as you may be, Bradshaw, you're certainly not wrong. But it doesn't change the fact that you're a deserter and an oath breaker, and I won't be discussing military strategy with the likes of you. Now, do keep your mouth shut. We cannot stay here, and your blabbering will only alert more of these animals to our presence."

It was supremely frustrating to be spoken to in such a manner and not have the ability to rearrange Conrak's teeth. In fact, Tylar had once beaten a man into a coma for far less of an insult. But there was nothing he could wield, save for his wit, something which Conrak seemed entirely immune from.

Despite his exhaustion, sleep that night was elusive. There were eyes all around the Blackthorn caravan, watching and studying, and perhaps even conspiring. Tylar was unsure if they were merely rodents or other animals which inhabited the Plainhold, or more Zylmacians waiting to strike. To him, it was all the same.

He curled up in the corner of the wagon, a dull, burning ache in his leg creeping back. There would be little point in worrying about another attack, as he would be helpless to do anything about it anyways. And not to mention, there was still the matter of his execution, which was awaiting in Bentmont.

EINARR

TEARS OF SPRING MOISTENED HIS CHEEKS, THOUGH HIS OWN HAD run dry long ago. A melancholy sky hung over Einarr Rolffson's head as he sat beneath the cherry blossom tree, cold and dreary, and devoid of light. Every day seemed just as bleak without Alina by his side, the love of his life who was called to Sjenohor all too soon. Despite years which now separated them, time still had not mended all of his wounds.

"I wonder… are you out there, somewhere? Are you waiting for me, as I am waiting to be with you again? Are you as lost as I am?"

There never was any answer; not now, and not in the weeks turned months he had spent at Skaginlef. Home was a place Einarr thought he might have been able to heal and forget the horrors of the past year, but his village seemed more foreign now than the lands of Betanthia. Even fishing the waters of the Teb felt different. While it was necessary in order to remain fed, there was little joy to be found in it anymore.

When once it was an activity he looked forward to, second only to carpentry, it was now little more than a tedious task. The fish certainly were not making Einarr's experience any more enjoyable, as his catches were becoming smaller and fewer in number. It felt as if the earth itself was abandoning him.

One particularly cold spring morning, he took a long, lonesome walk along the Teb. Its once vibrant waters were brown and still, and as lifeless as his heart. Dry autumn leaves blanketed its glassy surface, slowly decomposing against a backdrop of skeletal trees. Nothing was green. Nothing was alive. It seemed like death itself had followed him back to Skaginlef.

This was not what life at home was supposed to feel like. It was supposed to be his refuge, a haven away from the horrors of war. He was supposed to have returned to a hero's welcome. But now, inexplicably, it felt as if the battlefield was the only place where he truly belonged. Einarr sighed, shifting his gaze up to the heavens.

"Is this my reward for loyalty, and for seeing your justice served to those who slaughtered your people? Is this how I'm going to spend my days; living in torment, because I chose to do what was right?"

He received no reply, same as the last dozen times he asked the gods for answers. Dismayed, Einarr turned and started back home, following the Teb until he caught sight of the cherry blossom tree. It stood like a barren tombstone over the grave of his love, a somber reminder of everything he had lost. Each step forward brought with it more agony, until salty sorrow began stinging his eyes.

"Einarr… Einarr…"

A frigid gale came howling in from the north, rattling the branches of the cherry blossom tree. For a fleeting moment, Einarr thought he heard Alina's voice drifting on the wind, soft and distant and mournful. He sighed, his eyes fixated on the site of her burial, yet his gaze seemingly a million miles away.

It was becoming more difficult to picture her face, and recall the sweet, fresh scent of her hair. It seemed like the harder Einarr tried to remember Alina, the further from his memory she drifted, like a disappearing thought on the tip of one's tongue. The frustration was maddening.

"I don't blame you for leaving," he said with another sigh, running a hand through his short, brown beard. "You're free, and in the company of the gods. Would you even recognize me if you had stayed? Would you think of me as the man you called husband?"

The answer was one Einarr already knew, for there were many times in the months since returning to Skaginlef where he felt like a stranger in his own home. The Nothanek certainly seemed to look at him differently as of late, as it was his decision to bring their people into Damien Dreadfire's war. And now, here he was, alongside those who had returned wounded or too exhausted to fight on, the remainder of their warriors sitting wintered at Khorrtal.

Einarr kissed the palm of his right hand and pressed it against the trunk of the tree, whispering a few loving words before returning home. He saw many of the townsfolk tending to their properties, a few traces of snow having melted away. Some were preparing their land for the planting season, while others made repairs to their hovels, patching leaky roofs or filling cracked walls. Few paid him any mind. Those who did gave him only quick, spiteful glances before returning to their labor.

How quickly they've forgotten all I've done; all the hard-won victories, the glory, and the spoils. All meaningless to them because I returned home. Do they think me a coward? How can they judge me when they've seen none of the things I've seen, nor done the things I've done?

He was beginning to doubt everything: his decision to take the Nothanek to war, to leave the campaign and return home, the gods, his people, all of it. All Einarr ever tried to do was the right thing, by the Nothanek and by the gods. But he felt abandoned, as if Kholdyr had forsaken him entirely.

Is there no place in this world for men of conviction? Do the gods care only for men of war, and for the death and destruction they create?

His days were spent maintaining his neglected homestead and preparing for spring planting. The property had become overgrown and unsightly in the time he had been away, and there had been little oppor-tunity to tend to it upon his return. The next several days consisted of removing dead leaves and branches from the ground, scything over-grown grasses low, and organizing his seed stores for planting.

From dawn until dusk he labored, finding any excuse to remain out-side. While his abode was more comfortable than most, it drove daggers into his heart to be within those four walls. There were signs of Alina everywhere, from her knittings and decorations, to her handcrafted jewelry and more. Each item was another painful reminder of her loss, but Einarr could not bear the thought of parting with any of them.

I can still feel you here, as if you never left me. I don't know if I can bear it any longer.

Sleeping was next to impossible. For hours each night, Einarr would sit awake staring at the ceiling, his hand resting on the spot where Alina used to sleep. Oftentimes, he turned to the comfort of mead in order to drown out old memories, and in such great quantities it would put even the heartiest Rhivothi to shame.

One morning when he awoke, a once familiar scent lingered in the air. It was sweet and fragrant, which his nostrils remembered well. Einarr sat up in a flash, but quickly discovered his homestead was quiet and empty. Perhaps it was simply his mind playing tricks, it must have been, as Alina had long since returned to the earth. Sighing, he rose from bed, dressed in a simple tunic and trousers, donned an animal skin cloak, then stepped out to meet the new day.

A small marketplace sat beside one of several stone bridges which arched over the Teb. Its stalls had sat empty for months, as there were little goods to trade during the bleakness of winter. Hunters, weavers, and fur trappers sold their wares inside Skaginlef's large mead hall instead, but were now preparing to move their business back outdoors. There was almost a carnival-like atmosphere during the market months, a time Einarr had always thoroughly enjoyed.

I doubt any of them will buy so much as a shim from me, lest they be seen in my company.

But the stalls remained empty, for now. It would be some time yet before the villagers would begin hawking their wares to any who would buy them, be they local or traveler. But he had nothing of value to sell; no carvings nor furniture, no commissioned projects of any sort. Once one of the wealthiest men in Skaginlef, Einarr was left wondering if he would be able to earn any coin at all in the coming year.

But the lack of business mattered little, anyways. As badly as Einarr's fingers longed to work wood and create something grand and new, he had not the heart to even look at an axe, let alone pick one up. All of the creativity which flowed from his mind and through his hands had run dry, and only seemed to bring back terrible memories he would just assume to forget.

He could still see the hulking frame of Ruin, and smell the acrid smoke of Castle Morden as it smoldered. Despite the siege being months in the past, it was still difficult to acknowledge that such carnage had resulted from his labor. It made the thought of splitting a piece of wood nearly too terrible to bear.

Instead, continued on past the market, resigned to being absent this season. The mead hall sat with its doors open, a dozen or more locals already inside. The Nothanek adored their mead, and would savor its delectable taste day or night. Craving a mug for himself, Einarr entered wearily, trying to remain as inconspicuous as possible. He placed a dingy coin onto the wooden bar, then glanced casually out through the door. But Skaginlef knew him all too well.

"Coward," one of the patrons grumbled to another. "I lost my cousin at the Pass, and my brother is still out there fighting."

The tavernkeep set a frothy mug down with more force than was necessary. Einarr felt fiery gazes of those around him building in intensity, and moved swiftly to the other side of the hall. He swallowed nearly half of his mug in a few anxious gulps, stealing a moment to study carvings he had made in the thick wooden columns. Throughout the mead hall, he had etched runes and visages of the gods, and had hidden several dedications to Alina. It was their secret, one that made her smile every time they set foot inside.

Looking at them now was too painful to bear. Einarr felt his throat beginning to tighten. He coughed several times, finished off his mug of mead, then made for the door. He cast the empty vessel back onto the bar, ignoring the renewed mutterings of those around, and stepped outside.

Why did I bother to return if this is the sort of life I can expect?

The forest was calling his name, even though it was still deep in its winter slumber. Einarr started north, but not before passing by a small cellar where the hall's mead supply was kept. The doors were left open, a fresh haul of casks sitting inside. On top of several barrels were skins of mead, each filled near to bursting. Casually, he snatched up a skin, wrenched it open, and left Skaginlef behind for the rest of the day.

Hours came and went, and soon the setting sun cast its dying rays across the Teb. The air had grown cold, though Einarr felt none of it. There was only a comforting warmth coursing throughout his body, one which took away his sorrows. However, it left in its place a ravenous appetite, a reminder that he had not eaten in a day or more.

Einarr doubled over and groaned as hunger pains set in, and fought a violent urge to vomit. To his surprise, the ground was layered with an ever-thickening blanket of mist, rising up from below like spirits from the grave. A creeping chill prickled his skin and stiffened the hairs on the back of his neck.

The woods around Skaginlef became more ominous, though Einarr could not sense anything malevolent. It was as if a dream was taking hold of his mind, filling him with fear and uncertainty. He exhaled a cloud of wispy steam, realizing in his drunkenness that there were no terrors lurking in the darkness, at least none which could be seen.

As he turned and started for home, he noticed something from the corner of his eye. It was faint at first, perhaps merely the reflection of moonlight off the Teb. It was a white, hazy thing, which strangely enough appeared to move further into his view. Einarr Rolffson turned, brushed his long brown hair behind his ears, and nearly jumped out of his skin at the sight of her. She was garbed in a faded white gown, standing alone in the fog.

GARETH

THE HORSE REARED AND WHINNIED AS IT WAS BROUGHT TO A HALT, A haze of dust drifting in its wake. In an instant it wheeled about, breaking into a gallop in a sudden flash, its hooves rumbling over the parched earth. Clouds of sandy dirt kicked up behind the beast as it thundered forward with explosive speed. Horse and rider hurdled toward a mounted training dummy like an avalanche, a sharpened lance striking true at the center of the target. A plume of splinters erupted and showered into the air, the dummy rattling and clattering as it fell onto the ground.

"Well struck!" Sir Edmund Thomas said, clapping.

The steed grunted and shook its head as Gareth Bethard removed his helmet, a satisfied grin adorning his newly bearded face. He slid from the saddle, his sabatons landing with a crunch.

"It gets easier every time." Gareth walked over to the dummy to survey his handiwork.

"I think we found something you truly excel at. You may even be a better horseman than I am! Well, you *may*…"

"I don't exactly have a lifetime to master this," Gareth said curtly. "Spring is upon us, and soon the northmen will be on the march."

Edmund cocked his head curiously. "If I'm hearing you correctly, then…"

There was a fierce determination deep within Gareth's heart, one which he struggled to articulate. He looked at Sir Edmund with what could only be described as hatred, which burned deep in his eyes. "You heard me right. I'm not going to sit idly by while a horde of murderous savages and Ridley Vakaro fight one another for control of Betanthia and its destiny. No, not if I have anything to say about it."

Sir Edmund was clearly conflicted. On one hand, he was proud to have groomed Gareth into a proper warrior, but on the other, he was deeply concerned. "Are you sure that's wise? I understand your desire to protect what's yours, but—"

"But what?" he interrupted. "If I don't do something, if I don't show that I'm capable of fighting for my kingdom, then I'm doomed. The vultures are already circling, Edmund. I know you can see it as plainly as I do."

He motioned for a servant to bring water, then drank it down with a mighty thirst. Gareth retired from the training yard, his friend and mentor following close behind. Another servant assisted with removing his armor as they walked.

"Speaking of vultures, some news came to my attention just this morning," Edmund said.

"And you didn't think to tell me immediately?"

"I didn't want to interrupt your training, or fill your head with too many distractions. But I've received news of Lord Vakaro. It seems he's gathered a number of lesser lords under his dominion and summoned them to Bentmont. The information I'm getting is that he plans to coordinate a counteroffensive alongside the High Marshal of the Order."

Merely hearing mention of the Blackthorn made Gareth's heart sink. Memories of Madelyn Everly were cancerous, and only recently was he able to excise his wounds. It took time to accept that she was gone, and now all that remained was a festering hatred.

"Is there any word on when he plans to march?" Gareth asked, his mouth twisting.

Edmund scratched his chin, then dismissed the servant with a wave of his hand. "No, not yet. I would suspect it would still be a few months, since mustering an army requires a lot of time and effort. And, he still has to determine the whereabouts of the northern horde. With Morden gone, they have free rein to strike anywhere. They could come straight at us from the southeast, skirting the Plainhold. Or, they could shift hard east, then descend from the north. There's no telling what they might do."

Together they made their way past the barracks and to the doors of the Westwind Citadel. Trees throughout the courtyard were budding with thousands of tiny leaves, signaling the return of spring. Servants were scurrying about tending to the flowers and shrubs, and cleaning debris out of the stone fountain at its center. Life was returning to the palace, though it was sad to know the patriarch of House Bethard was still locked inside, slowly wasting what remained of his own. Gareth tried not to think of it too often, especially now, with everything that was transpiring.

"I would like to sit down with you and discuss this more in detail," Gareth said, "so nothing happens here while I'm away. I'm going west, Edmund, and nothing anyone says can change that."

"Aye, a discussion would be a sound idea. But I'm going with you, I hope you're aware."

Gareth stopped and shot his friend a sour glare. "No, I need you here to make sure the Citadel is safe from usurpers. Leave it up to Aldred to pull off a coup while I'm away."

"I have reliable men I can count on. There's no chance in hell I'm going to allow you, the future of House Bethard, to ride off to war without me by your side. Future king or not, you're just going to have to deal with it."

The Guardsman's face was deadly serious. It was a look Gareth knew all too well, and it would be a fool's errand to press the issue any further.

"Very well. I assume it won't be just the two of us going, am I correct?"

"That you are," Edmund replied. "I can't bring all of my men with me, as we're sworn to protect the palace, but I can bring a few along. I have a friend about a day's ride south of here, and he can gather a small force to bring with us. We'll serve as your personal bodyguard."

"Very well. Send word to your man at once, I want no delay in our departure."

"As you wish, I'll have him at the Citadel immediately."

"No," Gareth interrupted. "We can't risk being seen by Aldred, or those under his influence. Who knows how many eyes he has inside the palace. And I don't want Lord Vakaro knowing we're up to something. Have your man meet us somewhere more discreet."

"A sound idea." Edmund smiled. "And, if it's discreet you're looking for, then the docks are about the best place you're going to find. The busier it is, the easier to blend in."

The guards outside the great hall stiffened their backs and saluted as Gareth and Edmund entered. They were greeted by a strong yet pleasant scent of sandalwood and lavender, and the unpleasant approach of Lord Morgan Lawson.

"A good morning to you, my prince!" the fat lord simpered. "I trust you are well?"

"As well as one can be, given the circumstances. Tell me, Lord Lawson, what brings you to the Citadel? I've heard nothing about any upcoming council meetings."

"There are no meetings on the schedule, my prince, but I was hoping to discuss certain… um, contingencies in the unlikely event something were to happen to Lord Vakaro or yourself on the battlefield."

Gareth was nearly stopped in his tracks. How could anyone know of his intention to ride west and join the war effort, let alone a loathsome creature like Morgan Lawson? Something smelled foul.

"And tell me, my lord, how can you assume I'm going anywhere?"

"I've heard rumor, my prince. Word has it, you've been training diligently these last several months, and one can only assume you have intentions of putting your newly acquired skills to use."

Gareth looked at Sir Edmund, who pursed his lips and shrugged. Someone was informing on his movements, and if Lord Lawson was in the know, undoubtedly so was Lord Vakaro.

I know Edmund would never betray me. But can he be so sure the men under his command are trustworthy? Something is amiss, and I intend to get to the bottom of it.

"Rumors, and nothing more," he said curtly. "Sir Edmund will attest to the fact that he has been training me since before either of us were aware of the barbarian invasion. And after the loss of my dear friend Madelyn, I've needed the distraction."

"Ah, yes. I do understand, my prince. All of Betanthia mourns for Commander Everly and her knights. They were true heroes of the Kingdom. Em… my apologies for the interruption. Perhaps we can discuss matters further in private?"

The fat lord dabbed a linen cloth against his moistened forehead, then gave a bow and retired. Edmund and Gareth were left staring at one another incredulously.

"Did that really just happen?" he asked, turning back to the front doors. "How is he aware of our activities?"

"Someone's been keeping an eye on us, no doubt," Edmund said, scowling. "Someone who stands to gain from knowing your whereabouts. I don't like it, not one bit. I would certainly hope it isn't one of my men, but I fear a proper investigation would require more resources than we can afford."

"Who else might it be, if not a Guardsman?" Gareth scratched his hairy jawline. Together, the two men made their way back outside and strode to the center of the courtyard. Prying eyes might see them talking, but none could venture close enough to hear their words without being discovered.

"I would start with the most obvious candidates, then go from there. I wouldn't imagine Aldred is the one, he's far too old to be skulking around the hedges. No, I suspect we might start with Sir Tristan. He's been closer to you since autumn, and there isn't a soul around that doesn't know of his loose tongue."

Perhaps… Gareth pondered. *Bold of him to try and manipulate me while I'm in the process of manipulating him.*

He peered over one shoulder, then discreetly over the other. There was no servant or Guardsman in sight. "It certainly seems plausible. I wouldn't put it past Aldred to offer Sir Tristan all the incentives he would require to keep tabs on me. My only fear is what would happen if Aldred decides he's had enough of me."

"Well, you leave that to me. I take responsibility for this. I should never have been so lax with your security as to allow an eavesdropper to inform on your movements. I know a few men with certain clandestine skills which I could put to good use. If they see anyone poking around your business, we'll hear of it."

"Good," Gareth sighed. "In the meantime, I think perhaps a test of loyalty is in order for Sir Tristan. I'll need to think more on the matter, but not now. I'm exhausted from training. Go and arrange the meeting with your man, I'm in need of a nap."

Edmund nodded and dismissed himself, leaving Gareth to return to the confines of the Citadel. Setting foot inside the great hall felt as if it were a stranger's residence, and not the place he grew up in. There could very well be unfriendly eyes around every corner, each servant and Guardsman a potential spy. He cast each one a suspicious eye in passing, and quickly retreated to his chamber.

After wiping himself down with a wet cloth, Gareth laid down for an hour of rest. Rising heat from the afternoon sun soon woke him, a thick blanket of perspiration coating his body. Such a brief slumber did little to combat his exhaustion from training, but the chamber was growing insufferably hot by the minute. He spent the remainder of his day outside in the gardens, walking through maze-like hedges and thinking hard on the days and weeks ahead.

Every thought seemed to drift back to Madelyn, and the hatred brewing inside his heart. Though Ridley Vakaro was the closest and most immediate threat, Gareth would have liked nothing more than to have at Damien Dreadfire with every ounce of force Betanthia could muster.

I would kill him and every last savage with my bare hands if it meant she could return to me. Heavens, do I miss you...

There was a time and a place for vengeance, but now was neither. No, he thought, it would do little good to avenge Madelyn if it meant sacrificing the dynasty she died to protect. He had to deal with the threat closest to him, and quickly. But after arriving at his favorite alcove, old, uninvited memories began creeping back.

It seemed like an eternity had passed since Gareth laid on the alcove's wooden bench, drowning in bourbon and sorrow. He understood now why such pain was necessary, as it was the catalyst for every change he had made throughout the past year. It was nearly impossible to recognize the shell of a man he used to be, someone who was prepared to end it all to be free of his torment. But such isolation and misery turned out to be a gift in the end, something he would forever be grateful for.

Before long, the day had come to an end. Darkness descended over Cardale, and soon Gareth returned to his chamber reluctantly. Having missed supper, he instead instructed a servant to bring food and drink to his room. It was surprisingly pleasant to eat alone and enjoy the company of no one. After finishing the last swallow of a hearty beer, he turned in for a few hours of rest.

The next morning, a folded piece of parchment lay on the floor, a foot away from the door. Gareth shot out of bed as if it were ablaze, rushing over to grab the message and scratch off its waxy seal. He read the brief contents of the letter several times over, exhaling desperately each time. Plans had been set into motion, plans which could not be undone. It was now or never.

It's time. You know where to find me. -E

Gareth dressed in a set of modest clothes, a plain brown tunic and trousers, which he often wore when walking among the commoners. A sheathed dirk rested on his hip, and would be his only protection from Cardale's denizens. Though now, more than any other time in his life, he knew how to handle a blade.

Knowing there were potentially unfriendly eyes around every corner, he decided to leave through one of the Citadel's rear entrances. He preferred to use the stables whenever discretion was required, as the servants assigned there were absent after the morning feeding. With the aid of a hooded cloak, Gareth walked past stall after stall, until reaching the outer edge of the gardens. From there, he would make his way toward the barracks, tall shrubs and the Citadel's protective wall obscuring every movement.

Passing through the gatehouse was simple enough, and Edmund made certain to station his most trusted men at the checkpoint. It would be disturbing beyond belief if any of them were to inform on his movements, as it would mean the Royal Guardsmen were compromised at the highest levels.

But every plot must be rooted out one piece at a time, he supposed. None of the men gave any acknowledgement as Gareth strode out onto Auburn Row, nor did they give pursuit. As he shuffled through throngs of commoners, he paid especially close attention to those behind him. Thankfully, no one paid the slightest bit of attention, and he was able to move about freely without being accosted. Before long, an old, familiar scent from the docks greeted him like a long lost friend.

It seemed like only yesterday when Gareth last traveled down Crown Ferry Road. He had done so a million times before, yet everything about it felt different now. Gone were the days when he would stumble to the Hollow Stone and back, drinking away his despair until it returned, seemingly doomed to an endless downward spiral of suffering. It was difficult to imagine himself a year ago, or two, or even ten. If he had somehow happened to pass his younger self on the street, it would be nearly impossible to recognize the person in front of him.

There was one figure he did recognize, however. Sir Edmund Thomas was standing at the corner of an intersection where they would often summon transport back to the Citadel, when their drinking had become excessive. The elder Guardsmen said nothing, and made certain to trade only a brief glance in acknowledgment. Gareth moved toward him casually, pretending as though they were little more than strangers. After closing the distance, both men continued onward to the docks.

"He'll meet us here shortly," Edmund said softly, glancing over his shoulder. "More of a formality than anything else. He's reliable, and trustworthy."

"Good. Reliable and trustworthy may soon become currency, it'll be so rare. I have more faith in the northmen than I do Lord Vakaro; at least savages are honest with their intentions."

"An astute observation. But worry not, we'll put an end to both threats in good time."

A tall sailing ship arrived at port, floating gently to the dock before coming to a halt. Its mast was large and towered over the surrounding rooftops, its white sails nearly furled. A strong scent of salt and fish lingered heavy in the air, a pungent yet unmistakable smell Gareth had nearly forgotten. He wandered past one market stall after another, Sir Edmund at his side, eyeing the diverse wares of potters, blacksmiths, and trinket peddlers.

In short order, the faded wooden sign of the Hollow Stone came into sight. Old memories and emotions came drifting back, though most were unpleasant. Gareth's heart began to beat quicker, his brow moistening with perspiration. This was not a happy place, but it was one he knew could be trusted. Upon entering, his nostrils were reminded of the smell of must, his favorite spirits, and the old beer stained floors.

The tavern was more lively than he remembered, but the clientele had changed little. Four men sat at the bar, their elbows resting on its worn, discolored surface. A dozen other patrons sat throughout the room, some eating a fresh meal in peace, while others conversed and laughed among themselves.

"There." Edmund pointed. A man standing near the far corner of the room looked every bit as lordly as one might expect; middle-aged, distinguished, hair beginning to gray and thin, and well-clothed. A golden signet ring adorned his left hand, his right grasping the handle of a tankard.

He's early. And apparently not one for discretion…

The man took notice and made to raise his hand, but thought better of it. Instead, he sipped from his tankard and waited until Edmund was ready to call him over. Together, Gareth and the elder Guardsman sat at a table against the wall, carefully sizing up the rest of the room. After several minutes had passed and no threat presented itself, the two men lowered their guard, ever so slightly.

"Care for a drink?" Edmund asked, his old, mischievous grin emerging once again.

Gareth felt bile forming in the back of his throat. "No, I need to keep my head clear. You're welcome to."

"Fair enough, but keep this in mind; where we're going, there's a real possibility we may never come back. We might not get the opportunity to tip one in this place ever again."

For all his anger and determination, Gareth had scarcely considered such things. This was war, after all, and it had nearly claimed his father's life many years ago. Despite all of his best efforts, training, and well-crafted plans, he could very well be returning to Cardale on the bed of a wagon as Marcellus did, or perhaps not at all.

"You're right," he conceded. "A drink it is. But just one, for old times' sake."

"The usual?" Sir Edmund reached into his coin purse, licking his lips at the thought of the Stone's tasty house whiskey.

"You can, if you please. I think I would prefer an ale. It's been ages since I've had one."

"Ale is a proper soldier's drink! Very well. In fact, I think I'll have one too. Nothing wrong with a little variety in your life, I suppose." He motioned for the barkeep, who remembered their old routine well.

"Yes, Sir. Same as always?"

"No, not today," Edmund placed a pair of coins into the barkeep's hand. "Two ales, if you wouldn't mind. The best you have."

"I have just the thing!" The man grinned and hurried back behind the bar, fetching two tankards and filling them to overflowing from a large wooden cask. He brought the frothing vessels back to the table with lightning quickness.

Somberly, prince and protector tapped their tankards together and drank, neither breaking eye contact. The first mouthful was absolutely divine, and Gareth felt a pleasant and familiar warmth building inside his gut. While the ale was delicious, he could also taste fear and anticipation, the most bitter taste of them all.

He's right. This could be the last time we set foot in this place, one or both of us. I pray that isn't the case.

"Now," Edmund said, setting his tankard down. "Allow me to introduce you to Lord Kenfield." He motioned to the man standing in the corner, who had been staring at them conspicuously the entire time. He made his way to the table and slid a nearby chair next to it.

"My prince," the lord said softly, giving only the most modest of nods. "It's an honor to meet you. My name is Lord Anderton Kenfield.

My friends call me Anders. Sir Edmund has informed me of the situation, and I want to assure you, I am eternally loyal to House Bethard. My family has been faithful to yours for five hundred years, and I look forward to carrying on that tradition. I would fall on my sword this instant if you commanded it."

"Best not, I'm in need of every loyal man I can find," Gareth said. "I trust he's told you of our intention to ride west and join the war effort?"

"Indeed he has, my prince. My estate is less extravagant than most, but I command fifty of the best men you'll find anywhere. I took the liberty of bringing them with me, as I was unsure when you wished to depart. They're camped just outside the city walls, and ready to ride at your earliest convenience."

The man's diligence was impressive. Gareth pursed his lips and nodded in approval. "You have my thanks, and your rewards will be plentiful. There is another matter at hand that requires a more… nuanced approach. A certain lord in a high position of power apparently has aspirations far beyond his station. I believe him to be just as great of a threat as the northmen, perhaps even moreso."

Edmund took another long drink from his tankard. "We need to get our people close, as close to his inner circle as possible. We need to know what he's discussing and with who, and what his true intentions are. Can't go and arrest a man of his stature without solid evidence, not when he controls so many of our soldiers."

"You wouldn't happen to be talking about Lord Vakaro, would you?" There was a certain discomfort written across Lord Kenfield's face, as if merely speaking the man's name brought with it supernatural consequences.

"Indeed," Edmund replied.

"Have you heard anything about him recently?" Gareth interjected. "Any rumors or suspicious activities? Any sort of information could be useful."

It was sometimes said that rumors from the south tended to waft north like stink off a corpse, though thus far, the stench of treachery went undetected. Anders shook his head.

"No, my prince, unfortunately I have heard nothing. The south is a fickle place, as I'm sure you're aware. People there tend to be close-lipped, so I'm uncertain we'll be able to learn much."

"It's also my understanding that loyalties in the south tend to be quite firm, but not necessarily towards Cardale." Gareth shifted in his seat.

"Correct." Anders nodded. "Lordlings and their households are, I suspect, more likely to side with their lord over anyone, especially a lord like Ridley Vakaro. So, to your point, Edmund, I'm uncertain if we'll be able to slip a man into his inner circle. We may have to resort to more clever means of infiltration if we're to learn anything of importance."

"Nothing's impossible." Edmund shrugged. "My lads can make any-thing happen, though timing might be an issue. It might be relatively calm now, but once the army marches, things around us will begin moving exponentially faster. We'll have to be on high alert when it comes time for battle, and not necessarily for northmen."

"The fog of war does create certain… opportunities, I suppose," Anders said, glancing over his shoulder. "But perhaps we can continue this conversation later, in a less… public venue?"

Perhaps if Lord Kenfield had dressed in a less flamboyant manner, they could have remained a while longer, Gareth supposed. But with the times so uncertain, it was best to tread cautiously. The elder Guardsman nodded his head in agreement, looking to his prince for orders.

"Very well." Gareth downed the last of his drink. "Edmund and I will return to the Citadel and make our final preparations. We'll meet you outside the city before nightfall, Lord Kenfield. We've got to get the jump on this conspiracy before it gets the jump on us."

CHARLOTTE II

THE RIDE TO CARDALE FELT AS IF IT HAD LASTED FOR A LIFETIME OR more. With each mile, Charlotte Bethard began to feel old anxieties building within her again, familiar ghosts she thought to have vanquished. But there was another feeling as well, swelling and rising like the tide; determination.

The royal convoy traveled at a brisk pace, arriving at Cardale's outer wall in two days' time. Hot and humid air was growing more oppressive by the hour, but it was a welcome relief from the brisk and sometimes frigid Dellhaven weather. A breeze from the east carried with it a familiar scent of salt, seaweed, and rotten fish. Pollen from native trees and tall grasses made her sniffle.

Soon, crenellations of the massive wall came into sight, and not long after, the northern gate. One of the Guardsmen broke formation and rode ahead to announce Charlotte's return. Poking her head out of the carriage window, she saw a pair of guards scurry inside to alert the city watch.

"How does it feel to be back home?" Emilee Harper asked, taking notice of the Queen's fidgeting.

"To tell you the truth Emilee, I never thought I would see this place again," Charlotte said. "But this is something I need to do. I need to make peace with my past before I can move on and heal."

"What will you do, my queen?"

It was a question she had asked herself for days, one which she almost feared to answer. What would she do? Aside from gathering her most precious possessions, she had thought of little else, save for how Marcellus might react if he discovered she was back home.

We shall see…

Cityfolk were beginning to congregate as her carriage rolled through the large outer gate. A patrol of city watchmen arrived hastily and lined either side of the street, pushing back any commoner who ventured too close. The atmosphere was electric, much the same as the day she departed for Dellhaven.

"Make way for the queen!" a senior watchman shouted, his hand gripped tightly around the shaft of a spear.

Joyful shouts rang out from those who had gathered to see her home, some waving and others pointing, their children fascinated by the spectacle. Basking in the love of the people was comforting, and an experience from which she would never tire. She suddenly thought of Gareth, and how he rode alongside her carriage the day they left, and became overjoyed at the thought of seeing him again.

I wonder if he's been well, and how his time on the council has been? It feels like ages since we've seen one another.

Soon the looming majesty of the Westwind Citadel came into view, giving her heart a flutter. Though Charlotte would be within her right to turn around and head back to Dellhaven, she knew that now was a time to be strong, and to put her newfound courage to the test.

"You can do this, my queen," Emilee said, taking her by the hand.

Charlotte felt herself trembling every so slightly, and gave the servant girl's hand a gentle squeeze and smiled. "What would I ever do without you?"

When they entered the gates of the Citadel, the Queen was received by a large host of Royal Guardsmen, all standing at attention on both sides of the courtyard. She made certain to look for the familiar silvery hair of Sir Edmund Thomas, because wherever he was, Gareth was not far away. But to her disappointment, the elder Guardsman was absent. She was instead greeted by another senior officer, clad in a shining steel breastplate, pauldrons, gauntlets, and greaves. He opened the carriage door as a pair of servants placed a wooden stepping stool on the ground, their heads lowered in respect.

"Welcome home, my queen. The Citadel has missed your presence," the guard said, bowing.

It was a sentiment she wished she could share. "Thank you. Have you seen my son? Is he here?"

"No, Your Majesty, I haven't seen him since this morning. I suspect he isn't far, he's been training rigorously with Sir Edmund since his return."

Impressive! Charlotte thought while stepping out of the carriage. *I'm so happy to hear he's healthy and well.*

She might have stood in the courtyard for an hour or more, were it not for the throngs of Guardsmen and waiting servants. Confident though she was, the Citadel had a way of making her feel small and afraid. But for the first time in what felt like eons, she was strong. The palace doors were opened and awaiting her. Determined, albeit cautiously, she strode inside.

The great hall was undoubtedly just as beautiful as she remembered, but something about it felt different, like a distant memory from a time long passed. Despite the hall bustling with activity, it seemed as if there was not a soul to be found for a thousand miles. Charlotte glanced over at the grand staircase and swallowed hard, trying to keep her heart from jumping out of her mouth.

You can do this, Charlotte. You must.

With a flick of her wrist, she dismissed Emilee and the Guardsmen and carefully ascended the stairs one at a time, her pace slow yet deliberate. There seemed to be ten million steps before her, endlessly climbing into the heavens with seemingly no end in sight. Each one felt more exhausting to climb than the last, until finally she arrived on the floor where the royal suites resided.

The hall to her chamber was empty and quiet as a tomb. Charlotte continued on with great apprehension, like a soldier returning to the site of a bloody battle many years later. It was surreal and terrifying, and extremely difficult to believe this had ever been her reality. She paused outside the shut door to her chamber, her fingers stroking its aged and worn latch, as if to remind herself that this was, in fact, not a dream.

She opened the door slowly and looked around. Her room was the same as it had been left; it was tidy and filled with belongings and small treasures. The window was open slightly, allowing fresh air and afternoon sunlight inside. It was difficult to believe that at one point, she had contemplated throwing herself out of that very window and forever putting an end to her misery.

This place used to be my prison, but it can't hold me any longer, she thought, looking at the room as if it were some adversary in the flesh. "You did not defeat me, and you never will," she said aloud, her defiance growing. "I'm free of your shackles. I'm free now… I'm free."

"My queen?" Emilee asked, giving her a startle. "I'm so sorry to bother you…"

"It's quite alright," she said, taking a quick breath and exhaling deeply. "I'm happy you're here. I'd like you to gather all of my things and bring them back with us to Dellhaven. Summon a few of the servants to help you. I want all of my clothes, jewelry, and all of the keepsakes my children have given me. Leave nothing behind."

The few possessions she had were small joys, all of which had been sorely missed. Emilee curtsied and set off dutifully to gather the other servants. But there was something else weighing on her mind, hard as she tried to block it out. The King was just down the hall.

Any true catharsis would be impossible without a confrontation. Not that she wished to instigate a fight, not by any means, but Marcellus would have to be told of her intentions nevertheless. And besides, speaking her mind and ridding it of years of oppression was something she was owed. After all, he was graced with three children, and tended to by a faithful wife for decades.

Whether he listens or not, he's going to bear witness to what I have to say. I have to… for me.

As Charlotte approached the King's chamber, she began to tremble, a great, chaotic battle taking place inside her heart and mind. But something drove her forward, as if guided by an unseen hand. Surreal as it felt, there seemed to be a force greater than herself propelling her onward. Charlotte approached Marcellus' chamber, a pair of armed Guardsmen posted outside of it.

"My queen," one of the men said, each of them bowing at the waist then snapping back to attention. "I must caution you about entering, the King has become more erratic since you have been away."

"Open the door, please," she said politely. "And I would like for both of you to accompany me. I will not have my husband put his hands on me, not today, and not ever. If he steps out of line, you have my permission to deal with him appropriately."

"But, my queen—"

"No," Charlotte interrupted. "King or not, you will keep me safe from harm. I am the Queen of Betanthia. If you will not, then perhaps I will summon my son and Sir Edmund instead?"

Not like Marcellus will remember anything I have to say to him, or that I was even here in the first place.

"Very well, my queen. As you wish."

The door to the King's chamber opened, and Charlotte's nostrils were affronted by an old, stale, and familiar stench. The drapes were drawn shut as they always were, and she saw in the darkness a wasteland of utter filth and ruin which lay scattered about the floor. Discarded clothes, tankards, papers, and refuse lay in piles from one end to another.

Sitting in the corner, shrouded by shadows, was her husband. His frame was hunched and diminished, and in the darkness it was unclear if he was even alive at all. Charlotte moved delicately to the center of the room, looking over one shoulder to make certain the Guardsmen were following close behind.

"Marcellus," the Queen said, mustering all the strength inside her. "I have been away for a while now, and in that time I have done a great deal of soul searching. There was a time, once, when I loved you very deeply, and you were everything I could have asked for in a husband. But over the years you have turned into someone I do not recognize. I place no blame on you for your injury. We are all fortunate and grateful you survived. I shudder to think what would have happened to Betanthia if you would have fallen on the battlefield."

The King sat motionless, a hand clenched around a tankard on a table, his head drooped and gaze averted to the floor. It was unclear if he was even listening, but Charlotte knew she had to say what was in her heart. There would be no other opportunity to make peace with her past.

"I cannot continue to live my life like this, seeing you wither away with each passing day. I cannot subject myself to your cruelty, Marcellus. I cannot and I will not. My life is my own to live, and I have to be around for our children as long as possible. With you absent, I am all they have left."

Still, Marcellus Bethard sat idle, only a soft motion of his chest giving any sign that he was even alive. Charlotte considered peeling open a drape and letting light into the room, but doing so might only incite his wrath.

"By right and by law, I am still the queen, and your wife. Only death may separate us. But I have come back here to tell you that I am leaving you. Do you hear me, Marcellus? I will no longer stay in this prison. I am leaving, and I intend on spending the rest of my days living for my children and for myself. This is the last time you will ever see me."

Marcellus let out a deep sigh, a sign he was indeed listening. But whether or not his frail mind could comprehend Charlotte's words was anyone's guess. His gaze seemed to fall further, as if the weight of his shame was pressing down on him.

"I have said what I came here to say, and nothing is going to change my mind." She lifted her chin. "Please, if you have any love for me left in your heart, then I ask that you do not pursue me. If there is any trace of the man I married left inside you, then you will let me live the rest of my life in happiness. I hope, in time, you can become more like the man I swore myself to that day on the beach. But until then, I must say goodbye."

Charlotte was fighting back tears, both of sorrow but also of liberation. She took a step backward and made for the door, fully expecting Marcellus to explode with rage and storm after her. But he made no move in opposition.

"Goodbye, Marcellus."

And with that, she turned and entered the hall without so much as looking back. The Guardsmen followed closely behind, and it was not until she heard the sound of the door shutting that she was able to breathe a sigh of relief.

I did it… I actually did it…

Reality had not set in until she passed by her chamber once again. Emilee and the servants were busy gathering her things and storing them inside large, wooden trunks. She smiled, then laughed, then nearly cried tears of joy over what she had just accomplished.

She descended the grand staircase and immediately saw Gareth and Sir Edmund walking briskly across the great hall. Her heart felt as if it had stopped for a moment as she looked upon her son with pride.

"Gareth!" she called out, her voice echoing throughout the cavernous room.

The prince turned and stood in disbelief for a moment. Charlotte felt slightly guilty for not sending word of her arrival first, but it was fun enough to surprise him.

"Mother!" his shock quickly turned to happiness. He broke from Sir Edmund's side and trotted over, and they shared a long and loving embrace. "What are you doing here? I thought you'd never want to leave Dellhaven ever again! Is everything alright?"

"It is, it most certainly is. I came back to make peace with my past, and find closure. I just spoke with your father, and made my position perfectly clear. He knows now that I plan to leave for good."

Gareth's eyes grew as wide as wagon wheels. "You… you spoke to him? Alone?"

"No, the guards were with me to make certain of my safety, but your father said nothing. I wonder if he even heard me, or if his mind is still lost out there, wandering the Plainhold and the northern forests until his time comes to an end. But enough about me, how have you been? You look so healthy!"

From the looks of it, she was standing before a younger version of Marcellus himself. Gareth had grown a beard, though neatly cropped. His hair fell just past his shoulders, and was neatly put half-up. But perhaps the most noticeable change was his body; no longer was he the skinny boy she remembered, he was a man with arms as thick as tree branches, and a chest so developed his doublet strained to contain it.

"I've been at my training every morning, sometimes twice a day."

"Well, more like twice a day, and sometimes thrice!" Sir Edmund chimed in, smiling. As he approached, he bowed and offered his respects to the queen. "Your Majesty."

"How exciting!" Charlotte clasped her hands together. "I could not be more proud of you!"

"Mother," Gareth said, his face becoming somewhat grim. "Can we walk, perhaps through the gardens?"

Something seemed amiss, but Charlotte agreed without question. Gareth extended his arm and together they left the great hall, Sir Edmund mindful to keep his distance.

Servants were diligently tending to the grounds, scurrying about like worker ants. Some prepared flower beds for spring planting, while others began tilling soil and preparing it for a host of herbs and other delicious delicacies. Life was quickly returning to the palace. Gareth and Charlotte entered the gardens, and began traversing the maze-like hedges.

"So, what is it you wish to say to me?" she asked.

"I don't wish to alarm you, mother, but time grows short. I'll be as direct as I can. For the past year, our frontier at Castle Morden has been under attack from northmen. I'll spare you the unpleasant details, but… Commandant Valens and his field army were destroyed, and the castle sacked."

Charlotte gasped, stammering to find words. How could Betanthia be under invasion for the past year without so much as a word of it being mentioned to her? It felt like a deep betrayal, worse than Marcellus' nightly infidelities.

"How?" she asked, a slight tremble in her voice. "How could such a thing happen? I don't understand!"

"I came to learn of it after the invasion was well underway. I didn't wish to trouble you with such news, given everything you were going through. Aldred and the high council thought our western army would be enough to crush the invasion, but it appears they have vastly underestimated our enemies."

It was terrifying news, so fantastical she had difficulty believing it. Or, perhaps she refused to. But as her fear began to subside and the reality of the situation set in, the wheels in her mind began to turn. "Is there any plan to deal with this invasion?"

Sir Edmund could no longer keep his distance, nor hold his tongue. He strode over, the rings of his mail chiming against his steel breastplate with each step. "There is, my queen. Lord Vakaro has been dispatched to Bentmont and is rallying a large army there. The Blackthorn are mustering their full might as well. Gareth and I—"

The prince shot Sir Edmund a fiery glare, which Charlotte took notice of.

"Gareth!" she gasped. "Tell me you're not…" The words were almost too difficult to speak.

"Yes, mother. I'm going to ride west and join the war effort. This is something I have to do, for our family and our kingdom. I've trained as hard as I can, and Sir Edmund has taught me everything he knows. I'll be safe, and we won't be riding alone."

"No," Charlotte protested, tears forming in her eyes. "No, I cannot risk you. I cannot have what happened to your father happen to you, or worse. Don't go. Please, I beg of you. I forbid it!"

Gareth took hold of her hand. "This is what I was born to do, mother. This is an opportunity to prove myself not only to the lords, but to our people. This is my destiny, I know that now. I know you're worried about me, and I don't expect you not to. But please, this is my moment. Don't take it away from me."

It was bittersweet to look upon her baby boy. He was a grown man now, and a warrior in his own right. Despite her reservations, it seemed supremely unjust to keep him safe behind tall walls, especially when the Kingdom would soon be his by right.

"I won't be leaving his side, my queen," Sir Edmund stated. "We'll be stationed far from the front lines alongside Lord Vakaro, where the danger is the least. We won't be leading any charges, I can assure you."

It was a lie, of course. Charlotte was no fool, and knew if Gareth had the courage to ride off to war, there was certainly no chance he would remain out of the fight.

"I know nothing I say is going to change your mind, Gareth. I have only one command for you, one which you *will* obey," she said with stern determination. "Come home, and in one piece."

"I will, mother. I will leave Cardale a prince, and return a king."

With watery eyes, she gave a forlorn smile and nodded. A thought then emerged, and she remembered what Gareth had told her about the war. Aldred and the high council had remained silent, and chose to keep House Bethard uninformed about such matters. Charlotte knew that if her son was going to be protecting the realm from external threats, she would have to help protect it from internal threats.

"Sir Edmund," she called out. The elder Guardsman turned, and bowed. "Before you leave, there is one final thing I require of you."

"Yes, my queen," he said obediently. "Anything you desire."

"Send a group of your best men and fetch Lord Aldred, and bring him to me at once. He owes me answers."

LUCETTA II

A S SHE LOOKED UPON THE OUTER WALLS OF DELLHAVEN, AN unsettling feeling came over her. Lucetta had barely slept, if at all, since leaving the family estate, terrified at the prospect of being discovered. What she had done, or rather, what she had ordered Pavlos to do, was not nearly as thrilling as the day Sir Bryce Whitewood met his demise. Bile crept into the back of her throat at the thought of it.

Just as she began to nod off, her carriage arrived at the southern gate. The guards stationed there had come to expect her comings and goings as of late, or at least that was how it appeared. One of the men craned his neck to get a glimpse through the window, but Lucetta quickly recoiled. She felt a sharp pang of terror erupt from inside her body, fearful that perhaps word of the massacre had already reached Cardale.

Satisfied, the guards waved her driver through, and the carriage lumbered onward without further challenge. Lucetta gasped for air, unaware she had been holding her breath, relieved the encounter had ended.

"Be calm," the woman in black said, sitting cross-legged, opposite of her. "Everything is going precisely as planned."

It was a relief to hear the entity's reassurances, but Lucetta was not quite sold. She sat, picking at a large, red sore on the top of her wrist, the skin cracking and weeping blood. Her scratching worsened as the chateau came into sight, her breathing becoming quicker and more frantic.

None of the servants turned out for her arrival, though it was early and many of them were likely occupied with their morning duties. It was of little consequence, as she preferred to do without all of the pomp and ceremony, as was customary with her arrival. As the carriage came to a halt, she exited hastily, stepping out into a cool rush of air without any assistance. Discreetly, she began making her way inside, eager to avoid alerting anyone to her presence.

"My princess!" Devin Brandybrook exclaimed. "Welcome, and good morning to you!"

Lucetta cringed. *That damned man is everywhere. I'll wager he's been following me, or has sent men to follow me. He knows. He always knows.*

"And a good morning to you," she said as politely as possible.

"You look weary from travel. Breakfast is about to be served, if I could interest you."

Something treacherous lay underneath Devin's smile, she could sense it. His eyes were piercing and felt as if they could see clean through her, into the inner depths of her mind, where every dark secret from the last year resided.

"Yes, but I'm quite weary. I'm going to rest awhile. Have some food and wine brought to my chamber."

Without waiting for a reply, Lucetta turned and started off toward her quarters. Her heart was racing so fast it was a wonder it had not exploded by now. Even with her back turned, she could still sense Devin's judgemental gaze, peering through her like sunlight through thin morning clouds. When she reached her chamber, she shut the door and began gasping, as if the air itself had vanished.

The woman in black was sitting on the far side of the room, legs crossed, looking at her with a satisfied yet sinister smile. The entity had been her greatest champion, that much could not be disputed, but never in a thousand lifetimes would Lucetta have ever thought she would have found herself here.

"You have done well," the woman said, rising from her seat. She floated to the center of the room on a faint cloud of black mist, obscuring her footfalls. "There are none who suspect you, not that meddlesome servant, nor your mother. The fates are guiding your hand, and will not lead you astray."

"How could that be?" Lucetta protested. "I see the way they stare at me. Devin knows, and my mother is no fool. And if she doesn't know what we've done by now, she will soon enough. Nothing ever gets by her for long. Nothing!"

"You mean, what *you* have done. I am merely your guide. It is you that has undertaken this journey." The woman paused, her attention turned toward a nearby desk. She drifted to the drawers, opened them slowly and retrieved a map from inside. It was the same map Lucetta brought with her from Cardale, the one which outlined her plans for a new queendom.

"I couldn't have gone this far without you," she said, studying the entity curiously. "Tell me what the fates say. Please, I must know. How does this all end?"

The woman in black looked up from the map, smiling, the way a parent would to a child. "It ends with you standing before a massive crowd, reveling before all you have done. Your legacy will live on forever, in both the mouths of kings and commoners alike. History will remember you for all time."

Such words were as sweet as honey, nearly bringing her to tears. "That's all I ever wanted; to be remembered for my works… to leave the world in a better place than I found it."

"Your deeds will live on longer than your name. After all the pages of all the history books have crumbled to dust, after your name has been lost to the ages, what you will accomplish will be remembered for eternity. Generations yet unborn will live and die in the shadow of your labors. Now, take a seat. Your mercenary is at the door."

No more than a second later, there was a soft rapping at the door. Slowly it cracked open, revealing Pavlos' golden smile on the other side. "Princess? I trust I am not disturbing you, yes?"

"No. Please, come in. And shut the door."

The Droethien entered and let the door latch shut behind him. He strode over to a table on the far side of the room and poured a generous serving of wine into a crystal glass. With two mighty gulps, the vessel was nearly empty. He refilled it, almost to the brim.

"What brings you here, Pavlos? Any new information?"

"As a matter of fact, yes, princess. My scouts have searched in all directions around the village. The lands are, how do you say, empty of life."

"Uninhabited, you mean?"

Pavlos nodded. "Yes, uninhabited, that is it. We will find no more trouble from anyone. Perhaps we might bring with us some slaves to clear the land and make ready for your new kingdom, yes?"

"Queendom," Lucetta corrected, her face turning sour. "I do not intend for my new domain to be a slaver realm. I will not suffer to see families torn apart on the auction block. Not under my rule!"

The Droethien pursed his lips and thought. "Then would it not be wise to bring with you all of the slaves you can, and in exchange for their freedom, they work to build your new, as you say, queendom?"

It was a suggestion worthy of giving her pause. Despite being a simple-minded savage, Pavlos had proven surprisingly intelligent. His idea had its merits, and even seemed appealing, in a certain way. She could purchase the entire stock of slaves in Cardale and have them brought north, and would put an end to the practice of ripping child from mother.

"Pavlos, I do believe that is the best idea you've come up with. I think it's wonderful, and those who earn their freedom will be my most loyal subjects. Some of them may even rise to become my new nobility."

Perhaps she was getting a bit carried away, as she recoiled slightly at the thought. But a new aristocracy would have to be built somehow, and who better to do it than those who would owe her their freedom, their very lives?

"Very good, princess. I can have the arrangements made for you, yes?"

"Absolutely." She smiled. "There's also the task of bringing in builders and materials. We'll need to construct roads, houses, and of course, the palace. I pray it will be finished in my lifetime, if there are even any alive who could fulfill such a vision."

"As long as you have coin, princess, they will come. And they will work."

If there was anyone who had the coin for such expenses, it was her brother, Trace. He was doing exceptionally well these days, his profits from banking alone eclipsing all of his other ventures. Perhaps with some cunning, she might be able to siphon off some riches without arousing suspicion.

"I know just where to get it. Come, Pavlos, we must return to Cardale."

"Now? But princess, we have only just arrived!" he protested.

It was true. Leaving mere minutes after arriving would invite unwanted scrutiny. And besides, there was no plan of what to do once the slaves arrived in the north. What would they construct first? Where would they sleep? How would adequate food supplies be maintained? The more Lucetta thought about it, the more she realized how truly unprepared she was.

"I must be getting too far ahead of myself. You're right, Pavlos, which is why I value your company and your council. Perhaps in a day or two. But for now, we mustn't give anyone a reason to suspect us."

"As you say, princess." Pavlos bowed and strutted out of the room with confidence that bordered on arrogance.

Lucetta began to wonder if the Droethien was secretly manipulating her to his own ends, as his suggestions had become greater in number as of late. Perhaps he was even manipulating her for his own ends. It was certainly a possibility, given a Droethien's penchant for dishonesty.

"Are you sure he can be trusted?" she asked the woman in black, who had been watching their exchange from a sofa across the room. "I'm not so certain his ambitions are confined to what he is being paid to do.

"I have seen into the fates. The savage will meet his end one day, as all savages do. But not until he has given you everything you deserve. Trust in this divine plan, and you—"

"It's not that I don't believe you," Lucetta interrupted, much to the entity's surprise. "But… I just get this feeling when I'm around him. I feel as if he takes me for a fool, and is merely using me for my gold and influence. Like it or not, as my power grows, so too does his."

The woman in black stared menacingly, its orange-red eyes glinting with fire. The entity appeared irritated at being challenged, especially after all that had transpired. It stepped forward, its pale, dead skin turning so white and cold it brought with it a sudden chill.

"You continue to doubt me, child? Perhaps I have been wrong. Perhaps you are not the one to see this divine mandate to its conclusion. It would seem Lucetta Eldon is best served sitting behind high walls at her estate, shut out from the outside world while it burns."

"No, no," she stammered, gesturing frantically. "I'm absolutely the one you seek. I'm sorry, I just… I'm not as sure of myself as I know I should be. Please, I beg your forgiveness. Keep your faith in me."

The woman in black studied her curiously, teeth clenched and grinding like stones in a mill. "Then I will require a test of loyalty. At my discretion, you must execute my command faithfully, and see it through until the conclusion. Your lack of resolve is most troubling, but perhaps you can be redeemed."

Lucetta nodded in agreement. "Yes, whatever you say. I'll do anything!"

"Good. For now, go about your business. Worry not about planning your next move. Trust that the path before you has been determined. Everything shall fall neatly into place."

An interrupting knock came at the door, giving Lucetta a fright. She jumped, heart skipping a beat, and struggled to compose herself. The woman in black vanished as a teenage girl stepped into the room, informing her of lunch. Servants throughout the estate had learned to keep their interactions with her short and formal, thankfully enough.

The feast that afternoon was of typical fare; pheasant, boar, fresh fish, vegetables of every color, and wine of only the best vintages. Charlotte sat at her place at the head of the table, Devin Brandybrook and Emilee Harper close by. It was both frustrating and infuriating to see her mother keeping close company with filthy commoners.

Large glass doors inside the dining hall were propped open, a breeze of gentle spring air blowing inside. Scents from the gardens and ocean mixed with an intoxicating aroma from sandalwood incense. It was an otherwise pleasant day, if not for a crushing weight of anxiety building within her. Lucetta scratched at a row of small scabs on her neck, a ripping sensation helping to keep her mind from drifting too far away.

As the first course was served, she took notice of the attentive gaze of Devin, who made it no secret that he was watching. It seemed as if every time Lucetta glanced up from her meal, his eyes were fixated on her, peering, studying, and likely judging.

"Is everything alright, princess?" Devin asked, a coy grin dancing across his face.

Lucetta gave as convincing of a smile as she could, then quickly filled her mouth with a generous helping of fried and salted asparagus. It tasted simply divine, and for a moment, she was genuinely enjoying a proper meal.

"It's good to see you again," Brendon of Theeds said, smiling. "You look well, princess. Your time in Cardale must have done you some good."

It was comforting to hear the servants had not discovered her true whereabouts as of late, but Devin was acting suspicious. He was up to something, she was certain of it. There existed a real possibility that sooner or later, he would have to be dealt with.

"Yes, it has. As a matter of fact, I was considering going back for a few days. I have some business I left unattended."

"But you have only just arrived, princess!" Devin said, surprised. "It must be serious to be off again in such a hurry!"

She needed to come up with a lie, and fast. With all of her stress and uncertainty as of late, Lucetta had thought little about covering her tracks in all aspects. The woman in black appeared behind him, eyes glowing like two distant suns, each erupting with jets of fire. If she was to fail now, the Royal Guardsmen would be the least of her worries. Her mother would have her swinging from a rope for treason.

"I plan to finish a project I began last year, a new estate, if you care to know. There are some important matters I forgot to take care of before leaving, and I fear I need to return. I don't trust anyone else to handle such things."

"A new estate! How thrilling! Where will it be located, if you don't mind me asking?" Devin's gaze was becoming sharper by the second.

"In the countryside. As lovely as the chateau is here, I need a place of my own, designed with my mind and my hands from the ground up. I need a home away from home, a place I can escape to when life becomes too overwhelming."

Devin's suspicion seemed alleviated, at least for the time being. "Most certainly. The stresses of royal life can be quite the burden. Your mother knows all too well the struggles."

Her mother. The mention of Queen Charlotte sent a cold ripple down her spine, though she tried to play it off. Devin's incessant questions were growing bothersome, but lashing out at a time like this seemed most unwise. Especially with the Queen remaining eerily silent.

"Yes," she said. "And after spending years locked away at home, I've developed a sort of wanderlust, I must admit. It's hard for me to want to sit idle anymore. Enough of my life has passed by, I need to do something with it while I'm still able to."

"Most understandable, my princess. If you feel you must return to Cardale, then I will make the arrangements as soon as necessary. When did you intend to leave?"

"Tomorrow, or perhaps the day after. But for now, I must rest. I'm weary from traveling and I need to recover my strength."

It was supremely difficult to not sprint out of the room, but Lucetta kept her composure well enough. She hurried out into the hall, mindful of every step, and careful not to scratch at the sores on her elbow and neck. It was the itching that was most insufferable. It seemed that on some occasions, the only way to make it stop would be to peel the flesh right off.

How dare those peasants question me like some common criminal! I ought to have their heads for such an insult! The nerve of it!

Her pace began to quicken with each step, her shoes clacking off the polished marble floor. Thankfully, Pavlos was nearby, stepping out from a nearby lounging room. Discreetly, yet frantically, Lucetta motioned for him to follow into an adjacent room.

"Is everything alright, princess?" the Droethien asked curiously.

"No, not at all. Those meddling servants are asking questions, and I had no idea what to say. My mother is behind this, I just know it. She didn't say a single word to me at lunch. And I fear I might have only given their suspicions merit. We need to get out of here, and fast."

"Very well. Should I ready your carriage?"

"No, not yet. I can't be seen leaving the estate mere hours after I arrived. It would invite even more unwanted suspicion. Tomorrow, perhaps."

"As you say. Pavlos will make all of the preparations, and will keep a watchful eye open, yes?"

She spent the rest of the day indoors, pouring over maps and other documents. Building a new realm from the ground up was no simple task, and required precise planning down to the smallest detail. Food and shelter for her new workforce would be of utmost importance. Thankfully, the Siln River provided more than enough fresh water to sustain a settlement. The thought occurred to her to have Pavlos send word out west, and summon any man looking to start a new life for himself and his family.

The amount of administrators alone exceeds what the White Spear has. And that says nothing for security. How am I supposed to keep everyone safe?

"Worry not," the woman in black said from deep inside her head. "All of the answers will come to you in time. But for now, you must rest. You must leave before sunrise, and travel at speed."

Smiling contently, Lucetta shuffled her papers into a leather satchel, then placed it inside a bedside table drawer. She slipped into night clothes and slid into bed, pulling the linen sheets tight to her body. Even though Devin's suspicions were upon her, she was remarkably carefree, a deep drowsiness taking hold far quicker than usual. At least, as of late.

Moments before drifting off into the dream realm, Lucetta felt overcome with uneasiness. A soft shuffling in the hall drew her attention, the hairs on the back of her neck standing firmly at attention.

"H… hello?" she asked softly, a slight tremble to her voice.

There was no response. There were eyes peering, studying, watching, from somewhere. Lucetta could feel their gaze coming from the keyhole, or perhaps the gap at the bottom of the door. She thought to cry out for Pavlos, but if the person outside was hostile, they could burst in and remove her head before the Droethien could even rise from bed.

Terrified, she sat motionless, peering at the door without so much as blinking. After what seemed to be an eternity, a pitter-patter of retreating footsteps echoed softly, until they disappeared entirely. She exhaled loud and deep, nearly slumping over from lack of air.

"I have got to get out of here, before it's too late."

MADELYN II

"COMMANDER! COMMANDER! ARE YOU AWAKE?" DEVERELL AVELIO said, rousing her from a nightmarish sleep. The Elite was gracious enough not to shake her, or even touch her in the slightest. He had learned after their first night on the road the sort of terror a man's touch could invoke.

"I don't mean to wake you, Commander, but you're home. That's Bentmont just ahead. Can you see it?"

It was a long journey, and Madelyn had slept through most of it. It seemed as if she could have slept for a hundred lifetimes and still not recovered her strength, and it was only by some miracle that she was even alive in the first place. And to complicate matters, the baby inside was growing large and becoming more restless by the day, and taxing her already exhausted body even further.

She brushed a tangle of blonde locks from her eyes and squinted, light from the spring sun nearly blinding. Through a blurry haze she saw the tall peaks of Castle Thorn looming large in the distance, its dominion over the land unquestioned. Grief began to pour from her eyes like mountain waterfalls, for the sight was an unhappy reminder of her former life.

Her sorrow soon turned to awe as the encampments came into view. Surrounding Bentmont was a forest of white tents, tens of thousands of them, neatly placed into grids. She had never seen so many men gathered in one place before. Surely, this was the army which would stand against Damien Dreadfire and his horde of butchers.

"Quite a sight, isn't it, Commander?" Deverell grinned. He appeared nearly as surprised as Madelyn. "We heard reports there was an army assembling here, but I never expected something this large."

Sixty thousand men had gathered outside of the city, perhaps even seventy. In some small way, Madelyn felt humbled; such a massive army had been brought here to avenge her and the men who died at Castle Morden, or so she thought. But likely, none of the soldiers traversing the camps knew who she was; few outside the Order likely did. No, they were here to defend the Kingdom, nothing more, and nothing less.

A sea of curious faces looked on as the wagon passed through the camp. Madelyn could almost hear their whispers over the lumbering of the wagon, and pulled a pile of fur blankets over her head. There were even a few chuckles, though it was difficult to know if they were directed her way. Their amusement, and likely judgement, was nearly too great to withstand.

Part of her wished for Deverell to turn around and take her far into the wilderness, away from the High Marshal and those she called family, so they might remember her as she was; a warrior, fierce and determined, unconquered and unbroken.

"Wait..." she whispered, her throat as dry as the Plainhold. None could hear her plea, and even uttering a single word was enough to turn her vision to black. Exhausted, her head slumped against the wagon until the thumping of wooden wheels against uneven cobbles jostled her awake.

There were many eyes watching as the Blackthorn made their way toward Castle Thorn. For as solemn as everyone appeared, it might very well have been a funeral procession. Madelyn certainly felt as if she had died months ago and was only now being laid to rest, her spirit freed from earthly existence the day Castle Morden fell.

She pulled a blanket tight to her face, so only her steely-blue eyes were visible. It did little to disguise herself from Bentmont's locals; everyone knew it was her, and their whispers suggested they knew what had happened as well.

No, please... I can't do this. Please, let me die before the High Marshal sees me. Let me die and be buried as a hero...

The thought of seeing Jenson Powell's face after he attempted to dissuade her from riding west nearly drove her to tears. While she was loath to admit it, even now, he was right. Madelyn cursed herself for ever being so pigheaded. If only she had been more humble, she thought, and listened to those more experienced in the world, then perhaps this nightmare would have consumed someone else instead.

Castle Thorn was just ahead, the stronghold growing larger like a giant rising from its slumber. She was home now, and there was not an ounce of strength in her body to flee. Accepting the inevitable, Madelyn took several deep, panting breaths and prepared to face her brothers, and the man who was more like a father than anything else.

An ominous portcullis stood like the jaws of a great beast, teeth clenched and ready to swallow her whole. The wagon paused for no more than a few seconds before the iron barricade began to lift open, its mighty chains rumbling as they were strained under an immeasurable weight. As horse and wagon entered Castle Thorn, Madelyn's heart thrashed and fought and tried to force itself out of her chest, pounding so mercilessly her ribs felt as if they might shatter.

A glance around the courtyard revealed many faces, so many they were hard to distinguish from one another. Some she recognized, though most were unfamiliar, likely returned to Bentmont on rotation. Perhaps it would be a small mercy if few knew who she was.

"Take her to the infirmary, at once," someone said, their voice familiar.

Delicately, she was taken down from the wagon and placed on an old wooden stretcher, every eye in the courtyard staring intently. Madelyn turned away to shield herself from their judgemental gazes, and caught sight of the stables where her beloved Nora was once housed. It was a reminder of everything she had lost; her knights, Hunter, Nora, and Corbyn, and most distressingly, herself. Tears began to pool in her steely-blue eyes, turning them into a crystal lake.

A pair of knights carried her inside, where the air was a bit cooler, and smelled less like horses. The halls were as familiar as they always were, though far less inviting. It felt like she was an unwelcome guest in this place. Despite being her childhood home, it seemed as if the very walls themselves loved her not.

The bed was an uncomfortable thing, far from the luxurious cloud she slept on in her quarters. Madelyn wondered if she would ever be able to climb the steps to her sanctuary again, or have any semblance of life before the war.

Is there any reason to even try? I'll never fight again. I'll never lead again. I wish my breath would go out in my sleep. Peace... that's all I want now. I've served my time in hell.

She attempted to shift into a comfortable position, her belly making matters difficult. Even lifting a leg proved to be as insurmountable as scaling a mountain peak. She sighed, frustrated and already exhausted. But suddenly, the sounds of familiar footsteps came echoing down the corridor. There was a soft shuffle with every other step, a telltale sign of Jenson Powell's injured leg which had never properly healed.

Panic came over her in a near instant. The room became a sudden haze of blurry colors and fading light. The High Marshal's silhouette appeared just inside the doorway, his frame unmistakable. He stood motionless for a moment, then moved to the side of her bed. Madelyn could barely make his face out, but she saw it, or rather, the outlines of it. There was a peculiar look to his face, one of stony indifference, and perhaps even disappointment.

"Oh, Madelyn," he said, sighing. "Can you hear me? Perhaps not. I never should have sent you on that mission. I knew it would end this way. All of your life, I kept you safe. I protected you from harm. I guaranteed your success at every turn. And now look at what's come of it. Such a waste…"

"High… Marshal…" she croaked. Before another word could be uttered, Madelyn slipped into a deep sleep, the deepest one could go without succumbing to death itself. When she opened her eyes, a much different landscape lay before her.

The hilltop was a desolate thing, its trees brown and barren, the ground covered in a shroud of dry leaves. It was warm, with perhaps a slight hint of spring in the air, though there appeared to be no sign of life anywhere. From here, she saw the majesty of the forest, and dying rays of a setting sun filtering through its skeletal treetops.

It was calm and quiet, more serene than anything she had ever experienced. Madelyn sighed deeply in contentment, wondering if her breath had given out in her sleep and put an end to her pain forever. Thoughts of the afterlife, and if there even was one, had always seemed unsettling. But now, it appeared as a long lost friend.

She began to walk down a narrow deerpath, the hillside craggy and strewn with moss-covered logs and rocks. Their vibrant green hue was the only color to be seen among the endless expanse of gray and brown, aside from the occasional white cap of a forest mushroom.

Madelyn smiled contently, even though this was the last place she would have expected the afterlife to be, given the tales religious folk sometimes told. She had always heard stories of white walls and crystal seas, of sunlight which never faded, and great halls where beloved ancestors awaited the arrival of their kin. It certainly seemed like a pleasant way to spend eternity, but there was something to be said for the peaceful solitude of the forest.

If this is death, then I suppose it's not so bad. I would give anything to see Corbyn again. Maybe I'll find him out here, somewhere.

Hours came and went, the sun fading further until the last of its orange light bled into the approaching night, a banner of deep red trailing in its wake. Just when it seemed there was no end to the infinite desolation of the dead forest, she spotted something peculiar just ahead.

Through barren trees she saw a path wind down a hill, zigging and zagging to and fro, leading down to a narrow, snowy valley. A carpet of dry leaves was covered in a thick layer of freshly fallen snow, a well-traveled pathway iced over with footprints of those who had walked it before. Who or what may have come down this very same trail was a mystery, but perhaps there would be answers at the end of it, if there even was one.

There was a sudden, sharp drop in temperature as she approached, a misty haze of her breath becoming visible. The cold was refreshing, in an unusual sort of way, made even more unusual when she took a single step backward and felt warm air once again.

What sort of place is this? Where does this trail lead?

Instead of feeling distressed, Madelyn felt strangely at ease. With the cold came a distinctive smell, a smell she could only surmise was the scent of the forest itself. She had never been among the northern forests during a proper winter, only the rainy misery of Khorrtal, so there was no way to know if trees were even capable of producing such aromas on their own.

She found a large tree stump and stole a moment to sit and bask in the wintery landscape, her nostrils drinking in the intoxicating fragrance as if it were incense. There was magic in the air, an exciting, loving energy which rejuvenated her very soul. For hours she sat, comforted by a near total silence.

The path ahead had all but disappeared as darkness drank away the last rays of light. Madelyn found comfort in the night at first, lost in its blissful abyss as it swallowed the forest whole. Only outlines of tall oaks and pines were visible, standing like shadowy sentinels, silent and looming, and eternal.

But something seemed amiss. A cold tingle crept up her neck, the hairs standing stiff and alert. The energy of the trees had changed seemingly in an instant, filling her with an overwhelming sense of dread. A small speck of orange light flickered in the distance, barely visible at first, yet rapidly growing in size as if fanned by a swift gale. The pines suddenly erupted into a raging inferno, filling the forest with an explosion of flames. Tall columns of orange-red fire reached high into the blackened sky, clawing and reaching ever higher into the heavens.

Madelyn tried to run, but found herself paralyzed with fear. A figure stepped out of the fire and came into view. It was slender and shapely, clad in black from head to toe, the same figure she witnessed in a dream while in captivity. A single eye shone brightly like cold starlight, the other obscured by chin-length locks of black hair which hung down its face.

"Who are you?" Madelyn shouted, her courage waning. "What do you want with me?"

The figure moved forward, saying nothing, its footfalls on the frozen snow making no audible sound. While the burning forest was lit as brightly as day, it gave no illumination to the mysterious person. It reached behind its back and produced an object which appeared to be a crossbow.

Dumbfounded, Madelyn stood still, unable to process what she was seeing. The figure aimed the crossbow at her abdomen and squeezed the release. The barb of a quarrel sunk deep into her gut, the pain fiery and excruciating. She collapsed with a thud, clutching at the bloody wooden shaft and attempting to wrench it out, but to no avail.

"No, please! Stop!" she pleaded.

The cold, ominous eye stared back, emotionless and devoid of pity. The figure dropped its crossbow and produced two short swords, then marched with violent determination over to her. Madelyn tried to crawl away, clawing at the frozen soil, but her effort was futile. Raising an arm instinctively for protection, she grimaced as the shining steel blades were brought down, one after another.

She was suddenly jostled awake, the baby inside kicking wildly. Small beads of sweat moistened her brow, her breath quick and shallow. The room was very much the same as it always was, with no trace of the forest or the inferno which swallowed it anywhere to be found. Madelyn grasped her abdomen and groaned, the imagined pain from the crossbow quarrel nothing more than her baby, beating her insides into pulp.

Have I been driven completely mad? Has my mind been irreparably broken?

After a few deep breaths, her heart began to slow and beat at its normal cadence. She ran a hand down her face to wipe the moisture away, and noticed a peculiar smell emanating from her palms. Curiously, she sniffed her hand, front to back, then looked at her fingernails. Something seemed amiss.

Madelyn gasped, her hands trembling as if plunged into icy water. In the lambent candlelight she stared at the back of her nails, and at bits of ice and black soil caught underneath them. The dream, it seemed, was no dream after all.

CHARLOTTE III

S HE ENTERED THE THRONE ROOM, AN EMPTY PLACE WHERE ONLY ghosts and memories dwelled. It felt like ages since Charlotte last set foot inside it, or anyone else, for that matter. It was the crown jewel of the Westwind Citadel, spacious and elegant, and adorned with the most stunning artwork Betanthia had to offer. But despite all its splendor, the room remained vacant and nearly forgotten.

At the far end of the cavernous hall sat the throne. Chiseled from a slab of solid marble, it jutted upward like an obelisk, adorned with all the fineries one could imagine. The marble steps leading to it were long, platform-like things which gently ascended up to the throne, giving the royal seat a larger than life appearance to those in observance. One by one, Charlotte climbed them until she came upon her lesser throne to the right side of the king's, itself miniature in comparison. She sat in her old, familiar seat, running her fingers across a thin layer of dust on its armrest.

One final queenly act before I leave this life behind. I can do this. I must.

It was a mystery as to how many years had passed since she had last sat here, and the experience felt entirely surreal. Despite the passing of time, however, Charlotte could still picture the room filled with visiting dignitaries, servants, and guards. She could almost see her young children standing off to the side, fidgeting and toying with each other out of boredom.

Such memories made her smile, and feel a sense of pride and importance which she had only recently rediscovered. But then, Charlotte remembered her reason for being here in the first place; Aldred, her own son-in-law, had kept a terrible secret from her, and likely from Marcellus as well.

More likely than not. I do wonder when he was planning to inform me of this invasion.

She glanced to her left and studied the royal throne. Its red velvet was still plush, its gold inlays and gemstones glistening in pillars of light which filtered in through open windows.

I think Aldred has become a bit too emboldened since Marcellus became ill. Perhaps a reminder is in order, a reminder that House Bethard, not Eldon, rules this land.

Charlotte stood, smoothed out her skirts and moved slowly to the king's throne. Determined to exert what remained of her influence, she sat on her husband's seat, back straight and hands placed comfortably on its armrests. No more than a minute passed before the distinctive sound of Guardsmen armor filled the great hall. It echoed into the throne room, growing more thunderous with each passing second.

Soon she saw Aldred Eldon, flanked on either side by three Guardsmen. The look on his face was one of confusion, accented with perhaps a slight hint of fear. He must have wondered why she was seated in the king's throne and not her own.

"Good day to you, my queen," Aldred said with a lackluster nod. "I heard you were in Dellhaven for the winter. Had I known of your return, I would have—"

"Enough with the pleasantries. I have summoned you here today to provide me with answers." Her eyes scanned and studied him accusingly.

"My queen? I beg your pardon…"

"I have been informed of recent happenings on our western border. I am unsure which is more troubling, hordes of savages spilling into our lands, or your silence on the matter." Before Aldred could speak his slimy words, Charlotte raised a hand and silenced him. "Spare me any condescension, I am fully aware of everything which has transpired as of late. Were you intending to inform the crown of such a calamity?"

"Your Majesty, I serve at the behest of the King, and I can assure you, the council has—"

"Acted like a gang of incompetent fools. I have been told that our border has collapsed, and even now, northmen march across our lands unchallenged."

Aldred tugged at the collar of his silk tunic, glancing over his shoulder at the Guardsmen standing close by. "I must confess, the council was taken by surprise when Lord Valens was bested, but we have dispatched Lord Vakaro and his nobles to deal with the threat. We will meet them with overwhelming force and drive them back to the forests from whence they came."

Charlotte was unconvinced. She has always known Aldred to be a schemer, a man of cunning and self-interest. His marriage to Lucetta was one of convenience, admittedly for both houses due to his influence, but she never trusted the man. Not fully, and apparently for good reason.

"House Bethard will see to this matter personally." She lifted her chin in pride, studying Aldred's perplexion. "My son, Gareth, is heading to Bentmont, and will oversee the defense of our kingdom. If Lord Vakaro is as faithful as he is capable, as you say, then he will serve and obey without question. And I trust you shall do the same, when my son returns."

"Yes, of course, my queen."

Something was going on behind Aldred's eyes, she could see it, even as he simpered and tried to appear as harmless as possible. To a lesser woman, the subtle twitching of his facial muscles might have gone unnoticed, but Charlotte had grown accustomed to Marcellus' lies long ago. She could practically smell them as if they were body odor.

"You have yet to answer my first question," she said pointedly. "Why have you failed to inform the crown of these events in the west? I would assume such a matter would have been brought to our attention from the outset."

"I apologize for such a grievous oversight, my queen, truly I do. The council believed it was of the utmost importance to act first, then—"

"Lie to me again and I'll have your tongue," Charlotte interrupted. "Had you acted swiftly and in good faith, Castle Morden would never have fallen, and our lands would be secure, even now. Your arrogance and ignorance has cost us dearly enough. I plan to speak to my husband directly about this matter, and urge him to find a more suitable advisor."

Aldred's hands began to wring uncontrollably. "My queen, that is most unnecessary. I deeply apologize for my lapse in judgement, but I can assure you, all appropriate steps are being taken to quash the barbarian invasion. Lord Vakaro is amassing a host the likes of which Betanthia has not seen in a generation or more."

"I have no doubt the invasion will be defeated, and my son will see to it personally. In the meantime, Lord Eldon, I would recommend you find other endeavors of importance, if you wish to return to my good graces."

"Absolutely, my queen. You are most generous, and I will not disappoint you again."

With a bow, Aldred made a hasty retreat. The Guardsmen followed him out, their purple cloaks flowing behind them like windblown tapestries. Charlotte sat dumbfounded for a moment, unsure if the altercation was even real at all, or was instead a figment of her reminiscing mind.

No, she thought. *That really did happen. I showed that arrogant son-in-law of mine where the real power in this kingdom lies, and it's not with him.*

As exciting as such thoughts were, they were bittersweet as well. Charlotte had no intention of remaining in Cardale, or even speaking to her husband, for that matter. In fact, she was uncertain if she even desired to remain a sovereign, even though such powers would be bestowed until the day Marcellus Bethard died.

At least I can leave here knowing I did everything I could to keep Gareth safe. He's become the man I always knew he would be, and in such a short time. I suppose the time has come to let go, and allow him to lead Betanthia into whatever future he sees fit.

Smiling, Charlotte arose from the throne and made her way across a now empty room, her footsteps echoing like carpenter's hammers. As she entered the great hall, she motioned to a nearby servant. A young man presented himself and bowed deeply at the waist.

"Yes, my queen? How may I be of service?"

"Would you fetch my maidservant, and instruct her to bring up a small chest from the vault?"

The servant bowed again and scurried off, leaving Charlotte alone to bask in one final glance around the great hall. She stole only a few seconds to gaze upon its marble statues, large open windows, and looming grand staircase, because the gardens had been softly calling out her name.

Even though she had been among the expertly maintained landscaping many times before, this time in particular seemed more magical. Charlotte had always adored the fall, but there was something wondrous about springtime. Each year when the temperature was just right, the gardens would erupt with every color imaginable, like something out of a painting. It was sad to think of, however, knowing she would be back in Dellhaven before the bloom.

A small fountain nearby had been cleaned, and was bubbling with fresh water. Charlotte sat on its lip, her fingers dancing off the surface of the clear, cool water, smiling as little droplets flecked against her face. A songbird landed on the other side, stealing a quick drink for itself before fluttering off into a tree. Sadly, there were no squirrels or rabbits to be found, some of the many furry creatures which called the gardens home.

I sure will miss it here. This was my special place, a place where I could hide from the world and nothing could touch me.

A sudden thought came to her, which brought with it a smile. Perhaps she could commission a painting from one of Cardale's finest artists, and have them recreate the magic of the gardens on canvas. It would be a far cry from the real thing, but enough to keep her memories of this place fresh.

"So sorry to interrupt you, my queen," Emilee Harper said softly. "I brought the chest, as you requested."

"Thank you. Please put it inside the carriage. I'll have use of it." She closed her eyes and sighed, bidding a silent farewell to this storybook place. "I fear if I stay any longer, I may not have the will to leave. As torturous as the Citadel has been, these gardens will always be in my heart. Come, it's time to go."

Together, they made their way across the courtyard and to a waiting carriage. A detachment of Royal Guardsmen sat mounted and waiting for their queen, spears and shields in hand. Emilee placed the wooden chest inside as she was instructed, then stepped aside and waited for Charlotte to take her seat.

"Back to Dellhaven, Your Majesty?" the carriage driver asked.

"Not just yet. I would like to see my other children before I leave. Take me to their estate."

It would be a small detour, as the rooftop of Trace and Lucetta's residence could be seen from Auburn Row. A detachment of purple cloaks were the first to parade onto the avenue, clearing away the masses with little effort. Cardale's citizens knew well enough that to confront a Guardsman was to risk immediate injury or death.

Before long, she arrived outside of her children's estate. A pair of Guardsmen at the gate stepped aside and snapped to attention, then bowed as the Queen's carriage entered. Charlotte was greeted by a throng of servants, and spied the golden-white hair of Esma Bethard. She wore a gown of yellow silk, her dainty frame and fair skin giving her the appearance of a doll.

"My queen!" Esma smiled and curtsied.

Charlotte exited the carriage and held up a hand as Emille made to follow. "No, I won't be long." She turned to her daughter-in-law. "How lovely to see you! I would have expected you to be out on the town. Is Trace around? I would very much like to see him."

"Unfortunately no, he left early this morning and will likely return this evening. I could keep you company until then!"

It was a lovely offer, but Charlotte knew the longer she stayed inside Cardale, the more the city would try to keep her within its clutches. And besides, the chateau was open to all of her children and their spouses, who could come to visit at any time.

"I fear I must decline, sadly. I have to be returning to Dellhaven. Do let Trace know I stopped by, and tell him he can come visit me at his convenience. Today will be my last day in the capital."

Esma gasped slightly. "You… you intend to leave and never return? Why?"

"A personal decision, and not one I make lightly. As a mother and a wife, it pains me to have to be separated from my family and the life I have come to know. But as a woman, I know this is the only way for me to survive and thrive. I pray you never experience the things I have, and knowing Trace, you never will."

"I understand. Let me be the first to say you will be sorely missed."

"Worry not, my dear," she smiled. "Dellhaven is only a short distance away, and though it will be my permanent residence, you and all of my children are welcome at any time."

A sudden anxiety made Charlotte slightly lightheaded. Thoughts of Lucetta came drifting back. Judging by the meagre reception, it was unlikely her daughter was on the premises.

"Tell me, Esma, has Lucetta been home recently?"

"N… no, my queen, I cannot recall the last time she was here. Perhaps it was last year, if my memory serves correctly?"

Last year? The words were shocking to hear, but it truly came as no surprise. Charlotte's suspicions had been confirmed, though deep in her heart, she knew Lucetta had been deceitful. Being lied to by one of her children stung the most, but such disappointment was quickly replaced by worry. What had her daughter been up to this entire time? Was she involved in something nefarious, or some scandal which had now grown beyond her control? There were many questions in need of answers, and she would find none of them here.

"No matter, I'm sure there are many grand projects she is out fulfilling. You know how ambitious she can be. I would ask this of you; if she returns, could you inform her that I was here, and that I wish to speak with her?"

"Absolutely, my queen. And I will certainly let Trace know you were here, as soon as I see him."

Charlotte smiled, then gave the estate one final glance. It was likely the last time she would ever lay eyes on it. More than anything, she felt a crushing and nearly overwhelming sense of fear at the thought of what her daughter might be involved in.

"Very good, Esma. Come visit me soon."

Charlotte entered her carriage and began the long trek down Auburn Row. There appeared to be many more commoners on the street than before, some of them pointing and waving. Word traveled quickly when the Queen was out and about, and this time was no exception. Once again, she basked in warm love from the masses, though it was sad to know this would be her final moment in their presence.

Smiling, she opened the chest and plunged a hand into the coins inside, their golden faces smooth and cool to the touch. She clutched as many as her fingers could grasp, and without a second's hesitation, flung them out through the open window. The peasants were remarkably well-behaved, especially while receiving such charity, undoubtedly out of fear of the Guardsmen.

Marcellus would be livid if he saw this, but I don't care. I have more riches in Dellhaven than I could spend in several lifetimes, and it's been far too long since something was done for our people.

"That's very kind of you, my queen." Emilee's face beamed with pride.

"It warms my heart to do this for the less fortunate, truly it does. I want them to remember me as a queen of charity. When they look back on Marcellus' reign, I pray I'm remembered as one of the good things to come out of it. I will miss being their queen…"

"There will never be another Charlotte Bethard, that much is certain. Betanthia has been blessed to have you."

While she adored the admiration of the crowd, a small part of her wanted to leave as quickly as possible. Starting a new life could never come quickly enough, after all, and there were many things Charlotte looked forward to doing in Dellhaven. She continued throwing handful after handful of coins out onto the street until the chest ran dry. For once, it felt utterly satisfying to be without money, even though mountains of it sat waiting at the chateau.

The royal procession halted at the northern gatehouse with a mere motion of Charlotte's hand. There was another matter to attend to before departing Cardale for good, a matter which had weighed on her mind for some time. An uneasy feeling began to build inside Charlotte's bowels as her thoughts turned to Lucetta. She suspected something was amiss, as no report of her daughter's whereabouts had been produced. It was most unusual for Lucetta to be unaccounted for, especially for such a length of time.

"Captain," she beckoned a senior watchman forth. "I have an order for you and your men."

"What would you ask of me, Your Majesty?" He dropped to one knee.

"If at any time you encounter a royal caravan passing through this gatehouse, you are to inform me immediately. I want to know who is coming or going, and what their business is. But be clever about it. I'm certain that capable men such as yourself can glean information without becoming too conspicuous."

"Absolutely, Your Majesty. My men and I will remain vigilant, and send word to you immediately. I can order the other gates to be watched as well."

"Excellent. I will be taking up permanent residence at my estate in Dellhaven. Send a rider there if you must, but be discreet about it."

The watchman rose to his feet with a muffled groan, his men lowering their heads in near unison as the procession continued onwards. She looked up at the massive stone archway while passing underneath it, stealing a moment to marvel at its construction. At its center were two murder holes, though they had gone unused since their construction. There were so many little facets of Cardale that she never had the opportunity to explore. But leaving it all behind was a worthy sacrifice, and perhaps Dellhaven held a few secrets of its own, secrets which begged to be discovered. An encouraging thought for certain, but it did little to stave off a faint hint of tears.

"Is everything alright, my queen?" Emilee handed her a small handkerchief.

"Yes." Charlotte sniffled. "I cannot help but feel a sense of loss about leaving here, but I know life will never be any better for me if I stay. This city has been my home for decades, and now… no more."

"I once heard someone say, there is no creation without death or destruction. A fine piece of furniture was once a beautiful tree, cut down and shaped into something new. An elegant dress came from flax, growing wild and free in a field. I could go on, but you understand. Your new life requires your old life to end, but just like my examples, what comes next will be even more beautiful… and everlasting."

"Very wise words, Emilee. You surprise me more every day."

There was something profound in the servant girl's words, something which gave Charlotte pause. As hard as she tried to find fault in such logic, it was irrefutable enough. A part of her would have to die in order to be reborn into something new. The Queen continued to ponder on Emilee's words, long after Cardale became little more than a speck on the horizon, and disappeared fully from sight.

LUCETTA III

"**P**RINCESS, WE MUST GET OFF THE ROAD." PAVLOS' BARKED. THE Droethien glanced over his shoulder, scanning the nearby brush for a suitable hiding spot.

"What's happening?" Lucetta asked, unaccustomed to being addressed in such a manner. Her hands began fidgeting in anticipation of danger, either from bandits or perhaps vengeful northmen.

"A carriage approaches, princess. It flies your eagle banner, and there are many Guardsmen at its head. We must remain unseen."

At first, she could not comprehend what Pavlos was saying. Her first thoughts were of Gareth, though it seemed out of place for him to travel in such luxury. He was no better than a commoner in his transportation, preferring to ride on horseback. No, it could not be him. Perhaps it was Trace, she thought, coming to Dellhaven to visit their mother. It seemed the most plausible scenario.

"It's likely my brother. But it's best if we remain undiscovered. The last thing I need is for him to inform mother of my whereabouts. Heavens know she's prying into my business enough as it is, along with that meddling manservant of hers."

Pavlos said something in his native tongue, and in an instant the convoy retreated from sight with all haste. It was a regrettable decision, as the terrain was uneven and riddled with obstructions. Lucetta's carriage jerked and jostled violently, nearly causing her breakfast to erupt from her mouth. Fear of being discovered, however, kept her stomach well-enough in check.

A dense thicket of pines and tall shrubs helped to obscure the carriage and her Droethien companions. It seemed even their horses knew when to remain still and silent. As she watched the convoy coming up the road, a nauseating tightness began to form in her throat. Even though she was hidden and well-protected, there was an indescribable sense of dread and vulnerability which could not be overcome.

"Pavlos," she called out. "I think it would be best if we avoided the northern gate. Perhaps we can detour a mile or two to the west and use a different one. I feel it would be the best option, to avoid any suspicion. We cannot risk running into my brother, or whoever that might be."

"Why yes, princess. A sound idea indeed. I was about to suggest such a thing. We are becoming of similar mind, yes?"

Similar in mind to a cold-blooded killer? Yes indeed, perhaps.

The Droethiens waited until the unknown convoy diminished from sight before starting out again. Their pace was slow and measured, with a rider venturing far ahead to scout for any activity. After several hours of travel, they came to a fork in the road which bent and snaked westward, then southward. The added time from their detour was a nuisance, but a necessary precaution. One could never be too careful while conducting open treason against the crown, after all.

They arrived early the next day. The sight of the capital was as sickening as it was fear inspiring. Lucetta gazed at the outer walls of Cardale in disgust, her bowels churning as if suffering from a horrid case of indigestion. The sounds and smells only added to her revulsion.

A wafting stench of rotten fish and refuse was a reminder of her family's failings. It made her think back to the day she explored the streets of Cardale, and everything she had encountered. From dead men to starving children, the degeneracy of the capital was the rotten fruit of House Bethard's indifference. And from the look of things, very little had changed during her absence.

As her carriage rattled down a bumpy street, she was greeted by droning, indiscernible babble from the common folk. It was nearly insulting to watch the masses milling about, going about their insignificant, self-absorbed lives. There were pampered nobles, wealthy merchants, and commoners of every stripe and station, each oblivious to the northern wolves at Betanthia's door.

Fools, each and every one of them. Instead of peddling their worthless trinkets and seeking decadent pleasures, they should be defending their kingdom. But no, they have chosen lives of degeneracy and indifference instead. Maybe Betanthia does deserve to burn after all. Maybe I should let the barbarians have their way.

Such an idea seemed intriguing, but would require her to be prepared in time. Lucetta felt a sense of extreme urgency, an intense drive to focus and redouble her efforts. She cursed herself for not devoting every waking minute to the planning and execution of her grand scheme. Even sleeping seemed of little importance anymore, though she was already heavily deprived of it.

But as with any complex endeavor, there were certain obstacles to be overcome, obstacles which could starve her of precious time. The most glaring issue was money. She had a fair sum of it in her own right, but far more would be required, and quickly. Trace was the only man with adequate resources at his disposal, and the only one easy enough to manipulate into parting with them.

How in the world am I going to convince Trace to give me the coin I need to construct an entire city? That fat miser nearly soiled himself at the thought of building a new estate. But financing the birth of a queendom?

Lucetta scratched at the leathery, broken skin on her elbow, some of the scabs tearing and a faint weeping of blood collecting under her fingernails. The stinging of raw nerves was beginning to feel good, in an unusual sort of way. But even with Pavlos at her side, she dared not steal Trace's money, or else put all of her carefully laid plans at risk. No, there had to be a better way. But how?

"The solution is quite simple," the woman in black said, this time sitting beside her. "You must take what is yours, by whatever means necessary. You have come too far now to be stifled by your brother's insufferable money-grubbing."

"No, I mustn't arouse suspicion," Lucetta protested. "And if Aldred sees me at the estate, he's going to ask all manner of questions. His lack of inquiry over the last several months has been quite refreshing, and I would rather not subject myself to it."

Molten iron began churning behind the woman in black's eyes as it pondered, perhaps even searching the fates for an answer. It was an uncomfortable silence, one that seemed to last for hours. Testing the entity's patience, however, was never wise, and Lucetta devised a quick alternative.

"Trace has many ventures across Cardale. Surely he must be hoarding *some* of his wealth at one of them. I cannot very well steal from his stores at home, he keeps all of his riches under lock and key. Not even Esma can open his vault without permission."

"Continue," the woman said, the fire in her eyes fading.

"He said one night at dinner that he was adding another branch to the family bank. What better place to find coin than there? It would be simple enough to… adjust the numbers in his ledger, in order to avoid suspicion. And if the theft is discovered, it could easily be blamed on those under his employ."

"It seems a solution has presented itself. You are clever, Lucetta Bethard, more clever than you appear. You must take care to keep it that way. Give no one any reason to suspect you, and you will take them all by surprise."

The entity's words were poetry to her ears. Lucetta felt a comforting warmth wash over her body, the same sort of sensation she felt as a little girl, wrapped gently in her mother's arms. It made her sad to recall those precious moments from her youth, and to know the Queen could care so little about her wellbeing now. But at least she had the woman in black, a guardian spirit who would help guide her down the path to immortality.

"Driver," Lucetta called out. "Summon Pavlos, at once."

The man shouted something in his native tongue, and Pavlos presented himself within moments, sitting on the back of his destrier. "How may I be of service, princess?"

"A change of plans. I no longer wish to return to the estate. Instead, I have business at—" She paused, unable to recall where Trace had said the newest branch of the family bank was built. Her mind had gone completely blank, and with the Droethien looking on, she scrambled to produce its location.

"Eastway Street is where you wish to go," the woman in black interjected.

"Eastway Street, if you would please." Lucetta smiled, hoping Pavlos would think nothing of the request.

The Droethien appeared to become annoyed for a second, before remembering it was she who kept his purse filled with coin. He was a military man, after all, and military men seldom liked disruptions to plans. "As you wish, princess. If my knowledge of the city is correct, we will be there within the hour, yes?"

"You are correct."

They turned and traversed through one boulevard after another, cutting their way across the heart of Cardale. Were it not for the rising heat, the stench of filthy markets and filthy commoners might not have seemed so insufferable. Lucetta began to wonder how the city would smell if every inhabitant inside its walls were to simply disappear. She supposed soon enough, the northmen would make it a reality.

After another twenty minutes of meandering, Pavlos spied a wooden sign, painted white with the words "Eastway Street". He pointed at it, then thrust a finger down the avenue. As if guided by some unseen force, the convoy continued onward, passing one estate after another. They arrived at a large building, built of tan stone and capped with fired clay roof tiles. A placard displayed a symbol of a scale and gold coins.

This has to be the place. It certainly looks like something Trace would design. Absolutely hideous.

It was a gaudy, extravagant looking thing, with excessively tall columns jutting to the top of a sharply angled roof. It appeared to be five storeys or more, far larger than what was necessary for safely storing money. But it was a testament to Trace's success and his abundance. She could only imagine what sort of treasures lay inside the vault, or vaults, judging from the sheer size of such a monstrosity.

"Do you wish for me to accompany you, princess?" Pavlos asked, dismounting with a grunt.

"No, I wish to avoid any undue suspicion. Well, any more so than necessary."

The mercenary bowed, then said something in his language to his men. The riders milled about casually, themselves hoping to avoid drawing any unwanted attention. It would have been a lie to say she felt safe without Pavlos at her side. In truth, he was the only man she felt somewhat comfortable in the presence of.

Lucetta entered the bank alone, a warm rush of incense greeting her boldly. To say the smell was overpowering would have been an understatement. Thick, wispy clouds of lavender hung so heavy it was nearly suffocating. She shielded her nose with the back of her hand, exhaling the pungent fumes and growing lightheaded in kind.

Must Trace overdo everything? Does he have no concept of modesty?

The lobby was a cavernous place, filled with extravagant sculptures and paintings, likely the work of Cardale's many fine artists. On the far side of the room sat a desk, a lone man clothed in rich red silks sitting behind it. A pair of hired guards stood vigil behind him near a steel gate, spears and shields in hand, a short sword affixed to each of their belts.

"Greetings to you, Princess Lucetta! This is a most unexpected visit!" The man stood, smiling, and bowed his respects.

"And long overdue, if I may say so myself. Trace has told me for some time to get out into the city and see his works, and today seemed like as good a day as any."

"Indeed! He has mentioned you quite often in our conversations, and if he were here, I'm certain he would be overjoyed. Would you care for a tour, or perhaps some refreshment?"

This was the moment she was waiting for. Open sores on her elbow began to sting from sweat, and refraining from scratching them proved to be a nearly insurmountable task. "Absolutely. I would love to see what my brother has done with his time."

"Right this way! My name is Jacek, Highness. I apologize for not introducing myself, and welcome to Grand Summit Trust! We are Cardale's newest and largest institution. Not only do we safeguard the treasures of our nobility, but we serve the common man as well. Over here is our main vault."

Lucetta was led through an archway into another large room, with a lobby of its own. Against the wall was a counter, protected by a barricade of steel bars. Beyond it, she saw endless rows of small vaults mounted into the stone walls.

"All one must do is present their key, and an appropriate passphrase associated with their account." Jacek smiled. "Your brother is a visionary, my princess. Why should the common man not have a safe place to keep their wealth safe? We have already filled half of our capacity in recent months!"

Intriguing, she thought. It was peculiar why any peasant would want to store their money in such a place, given their penchant for debaucherous spending. Cardale's taverns and brothels likely held many times more gold than what was here before her. Still, such wealth, however meager, was better served in Bethard hands anyways.

"Come, my princess. As impressive as these holdings are, it pales in comparison to our grand vault! Allow me to show you!"

Jacek gathered himself and pattered back into the main lobby. Together they moved toward the guards behind his desk, themselves parted by a mere flick of his wrist. He produced a skeleton key, inserted it into an imposing looking lock on the gate, then opened it effortlessly. Lucetta followed, admiring the gaudy artwork, and feigning interest as best she could.

Her attention was drawn to a staircase behind the gate. It was triple wide, and ran both to the next floor above, and to a basement. Jacek started downward, his descent brightly lit by wall sconces. He was babbling something about the construction efforts, but Lucetta quickly lost interest. There was money down below, likely mountains of it, but not a single coin could be lifted from such a place without a careful plan.

Of which, I have none. How am I going to figure out how to pull off this heist in such little time?

"Worry not, child." The woman in black appeared alongside her. "You are proceeding according to plan. Give this fool your attention, for now, and mind your surroundings."

They arrived at the bottom, and were greeted by a massive, ornate iron door. It ran from floor to ceiling, nearly twelve feet in height, and looked to be able to survive any effort to breach it.

"Impressive, is it not?" Jacek spread his arms, basking in the magnificence of such a feat of engineering. "There are only two keys to the vault, one which your brother keeps on his person, and this one right here."

He produced a strange looking key, far larger and more misshapen than any she had ever seen. Smiling proudly, he placed it inside the keyhole, the tumblers inside clinking and clanking as their grip was released. The lock made a sudden, deep slamming sound, then lurched open about a foot.

"This is our vault, the first of its kind, and the most expensive part of the entire construction. There isn't a man alive who could breach it! At least, not without a considerable amount of effort. You would be better served demolishing the entire building first."

It may end up coming to that...

Jacek entered first, taking up an oil lantern on a nearby table and igniting it. Dull rays of light filled the cavernous space, which seemed to extend for miles. The vault's interior was unlike anything she had ever seen. Tall shelves made from thick wooden planks ran the height of the room, each holding chests of various sizes. The largest and heaviest sat on the floor, while the smallest, and quite possibly most valuable, were situated on top.

"Designed by the finest minds in Cardale. This is where the most elite families in the city store their riches. Dare I say, your brother Trace has outdone himself. This might very well be the greatest bank in all of Caldakas! But I'm certain you've seen more than enough gold and jewels throughout your life, my princess! Would you allow me to show you the lounges? We have fresh wine in plenty!"

"Lounges? In a bank?"

"Well, more like Trace's private quarters. He sometimes works long into the evening, and cares to have the comforts of home close by. Can't trust the streets after dark, after all."

Together they stepped out of the vault. Jacek extinguished his lantern, returned it to the table, then closed the massive door. After it was shut, he inserted the key and turned it, the tumblers clapping back into place. Smiling, he motioned for Lucetta to follow him up the stairs. Her mind paid little attention to his insufferable babble, but instead focused on a way to get back inside.

They proceeded up several flights until they came upon a spacious foyer. To the right and left were several shut doors, though a large set of double doors at the far end stood open. Lucetta scowled as she scanned the decor, shaking her head in disbelief at its gaudiness. Jacek finished rambling about whatever tripe he had been speaking, then motioned to a table with flagons of water and wine.

"Would you care for some refreshment, my princess?"

Lucetta nodded, eager to wet her palate. At least she knew Trace had decent taste in wine, or else she might have disowned him years ago.

"Now is your chance," the woman in black said, drifting through one of the closed doors and into the foyer. "When his back is turned, reach into his pocket and remove the key. Be swift about it, and act without hesitation."

She stared back at the entity with astonishment, voicing her disapproval silently. The woman in black's eyes glistened with an orange-red glow, then thrust a cold, dead finger at Jacek. He was already pouring out a chalice of wine, and time had grown desperately short. Carefully, she lifted her skirts and moved toward him as stealthily as possible.

With the chalice near to full, Lucetta waited until he bent over to fill another for himself. She extended a hand, then drew it back cautiously, then waited until the key was plainly visible inside his pocket. She reached in, snagged it, then stuffed it down her bodice as Jacek turned.

"Oh my, you startled me!" he chuckled, not expecting Lucetta to be so close.

"Forgive me, I have grown terribly thirsty after climbing all those stairs. Perhaps I might stay here for a little while and recover."

"Absolutely, my princess! You may come and go as you please, although you need not hear that from me! This is your brother's bank, after all!"

Smiling, Jacek took his wine and descended down the stairs. Lucetta exhaled a volcano of stress, retrieving the key from inside her bodice. She downed an entire chalice in several desperate gulps, gasping for fresh breath as she finished.

"Good," the woman in black said. "Now, remove your shoes so as not to be heard, and go and retrieve what you need."

"When should I—"

"Now." The entity began floating toward the stairs. "Time is of the essence, and no one will expect you to be leaving here in such short order. Go, that babbling fool has already returned to his station. Go, be swift, and be silent."

With no small measure of hesitancy, Lucetta removed her shoes, holding them in the same hand as the key, and hiked her skirts with the other. The floor was refreshingly cool despite the day's heat, though the rising temperature was likely radiating off her body. Step by step, she made her way down one flight after another, the woman in black floating ahead.

"Come, child. No one will come this way for some time."

When she reached ground level, Lucetta paused and glanced slowly out into the main lobby. The guards were still standing at their station, their backs turned. Jacek was sitting at his desk, pouring over a small stack of parchment, paying no mind to anything else. Holding her breath, Lucetta tiptoed cautiously to the next flight of stairs, then moved down them swiftly so as not to be discovered.

The vault door appeared to be several times larger than it did earlier. As intimidating of a sight as it was, she had come too far to turn back now. She set her shoes onto the floor, and fumbled with the key. The lock, however, proved exceptionally difficult to turn. Lucetta strained and grunted, trying with every ounce of strength to engage its tumblers, but it was to no avail.

"I… I can't do it," she whimpered.

The woman in black looked on, a deep scowl forming across its cold face. "This once, and just this once, I will assist you directly. Your pampering has left you weak." The entity grabbed hold of the key and turned it effortlessly, the vault door clanking before lurching open once again.

Lucetta's heart was racing so fast it nearly ruptured the stitching of her bodice. She looked over her shoulder once before stepping inside, swallowing hard. It was as dark as the inside of a casket, though thankfully the oil lantern was right where Jacek left it. She attempted to light it several times, huffing in frustration, but it was to no avail.

"You truly are helpless," the entity hissed. "Leave it, there is no time."

The woman in black raised her hands slowly, an ominous red glow radiating from deep inside the walls. Despite being in company with the entity for a year, it was still endlessly terrifying to witness its power. What else was the woman in black capable of? Lucetta dared not find out any more than what was necessary.

A wooden ladder sat nearby, propped against a tall shelf. Sensing time was growing short, she scurried up to the top, careful not to trip over her skirts. A small chest sat on the highest shelf, directly above her head. Lucetta reached up and opened it, closing a fist around what felt to be gems of some sort. When she brought her hand down into the otherworldly light, a bright glisten of diamonds filled her eyes.

A sudden rush of exhilaration was nearly as satisfying as sending Sir Bryce Whitewood to an early grave. Lucetta poured the diamonds back into the chest, closed it, then delicately brought it down. Never in a thousand years would she have thought herself both a murderer and a thief, but empires were often built on a foundation of unscrupulous means, after all.

"I did it!" she grinned like a child to their parents. "But how am I going to get this out of here? I can barely carry it, let alone sneak it out of here."

"Take the chest to the top floor, and with haste. Time is growing short."

The entity floated out of the vault, the red light fading like an exhausted candle. Lucetta lugged the chest out into the foyer, set it down, then muscled the large door shut. Turning the key back to its original position proved far easier, a task she was able to accomplish.

Tumblers clacked back into position, and the key was released from the door's iron grip.

"Come, we must leave this place," the woman in black said, making its way upward. "Leave it here, so that fool will think it slipped out of his pocket." She pointed halfway up the staircase.

Lucetta set her shoes on top of the chest, hoisted it with both arms, and clumsily carried it while holding the key in one hand. Setting it carefully in place proved to be difficult, the key slipping from her grip and landing with a rattle which echoed up the stairwell. She winced, expecting the entity to chastise her or the guards to come rushing down with truncheons in hand, but thankfully neither event occured.

Carefully, Lucetta climbed one flight after another, moving gingerly past the guards and back to the upper floor. Her heart was slamming so violently it was a wonder why the whole bank was not alerted to her presence. One upstairs, she set the chest down and doubled over, wheezing.

"Make haste, child," the entity commanded, standing near an open window. "There is no time to waste. Throw the chest outside, and be quick about it."

Such a command made little sense, but there was no use in arguing the merits of it. Lucetta lifted the wooden box with a grunt, struggling and straining with burning muscles to bring it to the window. Once there, she set it down onto the sill and craned her head out, seeing rows of neatly pruned bushes sitting below.

"Well, here goes nothing…"

With a shove, the chest slid from the sill and plummeted downward. Thankfully, there was only a soft rustling sound as it impacted below, easily mistaken for an animal or even the wind. No one was likely to be the wiser, she suspected.

"Good. Now, the time has come to leave this place. Go and secure your treasure."

Returning to the lobby would be impossible with such worry written across her face. Thankfully, the flagon of wine was still quite full. After putting her shoes back on, Lucetta marched across the room and over to the table, and drank directly from the vessel, a few droplets splashing onto her gown. Panting and huffing, she hurried back downstairs and into the lobby, past the guards still standing at attention.

"All finished?" Jacek rose from his desk, having heard the click-clack of her shoes.

"Yes. This is a lovely building, my brother certainly has his share of talents." Bile rose into the back of her mouth.

"I'll be certain to share your sentiments with him when he arrives."

"Thank you. I pray he will be as supportive of my endeavors, as I am of his."

She strode past Jacek and briskly exited the bank, and was finally able to breathe again. Lucetta gave pause for a moment, closed her eyes, and exhaled deeply, thankful the heist was over. Now, there was only the matter of retrieving her loot before it was discovered by someone else. She motioned for Pavlos, the Droethien sauntering over with a smile.

"Yes, princess?"

"I need you to go around the corner and retrieve something from the bushes. It's a chest about this large. Hopefully it hasn't been damaged. Be quick about it, if anyone sees us…"

"Worry not, my princess. Consider it done."

The mercenary disappeared from sight, each second he was absent filling her with dread. Without even knowing it, she had clawed open the scabs on her elbow, itching at her open sores until it hurt like bee stings. But Pavlos returned soon enough, the chest tucked discreetly under his cloak, his grin glistening with gold.

"Is this what you spoke of, princess?" Pavlos asked, tucking the chest into a saddle bag.

"Yes, we have everything. Or, as much as I could safely gather. It should be more than sufficient to secure the men and materials we need."

"We shall go to the slave markets, yes?"

"Yes, but I mustn't be seen. Remove the banners from the carriage, and your cloaks as well. We must appear as wealthy merchants or nobility, so none of this is traced back to me. Too many eyes are around the city, and word travels quickly."

"Worry not," Pavlos said reassuringly. "I have been to the slave markets before, princess. There are ways to acquire what you seek. Such men who trade flesh can easily be persuaded, and, how do you say it…"

"Discreetly?" she chimed in after thinking for a second.

"Yes." He nodded. "Come, I will take you there. The day is young and the markets will not be open yet."

The news was encouraging, and Lucetta eagerly entered her carriage. It was stripped of its adornments, and lumbered nakedly through Cardale's deserted streets. The city felt dead, as dead as the man she saw laying on the bridge over the Camsby that fateful day. A flock of pigeons fluttered overhead, cooing and searching for a morning meal. But to Lucetta's eyes, they appeared as vultures, feasting on the carcass that was once Betanthia's capital.

The woman in black sat silently across from her, a sinister and widening grin snaking its way across its pale, dead face. Fiery orange-red eyes seemed to burn a hole clean through her spirit, but there was no pain or discomfort. Far from it. Though the entity spoke not a word aloud, in Lucetta's head, she heard whisperings of events both past and future, of mysteries, and of good fortune. There were many voices, every one of them belonging to the woman, but each distinctly different.

An eternity had passed before the carriage was brought to a halt just outside of the slaver's market. Lucetta felt a tightness building within her chest as she glanced cautiously out of the window. Pavlos hopped down from his horse, saying something to his men in their foreign tongue and chuckling. It always made her feel slightly uncomfortable whenever he spoke his true language, as if he and the other Droethiens were somehow plotting against her.

Pavlos swaggered over to a three storey building with a massive tent canopy shrouding its front door. There were large wooden tables underneath, an old yet menacing looking man in rich yellow and black silks standing behind them. In front of him rested some sort of ledger by the looks of it, and a stack of papers as well. Pavlos approached, saying something in a *third* language, one even stranger than Droethien.

Who is this man, truly?

It appeared there was more to the mercenary than meets the eye. Both men conversed back and forth as if they had known each other for ages, but each was too stony to show any true emotion. Lucetta watched intently, though it was impossible to know what they were truly saying. The man in the colorful silks appeared to be growing more agitated, matching Pavlos' increasingly animated gestures.

They must be haggling, she thought, but it was difficult to be certain.

After throwing his hands into the air, the man in silks disappeared inside the building, and returned a few minutes later alongside another man, clad in a brown leather jerkin and trousers. He was a distasteful looking creature, long in hair and beard, with scars raking his face. On his belt was a ring of keys. They were large, black, rusted looking things that hung like daggers. After a few words, the man motioned toward a cage across the square.

Lucetta poked her head out through the window, eager to see where Pavlos and the other men were heading. They disappeared out of sight, another building nearby obscuring her vision.

"Patience," the woman in black said. "Everything is going according to plan. The fates have foretold this moment. All will be well."

The words were of some assurance, but did little to stifle a crippling anxiety building within her. Lucetta exhaled as she saw Pavlos returning a few minutes later, his golden smile wide for the world to see.

"Princess!" the Droethien exclaimed proudly. "It appears there are many slaves here for you to buy. Pavlos has struck for you a grand bargain, and the master is willing to part with all of them for a modest price. You will find this acceptable, yes?"

Exciting news indeed, but not surprising. Pavlos was a man of many means who could get things done, both quickly and efficiently. Perhaps she had underestimated him since the beginning, she thought. "Most acceptable. How soon will we be able to depart?"

"The master says all of the slaves are ours to do with, and ready to leave at your command, yes?"

"We must leave at once. Every minute we spend in Cardale is another minute we can ill afford."

Pavlos whistled so loud her ears nearly bled. Within moments, a long procession of men, women, and children bound in irons came funneling out into the courtyard. They were whipped and prodded into formation, and forced to stand silently until a long train of wagons were assembled. Lucetta's new workforce was unceremoniously stuffed into their cramped confines until not a soul was left uncaged.

One of the Droethiens produced the smuggled chest and carried it to the slave master. The man's demeanor quickly softened and turned to smiles and laughter as he looked upon its contents. Pavlos scooped out handfuls of sparkly gems and poured them into a pile on the slaver's table. They exchanged a few more words, along with an embrace of friendship.

"It is done, princess!" The mercenary then shouted something in his native tongue, and soon enough the procession was in motion through the streets of Cardale.

Finally, it's done. I cannot believe this actually worked!

It was endlessly relieving to have pulled off the near impossible. While Lucetta was still within the limits of the capital, she felt relieved and drowsy. Her eyes began to grow heavy, but even after they were shut she could still see. There were many wagons behind her armored carriage, though they were more suited for wild beasts as opposed to men. Instead of comfortable cushions and racks of refreshments, they instead had beds of hay and bars of iron. There were many dozens, snaking and stretching back as far as she could see.

But the most disturbing part was the fact that she could even see in the first place. Lucetta knew she was sleeping, or at least thought she was, but somehow the dream felt as real as anything she had ever experienced. She stared in wonderment at the sheer length of the wagon train, then turned and gazed off to the north. There was a forest ahead, not particularly dense, but one she had remembered seeing once before.

This is it! This is where Pavlos took me, the place near the river!

Something about the landscape felt different. As Lucetta leaned further out of her carriage window, she saw a glint of light catch her eye. Suspiciously she peered onward, the sight of large stone walls coming gradually into view. Beyond it loomed a tall tower, larger and more imposing than even the Westwind Citadel. It was her palace, she knew it, or at least, it seemed like it was.

As if being swept up like leaves in a sudden gale, Lucetta found herself flying toward the walls with frightening speed. She felt the most indescribable panic of her life as she sailed over the walls and flew to the palace, many thousands of buildings below seeming like little more than anthills. But before she could so much as marvel at the sight of her new city, she was unceremoniously dropped to the ground, though thankfully the fall was as painless as rolling out of bed.

Is this? Could it be? Could this be my queendom in its full glory?

There was a commotion around the corner of a residence which drew her attention. Curiously, Lucetta followed the disturbance, peeking around the freshly carved gray stone. She saw a long procession of commoners, six abreast, walking in lockstep through the street. Their gazes were fixed forward, though it was unclear what they were staring at. From their modest, roughspun attire, they looked to be the lowest form of peasant, possibly even slaves, but it was too difficult to tell. And besides, Lucetta cared little for the distinction.

"Hello?" she asked. To her bewilderment, there was no acknowledgement of her query, let alone her presence. Something compelled her to join the procession, though something else deep inside feared to see where the near endless mass of rabble was heading.

Onward she walked through the streets, themselves immaculate and nearly glowing in the sunlight. Lucetta basked in the wonderment of the city around her, and felt a certain kind of vindication that she had never experienced before. One would have come to expect the usual stench of a large city, but surprisingly, the air smelled like nothing at all. Some scents, like freshly baked bread and burning incense, were far more pleasant than rotting refuse which often blanketed the streets of Cardale, but here, there was only a void. It was if there was nothing beyond what her eyes could see and ears could hear.

The procession of commoners continued for what felt like a year. Lucetta had quickly grown bored and frustrated, and decided to take her leave and seek out the palace in the distance. But to her horror, as she tried to pull away, her body continued onward, rejoining the horde of unwashed peasants. Unable to control the movements of her legs, Lucetta began to panic and search all around for some manner of escape.

What in the heavens is going on!? What's happening to me?

There was a sudden change in temperature, and not for the cooler. A thick wall of heat and humidity slapped her dead in the face, immediately sucking what little energy she had out of her body. One final corner was rounded before it appeared, a giant, gaping pit at the central courtyard of the city. It was an endless chasm, glowing with a raging inferno, its flames leaping dozens of feet into the air and crackling like the falling of great trees.

Lucetta felt a sickening terror come over her as she saw where the mob of commoners were heading. Six abreast they marched toward the endless pit of fire, falling into it seemingly without a care for self preservation. The flames grew a bit brighter and a bit hotter with each body it consumed, melting the very stones of the buildings surrounding it.

"Stop! Please!" she pleaded in futility as a half-dozen men were enveloped by the fire with every heartbeat. Row after row of men and women were swallowed whole until it was finally her turn to face the hellfire. But something compelled her to look away, to scan the breadth of the square once more before her life was consumed like kindling.

The majesty of the Westwind Citadel suddenly appeared before her. It was a shock to see her old residence staring her directly in the face, but as Lucetta looked around once more, her surroundings suddenly became much more familiar.

This is Cardale. I know this square. I know these buildings. That palace is my home...

Bewildered, she searched around for some salvation that would likely never come. The heat was growing more intense with every heartbeat, and before she could reach out to the Citadel, the flames began to lick at her legs. Moments before they encompassed her entire body, she awoke, the nightmare coming to an abrupt end.

Her dress was soaked in sweat, despite the crispness of the evening. The inside of her carriage felt like a sauna, though far less enjoyable. Lucetta threw open a window, gasping and choking and nearly vomiting from the discomfort which wracked her body. With each passing minute it became more clear that it *was* just a dream, albeit the most real and disturbing dream she had ever experienced.

Perhaps it was some vision from the woman in black, but the entity had not revealed itself since setting out from Cardale. But nevertheless, Lucetta took the dream for some sort of ominous premonition, of which she was beginning to suffer under the weight of.

What could such a dream mean? And why would it come to me in such a manner? I'm doing everything she's asked of me, and I haven't failed yet. What could it mean?

It was then that she remembered something, something which might be the end of her. Panic stricken, she clawed at the side of her face until her skin turned a bright shade of pink.

Oh no… I forgot to adjust Trace's ledger…

SYLVIA II

B Y THE LIGHT OF THE FULL MOON THEY ARRIVED, SIXTY THOUSAND strong and baying for blood. In the darkness the warband crept, silent and looming, like shadows bleeding across a darkened landscape. Hok lay only a short distance away, its walls glowing softly with warm torchlight, the men patrolling it unaware of the impending doom drawing ever closer.

Sylvia Stormguard sat motionless, scanning the blackness like an owl, ready to strike at any moment. She felt the ancient magic of forest mushrooms taking hold, slowly filling her to the brim with an anger and anxiety which could barely be contained. But Damien's orders were clear, and despite the intoxication flooding her body, she remained idle.

"When?" Mikka asked for what seemed like the hundredth time, her face beaming brighter than the moon with excitement.

"We wait for the signal," Sylvia answered. "And not a moment before. Keep control of yourself."

Far too much time had passed since the warband last enjoyed a proper fight, and the warriors were growing impatient. She would have been lying if she was to deny having an itch to shed more Betanthian blood.

"I'm going to enjoy this," Hilde said, brushing a lock of short, black hair behind her ear. "Truly, I will. Perhaps I'll even knife a few Zylmacians when no one is looking."

Sylvia smiled, even considering such a prospect herself. The world could certainly use a few less wildmen, she thought, given how alarmingly their numbers had grown. As amusing as it would seem, however, there was more pressing business at hand. The Blackthorn Knights were no fools, or so they were led to believe, though their fighting prowess at Castle Morden left much to be desired.

Stay focused now. This is merely a detour, but a necessary one. We can't have Betanthians coming up behind us once we push into the Plainhold. We can't leave ourselves vulnerable.

The rest of the Rhivothi lay a short distance away, primed like a steel trap, ready to clap shut at a moment's notice. Somehow, she was able to sense the energy from Marvath Bonesplitter, a kindred bond which only grew stronger when danger seemed most apparent. The looming nomad warchief appeared alongside her, his long, sandy beard and hair loose and flowing.

"The fight will be here soon," he said in a soft yet gravelly voice. "Be patient."

"Easy for you to say. I feel as if my skeleton is going to claw itself out of my flesh."

It was becoming nearly impossible to sit patiently any longer. The mushrooms were taking hold, and strongly, her anxiety becoming so fierce that she felt like screaming. A glowing red sky over Hok began to spin and shift into a bleeding whirlwind of colors, nearly too nauseating to look at.

Marvath set his great axe onto the ground, then removed a small skin from his belt. He took a drink then offered it to Stormguard. She drank, but paused halfway through the first sip. It was not mead, to her surprise, but water.

"Drink, you're going to need it," he said. "You ate the mushrooms too soon. Only the gods know when Damien will order the attack. Who knows what condition you will be in once the horn sounds."

"He better do it soon," Mikka interjected. "I'm getting impatient!"

"Getting?" Sylvia snorted. "You won't seem to shut up about it. And don't worry about me, Marvath. I've never been more focused on anything in my life."

With a grunt, Bonesplitter retrieved his axe and disappeared into the darkness. Water did little to stave off the sickness and building battle rage. A sudden pain shot through her jaw, as if pierced by a flaming arrow. To Sylvia's surprise, her teeth were clenched so tightly they nearly burst like stones under a hammer. The pain only served to provoke her anger even further.

Come on Damien, give the order. By the gods, give the damn order!

Near to vomiting, Sylvia grunted and took a few deep breaths, before the rippling blow of a horn pierced the silence. It was an ominous, low rumble at first, but then erupted into a devastating blast so loud the ground felt as if it were shaking. This was it, the moment she had been waiting for.

As if the bowels of the earth had opened, the warband surged toward Hok's outer wall, wailing and screaming like pit demons. Sylvia found herself frozen in place for half a heartbeat, too awestruck to move, before her legs took on a mind of their own and began racing as fast as they would allow. Small mangonels hurled flaming pitch over the walls from across the field, leaving trails of flickering light and black smoke in their wake.

The energy was unlike anything she had ever experienced; not the fear and uncertainty many felt while storming Castle Morden, or fighting in the thick of the Hinterwood. No, there was something else in the air now. The warband was emboldened, and more fearless and ravenous now than ever before.

A pair of guards along the parapet struggled to raise an alarm, themselves too dumbstruck to realize what was happening. Before they could alert their brethren inside the city, the Rhivothi were already raising ladders against the wall and racing up them. There was little to no resistance, and soon warriors were cresting over the crenellations in frightening numbers.

"Azldyr!" Hilde screamed, keeping pace with Sylvia. She felt raw power emanating from her shieldmaidens as they charged in tow, like a pride of lionesses on the attack.

She was nearly out of breath by the time they reached the wall, the mushrooms rapidly draining her energy. After a few desperate gasps for air, she slogged up a ladder, each rung as demanding as scaling a mountain. It was only when she heard a clash of steel and wails of dying men that the fire inside her was rekindled.

The hunt was on. She reached the top at a frenzied pace, her body slowing despite yearning to join the fray. She reached into a small leather pouch on her belt and produced a fistful of dried mushrooms, and with little regard for the consequences, stuffed them into her mouth. With each chew, the potency of their ancient magic began to swell within her once again, leaving in its wake a paranoid rage which could not be contained.

Several buildings nearest to the wall were alight and crackling, illuminating the night sky with a warm, orange glow. Sylvia scanned the hellish scene, her pupils as wide as black, endless pits. She saw burning bodies strewn about, and men fighting desperately to keep the warband out of the city. Grinning, she took hold of her axe and descended onto ground level as more Rhivothi poured over the top of the wall.

A shadow emerged from around a burning building, approaching rapidly like some terror of the night. Wailing like a wild beast and with sword and shield in hand, the man charged Sylvia, winding up a powerful slash in hopes of claiming her head. But the shieldmaiden was too quick, her eyes taking in the smallest of details around her. She crouched and sidestepped the blow, raising her shield defensively and answering with a horizontal swing of her axe. The weapon cleaved only air, the soldier regaining his footing and slashing wildly yet again. His sword met her shield, steel biting down against the battered wood, jarring her arm from the impact.

As if possessed, Sylvia's axe arm swung again with blinding speed. The soft flesh of the soldier's stomach gave way as her blade split the skin and dug deep into his bowels. She wrenched the axe free, a torrent of blood and entrails spilling out of a gaping wound. A stiff shield bash sent the dazed and dying foeman to the ground, his groans faint and labored.

The mushrooms had taken hold of her so strongly that she began to panic. The world around her shifted and morphed into a bleeding maelstrom of lights and colors, the chaos of battle and the raging of fires playing the worst of tricks on her eyes. Sylvia fought back an urge to vomit as she panted desperately, cursing herself for consuming so many.

Even looking upon her own kin was nearly unbearable. The Rhivothi appeared to her as great beasts, their animal skins making them seem like creatures from another world. She stared in horror at a large warrior clad in bear hide, howling and whipping his axe around like a man possessed.

The visions were becoming too grotesque to stomach. A Blackthorn charged toward her with a spear, his skin turning to a foul liquid, like melting wax, and falling to the ground in clumps. Sylvia shrieked at the sight of his skull, mouth agape and dripping with gore, and stepped backward as if to flee. His spearpoint thrust toward her with blinding speed, but found only the face of her battered shield.

The armored skeleton grunted and tried to pry his spear loose, but it was to no avail. Sylvia quickly discarded her shield, then with both hands swung the axe downward with such force, the skull split and nearly turned to powder. It fell to the ground in a heap of bones, its steel cuirass clanking as it bounced several times. She frantically searched for a new shield, desperate to find another means of protecting herself from the terrors all around. A torrent of whizzing arrows overhead sounded like great clouds of locusts, leaving thin streaks across the night sky.

Another one-handed axe lay not far away, near the body of a slain northman. Sylvia dared not look upon the man's face, for fear that it may be familiar, but was quickly overcome with curiosity. To her horror, she saw Marvath Bonesplitter's face, his sandy-blonde beard soaked with blood. She blinked hard in disbelief, then saw the face change once more, this time back to its original owner. Likely a Nothanek, judging by his soft features and lack of facial hair.

It was then that Sylvia Stormguard felt an uncontrollable anger erupt inside of her. The nightmarish ghouls who fought against her animal kin no longer made her feel afraid. She screamed a violent, bloodcurdling scream, and charged at the first terror she saw. As if infused with the battle rage of Azldyr himself, she cleaved her way through one foe after another with frightening speed.

The air became a haze of misty blood as she dispatched one Blackthorn after another, each kill seeming to only fuel her ferocity. The nightmare creatures began to morph and fade back into their previously human forms, awakening a wolf's hunger inside her. She tried to curse them, but found she could speak only in tongues. A river of babble poured from her mouth, interrupted only by an ear-splitting shriek as her battle rage began to peak.

"Show them no mercy!" a northern voice called out, gruff and deep. "The gods are with us!"

Suddenly, Sylvia began to laugh. It was a mere chuckle at first, but quickly became an uncontrollable storm of hearty bellows. She found herself unable to control her laughter, which only seemed to grow after dispatching another Blackthorn, and then another. It felt so good to kill them, and she found it endlessly amusing, the way a child might find amusement in stepping on insects. Glowing light of the fires deep within Hok gave her pause, but only momentarily. Her eyes caught a glint of firelight off a knight's breastplate as he charged with an arming sword, both hands gripped tightly around its hilt. Without any control over her own body, Sylvia threw one of her axes, the blade parting the man's face in two. He ran another two paces then dropped like a fallen tree.

Incensed, she continued to carve her way through the enemy ranks. Each jet of blood that splashed her face made her cackle with glee, a warm excitement of ecstasy building within. It was only a short while until the sun began to rise over the ruin that was Hok. Rays of new daylight revealed the sheer devastation of their assault. Sylvia Stormguard paused, a sudden exhaustion doubling her over.

Gods, we did it. We've won.

The battle seemed to have lasted only minutes, time itself having slowed to a crawl. Hok was little more than smoldering rubble, its streets stained red with an ocean of blood. Bodies lay strewn about everywhere, some friendly, though thankfully most were foreign. The first battle of the new year had ended in a devastating success, and reminded her of their very first victory outside of Khorrtal.

A hearty chorus of cheers began to build in every direction. At first she thought the jubilation was little more than the revels of victory, but something about the commotion seemed different. Sylvia drew in a few deep breaths, the air tinged with smoke and death, and trudged over to a large gathering of warriors. She saw the hulking frame of Damien Dreadfire at the center of a crowd, towering over those around him.

What was peculiar was the smile on his face. In all of her time in the warband, she had never seen Damien smile. Perhaps a smirk, once, or even twice, but never a smile. Certainly not a smile of joy. His black steel plate armor was splashed with jets of blood, which shimmered

red in the rising sun. He was holding something in one hand, and the higher he held it, the louder the cheers became.

What is going on here?

Muscling her way forward, Sylvia entered a small clearing around Damien. There were wooden carts parked at the top of a long pathway which snaked down into a cavern, its contents piled near to overflowing. It was difficult to make out what was inside them, though judging from the expression on Damien's face, it was something of great importance. She approached with exhausted anticipation.

"Damien! What is it? What have you discovered?"

The warlord's expression turned stony. "It appears King Bethard was keeping a secret from the rest of the world. Hok is a greater prize than we could have imagined." Dreadfire tossed what appeared to be a crude rock at her feet, but upon closer inspection she discovered it was anything but ordinary.

Gold! This is gold!

She hefted the rock high, studying it, eyes growing ever wider. There was a glimmer to be found for certain, but before she could examine it further, Damien Dreadfire beckoned her to follow. She tossed the ore into a nearby cart, itself filled to capacity. Together, they started down the winding pathway, down into the large pit mine. But it was not the mine itself they were descending into.

Damien made an abrupt turn and headed toward a secure, nearly fortress-like structure with reinforced iron doors. The building itself was modest in size, and to the unaware, appeared to be little more than a warehouse of sorts, perhaps even an overseer's residence. Sylvia took notice of a score of Rhivothi standing at the entrance, its doors having been forced open.

Curiously she followed, her heart racing on ahead. As they approached, the warriors parted, themselves offering reverent bows of their heads. There was a soft glow of oil lanterns inside, though something appeared to shine out through the doorway. Damien paused, a sly grin drawing his mouth tight. He raised a hand and beckoned her to continue. Sylvia drew in a deep breath, then cautiously entered the imposing structure.

What she saw was something out of a dream. The room was cavernous, with no other rooms inside it. But the space itself was of no consequence; what it held within drew her immediate attention. Stacked from floor to ceiling was a vast collection of large, golden ingots. There had to be hundreds of them, likely thousands, each twinkling in soft rays of lantern light.

Sylvia stood breathless while Damien stepped past her. He held his arms out wide, basking in the glory of their plunder. "You see, Stormguard, what we have done here today will help to hasten Betanthia's demise. Iron is of great use on the battlefield, but gold is what commands armies. It is the lifeblood of any kingdom. And now, Marcellus Bethard will be bled dry. Come."

He gestured for her to follow back outside. She saw almost the entirety of the warband looking on intently, word of the discovery having spread like wildfire. Each man was grinning and baying for their chance to take a share of the spoils.

"Inside that cavern is where they mine for gold. We must not allow it to be retaken," Dreadfire said, before turning his attention to the warband. "Time is precious, and we must not linger any longer than is necessary. You have earned your fortunes today, my friends. Take all you can carry, but no more. We must set off across the Plainhold at once, and strike at the heart of Betanthia while they are weakest."

"Damien," Sylvia called out over an approving roar from the warriors. "What of Betanthia's northern army? Will they not be upon us by then?"

The warlord grinned. It was the sort of unsettling look she had seen on occasion, though not for some time, and only when he possessed some sort of knowledge that others did not.

"Worry not, Stormguard," he said. "Their northern army is leaderless, and fears to leave their stronghold at Brimnora. We shall not be encountering them any time in the future. Believe me when I say this."

"And how do you know?" she asked, apprehensively.

Damien Dreadfire lifted his chin, his eyes becoming vacant, as if replaying some distant memory. "Another story for another time, perhaps." He turned and disappeared into a sea of warriors, each of them pushing forward to claim their plunder.

Gold was of little consequence to her, though a few extra coins would warrant no complaint. Above all else, Sylvia yearned for rest, her strength utterly exhausted. An oak tree sat not far from the wall, its branches and trunk unphased by the fiery bombardment. She sat beneath it, slipping into unconsciousness in an instant.

Her dreams were a chaotic mess of colors and the memories of battle. Thankfully, the visions faded as quickly as they arrived. Sylvia then awoke suddenly, gagging and vomiting up a foul, brown liquid. The taste was something out of a nightmare, though it was thankfully cleansed away with a mouthful of mead.

Another horn blast pierced the air, and soon a procession of warriors began to slither out from the mine. Each of them was laden with pilfered weapons, armor, and above all else, gold. Many of the men struggled to carry their ingots, but none would be caught dead leaving them behind. Not only was the battle a success, but it had also made them fabulously wealthy. No doubt the camp followers would return to their villages and bring with them good fortune and word of victory, and likely return with more men seeking their own riches.

She smiled, encouraged by the merriment, and satisfied at the sight of plumes of black smoke which rose into the air. Hok's last vestiges were now burning, and with it went Betanthia's lifeblood. Sylvia stood on unsteady legs and began making her way out of the uninhabitable husk of a city. Along the way, she passed many dead knights, but even more northmen, each lying forever still on reddened ground.

It was an uncomfortable reminder of the warband's mortality. Their warriors fought well, but the knights were every bit as deadly as Damien had cautioned, as evidenced by their swordwork. Sylvia somberly looked upon the remains of every Rhivothi, every Nothanek, and indeed every Zylmacian, humbled by the true cost of things they sought more than riches: their lives, and their freedom.

TITAN III

T‍HE LONG SHADOW OF CASTLE THORN STRETCHED FAR AND WIDE, eclipsing the rising sun behind it. The sight of its ominous black tower came as a relief, in a macabre sort of way. It was a sign of inevitability, that his time upon the earth was growing short. It would have been a lie to say he was unafraid, as evidenced by a light jingling of his wrist shackles against one another.

It was not the sword Tylar feared, nor the rope, which was the more likely option. No, not even the prospect of death itself was frightening. He had stared it down more times than even the gods could count, if they were real. It was, however, difficult to know why his hands were even shaking to begin with. Perhaps he really was afraid, but if he had to be honest with himself, the sight of Castle Thorn brought with it somber thoughts of Madelyn.

The girl should have been here to see this, alive and on her horse, riding back to return with an army and avenge the others. But now here I am, by some cruel twist of fate, coming back here to die. Fuck it. If there's a life after this one, maybe I'll see her again. And if I do, I'll slap the shit out of her for not leaving when she had the chance.

The army was certainly here waiting, judging by what he saw. A tent city had sprung up around Bentmont's outskirts, populated by tens of thousands of men who marched under the King's banner. Titan supposed that soon they would be on the move, joined by his so-called brothers in the Order.

"You see that, Bradshaw?" Elite Conrak asked mockingly. "Take a good, long look. While you're rotting in a cell, waiting to have your day at the gallows, those men are going to bring this war to a swift end. The glory will be theirs, and Betanthia will forever be in their debt. You, on the other hand, will be remembered as a coward and a traitor, if you're even remembered at all. You could have died a hero, and had statues built and songs sung in your honor. But it seems you weren't man enough."

Tylar offered no retort nor challenge, not that it would do him any good in the first place. The Elite was not a man to rise to such bait, gutless as he was for it. Even though Tylar was weak from nursing a leg wound, he could still dispatch the whole lot of them with ruthless efficiency. But no, Conrak was too smart of a man.

It was impossible to not feel judgemental gazes from every soldier throughout the camp. It seemed Conrak made it a point to venture right through the heart of the army on their way to Castle Thorn, smiling and boastful and mocking. Tylar wondered if any of the men staring at him knew he was a survivor of Castle Morden. If appearances were taken into account, they likely thought him nothing more than a common cutthroat.

There seemed to be more important matters on the minds of the soldiers, thankfully. Most looked grim and determined, and likely had never experienced a real battle in their lives. It was easy for a man such as Tylar Bradshaw to know, as he could tell how much blood a man had spilled simply by looking into their eyes.

These men aren't killers. No, they're nothing more than conscripted rabble. I wonder if any of them will even make it out of this war alive.

The closer they drew to the streets of Bentmont, the more the army's composition changed. He saw banners of Ridley Vakaro, and the seasoned men who marched under them. The large white and red standards were emblazoned with a sword and shield, and commanded nothing less than awe at the mere sight of them. Tylar almost began to feel sorry for the barbarian horde, knowing what sort of vengeance was soon to come their way.

He had heard near countless stories about the southern Commandant, as his forces were tasked with defending Naxonnos and its surrounding lands from the Droethiens. On rotation, Tylar would often encounter Lord Vakaro's soldiers, and knew them to be nearly as ruthless as their master. These men had the look of killers in their eyes.

The wagon rolled through the cobbled streets of Bentmont, which he had come to know like the back of his hand. It was the same droll, narrow, cramped shithole he remembered it always being, except this time the streets were overflowing with soldiers. He saw many war flags decorating nearly every avenue, most of which were foreign to him. Judging from the well-tanned men carrying them, they were from the south.

At first the masses thought little of him, until some began to hollar and catcall. The insults were few at first, and Tylar paid them little heed. But gradually, the locals began to take notice. The mood shifted like the arrival of a sudden thunderstorm, erupting into a downpour of shouts and curses. All manner of projectiles and refuse were hurled at the wagon, pelting him mercilessly.

"You dumb shits!" he roared. "Who do you think I am, some northman? Don't you know your own kind?" His fingers gripped the wagon's steel bars so tightly he could have pried them apart, were it not for his weakened state.

"They don't recognize traitors, Bradshaw!" Conrak taunted, leaning his head backward. "You might as well be a northman, for all they care. You're going to die all the same anyways, so what difference does it make? You see that up ahead? That's your reckoning."

Tylar felt his throat tighten as he turned and saw the imposing mass of Castle Thorn staring back at him. The stronghold was not far away now, and as it drew closer, any hope of escape drifted further away. Before long, he was outside its front gate, hoping beyond hope the portcullis was rusted and seized and would never open. But such thoughts were foolish, and before long the massive steel barricade was lifted, and the wagon rumbled inside.

It seemed like only yesterday when he last stood in the courtyard with Madelyn and her soft little lover, and that insufferable old twat Northcott. He could almost see the four of them, even now, like ghosts from another era, about to embark on a quest doomed to fail. If only he could have done more to convince the girl not to leave, then perhaps she would still be alive and he would be back in the barracks drinking himself to death. It was the only sort of fate he desired.

"Take this coward to the dungeons. The High Marshal can't stomach the sight of him," a lean, young looking officer said, sizing Tylar up. A pair of knights opened the cage and dragged him out.

"Any idea when he plans to take his head?" Conrak asked. "I was hoping it would be soon, so I could see it for myself. I rode a long way, I think I'm at least entitled to a show."

"It'll be soon enough. The High Marshal is busy planning the offensive with Lord Vakaro. They're inside now."

"Lord Vakaro, eh?" Conrak stroked his chin. "Then it seems Cardale is finally taking this war seriously. Any word on who the High Marshal is bringing with him?"

"Not yet, but that's a discussion better had without the company of traitors."

Both men looked at Tylar, who found his gaze slowly falling to the ground. He would have liked nothing more than to rejoin the army and head back west to have his vengeance. But it was sadly not meant to be. Other men would have to avenge Madelyn, lesser men, he thought.

"Fair enough," Conrak conceded. "Let me take care of this first, then we can talk." He gave Tylar a shove, and they continued on into the keep, then turned and headed down toward Castle Thorn's dungeon.

Together, they descended a long, winding staircase, poorly lit by a few flickering lanterns. Conrak took up a lantern of his own, though the light did little to guide Tylar. He stumbled and nearly fell several times on unsure footing, much to the Elite's amusement. Soon, a warm glow of light from the dungeon filled the stairway. Tylar gulped, knowing his chances of escape were diminishing with every step.

"Don't even think about it, Bradshaw," Conrak cautioned. "I know what you're thinking; you think you're going to try and overpower me and make a run for it. But I would warn you against such foolishness."

"And how the fuck did you know what I was thinking? You some kind of mind reader?"

"Your body language, you dumb animal. Do you honestly think I can't size a man like you up, or have you forgotten how easily I dispatched those Zylmacians? Truth is, I could have handled twice as many and produced the same result."

The man's arrogance was truly astonishing, but his boast was nevertheless plausible. Conrak was a different breed of warrior entirely. He was not some rigorously trained soldier, fighting in formations and following gentleman's rules. No, he was a man who fought without constraint, on terms of his choosing, regardless of circumstance.

"Yeah, you can fight. I'll give you that much. So what's a man like you doing in the Order? You could be making a fortune as some lord's bodyguard, or as a hired sword."

"Because, Bradshaw… sometimes in life, we're called to serve a purpose greater than ourselves. But I wouldn't expect a deserter to understand."

They arrived at the dungeon, a dank, foul place from which no hope could escape. Many cells sat vacant with little more than old straw inside them. Some held prisoners, their occupants either asleep or staring vacuously into space. While the quarters were cramped and anything but luxurious, they were far from the dens of nightmares he had sometimes heard stories about. A pair of jailors fell in behind Conrak, each clad in mail and carrying short swords.

"No, not here," Conrak said, shoving him toward a dark, musty smelling cell in the far corner. " This is you. Enjoy it, while you can. I suspect you'll be dead within the week, if the High Marshal is merciful."

"Fuck his mercy," Tylar snarled back. "I'd rather he just take my head now and be done with it. Everyone I've ever cared about is waiting for me, everyone who died for this fucking Order in vain. As much as I'd like to tear your throat out, I pray you never have to experience the things I have. I can't describe how it feels to watch as the people you care about are cut down and butchered, then forgotten."

The Elite chuckled. "Come now, Bradshaw, who could ever care about a miserable old man like you? Your friends must not have been too hearty, or else they would still be alive. Perhaps if you and your lot focused more on your training and not on the wine cask, you all would have been better off."

Tylar ground his teeth until his jaw was quivering, his brow so furrowed his eyes began turning red with rage. "Madelyn, the girl you fuckers let ride to the far side of the world and die; what about her? Perhaps if more of you had the balls to come with us, we would have stood a fighting chance. The best Commander and—" He felt himself beginning to waver. "—one of the best friends I've ever had, dead. Are you going to be cruel and keep her waiting for me even longer? Come on, Conrak. Just take my life and be done with it."

Both men stared at each other in the dancing torchlight briefly, before the jailors shoved Tylar into his cell. The rusty hinges screamed as they were closed, a large skeleton key turning twice until the lock was secured tight. Elite Conrak turned and started down the hall, but paused halfway.

"That's where you're wrong, Bradshaw. Commander Everly lives. In fact, she's a few floors right above your head. I figured I would save that little piece of information until after you were in your cell. She's alive, and no thanks to you. Now, sit there and contemplate your actions."

Tylar's heart felt as if it were suddenly attacking him. At first, he was unable to believe what he was hearing. Madelyn? Alive? No, he thought. There was no way in hell she could have survived the siege, much less captivity. Conrak was lying, he had to be.

"You lie!" he shouted. "You can say whatever bullshit you want about me, but you leave the girl out of this! Don't you dare use her memory to torture me. She deserves better!"

"I'm many things, Bradshaw. A liar is not one of them. Slander me as such, and I'll come in that cell and cut out that insolent tongue of yours. She's alive, mark my words."

Time itself seemed to come screeching to a halt. He stepped back from the bars, falling onto the cold, slimy, disgusting stone floor. Each gasp for air became more desperate than the last. With every tear that filled his eyes, Tylar huffed and snarled louder, trying to intimidate his emotions away.

She's alive? How could this be? I was there, I saw how many northmen stormed into the castle. Nobody could have made it out of there, not if they weren't following me out through the window. How? How is this possible?

A sudden desperation took hold of him. Enraged, Tylar regained his footing and charged the door of his cell, jerking and straining to pull the steel bars apart. His effort, however, was futile. Even at full strength, it would be impossible to escape such an imposing prison. Instead, he slumped against the wall, eyes drifting off toward some distant point in space, and began reliving that fateful night at Castle Morden all over again.

EINARR II

NEED SOME TIMBER. WHAT GOOD ARE MY HANDS IF I DO NOTHING WITH THEM?
Despite his earlier efforts, the walls of his hovel were still bitterly drafty. Though, come summertime, it might not be so terrible. But to Einarr, the frigid sting of cold, dark nights was enough to compel him to make the necessary repairs. He remembered seeing a few fallen trees near the Teb, its banks eroding and the nearby vegetation diminishing as a result.

With axe in hand, Einarr walked down to the river, closing his eyes every so often to bask in its scent. There was something magical about it, something which felt rejuvenating to his soul. With the changing of each season, the water itself seemed to change in kind, offering forth a variety of sights and scents and energies which only the keen could pick up on.

It was almost enough to make him forget about the emptiness in his heart. Almost. The cherry blossom tree in the distance brought with it an avalanche of old memories, each of them tearing open old scars. As often as Einarr tried to remain stoic, there was something about the final resting place of his love that seemed to wither every ounce of his resolve.

As he walked, he approached the hovel of Nell, a neighbor only a few homes down the dirt road. She was a quiet woman, small in stature and not particularly shapely. Blonde of hair and gray of eye, she was neither beautiful nor homely, but a kind soul nevertheless. Einarr recalled Nell having a conversation or two with Alina when she was alive, and remembered her as being soft spoken, yet hospitable.

She stood in the doorway of her home, sweeping clouds of dirt outside, lost in whatever thoughts were running through her mind. Einarr glanced over his shoulder as he passed by, having sensed a gaze of what felt to be longing. Nell's gray eyes met his for half a second before falling to the ground, a shy smile creeping across her plain face. He thought nothing of it, giving little more than a nod of acknowledgement before continuing on toward the cherry blossom tree.

Once there, he brushed away some sticks and other debris from the spot where Alina lay. It was a ritual he had performed many times, far too many for his liking. Someone so young and beautiful was not supposed to be returned to the gods so soon. But no amount of begging, no amount of tears, and no amount of rage would ever bring her back.

"Another day without you is another day I count the moments until we are together again."

Einarr sometimes wished he had fallen on the battlefield, fighting for honor and for the gods. It would have been easy enough, as there had been every opportunity to taste death at Blackwolf Pass and Castle Morden. But the gods had decided otherwise, and here he remained. Frustrated, he left the burial ground feeling more alone than before arriving.

The further Einarr walked, the more he felt hostile eyes upon him, judging, even conspiring, for all he knew. He paid them no mind, as best he could, and continued on, following the bends of the Teb River. Even passing by Skaginlef's mead hall proved to be difficult, with all of the painful memories it provoked.

I can't take it anymore. I've got to get away from here. For the sake of my soul, I have to leave.

And so Einarr walked along the river's edge, further and further north, until the sounds and smells of Skaginlef faded away like morning fog. It was quiet, save for the bubbling waters and a choir of spring birds in the trees. While the land was still barren and dingy brown, soon it would breathe again and green life would return to the grasses and trees.

The serenity of isolation was something he was becoming dangerously accustomed to as of late. Leaving Skaginlef and its people behind and taking to the forests seemed more appealing with each passing day, and he suspected the Nothanek would miss his presence little. He began to understand the wanderlust of Marvath Bonesplitter and his kin, even envying it, in a way. But then again, the Rhivothi were never truly alone; they had each other. Einarr, on the other hand, wanted none of it.

What am I even doing here? There's nothing left here for me. How does it benefit me to remain in the company of memories?

He sighed, drawing a thick essence of pine into his lungs. He had always enjoyed walking among the evergreens, and found it to be one of the few things capable of calming his troubled mind. This was where the gods lived, and perhaps in their magnificent home there might be liberation.

Needles and dry leaves crunched underfoot as Einarr trudged deeper into the forest, his eyes scanning and searching its sacred groves. But for what, he could not be certain. Hour after hour, he continued onward until he had nearly lost all sense of time and location, wandering hopelessly until he came upon a peculiar looking pine tree. Its color was a deep blue, its trunk tall, with long, flowing branches which hung to the ground.

Curiously, Einarr approached, taking note of how different the tree looked compared to those around it. He spied a small opening between its branches and pushed them aside, and gave a sudden gasp at the sight of what lay beyond. There was a blanket of shaggy green grass, its blades thin and tall, and soft as feathers. Small, glowing orbs of what looked to be fireflies filled the enclosure with luminescent light, though as Einarr stepped inside, he saw they were instead some sort of spore, or other strange substance.

"Gods, how is this possible?" he asked in astonishment.

Such a place simply could not be real. Einarr knelt and ran his hand across the soft green carpet, which felt cool to the touch. How anything could grow in such an environment, devoid of sunlight, was a mystery unto itself. He walked toward the trunk, its bark nearly as blue as its needles. Cautiously, he extended a hand and touched its surface, and was awestruck at the warmth radiating from it.

"Thank you for bringing me to this place, oh gods. Thank you for reminding me of your presence. Forgive me for ever doubting your majesty."

For the first time in months, Einarr Rolffson had found his smile, and felt nothing but serenity. He sat, back pressed against the trunk, and watched as glowing green orbs fluttered to the ground, dancing and swaying playfully like falling flakes of snow. He laughed in disbelief, but then felt a sudden sadness deep within his heart.

I wish Alina was here to see this...

Einarr's eyes grew heavy in a near instant, and became more weary the harder he tried to stay awake. Something was compelling him to sleep, to enter the dream world and experience whatever the gods had waiting in store. He smiled once again before the light turned to black, but this time the darkness felt different. Since returning from Damien's war, his dreams were often filled with horrific images of fire and death, terrible things he had witnessed or done with his own hands. But now, he felt only love, and peace, and light.

A sudden brightness filled the thick canopy, not blinding, but warm, and as inviting as a morning sunrise. When he opened his eyes, bright pillars of yellow light filtered in through the branches, each boldly pronounced through a dense wall of humidity. Einarr rose to his feet, an unusual, soft prickling sensation covering his whole body, as if he could feel each and every hair standing firmly on end.

Apprehensively, he moved to the opening and brushed the branches aside. He jumped backward in surprise as he bore witness to the splendor of the forest all around. It was green and full of life, with a small pond sitting just ahead. Its waters bubbled and flowed over a slate rock waterfall, and were so bright and aquamarine they appeared to be glowing from deep underneath the surface.

"Kholdyr, what magic is this?"

Einarr was completely lost for words. He spied a pair of deer grazing nearby, their heads lifting as he stepped into the clearing, though they seemed not to mind. A flock of songbirds serenaded softly overhead as they flew from branch to branch, beautifully announcing his arrival to the forest. A refreshing northern breeze blew gentle, warm kisses across his face.

The air smelled of freshly burned incense, strong of sandalwood with a slight hint of perfume. Truly, this was the realm of the gods, Einarr could feel it deep within his soul. He approached the pond, eager to dip his hand into its waters and maybe even drink from them.

But there was a slight disturbance beneath the surface that drew his attention. With each step, the waters rustled and churned and eventually parted, and to his astonishment, he saw Alina rising from below, clothed in a slender gown of white silk. Einarr immediately fell to his knees, mouth agape as tears erupted from his eyes.

"My love, please don't despair," Alina said, a soft and inviting smile adorning her perfect face. She stepped forward on the water's surface as if it were glass, and slowly extended a hand.

"Is it… can it be… is it really you, Alina?" Einarr asked, choking on every word. He clutched his chest, heart pounding as strongly as a hammer on an anvil.

"It is, Einarr. It's alright. I'm safe and happy, and in the company of the gods. Come, come closer."

Though hesitant, Einarr moved to the water's edge and took Alina's hand. Her skin was warm and alive, exactly how he remembered it, not cold and devoid of life. She stepped gingerly from the pond and fell immediately into his arms. They held each other for what seemed like an eternity, tears of happiness flowing freely from his eyes.

"Alina… I've missed you so much. I've been so lost since you've been away," he said, sobbing. "I'm nothing without you."

"My love," she whispered, stroking his long, brown hair. "You know that isn't true. You're strong, wise, and loyal. You're a good man, and always have been."

"But I've done terrible things, my love, terrible things the gods have cursed me for."

Alina broke from their embrace, taking a step back, then softly placed both of her hands on his face. "No, the gods haven't forsaken you. You have done everything they have asked of you, and you never lost yourself along the way. Kholdyr forgives all, especially for those who lay down their lives in his service."

Einarr wiped water from his eyes. "It doesn't feel that way. I feel like I'm lost at sea, with no sail or paddle to save me. I don't know what to do, Alina. I cannot subject myself to more wanton butchery, and there's no peace for me at Skaginlef. And besides, I haven't sacrificed my life. I'm still here, and I'm more alone now than I've ever been."

"The gods haven't forsaken you, Einarr, and neither have I," she said, smiling. "You would not feel this way if your heart was impure. Do you trust me?"

The question seemed like an affront, but instead of being offended, he nodded.

"Good," she turned and started back to the water. "Then believe me when I say that Zifnir's mercy will come to you soon."

"But what am I to do?" he asked, trying to reach out to her, but his body was frozen in place.

"You must be strong, and remain true to who you are. The days ahead of you will be difficult, my love, and you will once more be thrust into the fires of war. You were chosen for this special time for a reason. Please, have faith, and trust me when I say the gods are with you always… as am I."

Alina began to sink into the bright blue waters of the pond, slowly, until she nearly disappeared from sight. Einarr felt a sudden panic deep inside him, and tried desperately to reach out to her. The gods were cruel enough to take her away once before, and he would be damned if he would allow it to happen for a second time.

Mustering every ounce of strength in his body and soul, he trudged forward, determined to save the love of his life as he could not before. But as he extended an arm, the brightness of the grove turned to black, and he was back underneath the canopy of the pine tree. Its magic seemed to have faded alongside the vision, the glowing spores and soft grass losing their allure and becoming dreary and lifeless.

When Einarr stepped out from under the pine, a soft wind rustled through the trees, sweeping dead leaves against his legs. He stood motionless, skin turned to gooseflesh, struggling to make sense of what had just transpired. The vision was real, the realest thing he had ever experienced, even more real than the moment he found himself in now.

Truly, the gods have spoken. But why me? I'm just a simple builder, not some great warrior. Men like me aren't meant to change the world.

It was frightening, yet exciting beyond belief to have had such an encounter, though it seemed to have left behind many more questions than it answered. The sun was beginning to fall, which helped to determine his way home. Einarr trudged back to Skaginlef, completely lost in thought, and before he knew it, the mead hall came into view just ahead.

A soft glow flickered from inside the windows, a thin wisp of smoke slipping from the chimney and into the sky. Sounds of merriment wafted throughout the village, though Einarr was not in the mood to partake in any of it. He returned to his hovel, shut the door tightly, and nursed one mug of mead after another.

He slept little that night, or not at all, it was difficult to know for certain. As the first rays of daylight began to glow in the eastern sky, he rose from bed, dressed, and retrieved two sacks of seeds from a storage closet. The weather had been exceptional, and Einarr supposed it was as good a time as any to begin his spring planting.

The ground was wet with dew, and a faint veil of fog lay draped over the village. As he stepped out into the crisp morning air, a disturbance near the river caught his attention. It was difficult to make out through the swirling mist, but it almost appeared to be some sort of fire. Einarr feared the mead hall might have burnt into nothingness in the middle of the night, likely the result of the drunken debauchery of a few hours prior.

Facing toward the unknown, he was brought to a swift halt as the fog suddenly parted. He saw the cherry blossom tree, its trunk glowing warm with radiant heat, its branches erupting with thousands of beautiful, pink flowers. A beautiful scent of vanilla, lilac, and rose was so thick Einarr felt intoxicated with each breath.

He closed his eyes and basked in the perfection, certain he was still dreaming. That was, until he felt a soft touch of familiar arms embracing him from behind.

"M… my love? Is… is that you?"

GARETH II

T HE OMINOUS PEAK OF CASTLE THORN CAME INTO VIEW AROUND midday, jutting high over the horizon. The sight was nearly as unsettling as it was unbelievable, and Gareth had to remind himself that these were still his lands, and the occupants of the imposing tower sworn to House Bethard's service.

"I never imagined I would see such a thing," he shouted over the pounding of his horse's hooves.

"I've seen it more times than I can count, and it still leaves me in awe," Sir Edmund Thomas said, his horse keeping stride. "Shouldn't be long now, we'll be there before you know it."

There was a nagging feeling in the back of Gareth's mind, a feeling which made him wish they would never arrive, for fear of what schemes Lord Vakaro and his lordlings were hatching. But despite such misgivings, he continued to drive forward, until the full breadth of Bentmont came into view. The city was much the same as he had imagined it, but now a cloud of tents blanketed its outskirts.

It was easy to imagine an army of such size, but seeing it was another matter entirely. Tens of thousands of men, more than sixty-thousand by the looks of it, moved about through the encampment like worker ants. It was sobering to behold, a reminder that this was war he was about to partake in.

If my father could do it, then so can I. I have to, there's no other way around it now.

A trumpet blast rang out as Gareth and his bodyguard approached the outer perimeter. The King's standard drew curious attention from the infantrymen, some of whom were tending to their weapons and armor, training, or performing whatever menial tasks their commanders had assigned. Many of them dropped to one knee and bowed to their prince respectfully, but the more seasoned soldiers looked none too impressed. Were he the king, every Betanthian in sight would have fallen to their knees without hesitation, but in that moment, he understood the name of Bethard would only carry him so far.

"Bow to your prince!" Lord Anders Kenfield bellowed. "You there! Bow, I say!"

While the sentiment was appreciated, Gareth preferred the soldiers under Lord Vakaro not think him an insufferable tyrant. Such men would be more apt to turn their swords upon him than fall on them, if ordered to do so.

"Anders…" Gareth silenced the lord with a flick of his wrist. "That won't be necessary. I know I'll have to earn their respect, as my father did before he became king. Besides," he said, softer. "It will help us learn which men are more loyal to our enemies than ourselves. Let them make their allegiances known."

"Very well, my prince," Anders conceded. "Call me old fashioned, but I never thought I would live to see the day when soldiers would need to be coerced into paying their respects."

Together, Gareth and his bodyguard trotted into the encampment. It was disconcerting to see so many men looking so grim. Gareth looked into the eyes of one soldier as he sat on a large stone, his gaze distant and fearful, as if he had just received news of a family death.

"Everything alright, soldier?" Gareth asked, bringing his horse to a halt.

At first the man was hesitant to speak, but after a hard swallow and a deep breath, he found courage. "Yes, my prince. Well… it's just… some of the men have been telling stories about the barbarians, and…"

"What sort of stories? Please, enlighten me."

"Many things," another wide-eyed soldier chimed in. "We've been hearin' stories about that Damien Dreadfire, or whatever his name is, and how he tore through Lord Valens' army with only a few hundred men."

"I heard they can transform into beasts," the first man interrupted. "Cruel, savage animals with all manner of scales, and claws, and teeth. I know a man who had a brother who survived Morden, and he said Damien Dreadfire shapeshifted into a dragon and burned it all to the ground!"

"That's bullshit," a third man said, muscling his way into the conversation. "Pardon the language, my prince, but Damien Dreadfire don't fly, that's ridiculous. See, I heard the northmen live in these huge underground caves, and they're expert miners. They burrowed under the castle and sank its walls from below. And I have it on good authority that—"

It was a terribly amusing exchange to witness. Gareth had to stop himself from chuckling at the soldier's embellishments, though it was easy to see why many thought the loss of Cedric Valens and his army was the work of some otherworldly force.

"I can assure you, men, whatever manner of beast these barbarians are, we will meet them in force and send them back to whatever forest, or pit, or swamp they came from. Have no doubt about that."

A lack of response from the soldiers was troubling, as fear had clearly taken root deep within them. Gareth would have been lying if he were to say he was absent of that same creeping sense of dread, but being in the midst of the army helped to strengthen his resolve. He would need it in the weeks and months ahead.

After riding throughout the encampment a while longer, he decided to head into the city. This would be his first visit to Bentmont, and knew it only through stories Madelyn and Edmund would sometimes tell. It was every bit as intriguing as he had imagined. It was an old city indeed, and it possessed a far greater charm than the capital could ever hope for. Its locals turned out in droves, lining either side of Bentmont's narrow streets as the royal procession made its way toward Castle Thorn. It was curious to note, however, their lack of enthusiasm.

Perhaps they had grown used to the comings and goings of military men, or perhaps it was simply fear of the unknown which gripped them. Surely, this was the first time Betanthia had amassed such a force in generations, and with Damien Dreadfire's location unknown, it was easy to understand their apprehension.

"They're terrified," Gareth observed.

"Can't say I blame them," Sir Edmund said, riding alongside him. "The northmen may never make it this far, but this war just became real for everyone living here."

"We'll stop them. We can muster ten times whatever force they send, without even trying."

"Be careful," Edmund cautioned. "They *did* best Lord Valens with just a fraction of what he sent out there. Never underestimate your foe, no matter how great the odds are in your favor. It's a mistake that can turn a certain victory into the most crushing defeat."

As they continued onward, a large, domed structure came into view. It was near blinding to look at in the light, its smooth marble surface reflecting the sun's rays like a mirror. Gareth had never seen such a structure before, and while its height was modest in comparison to Castle Thorn, it was every bit as awe inspiring.

"You're looking at the Ivornorium, my prince," Anders stated. "It's one of the oldest buildings in Bentmont, and perhaps even Caldakas, if memory serves."

"What is it?" he asked. "Some sort of temple?"

"It's a library, though I doubt men like us have use for such places."

As fascinating as the structure was, there was little time to explore much of anything beyond what could plainly be seen. Castle Thorn lay just a mile ahead. The ominous fortress grew larger the closer they came, its height and breadth rivaling the Westwind Citadel. From its towers flew black and gold colors of the Blackthorn Knights, each banner so large it nearly blotted out the sun.

A half score of guards stood outside the main gate, its portcullis lowered. Their discipline was a stark contrast to that of the city watchmen of Cardale, who were often seen lazing around their stations. Here, knights stood like statues, their eyes ever watchful. They saluted as Gareth and his host approached, a senior officer stepping forward to offer a greeting.

"Good day to you, Sirs. How may I be of assistance?"

"The only Sir here is me," Edmund Thomas said, smiling. "This here is Gareth Bethard, crown prince of Betanthia."

The knights immediately fell to one knee nearly in unison, their gazes averted to the ground. It was comforting to know the Order remained true to their vows of loyalty, even if it was merely superficial.

"Welcome to Bentmont, Prince Gareth. Castle Thorn is yours." The officer rose and moved briskly to the portcullis, shouting an order to open it with all haste. As the steel barricade rattled upward, he ducked underneath and entered the courtyard, shouting something indiscernible. The knights outside of the gate stood after Gareth passed by, his bodyguard following closely behind.

Castle Thorn's courtyard was impossibly large, though it had none of the adornments of the Westwind Citadel. It was every bit the fortress he had imagined, complete with stables, training dummies, and crates and barrels of newly arrived provisions. Rushing out from the officer's quarters was a man garbed in a fine black leather jerkin and boots, black breeches, and a flowing blue cloak.

"Welcome to Castle Thorn, Your Highness. We are privileged to receive you. My name is Commander Renald Fletch."

The stronghold was as impressive as it was intimidating. Its sheer scale was enough to give Gareth pause as he dismounted, stealing a moment to study its menacing architecture.

"Shall I give you a tour, my prince?"

"No," Gareth answered. "I fear the war might be over by the time we're finished. Perhaps you can give me an abbreviated version on the way to the High Marshal's quarters."

"Absolutely, Your Highness. But allow me first to present you with a gift, courtesy of the Order. The High Marshal welcomes you, and presents you with this Plainhold Strider." Renald motioned to a page, who brought over a large, black warhorse. "These mounts are the heart and soul of every knight. May it serve you well, as they have served us."

A fine gift, to be certain. Gareth studied the horse, whose fearsome size made his own look like a pony in comparison. He ran a hand across its mane, which was brushed as smooth as fine silk.

"You have my thanks, and my appreciation," he said, nodded in approval. "Now, if you would be so kind as to show me to the High Marshal's quarters."

"Very well, my prince, as you wish." Renald bowed. "Please, come with me."

A massive set of doors to the keep sat open, a faint echo of conversation filtering outside. Castle Thorn's interior was so vast and populated it appeared as if it were a city, complete with an armory, mess quarters, and a variety of other rooms and stalls. Gareth was uncertain if the stronghold appeared larger on the outside or on the inside.

Those in close proximity took notice of a multitude of purple cloaks and gave their sworn courtesies. Word spread rapidly throughout the keep, with each man vying for an opportunity to catch a glimpse of their prince. Commander Fletch was difficult to hear over the echoing of hundreds of knights, his introductory lesson on Thorn's origins going unheard.

"Impressive, is it not?" Renald boasted. "On the lower levels are the enlisted barracks, the infirmary, and armory, that latter you can see over there."

"I assume the High Marshal's office is in the tower?"

"Yes." Renald nodded. "All of the senior officers have quarters on various levels. Commanders such as myself are afforded suites on the highest levels with the best views."

Gareth sighed as they began a near endless ascent up a gargantuan staircase at the far end of the keep. "I was good friends with a Commander once. I wonder if her quarters are still there, or if they've been reassigned."

"Her?" Renald cocked his head. "You wouldn't happen to be speaking of Madelyn Everly, would you, my prince?"

"Yes. We were friends for many years, and unfortunately our last interaction left much to be desired. Now I'll never have the opportunity to set things right with her. I can only imagine how her passing has affected all of you."

"What do you mean, my prince?" Renald paused in his tracks. "She's alive, and returned to us just recently. She's in the infirmary as we speak."

His legs immediately turned to water. Gareth had to place a hand against the black stone wall to stop himself from tumbling down the stairs. There was a fierce tightness in his chest, as if his heart were attacking him. "You… you cannot be serious. Truly, is she here?"

"Absolutely, Your Highness. I would never speak a lie to you. Would you like me to take you to her? She's probably resting. The journey was long, and her road to recovery even longer. But she's very much alive."

Gareth nodded, and nearly stumbled down the stairs several times as he clumsily descended back to ground level. Time itself seemed to inch by as a million thoughts stampeded through his mind. She was alive, but in what condition? Had she lost a limb in the fighting, or perhaps was mutilated and horribly scarred? Each was certainly a possibility, but none of it truly mattered.

Renald moved at a brisk pace, sensing Gareth's impatience. The halls seemed to stretch for miles, with seemingly no end in sight. After what felt like a day of walking, they arrived outside the infirmary, though he was uncertain if he wished to enter. There was no telling what his eyes might bear witness to, but they began slowly filling with water regardless.

Gareth pressed an unsteady hand against the door, pushing it open slowly. The infirmary was a large room containing dozens of beds, each perfectly spaced from one another. Most were vacant, save for one on the end. On it lay a man, shirtless and sleeping, a white cloth resting over his feverish brow. Gareth scanned the room end to end, and only as he turned to leave did he see a golden head of hair, sitting in a cushioned chair facing a nearby window.

Is it? Could it be?

"Madelyn?" he called out, voice trembling ever so slightly. There was no response at first. Gareth stepped forward as Sir Edmund closed the door behind him, uncertain of what to expect. Had she been maimed by Damien Dreadfire's beasts and left blind or disfigured? It made little difference if it were true, as he would carve out his own eyes and give them to her if such a thing were possible.

"Madelyn, is that you?"

A pair of wooden canes sat next to the chair. With the strength of a woman in her twilight years, Madelyn gripped the leather-wrapped handles and rose slowly. She wore a simple gown of white linen, the same as the sick man across the room, her hair brushing the backs of her thighs as she stood. Gareth swallowed hard, his breath and heart slowing to a near halt.

Madelyn turned her head slowly, her face a collage of sorrow and pain, her red, swollen eyes distant and devoid of life. She seemed not to recognize Gareth in the slightest, instead staring through him as if no one was there at all.

He sighed and smiled, though it was sorrowful. Fighting back his tears proved to be more difficult than fighting back the thirst which nearly claimed his life. He moved closer, eager to wrap his arms around her and feel the warmth of her skin and smell the sweetness of her hair. But when he did, he saw Madelyn's belly, full and round and near to bursting.

"Oh Madelyn, what have they done to you?" Gareth moved to her side and reached out to hold her, but she began to shriek in terror and thrash with every bit of strength she had left. Clawing and spitting, Madelyn tried to push him away, but the effort was futile. Gareth placed his hands on her shoulders gently, trying to calm her.

"It's me, Gareth!" he pleaded. "Madelyn, Madelyn please! It's me! Don't you recognize me?"

Exhausted, she began to diminish, nearly collapsing onto the bed. Her steely-blue eyes met his, though they were dull and cold, not the shimmering gems he remembered. She studied the lines of his face, now obscured through a carpet of beard growth. But there was something in the depths of his hazel eyes, something which made her remember.

"Gareth!" She collapsed into his arms, babbling and sobbing so violently her words seemed little more than nonsense. Gareth held her gently, pressing her head against his shoulder and stroking her hair.

"It's alright, you're safe. Nobody can hurt you anymore. It's alright."

The stress was too great for her to bear. Madelyn's legs turned to water and began to fail, but thankfully Gareth's arms had grown strong. He delicately assisted her onto the bed, adjusting a pair of pillows and positioning her body just right. Within seconds, she grew faint and slipped into a deep sleep.

Oh my love... I'm so sorry. I can't believe this has happened to you. I'll make them pay, I promise you. Damien Dreadfire. Aldred. Lord Vakaro.

Each and every one of them, they'll all pay. I make this vow to you right here, right now.

A million thoughts raced through his mind, each one of them violent and dripping with blood. His tears of sadness quickly morphed into tears of rage. How anyone could do such a thing to someone like Madelyn was beyond comprehension. The northmen were every bit the cruel, murderous savages they were reported to be. Gareth vowed in that moment to slay Damien Dreadfire and his marauders, no matter what the cost. But for now, there were other matters to attend to.

A Blackthorn physician entered, his attention focused on the other patient inside. He was a man not quite middle-aged, but as weathered as any other knight of the Order. He wore a simple tan tunic and trousers, with a leather bag slung over one shoulder. Gareth stood dumbfounded as the doctor gave Madelyn not the slightest bit of attention.

"You there, come here at once," Gareth commanded. He strode halfway across the room in irritation.

At first, the physician paid no mind. He performed a brief check on the man in bed, who himself was asleep. It was only when the crunching of Sir Edmund's armor filled the room that his attention was given to Gareth.

"Oh, it really is you. I heard you had come to pay us a visit. Deepest apologies, my prince. How may I be of service?"

"Lady Everly. She's a dear friend of mine, and I wish to know her condition."

"Well…" The physician scratched the back of his neck. "She's pregnant, if that wasn't obvious enough. Near to full term, from the looks of it. Other than that, she has a few fractures, some of which haven't healed properly. Diminished muscle mass, lack of appetite, night terrors… it's a lengthy list."

"Is she going to be alright?"

"If by alright, you mean, is she going to survive? Absolutely. Although, if you're wondering if she's ever going to be able to *live*... well, that's another matter entirely. If you'll excuse me, my prince, I have other duties I must attend to."

The physician left nearly as quickly as he came, without so much as giving Madelyn a single glance. It was disappointing to see one of the Order's finest treated in such a callous manner. Gareth had always thought of the Blackthorn Knights as a close-knit community, a band of brothers who would lay down their lives for one other. Sadly, it seemed not to be the case. Instead, Madelyn was left to sit alone and unattended.

She's a Commander and should have her own quarters, with her own physicians to tend to her.

It was unlikely that Madelyn would be able to climb the stairs to her chamber in the tower, so suitable accommodations would have to be made. An infirmary was no place for someone like her, and keeping her in such a location was beyond infuriating.

Sir Edmund gave a soft smile and a nod. "I'm grateful she's alive. This is excellent news indeed."

"There's nothing excellent about what those northmen did to her," Gareth mumbled. "They're monsters. Savages. Animals."

"I didn't mean it like that, Gareth. She's here, and safe. I know what they did was unspeakable, but they could have done worse. Far worse."

It was nearly impossible to imagine a fate worse than what Madelyn had suffered. Death seemed like it would have been a kinder option.

"I know. Forgive me, but I'm angry, Edmund. I want to kill them, each and every last one of them. I want to see their villages burn. And I want to mount Damien Dreadfire's head on my wall for what he's done, not only to Madelyn, but to Betanthia as a whole."

"You'll get your chance soon enough," Sir Edmund said reassuringly. "You have to keep your wits about you, especially on the battlefield.

Fight angry, sure. But don't let it consume you to the point where you fight recklessly. That's how you get yourself killed."

"I know," Gareth replied. "Before we depart, I want to make sure Madelyn is taken care of properly. She's a Commander, and deserves much more than being shuttered away in a dank infirmary. To be honest, Edmund, I'm nearly as angry at the Order as I am the northmen."

"One thing at a time. You need to keep your head focused on the war effort, and whatever Lord Vakaro is up to. I'll make sure Madelyn receives all of the proper treatment, in a much more hospitable location."

Gareth gave her a sad, longing look, then stepped out into the hall. There was nothing more that could be done, for now at least. She was asleep, and from the looks of it, desperately needed the rest. One of the Blackthorn rounded a corner and approached, going about whatever menial tasks he was assigned to.

"You there," he commanded. "Does the High Marshal plan to find suitable quarters for Commander Everly? I would think for someone of her stature, the infirmary is quite unbefitting."

"My prince." The knight paused and bowed, paying his due respects. "It's my understanding that she has been relieved of command, and—"

"And what?" Gareth interrupted, his voice echoing down the hall and back. "Tell me the High Marshal isn't going to toss her out into the streets? After a lifetime of service? After everything she's sacrificed?"

"I'm unaware of what the High Marshal intends to do, my prince. I can certainly get an appropriate answer for you."

Gareth was nearly too stunned and angry to speak. "You'll take me to his chamber at once so I can have his answer for myself."

"As you command, my prince," the man stammered, his eyes darting between Gareth and Sir Edmund's sword, which the elder Guardsman was resting a hand on.

Together they walked down the hall and traversed another long corridor. Castle Thorn seemed to be an endless collection of them, with nearly as many rooms and staircases as the Westwind Citadel. It was only when Gareth spied a staircase leading to the upper levels that he became aware of just how large the stronghold truly was. Three dozen men or more could march abreast up the stairs, which were made from the same black stones as the walls.

Flight after flight they climbed, upward and onward toward the High Marshal's chamber. Sir Edmund was gasping and looked to be faring poorly, and Gareth's hair began sticking to his wet forehead. A servant descended past them, but was promptly stopped by his Blackthorn comrade.

"You there, is the High Marshal in his quarters?" the knight asked.

"No, sir. I have not seen him all day."

The answer came as a disappointment. Huffing his frustration, Gareth started back down the steps. Sir Edmund and the knight turned, giving him a curious look.

"Where are you going?" the elder Guardsman asked.

"I'm not going to wait around for the High Marshal. He's bound to turn up some time. I'm going to sit with Madelyn for now, and make sure she isn't left alone. I couldn't keep her safe before, but I'll be damned if I can't keep her safe now."

CHARLOTTE IV

A T LONG LAST, THE PRISTINE WALLS OF DELLHAVEN CAME INTO view. Queen Charlotte felt the very same excitement as a year ago, the excitement of liberation. However, her experience was not nearly as joyous, as Gareth was absent from her side. Still, returning to the family estate would mark the formal beginning of a new life, free from Marcellus Bethard's cruelty and the chains of the Westwind Citadel.

Thoughts of Gareth were never far away, though Charlotte tried not to dwell on them for too long. He was marching to war, and in war, nothing was certain. Part of her journey toward healing was accepting that some things were simply beyond one's control. She had to trust in Sir Edmund and the soldiers of Betanthia to keep Gareth safe, and she had to trust her son to make the proper decisions, for himself and the Kingdom.

Trust. It was a simple word, yet fraught with many complexities. It was a word that seemed so foreign once, but through love, Charlotte had learned to open herself to trust once more. Love opened many doors which hardship had closed, and behind each of them was an equally valuable possession: time.

With love, clarity of mind, and a newfound freedom, Charlotte would have all the time in the world to live the last decades of her life to their fullest. But what would she do with that time? The question began weighing on her mind, but the answer seemed obvious enough. She would never forget witnessing the joy and admiration of the people as she departed Cardale, and tears in the eyes of the poor and hungry as she tossed them golden coins.

Now that's what I should do! My life has been so blessed with abundance, yet there are so many who survive with so little. I should do my best to make sure no Betanthian goes to bed with an empty stomach.

There was certainly enough gold for such charitable works. With Marcellus forever shut inside his chamber, it was doubtful if he even knew how much money the treasury actually held. Even without state funds, House Bethard's coffers were overfull, and better served lifting the people out of poverty than collecting dust. It was an idea so exciting, Charlotte was unaware her driver had brought her carriage to a halt inside the estate courtyard.

Welcoming her home was Devin, Brendon, and the rest of their faithful servants. Though she had experienced ceremonial greetings a thousand times before, in Dellhaven, it felt much different. Each smile of the men and women in the courtyard was genuine, heartfelt, and nearly brought a tear to her eye.

"Good day to you, Your Majesty!" Devin Brandybrook could hardly contain his excitement. He rushed to open the carriage door, Brendon and another servant hastily hauling over a set of wooden carriage steps.

"And a good day to you, Devin!" She stepped out into the courtyard, the estate's keepers bowing their respects. "I want you all to know how very grateful I am for each and every one of you. I grew up on a farmstead, and my childhood was rather simple compared to my life now. Common, even. While I have enjoyed every day as your queen, I must confess, I long for those quiet, peaceful days once again."

"I trust your visit to Cardale was pleasant?" Devin asked, straightening himself out.

"I found peace… and enlightenment. I am free from the bonds of my husband, and I intend to spend the rest of my life doing for others, as they have done for me."

She stepped toward the servants, then paused, looking each of them in the face. Some were young, some old, but all were faithful in their duties. There was a stark difference in the atmosphere at the estate, as opposed to the Westwind Citadel. The servants at the palace sometimes appeared to be little more than soulless husks going about their monotonous duties on a daily basis. But here, there was love, and life.

"So I have come to a decision," Charlotte announced, smiling. "Some of you are here under free employment, some are indentured. But as of today, I have decreed that you are all free men and women, and shall be justly compensated for your services. You are all equally valued."

The servants were unable to contain their excitement. Many cheered and hugged one another, some wept softly, overcome by her unexpected charity. Charlotte nearly cried with them, her heart so full it was spilling over. She turned to Emilee Harper, her faithful maidservant of many years.

"And that goes for you as well, my dear. You will receive a proper salary, and back payment for each year you have been beside me. Without you, I might never be standing here now, a free woman."

Lost for words and for breath, Emilee gasped and stammered, clutching at her chest as tears spilled down her rosy cheeks. But there was no need for words. The gratitude reflected in her misty eyes spoke volumes all on their own.

"Come now," the Queen said. "I'm certain Devin has prepared a fine meal for us all."

And a proper feast it was. The dining table was crowded with so many dishes and delights it was impossible to know where to start. Tender backstrap, roasted duck, fresh greens from the garden, and fruits of every color were piled high, with wines of every vintage to match. Charlotte eagerly took a scat and welcomed all to join her.

The dining hall had never heard such laughter and lighthearted conversation. Royal protocols be damned, she thought. A moment such as this was infinitely more fulfilling than being among a thousand wealthy lords, laden with their trappings of wealth, simpering and prostrating themselves insincerely. There was much to be said of simple life and simple company, and if Charlotte wanted it this way, she was certain to get it. She *was* still the queen, after all.

She spent the day relaxing and trading stories with some of the servants. Each one of them had a tale of their own to tell, some so fascinating they hardly seemed real. Common folk lived such adventurous lives, at least compared to being locked inside a palace for years. Perhaps a good story was worth more than gold and jewels, she thought. Stories, after all, were the currency of experience.

You still have time, Charlotte... time enough to write a grand tale of your own!

As daylight faded into darkness, the Queen retired to her chamber. At first, it was difficult to find sleep, with thoughts and possibilities of the future dancing through her head. But eventually, she succumbed to slumber, and woke the next day with an ambitious excitement. Charlotte Bethard was eager to begin writing the first page of her story, a new story, one which might be passed down for a millenia or more.

The air was surprisingly crisp, the grass slick with droplets of morning dew. A chorus of song birds chirped softly against a backdrop of lazy tides splashing against sandy shores. Charlotte adored these Dellhaven mornings, though they were unlikely to last beyond the next fortnight. Summer would be approaching, and with it the agony of sweltering heat and suffocating humidity.

She found herself wandering the gardens before breakfast, enjoying the sights and scents of thousands of flowers as they began erupting into an explosion of bright colors and therapeutic aromas. While they paled in comparison to the majesty of the Citadel's, the estate's gardens were nevertheless an earthly delight. She often wondered how Devin was able to find the time to personally tend to the landscaping on top of his mountain of daily responsibilities.

The man truly is a wonder. I'm so blessed to have him here, along with Emilee.

Before sitting down for breakfast, Charlotte decided to go for a stroll. Leaving Cardale behind brought with it a sense of closure and relief, but being back in Dellhaven presented its own anxieties. Her thoughts drifted back to Lucetta, no matter how hard she tried to keep her worries at bay. Every piece of furniture, every tapestry, even the grounds themselves, reminded of her daughter.

A tall oak stood a fair distance from the chateau, its branches thick with new leaves. Many a day had been spent underneath its safe canopy throughout the last year, reading books or enjoying a picnic with Emilee, or simply watching the sea lap against the shore. It was a place of calm, and a reminder that even though the world was cruel and chaotic, there was peace and beauty to be found as well. Charlotte approached the ancient tree, smiling. She extended a hand and pressed it against its trunk, its bark old and cracked.

"Hello, old friend."

She sat beside the tree for an hour or two, listening to the sounds of the ocean. The crashing of foamy waves and squawking of gulls was like a soft lullaby, serene enough to put even the crankiest newborn to rest. Charlotte closed her eyes for a moment, basking in the serenity of nature, contemplating where she might begin her works.

Dellhaven is a wealthy place, so my efforts will be wasted here. Cardale certainly requires the attention, but perhaps I might start small, and get a better understanding of how to accomplish all this.

Betanthia's countryside was certainly not without its share of hardships. Growing up on a farmstead, Charlotte knew all too well the struggles rural folk often endured. Farmers were never more than one bad crop away from utter ruin, be it drought or an excess of rain, or wildfire. Perhaps digging new wells, improving aging roads, and providing aid to those who labored to keep Betanthia fed would be a good place to start.

"My queen!" Devin Brandybrook waved a hand above his head. From the wideness of his eyes, something appeared to be amiss. His sudden commotion made the Queen's palms moisten.

"Yes, Devin? Is everything alright?"

"Lucetta has returned to the estate, along with her bodyguard. I came to notify you as quickly as I could."

A sudden deep thump inside Charlotte's chest made her wince. "I see. Have we discovered anything about her whereabouts?"

"I'm certain my man has the answers you seek, my queen. I would expect him to report to us at a more convenient time. He's taken every precaution to ensure he remains undiscovered. Tonight, I suspect, we'll hear something."

Even an hour was too long to wait. Charlotte needed to know the truth of what was transpiring, and quickly. But despite an overwhelming urge for answers, she knew it was best to remain calm and patient. A premature confrontation might only serve to do more harm than good.

"Very well. Please, accompany me back. I need to see her."

Together they trekked back to the estate, though secretly, Charlotte wished they were miles away. It was the same nervous anticipation she often felt around Marcellus, but in those instances, beatings often followed. This was a different sort of danger altogether, for she was now interwoven into whatever unscrupulous deeds Lucetta might very well be involved in.

They arrived back at the estate just in time. Servants were hauling in various trunks and chests from the baggage train, the man with golden teeth looming over them like a taskmaster. She dreaded being in his vicinity, even with adequate protection. There was something about his eyes Charlotte could not trust.

Entering next was Lucetta, her steps labored by exhaustion. From across the foyer, the Queen saw how gaunt her daughter had become. While she was still beautiful, it was distressing to see how loose her typically figure flattering gowns had become.

"It's good to see you again, Lucetta." Charlotte forced a smile. "I trust your trip was comfortable?"

"Yes, mother. I would love to tell you all about it, but I'm weary from travel and in need of rest. Perhaps we can talk over dinner?"

There was something unsettling about the darkening circles under her daughter's eyes, as if she had not slept for weeks. To the uninitiated, a dusting of makeup underneath both lids might have been enough to stave off suspicion, but Charlotte knew better.

"Very well. Brendon will see you off to your quarters. I'll send someone to notify you when dinner is prepared."

With a subtle curtsy, Lucetta dismissed herself and strode down the hallway, her foreign looking companion not far behind. He smiled, his teeth shimmering like polished gold in the sunlight. Charlotte was unsure which was more unsettling, the darkness under her daughter's eyes, or the man's toothy smile. After watching Lucetta disappear into her quarters, the Queen cast a sharp glance at Devin, then stepped out into the courtyard.

"You must keep a sharp eye on her, especially tonight," Charlotte commanded. "I need to be made aware of her every movement, no matter what the hour."

There was an unspoken understanding between them both. Devin bowed and retreated toward the servant's quarters with a look of grim determination. Charlotte contented herself with retiring to her chamber for the rest of the day, secured away from whatever was transpiring behind her back.

To pass the time, she sat in a comfortable high back chair near the window and indulged in her books. Though poetry was often an escape from the worries of reality, today Charlotte found little solace in beautiful words. At times, she would set her book down and stare longingly out through the window, trying to make sense of the unfolding madness around her.

The night was long and restless, as neither Devin nor his associate had come with any news. It was an unexpected and disappointing turn of events, to be certain. Several days had come and gone with little difference between them. Lucetta appeared just as eager to avoid any interaction as she was, and the two had barely seen, yet alone spoken, to one another.

Charlotte was beginning to wonder how much longer she could maintain such a charade. Not knowing the truth was the most insufferable thing of them all. When left to its own devices, the Queen's mind had a tendency of running away with itself, despite all of the progress over the past year. Old habits, it seemed, were more difficult to break than expected.

Late one evening, however, her fortunes would change. After a pleasant dinner out on the patio, Charlotte returned to her chamber to relax with a goblet of wine. A small fire crackled in the fireplace, an aroma of dried, burning wood filling the room like incense. She sat in her high back chair, flipping through the pages of an old book she had read a hundred times before. Nothing seemed to take the edge off, despite her best efforts.

Perhaps there really is nothing to this after all, and Lucetta has been true to her word. Perhaps this is all in my head after all, and she really is just struggling with life, and nothing more.

A knock came at the door, just as her thoughts began to run away once again. Devin Brandybrook entered, his face long and solemn. His hands were clenched around something small, possibly a message from a rider.

"Good evening, my queen. Please forgive the disturbance, but I thought it necessary to come to you right away."

"Have you any news, Devin?" she asked, fiddling with her skirts. "Tell me."

"I do, as a matter of fact. My man arrived outside the city walls an hour ago, and gave a report to one of the Guardsmen." He handed over a small roll of parchment, its waxy seal emblazoned with a signet imprint.

Hesitantly, she took the scroll, unsure if reading its contents was wise. Slowly, she peeled the wax away from the parchment and unrolled it. With mouth agape, Charlotte poured over its contents, stopping more than once to process the news.

It seems my suspicions are correct.

While she was not one to overindulge in drink, Charlotte needed one, and fast. She poured out half a goblet of wine and drank it down desperately.

"Lucetta was at the slave market in Cardale," she said, "and apparently she purchased every last man, woman, and child on the block. They came back north, and after she returned to Dellhaven, the slaves and her guards continued on."

Charlotte was perplexed. How could her precious daughter do such a thing? Just when she thought the news could not possibly be any worse, the remainder of the message proved to be just that. The other details were too grisly to speak aloud. She handed the parchment over to Devin, who scanned it over with ever-widening eyes.

"Oh… oh dear," he said softly. "He then followed them north to a razed village near the Siln River. He saw the slaves clearing away burnt bodies and…"

It was a lie, the Queen thought, it had to be. Lucetta inherited a bit of a temper from Marcellus, that much was certain, but she could never be capable of such unspeakable acts. No, not her, Charlotte thought.

"I cannot believe it," she said in a near whisper. "I need to speak with this man right away. Now, in fact. I need to hear the words and judge the truth of it in his eyes."

"The hour is late, my queen, but I will summon him at once. If you would like to remain in your chamber for the time being, I will bring him here personally."

Hesitantly, Charlotte agreed. Against all hope, she prayed the news was nothing more than fabrication, and Lucetta's activities little more than mundane. Devin disappeared into the night with all haste, leaving her alone to ruminate on thoughts of what was, and what could be. Was this merely a bad dream, or were the words penned in black ink true after all?

Hours came and went, though it felt as if days had passed. Charlotte looked longingly out through the window, the light of a nearly full moon fading behind a wall of dark clouds. Perhaps it had all been a lie after all, and Devin would return empty handed. Such a hope was certainly possible, she thought. To help ease the unraveling of her nerves, Charlotte poured another serving of wine and nursed it delicately, all but giving up hope. It was only when despair began creeping into her mind that soft voices were heard outside, growing ever closer.

Devin lowered the hood on his cloak, then entered. Behind him followed another man, shrouded and burly, though nearly a head shorter. The man pulled back his hood, revealing a weathered face with a dark, bushy beard. His hair was combed back and tied, the sides of his head shaved.

"Your Majesty, allow me to introduce myself. The name is Giles. I'm most honored to meet you, but I do regret the circumstances."

"For your efforts, you have my thanks," the Queen said, then produced the scroll. "While I have no reason to suspect this to be a lie, I had to hear the truth for myself, and look you in the eyes as you tell it."

After taking a peek outside, Devin locked the door and drew a pair of long drapes shut. It was unsettling to know such precautions were necessary, especially because of Lucetta. The stress of it was nearly enough to bring Charlotte to tears, but she could not let herself cry in front of a commoner and a stranger.

Giles cleared his throat and sighed. "I'm afraid every word is true, Your Majesty. It troubles me greatly to bring you this news, and I swear to its authenticity with my life. I followed her day and night, as instructed. It's my sincere belief that those men she keeps around her are foreign, and perhaps are responsible for roping her into these schemes."

"Are you absolutely certain?" Devin asked.

"I would bet my life on it," Giles replied. "A foul plot is underfoot, Your Majesty. The only mystery is why, and what their goal may be."

The room began to grow unbearably hot and spin ever so slightly. Lost for words, Charlotte nodded and dismissed Giles with a wave of her hand, having heard enough. Devin showed him out, then secured the door and drapes.

"I knew it." Charlotte shook her head. "I just knew it. I knew from the moment I saw that man with the golden teeth that something was amiss. How could Lucetta do something like this? She's brought killers into my home, Devin! What am I to do?"

"I think it would be best for you to relocate your quarters to the second floor, and post guards outside your door, and in the stairwell. Best if we take every precaution until these villains are expelled."

It was a sound suggestion, though Charlotte would have preferred clapping all of her daughter's men in irons. Still, reacting too hastily might have unintended consequences. If those murderers were capable of performing such atrocities under her nose, it was anyone's guess as to what else they were capable of.

"We must think this through," she cautioned. "I cannot risk anything happening to Gareth or Trace. Who knows how deep this sinister scheme goes. We need to learn the full truth of this, and quickly."

"A sound strategy, my queen. I will send word to Sir Edmund immediately and inform him of the situation, so adequate protection is placed around your sons. I will also arrange a meeting of the city watch, and instruct them to monitor all movements coming in and out of Dellhaven. One way or another, we will get to the bottom of this."

As comforting as the plan sounded, it would be difficult to feel safe with foreign mercenaries sleeping under the same roof. Still, there was some reassurance to be found in the strength of the Royal Guardsmen, for they had yet to fail in their duties to protect House Bethard.

"One more thing," she said, raising a finger. "These other men of hers, where have they been camped?"

"I'm not certain, my queen, but I will find out and have their movements tracked. The answers will come in due time, rest assured. I will have Emilee bring all of your effects upstairs at once, and I will instruct the Guardsmen to shadow you both day and night."

Devin tried to remain stoic, but his face reflected the very same fear which had now shaken Charlotte to her core. He departed the chamber, shutting the door securely behind him. It was only a matter of minutes before there was a soft knocking, a pair of Guardsmen stepping inside.

"My queen." Both men gave a deep bow. "We have been instructed to show you upstairs, at your convenience, of course."

Truth be told, Charlotte could very well have sprinted upstairs with how dreadful the news had been. Still, it was important to maintain appearances, in case Lucetta and her strange partner had other eyes inside the chateau, eyes in their service. Such a possibility was once unthinkable, but now, Dellhaven had become even more treacherous than the capital.

Perhaps I should have stayed in Cardale after all. Better the devil you know...

MADELYN III

S THIS A DREAM? SHE THOUGHT, THOUGH THE DREAM SEEMED ANYTHING but. Ever since her return to Castle Thorn, life seemed like a blur of distant memories which bled endlessly into one another. The only true reminder that she was even alive was the pain. It was ever constant, and could rouse her from even her deepest slumber.

But not now. This dream was something different, more akin to what she witnessed in the grove with Marvath, before the day of her tribulation. What she experienced now was more real than reality itself. She felt whole again, both physically and spiritually.

If this is a dream, then I hope I never wake.

The heavens were a thick shroud of darkness, with no light from the moon or stars able to piece its veil. Somehow, Madelyn was able to see for miles across an open plain, its tall grasses swaying gently, though there was no breeze to be felt. Dry blades crunched gently underfoot as she set off in one direction, uncertain of what lay ahead. Hours came and went, but there was no real sense of time. Every step felt like it was merely a repeat of the last.

No, this couldn't be a dream, could it? Have I… have I died? Am I in the afterlife?

It was an unsettling notion at first. But at least here, wherever she was, there was no suffering, and no pain to be felt. However, an eternity alone in such a place would be lonely. Lonely beyond imagination, she thought. There was no life to be found; no animals scurrying on the ground, no birds flying above, and not another person anywhere in sight.

Frantically, Madelyn began to run as fast as her legs would allow, but there seemed to be no end to the vastness of the grassy plain. If this was indeed the afterlife, she wanted no part of it. She wanted to be among her old friends, and to be safe in Corbyn's arms once again. But no, there was none of that to be found, not here.

"Where am I?" she screamed, pausing only to catch her breath. Since her earliest days, Madelyn strove to be on the side of good, to live honorably, and protect those who could not protect themselves. This seemed a cruel reward for a lifetime of devotion to such selfless principles.

She slumped against the trunk of a large oak tree, its branches gnarled from the passing of centuries. Tears began streaking down her cheeks, the water quickly hardening into tiny crystals of sorrow. It seemed endlessly cruel to be separated from everything and everyone who mattered most in life, and to be stuck in a strange and foreign place as well.

Suddenly, there was a flickering of light up ahead. It was so faint it almost went unnoticed at first. Madelyn rubbed her eyes and squinted, unsure if the light was real or just some trick of her imagination. After a few steps it became apparent that yes, the anomaly was real after all. It was fire, an undoubtedly large one, burning bright against a pitch black sky.

"Over here!" she shouted, running toward the fire with all haste. The closer she came, however, the more apparent it was that something had gone terribly wrong. The flames were not some distant torchlight or bonfire. No, it was the roaring carnage of an entire camp ablaze.

Wagons burned like kindling, surrounded by dead horses and dead men. There were ten, perhaps even a dozen of them, each with a different manner of wound. Some had quarrels protruding from their heads, while others were without heads entirely. The dry grass was growing into an ever-larger inferno by the second, yet Madelyn felt no heat.

Orange light bled across the darkened plain, revealing a well-traveled pathway nearby. Madelyn peered ahead suspiciously, reaching for a blade on her hip out of habit, but finding none. She saw the silhouette of a corpse laying face down on the trail, its arms spread out wide, a large, red stain pooling underneath it. Swallowing hard, she started down the pathway, and spotted another, and yet another dead body.

Something happened here… this is the work of men, many of them.

Upon closer inspection, the corpses were not those of her Betanthian kin, but of northmen. Some had ragged clothes, or armor made crudely out of leather. Some were clad in animal skin cloaks, others bare-chested and decorated with runic tattoos. Her sympathies became a little less, as these were barbarians under Damien Dreadfire's command, judging from a banner of crimson cloth that lay tattered on the ground.

It seemed as if eyes upon her, cold eyes scanning her every movement from the darkness. Madelyn felt hairs on the back of her neck stand stiff, her hands clenching slowly into fists. Then she saw it. In the near distance was a figure garbed in black. It was slender and shapely, a figure she had seen before in a dream.

"Who are you, and what do you want?" she asked the mysterious person, but no reply was given. Light from the growing fire danced eerily off the figure, a single eye glowing like cold, bluish starlight. It extended a single hand, pointing directly at her. It was the most bone-chilling thing Madelyn had ever experienced, more so than even Lazilyth, the frightening barbarian crone.

"Don't come any closer!" she shouted in wavering defiance. "I know how to fight! I was a Commander of the Blackthorn Knights!"

She scanned the ground hoping to find a sword or a spear, but found nothing. A broken branch from a tree was the only weapon available, but would likely do little to fend off such a capable foe. The figure reached behind its back and drew two short swords, spun them around in each hand, and laughed.

It was a sort of deep, foreboding laugh she had heard once before, one menacing enough to shake the very foundations of the earth. In a panic, Madelyn turned to run, but the flames had grown too massive. There was nowhere to escape. She searched frantically for an exit, and saw a stone table standing behind her. The sight of it was startling, as there was nothing behind her moments ago. Curiously she stepped forward, an object on its surface obscured by smoke. The figure looked on intently, as if beckoning her to proceed.

Madelyn reached into the hazy abyss, curious to see what object lay resting on the table. Before she could touch it, a crippling, stabbing pain shot throughout her entire body. She let loose a howl of agony, clutching at her abdomen as the flames suddenly leapt inward, consuming everything in its grasp.

She awoke, screaming. Madelyn was wracked by the most intense pain imaginable, even more so than her days in captivity. The swollen mountain that was her belly was moving about, little humps emerging from underneath her flesh, then quickly disappearing, only to reemerge once again. The baby, it seemed, would be on its way soon. But there was something else that caught her eye. Sleeping on a large, upholstered chair near the bed was Gareth, his head hanging, eyes closed, and breathing rhythmically.

He… he's watching over me…

It was a beautiful and nearly overwhelming sight to behold. For the first time since the day Castle Morden fell, Madelyn felt an indescribable warmth inside her cold, dead heart. Here was the crown prince of Betanthia, on the eve of war, with so many other matters requiring his attention, sleeping beside her.

While basking in Gareth's comforting presence, Madelyn noticed someone standing in the doorway. It was one of the servants in the infirmary, his eyes wide and mouth hanging open. He looked as if he had just seen a ghost, and as she made eye contact, the man turned and fled with all haste.

Am I truly so hideous? Does the sight of me repulse anyone who dares to look upon me?

She shifted uncomfortably in bed, drifting back to an exhausted sleep as fresh tears dripped her eyes. But before the darkness of the dream realm took hold, she noticed something peculiar surrounding her. It was a black, wispy fog, much like smoke from inside her dream. At first Madelyn thought her eyes were simply hazy from exhaustion, but after rubbing them several times, it appeared the mist was no illusion.

As she reached out to touch the murk, it quickly disappeared. She wished Gareth was awake, and made to call out to him, but thought better of it. He might very well think she had lost whatever sanity she still had left. And besides, if the disturbance was indeed for real, there would at least be someone in the room to ward it off should it return.

Why is this happening to me? What did I ever do to deserve such torment?

Life seemed like little more than a cruel jape, one which seemed to only worsen with each passing day. Death at the hands of the barbarians would have been preferable to this. Instead of getting the honor of Damien Dreadfire's sword, she was instead subjected to a life of never-ending torment. Perhaps that was the warlord's plan all along, though it was difficult to understand why she deserved such a fate.

Such thoughts made little sense. Madelyn had never encountered Dreadfire or his Borjifan people before. She had sacked no villages, put no northmen to the sword, and transgressed against no one. Why her? It mattered little. It seemed futile to try and make sense of her situation, no matter how well it was rationalized.

She hated life and what it had become. Madelyn tried to roll over and drift back to sleep, but yanked hard on her hair. It was loose and caught beneath her body, and so long it was becoming bothersome to manage. Frustrated, she slowly slid out of bed like an elderly woman, and toddled to a nearby vanity.

It was distressing to see the size of her belly, her simple linen gown doing nothing to hide it. She tried not to look and instead focused on her bothersome locks. Madelyn retrieved a pair of doctor's shears from inside a drawer, gathered up her golden tresses in one hand, and held the sharp blades to her length, just at the base of her neck.

But something deep inside said not to proceed. The barbarians had taken so much from her, to the point where there was little reminder of what life was like before Castle Morden. She wanted to be healthy and strong and free, not the crippled shell of a person staring back through the mirror.

I've lost everything… my entire identity… my entire life. I cannot lose the one thing I have left, trivial as it may be. I need to keep this one last piece of myself.

With shaking hands, she clumsily returned the shears to the drawer. Slowly Madelyn shuffled back to bed, more depressed than ever. She began to cry, though it was a wonder how there were any tears left to cry at all. Her gentle sobbing was enough to rouse Gareth. The prince groaned and rubbed the sleep from his eyes, letting out a few deep breaths as he began regaining his bearings.

"Madelyn?" There was a hint of surprise in his voice, as if he had half expected her to never awaken.

While it was comforting to have someone familiar close by, there was another person inside the room which made her blood turn cold. Before Madelyn could utter a word, she caught sight of a figure standing in a dark corner, slender and shapely, with a bluish eye that cut through her very soul.

TITAN IV

"You alive in there, Bradshaw?" Elite Conrak clapped his riding crop against the cell bars, a shrill clanking sound jarring Tylar from his drowsiness.

"Eat shit, Conrak," he croaked with a parched throat.

"It must be surreal to be in a place like this, knowing what it means." The Elite grinned.

Castle Thorn's dungeon was not what one might expect from such an imposing stronghold. Its cells were small and rather simple in their construction, more suited for overnight holdings as opposed to harboring dangerous criminals for any length of time.

It's because they intend to execute me in short order.

Many souls had passed through these very same cells, and found their way to either the headsman's block, or the gallows outside. Seldom were prisoners kept for more than a fortnight, Tylar knew, and likely the High Marshal was personally tying the very noose he would soon hang upon.

"Go on, keep smirking," he snarled. "You think I give a shit what you do to me? If you're looking for me to beg for my life, then you're sorely fucking mistaken."

Conrak leaned against the bars, sighing and turning his gaze to the damp floor. "Actually, Bradshaw, I take no pleasure in seeing you like this. As hard as it may be for that primitive brain of yours to comprehend, I don't. And you want to know why? Because you were a part of the Order. You were a brother in arms to us all. You were a living legend, even though I believe many of the stories to be embellishments. And you stabbed all of us in the back when you tucked tail and fled."

Tylar sighed, hawking his throat to spit, but finding it too dry. "I don't expect you to understand why I did what I did, and I'm not going to waste the effort explaining it to you. If you'd have seen half of the things I have, you—"

"Spare me," the Elite interrupted. "We've all lost friends on the battlefield. You think you're the only one? It's the job we signed up for. What did you think, that serving in a military order would be easy? Heavens, man, tell me you cannot possibly be so dense."

"I actually gave a shit, hard as it may be for you to believe. I gave everything I had, and I'm not ashamed of it. I suppose life is easier for men like you when all you care about is your precious ego."

"Think what you want, Bradshaw, in the end it really doesn't matter." Conrak shrugged. "I suppose I should be leaving. Important business to attend to, after all. I'm likely the last friendly face you're going to see before they drag you out of here and sling a rope around your neck. It'll be in a couple of days, I'd imagine. In the meantime, consider this a parting gift; a token of gratitude for all your years of service."

Conrak slipped a large book through the bars, wrapped securely in gray linen. "It's the history of the Blackthorn Knights. Quite a tome indeed. But then again, you've nothing better to do before you die. I thought you might want to know more about the Order you betrayed, and what it's accomplished over the centuries. That is, if you can read. You *can* read, or am I mistaken?"

"Yes, I can fucking read," Tylar shot back. He glanced at the book several times before taking it reluctantly.

"Good. I've instructed the guards to make certain you have as many candles as necessary for your literary adventures. Goodbye, Bradshaw. Enjoy what little time you have left."

Fucking prick. Is he trying to bore me to death? He should have just given me a dagger to cut my own throat, at least that would have been more enjoyable.

Tylar flung the book onto his straw bedding, snorting in contempt. He stood, leaning against the bars, arms crossed, as if expecting Conrak to return for one final jape. But nearly ten minutes had passed before he realized the Elite was not returning. Frustrated, he slumped against a chilly, slimy wall, his back sliding down the stone until he was sitting. Tylar began to eye the book curiously, though he was loath to open it. Even touching it felt as if he would be giving Conrak another victory, however small.

That's what he wants. He wants me to rise to his little taunt. Well, he can ram that book firmly up his ass for all I care.

But at least the text could serve another purpose, he supposed. A wrist-thick book would make for a decent enough pillow, since the guards had seen fit to deny him the slightest bit of hospitality. There was also the overwhelming anxiety of being confined in such a manner. He wanted to run, to tear the bars apart with his bare hands and run until neither leg could go any further. But there was nowhere to flee to, and even if he could break out of the cell, escaping Castle Thorn would be an impossible task altogether.

He sat for hours, picking at a scab on his thigh. Small flecks of blood began weeping from the wound, a dull stinging sensation his only form of entertainment. When there were no more pieces left to scratch away, he stood and stretched, then retrieved a candle and flint from a small pile one of the guards had left inside. As the candle's wick ignited, it cast dancing light upon the book, which he had nearly forgotten about. He eyed it suspiciously.

"Alright, you son of a bitch. You win. You've killed me with boredom."

Tylar hefted the book from his bedding, then brushed away a few pieces of straw from its wrappings. He removed the cloth and glanced at the cover, its leather faded from the passing of countless years. A musty tinge escaped from its faded pages, the scent offending his nostrils for a brief moment. He flipped through the first dozen of what appeared to be several hundred pages, near to a thousand from the looks of it. Each one looked less appealing than the one before it, but reluctantly, he began at the beginning.

"The history and founding of the Blackthorn Knights."

At least there were pictures. Some even appeared interesting, to his surprise. There were many elaborate drawings of victorious battles and High Marshals from centuries past, but little else seemed appealing. It was only when he flipped past a few more that he noticed something peculiar. In the faint light, he noticed a slight difference in the hue of the paper. Curiously, Tylar compared the pages in the first chapter to those of the second.

The latter appeared more discolored and worn, and had the look of a text that had seen many decades of use. He peered at small, black specks which had formed on the parchment, and noticed wear from many hundreds of oily fingers. The beginning of the book contained no such damage, its pages appearing quite fresh in comparison.

As Tylar studied the book up close, he noticed the remains of pages which had been torn out, likely long ago. The newer pages appeared to have been put in their place, delicately, meticulously, but not expertly enough to evade his clever eyes.

"Interesting… Who would stand to gain from altering a book? Especially an uninteresting one such as this?"

There was a mystery surrounding the book, to be certain. But there was little time to find answers, even if he cared to find them in the first place. It was likely that come the dawn, or perhaps the dawn after, he would be dead. But it was difficult to shake the feeling that there was more to the text than he initially believed. Conrak was a clever man, likely the sort who would never make a decision without thinking ten steps ahead.

"Fuck it. I guess it doesn't matter one way or another."

Frustrated and hopeless, Tylar flung the book across the cell, then laid down on his foul smelling bedding. He stared up at a dingy ceiling, thinking of how many men he would kill for one last pint of ale.

ZANDER II

The march from Hok was long and grueling, though the detour had proven quite prosperous. Zander had collected enough gold to live in opulence for three lifetimes, but no amount of money could buy a place in the histories. No, there was something far greater he craved, and every day without a new victory against Betanthia felt like a day wasted.

The warband's pace was brutal, but spirits were high. As they marched south, they encountered no resistance, much to everyone's surprise. For a kingdom as formidable as Betanthia, their response to the invasion left much to be desired. It made Zander wonder why they had waited so long to go on the warpath in the first place.

If this is the best they can do, then I can't imagine how easy it'll be to snap everything up for myself.

A village came into view around noon. Jollkud and his marauders let out a roar of excitement, eager to put more of King Bethard's minions to the sword. From a distance it appeared to be a modest settlement, no walls or garrison to oppose their advance. It would make for easy pickings, no doubt.

"Here we go, mates!" Zander shouted, the Zylmacians behind him stirring into a frenzy. Many of the bare-chested wildmen began to smash axe against shield and howl and chant like beasts.

"Stay yourselves." Damien raised a hand in a bid to silence them. "These people are our kin. Should they seek liberation and our protection, they shall have it."

Dreadfire's pitiful sentiment made Zander's stomach turn. It was both amusing and infuriating to see him project such weakness on people fit only for butchering.

"Come now!" he protested. "These are Bethard minions. We ought to show them the price for betraying their ancestors."

"Can you not keep your fool mouth shut for once?" Marvath Bonesplitter interrupted. "Can you not see that every man we bring to our side only hastens Betanthia's demise? You Bymist rats are incapable of seeing anything beyond your noses."

It was endlessly infuriating to suffer yet another insult from the Rhivothi, especially in front of his own kin. If something was not done, and soon, not only would his warriors think him a coward, but likely Jollkud and his men as well.

"Bonesplitter is correct," Damien said. "We will find allies here. The deeper we venture into the heart of Betanthia, the less sympathetic our cause will be to whomever we come across."

The idea had its merits, though Zander was loath to admit it. He would have preferred putting a million men to death than bringing a single one into their ranks. A traitor was a traitor, after all. If they were too weak to resist the rule of Betanthia, then they were too weak to be allowed to live.

"If you say so," he conceded.

A pair of Nothanek rode ahead to the village, one of them waving an arm in the air. Damien brought the warband to a sudden halt, watching both riders intently as they delivered his message to the villagers. Zander secretly hoped the Nothanek would be killed outright, as it would mean the warband would be unleashed once again. Minutes passed before there was any activity.

Come on, come on… I need a proper fight.

To his disappointment, the villagers appeared to agree to whatever terms Damien had offered. The Nothanek raised their hands and waved, signaling to Dreadfire that the settlement had surrendered without a fight. Victorious cheers erupted from some of the warriors, while many were less than enthusiastic.

Damien rode at the head of his host, the village leaders coming out to pay their respects and surrender personally. The closer to the settlement they rode, the more it began to resemble Khorrtal. Many homesteads were modest places, each made of stone and wood, and capped with simple thatched roofs. Hardly the sort of place one would expect a pampered Betanthian to live. Judging by the smell, however, they were still in the north. The stink of farm animals was noxious, so thick it left a foul taste in his mouth.

The warband was brought to a halt, and camp was made around the village. While not a proper victory, the warriors contented themselves with feasting and drinking, welcoming their new brethren into the fold. Zander, however, would have none of it. These men were enemies, as much as the Rhivothi or Droethiens. Perhaps it was better if the wild-men kept to their own, he thought.

Merriment continued long into the night, the local mead stores likely run dry. Peals of laughter and droll murmurings of stories were like poison to his ears. The only antidote was found in a horn of strong Zylmacian brew, though it tasted like burnt grass. It mattered little, only the taste of glory could cleanse his palette.

He sat alone beneath a crescent moon, thoughts of murder dancing through his mind. Zander often thought about killing and the rush that came with it, and how nothing else could compare. It was disappointing to not put the village to the torch, as the massacre at Hok had done little to quench his bloodthirst. Though he was a cold-blooded killer, he was also patient, a rarity which set him apart from other Zylmacians. It made the payoff of a massacre so much sweeter.

If I were in charge, these Betanthians would be fleeing in terror, not marching alongside us. I was under the impression we were here to kill these men, not make peace with them. Seems Dreadfire isn't the beast everyone thinks he is.

Zander rose from beside a dwindling fire, lapped down the last mouthful from his horn, and began walking aimlessly. The camp was large enough to envelop the village several times over, though his accommodation would prove easy enough to find. The wildmen preferred to camp as far west as possible, an old superstition surrounding the mystery and allure of the Bymist. Its power was such that no outsider could truly understand it unless they were a native. It was as if the land was always reaching out to those who called it home, beckoning them to return.

While stopping to relieve himself against the side of a hovel, Zander thought it curious that he shared no such sentiment with his homeland. He was perhaps the only Zylmacian who had greater desires, greater even than Damien Dreadfire, if one could be so bold. The Bymist was simply not enough to contain such lofty ambitions; to be remembered as the greatest warrior to walk the face of Caldakas. The thought made him chuckle.

They may mock me now, but my name will be spoken for a thousand years or more, long after their bones have turned to dust.

Something caught his attention, dancing amidst the shadows of lantern light. After shaking off the last few drops and securing his britches, Zander scanned the darkness, wondering if it was some trick of the eye or perhaps the alcohol taking hold. His suspicions were soon confirmed when he spotted a dark, faint outline of a figure, followed by another, and then another two.

Now who would be sneaking around in the dead of night? Nothing worth stealing here, aside from a few chickens.

Curiously, he crept off in pursuit, stopping only to steal a cloak from a sleeping Nothanek. Its thick wool draped comfortably across his shoulders, a large hood shrouding his bald head from reflections of light. With the instincts of a lion, Zander stalked the unknown figures silently, with not so much as a twig breaking underfoot. Upon reaching the village outskirts, their true identities presented themselves, their concealment betrayed by the flickering of campfires.

Is it? Could it be?

At first, it was difficult to believe what he was seeing. The figures were bereft of hair and clothing, save for their roughspun britches. Thick scarring running down the length of their backs was evidence enough that these were Zylmacians, although not his clansmen. Upon closer inspection, they appeared to be Jollkud's men, but to make such an accusation aloud could prove lethal.

The mysterious men gathered outside of a hovel at the northernmost edge of the village, and sat whispering amongst themselves for several minutes. One of them crept toward the door, nimble and silent, a glint of moonlight flashing on what appeared to be a dagger clutched in one hand.

Oh? Up to no good, are you, lads? Shame you didn't invite me!

The door was pried open, its lock clearly no match for western steel. Five figures made their way inside one by one, their entrance undetected. Only moments passed before one of them returned to the door, looking one way, then another, before motioning for his brethren to follow. Two figures emerged with a body, grasped by the wrists and ankles. They made a hasty escape into the darkness with their prey, although their intentions remained a mystery.

Zander pulled the hood down across his brow and took off in pursuit, careful not to alert anyone to his presence. The band of Zylmacians retreated far from camp to a thicket of overgrown shrubs, enough to shroud whatever nefarious activities they were about to partake in. The ringleader was the first to enter, followed by the rest of his kinsmen. One of the men poked his head out through the dense vegetation, scanning the darkness to make certain they were not being followed.

But Zander was too skilled of a tracker, and even more skilled of a killer. If inclined, he could dispatch all five of them without so much as making a sound. However, these *were* his countrymen. Still, he wanted to know more, he wanted to see what such secrecy was all about. Crouching amidst the tall grass, Zander crept forward, discreetly drawing an axe in case the encounter turned hostile.

A gentle flickering of light filtered through the branches, alongside a soft crackling of wood. He spied a large cauldron, sitting on top of a roaring fire, wisps of steam snaking upward. The Zylmacians were saying something to each other, an occasional ripple of muffled laughter interrupting their preparation.

Crawling on his stomach, Zander drew so close he could nearly smell the sweat of his kinsmen. One of them sat crouched, peeling the flesh off a large helping of fresh meat, while another diced an already prepared portion with a one-handed axe. Bowls of meat were emptied into the bubbling cauldron, along with a helping of wild herbs and pinches of western spices. Were it not for a severed head laying unceremoniously on the ground, Zander might have thought the men were butchering a deer. But no, his kin had chosen to feast on the most dangerous game of all.

Cannibals, eh? It seems Jollkud brought with him whatever the Bymist shit out. This just made our campaign all the more interesting.

There were many things Zander could do which might turn the stomachs of lesser men, but eating human flesh was not one of them. Having seen enough, he slunk away undetected, eager to retire and sleep off the looming effects of the brew sloshing around in his stomach.

When morning arrived, the village was in an uproar. He awoke to the sounds of men shouting, and the shrill wails of women. Groggy and still slightly intoxicated, Zander stumbled from his tent, eager to make sense of the growing chaos all around. The Rhivothi were unusually heated, which was a sight in and of itself, given their perpetually agitated state. Jollkud's clansmen were on the receiving end of their wrath, though the wildmen returned every bit of animosity they received.

Zander might have chuckled at the exchange, were it not for accusations turning towards his own clansmen. It was a slight he could not ignore.

"What's going on here?" he demanded, but none seemed to take notice. "What's this all about?"

Arik Akselson was nearby, and had heard his questions. He appeared violently upset, a rarity for peaceful fisher folk. "You and your wild dogs are the matter, that's what!"

Zander chuckled, though affronted. "Might want to check your tone, mate. I just woke up. What's got you shitting your britches at such an early hour?"

He caught a glimpse of Damien Dreadfire from the corner of his eye. The warlord stood, face drawn tightly into a scowl as the villagers wailed.

"You assured us of your protection if we welcomed you into our homes!" one of the local men shouted, his voice drenched in anguish. "And now look at what's happened!"

"When Damien gives his word, he does not do so lightly," Marvath Bonesplitter interjected. "I can assure you this was not the work of any Rhivothi; we find no pleasure in murder. We prefer to kill a man when he has steel in hand. And our Nothanek friends are no butchers either, they would assume—"

"It doesn't matter who is responsible!" a woman cried out. "They're dead, and they wouldn't be had you not come! We swore ourselves to you in good faith!"

"And I have kept that faith," Damien responded. "It grieves me to hear of your loss, and I will give you my sacred vow to find those responsible and hold them to account."

A grin of half-rotten teeth was beginning to form across Zander's face, but he was quick enough to check it. Had anyone else seen the Zylmacians breaking into the residence and killing its unfortunate inhabitants? Likely not, as an alarm would have been raised moments after, he thought.

You mean… no one is aware of what happened, except for me? Interesting… most interesting indeed.

The situation was undoubtedly volatile. But perhaps it could be put to good use, not only with regards to his Zylmacian kin, but to the warband itself. The wheels in his head were turning, though so much as a smile might betray his knowledge of what transpired.

"It was likely one of those Bymist rats," Marvath Bonesplitter snarled. "It was a mistake to welcome more of them into our ranks. They will be the downfall of this alliance, mark my words."

"Is this how the north welcomes those who fight for their cause?" Jollkud called out, the agitation of his nearby fueling his boldness. "Tell me, Zander, is this the sort of insult you've had to suffer this past year?"

"Silence!" Dreadfire commanded. "I will have the truth of this matter, and I will have it at once!" He turned to one of his Rhivothi bodyguards. "I want our finest trackers to investigate these murders. I will not leave this village until the culprits are discovered."

Damien stormed off, leaving a volatile situation behind him. Were he a lesser man, the tribes might very well have turned on each other right then and there. But many feared what Dreadfire was capable of. Zander, however, was more convinced than ever that the crone, Lazilyth, was the one who held true power. How amusing, he thought, that such a powerful man was beholden to such a feeble old creature.

Amidst heightening tension and the hurling of insults, the alliance stood poised to fracture. While the thought of slaughtering the Rhivothi where they stood had him salivating, now was hardly the proper time. He would still need the northmen to break Betanthia's armies, and could not afford an utter collapse of the warband. Zander had intended to get closer to Damien and accrue greater influence for himself, but now, such chaos presented a unique opportunity.

Oh Zander, you evil bastard! He grinned. *Not only can you gain the favor of Dreadfire, but perhaps Jollkud can be diminished as well.*

Playing his own people off against the rest of the warband was a dangerous gambit, but one which might prove endlessly fruitful. If successful, both sides would be looking to him to keep the peace. Zander knew he had to seize the moment, or else such an opportunity might never present itself again.

He set off in search of Dreadfire, navigating an endless forest of tents. The warlord preferred to keep his command tent near the center of camp, regardless of whether they were in friendly territory or not. Finding it would not prove difficult. A black and crimson banner bearing the runic symbol of Dreadfire himself flew high, its colors unmistakable. A pair of Rhivothi guards had come to know his face well, and offered no challenge as he approached, though they likely fantasized about planting a spear in his guts.

"Damien," Zander said, peeking his head through the tent flap. "Might we have a word?"

Dreadfire cocked his head curiously, as they had not spoken in private since before the campaign, when the Zylmacians were courted into his alliance. "Yes, you may enter."

"I have something of dire importance I must share with you, but only if certain… assurances can be made."

It was bold of anyone to demand anything from Damien, but there was too much at stake and too much to gain without taking such a step.

"Speak plainly, I have not the patience for coyness," the warlord stated coldly.

"I have information as to the identities of those responsible for the killing." Zander glanced over his shoulder to make certain no unfriendly ears were listening. He snatched up a silver flagon and poured a generous serving of mead into a wooden tankard. "But first, I need to have your solemn vow that my identity will not be made known."

"I find your concern most curious. It was my understanding that you cared little for what other men thought of you."

"I need your word, because the perpetrators are my countrymen."

It was nearly possible to hear his heart beating, given how quiet the tent had become. He saw rage building behind Damien's black eyes, though it was expertly controlled.

"And how did you come by this knowledge?" Dreadfire asked, his voice low.

"The longer I spend here, the more suspicion I'll draw, so I'm going to be quick. I was sitting there, minding my own business, you see, when I noticed something creeping around in the shadows. At first I thought it was nothing, but nothing slips past my eye. I saw a handful of men break into one of the hovels and drag someone out, and carry them off to a thicket nearby. That's where you'll find one of the bodies, or whatever is left of it."

Damien Dreadfire took a sip of mead, swishing it around in his mouth before swallowing hard, masking a growing scowl. "I am uncertain as to your meaning."

"I mean they ate them. Cooked up all the parts into a stew and ate it. I saw it with my own eyes." He nervously gulped down mouthfuls of mead until little remained inside his tankard.

"And you allowed your men to perpetrate such a crime, against my explicit orders?"

The temperature inside began to rise sharply, and Zander knew that if he was not careful, Damien would have his head faster than he could flee.

"And why would you think that, after everything I've sacrificed for this alliance?" he protested. "I threw myself against the walls of Morden for you and your cause. But no, my men didn't do this. They obey me without question. No, these were men under Jollkud's banner, from deep in the Bymist. Some of the tribes there are cannibals, given how scarce food can be. It seems they haven't lost the taste for man."

Dreadfire ran a hand over his bald head, sighing deeply. "This is an unwelcome distraction, Zander, a distraction I have no patience for. Our time would be better spent taking the fight to King Bethard. Instead, we have this nuisance to address. Tell me, why would a man such as yourself inform me of the identities of the culprits? What benefits you to forsake your kin?"

"It benefits me greatly. I'm not here for your personal vengeance, Damien. It's not a concern of mine. No, I'm here to forge a legacy of my own, and I'll be damned if I let any man tarnish what's rightfully mine. I'm here for glory, and yes, for Zylmacia. But at the end of the day, I want the name of Zander to reverberate throughout history. How can I do that if my own kinsmen cannot control their impulses? How can I be remembered as I wish to be remembered if they're murdering and eating those we liberate? No, I cannot stand for it."

"You impress me. Perhaps we have judged you too harshly." Damien filled Zander's tankard near to overflowing.

He smiled in reply, taking a few mighty swigs. "You have my thanks. But there's an obvious issue, the way I see it. How are we going to seize the men responsible and not have it lead back to me?"

The warlord thought hard over a sip of mead. It seemed as if events from the future were playing out behind his black eyes. "I have an idea, one you will find satisfactory. I will gather the warchiefs and their closest retainers, and address this matter in an open forum. When there is no admission of guilt, I will call for Lazilyth, and instruct her to gaze into the past."

"She can see the past?" Zander asked incredulously. "I always heard she could see the future. Does she have more abilities than we were told?"

Damien gave a clever grin, the light itself seeming to flicker around him. "She cannot see the past, only what the fates have written for the future. But Jollkud and his minions are unaware of this, and I suspect Lazilyth's presence will be sufficient to force either a confession, or for the perpetrators to turn on one another. Either way, this matter will be concluded to my satisfaction."

"Very well," he said reluctantly. "I'm taking a huge risk by doing this, even by speaking to you. I do hope my good faith is rewarded, in time."

"Indeed it shall. You have proven yourself to be a man of honor. Your actions throughout this campaign have been noted, and what you have done here today has spoken volumes of your integrity. Zylmacia should be proud of all you have accomplished."

As he left the tent, the two Rhivothi bodyguards outside entered. They exchanged their typical indignation, though he was unable to hide a half-rotten smile. Whether this day or the next, this year or the next, revenge against the northmen would be had. But revenge was like a ripening fruit; only after sufficient time would it become succulent enough to feast upon.

For the next hour, Zander lingered near Damien's command tent, drinking a steady supply of mead, and sharpening his axes on grindstones. There was a strong possibility he would be in need of sharp weapons, if his scheme turned sour.

Before dinner that evening, Arik Akselson emerged, half a dozen spearmen at his side. "Damien Dreadfire has commanded all warchiefs to assemble, along with their retainers," Arik bellowed. Zander thought it amusing for a Nothank to be ordering anyone around. Still, they were seen as the most neutral people in the warband, which had its uses. Arik's command echoed throughout the camp and into the village, until one by one, each warchief began to emerge.

He stole a minute to admire Sylvia Stormguard. The shieldmaiden was looking quite delectable, her brown hair loose and flowing, the soft skin of her midriff showing beneath a short linen shirt. It seemed even at the most inopportune time, she was able to get a man's blood up.

Easy now, mate. Got to stay focused now.

With the warchiefs and their retainers gathered around, Damien Dreadfire emerged from his tent, Lazilyth following closely behind. The energy in the air suddenly shifted, an uneasy silence falling over the onlookers. Zander felt his skin turn cold as he caught sight of the crone toddling alongside a pair of Rhivothi, themselves diminished despite towering several feet above her. A tattered gray shawl wrapped across her head fluttered in an icy breeze, revealing a nest of thin, white hair and a face like dry leather.

While Zander displayed no fear, many of his kinsmen did, the old woman's presence manifesting an indescribable dread. Oftentimes there was a sensation that she was peering deep inside the most locked away places in his heart, even without making eye contact. Something about her was unnatural, not as unnatural as robbing a man or even cutting his throat, which many would consider as such, but unnatural like spending a night in a graveyard.

"For presenting yourselves here so timely, I give you my thanks," Dreadfire began. "Some who walk among us are responsible for perpetrating crimes against this peaceful village, and my response shall be swift and decisive."

Only a light rustling of tents and tall grass could be heard for miles. Thousands looked on in awe and fear as Damien beckoned the crone to join at his side. "Tell me, Lazilyth, tell me who perpetrated this crime. Can you see with your spirit eye?"

The old woman spoke not, but instead inclined her neck, the whites of her eyes facing up toward the heavens. She let out an ominous moan, though Zander knew it was false. It was difficult to hide a mischievous grin, but he remained as inconspicuous as possible.

"Someone… someone here has the taste of man on their tongue," Lazilyth croaked. "They carry the stink of flesh, burned and boiled, even now."

"Tell me, Lazilyth. Name those responsible." Damien immediately shifted his gaze toward the Zylmacians, who themselves began to stir. "Tell me who is guilty of this misdeed."

It was indescribably satisfying to witness their discomfort. Zander sat confident in the knowledge he possessed, eager to see the fruits of Damien's deception.

"The mist… the mist is upon them," the crone said. "I can smell it on the air. I can taste it." She turned and faced Jollkud and his retainers. "You… you harbor the stench of death. Your banner is stained red! The gods know your names!"

A sudden commotion erupted throughout the Zylmacian ranks. Men that Zander knew were innocent began flinging accusations at one another, each more fantastical than the last. Sylvia Stormguard, Marvath Bonesplitter, and Arik Akselson zeroed in on the excitement, their contempt plain for any man to see.

"It was him!" someone cried out, eager to absolve themselves of Lazilyth's condemnation.

"Yes, yes, I saw him!" another voice erupted. "He's the one!"

The Nothanek and Rhivothi stepped away, revealing a horde of Zylmacians, each pointing frantically at one another. Zander felt his stony face cracking with laughter. Such a sight was simply too amusing to behold.

"It was Lonak!" one of Jollkud's men shouted, pointing a finger. "He tried to get me to join, he said it would be quick and easy. Some of the men are getting sick, you see. He said we needed to feast on the natives to gain protection from the poison these lands hold!"

"Enough!" Damien roared, the intensity of his volume cutting effortlessly through the chaos. "The truth has been discovered, and before the sight of the gods, their justice shall be delivered. Seize them!"

Dreadfire's personal bodyguard muscled their way forward, the perpetrators unable to make an escape. They squirmed in the grasp of their kinsmen, begging and cursing for a reprieve. The Rhivothi tied their hands with lengths of rope, then shoved them forward.

You're a genius, Zander! Patience now, you have to remain patient. This is all going perfectly to plan!

Damien stared down the prisoners, teeth clenched, his eyes flashing a fiery red hatred. It was unclear what they were more afraid of; the prospect of facing the headsman's axe, or being in such close proximity to the crone. Their squirming made Lazilyth cackle, her voice deep like the rumbling of the earth. Dreadfire spat in disgust, then turned his gaze to the awestruck warband.

"The gods will be appeased for this treachery. Find me rope, and a sturdy tree to hang this filth upon!"

EINARR III

MILLIONS OF TINY STARS HUNG IN THE HEAVENS, BATHING THE snow covered forest in rich, heavenly light. It was a warm night, far too warm for snow, yet the land was blanketed in white. Einarr found himself beginning to sweat, yet the fluffy powder was as light and fresh as the moment it fell from the sky. He removed his animal skin cloak and scanned the barren trees, taking note of an absolute, eerie silence all around.

I know not this place, yet... it feels... familiar... so very familiar...

Einarr knew well enough that he was dreaming, yet everything felt strikingly similar to what he had experienced in the grove. More real than reality itself, if such a thing were possible. The thought of the gods speaking to him yet again made his skin crawl and turn cold, but in the darkness he saw nothing; no paths, and no sign of civilization anywhere.

Snow crunched softly underfoot as he began to walk, with seemingly no destination in mind. Tall pines towered a hundred feet or more into the air, and were aligned so perfectly it was as if the gods themselves had planted each one in rows. He saw no deer, no squirrels or rabbits, no birds, none of the furry creatures one might expect to find deep in the forest.

It was a pleasant enough experience, one that Einarr was grateful to have. His dreams could easily have been haunted by ghosts of the men he slew, or apocalyptic visions of Skaginlef wreathed in flames. But no, the gods were merciful on this night. He continued to walk, each row of pines looking no different than the ones before.

A good dream. Of that, I'm thankful.

Something felt different all of a sudden, and Einarr could sense a familiar presence nearby. He stopped, scanning the darkened pines for any signs of life, but found only the same empty desolation everywhere he looked. But still, something compelled him to go further, until a faint twinkling of light in the distance drew his attention.

Is it… could it be?

Even though he was unable to see what it was, Einarr felt a fluttering in his stomach. He raced through the snow, small, white clouds of fluff kicking up with each step. A dark shadow in the distance seemed to swallow all of the light around it, and only grew larger the closer he came. As the trees became more sparse, moonlight suddenly appeared, illuminating the land for miles in every direction.

A mountain? I've seen no mountains near Skaginlef, only some hills at Blackwolf Pass, and Castle Morden.

It was the largest thing Einarr had ever seen. Impossibly tall, the mountain stood commandingly over its surroundings, with none its equal. Its base stretched from horizon to horizon, with craggy slopes rising perfectly into a sharp, jutting peak which pierced the heavens like a spear.

The lightbearer came into view as well, though Einarr saw it was not one person carrying a lantern, but two. Racing on legs that were becoming numb, he continued onward as they began their ascent up to the snow covered mountainside. Squinting and straining, he was finally able to see light reflecting off the bald head of Damien Dreadfire.

"By the gods!" Einarr shouted in surprise. "Damien! Damien, it's me! It's Einarr!"

A smaller frame, that of Sylvia Stormguard, came into sight as well, her long, brown hair fluttering in a soft breeze. There was a moment when Einarr thought he heard her voice on the wind, and likely it was, but she was too far away to make out what was being said.

"Sylvia! Wait!" he screamed, his lungs burning with exhaustion.

The harder he tried to run, the more he began to slow, until Damien and Sylvia had nearly disappeared from sight. He watched them ascend the slopes until they became little more than dark specks against a backdrop of white snow. A fog of flurries then swallowed them whole. It seemed hopeless to keep up his pursuit, but Einarr continued to slog through a deep drift until he lost balance and fell.

A kiss from the cold wooden floor greeted his face as he fell from bed, flailing and shouting on the way down. Were it not for a thumping pain in his head, Einarr might have thought *this* was a dream, and his trek through the forest a reality. Morning light filtering through small holes in the drapes, which itself seemed dull and lifeless in comparison to the glory of the full moon. Truly, his dream was no ordinary dream.

He stepped out into a new day, rubbing a sore spot on his face. Skaginlef was abuzz with activity as the festival of spring drew near. It was a time to honor the gods and welcome new life into the world, and to celebrate the coming of age of a new generation. Soon, farmers would be planting their fields, and the markets would be bustling once more.

It was always Alina's favorite time of year, but ever since her passing, Einarr had enjoyed the festivities less and less. To him, it seemed little more than a pointless tradition, especially considering the death and carnage he had witnessed over the last year. Still, every man, woman, and child would be present at the opening ceremony. It would be considered a great disrespect to not attend, although it was hard to imagine being any more reviled than he already was.

Einarr stole a moment to place fresh flowers near the trunk of the cherry blossom tree and whisper a soft prayer. Music and laughter grew louder and more vibrant until it became impossible to even think. As he turned to join the festivities, he spied Nell approaching, dressed in a gown of white and red linen.

"She was a good woman," Nell said, smiling. "I always enjoyed our conversations."

Einarr nodded, his lips pursing. "Aye, she was. She was the best of me, and every day feels a little darker without her light in the world."

"I understand your pain, Einarr. When my husband Orrin died, my world came crashing down. We had plans to raise a family and build a new homestead outside of Skaginlef. But bandits came upon him one day when he was off in the Hinterwood. They killed him, killed him over a couple of silver coins."

There was a certain awkwardness that came between them. Einarr was unsure of what to say. He hardly knew Nell in the first place, and had spoken to her late husband only once or twice. Still, he offered what condolences he could. "I'm very sorry. The gods were cruel to take your husband from you."

Nell gave a melancholy smile. "No, they were kind to have given him to me in the first place. Such a man was truly a gift from the gods, and I cherish the time we had together."

It was difficult for Einarr to feel anything but resentment, and scoffed at Nell's misguided piety. "All I've ever done was try to please the gods; to worship them, to do their will, to live by their examples… and all I've received in return is suffering. I've seen the absolute worst in humanity, you know. I've seen men tear at each other like wild beasts. I've seen murder and butchery, cruel things that no one ought to see. How can the gods be real if this is what they allow?"

"Because they gave us free will," Nell answered sheepishly. "It's not up to them how the world is shaped, it's up to us."

She was right, in her own way. If Marcellus Bethard and the armies of Betanthia had never ventured north and never came to Borjifa, then the war might never have happened. That was the catalyst for all the death and suffering which had taken place since. But still, the sevelsej had been performed. Cedric Valens, the man responsible for the attack, had been put to the sword, alongside all of his soldiers. How could the gods not have been appeased?

"They should be wise enough to know the hearts of men are black, and thirsting for blood," he said. "Better that we were never created in the first place. Maybe the world would finally know peace."

There was an agony that manifested in Nell's eyes, the likes of which caused an inexplicable tightness in his chest.

"My Orrin's heart wasn't black, nor did he thirst for blood," she whimpered. "He was none of those things. How black is your own heart, Einarr Rolffson?"

She turned away, nearly sobbing. It appeared the loss of her husband had not eased with the passage of time, something he knew all too well. He felt shame and anger, and guilt for having lashed out like a wounded animal.

"Nell, wait," he pleaded. "My heart isn't black, it's empty. I suppose there's a part of me that wishes I would have died in battle, so I would be with Alina again. I apologize, I never meant to offend you. I've experienced horrors no man should endure, and I fear I may have lost my soul as a result of it. Please, forgive me."

Sniffling, and with a fire building in her soft, gray eyes, Nell turned and scowled, defiant as a lioness. "And what are you going to do about it, Einarr? Are you going to wallow in self-pity for the rest of your days? We've all lost someone dear to us. I can barely wake in the morning without crying myself back to sleep. But I get up and I keep going, because that is what my Orrin would want for me. What would Alina want you to do?"

It was a question that nearly broke him. Einarr felt his face twitching as sorrow began to pool in his eyes. "I know not, Nell. I've lost all sense of myself. Alina was my world, and it died that night in my arms. And each day that comes, I remember her face a little less. How cruel is that? To slowly forget the one who mattered to you most?"

"Then you must remember her in other ways," Nell said, nearly bowing up to Einarr, despite being more than a foot shorter. "If I had died, and my husband had lived, I would want him to be happy and healthy, and live the best life he could. And I would be waiting for him in Sjenohor, until the gods called him home. Do you not think Alina is waiting for you? What do you suppose she will think of you, seeing you like this?"

Gods... are you speaking to me through this woman? Are these your words instead of hers?

Einarr felt the skin on his neck turning to gooseflesh. "Knowing her, she would be disappointed." It was a difficult thing to admit, but also cathartic, in a way. "I know not what I'm supposed to do. All I feel is this endless longing, like a thirst I cannot quench."

"Maybe Alina would want you to save life, however you can," she said. "Most of our warriors are off fighting. If they fall, then Skaginlef will be defenseless. I fear what would happen should the Bethards come for us next. I think, knowing her as I did, she would want you to see this war to the end... and bring your people home."

Something sparked inside Einarr's mind. He could feel it now, as if a dark path had found sudden illumination. Perhaps the gods were indeed speaking through this woman after all.

"I know what I must do, though I hesitate to do it, even now."

"Follow your heart. Alina speaks to you, just as my Orrin speaks to me. They're in the company of the gods. Surely, they would not lie to us." Nell sheepishly looked Einarr in the eyes once more, but only for half a second before turning and starting back toward her hovel.

He sighed, weighing the gravity of their conversation. Perhaps the gods were indeed speaking to him through Nell, as they had through visions. Perhaps it was wrong to doubt and succumb to despair, he thought. If the gods truly found him unworthy, would they have ever sent him down such a path in the first place?

Each question seemed to produce even more questions, and few answers to boot. Einarr found solace in his homestead, meditating and sipping on mead until nightfall approached. Music and merriment drifted from the mead hall, along with a strong scent of the evening's feast. A strange feeling took root inside his heart, compelling him to reject his kinsmen no longer.

As if guided by an unseen force, Einarr willed himself outside, shutting the door to his sanctuary. The air was crisp and cool, a hint of warmth riding on the back of winter's waning touch. Mead gave him courage, courage to face the men who had shunned him at every opportunity for months.

Einarr pushed the door open, and was greeted by a rush of warm air, laden with roasted meat and incense. His ears were serenaded by a gentle plucking of strings, and the droll murmur of conversation. At the center of the hall sat a roaring pit fire, a billowing gray column of smoke snaking upwards. A long oaken table ran from one end of the room to another, with fifty high-back chairs flanking each side. Beyond it was a tall platform with nearly a dozen steps, and another table, itself reserved for the village elders.

At its head sat four weathered old men, each laden with fine silks, silver, and gold. They turned as the door opened and studied Einarr as he entered. It had been years since he last attended a proper feast inside the mead hall. Even after returning to Skaginlef, he could not muster up the courage to do so. He could nearly feel Alina's judgement and disapproval for what he had done on the battlefield, the shame overwhelming. But no longer.

"Greetings, Einarr. This is a surprise, I must say," Selbjorn said. He was the eldest of the four, once a strong and proud shield brother, now grown fat and soft. "Come, join us."

On the table sat a carved ox horn filled with mead, so large it might very well have been a cask. Selbjorn gestured toward the vessel, but Einarr declined. Instead he took up a seat on the opposite end of the table, its occupants looking at him curiously.

"What brings you to the hall after all this time?" Rosk inquired. "Your presence has been expected, since your return that is."

Einarr sighed. It was difficult to even make eye contact with the elders, especially Rosk. He was a thin, graying man who had seen better years, though anyone would be fool enough to cross him. It was he who convinced the other elders to give Einarr a seat at the high table, after everything he had done for the betterment of Skaginlef. But now, he could sense only frustration and disappointment emanating from the old man.

"I must admit that… I feel conflicted to be back here," he said. "After everything I've seen, and everything I've done, I feel unwelcome and unworthy. I built this hall in honor of my Alina, as a memorial to her life and everything she believed in. The truth is… it feels wrong for me to be here."

"Remember this, Rolffson," Rosk said. "Everything we do in life is at the behest of the gods, be it for good or for ill. Every action we take was etched into the fates long before our birth. Surely, Kholdyr would not curse you for what he himself foreordained you to do?"

"Come now, Einarr," Selbjorn interrupted. "Self pity is unbecoming of you. We have important matters to discuss, and as a member of this council, your input is needed. The Haalenhaad is nearly upon us, and we must finalize our preparations. Do you have any suggestions?"

It was a question with no easy answer. At the heart of the holiday was a ceremony for the gods, to give thanks and ask for a prosperous crop and a bountiful catch. One of the lesser rituals was the rites of passage for young Nothanek men, those who were coming of age. It was a rather droll affair, Einarr found it to be. Thanks was given to Olyndyr, so he might grace Skaginlef's young men with his blessings; skill with the plow, skill with the net, and skill with the hunter's bow.

But will Olyndyr come to our aid should Damien fail and Betanthia come seeking vengeance? Will he turn our plows into swords and armor?

He searched the faces of the elders, Finnvid and Geri remaining ominously silent. Einarr could sense their disapproval as well, but thankfully there was no hostility. At least, for now.

"I do have a few thoughts," Einarr cleared his throat. "This year, I think it would be wise to seek the blessings of a different god."

The plucking of strings came to an abrupt pause and was replaced with an audible gasp from the elders. They looked at each other stupidly, as if unable to understand what they were hearing. A few villagers inside the hall gave pause as well, some in the middle of a sip of mead.

"Einarr," Selbjorn said, rubbing his temples. "You know our traditions, we cannot simply—"

"No," he interrupted sternly. "You must listen to me, and heed my words. We are not living in normal times. This is not the age of peace and plenty, as we have grown so used to. Death sits on our doorstep. I have seen it. We cannot afford to remain aloof while Skaginlef's existence is in danger."

"Then what are you proposing, son of Rolff?" Geri asked, glancing briefly at the other elders.

"I think it would be wise to seek the protection of Azldyr."

"Einarr," Rosk pleaded. "We are not the Rhivothi. We do not pledge ourselves to the war god in such a manner. Skaginlef is a peaceful village, and seeks only the blessings of life and love. What you propose would bring ill fate to us all!"

"And I might very well agree with you, were it not for the hauntings in my dreams. The gods have spoken to me more times in the past days than they ever have. They have shown me wonders, and I believe, a vision of things to come."

"What have you seen, Einarr? Please, speak." Selbjorn pleaded. The other councilmen were leaning forward on the edge of their seats.

"Difficult to say for certain, I know not what any of it truly meant. But I do know this; we must seek the protection of Azldyr. Skaginlef needs sons. But more urgently, it needs warriors. Should Damien's fortunes on the battlefield turn ill, we will need to muster all of our strength to keep our lands safe against Betanthia's wrath. The fates have been kind thus far, but we all know how fickle they can be."

"Very well," Selbjorn conceded reluctantly. "I do believe the proper scrolls are still here. They should prove easy enough to find. But who would be the one to lead the ceremony?"

Silence came over the hall as the elders glanced at each other in uncertainty, the villagers looking on with bated breath. Slowly, gradually, Einarr felt the collective gaze of those in attendance shifting over to him.

"I think it should be you, Einarr," Geri declared.

Einarr scoffed and smiled, though he was the only one sharing in such amusement. "No, I am certainly not the right one," he protested. "Surely, there must be a far better man for such a task."

"But there isn't," Finnvid said. His voice was frail yet commanded authority. He was a scarred, husk of a man who had seen his share of hardship. He was missing an arm below the elbow, the result of a bear attack as a young man, the beast's claws forever marked upon his face and chest.

"Who among us has seen the things you have witnessed?" Finnvid continued. "Who among us has fought the battles you have fought?

You may not think of yourself as a great warrior, son of Rolff, but you have survived, and you are here now. Share with our young men what you have learned, and guide them through the invocation. Only you can do this."

It was a weighty responsibility, one he would assume not to have. But perhaps this task might serve as a form of penance, not only before the gods, but also before Alina. If he could keep Skaginlef strong and safe, then perhaps his soul might be cleansed.

"Very well," Einarr sighed. "In two days, I will perform the Haalenhaad. Bring me the totems, and I shall carve them. Now if you will excuse me, I must prepare."

GARETH III

HE SAT BESIDE THE BED AS MADELYN SLEPT, WISHING SHE HAD DIED. It was heartbreaking to see her this way, and to know of the unspeakable things the northmen had done. A reminder was plain enough to see, her belly grown large and near to bursting. The physicians said it would only be a short while longer before her baby was born, though it would be the most joyless of occasions. Staring down at her body, Gareth could not help but feel a great sadness, as well as a great anger. It was difficult to say which was stronger.

She never would have wanted this. Never in her entire life. Better that she would have died on the battlefield, so her honor would have remained intact.

Even watching her sleep was a painful exercise. As Madelyn slept, she twitched and jerked about, eyes relaxing and tightening every few seconds, as if witnessing her tribulation all over again. There were times when she would stop breathing altogether, then suddenly gasp for air as if being held underwater. For hours this went on, and as each passed by, Gareth continued to stand vigil.

He cursed the High Marshal for sending her out west. He cursed Cedric Valens for not having the fortitude to stop the barbarian horde in the first place. He cursed Aldred, Lord Vakaro, King Marcellus, and everyone else who facilitated the atrocity in the west. But most importantly, he cursed himself.

Were I a better prince, this never would have happened. My apathy caused this. I knew father was too far-gone to rule, and I should have filled that void instead of allowing lesser men to invite chaos into our lives. This is all my fault. I did this.

Delicately, Gareth brushed a lock of Madelyn's golden hair from her face, tucking the strands neatly behind her ear. There was a time when he would have felt elated at the thought of touching her. All he ever dreamt of was to hold her hand, share a passionate kiss, and spend a night tangled in each other's arms. But Damien Dreadfire had seen to it that none of those desires could ever be fulfilled.

Sniffling and dejected, Gareth took up a seat near the bed, his eyes heavy with exhaustion. Fighting off fatigue only made him more tired, until he slowly drifted off into slumber. Perhaps in a dream, he might find Madelyn as she once was, strong and determined, and full of life. And perhaps, she would love him with the same burning passion, free from the shackles of torment.

But he would not rest long. In an instant Madelyn's eyes shot open, a startled gasp erupting from her mouth. She was frantic, panicked, perhaps uncertain of where she was. Her screams were little more than babble, her wild thrashing that of a dying animal. Gareth rose from the chair and tried to offer comfort, but his presence alone seemed to worsen her delirium.

"Madelyn!" he called out, trying to gently restrain her. "It's me, Gareth! It's only me! Please, be calm!"

It took several moments before she was aware the nightmare had ended and was back in the waking realm. Still, the sight of Gareth brought with it little comfort, even as her gaze began to feel more familiar.

"G… Gareth…" she muttered, exhausted. Even mustering a single word seemed to drain what little remained of her energy, and within the blink of an eye she was unconscious one more.

"It's alright," he whispered. "Sleep now."

The next morning, he awoke to find Madelyn sitting propped up against the back of the bed, staring hopelessly at her mountain of a belly. Even now her eyes were disbelieving. She sighed, then looked away, trying to hide her tears.

"I'm so very glad you're alive, Madelyn." It was all Gareth could manage to say, though she appeared to be anything but pleased.

"I would rather be dead," she said in a near whisper.

"Don't say that," he pleaded, struggling to find the right words. "Please. I know you feel that way now, but please…"

"I never should have stayed behind," she lamented. "I knew it was hopeless, and I wanted to escape before we were surrounded. I should have run while I had the chance. But I was a fool. A fool blinded by duty and ambition."

"You were only doing what you thought was right."

"I don't even know what right *is* anymore." Madelyn's gaze drifted off to the opposite end of the room. She tried to roll onto her side, but the baby made such a thing far too uncomfortable.

"I would hope that if I ever found myself in such a situation, I would have your same courage." Gareth tried to sound reassuring. "Your dedication to your men, and to the fight, is unlike anything I've ever heard before."

Madelyn scoffed. "I've given my entire life to the Order, and how was I repaid for my dedication and courage? I was thrown out the second they no longer had any use for me. Goes to show you how men like the High Marshal feel about those under them. We're all expendable in the end."

Such words were especially painful to hear. Gareth had learned much recently, of how Madelyn and Jenson Powell came to know one another. It was both shocking and infuriating to hear how the High Marshal had unceremoniously stripped her of not only the title of Commander, but as a knight altogether. It was perhaps the greatest injustice one could inflict upon another.

"War is never kind to anyone," he said, "no matter how pure of heart. If there's anything I can do for you, Madelyn, anything at all, please, tell me."

"Go back to Cardale, Gareth. Just… go. There's nothing for you here."

What is she talking about? This isn't the Madelyn I know, not one bit.

Part of him wanted to grab her by the shoulders and shake a bit of sense into her, but doing so would most certainly make matters worse. Madelyn was in despair, and needed time, he told himself.

"Nonsense," he said defiantly, sitting back down beside the bed. "You are a wonderful, strong, brave, and kind person, and very dear to my heart. And I'm not going anywhere."

With a sniffle, Madelyn drifted back off to slumber, where hopefully the terrors of the night would not follow. However, it was only a matter of time before brutal memories of that fateful night would return, as such trauma was like to do.

Knowing there would be no sleep for himself, Gareth rose from his chair delicately, then stepped out into the hall for some fresh air. There seemed to be little change in the heaviness of the atmosphere, as if a cloud of sorrow was hanging over Castle Thorn. The only distraction he found was in observing various paintings and tapestries which hung throughout the hall.

"Ah, there you are," a familiar voice said. Sir Edmund Thomas strode toward him, looking equally as exhausted. "How is everything in there?"

"Quite sad, to be honest. I never would have imagined Madelyn in such a condition. She's more upset to be alive than anything."

"Aye." The elder Guardsman nodded. "Sometimes all a soldier can hope for is an end to their suffering. I don't expect you to understand, lad. At least, not yet, though hopefully never. Give her time."

Time was a commodity in short supply. At any moment, the army could begin their march to confront Damien Dreadfire's horde. At any moment, Ridley Vakaro might decide to unleash the full weight of his treachery. In either event, Gareth would be powerless to protect Madelyn, should some ill fate befall him.

"Any developments?" he asked. "Has Lord Kenfield learned anything more?"

"Not yet, but we're getting closer every day. It's not easy to infiltrate such a tight inner circle, but we'll learn Lord Vakaro's secrets soon enough. Of that, I have faith."

A soft clinking of chains rattled up the stairs. Gareth saw a pair of knights escorting a tower of a man, the most intimidating man he had ever seen. He was clothed in filthy roughspun and had a slight limp, but appeared to be anything but a common criminal. His face was perhaps the most terrifying thing of all. It was a patchwork of scars and pits, and wounds acquired from likely hundreds of battles.

"And who might this be?" Gareth pondered out loud. He could sense something about the prisoner, something which could not be explained.

"Nobody, my prince," one of the guards said. "Just a traitor headed for the rope. Apologies for offending you with his presence."

"A traitor, you say?" he asked quizzically.

"Yes, Your Highness, we caught him thieving out in Mor Seveht after deserting his post. Nobody you need to concern yourself with, justice is about to be served."

The name of the city, or village, or whatever it was, sounded strange and foreign. Gareth turned to Edmund. "Have you ever heard of Mor Seveht?"

"Indeed I have," Sir Edmund answered. "It's on the far reaches of the western border, about two weeks from Naxonnos, and about the same to Castle Morden."

Gareth cocked his head curiously. Could the prisoner have been one of Cedric Valens' men, either from the army or perhaps the castle garrison? No, he thought, the guards said he was a traitor, so he must have been a Blackthorn.

He couldn't have been there, could he?

"You there," Gareth asked the ragged man. "Tell me, were you at Castle Morden?"

The colossus said nothing, his eyes staring down in shame. When he failed to respond, one of the guards gave him a stiff elbow to the ribs.

"Yeah, yeah, I was there."

Gareth felt his heart flutter. Having a survivor of the battle could prove most valuable, and give him an unexpected advantage not only against the northmen, but against Lord Vakaro as well. Perhaps with the right knowledge, he would be able to defeat Damien Dreadfire and undermine the treacherous Commandant on the battlefield, and win the glory for himself.

"Tell me, tell me everything you saw. I need to know." He could hardly contain his excitement. "Please, speak!"

"We rode out, understrength and far too late, and were slaughtered for our effort. Not much more to tell than that."

"There has to be more to the story," Gareth insisted. "If you tell me, perhaps I can spare you from the rope. Give me your name, at least."

After a moment of silence, one of the guards answered. "This here is Tylar Bradshaw, once known as Titan."

The large man spat, then lifted his eyes. They were cold, empty vessels, devoid of light and life. "Spare me? Fuck all of that. I'm ready. Let these cravens hang me, I don't care. Leaving wasn't my crime; the only thing I'm guilty of is letting the one friend I had in this world die. I was stupid, and should have made her leave first. But no, I listened to her, and not my gut. And now she's dead. Dead and rotten to the bones by now."

"She?" Gareth asked. "You wouldn't happen to be speaking of Madelyn Everly, would you?"

Mentioning of her name ignited a fire inside the man, not of fury, but of sorrow. His eyes turned hazy with water in a near instant, his teeth clenched like a steel trap to keep his heartache at bay. "Yes," Titan croaked.

"She's a good friend of mine, and has been for many years. It'll relieve you to know she's alive, and here, resting in the infirmary."

Tylar Bradshaw roared, trying valiantly to ward off an avalanche of emotions, his eyes falling back to the ground one more. Gareth almost thought he saw tears dripping down his ravaged face.

"Come, I'll take you to see her," he said, motioning for Titan to follow.

"My prince," one of the guards protested. "That would be most inappropriate. This one is—"

"There seems to be a real problem within the Order these days," Sir Edmund's voice thundered in a rare display of agitation. "You lot don't seem to understand that this is Gareth Bethard, your soon-to-be king. It's not your duty to question him in any way, shape, or form. It's your duty to obey. Now, are you going to obey?"

Both guards glanced at each other, then reluctantly nodded.

"Good." Gareth turned and stared down the hall. "This is a new day in Betanthia, gentlemen. The days of my father's indifference have come to an end. Act accordingly."

The confidence he felt inside was building to the point of arrogance. There were times when Gareth could hardly believe the words coming out of his mouth, words which only a year ago would have been impossible to speak. But he reminded himself of the men he was dealing with, men who would only respect strength. As distasteful as he found such forceful language, it was nevertheless necessary.

Briskly, the entourage made its way to the infirmary. Were it not for his chains, Titan might very well have shoved past Gareth and sprinted onward, given how closely he was following. They paused outside the door, emotions rising from both men.

"I'm going to warn you," Gareth cautioned. "She's in rough shape, nothing like how you remember. Are you prepared for this?"

Titan grunted. "I have to be. This is my only chance before these cowards hang me."

"Very well, you may enter."

Gareth opened the door, and the two men stepped inside. Instead of looking upon Madelyn, he studied Tylar's reaction. The large man's jaw tightened, his wrist shackles jingling ever so slightly. Seeing Madelyn lying asleep in her condition nearly broke him.

"I did this," Tylar said, shaking his head. "I should have thrown her over my damn shoulder and climbed down that fucking rope. I knew I should have."

"I don't blame you," Gareth said in a near whisper. "I blame Damien Dreadfire. You followed orders, like any soldier should. It's not your fault."

"No… it is. You weren't there. You'll never understand how it feels to be trapped and to know your death is only moments away. There's little in this world that scares me, practically nothing. But that night, I felt fear for the first time in years. I wasn't thinking properly. I should have stayed behind and fought for as long as I could, and died to keep her safe. But I didn't. I followed orders when I shouldn't have."

"You're right," Gareth conceded. "I've never been in such a situation before. As a matter of fact, I've yet to be in a battle."

Titan turned and gave him the most haunting look he had ever seen. It was the look of a man who had seen too many horrors, someone who had witnessed things no mortal man ought to. "There's nothing glorious about it, and anyone who tells you otherwise is full of shit. And every time you set foot on a battlefield, even if you survive, a little piece of you dies and is left behind."

"I know. Well, I *don't*, but soon enough I suppose I will."

"Well then, I hope for your sake you have a short memory," Titan grunted. "Because me, I remember. I remember it all. Every friend I've ever made. Every man I've lost. And every mistake that put me here. I suppose it doesn't matter, though. I'm not long for this world anyways."

Titan walked slowly toward the door, his chains chiming softly, the guards entering to retrieve him. Gareth watched Madelyn sleep for a moment, her eyes darting back and forth beneath the lids. Was she still there, on the battlefields of western Betanthia, reliving her nightmares? He certainly hoped not.

He closed the door gently, giving one last peek inside before the latch clicked shut. It was heart wrenching to see Madelyn in such a state, barely clinging to the edge of life, her hopes and aspirations for the future likely gone forever. But she was alive, something he was immeasurably grateful for. Hopefully soon, she would recover enough strength to awaken.

"Madelyn is very special to me," he said, drawing Titan's attention, "as she is to you. And when she wakes, how am I supposed to explain that her friend was executed for grief? Executed for despair, thinking she was dead? No, I cannot do this, not to her or to you." He flicked his wrist toward Titan's chains. "Remove them at once. And not a word from either of you."

Both guards compiled without protest, which was a first. They inserted small keys into the keyholes, turned them, and freed Tylar Bradshaw from his restraints. The large man rubbed his wrists, which were horribly red and raw.

"You fought bravely," Gareth continued. "And against odds no man could best. And what's more, any friend of Madelyn's is a friend of mine. I will hereby extend to you a royal pardon, and draft you into the service of the Royal Guardsmen, should you choose it."

The guards gasped in unison, then looked at each other incredulously. Gareth drew his silver sword, a firm grip on the hilt, its blade singing as it was freed. "Where I'm going, I'll be in need of brave and loyal men. Madelyn's fighting days are likely over, but perhaps you can find redemption in keeping me safe."

"I... I cannot accept such an offer," Titan replied, looking nearly as stunned as the knights. "I failed her, and I fear I would only fail you as well,"

"Well, then you had better not disappoint her a second time. I'm sure Madelyn would be more than grateful to know you'll be standing at my side."

Sir Edmund grinned, nodding in approval. Titan appeared lost, as if he was unable to process his sudden change of fortune. He glanced at his now former captors, then quickly at Gareth. With a sigh, he dropped down to one knee, on his uninjured leg.

"Tylar Bradshaw," Gareth announced. "You are hereby absolved of all crimes against Betanthia and its people, and released of all oaths to the Order of the Blackthorn Knights. I hereby announce under royal decree that you are inducted into the ranks of the Royal Guardsmen, and will serve as one of my personal bodyguards." He placed the blade on Tylar's right shoulder. "Rise now, Guardsman."

The man known as Titan stared deep into his eyes. It was a look Gareth had never experienced before; one of shame, gratitude, determination, and of unyielding wrath. Once healthy, such a man would certainly be a force to be reckoned with.

"Sir Edmund," Gareth continued, "if you would be so kind as to find our newest Guardsmen some more suitable attire. And see to it he receives proper attention for that leg. A gimpy Guardsman simply will not do."

Edmund Thomas chuckled victoriously, gave a bow, then motioned down the hall. "Right this way, recruit. I'll give you my introductory briefing along the way. In the Guardsmen, we do things a bit differently. I believe a man with your attributes will be right at home with a purple cloak around your shoulders."

"I'll join you," Gareth interrupted. "I could use a break from this place."

After making their way clear of the guards, Gareth motioned for Titan to move a bit closer. "There are many things we need to inform you of, if you're to be one of my bodyguards. The realm isn't only under threat from northmen, as shocking as that might be to hear. But I don't dare speak a word of it inside these walls. Heavens know who might be listening."

"With the things I've seen in the world, nothing surprises me anymore." Titan grunted, his leg throbbing. "And with how those guards questioned your order, I can only imagine what—"

"Not here," Edmund whispered as they neared the heart of the keep. "Say nothing until we're clear of this place."

"If you say so," Titan muttered. "I know somewhere we can go. Somewhere these uppity twats won't follow. But what about the girl? Can't just leave her like that. She'll never get proper care here."

"Worry not," Gareth said. "I'll have Sir Edmund move her to a better location, and have midwives look after her."

All three men winced as they stepped out into a warm, cloudless day. Summer would be upon them soon enough, as the sun was quickly building its strength. Gareth wondered how the army would fare marching through the blistering heat, especially across a land as unforgiving as the Plainhold. He glanced over at Titan, who was grimacing in pain, and wondered how he would ever manage such a journey.

"We should really have that leg treated before it gets any worse," Gareth suggested.

"The only thing I need right now is a proper drink," Titan said, licking his lips in anticipation. "Come on, let's get the fuck out of here before any of these cunts start asking questions."

It was most amusing to hear the steady stream of profanities coming from Titan Bradshaw. Gareth had rarely heard such words uttered in his presence, though he was not the least bit offended. If anything, it made him feel more comfortable around men of war, men who cared little for manners and formality.

"Can you ride?" Edmund asked Titan.

"I suppose I don't have much of a choice."

They passed through the gatehouse to Castle Thorn, the guards gawking in utter confusion. Thankfully, most of the other knights were more respectful than their brethren, and raised no protest as Titan Bradshaw lumbered past. Gareth saw just how badly Titan wanted to accost those who he once called brother, but his desire for a tankard of ale was that much greater.

A pair of squires brought Edmund and Gareth their horses, and another for Titan, though they appeared reluctant to do so. The large man thought twice before mounting, carefully weighing how to climb into the saddle with only one good leg. It was obvious the pain was more bothersome than he was letting on. Titan put a foot in the stirrup and hoisted himself onto his horse with a deep grunt.

"If you wouldn't mind." Edmund gestured down the road, bidding their newest Guardsman to lead the way.

Titan needed little convincing. With his good leg, he prodded the destrier into a trot and left Castle Thorn behind. Gareth was happy to be free from such a place as well, though leaving Madelyn alone was already beginning to weigh on his mind. Fortunately, the ride was short, and soon enough a fresh whiskey would be in his hand.

"This here is the lowest of the low, as far as Bentmont goes."

The tavern was unremarkable, as taverns often were. Gareth had been in his fair share of shady establishments before, and had come to know both the environment and the clientele well enough. A weathered hitching post sat outside of an equally shabby door. The windows were opaque with years of grime, so filthy it was a wonder if any light was able to penetrate them at all.

After dismounting, Titan was the first to enter, Gareth and Edmund trading glances before following. The tavern's interior was quite different from what they were expecting. While it was certainly an establishment for those of low birth, it was surprisingly similar to the Hollow Stone in Cardale. A tall wooden bar ran the length of the room with nearly two dozen stools pushed up against it. Less than a third of them were claimed, their occupants already thoroughly inebriated despite such an early hour.

Crude sets of tables and chairs pimpled the dingy stone floor, which itself was so tarnished it appeared as if it was dirt. A plate of bones sat discarded on one table, every trace of meat picked clean. On another, a pair of tankards, one empty and the other still quite full. Judging from the positions of the chairs, a conversation which began with ale likely ended with fists out in the street.

Near one of the corners sat a table with a lit lantern at its center. Titan snapped his fingers at the barkeep then took up a chair. Edmund sat facing the door, should any unsavory characters make an entrance. Gareth preferred to sit with his back turned, so as to not be immediately identifiable.

"What can I do for you today, sirs?" a barkeep said, drying his hands on a stained apron which appeared more gray than white.

"An ale, and whatever you've got on the fire," Titan said, his stomach roaring.

"And for you two?"

Edmund looked at Gareth and smiled. "Two mugs of your finest whiskey."

"If it's fine you're looking for, then I'm afraid you've come to the wrong place," the barkeep quipped, his expression anything but friendly.

"Give us your best," Gareth interjected. "Something that won't leave us pissing ourselves and fighting everyone in here."

"I don't know, sounds like a good enough time to me!" Edmund chuckled. "Haven't had a proper tavern fight in ages."

The barkeep looked none too amused, and returned to his station. Several patrons at the bar glanced over their shoulders, annoyed at the banter. Commoners as they were, they seemed to take exception to high-born trespassers in their establishment.

"Whiskey, eh?" Titan raised an eyebrow. "Never cared for it, unless there was no other option."

"Ale is good, no argument there." Edmund pursed his lips and nodded. "But if you're going to be around men like us, you had best learn to acquire the taste. Hopefully your liver is as strong as the rest of you."

Gareth and Titan snorted, the former in amusement and the latter in what seemed like contempt. The barkeep returned in short order with a plate of boiled potatoes and roasted chicken in one hand, and three mugs in the other.

"Now," Titan said after taking a sip. "What's this business with the Order? I mean, I know they're nothing but self-serving cunts, but…"

"Well, here's the situation, in as few words as I dare speak." Gareth took a long pull from his mug, eyes locked with the behemoth. "It's come to our attention that a certain lord and high council member have greater aspirations than the defense of the realm."

Titan appeared confused for a moment. "Not sure if I get your meaning. You're telling me that even as the northmen are invading, a coup is underway?"

"Not underway," Edmund pointed out. "At least, not yet. But we're aware of its development. As concerning as it is, the reception we've received from the Order is even more troubling. The High Marshal has yet to receive our prince, and the contempt I've seen from your former brothers leaves me concerned."

"As you can see by how they've treated me, their brotherly loyalty only goes so far." Titan paused to stuff a generous helping of chicken into his mouth. By the look of his frantic chewing, it appeared as if he had not eaten in a lifetime.

"Indeed." Gareth sighed. "To be quite honest with you, I'm not certain which is the greater threat, the barbarians or our own lords. Which is why I'm here in the first place. House Bethard cannot afford to remain in Cardale while our lords further their own influence. And this is why I need you. You're a man who looks like he can get things done, and doesn't back down for anyone."

"Damn right," Titan Bradshaw grunted. "But if you're looking for me to somehow command respect from the Order, you're sorely mistaken. I'm an outcast. If you hadn't showed up, my corpse would be swinging from the end of a rope by now. The only ally I have left in the Order is Madelyn, and…" His gaze fell to the table. "It looks like her fighting days are over. I doubt that cunt of a High Marshal will even keep her around now that she's of no use to him."

"That's preposterous." Gareth huffed. "She's given her entire life to the Order! You can't tell me—"

"Be warned," Titan interrupted, his gaze deadly serious. "In Bentmont, nothing is as it seems. If you came here searching for loyalty, then you're in the wrong town. Yeah, I can tell by how you're looking at me that you think I'm full of shit. But think about it, you never would have thought one of your Commandants could turn on you, and now here you are, hoping to end a coup before it begins. Don't make the mistake of thinking anyone outside of your circle has your best interests in mind."

Such a revelation was troubling, to say the least. Gareth cursed himself for not taking charge of his life sooner and building a reputation so strong that none could challenge it. Now, he was faced with what appeared to be insurmountable treachery. If Lord Vakaro and Aldred were to be outed for their treason, would it even be possible to arrest them? Who would stand up for House Bethard, aside from the Royal Guardsmen? Their numbers were too few to make any meaningful difference in the grand scheme of things.

"That's why I brought a few loyal men with me," Gareth said. "Lord Kenfield and his best soldiers are here."

"Here?" Titan sneered. "Where exactly is *here?*"

"They're at our campsite outside the city." Gareth lifted his chin. "I thought it best to spend time among the army. I want the men to see their prince as a leader, not a pampered monarch who commands from afar. I want them to know that I have every bit as much to lose as they do."

It was a stretch of the truth, to say the least, as most of his time had been spent at Madelyn's side. But still, the King's standard was represented at the camp, itself a sight of inspiration, or so he hoped.

Titan downed a mouthful of ale and nodded, a few drops speckling his chin. "I'm impressed, but I'll believe it when I see it. If you're every bit the man you say you are, then you're a rarity, especially around here. But let me tell you something. It's easy to have convictions, but when you're knee-deep in other men's guts, your mind tends to change. Now, onto the real business. Who is this lord you speak of? The one plotting against you?"

Gareth glanced over his shoulder, then leaned in close. "Lord Ridley Vakaro."

His reply was silence, and a piercing gaze. Titan downed the last of his ale without breaking eye contact.

"Then it seems like northmen are the least of your problems. Fucking hell, you sure know how to pick your enemies."

"Hence why we're here," Edmund chimed in. "If it was some upstart lordling, he'd be rotting in the dungeon at the Citadel. But this situation requires a much more delicate hand. Lord Kenfield is assisting with getting a man into their inner circle, but Lord Vakaro is very strict about the company he keeps."

"Well, I'm certainly not the man to help you with that." Titan bit into his potatoes, though they appeared none too appetizing. "But if you need a few skulls broken, then I'm your man."

A thought entered Gareth's mind, since a clandestine approach was likely to produce little in the way of results. Perhaps instead of seeking to catch Lord Vakaro in the act, he would be better served building a sphere of influence of his own.

"We could be going about this all wrong," he said, drawing both men's attention. "Instead of currying favor with lords who would just assume cut my throat, perhaps we should be focusing our efforts somewhere else."

Edmund stroked his chin. "I think I know where this is heading."

"Tylar, you and Madelyn have tremendous reputations within the Order. Whether they love you or hate you, they know your name. If I can build a similar rapport with the army, then this little plot will fail before it truly begins."

"Now there's a thought," Sir Edmund said. "The love of the common man is often underestimated. Your father had the people's devotion once, as did King Torbin, his father. But in order to achieve that, you'll need to put yourself in the greatest danger. Sitting back and watching from afar as the men fight will gain you nothing. You'll have to be in the thick of it."

It was quite curious, Gareth thought, that to secure his safety, he would have to openly flirt with death. But death would be most certain if Lord Vakaro succeeded in overthrowing House Bethard. There was truly only one option to choose from.

"Then so be it," Gareth Bethard said in growing solemnity. "And if I should die, then I'll die fighting for my lands and my people. At least my life would have been for something. What say you two? Care to join me in a dance of death?"

LUCETTA IV

T HE CONVOY STRUCK OUT BEFORE SUNRISE, RAYS OF A NEW DAWN glowing bright in the distance. Behind her carriage marched nearly one hundred and twenty souls, bound to one another in chains. Lucetta had allowed them to walk unshackled the first day, but mere hours after leaving Cardale, six of the slaves had escaped. Four were recovered, one was killed in a struggle, and another had gone missing.

It was disheartening to keep men, women, and especially children in restraints, but such precaution was necessary. They should be grateful, she thought, as they would soon be free to build a new realm from nothingness. Chains were little more than a temporary inconvenience, after all, one which would be forgotten in due time.

They look so miserable… so lost for hope. If only they could see what wonders they will be part of, as I do. I'm certain they would rejoice.

On the first night, several of the slaves attempted yet another escape. The Droethiens, however, were every bit as vigilant as they were dangerous. Three men were apprehended at spearpoint not long after breaking their iron shackles open, and were immediately brought to Pavlos for proper punishment. A sharp crack of a whip was enough to rouse Lucetta from her slumber, its tails snapping and filling the air with flecks of blood and screams of agony.

At first she was horrified, and impulsively attempted to stop Pavlos, but quickly thought better of it. Witnessing the man's cruelty, and the joy he took in it, made her blood run cold. The scourging seemed to last an eternity, but after the skin on the third man's back was sufficiently shredded, the ordeal abruptly ended. Perhaps most disturbing of all, she thought, was how easy it was to drift back to sleep.

Early on the second day, while miles away from Dellhaven, the convoy came to a halt. This was where the White Spear would break ranks and lead the slaves westward and around the city, lest the watchmen discover them. Pavlos, on the other hand, would not be going anywhere. Despite his barbarism, Lucetta felt safe in his presence, as if she was somehow shielded from every horror in Caldakas.

The Droethien said something to his men, then rode to her carriage. "Princess! Everything shall proceed as you have ordered, yes? My men will see these slaves to the village and begin clearing the land."

"Excellent. They know to stay as far west as possible, correct?"

Pavlos nodded. "Worry not, princess. Everything shall be as you desire. The White Spear has never disappointed in the whole of their existence, yes?"

There was almost a hint of annoyance behind the Droethien's dark and ominous eyes, though his golden smile was reassuring enough. Reliable men were difficult enough to come by as it was, and Lucetta had to remind herself that he was a mercenary, a man of silver and gold, and was loyal to those who provided it.

After watching the White Spear depart, the convoy continued on towards Dellhaven. They arrived mere hours later, and were shown through the outer gates without incident. Lucetta noticed the guards eyeing her more suspiciously this time, but none dared to offer any challenge of any sort.

The people were another matter entirely. They seemed to have grown used to the comings and goings of House Bethard, and few turned out to witness the royal arrival and offer their courtesies. Not that it mattered, the less eyes watching her every movement, the better.

I pray the servants at the estate are just as disinterested. Heavens know they'll probably run off to inform mother of my arrival, even before assisting me out of my carriage…

When Lucetta caught sight of the chateau, her heart began to flutter and take flight. She looked to the woman in black for comfort, but the entity was nowhere to be found. A bottle of wine on the refreshment rack was more than sufficient, however. She pried it open and drank several desperate gulps, a few drops dribbling down her chin. The bottle was nearly halfway empty as her carriage rumbled into the estate's courtyard, the Guardsmen snapping to attention and saluting her arrival.

Be calm, Lucetta, you're safe here. They suspect nothing. Just breathe.

The carriage door creaked open, and Pavlos was the first to offer his hand. She climbed out slowly, so nervous that walking straight was nearly impossible. Each step was filled with an impending dread, her pulse quickening so rapidly it was difficult to remain conscious. The doors to the estate opened, and out stepped Devin Brandybrook, diligent as always.

He gave a grin and a slow bow, his eyes never once falling to the ground. "Welcome home, Princess Lucetta. I trust your travels were well?"

"Yes, the countryside was lovely." She made to move past Devin, but he stood firm in the doorway.

"And Cardale?"

The inside of Lucetta's dress became a hot, swampy mess in a near instant. She felt beads of sweat forming across her brow. "I wish I could have stayed longer, but I'm simply not ready to be back home. I felt stress beginning to overwhelm me after only an hour, and so I returned here."

"I see." Devin stepped to the side, motioning for her to pass. "Excellent to have you back with us. I pray your business was successfully concluded."

Lucetta entered the foyer, the servant man's gaze studying her intently. Swiftly, she started off toward her chamber, her heels clacking like carpenter's hammers. There was another sound approaching from behind, an amalgamation of crunching and jingling, the sounds of familiar armor.

"Princess," Pavlos said in a near whisper. "Have you further need for me this day?"

"Stay close to me, I don't feel safe here. And keep some of your men nearby as well. We may need them in short order."

"As you say, princess. If any man dares to lay a hand upon you, they shall lose their hand. You can trust I will be close by, yes?" The Droethien gave a nod of his head, then dismissed himself as they arrived at her chamber.

Nearly consumed by panic, Lucetta shut the door and locked it, then rushed to draw all of the heavy drapes shut. Having overseen the estate's renovation personally, she was certain that no prying eyes could see inside. She hurried to a table against the wall and poured out a chalice of wine, and proceeded to guzzle it down with furious desperation.

As drunkenness was beginning to take hold, there was a soft rapping at the door, followed by an announcement of lunch. A sudden snarling of her stomach was enough to convince Lucetta to attend, as she had not eaten properly since setting out from Cardale. Before heading to the dining room, she gave pause in front of a mirror, taking note of the ever-darkening circles around both eyes. It was distressing to see the effects of sleeplessness creeping across her face.

A worthy sacrifice. I pray every minute invested will bring a year of peace.

After gathering herself, she started off down the hall. It felt as if eyes were around every corner, behind every curtain, each one studying her intently. Wine helped to blunt her anxiety, but nothing could prepare her for what was waiting in the dining room.

"Lucetta," Charlotte said, sitting at the head of the table. "Come in. Sit."

It was the most terrifying and helpless feeling yet. "It's good to see you, mother. You look well."

In days past they would have traded friendly banter, but this time, Charlotte appeared more distant. There was a different aura to her mother, a firmness and strength she had not witnessed in years.

Devin Brandybrook pulled out a chair and beckoned her to sit. His grin was more sinister than usual, as if he was hiding unspoken knowledge. Lucetta tried to act casual, smiling at her mother and smoothing out the length of her skirts as she sat.

While the feast was bountiful, conversation was in short supply. Such awkwardness around the table was maddening, but she was too terrified to speak first. Likely, anything she would say would most certainly be used against her in some fashion. She scratched at scabbed flesh on her wrists, fighting a compulsion to scream.

Someone say something, please! Anything! I cannot take this silence any longer! I beg you, someone, speak!

Thankfully, Charlotte dabbed her mouth with a clean linen napkin and cleared her throat. "I take it you will be leaving us again shortly?"

While it was a worrisome question, she was thankful the torment of silence was over. "No, mother, I intend on relaxing for a while. My travels have left me weary."

"You certainly seem to be getting around these days." The Queen eyed her without any hint of emotion. "It seems every other day, you disappear off somewhere. Tell me, what is going on with you?"

Lucetta nearly blacked out from panic. They were onto her, that much was certain. If not, then why were Devin and the other servants permitted to remain in the room? Why was this not being discussed in private?

Help me! Save me, wherever you are…

But the woman in black was nowhere to be found. If there was any time when she needed the entity's assistance, it was now. Lucetta glanced around, desperately searching for the woman, but doing so only seemed to heighten the Queen's suspicions.

"I've been busy planning my new estate, mother. Life has become too tedious for me to remain shut inside every day. For once, I'm enjoying my life."

"The weather must be quite frigid up north," Devin chimed in.

"We *are* up north," she snapped back. "It's always cold up here."

Sweat was rolling from her armpits and down the inside of her dress. How could anyone have known about what transpired in the northern riverlands? Her mind was racing a million miles a minute, panic, anger, and fear overwhelming her senses. She pushed a half-finished plate aside and rose from the table, eager to retreat to her quarters where Pavlos could keep watch.

"Stay," Charlotte commanded. "Tell me and tell me the truth, Lucetta. Are you having an affair?"

"No!" she whimpered. "Is that what you think of me, mother? You think me to be an unfaithful whore? That's what you think of your only daughter? Perhaps I should have stayed shut up in Cardale, never to see the light of day. Perhaps I should have been Aldred's trophy and nothing more."

"You're overreacting," Charlotte said. "I simply wish to know why you have been acting so strange lately. Your behavior and your travels have been quite suspect. You have the look of guilt on your face."

"No, mother," she protested. "I am not having an affair. I'm simply trying to find a reason to make it to tomorrow. I hate my life, and I have for many years. I cannot have the family I always wanted, with children of my own blood, so I try to distract myself with projects. But I always feel the same emptiness. Some days, I just wish I was dead."

Sobbing, she fled from the dining room. Her ruse seemed to fool everyone well enough, as neither Devin nor any of the guards gave pursuit. She ran into her chamber and slammed the door, locking it securely. In an instant her faux tears of sorrow turned to tears of rage, both hands balling tightly into fists.

Lucetta lit a single candle on her desk, and stared intently into its soft flame. What knowledge she sought from the fire, she could not tell. There were no visions, no premonitions, no guidance of any sort to be found. Its warm glow reminded her of the woman in black's eyes, and not only the terror, but the confidence they could inspire.

Please, speak to me. I don't know what to do. I fear I've made a terrible mess of everything. Please, save me!

But no reply came. Frustrated, Lucetta slipped into bed, but could find no slumber. She stared at the wall for hours, pretending to sleep as Brendon of Theeds opened the door to announce dinner. The young man left nearly as quickly as he arrived. As the door shut, she shot up from bed and desperately drank down an entire flagon of wine until the sun departed from the evening sky.

Despite a wall of warm, humid air outside, Lucetta found herself shivering violently. She sat on the floor near the patio doors, rocking back and forth, searching an overcast sky for starlight to wish upon. But there was no light to be found.

All of her well-laid plans were falling apart by the second, she knew it. And worse, there seemed to be no way to salvage any of it. Likely, the Guardsmen would clap her in irons and haul her off to some dank prison, with only rats to keep her company. She wept like no other time in her life, sobbing so violently she nearly vomited.

"Do not despair," the woman in black said, sitting on a chair across the room. It was relieving to finally see her guardian spirit. "You are precisely on the path you must travel down. The fates could not be more clear. Your weeping serves no purpose."

"No, no you don't understand!" Lucetta pleaded. "Devin knows, I can see it in his eyes! This was a terrible idea, I never should have done any of it. I never should have left home, or—"

"Enough of your sniveling!" The entity suddenly manifested mere feet away. "Must I show you again what fate awaits Betanthia and your family should you fail? Have you learned nothing?"

Gasping in fright, Lucetta raked her fingers through her scalp, clumps of hair torn free. "But can you tell me with certainty that Devin does not know? Can you?"

The woman in black paused, her orange-red eyes swirling with fire. "Indeed he does, and he has been watching you closely for some time now. He is a threat, and must be eliminated before your plans can be foiled."

"And yet you saw fit not to inform me of this?"

"All in good time," the apparition said. "Information I disclose to you must be done so at the appropriate moment, lest the fates be circumvented. Should you learn too much about the future, it could very well alter the fabric of existence, and send you down paths even I cannot foresee. For now, trust in me, and the guidance I have given you. Now is the time to act."

"Tell me one more thing, you must," Lucetta pleaded. "Is anyone else watching? Who else is aware of what we've been up to? Does my mother know? She suspects I'm having an affair, but does she know what I've truly done?"

It was the first time the woman in black appeared sad, its fiery gaze subsiding and falling to the floor. "I say this with no pleasure, as it will hurt you terribly. But yes, your mother is aware. Devin Brandybrook has been watching you at her behest. She suspects you have done terrible things, and has utilized every resource at her disposal to gather information. I am sorry, my dear child, truly I am, but your mother knows everything."

There was never a time in her life when she wanted to die more than in that moment. Lucetta crumpled into a ball on the floor, buried her face into her hands, and erupted into an apoplectic fit of tears.

"I cannot do this," she cried out. "Please, make it all stop. Take this burden away from me. Please, I'll do anything!"

"There, there," the woman in black said comfortingly, kneeling down and stroking her auburn hair. "Your distress is only natural. Your own blood has betrayed you. Better for you to realize it now, while steps can be taken to protect yourself."

It was all too much to take it at once. Lucetta leaned forward, panting like a dog and nearly vomiting, a million thoughts polluting her already troubled mind. If the Queen knew of her activities, then it would only be a matter of time before men in purple cloaks would arrive to arrest her. And she knew what the punishment was for treason, even for a member of the royal family.

"What would you have me do? Please, tell me! I'll... I'll do anything! Please!"

The entity returned to its seat, crossed its legs, and pondered for a moment. "This will be the most difficult trial you will face, far more difficult than your encounter with Sir Bryce. But if you wish to remain alive and free, you must do exactly as I instruct. Are you willing to do whatever it takes, no matter what the cost?"

"I am..." she whimpered.

"You already know that Devin Brandybrook must be stopped. He is an imminent threat, and if not eliminated, will be directly responsible for your downfall."

"Eliminated?" Lucetta scrambled to her feet. "No, I... well... I mean, he *is* onto me, as you say, and... yes, yes I agree. But how will Pavlos ever be able to pull off such a feat without being caught? Devin is surrounded by the other servants day and night."

"Your mercenary is capable enough, but I am afraid there is another task you must complete as well, if you are to survive. Come and sit, child."

The woman in black stood and motioned for Lucetta to take a seat. Apprehensively, she made her way across the room and nearly collapsed onto the chair from utter exhaustion.

"I fear there is no easy way to say this, but as a future queen, you must acclimate yourself to making life and death decisions. Not only must Devin Brandybrook be silenced forever, but so must your mother as well."

Lucetta gasped and nearly fainted, but the entity held her upright by the shoulders. Liquid churning inside her stomach finally let loose, a jet of brownish water erupting onto the floor. Coughing and sobbing, she babbled only an incoherent response. The woman in black embraced her, the way Charlotte used to when she was little. It brought back memories of happier times, when the bonds between mother and daughter were as strong as steel.

"There, there, child. Everything will be alright. Do not let your heart be troubled. I have seen into the fates, and should you not do this, your mother shall be the one to take your life. Do you wish to see with your own eyes? I can show you this vision of the future, should you choose it."

"No!" she cried out. "This has all gone wrong, so terribly wrong. I never wanted—"

"Hush now," the woman in black interrupted. "I understand the pain you feel inside. But you chose this path, and pledged to do whatever was necessary to see it through to the end. Remember, countless generations yet unborn are relying on you. This is the greatest sacrifice you will have to make, Lucetta Bethard, but your rewards will be limitless. And fear not, your mother will be waiting for you in the afterlife, when your time comes. And she will understand, and applaud you for everything you have done. Trust me when I say this is your destiny."

An unusual calmness suddenly came over Lucetta, her tears quickly drying like desert rain. She felt a soothing warmth inside, the sort of reassuring sensation one might feel from a loving embrace. The entity was looking on, her orange-red eyes swirling and pulsing with a white-hot energy.

"Very well then," she whispered. "Tell me how I need to proceed."

The woman turned and drifted to the window overlooking the courtyard. "We will act tomorrow night, you dare not wait a day longer. Devin must be the first target, as he is the one watching you most closely. You must devise a way to lure him away from the other servants, some place where your Droethien can seize him. Come, have a glass of wine."

At first, Lucetta appeared hesitant, knowing the large silver flagon was empty. But upon closer inspection, it was mysteriously full. Her skin felt as if it were crawling off her bones, but the wine was too inviting to sit untouched. She filled a crystal chalice near to overflowing, then joined the woman in black at the window.

"I'm certain Pavlos and I can devise some distraction," she said, taking a sip.

"You are too clever for some simple-minded servant to best you. Be cautious, as this will be the more difficult task of the two."

It was heart-wrenching to think of Queen Charlotte and what was soon to befall her, but Lucetta forced herself to feel nothing, to clear her mind of all other thoughts. Devin was the sole focus of her attention for now, and would be until Pavlos could do his handiwork.

"You know what it is you must do," the woman said, slowly dissolving into the shadowy corner. "I will rejoin you then. Sleep now, you will need every ounce of strength come tomorrow."

As she watched the entity fade out of sight, a swift drowsiness took hold. Lucetta set the chalice down and stumbled to her bed, barely reaching its edge before falling into a deep, restful, and thankfully dreamless sleep. Breakfast came and went the next morning, though she was conspicuously absent. The servants had come to expect such behavior, but one of the girls came by to check on her regardless. There were several soft rappings on the door before its hinges creaked open.

"My princess? Are you here?"

"Yes," Lucetta croaked, feigning discomfort.

"Are you unwell?" A servant girl stepped inside, hands fiddling with one another.

"I am. Fetch me water and a clean cloth. And bring Pavlos to my chamber." She coughed and groaned, wincing as if suffering from a rampaging migraine.

"Right away, princess. I do hope you feel better."

She returned nearly ten minutes later, likely from having to locate Pavlos. But the Droethien was never too far away, and entered immediately after the servant girl brought cool water and fresh cloth for her forehead. He dismissed her with a flick of his wrist and a hissing sound.

"Princess." Pavlos moved to the side of the bed, then dropped to one knee. "I was told you were ill?"

She waited for the door to close. "No, I'm fine," she whispered. "There's something I need you to do, and it must be done tonight."

"Absolutely, my princess." The mercenary grinned, amused at the charade.

"Good. Devin is onto us, he knows everything! He's simply waiting for the right opportunity to set the Guardsmen on us. We have to do something, and fast."

Pavlos ran a hand across his chin. "This is… a most unwelcome distraction. Let me cut this man's throat in his sleep and blame it on one of the servants, yes?"

"No," she replied. "We cannot be so obvious about it. I will write a letter anonymously, pretending to be one of the servants, and informing Devin that I have damning information to share. The instructions will be to come alone and meet behind the gazebo after dark. Then, I want you and several of your best men to capture him."

"Ah, you wish to avoid raising suspicion, yes? Worry not, my princess, Pavlos was able to kill Bryce Whitewood without ever raising an alarm. You want me to kill this man, this Devin, yes?"

"Well… yes… I do." Fortunately, Lucetta was still in bed, or else her legs might have given out. "And he has to disappear somewhere he'll never be found. Everyone must think he fled the estate."

"Princess," he chuckled. "I would think by now you would know Pavlos, and what he is capable of doing. Worry not, it will be done, as you wish it to be done. Now, shall I have some food brought to your room?"

Merely mentioning food immediately set her stomach to groaning. She nodded, running a hand across her rumbling midsection. "Yes, and some more water."

Brendon of Theeds returned a short time later with a platter of freshly baked bread, fish, and vegetables which looked none too appetizing. It was only after the first bite that Lucetta realized just how starved she truly was. Within minutes, the plate was wiped clean and discarded on her disheveled desk.

Lucetta spent the afternoon staring at the sun as it drifted slowly across a cloudless sky. Every minute crept by like the passing of years, her mind racing through every possible scenario. Would Pavlos succeed, or would Devin somehow thwart their plans and have them both arrested?

I'm going mad, and not even wine is helping. I cannot believe this is truly happening.

Lucetta remembered keeping several small vials of sleeping tonic in her desk, for nights when her anxiety was too ferocious to permit slumber. She retrieved one, carefully pulled out its cork, and held it to her lips. The liquid inside smelled foul, and tasted even worse, but within a short while, a heavy drowsiness took hold. She shambled over to her bed and flopped down onto the mattress, a deep and dreamless sleep proceeding.

When she awoke, it was evening, and nearly time to execute her plan. Frantically, Lucetta shot out of bed and began scrambling to prepare, though she had little idea of what precisely to do. A simple, thin black silken gown would help her to move about the shadows without being detected. She tore off her sweat-drenched clothes, hastily donned the gown, then put her hair up into a lazy updo. The sun was setting faster with each passing minute, and soon the room filled with darkness. It was another overcast night, one of many, which gave Lucetta pause. Perhaps the woman in black could exert her influence over nature itself, she thought, shuddering at the possibility.

For an hour she waited by the window, back pressed firmly against the wall, peeking occasionally outside. At first she saw nothing, until a figure appeared in the distance, slinking from tree to tree, careful to remain only in the darkest of shadows. It was Pavlos. It had to be.

As the Droethien drew closer, it became apparent he had something large slung over one shoulder. Lucetta squinted, curiously studying his unknown baggage, until Pavlos dumped it unceremoniously onto the ground. She spied the pale skin of an arm, hanging from the linen sheet it was wrapped in.

Heavens! Pavlos, what have you done! You were supposed to make Devin disappear far from here!

As the sheet was thrown back, Lucetta saw the body of a girl lying dead, her clothing indicative of those worn by the estate's servants. Pavlos propped the corpse against the gazebo, making it appear as life-like as possible, then draped the sheet over its shoulders as a sort of crude cloak. He then scurried around the gazebo and disappeared from sight, mere moments before another figure made its approach.

She spied Devin Brandybrook, clutching a piece of folded parchment, his eyes cautiously scanning the darkness. Carefully, Lucetta cracked the window open an inch, eager to bear witness to what was about to happen. Devin approached the gazebo, glanced over each shoulder, then proceeded onward.

"There you are!" he said in a hushed voice, but loud enough to be heard. "I've come alone, as you said. You have my word, no one will be aware that you've come forward."

There was no response. Lucetta felt pleasure building within her, the same pleasure she felt when Bryce Whitewood's life was snuffed out. Smiling, she watched as Devin stepped forward, peering down at the body suspiciously.

"Is… is everything alright?"

Before he could manage another step, Pavlos crept around the other side of the gazebo, as swift and silent as a shadow, and set upon him. The Droethien wrapped his mighty hands around Devin's head and jerked, a resulting crack sounding as if a tree branch had broken. It felt surreal to see his lifeless corpse fall to the ground, as if she was watching from outside of her own body.

He's done it. Devin is… really dead… I can't believe it…

Two more figures scurried through the near pitch blackness, making their way quickly to the gazebo. Pavlos wrapped the servant girl back into the sheet as they arrived. Both mercenaries snatched up the bodies and made a hasty retreat like thieves in the night. They moved at speed away from the estate and disappeared nearly as quickly as they arrived.

Pavlos, on the other hand, was going nowhere. After making certain his men had fled the grounds, he slunk over to Lucetta's door, sliding it open without so much as making a sound. Once inside, he drew the drapes shut and threw back the hood on his cloak. Smeared across his face was what appeared to be soot, his arms and neck also camouflaged.

"It is done, princess," he said proudly.

"Who was that out there? That girl? Was it…"

"I took the liberty of kidnapping one of the servants after they had gone to bed. I killed her quickly, it was as easy as snapping my fingers. This Devin is... *was* a thorough man, and he would have checked the servants quarters before coming, yes? After seeing one of the girls missing, his guard was lowered. It was the only way, princess."

Not that it mattered. Lucetta found herself unconcerned over the loss of a servant, as they had become little more than nameless, faceless nuisances in recent months. The Droethien's diligence had once again proven impressive to behold. It also made her bowels quiver, as it would undoubtedly prove fatal to see such a man turn disgruntled.

"I applaud your... creativity, as always. You have yet to disappoint me, Pavlos. Well done."

But there was another matter at hand, one which she dared not speak aloud. Lucetta stared long and hard into his blackened face, hesitant even now to give the order. But the woman in black had not deceived her yet. If she faltered now, when it mattered the most, it could be a life-threatening mistake.

"If you have no further need of me, princess, I will take my leave and rejoin you in the morning, yes?"

"Wait, Pavlos. There's something else I need you to do." She began scratching the scabs on her elbow. "I... I need you to kill one other. Tonight. Now, in fact. Right now."

"You have made many enemies it seems, yes?" The tone in his voice was that of annoyance.

Lucetta reached into a nearby desk drawer, produced a sack of gold, then tossed it to him. A soft clinking of coins was all the motivation Pavlos needed, a contented, golden smile emerging.

"I need you to kill my... my..." The words caught in her throat. If not for a soft glowing of orange-red eyes outside the window, she might not have spoken any more. "My mother."

"The Queen? A most unusual request. Why, yes... if you say so, princess."

"She's taken to sleeping on the second floor, with guards posted outside the doors. I'm uncertain how we can make it inside, but it's imperative we do this tonight."

The mercenary chuckled. "It would not be the first time Pavlos has had to scale a wall. Trust me, princess, I can climb to the second floor from outside, then enter the room undetected."

Such a plan seemed simple enough, and there was much to be said about the man's capabilities. But there was a nagging, unsettling feeling she could not ignore. It was not of fear or anxiety, but of sadness. Tears filled her eyes as hesitation began to fill her heart.

"Be strong, child," the woman in black said, stepping out from behind Pavlos. "It would seem only proper for you to be present. While the death of your mother is necessary, it need not be cruel. She deserves more than the company of a foreigner in her last moments. She saw you into this world, and it is only right for you to see her out of it."

Even if I can get inside, the guards will storm in the second they hear the slightest disturbance. How am I to do this?

"Leave everything to me. Go now, follow your Droethien." The woman drifted across the room and vanished into a wall.

"I'm ready, Pavlos," Lucetta said reluctantly. "I'm coming with you. It's only right that I be there. But I'm uncertain if I can make the climb."

"Worry not, princess." He pulled back his cloak, revealing a utility belt with pouches, poison darts, several sheathed throwing knives, and a length of rope over one shoulder. "Pavlos is prepared for any possibility, yes?"

Not only was he a reliable mercenary and a proven commander of men, he was also a capable assassin, she was beginning to realize. This must have been how he dispatched Sir Bryce Whitewood with such efficiency, she thought. If it worked once before, it could work again.

Is it wrong for me to hope he fails, and the Guardsmen catch him before it's too late? Yes... and no. If he fails, then mother will have me arrested immediately.

Together, they slipped outside and moved cautiously against the wall. Charlotte's new chamber was on the other side of the building, but not difficult to find. They paused underneath a large, ornate balcony. Pavlos looked around briefly, and once satisfied, removed his cloak and stashed it in the bushes.

"Wait here, princess," he whispered.

Pavlos backed up several dozen paces, surveyed the area once again, then sprinted toward the wall. Lucetta thought he had gone mad, until he lept, propelling himself up the wall with a giant bound, then another in the blink of an eye. He grabbed hold of the balusters, then effortlessly pulled himself up and onto the balcony. Such an acrobatic feat was unlike anything she had ever witnessed before.

I never knew men could run up walls like that!

After carefully peeking into the Queen's chamber, Pavlos removed the rope from around his shoulder and began tying a large loop, which he began feeding down below. He gestured for Lucetta to wrap it around her midsection, which seemed simple enough. She did so, nearly sitting on the rope like a basket, then took hold of the length.

As if she weighed a feather, Pavlos hauled her up the second storey with several powerful pulls. She grabbed the balustrade with moistened palms, trying desperately not to look down, and was gently assisted onto the balcony. A glass door was cracked open, its silken curtains rustling gently in a cool breeze. This was the moment.

Now or never…

The woman in black was standing in the center of the room, her orange-red eyes appearing as little more than flickering candles in the night. She smiled, then gestured, beckoning Lucetta forth. At first, she was uncertain, even more so after hearing muffled voices beyond the chamber door.

"Worry not," the entity said. "The guards are investigating a noise I made in another room. Should they start back this way, I will create another distraction. Go now, do what must be done, for your sake, and for millions of your subjects yet to be born."

Cautiously, Pavlos drew a throwing knife and readied it, tip-toeing inside and scanning the darkness. He moved to the side of Charlotte's bed as silently as a cat, the Queen lying peacefully and unawares. A slight whistling sound emanated from one of her nostrils. Knowing the coast was clear, he sheathed his knife, and motioned for Lucetta to follow.

The woman in black took her by the hand and moved closer to the bed. Her heart was pounding so violently it nearly shattered her ribs into fragments. Pavlos turned back and waited for the order, which even now she was hesitant to give. Reluctantly, Lucetta swallowed hard and nodded, tears pooling in her eyes until they flowed like rivers down her cheeks.

Pavlos picked up an unused pillow next to Charlotte's head, careful not to disturb her slumber. Decisively, he pressed it down onto the Queen's face and held it firmly in place. Charlotte began to thrash about, clawing at his hand and attempting to wriggle free. Lucetta began sobbing softly, her other hand clasped over her mouth. Memories of happy moments from her childhood began manifesting and playing out before her very eyes.

Every birthday, and its lavish celebrations at the Citadel. Every night she lay in bed, frightened of the dark and too terrified to sleep. Every time she fell while playing, and crying at the sting of scuffed skin on an elbow or knee. Throughout all these moments, her mother was always there with loving words and warm hugs. Panic swept over her as the Queen's movements began to grow still, the last of her life rapidly fading away.

No, mother! she thought, whimpering. *I cannot do this! No, please! Mother!*

She made to move and rescue Charlotte, but the woman in black stood firm. The entity's grip was strong and felt like frozen leather. It squeezed, keeping Lucetta firmly in her place.

"Shhh, be still now. This is the way it must be. There is no going back now. Soon she will be at peace, and will come to know the full breadth of your works from the next life."

Pavlos continued pressing down onto the Queen's face, though careful not to fracture her nose. Charlotte swatted at his hands, but each attempt was more feeble than the last. Her body thrashed about violently, struggling to draw breath, but the effort was in vain. Her last strike hit with the might of a newborn child.

Charlotte Bethard's arm fell limp down the side of the bed, her body twitching one final time before becoming still. Pavlos removed the pillow slowly, ready to clamp it back down onto her face if necessary. But it was not. The Queen was at rest, an eternal rest from which she would never wake. Lucetta grit her teeth harder and harder, struggling to contain her anguish. The strongest and most beautiful woman she had ever known was dead, not by her own hand, but by her command. Such distinction mattered little; it was all the same in the end.

"Mother..." she whimpered, reaching out in desperation. She stepped toward the bed, the room spinning and turning blurry.

Before her vision turned to black, Lucetta remembered Pavlos scooping her up like a small child, and reaching out helplessly as if to take back what could not be undone.

"I'm sorry, mother," she whispered in anguish. "Please, forgive me."

ZANDER III

"I WILL NOT ALLOW IT!" JOLLKUD SLAMMED HIS FISTS ONTO THE TABLE.

The mood inside Damien's command tent was growing more sour by the second, and it was becoming increasingly difficult for Zander to control himself. He masked a growing sneer by tonguing at his half-rotten teeth.

"Mind your tone, Bymist rat," Marvath Bonesplitter snarled, stepping forward with a puffed out chest.

It seemed everything was going perfectly to plan. The Zylmacians responsible for the murder were awaiting their due hanging, though Jollkud had hoped for a last minute reprieve. Tensions outside the tent were growing in kind as warriors began to congregate in increasing numbers.

"I will not be spoken to in such a manner, not by you or by anyone!" Jollkud spat, hand drifting down to a short sword on his hip. "Say another word and I'll have your tongue for tonight's stew."

"Step outside." It was all Bonesplitter could utter, his jaw clenched so tightly it could crush stone.

Zander had taken plenty of swipes at the Rhivothi warchief before, to be certain. But he had never seen Marvath so violently angry before, at least off the battlefield. He stepped over to Jollkud, pulled him back a few paces, and whispered in his ear.

"Now isn't the time, mate. As badly as I'd like to see it, we cannot—"

"What sort of man are you? Hm?" Jollkud snapped back. "Who are you to allow this treachery to stand?"

"A smart one," he answered, glancing over his shoulder. "Remember what you said, this is my hunt. And I say, now is not the time. Five men is a small price to pay for what lies ahead."

Jollkud wrenched himself free from Zander's grasp, spat across the tent, then stormed outside. His absence did little to quell Marvath's rage, which was restrained only by the staying of Damien's hand. Zander found the spectacle quite fascinating. For such a savage man, Bonesplitter sure allowed himself to be ordered about like a dog. Perhaps one day, he too might command such authority.

"Is everything in order, Zander?" Dreadfire cast him an icy glare.

"Most certainly," he smiled. "You'll hear no objection from me or my people. They understand the greater good."

"Hard to believe murderers can know anything about good," Arik Akselson said in uncharacteristic courage. "Especially murderers who feast on their fellow man."

"And yet justice is being served," Zander retorted. "What more can you ask for?"

There was little the other warchiefs could say, though each of them likely wished to heave their own share of insults. They stood motionless and silent, knowing any outburst would garner a swift rebuke from Dreadfire. Zander's scheme was unfolding perfectly, almost better than he could have anticipated.

"I will hear no more of this," Damien said, making his way to the tent flap. "Justice shall be served, and that will be the end of it. We cannot have such distractions undermining our efforts against Betanthia."

"Then we should end this quickly," Zander suggested. "The longer this drags out, the more… feisty Jollkud and his men will become."

Damien Dreadfire turned to Bonesplitter, who appeared all too eager to kill a few Zylmacians. With a nod, the warlord made his exit, his band of warchiefs following closely behind. Surrounded by loyal Rhivothi bodyguards, they walked a short distance to where the execution was to take place.

A large crowd had gathered around a tall oak tree, its branches thick and sturdy. The five Zylmacian cannibals were set on top of horses, hands bound and lengths of rope around their necks. Zander felt a slight pang of guilt deep inside his black heart, for these were his kinsmen, after all. But their deaths would serve a grander purpose, he reminded himself.

"Jollkud!" one of the wildmen cried out. "You have to save us!"

"Kill them!" another screamed, trying vainly to free himself. "You can't let them do this to us!"

It was endlessly amusing to watch Jollkud grind his teeth, knowing there was nothing he could do. However, there was always the possibility he could turn on the warband in an instant. Zander made certain to inch a bit closer, should such a rash order be given. In fact, he almost hoped Jollkud would do just that. Putting down a fellow chieftain would certainly elevate him even further in Dreadfire's eyes.

Remaining family members and loved ones of the slain gathered near the tree, weeping softly and embracing one another. They were flanked by Marvath Bonesplitter and his companion, Valerick the Red. Both waited eagerly for Damien to give the order, each man practically salivating in anticipation of performing the execution.

"Relax, mate," Zander whispered to the marauder. "We'll get our chance."

"You had better be right," Jollkud seethed. "Mark my words Zander, it will be your head for this! Vengeance will be mine!"

"All in good time, mate. All in good time."

Damien Dreadfire stepped forth, his armor as black as an eclipse. He raised a hand in a bid to silence the warband, then looked over the prisoners. While it appeared he took no pleasure in what was about to happen, Zander suspected otherwise.

"Let all who have gathered here be reminded of our purpose. We have come to free these lands from the tyranny of King Bethard. We have come to bring our kinsmen back into the fold, not put them to the sword. The people of this village are not counted among our enemies, and what was done here cannot be forgiven."

Bonesplitter and Valerick moved toward the prisoners, ready to carry out Dreadfire's order. Zylmacians had massed in great numbers, many cursing and protesting, beseeching their chieftains for a reprieve. Zander felt their hatred brewing, even with his back turned.

"May the gods bear witness to this judgment," Damien continued, "And may they forgive us for visiting such horror upon our own people."

With a flick of his wrist, the order was issued. Marvath and Valerick gave the horses nearest to them a smack, the beasts slowly walking forward. The cannibals cried out as they slowly slid from the horse's backs, the length of rope growing tighter until there was only air beneath them. Choking and thrashing, the Zylmacians slowly strangled, their eyes bulging and bloodshot.

"No! Zander! Jollkud! Please!" the last of the prisoners cried out.

Marvath stood beside him, adorning a satisfied grin. "All of you Bymist rats deserve to hang. Good riddance." He spat a thick gobbet onto the prisoner's face, then slowly walked the horse forward.

Dozens of Zylmacians lurched forward, desperate to try and save their brethren, but were met by nearly a hundred snarling Rhivothi. Both parties were coming dangerously close to blows, the Rhivothi drawing steel and preparing to scrap. Jollkud's wildmen responded in kind, axes and short swords at the ready, eager to drink their fill of blood.

Zander nearly cackled with glee, but knew something had to be done at once. Now was not the proper time for the northmen to be disposed of. Brazenly, he stepped between both clans, raising his hands in a bid to ease their hostility.

"Enough! Enough, I say!" he roared to his kinsmen. "I ought to kill every last one of you for this disrespect! Did you forget this is my hunt? Did you not swear to follow and obey? I'll be damned if I allow any man to put my glory and my legacy at risk!"

"They're killing us!" one of the Zylmacians cried out. "Have you no loyalty to your kin?"

"Have you no loyalty to me?" he answered. "Have you no respect for this hunt? Doesn't look like it to me, mate. You're here at my invitation, and anything you do is done in my name. This, I don't approve of."

The Rhivothi looked none too amused, and most likely suspected treachery. But Damien was content to look on, and had thus far remained silent. Jollkud stepped forward, the eyes of the wildmen turning to meet him.

"This day will never be forgotten, Zander!" the marauder roared. "But our customs are our customs. This hunt is yours, by right, until you are slain or retire. Therefore, my men will stand down."

Thankfully, the hordes dispersed before it could come to blows. Zander felt relieved, knowing his carefully laid plans were intact, at least for now. With a nod from Damien Dreadfire, he retired from the execution site, the bodies of his slain countrymen swaying gently.

There was little merriment to be found around the fires that night. Though Zander chose to forgo company on any given evening, he was especially hesitant to walk the Zylmacian camp. There was murder in the air, to be certain. He could nearly taste it.

I pity the unfortunate soul who looks at those men the wrong way. They'll be carved into fillets in an instant.

It was safer to watch his kinsmen from afar, at the foot of a hearty fire, with a mug full of mead. For all Zander knew, they could very well be plotting his own demise, given his position on the execution. It was certainly within the realm of possibility, and would be dangerous to leave unacknowledged. They would need a taste of Betanthian blood, and soon, if their wrath was to be contained.

A cloaked figure approached in the darkness, his face shrouded behind a wall of dancing flames. Zander squinted, eyes adjusting, and recognized the man as Arik Akselson. It was a wonder why any of the soft Nothanek would dare to venture this far from their camp.

"You're a brave one, mate." Zander chuckled. "Any one of these men would have your guts right about now, and it wasn't even your people who did the killing. Imagine if they got their hands on a Rhivothi."

"That's why I came," Arik said, looking none too easy. "There's a lot of talk throughout the camp right now. Everyone is on edge."

It was a most interesting revelation indeed. It appeared the warband had a much greater fear and respect for the Zylmacians than he had thought. Zander masked a widening grin behind the lip of his mug, drinking down a large mouthful.

"And they should be," he said. "Five of our people are dead, and at northern hands, no less. You have every right to be fearful, fisherman. My people are not the mindless animals you tree-dwellers think we are. We have a rich and complex culture. We can survive and thrive in the harshest climates. There's a lot more to Zylmacians than you think, mate."

The northman took a seat beside him, still stinking of fish. Perhaps Nothanek had the waters of the Teb flowing through their veins instead of blood, given their peculiar aroma. Zander was half tempted to slit Arik's throat and find out. The thought made him snicker.

"Well, I for one am grateful for your leadership." Arik gave a half-hearted smile. "And Zifnir is grateful for your peacemaking as well."

While such gratitude was pleasing, Zander was already growing irritated by the conversation. Still, the possibility of having a new ally in another clan might prove even more fortuitous. He stood and retrieved an empty mug, then filled it to the brim with mead.

"Then let's drink to peace, mate. Peace, before we continue the war."

He watched Arik intently as they drank, studying every mannerism as only an apex predator could. Even now, Zander could sense discomfort and fear, the scent of which was as enticing as roasted boar.

"Now, if I were you," he continued, "I'd best be heading out of here. It's only a matter of time before someone spots you, and… well… I'm sure you have an imagination as to what will happen next."

Arik swallowed hard, having heeded the warning. He threw over the hood of his cloak and slinked away into the darkness, much to Zander's amusement. Though, he supposed a fair bit of credit was due for coming into the Zylmacian camp in the first place, something many would consider downright suicidal. It was unlikely, however, that any further commotion would take place tonight.

By morning, Zander awoke to scuffling and shouting which grew louder by the second. Fearing a possible Betanthian attack, he took up axe and shield and emerged from his tent, bare-chested and prepared for battle. A small band of Rhivothi had ventured over, boisterous and insufferable as ever. Their presence was ill-received by the nearby wildmen.

Insults of every manner were hurled back and forth, each louder and more distasteful than the last. Fists soon followed, and Zander knew it was only a matter of time before weapons began flying as well. He watched a vicious brawl break out, half a dozen men clubbing each other mercilessly. Others quickly joined in, until the scuffle exploded into a full blown melee.

He watched a gangly Zylmacian break the nose of a Rhivothi with a sucker punch. The northman appeared more agitated than injured, and immediately set about beating the wildman to within an inch of his life. Thunderous blows rained down, one after another, until another Zylmacian jumped onto the Rhivothi's back in a bid to save his kinsman.

While Zander chuckled with delight, he knew it was only a matter of time before someone was killed. He stepped forward, cupping both hands and bellowing so loud his throat burned.

"Alright mates, that's enough! Save some for Betanthia!"

His command went unheard. More and more men were flooding into the fight, their screams of hatred reminiscent of a proper battle-field. Again, Zander tried to bring an end to the chaos, but was utterly ignored. After a sigh of frustration, he was startled by a sudden blast from a warhorn.

"Enough of this madness!" Damien Dreadfire's voice erupted. "Do you not remember why we are here? Do you wish to be divided when King Bethard unleashes his wrath? You would doom all of our peoples and all of our lands to destruction for the sake of a few drops of blood?"

A hush fell over the warriors, though it was not Dreadfire's anger which silenced them. Standing next to the towering warlord was a frame diminished, a woman so old she appeared little more than a corpse. Lazilyth toddled forward, her glassy eyes scanning the unruly mob with contempt. While feeble of body, her spirit was undoubtedly powerful.

"Doom," she croaked, pointing a gnarled finger accusingly. "Doom unto you, fools for men! You are petty and weak. You squabble like children while the adversary gathers strength. Stray from the grace of the gods, and your corpses will bloat and stink under the sun!"

The old woman chuckled, a low rumbling sound building in the back of her throat. Zander found the spectacle strangely fascinating. How a decrepit creature could instill such fear into the hearts of blood-thirsty killers was impressive by itself, but he still suspected it to be a ruse. Were he to plant an axe in her forehead, her carcass would crumple to the ground like any other.

Best not to put that to the test. At least, not yet. I suppose she has her uses... for now.

The Zylmacians stood down first, the mere sight of Lazilyth enough to scatter many of them like frightened cats. Western superstition was a strong thing, stronger than their blood feud with the northmen. It would be enough to keep the warband from tearing itself apart, he supposed, which was all for the better.

"Why do we pretend to be allies to these dogs?" a Rhivothi called out, his eye already swollen shut.

His question was met with a flurry of agitation, the wildmen baying for their share of blood. Damien raised a hand, though it took a second horn blast to silence them.

"Enough!" Dreadfire stepped between the two feuding parties, glaring at each of them. "I do not expect you to trust one another, nor keep company. We march together because we must. Who will stand against the might of Betanthia, if not us? Would you pass this burden onto your sons and daughters?"

There was no response, save for a few muffled whispers. The warband knew why they were here, having traveled so far from home.

"Good," Damien said, taking note of the silence. "King Bethard and his armies may be upon us at any moment. Should we be caught in disarray, we will never see our families or lands ever again. Your grievances with one another are real, and no man is asking you to forget them. But now is neither the time nor place to seek vengeance."

Zander smirked, feeling emboldened by an ever-widening divide between the tribes. He stepped forward, bold as you please, upstaging Dreadfire.

"Come now, mates! Why let bad blood stand in your way of riches and glory? Does anyone remember Hok? I do, and my great-grandsons will live like kings because of it!" He turned to the Zylmacian horde. "Is a dead tree-dweller a prettier reward than gold? I don't think so!"

Surprisingly, the mood among Jollkud's wildmen began to lighten, though many were still drunk for combat. They could see spoils from

Hok throughout the baggage train, wagon after wagon of solid gold, and were undoubtedly jealous of Zander and his kinsmen.

With a smile as wide as the Plainhold, he held both arms outstretched and stared down Damien Dreadfire. "Well now, when do we march?"

GARETH IV

"You're still here," Madelyn uttered in surprise, her eyes barely open. "It's night time, you know."

His vigil had been long and tiresome, but Gareth remained undeterred. He sat, face long and weary, head bobbing in exhaustion. But such a sacrifice of time was a worthy one. The people who mattered to Madelyn, the people she had known since childhood, had all abandoned her when needed most. The thought of it was unconscionable.

"I'm still here." He smiled, dark bags under both eyes puffing up even larger. "Are you feeling any better?"

It was a stupid question to ask, given her condition. But above all else, Gareth wanted Madelyn to know that at least one person genuinely cared for her wellbeing. She was in a more suitable location now, a two storey residence under the ownership of a pair of midwives.

"No. The pain is constant." She shifted around and grimaced. "I just want it to be over with."

Finding comfort with a belly so large was utterly impossible, despite having a soft cloud of a bed. One position seemed as good as the last, and every movement caused her to clutch at either hip in agony. Her joints still had not fully healed, despite weeks of rest.

"It will be," Gareth said reassuringly. "Soon enough you'll be out of here, and getting back to your old life."

"You're wrong." Madelyn's mood quickly soured. "Part of me is scared to have this baby. At least now, I know what to expect. Pain and lack of sleep, and days spent staring out of the window. Once this is over, then what?"

It was a good and fair question. While many doors had closed, some were perhaps still open. Gareth thought hard, trying to manifest some solution, but his mind had grown weary.

"I could always bring you back to Cardale. You can start a new life there, and do whatever it is you wish to do. I'll make certain you're never left wanting for the rest of your life. It's the least I could do for such a dear friend."

Through her despair, Madelyn gave a forlorn smile. The sentiment seemed to touch a small place in her soul, a place where embers of her inner fire still remained.

"You're very sweet, Gareth, and you have a big heart. The world needs more men like you in it. But I refuse to be a burden on you or anyone else. I could never accept your offer and feel good about myself."

"I know, you're a proud person. I mean, you've achieved so much and now…" He grew flustered, one foot after another planting itself in his mouth. "I'm sorry, I can barely think. I'm so tired. I would ask you to keep my offer in mind. Who knows, you could always become a Guardsman. I know Edmund won't be able to command forever. Life is full of possibilities, if you're open to them."

Despite good intentions and best efforts, Madelyn seemed disinterested. Perhaps it was simply pain overwhelming her senses, or despair which held her tightly in its grip. Either way, the time for such a discussion was most certainly not now, Gareth deduced.

"Perhaps." Her steely-blue eyes met his, though they lacked their natural sparkle. "You should get some rest, Gareth. You look beyond exhausted. Go, I'll be fine. I'm not going anywhere."

The thought of a soft pillow beneath his head was most enticing. Merely mentioning rest was enough to make Gareth's already light head feel as if it was swimming. He nodded, offering little in the way of protest.

"Very well. If you need anything, don't hesitate. My door will be open, just in case."

For a moment, Gareth considered kissing Madelyn's forehead, but decided otherwise. The touch of a man, however genuine or loving, might be enough to reignite the terrors which once tormented her. All he could offer was a warm smile and a bow of respect. Madelyn pursed her lips, thankful for such a kind gesture.

Wearily, he slogged into the next room, nearly tripping while unlacing his boots. Never in his life had a freshly made bed appeared more inviting. After opening the shutters on a nearby window, Gareth threw himself into bed, its linens soft and smelling of spring air. No more than a minute went past before his eyes slammed shut. But the relaxing realm of the dream world would not last long.

A shrill and agonizing scream rang out suddenly. Gareth Bethard shot up in alarm, a sharp pain in his neck causing him to wince. Instinctively, his hand reached for steel, ready to fight off whatever would-be assailant was in the room. But no intruder was to be found. The screams were in fact coming from inside Madelyn's room. In a flash, he bolted into the hallway, and saw her sitting up in bed, face tightened and breathing hard through clenched teeth.

"Are you alright?" he asked, utterly flummoxed. "What's the—"

In an instant, the answer became clear. Madelyn was about to give birth. He stumbled down the hall, praying the midwives downstairs took heed of the commotion.

"Come quick! Hurry!" he shouted breathlessly.

Moments later, frantic footsteps thundered up the stairwell. Both midwives were in their nightclothes, Jann's hair a mess of tangles, Wilka still half asleep. They burst into the room and rushed to the bed, quickly examining Madelyn and making preparations. The child was coming, and quickly.

"Bring water and linens!" Jann shouted over a chorus of screams. "Do it quickly!"

Were it any other scenario, Gareth might have taken offense at being addressed in such a manner, but time was of the essence. He flew downstairs as hastily as his legs would allow and ran into the kitchen. A bucket of fresh water sat on a stone hearth at the center of the room, a large wooden bowl not far away.

Gareth snatched up both of them clumsily, tucking the bowl under one arm. Fresh, folded linens were piled nearby. Uncertain of how many to take, he awkwardly snatched up the entire stack, several pieces falling onto the floor. With supplies in hand, he trudged back upstairs, huffing and straining for breath.

"Here! I have everything," he wheezed, setting the bucket down next to the bed. "Is she going to be alright?"

Wilka shot him a brief glance. "In her condition?"

Thankfully, Madelyn was unable to hear such an unsettling response. Her screams grew louder as the contractions became more severe. It was distressing to be so powerless in such a situation. Gareth stepped back from the bed, mind racing in every direction, unsure of what to do next. As the midwives began their work, he moved to Madelyn's side and took hold of her hand.

"It's going to be alright. Here, squeeze my hand. As hard as you need to."

Despite being so frail, there was enough force in Madelyn's grip to crush a stone into gravel. Gareth grit his teeth and blocked out the pain, knowing hers was far worse in comparison. She looked at him in desperation and disbelief, as if wondering how this could have ever happened in the first place.

"Don't speak," he said. "Just breathe. Breathe now. Good, just like that."

Deep, thumping footsteps raced up the stairs, rattling the upper floor. Gareth turned and saw Titan Bradshaw, looking inside in utter bewilderment.

"What the fuck is happening?" Titan asked, knowing how stupid of a question it was. He too must have felt just as helpless as Gareth, knowing the situation was out of their hands.

Madelyn released her crushing grip and motioned for water. Jann took a wooden cup from a bedside table and dipped it into the bucket. It was snatched away and emptied in the blink of an eye, though Gareth suspected something stronger might be needed to dull out the pain. Uncertain of what more could be done, he left the bedside and hurried over to Titan.

"The baby's nearly here," he replied, stepping into the hall. "So far, there's no complications. But she's not out of danger just yet." Titan tried to enter, but Gareth placed a hand on his massive chest. "No, there's nothing you or I can do. Best to give the womenfolk their space. This is a battle you and I are powerless to fight."

"Fuck…" Titan grunted, appearing equally as frustrated. "Mark my words, I'm going to pull Damien Dreadfire's guts out through his cock for this. Give him a taste of what true pain feels like."

There was little doubt in Gareth's mind that Titan could do just that. He was fiercely protective over Madelyn, like a lion watching over his pride. But there was an absence of any longing in his eyes, as lovers often had. No, their companionship ran deeper than such things. They shared a bond which could only be forged in the crucible of battle.

"I see the head," Wilka said.

Gareth rushed back to Madelyn's side, tears rolling down her cheeks. She looked at him, exhausted and weary, hoping the pain was at an end. It was heartbreaking to stare into the steely-blue depths of her eyes. Despite the tribulation of birth, this should have been a happy occasion, one which Gareth hoped to have shared with her as husband and wife. He sighed, taking hold of her hand, trying to tamp down thoughts of what might have been.

Suddenly, Madelyn roared in agony, her body tensing and trembling. Her cries were then replaced by the cries of another, the baby which was now resting in the hands of Jann. The old woman smiled at the sight of new life, wiping the child clean with a fresh linen.

"Here, my prince." Jann delicately passed the baby to Gareth, then nodded toward Madelyn. He looked at the newborn incredulously, still taking in the totality of the experience. He stood motionless, staring in disbelief, uncertain of how to feel.

"It's a girl," Wilka said.

Madelyn erupted into a fit of sobbing, though they were the most joyless tears of all. When Gareth offered forth her child, she instead turned and looked away, as if she could see Damien Dreadfire's face reflected in that of the newborn. It was a tragic thing to witness, but her distress was easy enough to understand.

This was not a child made of love, but of events most unspeakable. But such acts of brutality were no fault of the baby. The infant girl was innocent, just as Madelyn was the night the northmen defiled her flesh. It seemed supremely unfair for a new life to be cast away so callously, but perhaps all that was needed was time.

Gareth turned to Jann, child in hand, and nodded toward the door. "I cannot begin to imagine what she's feeling right now. We cannot force her to do anything right now, but the baby needs to be cared for. Please, see to it that—"

"Rest assured, my prince," Jann interrupted, gently taking the child from his arms, "everything will be taken care of. There's an orphanage in town I can take her to for the time being."

"Thank you. I have a feeling we'll need to find an appropriate home, should… she…"

Each word felt like hot coals in his mouth. But thankfully, the midwives understood well enough, and nodded in agreement. To them, this situation appeared to be one of many they had dealt with before.

"Wait," he whispered. "I have a task for you, but only if you are willing."

Jann nodded without hesitation. "Whatever you ask of me, my prince, it will be done."

"I want you to personally look after this child. See to it she's taken care of properly, and that no harm comes to her. I would hate for Madelyn to have a change of heart, then be unable to reunite with her child. Do this, and the rewards will be plentiful. I'll see to it you're never left wanting for the rest of your life."

"It would be my highest honor, my prince." Jann curtseyed and took the baby downstairs.

Madelyn's exhausted body could no longer cling to consciousness, and after a few heavy blinks, she slipped into slumber. Gareth thought of remaining by her side, but supposed it would be better to give her adequate space. Watching her sleep was a reminder of how little he himself had slept recently, and quietly shut the door and retired to his chamber. No more than a minute after flopping down onto his bed, he immediately fell into an exhausted slumber.

Rays from the rising sun roused Gareth. Though only an hour, maybe two, his nap was sorely needed. He shuffled out of bed, straightened out his tunic and trousers, then quenched a parched throat with a chalice of water. A scent of what appeared to be lamb and spices wafted up from the lower level, setting his stomach to grumbling.

He stepped into the hall, glancing over at Madelyn's chamber. The door was shut, and while it was tempting to peek inside, he decided against it. After such an ordeal, her battered body would be in need of proper rest.

Wearily, Gareth shambled downstairs for a bit of breakfast. However, an unexpected visitor was sitting near the fireplace. Sir Edmund Thomas had arrived, and was helping himself to a heaping plate of piping hot food.

"Edmund!" Gareth smiled. "I didn't expect to see you here. Thanks for coming, I could use some company."

"Aye, I figured you could do with a little entertainment. How's everything upstairs?" The elder Guardsman poured himself a mug of water. It was strange to see him drink anything other than whiskey, but the day's heat was becoming bothersome.

"She's alright. Sleeping when last I checked. I don't know how she managed to make it through. Even the midwives appeared stunned."

"That's excellent news." Edmund nodded. "She's a fighter, even now. And you're a good man for looking after her. Just be careful not to become too distracted. There's a reason why we're here, after all."

"Anything to report?" Gareth poured himself some water, though what he really wanted was an ale.

"Lord Kenfield has a few of his best men making their way through camp. Getting close to Lord Vakaro is proving difficult, but not impossible. Word has it the army won't be moving for some time yet. He's waiting for more of his southern lordlings to arrive, and apparently still has no idea where Damien Dreadfire is. Hundreds of scouts are lurking around up north, so it's only a matter of time before we hear something."

The news, or lack thereof, was more frustrating than informative. At some point, the upstart Commandant would have to be confronted, and soon. Progress was painfully slow, but perhaps it was simply Gareth's own impatience. While he had little experience in such matters, the men around him seemed to be equally as stymied.

"It's all the waiting that's killing me," Gareth said. "It's hard to sit idle when your life hangs in the balance. And not only my life, the life of my entire family."

"You've done well so far, lad. Everything a man can be asked to do, you're doing. And these are valuable lessons to learn for when you're king. You're going to need to be as patient as a hawk, and as swift as one when the occasion arises."

They were interrupted by sounds of commotion down the hall. Edmund and Gareth looked at each other, then approached the disturbance together. Titan Bradshaw was standing near the front door, holding back another man with a single arm.

"I told you, you're not getting in here!" Titan snarled. "Now get the fuck out of here before I—"

"Easy there, big fellow," Edmund said, raising his hands. "This here is a Guardsman."

"Don't look like no fucking Guardsman to me. Where's his cloak?"

"Messengers ride without their cloaks." Edmund pointed to an insignia pin on the man's doublet. "A single man riding with a purple cloak is ripe for being intercepted. Come, lad, let me see what you have there. What business does Cardale have?"

The rider handed over a tiny roll of parchment. "I'm not certain where this message is from, Sir. It arrived at our campsite via carrier pigeon."

A deadly serious look formed across Edmund's face. He wrenched the dispatch away and shooed the man outside, slamming and locking the front door behind him.

"What is it, Edmund?" Gareth asked incredulously.

"These sorts of messages are only sent under the direst of circumstances." Edmund handed the roll of parchment over.

Direst of circumstances? Gareth thought, his mind harkening back to last year. Lord Valens had sent riders, not pigeons, to inform of the barbarian invasion, and it was difficult to imagine a situation more dire than that. Hesitantly, he opened the dispatch.

"Prince Gareth," he said, struggling to read its small, scratchy writing. "I regret to inform you of the death of... your... m... mother..."

It was if time itself came to an abrupt halt, and all understanding had left him. The words were simply too fantastical to speak, let alone believe. Was this some cruel joke, perhaps perpetrated by Lucetta? He read the message again, skimming over every detail and looking for the person responsible for crafting it. To his dismay, it bore the signature of Emilee Harper.

"No… this… this cannot be…"

The parchment slipped from his hand and fell like a dry leaf in autumn. Edmund shot over and snatched it up, squinting and frantically reading as quickly as his old eyes would allow. Gareth felt a burning tightness in his chest, and for a moment was unable to draw breath. He stumbled over to a chair and slumped into it, clawing at his heart, grunting in discomfort.

Uncertain of what to say, Titan's eyes fell to the floor. He quickly dismissed himself from the room and retreated to the second floor, each step groaning under his weight. Edmund ran a hand through his silvery hair, eyes turning misty and red. The matriarch of the Bethard dynasty, whom he had served for decades, was gone. And to make matters worse, there was nothing he could have done about it.

"Gareth… I'm so sorry, lad. I'm so, so sorry…"

They shared a long, sorrowful embrace. When he was finally able to regain his breath, Gareth broke down into a fit of sobbing. He poured out an avalanche of agony into Edmund's shoulder, with fists clenched so tightly they were shaking.

"Mother… why? Why? Why did this happen?"

"I wish I had words for you." Edmund sighed.

All the words in the world would do nothing to ease the devastation in Gareth's soul. Charlotte had only recently rediscovered the joys of life, and now her own had been snuffed out by some cruel twist of fate.

"I need to return to Cardale," Gareth said, panting. "I… I have to be there. I have to be at her side when… when… they bring her home."

"You do whatever it is your heart tells you." Sir Edmund thumbed at the corner of his eye. "I'll have the horses ready to go whenever you decide to head out."

"No, I need to travel alone. It'll be much faster that way. I have to make it to Cardale before it's too late, and I cannot have anyone slowing me down."

Edmund Thomas chewed his tongue, uncertain of how to reply. It was his responsibility to look after the security of House Bethard, and now with its matriarch gone, he appeared reluctant to let Gareth out of his sight for an instant.

"I could start an argument with you over it, but at the end of the day, you're my prince. I have to obey whatever command you give me, regardless of how I feel about it. When do you plan on leaving?"

"Right away. Every minute is vital."

Gareth hurried upstairs to fetch his sword and provisions. Though he would be traveling light, it would be foolish to take to the roads unarmed. His chamber had been kept tidy, and locating his silver blade and other necessities took only seconds.

Rushing into the hall, he noticed Madelyn's door was still shut. The midwives were likely still tending to their work, as evidenced by a pair of muffled voices inside. While this was an occasion that all of Betanthia would mourn, he decided now was not the proper time to break the news.

He stole a moment to stare at the closed door, deciding through grief and exhaustion if leaving was the right thing. There was a burning inside Gareth's heart for Madelyn Everly, a deep, heavy passion so hot it could scorch the sun. Despite all the horrors inflicted by Damien Dreadfire's savages, she still appeared every bit as beautiful to him.

I do love you, Madelyn. I can't make my feelings go away even if I tried. But I have to be there for my mother now. I hope you understand, and forgive me.

Fighting back more tears, he hurried down the hall and back downstairs, determined to leave before doubt could overcome him. Sir Edmund was waiting by the front door, arms crossed and looking equally as dejected.

"Be safe out there," the elder Guardsman said. "And don't put yourself in any situation where—"

"I'll be alright, Edmund, don't worry about me. Make sure Titan doesn't leave Madelyn's side for a second, I cannot have anything happen to her. Not now."

"Consider it done." Edmund placed a hand on his shoulder. "Anders and I will stay on top of Lord Vakaro and his ilk, so don't waste any of your thoughts on that. Go now, before I change my mind and saddle up and come with you."

There was precious little time to waste. Gareth hurried over to a hitching post and stuffed his belongings into an empty saddlebag. One of the other bags had been filled with food and fresh water, even a skin of wine. It would be a week under normal circumstances to reach Cardale, but he was determined to make it half the time.

I guess it's time to see if these Blackthorn horses are all they're made out to be.

Gareth Bethard climbed into the saddle, then glanced up at the window to Madelyn's chamber. He prayed she would forgive his absence, just as he prayed Charlotte would do the same. The road to Cardale would be long and fraught with despair, same as the road to redemption.

I'm coming, mother. I won't fail you again.

TITAN V

"About fucking time you woke up," Tylar Bradshaw grinned as Madelyn's eyes opened. She sat gasping for a moment, a river of sweat snaking down her face.

"Tylar?" she groaned, still disoriented from another night terror. "Is that you?"

Admittedly, he was quite a different sight from last they saw each other. His silver breastplate shimmered with rays of candlelight, the length of his purple cloak draped over one leg.

"Yes, girl, it's me. Who else would it be?"

They stared at each other in silence, each viewing the other's pain through their vacant eyes. It was obvious from the look on Madelyn's face that she had gone far beyond feeling nothing. Quite the opposite. In fact, it appeared as if she had lost the desire to live, which was the most troubling look of all.

"I thought I saw you standing outside the door when I was…" she whimpered. "But I wasn't sure. I'm so glad you're alive."

"Well, at least your eyes work." The comment was an insensitive one, considering the rest of her was broken. Tylar chewed the inside of his cheek, but Madelyn smiled wearily at his gruff wit.

"Tell me, what happened to you?" she asked.

"I went down the rope, as you said, and made sure the area was secure. When I heard you weren't coming, I… I could have killed you myself right then and there. But I got the men out of that hellhole. We found some horses, and I sent the others back to Bentmont. I waited for you. I waited until the very end, but… I…"

Each word was a separate dagger into his cold heart. Tylar gave a rumbling growl, rousing his agitation to halt a sudden rush of emotions. "I'll spare you the details, but I made my way to Mor Seveht. Stayed down there for a bit, scrounging up what I could. But some cunt named Conrak found me and dragged me back here. Thankfully, a certain prince saved my ass as I was heading to the gallows."

"Gareth?" She perked up ever so slightly. "He saved you? How? Where is he?"

"That he did. He's on his way back to Cardale. I'm not sure if you heard the news, but his mother died."

Madelyn's pain and trauma seemed to clear, like the parting of storm clouds. "Queen Charlotte? She's… dead?"

"Afraid so. I owe him my life, and he in turn commanded me to keep you safe while he's away."

As tears began to roll down her cheeks, Tylar turned away. The girl had ways of conjuring up strange emotions within him. It was a peculiar feeling, given how dead he felt inside.

"I wish I had known before he left," she said. "He loved his mother so much…"

"With everything you've been through, he thought it best to let you sleep. Be thankful you weren't there when the news came in, it wasn't an easy thing to witness. But in a way, between that and finding out you're alive, it made me realize something."

He reached over to a nearby table and picked up a mug of ale, taking several large gulps, his gaze drifting off into the distance. "It made me realize how precious time is, and how much of it I've wasted on despair.

Time… such a small, stupid thing… but it's more valuable than anything. You can always get more gold, or more land, or more glory… you can never get more time."

"So, what are you going to do?" Madelyn cocked her head, still groggy and fatigued.

"I'm not the young man I once was. I've pissed away years of valuable time when I could have been out there doing something with it. I'm going to use what time I have left and leave a legacy worth remembering. Gareth saved me from the rope and made me one of his personal bodyguards. I'm going to help him win this war. What about you? Want to spend your time killing northmen, or do you want to stay in this bed forever?"

"I'm of no use to anyone. I've lost my command and my place in the Order. My body is broken, and I'll never have the strength to fight again. I have nothing left to live for."

Self-pity was something Tylar had little stomach for. He spat his contempt onto the floor. "Fuck that, there's plenty for you to live for. Live for vengeance. Live for hate, if you must. Live to reclaim everything they took from you."

"Look at me, Tylar," she pleaded. "How can I? I can barely move around on my own. How am I supposed to return to my old life in this condition?"

"You want to know how? You get out of that bed, and you go take your life back. Every single last bit of it. The only thing stopping you right now is you. The Madelyn I know would never back down from a challenge, even when the odds were fucked."

"The Madelyn you knew died at Morden with her men."

When she attempted to pull the blankets tighter to her body, Tylar rose in sudden agitation. He snatched the sheets with one hand and gave them a sharp yank, pulling them clear off the bed.

"That's good! And you want to know why?" He grinned insidiously.

"Please, do tell," a familiar voice said from behind. Elite Conrak stood in the doorway, arms crossed and leaning on one shoulder. His face bore the same insufferable smirk Tylar had learned to hate.

"What the fuck are you doing here? Don't you know I have no business with the Order any longer? You see the cloak? I'm a Guardsman, unless you're fucking colorblind."

"Easy there, I heard you were skulking around here. Figured I'd come see if the rumors were true, that's all. You really need to learn to control that temper of yours, Bradshaw." He strode into the room, bold as you please. "I'll answer that question of yours." Conrak's icy gaze turned toward Madelyn. "It's because you no longer have any fear inside you, Lady Everly. You're ready to become a true instrument of death."

"If you don't turn around and get the fuck out of here, you're gonna see how bad my temper can really get," Tylar cautioned. "And I won't be fighting outnumbered and wounded this time."

"And as for you, Bradshaw," Conrak said. "I meant it when I said you need to learn to control your temper. But this is your lucky day. As much as you think I despise you, it's quite the opposite. I'm willing to teach you how to control that anger of yours, to refine it, and use it to your advantage."

"Heh, like I need to take advice from you. I fight with hate. Pure, unrelenting hate. And when my blood gets up, no man dares stand in my way."

"Oh believe me, I fight with hate as well." Conrak grinned, then stroked his short beard. "But yours is reckless, mine is focused. And there is nothing more dangerous than a man who has mastered his emotions. You saw how easily I dispatched those Zylmacians. Truth is, I could have killed twice as many without a second thought."

"Excuse me, but who are you?" Madelyn asked, propping herself up.

As Conrak made to speak, Tylar interrupted. "This here is the man who captured me and sent me back here to die. He put an arrow in my leg and damn near had me hung. He's lucky I don't pound his face into pulp with my bare hands."

"You can save the theatrics for lesser men." The Elite waved a lazy, dismissive hand. "I heard the news and had to come see it for myself. The great Titan Bradshaw, rescued by Prince Gareth Bethard. How fortunate! You really ought to be down on your knees thanking the gods."

"Gods? Don't tell me you believe in that shit." Tylar spat. "Now get the fuck out of here, and be quick about it. The girl needs rest."

"No, I won't be leaving just yet. I meant it when I said I'll teach you what you need to know. Amusing as it is for me to rile you up, the truth is, I see something in you. I saw it that day in the tavern, when you stood your ground instead of surrendering."

It felt like the setup to yet another insult. Tylar rolled his eyes and turned away, hoping Conrak would lose interest and leave.

"This war needs heroes, if it's to be won," the Elite said. "It needs soldiers who can inspire the rabble, to rally them to defend Betanthia. You know what I see when I look around the camp? Fear. And who do the men have to look to? Commander Fletch? Ha! The man is an imbecile. The High Marshal? He won't set foot anywhere near the battlefield. A real inspiration to the men, is he not? Lord Vakaro? Perhaps, but he's a man chasing his own legacy."

Conrak picked up a flagon of wine and drank directly from the vessel. There was a fierceness in his eyes, though a sly grin was able to distract from it well enough.

"The northmen certainly have heroes," he continued. "Look at Damien Dreadfire. The man is legendary all throughout the north because he fights for his people. And who knows how many famous warriors he has in his horde. I'm sure you've met some of them, Lady Everly. Like it or not, you two are the closest thing we have to heroes. You already have reputations as fighters. Now, we just need to make you legendary as well."

Tylar was growing irritated with the conversation. He saw discomfort on Madelyn's face, which only fueled his agitation. "As you can see, Conrak here loves the sound of his own voice. He never shuts up, no matter how many times you tell him to."

"But am I wrong? Have you not listened to a single word I've said?"

It was nearly possible to feel Madelyn's distress filling the room. In the short time since they were reunited, Tylar felt an even deeper connection to her, a protectiveness with no limits to its savagery.

"My fighting days are over," she muttered dryly. "I'll never be able to lead again. I'll never be able to ride. I won't be able to even lift a sword anymore. Don't waste your time, Conrak. Leave me be. Go fight your war. Go win your glory."

"The girl's right," Tylar snarled. "Leave her alone. She's been through enough. I'm not going to tell you again."

The Elite shook his head slowly. There was something sadistic about him, that much was certain. Tylar remembered the day he was captured in Mor Seveht, and the enjoyment Conrak seemed to take in his suffering.

Ruthless though he was, he was nevertheless correct. With some of the Order's finest now dead and rotten to the bones at Castle Morden, there were few left to galvanize their ranks. The thought was even more disturbing when turned toward the Betanthian army, as the common soldier looked upon Blackthorn Knights as indomitable beings. Such a notion, sadly, was far from the truth. The uneasiness around Castle Thorn was thick enough to cut with an axe, and written plainly on the faces of every knight he laid eyes on.

"Tell me, Lady Everly." Conrak cleared his throat. "How many more men will die while you lay here in this bed, wallowing in your misery? How many families will be wiped out as the northmen rampage across Betanthia?" He drew his sword and threw it onto the bed, its hilt landing mere inches from Madelyn's fingers. "And what do you think they're going to do when they reach Bentmont? What are *you* going to do when they find you? Do you think they're going to kill you quickly? No, I think not. They'll take their time, and perhaps even put another mongrel bastard inside your belly."

Shrieking in fury, Madelyn clutched the sword and shot up from bed, her legs failing almost immediately. She landed in a heap on the floor, howling in pain while tears of pure hatred erupted like a geyser. Tylar instinctively lunged forward to protect her, but was unable to move further. Some curiosity inside him said to stand down and observe.

"That's it, girl," Conrak taunted, beckoning her forth with an extended hand. "Come on, strike me down. You know you want to. Put that sword through me as if I was Damien Dreadfire himself! Or perhaps I'll put my own sword into you later!"

Madelyn lurched forward, lifting the blade with frail, trembling arms. Her swing was pitiful and cleaved only air. Her second strike was a thrust, but Conrak gracefully slipped to the side, then wrenched the sword free by its blade with his bare hand. With the other, he pulled Madelyn close, their noses nearly touching.

"There you are!" he exclaimed, half taunting and half in awe. He stared deep into her steely-blue eyes, studying them. "You're a killer, Madelyn Everly. It's who you are. It's what you're meant to be. And at the end of the day, we're all dead men. Time has never lost a single battle. Do you want to die alone in your bed, or do you want to take as many northmen to the grave with you as you can?"

A look of rage in its purest form was enough of an answer for Conrak. Tylar stood awestruck as the Elite loosened his grip on Madelyn's linen bedclothes and took a step back, having stirred something unsettling inside her. He could nearly feel her hatred in the air, as if it had become a thick, poisonous fume.

"Very well then." Conrak retrieved his sword, then started for the door. "Follow my every command, and by the time the army is ready to march, you'll be back in fighting shape. We'll start with stretching and basic exercises to awaken your muscles, and we'll get you on a proper diet, instead of this gruel they've been feeding you."

Madelyn suddenly grew faint, her body having spent what little energy it had. Tylar rushed to her side, his large arms cradling her gently.

"If you think I'm leaving her side for one second, you better think again," he said.

Conrak stopped just outside of the hallway, turned and grinned mischievously. "Oh don't worry, I'm not finished with you yet. I have plans for you, Titan Bradshaw. Since I can't kill you, that is."

Such sheer arrogance radiating from the Elite was enough to give Tylar pause. Many a man had shot off their mouths to him in the past, and each of them were left spitting out fragments of teeth, or worse. But this man was a different case altogether. Tylar could only wonder what the coming days would hold in store for himself, and for Madelyn.

"Tell me, Conrak. Who the hell are you?" he asked quizzically.

"Did you bother to read any of that book I gave you?"

"Yeah, I did." Tylar said. "But there were pages missing from it. Obviously, something was in there that someone doesn't want the world to know. What did they say?"

"You're not as dumb as I thought, Bradshaw." Smiling, Conrak made his exit into the hall. "You're finally asking the right questions. I'll see you in the morning."

LUCETTA V

A WINDING PROCESSION THROUGH THE NORTHERN GATE WAS SLOW and somber, with not a voice to be heard for miles. Word had reached Cardale with lighting speed, thanks to the swift wings of carrier pigeons. Likely the entire kingdom knew by now, and a staggering turnout of the cityfolk seemed to confirm as such.

Charlotte Bethard's body lay on the bed of an elegant wagon, laden with hundreds of flowers, and towed by a team of white horses. Lucetta sat beside the driver on her own carriage, opting to make herself known for the mournful occasion. But none who were present paid her any mind. Many looked on with despair. Some openly wept.

Dark circles and dry tears adorned her face. Lucetta wore a flowing dress of black linen, the opposite of the Queen's white silken gown. Though Charlotte had been dead for days, she appeared to have the warmth of life still within her. It looked as if she was merely sleeping, and being returned to the Westwind Citadel after a long vacation. But there would be no returning from the journey Pavlos had sent her down, a journey to the world beyond.

As the funeral procession made its way through the streets, commoners stepped forward to throw flowers ahead of the Queen's body. Such respect from every man, woman, and child in Cardale was heartwarming, but Lucetta knew she could never receive such love for herself. Not that it mattered, as she supposed that in years to come, most of these very same people would either be dead or subjected to her dominion.

Instead of returning to the palace, Charlotte's body was taken to the Temple of the Dawn, an ancient structure once reserved for the gods and their worship. Throughout the last several centuries, it was converted into a meeting ground of all sorts, though weddings and public funerals were most common. There, Charlotte Bethard's body would rest and be given the proper funeral rites before being taken to the Citadel, to rest beside Bethard monarchs of old.

The temple was located at the city square, where Lucetta was set upon by a vicious mob the year prior. Thoughts of that day still filled her with dread. But in many ways, the attack was a catalyst for a long series of changes which had reshaped her life. She was grateful, but the price for discovering her destiny was nearly too great to bear.

After traversing through familiar neighborhoods, the square came into view. It was no longer a pit of squalor as it was when she last visited. The city watch had turned out in force, and driven every vagrant and scoundrel from sight. Hundreds of them stood shoulder to shoulder, spears at the ready, making certain the area was secure. A detachment of Royal Guardsmen was nearby as well, and joined in the procession as it approached the temple.

I'm so sorry, mother. I never thought we would be parted so soon. And I feel ashamed I was never able to give you grandchildren. But I can still feel you here with me, as well as your pride in everything I've accomplished.

The procession entered into the square, which in turn was sealed off by the city watch. Pavlos assisted Lucetta in stepping out of her carriage. He brought a score of his men along, all of whom were clad in the King's colors, some with their faces shrouded. Despite their capabilities, it was unlikely they would be able to fend off the entire city, should Queen Charlotte's demise be discovered.

"Be calm, child," the woman in black said, stepping around Lucetta's left side. Somehow, the entity could always sense when her anxiety was at its worst. "Your plan was executed perfectly. Not a soul alive will suspect what you have done. Remain on your path. Everything is unfolding according to plan."

She made to speak, but thought better of it. There were too many people around, though all of their attention was diverted to the temple. The Queen's wagon came to a halt, her body carefully removed and carried up a length of marble steps with the greatest of care. Lucetta had always known such a day would come, a day when she would have to bury her mother, but never would have thought it would be under such circumstances. Remembering the night Pavlos extinguished the Queen's life brought tears to her eyes.

"Good," the entity said. "Let your grief flow. It is, after all, expected of a child to mourn the loss of their parent. It will only help to diminish the possibility of suspicion."

While the woman in black was right, her tears were entirely genuine. Charlotte was the one who gave her life and unconditional love as a child. There were thousands of happy memories, each one of them driving daggers deep into her soul. Murdering her mother was necessary in the grand scheme of things, but was heartbreaking nevertheless.

"My sincerest condolences, my princess," a wealthy nobleman said, bowing deeply.

Only Cardale's aristocracy was permitted to be inside the square. Everywhere Lucetta turned, there was another pampered lord or noble, simpering and offering their respects. In a near instant, there were seemingly hundreds of faces all around, so many they appeared indiscernible from one another.

The sound of their voices rattled inside her head, each growing louder and more garbled than the last. Lucetta had felt such feelings of utter panic before, but could do nothing now to stop it. She was helpless, and knowing just how helpless she was only served to worsen her terror.

"Pavlos!" she uttered. It was unwise to use the Droethien's name out loud, but she had grown dizzy and near to vomiting. Thankfully the mercenary was close by, and threw an arm around her and trudged through the crowd. It was easy enough to disperse the fat, privileged aristocrats. Pavlos brought her to the steps of the temple, which was protected by a detachment of Royal Guardsmen.

"Princess," he said in a hushed voice. "You should be with your mother now, yes? Never mind these lords and nobles. Say your good-byes, Pavlos will keep you safe."

Timidly, she agreed. A pair of imposing doors to the temple were cracked open, and Lucetta heard conversation and sobbing filtering out from inside. She entered and immediately became awestruck. A cavernous main hall was decorated with thousands of flowers, and hundreds of lit candles. Large purple banners hung from the upper balconies nearly to the floor, their pristine cloth swaying ever so gently in a western breeze.

Trace, Aldred, and Esma were inside, a half dozen of Cardale's wealthiest around them. How long they had been waiting for the procession to arrive was anyone's guess. Trace held his wife and bawled, while Aldred stared down at the floor. Lucetta felt a sudden tightness in her chest at the sight of her husband, but it was unlikely any of them knew the true cause of the Queen's demise. The woman in black had assured her so.

"Lucetta!" Trace said, sobbing. "Our… mother… our poor mother…"

"There you are!" Aldred said, astonished. He rushed to her side and they embraced, though his touch was enough to invite nausea. "Are you alright? It's been so long since I've seen you. I've grown sick with worry."

Lucetta shook her head, for she was clearly not well in many ways. "No, no I'm not. My poor, sweet mother… I… forgive me, the shock still has not subsided."

"I never thought I would see the day," he mumbled. "I regret that my last interaction with her was so hostile. She was always a kind woman, and strong. But now there will never be a chance for us to reconcile."

The royal maidservant stood beside the Queen's body, crying uncontrollably. While common folk were insufferable more often than not, Emilee Harper was a kind and dutiful servant, and adored Charlotte. It was difficult to even look at her, knowing the kind of anguish in her heart.

"How could this have happened?" Trace said, near shouting. "You were there, tell us! Was she ill? Did she—"

"I don't know!" Lucetta screamed, her hands trembling. "She was perfectly fine the day before. We went to bed that night, and the next morning the servants awoke me with the news. I thought Devin would have informed me, but he's been missing since that evening. I bet he had something to do with it!"

"Now is neither the time nor place for this," Aldred cautioned. "Rest assured, I will launch a full investigation into this matter. I brought a team of physicians here, and after our viewing they will examine her body. If there's any truth we can learn of what happened, we will uncover it. Hopefully."

The thought of being discovered made her shiver. But she had personally witnessed Pavlos suffocating the life out of Queen Charlotte. He was both swift and efficient, and left not a single trace of his handiwork. If the kill had been sloppy, or if there was a struggle, she would have seen it with her own two eyes.

No, it was perfect. It was! No one could possibly detect anything otherwise.

Trace's composure was beginning to melt like wax in the summer sun. For a grown man, he shed the tears of an unnerved little boy, clinging desperately to Esma like a blanket. It was a pitiful sight to behold, but not unexpected given the weakness of Bethard men.

"I… I can't do this…" he sobbed. After another brief glance at the Queen, he departed with Esma in tow.

"Can your examination not wait another day?" Lucetta complained. "Give us at least until tomorrow before your damnable doctors go poking around her body. Let me stay with her a while longer."

It was a request not even Aldred dared to refuse. He pursed his lips, nodded, then planted a kiss on the top of Lucetta's head. It was a kind gesture, but one which went unreciprocated. Even the click-clacking of his boots as he started for the door was enough to make her want to scream. But finally, Aldred had departed, a few remaining priests following behind.

The chamber was empty now, save for a soft chirping of birds and droll mumblings of the crowd outside. Lucetta let out a deep sigh, nearly gasping for air, as it was the first time all day she felt able to breathe freely. Though the Queen was peacefully at rest, there was something disturbingly unnatural afoot. Even now, after days of travel and now an entire day under a stifling sun, her body had yet to show the slightest hint of corruption.

Cautiously, Lucetta moved to Charlotte's side, sniffing at the air suspiciously. There was only the scent of incense and smoke from a thousand candles, but not death. No, the Queen's skin had not even turned a hint of blue, which Pavlos told her to expect.

She looks so peaceful, as if she's still sleeping. Is my mind playing tricks on me? Is she actually alive, and I'm merely imagining what happened in Dellhaven? Is such a thing even possible?

Standing mere feet away, she looked down at her mother, but was unable to muster a single tear. No, something was wrong, terribly wrong. And to make matters worse, the woman in black was nowhere to be found.

"I'm sorry it had to be this way, mother. But I do hope you under-stand why I did what I did. Now that your spirit is free, I pray you can see my intentions and the glorious future I plan to usher in. I know you would have done anything for your children, and you must believe me when I say that this is the greatest gift you could have given to any one of us. Your sacrifice will be the beginning of something beautiful, and eternal."

She turned from the altar, descending the long, platform-like steps slowly, and headed toward the doors. Before she managed to make it halfway, there was a sudden disturbance which froze her in place. A sound of joints and cartilage snapping and popping filled the chamber, and the wet twisting of flesh, followed by a deep grumble of sorts. Apprehensively, Lucetta turned to see the source of the noise, and looked on in horror at the corpse of Charlotte, sitting upright, staring back through glazed white eyes.

A deep groan built inside the Queen's chest as a putrid stench befouled the air. A slow smile formed across her dead face, revealing teeth as black as pitch. But perhaps the most disturbing thing was her laugh. It was the sound of timber flexing, stones grinding against one another, and an indescribable cackle melded into one. Such a noise was unlike anything Lucetta had ever heard before.

The terror was so great, she nearly lost consciousness. Lucetta stood motionless, unable to breathe at first, but then let loose a bloodcur-dling scream. Racing for the door, she nearly tripped over her skirts and fell onto the marble floor, but was able to regain solid footing. She reached for a large brass door handle and prepared to wrench it open, but turned one final time to see if her mother's corpse was in pursuit.

Lying on the altar was Charlotte Bethard, hands folded neatly, and resting as peacefully as the moment she was brought in. Lucetta gasped, unable to believe what she was seeing. But suddenly, the candles in the room were mysteriously extinguished in an instant, and the noise from outside fell silent all at once. Sunlight swiftly dimmed to darkness, as if thick storm clouds had manifested overhead.

Lucetta could spy a faint haze of breath with each exhale, an icy chill filling the chamber. Shivering, she tried to wrench open the door handle, but the metal was so frozen it nearly burned when she took hold of it. Screaming and beating against the wood, she called out to any who might hear her, but it was in vain.

"I've got to get out of here! Please, help me! Help me!" she called out frantically to the woman in black, but the entity still had not manifested itself.

She began searching for another way out, but before taking so much as a single step, the candles erupted with explosions of fire. Flames shot to the ceiling, a furious roar of the inferno nearly deafening. The corpse of her mother became wreathed in fire, then slowly sat up once again.

Terror-stricken, Lucetta watched as the remains of Queen Charlotte stood and lurched forward. Her gown was quickly consumed and burned away, orange flames licking at her bare skin. Her flesh boiled and turned black, until large pieces began to slough off and fall away. The corpse reached out, bony fingers clawing at the air.

"Please, stop!" she cried out. "I'm sorry, mother! I'm sorry! Please, leave me!"

Sobbing, she covered her eyes and winced in anticipation as her mother drew closer. The smell of burning flesh and hair was thick and nauseating, and only grew more intense with each wet footfall. Lucetta screamed, took hold of the handle once more, and pulled with all of her might.

The door opened, revealing a warm, sunny day on the other side. Hundreds of commoners were standing vigil outside, looking on curiously as she stumbled out into their midst. Cautiously, she glanced over her shoulder, but was relieved to see the chamber the same as it had always been. The Queen was still at rest, candles and incense burning softly, and the nightmarish vision nowhere to be seen.

Thankfully, Pavlos was waiting nearby, and had taken notice of her distress. He hurried over with a half-dozen Droethiens, throwing a hooded cloak over her shoulders and whisking her through the crowd with all haste.

"Come, princess. Pavlos will bring you home safe, yes?"

Home. It was the one place she never wanted to return to. The thought of being in such close proximity to Trace and Aldred again was nearly too stressful to contemplate. There would undoubtedly be many questions about her whereabouts and activities over the last several months, all of which she had no intention of answering.

"No, we cannot," she protested. "There must be some other place in Cardale where we can lay low, somewhere safe."

It was embarrassing to know so little about the city she had grown up in, but such was the life of a princess. A woman of royalty had no business in common quarters, after all. But a man such as Pavlos likely knew Cardale from its wealthiest enclaves to its lowliest alleys. Thankfully, the Droethien once again proved his resourcefulness.

"As you say, princess." He scratched his chin, head cocked to the side. "Pavlos knows of such a place. However, it may not be to your liking, yes?"

"Not to my liking? Do tell me, you are not intending to take me into some squalor-ridden shanty, are you?"

"Not quite, princess. You will find it suitable enough. Come, we must leave quickly, yes?"

Pavlos motioned to one of the carriages from the funeral procession. Together they made their way toward it, the Droethien assisting Lucetta inside effortlessly. Travel was difficult on her emaciated body, but it made her feel safe to know that soon the temple, the nobles, and her family would be far enough away.

With a snap of leather reins, the carriage wheels began to turn. Lucetta let loose a sigh of relief, and glanced once more at the temple. A cold tingle nipped at the back of her neck as she spied the woman in black standing in the doorway, eyes glowing orange-red, a dark smile ever-widening.

SYLVIA III

THE VILLAGE WAS A SCANT THING, THE FIRST OF MANY THEY WERE likely to see. It was peculiar to note how common folk lived in Betanthia, in stone and wooden hovels, much the same as her northern kin. If not for a lack of tall pines and frigid air, one might not be able to detect much of a difference between their people. But Sylvia Stormguard cared little for similarities. To her, every Betanthian was an enemy, a lurking threat which could not be trusted.

She sat mounted, surrounded by Damien Dreadfire and the other warchiefs. Marvath was never far from her side, as she had come to expect. Arik Akselson, the reluctant Nothanek warchief, lingered behind them, himself looking on in uncertainty. Perhaps he felt safe in the presence of Rhivothi, proper warriors in their own right. Not that she could fault him for such a sentiment. It was the furthest south the Teb dweller and his kin had ever ventured, and Sylvia could not help but sense a longing for home in his gaze.

At least there's one man here who understands his place in all of this. Bless them though, the Nothanek. Sometimes I feel they're too pure for this world.

Thinking of the Nothanek brought back memories of Einarr, a face she had not seen in ages. She wondered how he fared throughout the winter in Skaginlef, and if he had found peace after a bloody year at war.

The memories brought with them a certain bittersweetness, something difficult to describe. Sylvia felt deeply conflicted, both with her desire for his company, and resentment for his absence.

A man of his convictions should have more resolve. We've all had to do terrible things to appease the gods. Maybe his faith isn't as strong as he lets on...

Her tangled web of thoughts was soon soured by the presence of Zander and his ilk. Unlike her complicated feelings for Einarr, Zander instead provoked only disgust, her face tightening into a ball at the sight of his filthy bald head.

"So, what are we waiting for?" Zander's half-rotten teeth emerged like decaying fruit on the vine, bringing bile into the back of her throat. "There's bound to be a little gold or steel hidden away here somewhere."

"Patience," Damien commanded, raising a hand. "We no longer have the safety of the Hinterwood at our backs. Here, there may be enemies lurking in every direction. We must find allies wherever possible."

"Are you suggesting we treat with them?" Marvath Bonesplitter asked incredulously.

"Yes," Damien answered confidently. "Every village and homestead under King Bethard's thumb is a potential safe haven for our enemies, and we must take care not to leave ourselves vulnerable. There is no telling who may take us by surprise at an inopportune moment."

"So let's kill them all and be done with it," Zander chimed in.

Overcome with irritation, Sylvia wheeled her horse around. "Do you listen to nothing Damien tells you, or are you too stupid to comprehend? If we raze this village, word will spread far and wide, and every village we come across will be openly hostile toward us. Every ally we gather is another ally Marcellus Bethard will be lacking."

"Be at peace, Stormguard," Dhuuld Lurrson chimed in. "There will be no killing today, from the looks of it. This village has been abandoned."

At first, she brushed off the Khorrtalli chieftain's words, but upon closer inspection, something indeed appeared amiss. There was an odd stillness to the village. No sounds of terror. No panicked fleeing of its inhabitants. It was if they had stumbled across a settlement long forgotten.

"It appears word of our travel precedes us," Damien said bitterly.

"Good." Marvath nodded. "Less time wasted on distractions. Our strength will be preserved for when the real battle comes."

"Indeed," Dreadfire conceded. "I would have expected such a thing far deeper into Betanthian territory. If villages are already emptying before us, then surely they have cast their lot with King Bethard. I had hoped to bring as many men under our banner as possible, but I can see now such a thing is not possible."

His disappointment was not shared among the Zylmacians. While they undoubtedly craved blood, the idea of looting the village empty appeared to please them just as well. Jollkud's men were whipping one another into a frenzy like rabid dogs.

"My lord," Zander said with unusual formality. "It might be a good idea to let our western friend as his men take this one. I'm sure a little treasure will take their minds off the hanging. Could do well to lessen the tension a bit."

For once, the wildman appeared to have a sound suggestion, one devoid of stupidity and bravado. Sylvia found herself impressed that such a simple creature was capable of rational thought.

"A sound idea indeed," Dreadfire said. "Give word to Jollkud. Take this settlement, and kill any who remain."

Zander grinned, then rode off to spread the good news. Shortly after, the wildmen let loose a howling fury, then charged forth with reckless abandon. They appeared just as content to set upon an empty village as they were to slaughter masses of Betanthians. Zylmacians were simple creatures, after all, and as easily amused as a dog with a stick.

There was little in the means of spoils, most homesteads having been stripped of anything of value by their fleeing owners. It was the same story at the next town they encountered as well, much to the irritation of many. While Hok and its glorious sacking was still fresh in Sylvia's mind, to the warriors it seemed like ages since their last real plundering.

She unfurled a rolled piece of animal hide, a map of Caldakas scratched onto it. According to their position, they were drawing ever closer to Greenwood Forest, itself on the doorstep to Bentmont. Surely, it would only be a matter of time before the armies of Betanthia offered a challenge.

And when they do, I pray we're ready. Gods protect us. Keep our steel sharp and our minds focused.

That night, she awakened to agonized screams and pitiful groans, and the flickering of torchlight outside her tent. Sylvia rose and rubbed the exhaustion from her eyes and peered outside. She saw Zylmacians, dozens of them, likely hundreds, stumbling around in the darkness.

What are these filthy westerners up to now?

While the spectacle was an annoyance, it was nevertheless a cause for concern. The men appeared to be sick, some retching and coughing, their movements stiff and labored. Some of the Zylmacian camp followers were bringing the afflicted fresh water, and rendering whatever aid they could.

At first she dismissed their plight, but soon the truth became clear. The wildmen were truly unwell. Sylvia passed by one man curled into a ball on the ground, shaking violently and nearly in tears. He was bald and burly, and looked equally as savage as the most bloodthirsty Rhivothi. To see such an imposing warrior reduced to a blubbering mess was perhaps more disturbing than their typically unsavory behavior.

"Summon the healers!" a warrior cried out, tending to a stricken brother.

Wails of agony and pleas for help pierced the darkness. Before long, the entire warband had stirred, many believing they were under attack.

Bonesplitter and a band of Rhivothi arrived with axes in hand. They looked on in disbelief, certain a fight was nearby. But no, the only battle taking place was against an unseen enemy.

"Leave it to these Bymist rats to create such a stir," Marvath grumbled. "Let the gods take them all, I say."

"If we were in the north, I might agree with you," she said. "But this could spell disaster for us all! This racket will be heard all the way in Bentmont!"

Marvath grunted, but held fast as a group of torches drew close. In the darkness, Sylvia saw Damien Dreadfire and his bodyguard making their way to the site of the disturbance. He was without armor, but with bastard sword in hand, equally as perplexed as she was.

"What is the meaning of this?" Dreadfire barked, his black eyes half open. "Where is Zander? Why are his men shambling around like the undead?"

"I will send for him at once, my lord," one of the Rhivothi said before hurrying off.

Only a short while passed before the Zylmacian warchief arrived, himself having walked among the chaos. He appeared the least concerned of them all, which served to bewilder Sylvia even further. With a horn of mead in hand, the wildman strode to Damien's side and presented himself.

"You'll have to forgive the lads." Zander grinned. "Many of Jollkud's men have never ventured outside of the Bymist. We call it root foot, it's a sickness we get our first time in new lands. Quite painful, actually. First comes a fever, followed by excruciating pain in the body. And to make matters worse, the pain only subsides when you stand or walk. Sitting or laying down is... well, pure torture. Feels as if your feet are being rooted into the ground."

"And how long does this affliction last?" Dreadfire planted his sword into the ground, then crossed his arms.

"Hard to say. Once the sickness takes hold, most men recover in days. For me, nearly a week. A witch doctor said it was a curse from the land itself. And to cure the condition, one must eat of those who dwell on the land, to gain their strength."

It was a disturbing revelation, but served as an adequate explanation for the recent cannibalism. However, eating human flesh was hardly a thing to make sense of. It was a reminder of how different Zander and his kin were from northmen. A Rhivothi would feast on his axe handle before ever considering such an unthinkable act.

"Send for our healers at once," Dreadfire commanded. "See to it these men are cared for. We can afford no further delays, not in these lands."

For the next hour, Sylvia watched as shamans and medicine men tended to the stricken Zylmacians. Thankfully, the warband was secure and away from hostile eyes. Hundreds of scouts maintained vigilance in every direction, in case Betanthia sought to capitalize. But with no attack imminent, she decided to retire and claim what little sleep there would be before dawn.

An unexpected scent of pipe herb wafted throughout the tent city, instantly flooding her mouth with water. With a new day fast approaching, and with the camp already awakened, she set off in search of the delectable odor. A small haze drifted out from a tent near her own, which could only belong to one of three people. It glowed with the flickering warmth of lantern light, and cast shadows of three bodies against its canvas.

Those harpies didn't invite me?! How dare they!

Sylvia giggled as she approached the tent, her shieldmaidens cackling inside. There had been precious little time to relax and unwind with her companions during their march south. It seemed there was no better time to steal a few moments with Hilde and the others before the long trek resumed. Smiling, Sylvia threw open the tent flap, a thick cloud of herb greeting her accordingly.

All three women were in fits of laughter, passing a wooden pipe in a small circle. Wooden mugs of mead and beer and leftover meat from supper sat around them. Even Ingryd Bjornsdottir was smiling, at rarity to be certain. Her thick blonde hair was loose and wild, shrouding a map of blue runic tattoos on the side of her head. It was endlessly relieving to be among such familiar company once more.

"Why, look who decided to join us!" Mikke said, tipping over onto her side.

"Yes indeed," Hilde said, her cyan eyes stern. "Our fearless warchief, come to visit at long last."

It would be unwise to trade barbs with a fanatic of Azldyr, Sylvia thought. She had always thought of her shieldmaidens as blood sisters, and Hilde an older sister at that.

"I do apologize," Sylvia said, inserting herself into the raucous circle. "This march weighs heavy on my mind. These Zylmacians never give me a moment of rest."

"They certainly appear to be getting what they deserve," Ingryd said, sipping beer from a mug. "I would sooner care for a rabid dog than give them an ounce of sympathy."

Nothing about Bjornsdottir's sentiment seemed unreasonable. Sylvia would be content to watch every last Zylmacian die a slow and agonizing death, there could be no disputing that.

"My concern for the wildmen only goes so far," she said. "I enjoy watching them suffer as much as you, but their affliction leaves us all vulnerable. Should the Betanthians find us come morning, I shudder to think what it would mean for our people."

"Which is why we're enjoying the night!" Mikke passed Sylvia the pipe.

A thin line of smoke slithered up from a wad of burning herb, saturating her nostrils with its enticing aroma. Sylvia licked her lips and wasted little time in taking a long, deep hit. The smoke burned her lungs, but was otherwise pleasant. An immediate rush of euphoria made the world outside of the tent seem so distant and trivial.

She coughed out a large white cloud, then laughed. It was the first time she had shared a genuine laugh in what felt like an eternity. There was little to be happy about these days, but moments like these were to be treasured. Sylvia motioned for a mug of beer, and toasted her sisters in arms.

"And to that, dear Mikke, we will drink!" She hoisted a frothy mug, and the shieldmaidens crashed theirs together. "I've missed this… these moments together. I pray they never end."

Together, the shieldmaidens laughed and drank their cares away until sleep claimed them one at a time. Though her own tent was larger and more comfortable, Sylvia could not very well part with the company of her sisters. It was difficult enough to remain awake, her eyelids as heavy as boulders. She waited until they were all fast asleep before downing the last drops of beer, and joined them soon after in the dreaming.

After what seemed to be only minutes of rest, a horn blast rang out, rousing Sylvia in an instant. It felt as if a band of horses had trampled across her head, the spinning and a dull ringing sound enough to sour her stomach. Even rolling from one side to another was enough to bring liquid up and into the back of her throat.

Has it truly been so long since I've drank so much?

Fortunately, her shieldmaidens fared far better. They were outside preparing breakfast, laughing and boasting as if last night's drunkenness had never happened. Sylvia willed herself to standing then stumbled through the tent flap, desperate for water and fresh bread.

"You're alive," Hilde said, brushing a lock of black hair behind one ear. "I haven't seen you drink like that since… the solstice, five years ago. You remember?"

"How could I forget," she groaned.

Twice every year, the natives of Rej Rhivoth would lose themselves in celebration. There was enough feasting, drinking, fighting, and debauchery to put the entirety of Caldakas to shame. It was a time for unrepentant merriment, to be certain. At one particular festival, Sylvia drank every shieldmaiden unconscious, and even some of the men. Few dared to challenge her iron stomach from that day on.

Even the memories were enough to make Sylvia retch, however. She poured out the contents of her stomach into a nearby pail, Hilde looking on in amusement. Rhivothi women had a certain reputation to maintain, and thankfully, none outside of their small circle would witness her shame. To be conquered by drink was to be considered unworthy, especially among the menfolk.

"We're heading out soon." Mikka crouched down and moved Sylvia's hair out of the way, then reached for a cup of water. "Here, drink."

"Be sure to wrap me in the tent and throw me in the back of a wagon," she jested, to the shieldmaiden's amusement. "Has anyone been by this morning?"

Hilde nodded. "Arik was here, asking for you. Damien called a meeting in the early hours, and—"

Sylvia groaned. What would the other warchiefs think, now that she had proven incapable of handling her drink? It was an embarrassment she could ill afford around such deadly serious men.

"Tell me, what did he say?" she asked, sighing.

"Damien ordered us to break camp," Hilde said. "I hope your stomach recovers soon, we're about to cross into the Plainhold. The real fight is just over the horizon, and you better be prepared."

EINARR IV

Furiously, Einarr Rollfson toiled, his leathered hands blistered and broken. With the aid of a cask of mead and potent pipe herb, he slowly carved and chiseled half a dozen barkless tree trunks until they began taking form. Whenever exhaustion arrived to claim him, Einarr ingested a small amount of forest mushrooms, similar to those the Rhivothi foraged.

By the light of bonfires he labored, their tall, dancing flames fueling a paranoid hunger. Each hammer strike against chisel, each stroke of a sanding stone, seemed to bring with it an unexpected catharsis. Every shaving which fell to the ground felt like it was another sin forgiven, another weight lifted from his shoulders. It was a feeling of bliss he had not experienced for some time.

That evening, the Nothanek curiously emerged from their hovels. Einarr's incoherent ramblings and frantic flailing inspired some to beat drums and sing, while casks of fresh mead were rolled out for all to enjoy. While the festival was still a day away, Skaginlef indulged itself in early celebration.

When daylight arrived, the villagers of Skaginlef offered meat and bread, enthralled at his near supernatural diligence. Such offerings were kind, but went unaccepted. Instead, Einarr contented himself with more mead, cursing and demanding the beating of drums and blowing of horns.

"More!" he belched, the rest of his words incoherent babble.

And more there was. Dancing and feasting throughout Skaginlef had grown twofold from the day before, all driven by Einarr's intoxication. There were times when he was barely aware of what was transpiring, his body seemingly possessed by an all-consuming energy. As the nightly bonfires grew in size and number, he swallowed another handful of mushrooms, their effect soon jolting him into another plane of existence.

Einarr's hands began moving with otherworldly guidance, slamming hammer onto chisel seemingly on their own. With each passing minute, he began to feel less connected to the world of the living, and more at peace with the world beyond. Were Kholdyr to call him home at that moment, he might very well have smiled.

Something appeared in the darkness, two small orbs of light reflecting the glow of bonfires. Einarr squinted, unable to make out the anomalies in such condition. The tiny lights drew closer and grew larger, until their host revealed itself. Standing behind a wall of fire was a giant beast, long of tail and large of mane. At first glance, it appeared to be a mountain lion, though far larger and fiercer.

No. This beast is something else entirely.

A great cat stared through the flames, its gaze unflinching. Instead of fear, he felt only strength welling within him. Gracefully and silently, the beast stalked around the bonfire, until it was standing mere feet away. Their gazes remained locked in a contest of wills, each vying to see the other break first.

The gods have tested my spirit, beast. They could not break me, and nor shall you!

A low rumbling began building inside the cat's maw. Still, Einarr remained unshaken, his face tightening into a snarl. Like a clap of thunder, the large beast let loose a mighty roar, enough to make cowards of even the mightiest warriors. Einarr responded with a fierce battle cry of his own, teeth bared and fists clenched, ready to fight to a violent and bloody death.

There was no fear in his heart any longer. Every last ounce of it had melted away in the fires, leaving behind a tempered instrument of war. Even the beast seemed to notice, and quietly slunk back into the darkness, though its gaze remained fixed.

His vision became a swirling mess of light and colors smeared into one another. As the drums beat louder, Einarr felt the contents of his stomach erupt. A stream of black vomit sprayed from his mouth moments before he crumpled to the ground, a whirlwind of lights and sounds fading into blackness.

"Wake up, son of Rolff," Selbjorn said, giving a nudge with his foot. "I see you've completed your work. And not a moment too soon."

The elder ran his hand across a finished totem, its surface sanded and smooth. His fingers danced around intricately carved runes and a masterful visage of Kholdyr emblazoned at its center. Einarr sat up, his head so light it nearly drifted away into the heavens.

"I might never create another thing after this," he groaned. "I have given these totems all of my life force. I only pray it's enough to appease Azldyr."

"Of that, I have no doubt." Selbjorn produced a faded book, one which had not seen the light of day for centuries. "You will need this, son of Rolff. I pray you find the will to complete what you have begun. You must, for all of our sakes."

Einarr took hold of the text, but there was no strength in his arms. He grunted, struggling to crawl toward a skin of water a villager had left. It was both cool and refreshing, the waters of the Teb running clean. With a dozen desperate gulps, he drank the skin empty.

Some of the Nothanek emerged from their hovels, curious to see the result of his labors. Einarr could feel their awe and admiration as they pointed and whispered. It was the first time since returning home that he felt respected, the mystique of his craftsmanship having returned.

After gnawing down a heel of fresh bread, Einarr stumbled to his feet, surveying the results of the last two days. Astonishingly, the runes and carvings were magnificent beyond anything mortal hands could rightly produce. Every detail was so minute and perfect, it appeared as if the gods themselves had guided his hands.

This… this cannot be. Even on my finest day, I could never create anything of this magnificence.

The gods, it seemed, were with him once again. Or perhaps they had been with him all along, given the wonders he had seen in visions. Merely looking at the totems was enough to send a cold tingle up his back, a strange energy emanating from within them. Einarr took his leave, book in hand, and shambled toward the cherry blossom tree to rest and reflect.

"Alina, I know what I must do, but I fear what it will mean," Einarr whispered, setting the ancient tome beside the tree.

He sighed, closed his eyes and leaned against the trunk, its branches blooming pink flowers. It was always a bittersweet time of year, to see the cherry blossom in its full majesty. It was comforting to know that Alina's body had returned to the earth and her essence taken into its branches, but seeing the blossoms only worsened his longing. And he had missed the last two seasons, having been away with Damien Dreadfire, first with forming the warband then with striking back at Betanthia.

For hours Einarr Rolffson sat beneath the tree, focusing his mind, hoping that Alina would speak to him. As hard as he tried, there was no response. It was difficult to contain his frustration and the sorrow, which soon began to boil into anger. He sat agitated, fists clenched, jaw tightening, ready to be done with such folly. Einarr grunted and made to open his eyes, but an unexpected breeze blew in from the north, shaking the cherry blossom's branches, its cold crispness cutting through him like a sword.

Is that you, my love? Are you out there, somewhere?

A strange, warm sensation washed over his body. Einarr felt drowsy, yet surprisingly alert as his vision blurred and spun and morphed into a dream-like haze. He felt separated from his body, as if observing himself through a windowpane. There was a grove set beside a river, not in Skaginlef or any place he was familiar with. Warm rays peeked through a canopy of gray clouds, a soft and waning rainfall refracting gentle light. The land around was bright and green, and teeming with life.

At the center of the grove stood Alina, in a gown of white silk, her brown hair loose and flowing. She smiled so lovingly it made his knees quiver, and brought him to tears.

"I feel so uncertain, Alina. I'm not the one to usher these boys into manhood. Surely there must be another."

She stepped forward, touching his soft, dark beard. "No, it must be you, my love. You have strength within you, and it saddens me that you cannot see it. You've survived three battles. You're a leader. You're a warrior, whether you would believe it or not."

Warrior. It was a strange word to hear, especially with it attributed to himself. But the more Einarr thought about it, the more sense Alina made. Only the bravest men of Skaginlef had dared to venture from their ancestral home and into the fires of war. Though reluctant, Einarr was still counted among them, and had witnessed more warfare than any Rollfson since the days of Kuggvord the Grim.

"You're right," he conceded. "I need to stop running from my destiny. I know what I must do."

He reached out to offer a kiss, eyes shut and lips wanting. But there was nothing. No Alina, no warmth, and no grove. He was back where he had been the entire time, in Skaginlef, near the bubbling waters of the Teb. But the sun had grown low, and the festival mere minutes away from beginning.

"Good people of Skaginlef!" Selbjorn shouted, both arms raised in the air. "Gather 'round!"

The villagers began to congregate in excited anticipation, though it served to only moisten Einarr's brow. It was curious to feel his pulse quicken and nerves fraying, the same as before a battle. While there would be no combat here, he was about to begin fighting another kind of war entirely: a spiritual war.

"Today marks the first day of spring!" Selbjorn said to raucous applause as he approached a dais. "With this most joyous of occasions comes the renewal of our lands. By the blessings of the gods, the trees and flowers have bloomed once again. Our crops will grow and give sustenance to those who call these lands home. And we will welcome new life into the world!"

Several pregnant women smiled, their men and elders giving them a hearty cheer. Scores of young men began growing restless, waiting for their moment of acknowledgment. Einarr studied their joyful and innocent faces, knowing what he was about to subject them to.

"And finally." Selbjorn raised his hands again. "We welcome the boys of our village into manhood. The Haalenhaad is a ceremony older than Skaginlef itself. Every year we give thanks to Olyndyr, and seek his blessing so these boys made men can prosper from his bounty, and provide for families of their own."

Rosk looked over to Einarr and gave a gentle motion of his hand. Clutching the ancient book, Einarr approached the dais. Jubilation quickly turned to silence, many staring incredulously while some pointed and whispered.

"Be still," Selbjorn continued. "As all of you know, Skaginlef has pledged itself to our Borjifan neighbor, Damien Dreadfire, in his quest to seek vengeance for the massacre of his people. For the past year, our brave men have joined the war effort against Betanthia. We have been blessed to have lost so few. However, it is the belief of the elders that, given these circumstances, this year we should perform the Haalenhaad in honor of another god."

Selbjorn stepped aside, motioning for Einarr to approach. Every eye was watching, though some of their gazes appeared ill-favored. Even now, the village bore little love for him, but perhaps the gravity of his words might have a different effect.

"Sons and daughters of Skaginlef," Einarr began, clearing his throat. "I know many of you here bear resentment, even hostility toward me for returning home while so many others fight on. I cannot blame you, as I was the one who championed Damien Dreadfire's cause, and took our people to war."

The Nothanek began to stir, some in disinterest. Einarr straightened his back and mustered every ounce of courage within his wounded heart. He thought of Sylvia Stormguard and Marvath Bonesplitter, brave friends who had not lost heart. Perhaps in remembrance of their heroism, he might find words to honor their commitment to the cause.

"I returned because I lost the stomach for killing… and killing there was. I could never have imagined death on such a scale, but it was Betanthia who suffered the most. However, I believe such fortune is not limitless. In my heart, I believe that this year, we must give our thanks and praise to another… another who will see our warriors home, and give strength to these young men to keep Skaginlef safe."

Confusion swept over the Nothanek, as if Einarr was speaking in tongues. For generations, the Haalenhaad had been performed in honor of Olyndyr, god of the harvest and fertility. In fact, many had thought the festival to originally be in his honor alone.

Einarr cleared his throat. "I have proposed to the council of elders that this year, we honor Azldyr."

A near panic washed over the villagers. Merely mentioning the war god's name was enough to strike fear into their hearts.

"Be still now!" Selbjorn said, raising a hand into the air. "What Einarr says is the truth. We cannot continue to take our safety for granted. Neither the Teb nor the Hinterwood will keep Skaginlef from harm, should the tide of war turn against Damien Dreadfire. We must seek the protection of Azldyr."

Some of the mothers began pulling their young men closer, but even in their youth, they knew what had to be done. Fathers who had seen many winters had difficulty understanding the need for such precaution, but grandfathers in their wisdom knew otherwise.

"I understand your reservations," Einarr said, stepping to the edge of the dais. "Skaginlef has known nothing but peace and prosperity for generations. But I tell you now, what takes place beyond our lands could be the death of us all, should Damien fail. We must prepare ourselves for any eventuality."

"And what are you doing to keep the wolves of Betanthia at bay, coward?" a voice called out. There were a few soft murmurs of agreement.

"I have resolved to return to the fight, and see this war to whatever end," he answered. "Perhaps it was Kholdyr's will that I return to both warn and prepare you. It is my deepest regret to have involved you good people in this, but we are too far down the path to turn back now. The gods have willed us toward this moment in time for a reason, even if we cannot understand why."

While his words were true, many were reluctant to agree. Even now, the horrors of war seemed so far away, even with Skaginlef's bravest in the heart of the fight. Still, others knew what had to be done to ensure the survival of their people.

"Having said that," Selbjorn said, "Einarr will be performing the Haalenhaad this evening. All of the arrangements have been made. Only those who are to partake in the ritual, and their fathers, are to attend. To those young men who will cross into manhood tonight, I say this: be not afraid, for the gods will walk beside you. Have courage and faith in your hearts, and not even the mightiest foes will best you."

Night had fallen over Skaginlef, and time enough to begin the ceremony. Each of the carved totems had been erected and placed in their precise locations, coinciding with the stars above. It was a cloudless night, devoid of wind or rain, and deathly quiet. Not even crickets dared to pierce such holy silence.

Einarr stood alone at the center of the totem circle, his face raked with lines of green paint and wood ash. Bare-chested and loose of hair, he waited in silence until glimmers of torchlight emerged from the forest. The ancient procession had begun, starting first among the trees where Kholdyr and his brethren lived.

By twos, a column snaked out from the darkness, the fathers of each boy carrying their own torch. Rosk marched at the head of the procession, adorned with animal furs and deer antlers, his face painted dark as the night. A slow, steady beating of drums followed, beckoning spirits of the woods to awaken. At the end came Selbjorn, dressed in his finest robes and laden with gold and talismans.

Hairs on Einarr's arms and neck began to stiffen as he felt Skaginlef's ancestors rouse from their eternal slumber. He could nearly see them congregating around the totems. To his sadness, Alina's loving presence was nowhere to be found among them, but alas, this night was not for her. Einarr knew he had to remain focused and pure of heart and mind. The future of his people might very well depend on it.

A chorus of chiming bells joined an ancient melody, accented by the clicking of bones against one another. As the procession drew closer, Einarr saw each boy clutching a spear. Their hair hung loose against their bare chests, themselves painted and adorned to represent various animals of the forest.

It was a scene more familiar to the natives of Rej Rhivoth as opposed to that of a peaceful fishing village. But Stormguard and Bonesplitter would be proud nevertheless, to know the Nothanek had not forsaken their Khorrish warrior spirit. The procession came to a halt in a perfect circle within the totems, dozens of torches illuminating each delicate carving in the wood.

Einarr opened the dusty tome, its binding crumbling to pieces from the passage of time. It contained runes of Azldyr and incantations associated with his protections. Though he spoke the ancient Khorrish tongue, many within the village sadly did not. Thus, a translation would be necessary. He only prayed the words still held their same mystical energy when spoken.

"From the earth, we arise!" Einarr began. Selbjorn followed behind with a bowl of burning incense, a cloud of pungent smelling herb trailing behind. The fathers gave a roar in reply, then fell silent.

"From the waters, we are sustained!" He began a slow walk around the circle, staring each boy in the eyes.

"From the winds, we are renewed!" The boys thumped their spears against the dry ground. Rosk blew a cloud of smoke into each of their faces, some fighting to not recoil as it stung their eyes.

"By the stones, we build!" A thundering of drums grew louder and louder until it sounded as if earth itself was splitting in two. Some of the men began howling and huffing, an intense energy within the circle building like the coming of a lightning storm.

"By the fires, we destroy!" Einarr shouted, fathers and sons replying with their fiercest battle cries. Rosk hefted a large war horn with both hands, then let loose a blast so powerful it nearly extinguished the flaming torches.

"Azldyr, god of war, hear us!" Einarr lifted his arms toward the heavens. "We call out to you with axe and torch, with spear and shield. We have gathered here on this night to honor you and seek your protection.

We bring before you these young warriors, these faithful servants who will bear your runes. We ask you to guide them from the innocence of childhood and into manhood. Gift them with strength to wield the spear and protect your people unto death!"

A pair of elders brought forth a cow, a giver of life and sustenance. Its hide was painted with the symbols of Azldyr in woad and wood ash. The animal was led by rope into the center of the circle. Einarr drew his sword and hefted it high above his head, its steel shimmering with orange fire.

"We make this sacrifice to you, god of war, to grant these men of the Nothanek your favor. Keep their sword arms strong, and their steel sharp. Give them the courage and savage will to defeat your enemies! May their adversaries drown in their own blood!"

Einarr placed the sword beneath the cow's neck, then drew it upward with every ounce of strength. A jet of blood erupted from the animal as it groaned and stumbled, then fell to the ground with a thud. Red liquid began pooling beneath it, and was collected into another bowl by Selbjorn. Einarr dipped his thumb into the blood, then drew a line across the forehead of each boy.

"With this marking, you leave behind your innocence, and step forward into the life of a man… a man of the Nothanek!"

Celebratory cheers and vicious war cries erupted, a fierce beating of drums quickly following suit. Casks of mead which had been prepared were opened, and a large bonfire outside the circle lit. The new men of Skaginlef danced around the flames like their warrior ancestors once did, lost in jubilation. With the Haalenhaad concluded, Einarr gracefully took his leave. This night was for the young and hopeful, not weary men who had seen the horrors of war.

I have done what is necessary, Alzdyr. Protect them when the time comes. Give them courage. Heavens know, they will need it.

TITAN VI

"Get up, girl," Conrak said dryly. "Come on now. Try again."
For something as simple as squatting down, the pain seemed excruciating. Madelyn picked herself off the ground using a nearby chair, then attempted to stretch again. Slowly she squatted, joints popping and protesting, and sounding like the crunching of walnut shells. Gritting and growling, she raised her arms into the air and attempted to rise, but her strength had been exhausted.

"Push! Come on now," Conrak taunted. "Prove to me you're not entirely worthless."

Madelyn shot Conrak a distasteful glare, then began to rise. Inch by inch she stood, a searing agony rippling through muscle and joint alike. But the pain was too great to conquer. She fell once again, unable to complete the exercise.

"I… can't…" she panted.

It was a pitiful sight to behold, but even witnessing a failed attempt was encouraging enough. It was only a few days ago when Madelyn was confined to bed, chained down by the weight of her sorrow. Tylar looked on, hopeful and perhaps even a bit proud.

"Enough for one day," he said. "The girl needs to rest."

"Nonsense. She'll have plenty of time to rest when she's dead." Conrak crouched down in front of her. "You planning on dying, Lady Everly? Hm?"

"Fuck you," Madelyn wheezed.

Both men chortled.

"Seems she's becoming more like you by the day," the Elite said with his typical, shitty grin. "I have yet to decide if that's a good thing or not."

"It means she's a fighter," Tylar said. "It means she's the hard bitch everyone remembers."

He offered a hand, but Madelyn swatted it away. Groaning and straining, she rose on watery legs, then slumped onto a nearby chair.

"Do they really?" she asked. "Do they remember me?"

It was a question more difficult to answer than it should have been. The men who knew her best were dead, and those who knew her by reputation had seen only an empty shell of a person. But all of that was soon to change, Tylar was certain of it.

"If they don't already, they will." He poured out a mug of fresh water and offered it. "The men could give two shits about me. Thanks to this twat over here, they still look at me like some kind of coward. But you? No, they remember you well enough."

"And how do you know that?" Madelyn's eyes began growing glassy.

"I may not be a part of the Order anymore, but I still hear them talk. I was in a tavern just yesterday, minding my own business. A few of them were at the bar, green and smooth-cheeked… probably not a hair on their balls either. They're scared. They've seen what the northmen can do to our best. What they did to you."

"So they remember me as a broken woman, and a failure on the battlefield? Very reassuring, Tylar."

Conrak chuckled. "I believe what our scholar of a friend is getting at is, once you make your return, it'll ignite a fire in the hearts of every knight. It's quite the story, after all. Madelyn Everly: Commander turned prisoner, turned indolent, then returning to glory. But I suppose you've done enough, for today. We move to twice a day real soon, so eat hearty and rest up. You're going to need it."

The Elite strode from the room, leaving the door half open. After his footsteps disappeared downstairs, Madelyn flopped onto her bed, unable to mask her exhaustion any longer. Tylar was growing fatigued even watching her.

"I'm growing bored with these exercises, Tylar. This is what I really want." She nodded at the sword on his hip.

It seemed unjust for a warrior to be without their weapon. Titan loosed his blade, the steel singing and shimmering in the light. "Here. Take a few swings. Your muscles will remember."

Apprehension was hiding behind her steely-blue eyes. With a hint of hesitation, Madelyn stood and reached out and took hold of the sword, but nearly dropped it. Though light in his hands, in hers it was like lifting a boulder. Tylar moved around behind her, assisting her frail arms ever so delicately.

"You remember the motions, right? Close your eyes. Breathe. Breathe and remember."

She filled her lungs slowly, and with Tylar's assistance, lifted the blade and held it outstretched. Together they moved the sword side to side, each movement accented by a grunt of discomfort and the popping of a shoulder joint. Each pass became faster than the last, until the strength in her arm diminished and departed.

Tylar took hold of the hilt, then returned the blade to its scabbard. "Good, you can still cut a man. Just need to put some meat back on your bones, then you'll be slaying northmen in no time."

His encouragement seemed to have little effect. If anything, it appeared to lower her spirits even further. Madelyn sighed, staring off into empty space. "I remember something the High Marshal said to me when I returned to Bentmont. Or at least, I think I remember. It's difficult to say, I was barely awake. He said something about how he made certain I would be successful at every turn."

Tylar cocked his head, scowling. "What in the bloody hell did he mean by that? You won your glory with your own two hands, he—"

"No, he's right," she interrupted. "The more I think about it, the more sense it makes. In all of my battles, save for Morden, the odds were overwhelmingly in my favor. He knew he couldn't keep me locked away my whole life, so he gave me the easiest missions with the highest chance of success. He tried to keep me safe, and it only did me a disservice in the end. I was so accustomed to victory that I didn't know when to retreat."

Whether true or not, it was one more reason to despise the High Marshal. Something about Jenson Powell never passed the smell test in the first place, but his feelings about the man were beginning to make more sense.

"You still learned to fight and lead, didn't you?" Tylar huffed. "No amount of nepotism could compensate for that. Look at Renald Fletch, the man has shit for brains, and he'll end up spilling them all over the place if Powell pits him against the northmen."

"I wonder if your friend Conrak can offer any insight." Madelyn shrugged. "He seems to know a lot more than he's letting on."

Such sentiment was certainly mutual. Tylar remembered the book Conrak gave him in prison, and the pages missing from inside it. He also recalled their showdown at Mor Seveht, and the long journey across the Plainhold. While there was certainly a price on his head, the Order's bounties were often dead or alive. Returning his head in a burlap sack would have sufficed. Why was he spared? What did it all mean?

"He's not my friend, first of all. But you're right, the more I think about it, the more I feel like he's leaving doors cracked open for us. Care to walk through them and see what's on the other side?"

They stared into each other's cold, lifeless eyes, until an understanding came between them. Madelyn limped over to a chair, groaning as she dropped herself onto it. She stared longingly at a dreary sky, wishing she was any place but here.

"You'll have to do the walking for now, until my legs return. Aside from Thorn, I have no idea where to find him. And if you go gallivanting around in there, you'll end up back in—"

Tylar raised a hand, silencing her. "If he's any bit the man I suspect he is, I know where to find him. I'll let you know what comes of it. In the meantime, eat and get some rest."

Taking up his purple cloak, he stepped out into the hall and lumbered downstairs, the wood squealing its disapproval. He gave pause as Madelyn called out, her voice straining to find volume.

"Tylar! When you find him, ask if he's familiar with the word, Eveldanyr. Will you?"

With a grunt, he continued onward. Once in the streets, he paused and thought for a moment. Where *would* he find a man such as Conrak? Certainly, he was not the type to laze around Thorn all day, and the taverns around Bentmont were too low for his liking. No, such a man would undoubtedly prefer a finer establishment. For some unknown reason, Tylar knew exactly where to look.

The northeastern corner of Bentmont was quiet, and more affluent than the rest of the city. Here, the architecture retained its classical appearance, but was more refined in many ways. Lantern posts lined both sides of a wide, cobbled street, itself cleaned to near perfection. It was the sort of place where privileged men of gold and fine silks would congregate to fellate one another over their latest venture.

I should have done a bit of thieving around here instead of Mor Seveht. Fucking pricks deserve it.

At last, he arrived at the tavern, though tavern was perhaps too lowly a word to describe it. The establishment's exterior was elegant, made of burgundy bricks and black painted timbers. Its shutters were closed, as they always were. No sign hung outside its entrance, and to the common man, it looked to be little more than a residence for some wealthy Bentmont noble.

Tylar approached the door, recalling the last time he tried to enter. He was particularly drunk that evening, and had shambled from one watering hole to the next. He barely managed two steps inside before a burly guard threw him back outside, with a stern warning to never return.

This time, he would not be taking no for an answer. Tylar threw open the door and stepped inside, and again was stopped almost immediately by the same man as before.

"I don't think so," the guard said, placing a hand against his breastplate. "I told you to stay out of here. This establishment isn't for your kind. There's plenty of taverns around this town for you to piss yourself in. This ain't one of them."

"Seems I've had a bit of a reversal of fortune as of late." He tugged at the collar of his cloak, its purple fabric rippling. "You see this? I'm the crown prince's sworn bodyguard now, and I won't be taking any shit off the likes of you."

"You probably killed a Guardsman to get that, I reckon." The burly man lifted his chin. "Am I supposed to be impressed?"

"If that were true, and I really did kill a Guardsman, then I hope you'd be smart enough not to fuck with me. But no, I earned this cloak rightwise. The Prince is in town, here to lead the war effort. If you'd like me to explain to him that some miserable doorwatcher denied one of his most privileged men entry into—"

"No, no. That's not necessary. Be mindful of your manners here, these aren't the sort of folk that take kindly to drunken antics."

Tylar stepped through another door and into a foyer. Immediately, his senses were overwhelmed. A thick wall of sandalwood incense greeted his nostrils, distracting momentarily from a warm glow of sconces throughout the room. The floor was adorned in an elaborately designed red carpet, its threads new and unworn. A massive bar carved from dark walnut sat commandingly at the center, with wide hallways branching off from either side.

It was difficult to know where to begin. Tylar thought about fetching a quick drink, but supposed he lacked proper coin for it. The barkeep was a pretty man, his hair oiled and mustache well-groomed. He gave Tylar a quick glance while cleaning a crystal glass, then looked away. Perhaps it was the sight of his purple cloak which made the man nervous, or even his battle-scarred face. This was the sort of place for men of wealth and privilege, after all, not steel.

Fuck me... I never would have guessed there was a place like this in Bentmont.

The smell was becoming nauseating. He would have preferred the stench of stale beer and piss in one of the city's common taverns, but his stay would be short enough. He moved past doorways with curtains drawn, and private booths where patrons enjoyed a proper drink, as well as herb and tobacco from their pipes.

He searched about the room from end to end, and quickly grew frustrated. It seemed a stupid idea to come here looking for a knight, but just as Tylar turned to leave, a familiar silhouette appeared in the corner of his eye. The smoky haze had cleared long enough for him to see Conrak, sitting in a booth against the far wall. He had a wooden pipe between his teeth and a book in one hand. He exhaled a thick cloud of smoke, then promptly disappeared behind the fog.

Tylar strode over to the booth and dropped himself down onto its red velvet cushions. Conrak lowered his book and grinned in surprise.

"Bradshaw! What in the heavens are you doing here? Or better yet, how did you manage to find me here? This isn't the sort of establishment I would expect the likes of you to frequent."

"I don't." He immediately eyed a frothing tankard at the center of the table, flanked by a small silver plate of dates, and an open canister of tobacco. "Only been here once, and it wasn't for long. I figured it would be the perfect place to find a twat like you. And here you are. I never took you for much of a book reader."

"As a matter of fact I am!" Conrak exclaimed, closing his book and setting it down. "It's important to keep one's mind sharp."

"And what does a man like you care to read? Hm? Histories of the Order?" Tylar again glanced at Conrak's drink, unable to mask his thirst.

The Elite reached for his refreshment, but paused. "Finish it. I haven't the stomach for more ale. As to your question, I prefer to indulge in philosophy mostly. I know more of the histories than I care to remember. I often think about the nature of our world, of life, and what this existence means. But I suspect you'd care little for such a lesson."

Tylar guzzled down the tankard, setting it down with a soft thump. "As a matter of fact, I would. But not about whatever's in your little book. I need to get the truth out of you, and don't bullshit me. You seem to be leading me on, and the girl as well. What do you know that you're not telling us?"

Conrak picked up his pipe and tapped out the remaining tobacco inside it, then placed it in a small wooden box. "The truth is actually quite mundane, Bradshaw. I was the closest Elite to Mor Seveht when your warrant was issued. I was authorized to bring back your head, but I thought it better to see you swing from a rope for your betrayal. And the book I left you was a mere parting gift, so you would better understand what you walked away from before you died. No motive, no plan. It simply is what it is."

He rose from the booth and smoothed out the length of his black tunic. Tylar looked at him incredulously, expecting a far different answer. But the man was no liar, or at least seemed as such, given his frightening capabilities.

Lies are the tools of cowards, and as much as I'd like to pound his smug face into pulp, he's no liar.

There was an uneasy feeling lurking in the depths of Tylar's heart, a feeling which he could no longer ignore. As his thoughts raced to make sense of it, Conrak was beginning to slip into the haze of the lounging room. He stood in a hurry, his knees slamming against the edge of the table. With a grunt, he gave chase, straining to see through the blurry fog.

"You're wasting your time, Bradshaw. I have no revelations for you, truly I—"

"What do you know about the Eveldanyr?"

Conrak spun around in a near instant, clutched Titan by the shoulders and shoved him into an adjacent room. After checking both ways, he threw a pair of curtains closed.

"Where in the world did you hear that name? Tell me, and speak true."

"The girl told me to ask you." Tylar tugged at the collar of his cloak, loosening it a bit. "I have no fucking idea what it means."

Conrak's face was enough to confirm the strange feeling still rumbling throughout his insides. It was the look of foreboding and perhaps fear, though most certainly it was that of worry.

"Alright, look," Conrak cleared his throat. "We can discuss this further, but not here. And I'm going to need some time to—"

"There's no better time than now. But I'm willing to wait until tomorrow. Provided you stay true to your word."

"Very well. But do yourself a favor and keep that big mouth of yours shut. Do not even think about uttering that word anywhere, do you understand me? I'll have your tongue if you do."

Having come to an agreement, Conrak disappeared into the haze once again. Tylar felt a chill biting at the back of his neck, and uneasiness he had seldom experienced. A fresh tankard of ale was in order, even though his pockets were still empty. He moved to the bar, leaned against its smooth and ornate surface, and cast a menacing glare at the barkeep.

"Can I… help you?"

"How about a pint for one of the King's men? Protecting Prince Gareth and defending the kingdom is a thirsty business, after all." Tylar grinned, his scars twisting and folding.

The scrawny bartender received his message well enough, and wasted little time in pouring out a frothy mug from a cask of house ale. He set the drink down with a smile, though it was the smile of a coward. Tylar gave a nod and headed back to the corner where Conrak had sat, plopping himself down onto a cushioned seat.

He stared long and hard at the foam inside his mug, a million thoughts fighting themselves for supremacy. It seemed there were forces at work within the world, forces greater than a single man or even an army of them. Such things made Tylar feel unsettled, nearly to the point of fear. It was never easy to admit one's destiny was in the hands of something which could neither be seen nor touched. Nor killed. With a sigh, he drank down half the mug, the amber ale inside both smooth and refreshing.

Just when I thought my life couldn't get any fucking crazier. What have I gotten myself into?

GARETH V

THROUGH DARKNESS AND LIGHT HE RODE, DESPERATE TO CROSS every mile between himself and Cardale. It was a journey which most certainly would have killed a lesser beast, but his Plainhold Strider was impressive in its endurance. Would it be possible to make a week-long trek in half the time? Gareth was determined to find out.

The barren roads were long and lonely, and as empty as his heart. It was likely news of his mother's death had spread throughout all of Betanthia, and every citizen of the Kingdom had already flocked to the capital. Gareth prayed he was not too late. The thought was too distressing to even comprehend.

I failed you, mother. I wasn't there for you when it mattered most. Please, let me make it in time to say goodbye, at least.

He sat hunched over a small fire off the road, his weary Strider grazing nearby. The moon was little more than a sliver, sitting delicately among an ocean of constellations. Perhaps Queen Charlotte was in the heavens somewhere. Perhaps one of the many billions of twinkling orbs of light was actually her, looking down from the endless plain of eternity. It was a comforting thought, but not nearly as comforting as being in her presence once more.

A skin of wine helped to ease his agony, its warm embrace all too familiar. Gareth drank until his stomach began to relent, the drink's comfort quickly turning to torment. He laid next to the waning flames, sobbing, begging his mother to come back.

"Please, mother… don't leave me. I'm sorry I wasted so much time in despair. I should have been a better son and a better prince, and not become so lost. I hate myself for it. There's so many things you never got to see because of me. You never got to see me marry, and give you grandchildren. You never got to see me ascend to the throne. You… never…"

An avalanche of distress began to break him. Gareth shot up onto all fours, his stomach heaving and churning, wine suddenly erupting from within him. His vision blurred and went to black for a short while, replaced with an empty, dreamless void. A few hours passed before his Strider began to stir, rousing him awake.

Thirsting for water, Gareth rose and stumbled to his horse, removing a skin and drinking it nearly dry. Dawn had not yet arrived, but there was light enough to resume his journey. After packing up his makeshift camp, he continued onward down the highway, solely focused on the task at hand.

Day and night came and went, as did the following day. His pace was grueling beyond comprehension, and was beginning to break him. Even his Strider was beginning to show signs of fatigue, though its resilience was impressive enough. Betanthia's rural landscape was bleak and changed little, but thankfully civilization was never more than a few hours away. Gareth opted to stay on the road, however, as a warm bed inside an inn might entice him to sleep an entire day away.

No, I cannot afford the risk. Even an extra hour of rest might mean I arrive an hour too late.

That night, he made camp under the stars, a small cook fire crackling away into embers. His quest had been a lonesome one, but such isolation was a lifelong companion. Another old friend was the sweet taste of wine, though he would have preferred whiskey. Still, one drink was just as good as the other, but the skin was nearly empty.

As Gareth went to douse the remains of the fire, he heard a faint clopping of horse hooves in the distance. They were coming from the west, the same direction he had traveled. Cautiously, he gathered his silver sword and kept it close, ready to answer any potential treachery with steel. A mysterious rider drew closer, the moon at first revealing only a shadowy silhouette. Squinting and straining, Gareth began to make out features most familiar, until he rose in astonishment.

"Edmund!?" he shouted incredulously. Sure enough, it was the elder Guardsman, his best friend. "How? Why? I thought you were staying behind?"

"Did you really think I was going to let you ride all the way back by yourself? The Order must have given you one hell of a horse, I thought I would have caught you the day you left. Don't worry, lad, Lord Kenfield and Tylar are keeping a close eye on things for us. There's no way in hell I—"

Unable to control his emotions, Gareth stood and shambled over to his friend. Edmund dismounted in a hurry, his own discomfort evidenced by a labored gait. They embraced each other, though it was the most unhappy embrace of all. Gareth felt a slight tremble building within Edmund's chest, his fingers clenching tighter and tighter.

Were it not for the two other Guardsmen who emerged from the darkness, they might have completely lost themselves to despair. Gareth himself was too grief-stricken to think clearly, but he knew well-enough to maintain composure around the men. It had become more of an instinct than anything, his months of rigorous training propping him up appropriately.

"Thank you for coming," Gareth whispered, discreetly wiping his eyes. "I can't believe this has happened, Edmund. And why now? Now, at the worst possible moment?"

"Most people cannot choose the moment of their passing. And when that moment might be, not even the wisest can tell. But for soldiers, for men like us, that moment could arrive at any time. It's something you have to make peace with, or else it'll drive you mad. But there's also a great freedom that comes with not living in fear of death."

It was a sentiment Gareth had come to know well. There were many moments during his training where death or bodily harm seemed imminent. When staring down the point of a sword or lance, there were times when events of his life suddenly played out before him. He had never put much stock in the idea before, seeing one's entire existence flash before them. Not until the first time it happened.

"You're right," he said. "You've always had this way of cutting through the darkness in my head and making things clear."

"Aye, but soon enough you won't need my old parables and rants anymore. You'll be telling your own sons about the things you've experienced."

Gareth sighed, fighting to rebuild his emotional defenses. "I only wish my mother could have lived to see such a thing. I wasted so many years of my life not knowing who I was. I could have had it all, Edmund. A family of my own. A legacy. I feel like I let her down. If I weren't so lost, perhaps I could have helped make certain these last few years weren't as terrible for her."

"Ah, but you did," Edmund squeezed his shoulder. "In the end, you helped set her free. And a bird flying free thinks not of its old cage, only the open skies before it. Wherever your mother is now, trust that she is flying, and looking down on you with pride."

With a forlorn smile, Gareth nodded and returned to his makeshift campsite, too exhausted to remain awake. Edmund, however, would not let him off without at least sharing a drink. Together, they toasted the memory of Betanthia's most beloved queen, then drifted off to a brief slumber underneath the stars.

By the following morning, their exhaustion was becoming insurmountable. As Gareth nearly slipped from his saddle and into unconsciousness, a familiar landscape presented itself. He had seen the rolling hills and lush trees once before, on the way to Bentmont. Gareth sat up straight, sniffing at an all too familiar scent of salty water and fresh fish as it danced on a warm breeze. The crisp, refreshing air also brought with it a faint chiming of bells, soft at first, but growing with each passing second.

"You smell that?" Edmund inhaled the aroma. "We made it."

Like an emerging sunrise, the peaks of the Westwind Citadel came into view, jutting up into the sky, nearly piercing a cover of fluffy white clouds above. He was home, but the ringing of golden bells was the most joyless of welcomings.

"But are we too late?" he asked. "I don't know if I could live with myself if I missed my chance to say goodbye."

"Then let's see what that Blackthorn mount of yours can do."

Edmund roared and cracked the reins violently, his horse taking off at speed. Gareth slammed a heel into the side of his Strider, the beast wailing as it broke out into a full gallop. Both animals jockeyed for supremacy as they raced toward the outer walls of Cardale. Its gates sat open, and what appeared to be the last of a long procession was filing inside. He prayed there was still time.

A handful of guards took notice of his approach and stepped forward to offer a challenge. Gareth brought his Strider to a halt just outside their post. "Is it… am I too late?" he asked, breathless, fumbling with the clasp on his weathered brown cloak.

A watchman gave him a curious look. "Sir, you cannot come into the city mounted. There is a procession that—"

He was interrupted by another, more senior looking officer. "Silence, you oaf. Do you know who you're talking to?"

Gareth's exhausted fingers were able to free the clasp, his dingy cloak fluttering to the ground. Beneath the garment was revealed a purple surcoat and deep blue tunic, finely stitched and adorned with silver trim. The watchmen immediately fell to one knee, having come to recognize their prince.

"We need to get to the temple, and fast," Sir Edmund said impatiently.

"We are happy to serve, Your Highness. If I'm not mistaken, the service has not yet begun. The bells are still chiming. We'll get you to the square straight away."

The watchmen abandoned their posts and retreated inside, fetching their horses from a nearby hitching post. Together, they thundered through the streets of Cardale, screaming for the common folk to make way. But the further they rode, the greater the congestion became. Thousands of citizens were becoming so bottlenecked it became impossible to ride any further.

"This way, my prince!" a watchman hollered.

They detoured down an alleyway, barely large enough for a horse to fit through, then down another. After a winding series of turns, they managed to emerge just outside of the city square. Gareth had never seen so many people gathered in one place in all of his life. Tens of thousands of commoners were packed shoulder to shoulder, with barely an inch between them.

The Temple of Dawn was ringed by hundreds of city watchmen, themselves bolstered by a heavy presence of the Royal Guardsmen. Even from such a distance, Gareth could see the body of his mother, lying peacefully on an altar, surrounded by red roses. A priest in a flowing robe of silver linen stood behind her, hands folded and eyes closed in prayer.

"We're not too late." Gareth exhaled, but reaching the temple was another matter entirely. Edmund opened the clasp on his cloak and waved the purple fabric overhead in hopes of alerting the Guardsmen.

"Come on lads, come on," Sir Edmund said through clenched teeth.

By some miracle, the vigilant guardians of the Citadel took notice, and a detachment of some fifty swords formed up and pushed forward.

The sea of rabble was parted, though it was by no means a simple affair. The Guardsmen resorted to shoving on more than one occasion, but the masses took notice of their objective, Gareth and Edmund having drawn their share of attention. Silence filled the square as the common man looked upon their prince, their eyes as sad and remorseful as his own.

"My prince," a Captain of the Guardsmen said, bowing. They formed a protective ring around Gareth and Sir Edmund, their shields locked into an impenetrable barrier. "Please, right this way."

All eyes were upon him, riding tall with columns of purple cloaks on either side. Gareth Bethard rode to the steps of the temple like a returning king, but the occasion was anything but celebratory. He took notice of Trace and Esma, standing behind the Queen's body. They too were watching his arrival in astonishment, though Lucetta's expression was vacant. Looking upon his siblings brought with it a rush of resentment and anger, as well as regret. Gareth was the oldest of three, but in many ways he felt like a lesser child to them all.

He recalled their last moment together with the Queen, and how terribly it had all ended. It was regrettable to have Charlotte's final day with all of her children go so horribly wrong, but he was thankful to be an important part of the closing chapter of her life. In Dellhaven she found peace, and were it not for him, such a thing would not have been possible.

The city watchmen surged forward as they neared the temple, creating a safe perimeter to dismount. Gareth climbed down from his mount, careful to mask a sharp, searing pain in his body. This was a time to be strong, both inside and out. His people were looking upon their future king, after all. Gareth was led past the defensive perimeter and up the stairs, Sir Edmund close behind.

You have to show them you can be strong. You have to show them all the stories about you were false. You have to. You can do this.

He was greeted with a bow from the high priest, who then retreated back several paces. Charlotte Bethard was garbed in the most elegant purple dress he had ever seen, accented with golden trim. Her hair was loose and slightly curled, but perhaps the most striking observation was how lifelike she appeared. Charlotte's skin still looked flush and warm, and alive.

For a fleeting moment, Gareth thought she might have been sleeping, but his eyes betrayed him little. The Queen was truly dead, but the priests had made an astounding effort in making her appear every bit as beautiful as she was in life. It was a small consolation, perhaps the smallest one of all.

"Welcome, my prince," the high priest said softly. "My deepest condolences to you and your family."

"Have I missed the service?" he asked softly.

"Only the opening prayers, my prince. Worry not."

The priest turned and addressed the gathered masses, thanking them for paying their respects to the matriarch of House Bethard. His words seemed as distant as Bentmont, however beautiful they might have been. Gareth instead looked upon his mother, jealously holding onto every last moment.

There had never been a time in his life where he felt more empty, which, up until now, seemed impossible. He could feel the grief of Trace, Esma, and Sir Edmund all around him, like heat radiating from a torch. He glanced to the side, watching as a single tear slipped down his brother's jowls. Esma's face was shrouded by a black veil of lace, though her grief was able to pierce through it.

Gareth tightened his jaw, fighting to not weep at the sight of their despair. He turned and glanced at Lucetta, standing beside Aldred, her reaction more bewildering than anything. She seemed distant, and not particularly invested in what was taking place. Instead, she appeared to be lost in a daydream, or listening intently to a conversation which none could hear.

It was a sickening and disrespectful sight, given the occasion. Gareth wanted nothing more than to grab Lucetta by the shoulders and shake the daylights out of her. This was their mother, the woman who saw them into the world. She was at least owed the courtesy of her children's attention, he thought. But in the end, Gareth knew better than to create such a spectacle in front of the cityfolk.

How could you be so distant at a time like this? Do you care about nothing except your own selfish interests? Mother doesn't deserve this, not from you or from anyone.

"Good citizens of Cardale," the high priest said, arms raised to the heavens. "I ask you to bow your heads, and offer your final respects to our most beloved queen, Charlotte Bethard."

Gareth had been so lost in thought, he had missed much of the eloquent service. The demons which continued to lurk in dark corners of his mind and heart were winning, stealing his attention away when it was needed most. After cursing himself, Gareth lowered his head as the bells of the temple began to chime once more.

I'm sorry, mother. I'm sorry I couldn't put my petty grievances with my siblings aside for one day. Please, forgive me. I'm so lost without you.

As the bells tolled one final time, the square began to empty. The good people of Cardale somberly returned to their daily routines, though some lingered. A few of the wealthier nobles who had known the Queen in life looked on, grief pouring from their eyes. With a nod of his head, the high priest and his brethren delicately lifted the wooden table off the altar, and carried Charlotte Bethard into the temple.

"I would like a moment alone with her," Gareth said to his siblings. "Please."

Trace nodded, while Lucetta answered only with silence. Esma was kind enough to offer a loving embrace, her arms shaking from bereavement. It was a kind gesture, and Gareth held her lovingly for a moment, fighting back his sorrow.

"I won't be long," he said, rubbing Esma on the shoulder before heading inside the temple.

Charlotte was laid out on another altar at the center of the chamber. A group of priests and guards bowed in reverence, first to mother, then to son, before departing. The doors to the temple were clapped shut, leaving only Gareth and the Queen inside. It was quiet, save for a few distant murmurings outside. Incense smoke and a gentle aroma of flowers lingered pleasantly in the air. Hundreds of bouquets surrounded the platform, so colorful they appeared like an endless field of wildflowers.

Slowly, Gareth approached the altar, his legs turning to water. It felt as if he was walking through a nightmare, beautiful though the scenery was. It was a reminder of times long ago, when he was young and frightened of the dark. Gareth would run into his mother's chamber at night seeking comfort, and would find her sleeping just as peacefully.

"It's lovely," he said, glancing around. "Colorful flowers, incense… quite lovely indeed."

He reached down and touched Charlotte's hand. While her skin looked warm and flowing with life, it was as cold as a Dellhaven winter. Gareth pulled back his hand, shocked and saddened by what he already knew. Charlotte Bethard was gone, regardless of the lies his eyes were telling.

"I'm sorry I wasn't there for you when you needed me most. I only hope I didn't let you down. I hope… I was able to make you proud."

As he teetered on the edge of despair, another memory came drifting back. It just so happened to be the last time they saw each other, at the Westwind Citadel. When Charlotte learned of his intention to ride west and lead the war effort, she might well have forbidden it. But when she looked upon Gareth, bearded and burly, she saw him not only as a son, but as a king.

A soft breeze blew through an open window high above the ground, rustling dozens of large, purple banners which ran to the floor. While he could feel the cool kiss of the wind, not a single candle flickered in its presence.

"Is that you, mother? Are you reminding me of something?" He smiled. "I know you would never want me to give up, in anything I do. That's why I'm going back west to lead the army. And I swear to you, right here and now, that I will make good on my promise. I *will* return alive, and in one piece. And not only that, I'll put an end to this threat and restore peace to Betanthia. You can count on me to keep our family's legacy alive."

He sighed, knowing time was growing short. Soon enough the army would be on the march, and he had to regroup with them before it was too late. But he hesitated, as this would be the last moment he would ever lay eyes on his mother. By dusk, she would be laid to rest in the family tomb, never to see the light of day again. Gareth leaned down and placed a delicate kiss on her forehead.

"Goodbye, mother. Thank you for everything. Thank you for being a guiding light in my life. I'll make certain that every sacrifice you made for this family will not have been in vain. I'll make you proud. And I'll never let that light inside you, which you passed onto me, die."

With grim determination, Gareth Bethard gathered his wavering emotions and locked them away deep inside. The time for mourning was over, and now would be a time for strength. Betanthia and House Bethard would need it, if they were to weather the storm which was quickly descending from the north.

Each step toward the doors was as exhausting as riding from Bentmont. Gareth's inner child was crying and begging for more time, refusing to be torn away from Charlotte so soon. But there would never be enough time, and each moment spent in mourning would put her legacy further in jeopardy. It was necessary. It was what she would have wanted.

The square was nearly empty now, save for the Guardsmen and city watch. His siblings were waiting nearby, Sir Edmund off to the side and discussing matters with his men. Trace appeared eager to speak, though merely thinking about conversation was enough to exhaust Gareth's weary mind even further.

"Thank you for being here," Trace said, wiping his red and swollen eyes. "It would have meant the world to her to have all of us here."

"I would rather be thrown into a thousand pitched battles than be in Cardale under these circumstances," he replied, sighing deeply. "I cannot believe she's gone."

Esma reached out and touched him on the arm. "You're very brave for riding to war. I want you to know how proud the family is of you."

Proud. The word itself was enough to twist Gareth into knots. Rarely had anyone in House Bethard said such a thing, aside from Charlotte, of course. He felt a slight quiver in his cheeks, a misty haze filling in the corners of each eye.

"Thank you, Esma. I know I should stay, but I'm needed back in Bentmont. The army could be marching at any moment, and I have to be there. For all of us."

"Come now, brother," Trace said. "Surely you can stay the night. You look utterly exhausted. Please, it would mean a lot to all of us if you would stay. We were going to have a feast in mother's honor."

A good night's rest in a familiar bed certainly sounded enticing. Edmund would undoubtedly be grateful, given how weary he appeared. The Elder Guardsman nodded, letting him know a single night at home would be time well spent.

"Very well," Gareth said. "Perhaps we could feast before I leave tomorrow?"

It was curious to note how silent Lucetta had remained, and how dramatically her appearance had diminished. Had grief taken such a devastating toll so quickly, or was there another condition afflicting her? Gareth was tempted to inquire, but decided against it. This was neither the time nor place to risk stoking Lucetta's unpredictable temper.

"A fine idea, brother," Trace said. "I understand if you need time alone. We all process grief in our own way."

Time was a peculiar thing. There never seemed to be enough of it when it was needed most. But a night in Cardale would not be the worst thing, he supposed. It was only proper for all of the Bethard siblings to come together, just this once, to give thanks and reflect on the life of the woman who brought each of them into the world.

"Let's go home," Gareth said, staring longingly at the towering peaks of the Westwind Citadel. "Together, as mother would have wanted it."

As they made to leave, Sir Tristan Conway approached, the bulbous Lord Lawson keeping his distance. Both were clad in the finest silks, and laden with jewels. Gareth had barely noticed the councilmen in his grief, and supposed they had made to offer their condolences.

"My deepest sympathies for your loss," Sir Tristan said, bowing deeply. "We are all shocked and saddened by the passing of your mother. Truly, Betanthia will never be the same without her."

"You have my thanks for your kindness," Gareth said, studying the young councilman intently.

It was curious to note how timid the typically boisterous Lord Lawson appeared. His meaty fingers fumbled with one another, an occasional glance shooting over Gareth's shoulder.

"The council wishes to assure you that we will continue to work diligently in your absence." Tristan smiled. "The King has expressed his approval for your fortitude during this trying time, and we all stand firmly behind you."

A lie, to be certain. The only thing Marcellus Bethard could express was his desire for more women and more wine. Were Gareth's senses not already heightened, he might very well have taken the young councilman's simpering as genuine. But no, something about the exchange felt unnatural. He glanced over his shoulder and saw Aldred staring back, cold and stony as ever.

"How kind of you to put my family's interests so high above your own," Gareth said. "I trust the Citadel will be in good hands until I return."

As he walked away, Gareth felt their gazes upon him. Were Sir Tristan's words a veiled threat in some manner? Would he return from besting Damien Dreadfire and Lord Vakaro only to see the banners of House Eldon flying from the Citadel? It was certainly a possibility, given how unpredictable life had become as of late.

Let them try to steal my throne while I'm away. Perhaps I'll send them to an early grave, to face my mother in the next life. Heavens help them if I do.

EINARR V

I T WAS A LONG AND RESTLESS NIGHT, AS NIGHTS OFTEN WERE. EINARR rose before dawn, passing the time in his favorite chair. Thinking was an activity he was doing far too much of these days, each thought gnawing at him like an insect burrowing into a tree. Every vision, every dream, every instinct was leading toward the same conclusion.

He took a long look around the homestead, studying every detail. There was not an inch of space where Alina's ghost did not lurk. Her presence was everywhere, and only grew stronger with each passing day. Einarr's mind drifted back to the previous year, and his time with the warband. All he could think of was returning home and being close to his love once again, and to feel close to her loving essence.

But the more time that passed, the more foreign Skaginlef began to feel. Familiar sights and familiar routines became nearly suffocating. The battlefield and all of its terrible wonder seemed more like home than home itself. Something about the fight, about steel and spear, death and glory, felt more exhilarating than a lover's touch.

With the rising of the sun came a stark realization, something he would have been terrified to admit even a week ago. Skaginlef was not the place he was meant to be. While peace was the desire for any man, Einarr began to wonder if now was simply not his time to enjoy such a luxury.

Every path I've walked, every decision I've made, has led me to this point for a reason. I cannot ignore that. For better or worse, I was meant to join Damien. I was meant to do the things I've done. I cannot waver now.

Perhaps it was what Alina was trying to tell him all along. The ghostly visions were not without a purpose, it seemed. A quiet life of fishing and farming was not what the gods had planned for him, at least, not yet. There were great works to be done.

Einarr hastily gathered his weapons and armor, and whatever provisions his horse could carry. It was strange to feel his unyielding homesickness fade away, as if Alina's spirit had vanished and taken memories of love and better days with her. He stepped outside and shut the door without daring to look back. Nell was tending to her garden and took notice, and curiously ventured over while he prepared his horse for the journey ahead.

"Where are you going? You're not leaving, are you? After everything you said?"

It would have been easy to lash out at Nell, with all of her constant antagonizing. But she meant well, and was undeserving of such harshness. Einarr nodded and sighed. "Yes, I am. I intend to rejoin Damien and see our people safely home. And besides, I don't belong here."

"But you do belong! The elders listened to you. The village listened to you. Our boys went through the rites of passage you decided on, and became men. You have to lead them now, you have to show them the way forward."

"Such a task is better suited for greater men." He tightened down straps on the saddlebags, securing them in place. "There are plenty here who can teach them what it means to be a man of the Nothanek. My place is out there, at least for now. The gods chose me for this time, and for this task. I must return to the fight, and see it through to whatever end."

When he turned, the eyes of the village were upon him. So many had turned out that it was difficult to distinguish between them all.

They stood silent, likely in disbelief, though their uncertainty was plain enough for anyone to see.

"Well, this is a sight," Selbjorn said, looking cross. "You must forgive me, son of Rolff, but I am confused. To my eyes, it would appear you are leaving. We were not expecting your departure so soon."

"Your eyes betray you not," he sighed. "I owe you my thanks for the trust you and the other elders have instilled in me, but I must be leaving now."

"Please, explain." Selbjorn spread his hands. "Explain to your people why you leave so suddenly? Surely a fortnight would suffice. We have barely spoken on these matters between us."

"I understand your reservations, but in my bones I know I cannot stay. Every hour is precious, and I dare not linger any longer."

"Then who will protect our village in your absence?" the elder asked. "What are we to do if the wolves of Betanthia come baying for our blood? You were so passionate to beseech the war god, but you make no plans for what comes after?"

These were questions he had asked himself many times before, though a proper answer was always fleeting. Einarr was uncertain of how to respond, knowing any explanation he gave would be met with scrutiny.

"Skaginlef survived while I was away, and will continue to do so. There are men here who fought alongside me on the campaign. They have seen not only how Betanthia fights, but how our northern kin do as well. I would trust my life to any man who bled with me on the battlefield last year, and you should too. Seek their knowledge. It will serve you well."

It was an unsatisfactory answer, as anticipated. Einarr's words did little to assuage the villager's worries, but it was surprising to see how many truly cared. After being shunned all winter, the people of Skaginlef were now hesitant to see him leave.

"You are a complicated man, Einarr Rolffson," Selbjorn sighed. "Far be it from any man to deny you your freedom. The gods have spoken to you plainly, after all. If you believe this is the way, then so be it. May Kholdyr protect you, and Azldyr guide your sword."

Slowly the villagers began to disperse, some glancing back over their shoulders. Nell stood firm, staring down at the ground, fiddling with her fingers. It would have been easy to disregard her worry, but it was a wonder why she even cared in the first place.

"Why are you sad, Nell?" Einarr cocked his head.

"This war has claimed many good men, and many still fight," she said, gaze averted. "I don't want yet another good man to die."

"The gods have shown me many things since returning. They would not do so if my destiny was to die in battle, I know that now. Have faith, as I do again. Have faith we will all return home."

Without hesitation, he climbed into the saddle and set off at a gallop, leaving the serenity of Skaginlef behind. A year prior, returning from war and to a normal life was the only thing his soul craved. But alas, the fates held something different in store for Einarr Rolffson. He saw apprehension on the faces of the Nothanek, a stark contrast to their utter contempt upon returning home.

It was difficult to know where to track down the warband, but perhaps answers might be found in Khorrtal. For days he traveled west, riding from dusk till dawn. On the third day, a group of ominous, looming pines near the heart of the Hinterwood appeared, their shadowy silhouette blocking out the setting sun. Einarr's pulse quickened at the sight of it.

He feared to venture any further into the forest, knowing what lay ahead. Blackwolf Pass would not be far, and taking it would cut days off the journey. But memories of the battle still haunted his mind, so vivid he could hear the rattling of steel and wails of dying men even now, the stench of their demise still fresh in his nostrils.

I can still make it without taking the Pass. Gods, guide me true. See me to Khorrtal without bringing me back to that accursed place.

Einarr spent the night under a cathedral of pines, nestled near a fallen log. A soft chirping of crickets serenaded him off to a restful sleep. He awoke several times to the biting of mosquitoes, and after being roused a third time, he decided to continue onward. There was magic to be found in the forest, to be certain, though the rainy season always made the insects unbearable.

By the fourth day, the scenery was becoming disturbingly familiar. Einarr had traveled through the Hinterwood enough times to know its major landmarks; certain hills and unnaturally large trees which pimpled the forest. He had taken care to stay south, away from the one place he wished to avoid. Every course correction seemed to put him closer to Blackwolf Pass, curiously enough. It was if the gods were compelling him back to that dreadful place, their reason however uncertain.

That evening, the energy throughout the forest suddenly shifted. No longer could Einarr hear the chirping of birds nor the scurrying of furry things. Utter silence befell the Hinterwood, an unnatural silence one might find inside a tomb. Something about the trees felt menacing, as if their will had been turned against him.

The mouth of Blackwolf Pass lay just ahead, its mere sight inviting terror back into his heart. Einarr looked on in utter disbelief as he scanned the site of the massacre. He took note of where the cavalry sat, himself alongside Damien Dreadfire on that fateful day.

"Gods, why have you brought me here? What purpose does this serve?"

The forest looked much the same as it did the year prior; green and alive, its trees bursting with leaves. He saw the remains of horses, their bones picked clean and bleached by the sun. Next to them were skeletons of their former riders. All of their clothing and effects were long since pillaged, with no evidence remaining of who they once were. But Einarr remembered.

His horse reared and whinnied, itself knowing well-enough to stay clear. He dismounted and took hold of the reins, compelling the beast to follow. It offered surprisingly little resistance, as if somehow calmed by an invisible hand.

"Alright Kholdyr, I'm listening, and watching. What lessons do you have for me to learn?"

Blackwolf Pass had become an open burial pit, just as Damien had left it. Einarr stood dumbfounded at the sight of tens of thousands of bones, blanketing the ground so heavily it became impossible to venture further. Unsettling memories of that day played out before his eyes, the ghosts of friend and foe alike reunited for another battle to the death.

Frantic memories manifested into a hazy vision, where he could see the battle unfolding all over again. There was something different about its outcome, however. He watched as the last of the warband was cut to shreds, a victorious Cedric Valens standing tall atop a pile of northern corpses. He thrust his ornate sword into the air, the blade washed with warm blood. It was the outcome Einarr had feared most that day, but the fates had decided otherwise.

No... we won the battle. Us, not them!

A cold wind rippled through the pass, stirring the trees and turning his skin to ice in an instant. Ghosts of the victorious Betanthians ceased their revelry and turned slowly, their eyes focused solely on him. Cedric Valens lifted a cold, bony finger and pointed, as if to loose the undead army for a final kill.

Einarr felt his heart come to a swift halt as specters of his enemies looked on, their lifeless eyes burning deep into his soul. Hastily, he jumped into the saddle and galloped back in the other direction, desperate to flee. It was the greatest fright of his life, far more dark and disturbing than the visions he had witnessed back home.

Despite retreating in the opposite direction, Einarr miraculously arrived once again at the mouth of the pass. Some foul magic was afoot, keeping him locked in the grip of the killing grounds. He drew steel and hefted his blade overhead, seeking to challenge whatever force was lurking in the forest.

"Whoever you are, whatever you are, know that you face Einarr, son of Rolff, and the gods are with me! Do you hear? The gods are with me!"

As if awakening from a dream, Einarr suddenly found himself back in the heart of the Hinterwood, and far from Blackwolf Pass. Days, in fact, judging by his position. The experience left him shaken, yet strangely unafraid. It was curious and unsettling how real the vision was. In a way, it seemed more real than reality itself, much the same as what the gods had shown him in Skaginlef.

Nudging his horse gently, Einarr set off once again toward Khorrtal. Perhaps there, he would find not only the location of Damien, but answers to many haunting questions as well. With the rush of fear beginning to subside, he took notice of a pair of glowing orbs in the distance, like two eyes reflecting faint light. They sat nestled between a pair of tall trees, silent and watchful, and unflinching, like a great cat sizing up its prey.

MADELYN IV

A FIERCE BANGING AT THE FRONT DOOR ROUSED TITAN FROM HIS sleep, the noise filling the building from floor to ceiling. Madelyn shot awake and saw an outline of his hulking body race from his room and downstairs in a flash. She sat up, gasping and terror-stricken, nearly unable to breathe. Had she slept through the war? Had the northmen destroyed Betanthia's army, descended on Bentmont, and arrived to reclaim her? Such an irrational thought seemed to be the only logical conclusion.

I'll never let them take me, never! I cannot! I will not!

A soft rumbling of deep male voices echoed upstairs, followed by heavy footsteps. Madelyn pulled herself out of bed, every aching muscle searing with pain. She searched frantically for a blade, or any manner of weapon, but found none. Fighting a gang of barbarians in such shape, with no sword in hand, was not an option. The only possible alternative would be to throw herself from the window, and deprive them of their satisfaction.

As she turned to make her final escape, a familiar voice broke her from a downward spiral of madness.

"Madelyn," Tylar said, stepping into the room. "Everything alright? You look like you're about to piss yourself."

A droplet of water slid down her nose and dripped onto the floor. It was not a tear. No, her eyes were dry. It was perspiration, a sort of anxious reaction she was not accustomed to. It was the most supremely frustrating sensation, one which dredged up feelings of sadness, anger, and uselessness.

"There's somewhere we need to go." Tylar marched to the wardrobe and opened the doors. "Come, get some clothes on."

"No," she protested. "I can't go anywhere. Please, not like this."

Stepping into the room was Conrak, who had been lurking just outside. He wore a hooded cloak and clothes which seemed beneath him, the sort of garb a commoner might wear.

"This is important," the Elite said gravely. "I believe a chain of events has been put into motion, one of which we are mere observers. Get dressed, Lady Everly. We cannot discuss such matters here. I've summoned a carriage to take us to our destination."

There was something unsettling about the man, though not in the way one would find barbarians unsettling. It was easy to fear uncivilized men, men of steel and fire, who rode on wings of death. But Conrak was another matter entirely. He was the sort of man who could know the exact hour of your death and look you in the eye and smile, content in such knowledge.

With the assistance of Jann and Wilka, Madelyn dressed in a modest linen gown, her hair braided and hidden beneath a dark shawl. The garment was not to her liking, but dressing in her usual corset and leggings was too difficult to manage. She supposed it was for the better, as it would allow her to remain as inconspicuous as possible.

Stepping outside was another challenge altogether. The sun was blinding, so bright and overwhelming it pained her steely-blue eyes to open. Thankfully, Tylar took notice and assisted her into the waiting carriage. It was both upsetting and depressing to notice how exhausted she had become already. The only thing Madelyn craved now was to return to bed and sleep the day away.

They rode through lesser traveled streets of Bentmont, though these days, every street was more congested than usual. Thankfully, there was anonymity to be found among the masses, especially with tensions so high. The many soldiers who gathered from across the south seemed more interested in the local taverns, brothels, and jousting lists as a way to keep their minds off the impending march north.

Soon, the Ivornorium came into view, its dome nearly blinding under the ferocious sun. She became confused, wondering why a man such as Conrak would be taking her to a place better suited for scholars and old men like Willard. Their carriage rumbled into the courtyard, past the ornate fountain where birds had only recently returned.

Seeing the old Chronican again sent nervous shakes throughout her body. It was difficult to have anyone from her past look upon her in such a condition. After all, the High Marshal welcomed her home with discharge papers and a callous disregard for what the northmen had done. Would Willard forsake her in the same way?

"What are we doing here?" she asked, fingers toying with each other.

"Not a word, not until we're inside." Conrak replied sternly. "Then, all will be revealed."

They came to an abrupt stop, the horses whinnying. The driver dismounted and assisted Madelyn out, her body aching with every movement. For his service, Conrak produced a small pouch of silver, then whispered a few words into the driver's ear. Both men nodded in whatever understanding they had reached.

Conrak scanned the area briefly, searching for unfriendly eyes. Once satisfied, he motioned for Madelyn and Tylar to follow. He approached the Ivornorium's massive wooden doors and rapped its iron handle several times. It felt as if hours had passed before there was any response, but eventually, one of the doors cracked open, the old Chronican struggling to push it.

"Sir Conrak!" Willard's frail voice was more raspy than usual. "Come in, come in. Quickly now."

Madelyn stood huddled behind Titan, his hulking frame keeping her from Willard's sight. A nauseating tightness grew inside her chest, slowly squeezing every breath from her lungs. She stood motionless for a moment, contemplating an escape. But it was of little use, Tylar had already entered, and now all three men were staring at her.

"Maddie?" Willard squinted. "Is that you? Why, yes! You've returned home!"

It was relieving to know the old man took no notice of her diminished state, and cared only for seeing her again. It made the crippling tension throughout her body ease, and allowed her to enter the Ivornorium without succumbing to panic.

"What's going on here, Willard?" she asked, eyeing him suspiciously. "How do you know Conrak?"

He glanced uneasily at the Elite, who himself held up a hand and nodded.

"It's alright, Willard," Conrak said, "I'll explain. Come, there's much to discuss, and time is certainly not in abundant supply."

Madelyn had wandered through the Ivornorium more times than she could count, but this time seemed strangely different. Something about the ancient library felt just as cold and uninviting as Castle Thorn. But thankfully, the old library was empty, save for the four of them.

"How best do I explain this to you?" Conrak's pace slowed as he let out a deep sigh. "When Bradshaw and I concluded our most recent discussion, he mentioned a name which I have not heard spoken aloud in ages. The Eveldanyr."

Merely mentioning the word brought back a tidal wave of emotions and memories, though all were tinged by the horrors of her tribulation.

"Now," he continued, "do either of you care to tell me how you came by this name?"

"I was held captive by the northmen after Morden fell," Madelyn said reluctantly. "Their leader, a vile, cruel, beast of a man, claimed I was a descendent of the Eveldanyr. At first I thought little of his boast, until this... this old witch he keeps at his side..."

She began to shiver again, eyes growing moist and sorrowful.

"I see," Conrak stroked his short, gray-speckled beard. "Mystics are powerful beings, and the fact he has one makes our situation all the more dire. I'm a very direct man, as I'm sure Bradshaw has told you. So let me say this, everything the barbarian said about the Eveldanyr is likely true. They existed, and were every bit as powerful as he claimed."

Together they arrived at the far side of the Ivornorium, then turned right down a short corridor. They entered another smaller room with large bookshelves lined against the walls, and several reading tables at its center. Conrak moved toward a shelf near the far corner, gesturing for them to follow.

"And how exactly do you know all of this?" Titan inquired. "You some kind of historian? I thought only old men and eunuchs dabbled in such things."

"I'm a guardian of forgotten knowledge." Conrak pressed his shoulder against the end of a bookshelf and pushed, a click-clacking sound filling the room. "The last of my kind, in all likelihood. The last of an order within the Order, you might say."

The bookshelf gave way and slid open, revealing a darkened staircase behind it. A cool air escaped from inside, though it smelled stale and uninviting. Madelyn could only wonder what horrors might await in the black unknown, but thankfully Tylar's presence helped to stifle her fear.

"Are... are you sure this is wise?" Willard protested. "We are not at liberty to discuss such matters with—"

"With who, Willard?" Madelyn's heart began to race, her vision blurring for a moment. "Me? You've known me since I was a child! I was a Commander in the Order! And now you treat me as if I were some loose-lipped drunkard in a tavern?"

"N…no, Maddie, it's… not so simple…"

"Willard," Conrak interrupted. "Be still. They know of the Eveldanyr. In fact, you're looking at one, if what they've told me is indeed true."

He pointed not at Tylar, but at Madelyn. The old man's eyes grew wide with an uncharacteristic fear. It was the first time she had ever seen him look such a way, having always been a kind and cheerful soul.

"He is right, though," the Elite continued. "What I'm about to show you could get all four of us killed on the spot. So, let me make myself abundantly clear." He paused and scanned their faces, pointing a stern finger in their direction. "If either of you speak so much as a word of what you're about to see, I'll kill you. Even on your best days, I could kill both of you at the same time with ease, and you know it."

Tylar's lack of response made the boast seem all the more ominous. She had known many knights throughout the years, and from experience, it was the quiet ones who were the most dangerous. But there was something particularly menacing and bone-chilling about a man who could not only make such claims openly, but also silence the meanest, most violent person in the room.

"You have my word," she said. "Does the Order know about this? Or, the High Marshal, at least?"

"The High Marshal, yes. But that, I believe, is where it ends. The Order you know, the Order you've served for your entire life, is built on a foundation of lies. Each lie is its own separate stone. Over the centuries, they've been stacked atop one another until it grew into a fortress of deceit. And now, everyone forgets the individual lies and sees only what they have grown into."

Surely, Conrak must have been speaking about a different Order, Madelyn thought. How could the most noble and selfless organization, dedicated to protecting the people of Betanthia, be built on lies? She had to know more, though not without a small measure of uncertainty. Conrak motioned for an oil lantern at the center of one of the tables, and Willard toddled over with it in hand.

"Follow me, and mind your footing. We are about to descend into one of the oldest parts of the building. It's built around a cave, once used to worship the gods. To some, this is one of the most sacred places in Caldakas."

They descended a spiral staircase, its stones faded and dingy. Madelyn held tightly onto Titan's tree trunk for an arm as they slowly made their way to the bottom. Once there, they were greeted by pitch blackness, the air as dry as a desert. Conrak's lantern pierced the darkness, and as he brought light to sconce after sconce, the breadth of the sanctuary came into view.

"Here is where Betanthia's true history is kept, where all of our darkest secrets live eternal. What you see around you is ancient, some of it written a thousand years ago, or more."

Sitting on crude stone tables and old wooden bookshelves were scores of chests, large jars, and heavy leather-bound books wrapped with linen. Together, the documents numbered in the hundreds, likely thousands. Conrak set his lantern on a large stone slab at the center of the cave, likely used as an altar at one time.

"Willard has spent his life translating these documents, to the best of his ability, as did his predecessors. Some of what you see chronicles the founding of the Order, others the traditions of the northmen. Yet others are sacred texts, which speak of powers so great and terrible that even after all this time, it still makes me shiver."

It seemed odd for a collection of the Order's historical documents to be littered with tales from the north. Madelyn furrowed her brow, uncertain of what to make of it.

"The truth is," Conrak continued, "the Blackthorn was not founded as some sort of mercenary force or border guard. No, it was founded by northmen, ancestors of the very men we find ourselves in conflict with now."

A deep guffaw filled the cave. It was one of the few times she had ever seen Titan Bradshaw legitimately laughing, perhaps the only time.

"You're so full of shit," Titan said. "A horde of bloodthirsty tree-fuckers founded the Order? You've either gone mad, or have been this whole time."

"I'm serious." Conrak's brow furrowed. "They were originally adventurers, called Sanvalldin, who came down from the north seeking plunder. When they saw the expanse of Bentmont and what Betanthians could build, they were in awe. Even more so when they came to Cardale. They soon pledged themselves to the service of King Leopold, in return for riches beyond their imagination."

Conrak scanned the shelves, searching for a tome he had been referencing. After throwing back linens on several books, he found the correct one, and set it down on the altar.

"They brought with them not only their superior fighting skills, but knowledge of the untamed north. They told tales of the King of the Eveldanyr and their otherworldly abilities, and how they could not only commune with the gods, but also channel some of their power. Leopold knew he would not be able to conquer the north with the Eveldanyr standing in his way, so he devised a plan."

The old book crackled as it opened, its spine dry and worn. Conrak flipped about half of its dusty pages over, then a few more, before jamming a finger down onto one.

"The Sanvalldin were sent back home to share their newfound fortunes, and return to Cardale with those seeking riches of their own. One fateful night, after much drinking and feasting, they killed the Eveldanyr in their sleep, stole their sacred texts, and fled. For their efforts, King Leopold gave them the city of Bentmont as their own, and an unending supply of treasure, so long as they remained loyal. The Order you serve was founded by kinslayers."

It was a revelation so shocking, Madelyn could hardly believe it. She glanced down at the book and saw a colorful drawing, depicting the night the Eveldanyr were murdered.

"Nothing surprises me about the Blackthorn," Titan grumbled. "But what are you still doing serving them, if you know all this?"

"Throughout the years, this knowledge has been passed down to a chosen few within the Order. We're known as the Sacrithon, and our mission is to keep the truth alive. And that's because the truth matters, Bradshaw, unpleasant as it may be. But the gods are not without a sense of justice, it seems. The last of the Eveldanyr is here."

"So, what the fuck are we supposed to do now?" Titan crossed his arms. "March into Thorn and stab the High Marshal in his face? Now, don't get me wrong, that sounds pretty fucking entertaining, but…"

There was a sudden searing, piercing sensation in the center of Madelyn's head. It felt as if her skull was splitting apart from inside. The conversation seemed to fade into nothingness as a deep rumbling sound filled the cave, though none seemed to take notice. Small slivers of silver-blue light began to emanate from several of the texts, soft at first, but quickly becoming so bright it was nearly blinding to look at. She recoiled, eyes closed and hands clasping her ears, her senses overwhelmed.

"Is… is everything alright, Maddie?" Willard asked, stepping out from the stairway cautiously. He extended a hand toward her shoulder, but recoiled slightly.

"No…" she said. "I feel… ill…"

Titan held up his hand to silence Conrak, who was berating him for not taking matters more seriously. They stared incredulously, studying her strange, nearly debilitating reaction.

"What's going on with you?" Titan asked, moving to her side. "We need to get her some air."

"Wait." Conrak stepped between them, pushing Titan back a pace. "Tell me what's happening. Describe it."

The room was spinning and pulsating with an unfathomable energy, churning her stomach to the point of heaving. "It's… bright, so bright. Can't you see it?"

"Then it really is true, you are an Eveldanyr. You can feel the power of the texts, can you not? Your senses are awakening for the first time! These books are much more than parchment and ink, after all. They are a living, breathing conduit to the gods. This is how your ancestors honed their abilities. As painful as it may be, you need to stay and bathe yourself in its aura. Come, we need to leave at once!"

Conrak motioned for Tylar and Willard to follow, but both appeared hesitant. Despite their reservations, both men relented, and soon Madelyn found herself alone in the cave. It was nearly as difficult to breathe as it was to move, the sheer intensity of unknown energies pressing down on her like a giant weight. But the stress was too great to bear, and she stumbled onto the ground and lost consciousness.

Hours came and went, and it was impossible to tell how much time had passed. When she awoke, only darkness remained. But Madelyn saw perfectly, as if the cave had opened its ceiling and pure sunlight was shining down from above. She rubbed her eyes in awe, unable to make sense of such otherworldly wonderment.

Is this really happening, or am I still dreaming?

Hundreds of books scattered throughout the cave glowed like pure starlight. One in particular drew her attention, its aura not a silver-gray, but a warm, yellowish-white. Its cover appeared as rough as dry tree bark, the rot of centuries having exacted its toll. Delicately she removed the book from an old wooden shelf and set it on the altar, opening it with the greatest of care.

To her astonishment, its pages appeared to be moving, its ink swirling and coalescing, then scattering as if it were a living, breathing being. Pictures depicting scenes of glorious battles and mysterious rituals played themselves out on the page as they had thousands of years ago.

One of the depictions, a man clad in a wolf pelt and painted from head to toe, turned and stared directly into her eyes. In one arm he clutched a silver sword, a blue gem set in its crossguard. The blade seemed oddly familiar at first, but she was unable to place it. He raised a finger and pointed, appearing to reach out from beyond the parchment and toward her. The shock was so great that Madelyn stumbled backward, gasping and panicked, then fainted.

It was not until the next morning when they found her, sprawled out on the ground. Titan's shouting was enough to wake the dead, but he seemed to calm after seeing her sit up. Willard was nearly in tears, wringing his old, gnarled hands together.

"We never should have come here," Titan said, kneeling down. "Are you alright?"

The answer was a surprising yes. Madelyn was taken aback by how refreshed she felt, and how easy it was to stand. While not fully renewed by any stretch of the imagination, it was progress nevertheless.

"Yes, as a matter of fact." She looked down at her arms, studying them in disbelief, their strength beginning to return. "I haven't felt this rested in…"

It was difficult to describe just how different her body felt. Perhaps it was more of a spiritual rejuvenation, she thought. Regardless, the brief slumber seemed more refreshing than any she had experienced since arriving at Hok. Conrak stood at the entrance to the cave, nodding and smiling.

"This bodes well for us," he said, moving toward her. "However, I would caution you against speaking a word of this outside of here. I'll arrange for a driver to bring you back here whenever you're ready to learn more."

The thought of leaving the cave filled Madelyn with an overwhelming sadness. It felt as if she was being torn away from her family, even though she had never known her true parents. Somehow, the energy radiating from the texts had the same warm, familial feeling she had experienced throughout life with Corbyn, Hunter, and others.

"I think I might stay awhile longer," Madelyn said. "I don't know why, but I have to be here right now."

"Good!" Conrak smiled. "Far be it for me to pull you away at a time like this. Bradshaw and I have business to attend to, but we won't be far away. You've become my mission now, Madelyn Everly. The last of the Sacrithon, protecting the last of the Eveldanyr. The gods certainly know how to make themselves known, do they not? Our destinies, it seems, were written long ago."

Madelyn felt a comfort she had not experienced for more than a year. It was reassuring, albeit slightly unsettling, to feel the hands of the gods guiding her forward. She had never been a believer in a higher power, but there was little denying the obvious now.

"It certainly appears that way," she said. "I'll be awaiting your return. Willard, would you mind doing something for me?"

The old man came closer as Conrak and Tylar took their leave. His face was long and weary from an exhausting, sleepless night. "What can I do for you, my dear?"

"There's something I need to do, and I require your assistance." Madelyn paused, her mind harkening back to her first unforgettable experience. "When I was held prisoner, I was taken to a grove of trees and given a strange concoction to drink. Soon after, my mind began to… drift away, and I saw things. Strange things. Are you aware of any potions or tonics the northmen partake in?"

Willard rubbed his wrinkled chin and squinted. "Hmm… perhaps. To my knowledge, the northmen use a particular brew to commune with their ancestors, and perhaps even the gods. I do believe I have a translation of a recipe somewhere."

"If it's not a burden to you, would you be able to prepare some for me? If you can find the proper ingredients, of course."

"Why yes, Maddie." Willard said, though he appeared anything but happy. "Some of the ingredients might prove difficult to locate, but the Droethiens are known to hawk all manner of strange wares. Perhaps one of them has the items we seek. I'll send for them right away, as soon as I can find the proper recipe."

It would have been a lie to say she was not terrified of what she saw that day with Marvath, even though the ghostly presence there was comforting. Madelyn had been bombarded with an avalanche of life-altering information in such a short time that it was hard to wrap her mind around it.

How could she be anything other than a simple soldier? How could the events of her life lead to such strange and unbelievable places? The notion of an invisible hand guiding her every movement was unsettling, but also brought with it a small measure of comfort. If there truly were gods, which there most certainly appeared to be, then they would undoubtedly keep a watchful and protective eye over her.

Madelyn returned to the cave, eager to feel its intense energy soaking into her body. After only a few steps, she already began to feel lighter and more like the Commander of old. Painful throbbing of aching joints and the atrophy in her muscles felt a little less, but the road to recovery was still long, far too long for her liking.

She sat on the edge of the altar, its stone cool to the touch. A low humming vibration began building in between her ears, but it was far from unpleasant. It felt as if gentle hands were wrapped around her head, soothing away the aches and worries of a troubled mind. As horrors of the past year slowly began melting away, only silence and serenity remained.

Hours went by until Willard came toddling down the stairs, a steaming wooden mug shaking precariously in his hands. The smell was strong, and quite off-putting, even from where she stood. It immediately brought back memories to the grove where Marvath Bonesplitter had taken her.

"Was it prepared according to the instructions?" Madelyn asked, her pulse quickening in anticipation.

"Yes, I followed the directions to the letter. Are you sure this is wise?" Willard slowly offered her the vessel, a few drops splashing against its lip.

Was it wise for me to ride west? Was it wise for me to stay at Morden? No, but I did it anyway.

She felt conflicted, but only for a moment. It was impossible to be harmed any more than she already had been, after all. The concoction tasted as foul as it smelled. Madelyn nearly spat out the first sip, but forced it down with a sour face. She drank again and again, swallowing quickly until nothing remained.

"Willard, I need to see the page the recipe was written on. The original one, not the translation. I need to feel the words for myself, if that makes any sense."

Fortunately, the Chronican knew exactly where to find it, though he was not without a healthy skepticism. He fumbled around a few old jars until coming across the desired parchment. It was dry and felt like it could crumble at any second, but already she could sense power emanating from it. Willard passed the page over slowly, careful not to damage it any further.

In a span of mere minutes, the potion began taking effect. Madelyn held the ancient parchment in her hand and studied it intently. Its words were already beginning to melt, then slither and congeal into a mass of black ink. It mattered little, as she could neither read nor pronounce any of the words correctly in the first place. Willard had spent his entire life among every text in the Ivornorium, and even he was baffled about how to speak the ancient tongue.

Forget it, I'll do this alone.

Sitting crossed legged on the cool ground, Madelyn shut her eyes and drew a deep breath, gripping the old page in both hands. All she saw was darkness. Even after everything she had seen, after witnessing Lazilyth's unsettling power, she still could not believe in the gods. At least, not fully. How could any divine being subject her to such cruelty? Still, the bizarre visions that day in the grove were real, and there was no other explanation.

Gods... I reach out to you now. Hear me, and answer my call. Come to me. Speak to me.

There was silence, save for the soft thumping of her heart, and an endless darkness from which she could see no light. Minute after minute passed by until they had accumulated into what felt like days. Still, there was no response.

Please, gods. Ancestors... Will any of you hear me?

The potion was taking hold, stronger and stronger, she could feel it. When all hope seemed to have been lost, there was a pinprick of light in the distance, small at first but growing quickly in size and intensity. Madelyn clenched her eyes tighter in surprise, but exhaled slowly and relaxed. The light grew larger and larger, until she felt warm rays caressing her soft skin.

Suddenly she felt separated from her body, as if her consciousness had become disconnected from time and space, from life and death itself. Madelyn could no longer sense any part of her physical body. Instead, she felt connected to a greater whole, an eternal energy that was one, but also many at the same time. It was unlike anything she had ever experienced, as if life was merely a dream and this was the true reality.

An infinite, pitch black sky hung overhead, penetrated by neither starlight nor moonlight. Below was a field of tall, soft grass, and a large and barren tree with many limbs. On the limbs were many branches, and on the branches were many twigs. Each twig held what seemed to be millions of tiny buds, though all appeared dormant.

Madelyn felt sadness, but it was difficult to understand why. She watched from her formless essence as the tree stood motionless and in solitude. A single tear fell from her eye like rain from a stormcloud. It spattered onto the earth and was lapped up by the tree's ancient roots, themselves thick and gnarled.

In the space of a second, the tree suddenly sprang to life, its buds bursting forth with bright leaves of every color. A swift gale blew from out of nowhere, shaking its branches and rustling the leaves and tall grass, their song sounding like millions of faint whispers. A brown acorn fell and plopped onto the ground, then melted away until it disappeared entirely.

A lone root wiggled from the loose soil, piquing her curiosity. As Madelyn's essence drifted closer, the root exploded forth, thick as a rope, wrapping itself around her with lightning speed. There was an immense pressure which gripped her spirit tightly, as if being squeezed by a serpent.

Let me go! No, please! Leave me be!

The root slowly began dragging her into the ground, besting any attempt to break free. Madelyn disappeared into darkness, and felt only warmth from the earth and a deep, beating pulse emanating from the tree. Millions of tiny tendrils began embedding themselves in every fiber of her being, leaving nothing unmolested.

Searing pain and sheer terror drove her toward escape, but the entanglement was unbreakable. Madelyn fought until there was no energy left, her essence diminishing like spent candles. Moments before succumbing to oblivion, the earth began to rumble from underneath, then from all around. The root began pushing her upward, faster and faster. She felt wet dirt and small stones rubbing against her pristine skin.

I have a body? Wait… yes, yes I do! I remember now!

A sudden eruption blasted Madelyn to the surface, her naked body landing with a thud. She had been born anew, not only from within but also from without. The agony of her tribulation and the scars it left behind had been wiped clean.

I'm… I'm whole again! Oh gods, this must truly be your work. I've never felt so alive!

Standing beside the massive tree was a figure in black, the same slender and shapely figure which had plagued her dreams as of late. A cold, blue eye peeked from behind a chin-length lock of black hair. The figure then thrust a gloved finger, pointing directly at her. Madelyn felt a jolt of panic, and was blinded by an explosion of white light.

When the brightness faded, she found herself back inside the cave. The warm serenity of the realm beyond realms had faded as well, and she felt an unusual calmness in its wake. Something about the cave seemed black and hazy, but as Madelyn blinked, the murk began to diminish.

"Your… eyes…" Willard croaked, drawing a hand up to his mouth. Terror-stricken, he fled upstairs as fast as his old legs would allow.

Standing proved remarkably effortless, and walking even more so. Perhaps her otherworldly transformation was more than just spiritual, she thought. Or, with her spirit renewed, her body could simply be following suit. Knowing the full truth of the matter would be impossible, and there was precious little time to seek it out.

As she made to leave the cave, something beckoned her to remain. It was the sensation of being watched, of eyes silently studying every movement. Frightened though she was, Madelyn turned and glanced around the cave, and saw in the black distance a single point of blue light, cold and ever watching.

LUCETTA VI

S HE LOOKED UPON THE FACADE OF THE WESTWIND CITADEL, A SUDDEN queasiness twisting her bowels into knots. Lucetta Eldon could hardly believe she had agreed to come back to this place. She would have preferred being carted off to the family crypt as opposed to spending another moment inside. At least, not until she became the sole resident of the palace.

It was only proper, she thought, to hold a feast in celebration of Charlotte Bethard's life. The Queen made many sacrifices throughout her years and deserved nothing less in return. As Lucetta crossed through the courtyard, she took notice of an unusual stillness all around. Even the Guardsmen, so eager and diligent in their duties, seemed as lifeless as her mother.

When she entered, she was amazed at how vacant the great hall was. The palace was always bustling with servants and visitors, and conversation was never in short supply. But not today. Today, there was only a painful silence. Even the air was thick with grief, as if the Citadel itself was in mourning.

She set off toward the banquet hall, eager to get the feast underway. A pair of servants moved large platters of roasted meat and fresh vegetables from the kitchens. They paused as Lucetta approached, eyes falling to the floor somberly.

"Welcome back, my princess. You have our deepest condolences."

"And you have my thanks," she said. "A terrible time for the realm, indeed."

Muffled voices drifted out from the banquet hall. Lucetta craned her head curiously, straining to identify who was speaking.

"Your brothers are awaiting your presence, princess," one of the servants said.

If only you could see and hear their pain, mother. Then you would know you were truly loved.

When she entered, the conversation quickly died. The remnants of House Bethard were seated around a large dining table, absent its patriarch. What King Marcellus was doing in his chamber was a mystery, but it was likely the same routine of drinking and degeneracy as it was on any other day.

Trace raised his wine glass. "How proud mother would be to see us all gathered here once again, like in the days of our youth. It truly is good to see you all here."

A servant pulled out a chair, and she was seated. Lucetta instinctively reached for a wine glass and gulped it down. Being in such close proximity to Gareth was akin to having fingernails torn out one by one. He was beginning to look more like Marcellus by the day, albeit a younger, less disgusting version.

They certainly share the same thirst, those miserable drunkards.

"Yes, indeed," Lucetta said, feigning a smile. "How splendid it is to be here again, but I do regret the circumstances."

Platters of food were brought out, nearly a dozen at once. Each course smelled absolutely divine. It was enough to rouse her hunger for the first time in ages, but the idea of eating felt torturous. Her stomach had likely shrunken into nothingness by now, she supposed.

"Before we begin this feast," Trace said, "I would like to raise a toast to our dear mother and queen. May her memory and deeds live on forever in the hearts of every Betanthian, and may we continue her legacy of kindness and charity."

Together, the Bethard siblings drank, Esma and Aldred keeping their silence. They were family by marriage, not by blood, and knew well enough to allow Charlotte's children their moment together.

Servants began expertly placing generous helpings of seared lamb with potatoes and fresh greens onto their plates. It was a favorite dish of the family, and quite fitting for it to be served first. Lucetta could hardly contain her hunger, and immediately began gobbling down one mouthful after another.

The taste was enough to make her want to cry. Almost instantly, her stomach pain and queasiness disappeared. She washed it down with a few sips of fine wine, smiling contently. Both brothers followed suit, digging into their meals with little regard for formality.

"And how good it is to see you, brother," Trace said. "Truly, you have been missed. Esma and I do hope you stay awhile longer. Perhaps one more day?"

"I cannot." Gareth looked up from his plate. "I'm afraid I must be leaving within the hour. I have to be back in Bentmont when the army breaks camp."

It was curious to know where Gareth had acquired his newfound courage, though Lucetta suspected it was merely a front. While starting a conflict at the table would be distasteful given the occasion, the temptation to do a little prodding was irresistible.

"I never took you for a general," she said, smiling. "What made you decide to take up the sword, dear brother?"

"Duty," he answered. "Something I should have done long ago. It's what father did, before he was crippled. And it's what grandfather did as well, when he was a young man. Someone has to see the realm through this dark time."

Lucetta nearly exploded with laughter, but had learned to expertly control her emotions. While Gareth had grown both beard and muscle, he was still every bit the drunken boy he always was.

"I see." She picked at a few pieces of fresh broccoli. "I applaud your bravery, truly. Seeing such things would put fear into the heart of any man."

"I won't be a mere spectator, sister." Gareth straightened up in his seat. "I will be leading the men from the front, as father once did."

Trace and Lucetta nearly choked at the same time, the news most unexpected. They stared at each other incredulously, while Aldred guzzled down a nearly full chalice of wine.

"Surely, you cannot be serious!" Trace protested. "Why… why would you—"

"Because it must be done!" Gareth's brow furrowed, the look of steel and fire in his eyes. "Because our enemies think us weak. They're everywhere, brother. And something must be done to put the fear of House Bethard back into those who would tear this kingdom to pieces. How can I do that without getting my hands dirty?"

Clearly, Gareth was boasting. At no point in his life did he ever display anything akin to courage or responsibility. Lucetta began scratching a scaly, red patch on her wrist, trying not to grin.

"Your brother is in good hands," Aldred said, clearing this throat. "Lord Vakaro is the finest military mind in Betanthia, and our forces will outclass anything the northmen send our way. Worry not."

Lucetta was reminded of a revelation the woman in black shared but a year ago. The entity said Gareth would not inherit the kingdom, she remembered it plainly enough. Perhaps this could be another piece of the grand puzzle. Perhaps he was destined to die in battle. Such a possibility was quite plausible, especially considering the woman in black's untarnished record of prognostication. If anything, Gareth needed further encouragement, in case the prophecy was indeed true.

"Well, I think it's a fantastic idea," she said, drawing confused stares from across the table. "This duty is rightfully yours as the first born. I for one wish you good fortune, as our fate is directly tied to your success." With a snap of her fingers, fresh wine was poured out by the servants. Lucetta raised a full glass and stood, smiling slyly. "To victory."

Both brothers stood and hoisted their glasses, toasting to Betanthia's victory. The three siblings drank their fill of wine, and continued with their celebration of Charlotte's life for the next hour. All Lucetta could think about was seeing Gareth's corpse on a battlefield, butchered and bled dry.

Imagining such a thing was difficult, because he was her eldest brother, after all. But Gareth was also an obstacle, a barrier standing in the way of a new queendom and immortality. Family or not, such a thing would simply not be allowed to pass.

I have spent my entire life yearning for this opportunity, while you squandered yours with drunkenness and self-pity. Why should I return to obscurity now? No, I will not. You had your chance, Gareth, but now is my time. Stay out of my way.

After the feast was concluded, Lucetta slipped out of the palace with little fanfare. Thankfully, Aldred was tied up with more council business, and offered no protest when she departed. It mattered little, as what she truly wanted was to be free of the Citadel and its dreary influence as quickly as possible.

Pavlos sat waiting on Auburn Row, not far from the palace gate. The Droethien appeared to be more loyal and dutiful than her own husband, though it was of little surprise. It was easy enough to purchase a common man's unwavering loyalty with a few pieces of gold, after all.

"There you are, princess!" he said, drawing back the hood of a plain brown cloak. "You wish to return to Dellhaven soon, yes?"

"Without delay," she sighed. "But perhaps we can leave in the morning, I've grown tired. You know this city well. Tell me, is there a suitable inn where we could spend the night? I have no desire to return to the estate."

Pavlos scratched his chin. "Why yes, there is such a place, princess, and not far from here."

Thankfully, Auburn Row was never short of carriage drivers looking to earn a few coins. Pavlos flagged down the first one he saw, then together they set off down the avenue. It was a poor mode of transport, with little more than a simple wooden bench to sit on. Its interior smelled strongly of body order and some other pungent stench, but thankfully it had an open window.

After only a short ride, the driver came to a halt. Pavlos was the first to disembark, and offered Lucetta a hand. Her gaunt body ached as she stood, the bench nearly bruising her tailbone. Such an extreme loss of weight was taking its toll, and had become more frustrating than anything. While the thought of food was still unsettling, she resolved to force it down whenever possible.

The inn was a travesty by her standards, but to the common man it might seem a paradise. Lucetta spent the rest of the day in a third floor suite overlooking Cardale's wealthy merchant district. Fear kept her locked away until dusk, and fear brought with it another restless night.

It was disconcerting to realize how comfortable she had become with sleep deprivation. The sensations inside her head were unlike anything she had ever experienced, especially when paired with a wine of sufficient vintage. It was the one thing she could stomach without issue, and so Lucetta drank until the new day arrived.

Cardale was abuzz with activity that morning, strange considering how somber the day prior had been. It sounded as if life had returned to normal in the capital, the clopping of horse hooves on cobbled streets and faint murmurings of the common folk growing louder as the sun rose.

A servant girl knocked on the door and announced breakfast. She set a tray of some unsavory gruel on a desk and made a hasty retreat. Pavlos had made it clear to the innkeep that Lucetta was to be spoken to only when necessary, and briefly if it was deemed so. The food smelled worse than it looked, which made wanting to eat all the more difficult.

Where is Pavlos? We need to get out of this wretched city at once. I have a queendom to build.

Another hour passed before the sound of heavy footfalls echoed outside her door. Pavlos rapped gently several times to announce his arrival. When the Droethien entered, Lucetta noticed there was something unusual about him. Gone was his customary smile and arrogant swagger. He glanced toward the window, and an insufferable racket outside which was building in intensity.

"Is everything alright, Pavlos?" she asked, heart racing. "There sure seems to be a lot of chatter out there. What in the world is going on?"

"Princess." Pavlos cleared his throat. "How do I say this? The people, they speak of your mother. I have heard this, just this morning."

"And tell me, what do they say? Do they remember her as fondly as I'm told?"

"Em… princess." The Droethien pursed his lips and sighed. "At the funeral, the people could not help but notice the immaculate state your mother was in. There was no corruption to be found, yes? The people say it is a miracle! They say it is a sign from the gods!"

The more she thought of it, the more disturbed she became. Charlotte did indeed look beautiful, and gave no indication she was even dead. But then again, the only corpses Lucetta had ever seen was a dead man on the bridge of the Camsby River one year ago, and charred remains in the northern barbarian village.

"Tell me, how… how should a body look after it's been… dead?"

"Pavlos will spare your appetite, my princess. A body will turn colors and begin to bloat, yes? Your mother should have shown signs of corruption by now, I believe."

"What does it mean, then?" she asked, holding her breath. "Do you believe what the people are saying?"

"It is difficult to say, princess. My people revere the old gods, and I have seen many signs of their presence before. But this, I must say, I believe it to be a sign."

"A sign? What sort of sign?" She felt her heart beginning to slam violently, the room growing intolerably hot in an instant. Pavlos remained silent, clearly unsettled by their conversation, much to her frustration.

Lucetta snatched up her cloak and pushed past him, eager to hear for herself what the peasants were saying firsthand. There were throngs of people flowing down the avenue, like a river during the rainy season. A score of city watchmen came rushing by, giving her a startle as she opened the door.

It was difficult to make out what the crowd was saying, but they were animated to the point of agitation. Stepping out into such chaos might prove treacherous, especially if they thought Charlotte to be a witch or some other dark entity. The last thing Lucetta wanted was a confrontation with a rabid mob, especially one filled with religious zealots. She turned and moved briskly toward the innkeeper's office, where another door led to an alleyway. Pavlos followed closely behind, shouting something to several of his men inside the lobby.

Together, they made their way into the alley, the Droethiens alert and scanning for potential threats. The mob's roaring was so thunderous it rattled her insides. Lucetta put a hand to her chest in an effort to protect her heart from heavy vibrations pulsating off the buildings.

"What on earth is going on here? Where are they headed?" she shouted, her throat burning.

"They are headed east, princess. Either to the temple or to the palace," Pavlos replied, moving around in front of her. "We must get you back inside, princess. It is not safe here. We cannot protect you against—"

"No!" she protested. "I must know where they're going and what they intend to do!"

Admittedly, the mercenary was correct. Being caught on the streets with a riled up mob was near suicidal, but a morbid curiosity compelled her onward.

"Very well, but Pavlos does not approve of this! We must remain out of sight, yes?"

She nodded. Cautiously they began heading east, maneuvering through alleys and side streets, shadowing the masses from afar. A sudden ringing of bells caused her heart to nearly explode. There was chaos brewing in Cardale, that much seemed certain.

Heavens… they're not going where I think they're going… are they?

Gradually, the cityscape was becoming more and more familiar. Just as Pavlos had surmised, the mob was indeed heading to one of two possible locations; the Temple of the Dawn. She saw tall spires poking over nearby rooftops, and as more of the ancient building presented itself, the furor of the people grew in intensity to match it.

She was awestruck by the sheer number of people. Thousands, perhaps even tens of thousands stood shoulder to shoulder, tightly packed inside the square. They were held at bay by several dozen city watchmen, spears lowered and shields locked, though their courage appeared to be wavering.

The protectors of Cardale were attempting to force the commoners back, shouting and cursing, and on occasion, thrusting a spear point at any who ventured too close. A detachment of reinforcements were attempting to make their way through the horde, but with little success. Lucetta had never seen such disorder in her entire life. She wondered if Aldred had been informed of the situation, and what he might do to help restore the peace.

"You must go," the woman in black said from inside her head, the entity shouldering through a group of peasants. "You must go and speak to the people. They must hear your voice."

"What do you want me to tell them?" she asked aloud.

"Whatever they wish to hear. This is an opportunity to put your name on the tongue of every man, woman, and child in the city. Come."

The woman in black's eyes flared with orange-red fire, small embers erupting and fading into the sky. It turned and began heading into the crowd, the peasants parting and taking hold of themselves as if a winter gale had swept through. Lucetta was awestruck to witness the effect the entity had on people other than herself, and began to shiver.

"Princess!" Pavlos called out, taking hold of her by the arm. "You must not! It is not safe!"

Inciting the wrath of the woman in black was more terrifying than any assault from a mob, she thought. Lucetta pulled away and continued on, giving the Droethien a fiery glare of her own. The mercenaries followed reluctantly, though ready to strike at any moment. Oddly enough, despite being immediately recognized by the commoners, none made so much as a more to accost her.

The city watchmen were equally as perplexed as Lucetta approached. They lowered their spears and allowed her through, but refused passage to any who dared to follow, save for Pavlos and his men. The square suddenly grew quiet, the citizens curiously anticipating what Lucetta might do or say next. Each step to the temple door brought back painful memories of her mother's funeral, but she remained stoic.

"Princess Lucetta?" a Captain of the city watchmen called out, standing near the entrance.

"What in the world is going on?" she asked, bewildered. "Why have all these people gathered here?"

"It's…" he glanced at the crowd, then back at her. "There's no easy way for me to say this, princess, so I'll just say it. They're here for your mother."

Lucetta cocked her head. "My mother? What could they possibly want with her? My mother is…"

"I know, but—"

A stranger stepped out from the crowd, making his way toward the watchmen. He was an older man who wore a robe of black and white linen emblazoned with strange runes, a long, stringy beard running the length of his torso. He approached the wall of spears, arms spread wide. The masses began to stir, but were quickly stifled by the unusual looking man. He walked onto the highest step the guards would allow, then turned and faced the people.

"Good citizens of Cardale! Behold, the daughter has come! She has come!"

"You there!" Lucetta called out. "Who are you, and what business do you have here?"

"My birth name belonged to a man who is now dead and reborn! My name bestowed by the gods is Hesgrin, and you may refer to me as such."

Emboldened by the crowd's growing fever, the old priest turned his back to Lucetta. With arms held aloft, he commanded an obedient silence, the people clamoring for his every word.

"The gods have returned to these lands, and they have given us a sign of their presence! We have been wicked in our ways, and they have taken our beloved queen from us. This is our punishment. But in their magnificence, they have left her body uncorrupted!"

Perspiration began to flood the inside of her gown. She had taken notice of Charlotte's remarkable condition, but thought little enough of it. Perhaps the undertakers had excelled in their craft and had managed to preserve her body far beyond expectations. It was difficult to be certain, as Lucetta had no knowledge of death outside of what her eyes had only recently witnessed.

"I'm grateful for your devotion to my mother," she said, "but it's time now for me to return her to the palace so she may—"

"You mustn't!" Hesgrin called out, looking aghast. "The Queen has been touched by the hands of the gods themselves! The people must be allowed to worship before her, and bear witness to this miracle! You cannot take her away!"

Such audacity made Lucetta's head feel light. Had her ears betrayed her? Could this mob of peasants truly be after the body of her mother? Such a demand was nearly as fantastical as it was revolting. Were it not for the growing horde of unwashed peasants surrounding them, Lucetta might very well have ordered Pavlos to put a spear through Hesgrin's guts.

"I can assure you," she said, "there will be a monument erected to my mother, where all may come to offer their respects and honor her memory. Please, return to your homes now. Go in peace, and with my gratitude. The Queen would truly be flattered by your unyielding affection for her."

More watchmen were flooding into the square by the minute, spears at the ready. Their numbers were enough to force Hesgrin's compliance, though his face bore reluctance. With the common folk looking on, the so-called holy man relented.

"You have not heard the last of me!" Hesgrin barked. "This travesty will not be permitted to stand! The Mother shall be exalted!"

The old priest took his leave without further incident, much to her relief. Lucetta let loose a deep sigh, thankful for the diligence of Cardale's protectors. Had they not arrived in force, there was no telling what sort of carnage might have unfolded.

I ought to paint the square red with their blood! The nerve of these filthy peasants, thinking they can lay claim to my mother's body?

Irritating as the situation was, she was reminded of her true objective, the one awaiting her return in the north. Lucetta would need only one final day in the capital, a day to take Charlotte's body home to the Westwind Citadel and to its ancient crypt. Moving the Queen right this moment would prove most unwise, she determined.

One more night in this accursed place. I say let the rabble do what they will with Cardale once I'm gone. The next time I return, it will be with an army at my back, and a crown upon my head!

406

TITAN VII

H E ARRIVED AT HALF PAST NOON, JUST AS THE SACRITHON HAD SAID. The building was a supply storage, one of countless many throughout Bentmont. This place, however, had not seen use in some time, judging by a healthy layer of dust throughout. Large wooden crates sat in rows, some stacked on top of each other. What these containers were used for was a mystery, but not one Tylar particularly cared to solve.

"About time you showed up," Conrak grinned, leaning against one of the crates.

"I'd have been here sooner if you didn't insist we split up on the way here," Tylar grumbled. "And why the fuck would you bring me to a dingy old place like this? Seems like a waste of time to me."

"Relax, Bradshaw. You're always so uppity."

And for good reason. The High Marshal's ire was upon not only himself, but Madelyn as well. Being pried away from her side for even a moment was a risk Tylar was reluctant to take, especially knowing her only protection was a feeble old man.

"Well then you better get to the point real fast," he demanded. "I'm not keen on leaving the girl alone."

"It's no accident that I brought you here." Conrak's eyes scanned the room in wonderment, though there was little to be enthralled about.

"You may see a dusty old building, sitting long forgotten. But the truth is, this is one of the most important sites in all of Caldakas."

The Sacrithon picked up a lantern, then motioned for Tylar to follow. They made their way past a workshop, its tools beginning to show rusty orange blemishes of time. At the far end was a series of smaller rooms, most of which were empty or contained items of little importance.

"Bentmont is an old city, Bradshaw. Far older than most are even aware of." He produced an old skeleton key and approached a small wooden door, its frame nearly a foot smaller than what was considered standard size. "I'm certain you've heard the tales of when the first Khorrish explorers came to Caldakas."

"I heard a few bedtime stories when I was young," Tylar sighed, disinterested.

"We all have." Conrak smiled, then opened the door. A faint stench of mildew wafted from the other side. "Come, there's something I need to show you. Be mindful of your footing."

After igniting the lantern, both men ducked down and stepped through the ancient door. On the other side was a small room, which appeared to have no practical use. A narrow passageway appeared in the flickering light, heading down into a dark unknown. While he was unafraid of dark places, Tylar felt an uneasiness beginning to take root in the depths of his heart.

"Many of the stories are true, Bradshaw. When the Khorrs first landed, they encountered no one. These lands were devoid of any human life, but that's where the stories typically end. What they don't tell you about… is what they discovered."

The passageway descended on for a short while, but then ended abruptly. Their path was obstructed by a wall of solid stone. Conrak approached it slowly, then placed a single hand on it. For a moment, Tylar thought he could sense the Sacrithon becoming emotional.

"So, why the fuck did you bring me down here?" he huffed. "There's nothing here."

"You couldn't be more wrong." Conrak held his lantern closer to the stone. In the dancing light, there appeared to be faint carvings in distinct shapes, most likely the work of mortal hands and not mother nature.

"You see, Bradshaw, there was something here before the Khorrs arrived, something older. But what, or who, no one knows. Some of the old texts in the Ivornorium tell of a circle of standing stones, right in this very location. Whether it was a shrine or a monument, or a gathering place, we'll never know."

If there was one thing Conrak excelled at besides fighting, it was telling a good story. Even though Tylar cared little for books and history, the tales were certainly enough to keep his attention. He found it oddly fascinating to know that on this very ground, thousands of years ago, men like him once stood.

"So, why is it buried beneath a shitty old warehouse then?" he asked, peering at the carvings in the stone. "If this place is so important, what's it doing in ruins?"

"From my understanding, the first Bethard kings pulled the whole thing down and buried it. They were determined to erase all potential threats to their legitimacy. We've all heard the stories of how House Bethard tamed these lands, bringing civilization and prosperity and all that. But the truth is… much different. I fear to speak it, even now. Even here, in this place where no one would ever find us."

It was most curious how a cocksure braggart could profess to feeling fear of any sort, especially in such a forgotten place. Perhaps there was truth to what he said. There was little reason for a man such as him to lie, after all.

"So, are you telling me those fucking barbarians are actually the just ones in all of this?" Tylar huffed. "I'll have a hard time believing you if you say yes. I've seen them do things to men that only rabid animals are capable of."

"Who is good? Who is evil?" Conrak shrugged. "These are questions only the gods have answers to. I've seen wicked men do great things, and great men do wicked things. All we can do is try to live with honor, and leave this world in a better place than we found it. And that's why I take my vow as a Sacrithon so seriously. And because of that, I would like to extend you an invitation to join me. The world needs men of conviction to stand tall and do what's right, and regardless of your insufferable attitude, you seem like just the sort of man for the task."

Tylar broke out into a fit of laughter, his guffaws echoing loudly throughout the passageway. At first, he thought Conrak was having a laugh at his expense, but a deadly serious look he received in reply said otherwise.

"You mean, you want me to join your little one man order?" he asked incredulously.

"I think it's been your destiny this entire time." Conrak grinned. "And even though you could care less about ancient truths and history, you're loyal to the one person who matters in all this; Madelyn. And that will do well enough. Perhaps one day I'll tell you more about the Bethards and the barbarians. If you want my opinion on the matter, ask me when the time is right."

Conrak peered once again at the ancient carvings, then closed his eyes and mouthed a silent prayer of sorts. He placed an outstretched hand on the stone once again, head bowed in reverence.

"If you think I'm going to go through some sort of fancy initiation, you're dead wrong." Tylar crossed his arms. "I don't have to prove shit to anyone, much less you. And I could care less about this musty cave and that old cruddy stone. Madelyn is my concern, not your old wives tales."

"Don't you see, Bradshaw? This *is* your initiation. You can fight well enough on your own, though I can teach you some of the more advanced techniques I know, if you so desire. But this place, the cave, the Eveldanyr… that's why the Sacrithon exist. If we don't preserve this knowledge, then who will?"

"What good is knowledge if nobody fucking knows it?" he grunted. "Why not just tell the world and let everyone decide the truth of it? Because if we're both killed fighting the northmen, then what? Your old Chronican friend doesn't have a whole lot of time left to pass on what he knows."

Conrak motioned back up the passageway, then took the lead. It was a relief to be heading out of such a cramped and unpleasant smelling place. After a brief walk, they ducked underneath the old door and closed it, the skeleton key once again shutting off its ancient secrets from the outside.

"Because the world isn't ready. But that time is nearly over. If Madelyn can realize her true power, then everything is about to change. She'll show us wonders, to be certain."

"And what about us?" Tylar furrowed his brow. "Will we be capable of doing the things she can?"

Conrak lowered his gaze with pursed lips. Despite his wealth of knowledge, he appeared regretful in a way. "No, Bradshaw. We can read the texts a thousand times, but we'll never be capable of the things she is. Madelyn has something we don't, and it's imperative we keep her safe and alive at all costs. *That's* our purpose, to serve something greater than ourselves."

It was the same sort of babble Tylar had heard many times in his youth, especially when joining the Blackthorn Knights. At first he believed in such sentiment, but the perilous, bloodsoaked years afterward made him doubt every word of it. But now, here in a dank, rat-infested shithole, he began to believe once again.

"My mind was already made up a while ago, Conrak. I would have died for the girl that day at Morden, and I'll die for her right now if I had to. I always knew she was more important than me, but I guess I never realized just how right I was."

"So, now you've come full circle. Are you ready to do what you were made for, and take up the mantle of the Sacrithon?"

It was one of the more surreal moments in Tylar Bradshaw's life, nearly rivaling the day Prince Gareth made him a member of the Royal Guardsmen. The past year had taken so many strange turns, some for the worse, but all leading to this moment in time. All he could do was marvel at yet another bizarre position he found himself in.

"If you expect me to kneel and swear a fancy oath or some other dumb shit, you can count me out. This knee bends for no man."

Conrak chuckled, then slapped him on the shoulder. "Fortunately for you, there's no ceremony or anything I'm aware of. Protect Madelyn. Protect the sacred sites. And protect the knowledge. This is what men like you and I have done for generations. If we do our part, and the gods have not forsaken us all, Madelyn will set things right. She will restore balance to these lands."

"Well, you're going to have to do your part when I'm unable to. I'm sworn to Prince Gareth, since he saved my ass from the gallows. Whatever he commands me to do, I'll do. Can't go betraying a man for saving your life."

"Fair enough." Conrak sighed. "An oath is an oath, especially one made to a prince. Seems you have a lot resting on your shoulders, Bradshaw. You know, you really ought to allow me to teach you a thing or two. I could serve you well."

The thought of clubbing Conrak senseless was beginning to cross Tylar's mind, as then it would leave little question as to his capabilities. "Teach me a thing or two?

"Hear me out. Do you remember the night on the Plainhold when we were ambushed? Do you remember how effortlessly I dispatched those Zylmacians? I could have fought twice as many and not broken a sweat."

Such a boast was one of the less impressive things he had ever heard. Tylar could remember a dozen battles in which he faced nearly insurmountable odds and came out on top. "I could kill twenty of those dogs at the same time with a fork. What could you possibly teach me that I don't know already?"

"Allow me to explain." Conrak drew in a deep breath, likely to keep his annoyance in check. "I'm not questioning your skill at arms, Bradshaw. All I'm offering is advice. I know you're a man who likes to fight angry. I've heard the stories. But all that roaring and snarling is going to tire you out. Focus on your breathing, and keep from talking or screaming unless absolutely necessary. Your endurance will last longer, and there's also something endlessly terrifying about fighting a man who remains silent."

"Alright," Tylar said, intrigued. "What else you got?"

"Use your opponent's momentum to your advantage. We're fighting northmen and Zylmacians. They fight with reckless abandon. It's quite easy to redirect their energy and use it against them. Keep your enemy focused in front of you for as long as you can. Deflect an incoming blow into another opponent. Use their bodies as shields. You can improvise in so many ways."

Tylar rolled his eyes. While it was sound advice, he would never admit it aloud. "Yeah, yeah. You can have all the plans you'd like, but when shit falls apart and you have another man's guts splattered all over you… plans matter little."

Conrak smiled and shook his head, then motioned for the door. Together they stepped back out into the streets of Bentmont, the old warehouse locked tightly behind them. So much had transpired in such little time it left Tylar's head spinning. He was beginning to realize his agitation was a suit of armor, a means of protection against the unknown elements in the world.

And from what Conrak had revealed, there appeared to be a good many things he still had yet to learn. Intriguing as the mysteries were, none of it would matter if Damien Dreadfire was successful in razing Betanthia to the ground. It was a fact Tylar Bradshaw was keenly aware of, perhaps more so than most.

"Speak nothing of what we discussed to anyone," Conrak said, his eyes scanning the streets ahead. "You and I can work on a few more tricks and tactics later. We best be getting back to the Ivornorium. There's work to be done."

ZANDER IV

A T DAYBREAK THEY ARRIVED, THE VILLAGE OUTSKIRTS JUST AHEAD. IT was yet another in a long list of settlements the warband had encountered, except something was different about this one. Instead of being greeted as liberators or welcomed by the ghostly emptiness of abandoned streets, they were met with spear and shield.

"They mean to fight," Marvath Bonesplitter grumbled.

A crude shield wall was forming across the main avenue, dozens of villagers frantically scattering behind them. A few warriors let out chuckles of amusement, knowing that such a force could not stand before the warband's might.

"Indeed," Damien said. "Kill those who resist, but spare those who do not. This village too shall become part of our domain. Go now, and make quick work of it."

The Rhivothi and Zylmacians were all too happy to oblige. They let loose rousing war cries and began forming ranks, eager to charge headlong into their hapless enemies. Many of the Nothanek, however, seemed uncertain. Putting a Betanthian army to the sword was one thing, subjugating a village and killing the men defending it was another.

Once in formation, Marvath gave a mighty blast from a large warhorn. The ravenous horde of warriors charged, the ground shaking like a great earthquake. Some of the village soldiers broke ranks and fled, but most stood their ground courageously. The Rhivothi crashed headlong into the shieldwall, their massive, lumbering bodies pushing it back effortlessly.

Zander watched as his Zylmacian kin changed course and began circling around to the side, content to find another avenue. They were met with little resistance, and began flooding into the unprotected square. Women shrieked in terror, corralling their children and attempting to find sanctuary. Many were caught out in the open and set upon with beastlike ferocity. They were given the courtesy of the axe, and left to die in the dirt streets like dogs.

Hearing sounds of slaughter taking place behind them, the men of the shield wall quickly lost heart. The skirmish immediately descended into a full blown rout as they fled to save their families. Zander watched from afar as a massacre unfolded, chuckling softly to himself. While he would have contented himself with a bit of bloodshed, it would be better to let the Zylmacians satisfy their pent up frustrations.

A few dead cannibals was a small price to pay, and the investment was beginning to return interest. Their savagery was breathtaking to behold, and all resistance was obliterated in short order. Zander had never seen his kinsmen fight with such unadulterated hatred before, a sight which left him awestruck.

A wildman pounced on top of a defenseless villager, raining down blow after blow from a one-handed axe. The man's head was little more than soup by the time the Zylmacian lost interest, his bloodlust not yet sated. A pair of bald fanatics were dragging a woman into a hovel, laughing and taunting as she cried out in terror.

The sights and sounds of death and glory played like sweet music. While this was not the army of Marcellus Bethard, these were enemies nevertheless, fit only to be butchered. Zander could barely contain his excitement, and wanted nothing more than to join in the slaughter and earn a bit of glory for himself.

His desires were cut short by another blast from Bonesplitter's horn. Damien Dreadfire decided the village had seen enough, and signaled an end to the attack. However, controlling wildmen when their blood was up was often an exercise in futility. But Zander decided to make a show of it, riding at speed down the red-stained street. He shouted and cursed those who had not relented, rearing his horse and threatening the lash if they refused to comply.

"Enough! This village is under our domain now. The killing is over! Come now, mates, take what you can, while you can!"

The Zylmacians under his command complied without incident, but those under Jollkud's banner were another matter entirely. It took a concerted effort to restrain many of them in their butchery, their rage for the loss of their brethren still an open wound. He dared not intrude on their axe-work, however. Not out of fear, but out of calculation.

Can't let them think I'm Dreadfire's lackey. Let them chop up a few villagers, it means nothing to me.

Sylvia Stormguard thundered down the road, her anger keeping pace. Behind came Damien and the other warchiefs, surveying the destruction up close. For having just won a decisive victory, they appeared none too pleased.

"Tell your men to stand down, Zander!" Arik Akselson barked. "Have you not heard the command?"

"Oh I have, mate." He grinned. "But these are Jollkud's men, and they thirst for retribution over the loss of their kin. These men are simply collecting their due payment. Would you deny them what's rightfully theirs?"

"One Bymist dog is no different than the rest, it seems," Sylvia huffed.

Such constant prodding from the Rhivothi was becoming ever more insufferable, and a lesser man might very well rise to their bait. But Zander knew better. And besides, how could he possibly become cross with such a delectable woman? Sylvia's fiery agitation only served to make his appetite that much stronger, his mouth nearly watering at the sight of her.

"Be still, Stormguard," Damien Dreadfire said. "This village chose to stand defiant against us. For their loyalty to King Bethard, they shall pay the blood price."

"My lord!" Arik protested. "These people are beaten and have surrendered. Do we not owe them their lives for submitting?"

Dreadfire's black eyes scanned across the village, cold and emotionless. Neither the sight of headless men nor butchered women drew the slightest reaction, aside from what Zander suspected was disgust.

"Conquered people are owed nothing." Damien grumbled.

Those within earshot sounded their approval, then set about ransacking every hovel in sight. It was a rush the likes of which he had not experienced for ages. Battling armies and sacking castles was an adventure, to be certain, but there was something indescribably satisfying about putting a village to the torch.

The first house he entered contained only basic accommodations. A small hearth sat against the far wall, a simple table and pair of chairs at the center of the room. Zander poked around but found nothing of interest. In an adjacent room there was little more than a straw bed and a small wardrobe. There was a curious absence of gold and jewels, or even usable steel for that matter.

For Betanthians, this sure is pitiful.

Zander had always pictured the Kingdom as a place where wealth was in abundance, a land of plenty, even for the destitute. But what he had seen, yet again, was little more than squalor. Some homes were certainly better than others, but the village seemed to be a modest place, for people of modest means. Hardly worth his effort, he thought, especially after the glorious sacking of Hok.

He stepped outside and noticed a commotion echoing down the avenue. A woman was screeching something awful, enough to pique his curiosity. As Zander moved closer to the disturbance, he spied a local tavern, and hordes of Zylmacians pillaging their supply of mead and beer.

Casks were looted by the dozens, so many in fact there seemed to be no end to them. The tavernkeep's wife was a stocky woman, near to sixty, with yellow hair and with a voice so shrill it could make a man's head explode. She swiped at the wildmen, cursing and spitting, and screaming.

"What do you think you're doing, you bloody savage? Put that back! Put that back right now, I say! You damned beasts think you can just come here and steal my livelihood?"

She disappeared inside, her screams echoing out behind her. Chuckling, Zander made his way inside to witness the spectacle, and perhaps have himself a cask of Betanthian beer as well.

Wildmen filled the tavern from end to end, and even a score of Rhivothi as well. They laughed and boasted and drank their fill, much to the owner's dismay. The shrill woman's husband was set on his knees in a far corner, a large and expanding dark spot running down his leg. She, however, had not relented in her attempt to stop the ransacking of their stores.

"Who do you people think you are?" She spat and clawed at those close by. "Get out of my tavern! Get out right now, I say!"

"Why don't you shut your mouth already?" a burly Rhivothi muttered, his beard wet with mead droplets.

Laughter filled the room, though it set the woman to seething. She grabbed the only thing at hand, a wet linen rag, and tossed it at the near drunken warrior. "How dare you! You think you can come into my tavern, steal whatever you want, and insult me? I'll have your eyes out, you bastards!"

She again screeched in rage, and attempted to wrestle a cask away from a passing Zylmacian. Having seen enough, Zander drew a one-handed axe and shouldered past his brethren, the weapon hidden behind his back. When the irate woman was not able to reclaim her property, she instead searched for whatever else could be hurled at her unwelcome patrons.

"Excuse me," Zander grinned in amusement. "The men are trying to enjoy a drink. Do yourself a favor and shut that hole in your face."

For a moment, it appeared the woman's head might very well have ruptured from rage. Her face had turned from white to maroon, a deep scowl revealing teeth clenched tighter than fists. "If you don't get out of here right now, I swear I'll—"

With the swiftness of a falcon, Zander raised and brought his axe down, the blade biting deep into the bitch's head from eye to mouth. A loud crack was followed by a jet of blood, her body jerking and stumbling before collapsing in a heap.

"Well now, it looks like that hole in your face just got a bit bigger!"

His quip was met with hearty laughter and roars of approval. The barkeep, however, was beside himself with grief. Sobbing and screaming, he began crawling toward his slain wife, but was promptly hauled upright by a pair of wildmen.

"Zander!" one of the Zylmacians called out. "He looks thirsty. Perhaps a toast, for his fallen love?"

Still grinning, he nodded in anticipation. Several wildmen took hold of a medium sized cask and a funnel, then wrenched the man's mouth open. Its contents were poured down his throat by the gallon, though most found its way down his face. Coughing and choking, he thrashed about like a stuck pig before falling limp, his lungs filled to the brim.

The Rhivothi found the execution most amusing, much to Zander's surprise. It seemed the only thing which might bring their people closer together was an elaborate and grotesque killing. While it would be wise to maintain peace for the time being, he suspected it would spoil as quickly as milk under a hot sun.

As he made to leave, Zander heard a gurgling sound coming from the tavernkeep's wife. It was surprising the old bitch was still alive, given how deep the axe was planted in her skull. She lay on one side, a pool of blood growing ever larger. Perhaps it was simply a death rattle, he thought. Even a man as hearty as Bonesplitter could not survive such a grievous wound.

"Well now!" Zander said, kneeling down beside her. "Still alive, eh? Well, probably not for much longer. Look at you now. You seriously thought you could stop us, after what we did to your men? Ha! Betanthian arrogance knows no bounds, it seems."

Smiling, Zander wrenched his axe free, a waterfall of blood running across the floor. He took up a mug of beer, one of many being passed freely around, and drank it on the way back outside. It was quiet now in the streets, save for heavy footfalls of thousands of men. The full weight of the warband had marched into town, eager to secure a perimeter and set camp for the evening.

If the tavern's stores were any indication, then the village would most certainly have an abundance of food. The thought of fresh meat roasting over a roaring fire set his mouth to watering. But before Zander could venture off in search of food, he was approached by a young Nothanek.

The only thing these fisher folk are good for is delivering messages, it seems.

"What is it now?" he asked in annoyance. "Can't you let a man enjoy his drink in peace?"

"A thousand pardons, but Damien wishes to convene a meeting, at once. He's with the other warchiefs, up that way." He pointed at a longhouse up ahead, likely where the local chieftain resided. Judging by its weathered appearance, it looked to be centuries old, and perhaps one of the last Khorrish buildings in the village.

"Meetings and more meetings," Zander muttered. He drank down the last of his beer, then tossed the empty mug over his shoulder. Irritated at having to abandon the merriment, he trudged off toward the longhouse.

As he entered, a cold tingle ran the length of his spine. There was an ominous presence in the room, despite only familiar faces around a large oaken table. Arik Akselson, Bonesplitter, Stormguard, and the rest were present, but so was the crone.

Lazilyth stood next to Damien Dreadfire, her frame crumpled and diminished. Though she appeared to be near death, there was a strange and powerful aura radiating about her. Her glassy eyes shifted slowly across the room until they looked upon him.

What in the hell is she doing here?

Damien seemed to dig up the crone only when matters were most serious, and Zander supposed this was one of them. He approached the table, its surface littered with mugs and tankards, and an unrolled map scrawled on a piece of animal hide.

"Let us begin," Dreadfire said, scanning the faces of those present. "The time is now upon us, honored friends. We have made significant progress against King Bethard this year. Surely, word of our victories has spread to every corner of Betanthia by now."

"Hear hear!" Arik Akselson lifted a drink into the air. Bonesplitter and Valerick the Red slapped the table, their mighty palms clapping in approval.

"We have fought well," Damien continued. "But now, we begin our march into the heart of Betanthia. Their army is waiting patiently, and we will be on their doorstep soon enough. And when we find one another, it will be a battle the likes of which have not been seen in centuries."

Damien's finger slid across the map, from their current position to the lands outside of Bentmont. It appeared Dreadfire was finally ready to strike Betanthia at its core, and not content himself with sacking defenseless settlements.

"We have momentum on our side!" Zander grinned. "I say we hit them so hard! They won't have the stomach for a proper fight!"

While the others appeared to share his sentiment, Bonesplitter instead cast him a distasteful glare. It was an annoyance at first, but the Rhivothi nomad's animosity was enough to make his blood boil.

"You disagree, Bone-shitter?" he taunted.

The insult was nearly enough to spark a battle of its own. Marvath's face turned a shade of crimson, his hand drifting down to a great axe propped against the table.

"I will suffer your insults no longer, you Bymist rat!" Bonesplitter snarled. "Come outside and face me, coward!"

"Enough!" Dreadfire bellowed. "I will not allow these hostilities to continue. You men must make peace with one another, or risk tearing this alliance apart when we are closest to the real danger."

As amusing as the exchange had become, Zander quickly reminded himself of all that was at stake. He had come too far to see such carefully laid plans come to ruin thanks to a witless oaf like Bonesplitter. Instead, he grinned and nodded, content to bide his time.

"Now, continuing," Damien grumbled. "We will skirt the edge of the Plainhold to protect our western flank. When the time is right, we will head east, and lay waste to their stronghold at Bentmont. There can be no victory if we cannot conquer this city."

As the warchiefs studied the map, reality began to set in. Marching on a proper Betanthian city was enough to humble even the fiercest warrior, Zander included.

"Who knows how many millions of Betanthians stand in our way," Arik said, his weak Nothanek stomach likely in knots. "Is this a war we can even win, Damien?"

"Yes, we can… and we will. Lazilyth has seen it."

The old woman grinned, her toothless mouth creaking open like a crypt door. An icy chill kissed the back of Zander's neck, then slipped down his spine at the sight of it. Even though he believed her powers to be little more than parlor tricks, there was something unsettling about her, something which could strike fear even in the hearts of the dead.

"Blood…" Lazilyth groaned. "Oceans of blood. I have seen it in the fires… I have seen it in the fates. A great victory shall there be! Our foes will lie broken before the gods, their corpses piled to the heavens. I have seen this. It is inevitable."

None had the courage to challenge Lazilyth, her prognostication lingering throughout the now silent hall. For all their enthusiasm, Zander might have thought the warchiefs had been told of a crushing defeat instead of victory.

"Well, that certainly sounds like music to my ears," he grinned. "Zylmacia is ready to march at your command, my lord."

With a bow, Zander took his leave. As he passed through the doorway, he heard a faint whisper of conversation from inside. Curious, he crept around to a nearby window and put an ear near the glass.

"Marvath, you mustn't!" Sylvia said, mindful of her volume.

"I will not tolerate such disrespect, Stormguard!" Bonesplitter shot back. "I have suffered that man's insolence long enough. I have my honor, and I will kill to protect it."

It was difficult not to snicker, but Zander held his tongue. He knew there was nothing the Rhivothi could do, or risk fracturing the warband beyond repair. He knew Damien would not risk a schism this deep in Betanthian territory.

"You have sacrificed much in the service to this cause," Dreadfire said. "Should Zander continue to provoke you, I will take steps to ensure it will be his last offense. Perhaps Jollkud would prefer to take his place as warchief."

"As if such a threat would stop that greasy rat!" Marvath growled. "Do not make the mistake of thinking he will disappear without incident. No, he would just assume stab us in our backs when we least expect it, since he lacks the courage to attack from the front."

Having heard enough, Zander started off toward the tavern once again, smirking in amusement. Regardless of their hatred, each of the northmen knew just how indispensable he truly was. Not that their approval mattered, as soon enough they would be liquidated, and the warband firmly under his control.

See, that's where you're wrong, Bonesplitter. So very, very wrong...

MADELYN V

T HE DAYS' TRAINING SESSION WAS ESPECIALLY GRUELING, EVEN FOR A healthy knight. Madelyn's body felt as if it had been trampled by a herd of wild horses, every joint stiff and popping, and burning like fire. Her discomfort only seemed to embolden Conrak, who was every bit as sadistic as Titan had said.

It was endlessly frustrating to have the will to maneuver and fight like the Madelyn of old, only to be hampered by a broken body. At times she wanted to scream at Conrak in frustration and put an end to their sessions. The chances of being in proper fighting condition seemed hopelessly overwhelming. But Madelyn's heart was branded with a hatred so fierce it could not be restrained. Damien Dreadfire had to die, and by her hands.

After a hearty meal of seared beef, potatoes, and fresh vegetables, she retired for a much needed rest. Trudging upstairs to her chamber proved equally as treacherous as sparring. Grunting through clenched teeth, Madelyn limped down the hall and flopped onto a freshly prepared bed. The linens felt cool and smelled of clean spring air, and within seconds her eyes slammed shut.

When she awoke, there was only darkness in the room. Daybreak was likely another hour or so away, and soon enough another training regimen would begin. Even thinking about her next session was exhausting, but Conrak was seemingly a man without sympathy.

Sometimes I think he's really a northman, sent here to finish me off. He might very well accomplish it at this rate.

A soft creaking of floorboards in the hallway drew her attention. Perhaps it was one of the midwives coming to look in on her, she thought. It was only when the footfalls stopped outside of her door that something felt amiss. The steps sounded heavy, certainly not those of a woman.

"Tylar?" she called out.

There was no response. It was too early for Conrak to have arrived, and whenever the Elite was around, the entire household was aware of it. Again, she called out to Titan, but again there was only silence. Madelyn sat up in bed, grunting and wincing. There was a dagger nearby in the desk, and a sword propped against the wall across the room. Delicately she shifted toward the side of her bed and made to stand, but before she could, the door crept open.

"Tylar? It's too early. What do you want?"

A male figure stood in the doorway, not large and imposing like Titan, his features obscured by darkness. Madelyn shot to her feet, frantically trying to reach the desk and retrieve the blade inside. The intruder lunged forward, pouncing on her and wrapping both hands firmly around her neck.

In a faint sliver of moonlight she saw him. He was bald and scarred, an ugly and brutish man if there ever was one. There was a look of both hatred and satisfaction in his eyes, a cocky grin forming across his face as he squeezed harder. Madelyn gasped and tried to call out for help, but the words could not escape. She clawed and slapped at his hands and face, then reached around for some manner of weapon.

An empty chamber pot sat underneath the bed, just within her reach. With as much strength as she could muster, Madelyn swung the pot against the assailant's head, ceramic shattering into dozens of sharp pieces. She gasped, drawing in several desperate breaths, then made to scream. But the man was seemingly unphased by the blow, despite a trickle of blood running down his face.

Again, he set upon her. This time, there seemed to be no escape. Madelyn's strength was all but spent, and as the light in her eyes began to dim, death seemed inevitable. That was, until she heard a sudden loud thumping of footsteps charging into the room. With an uncontrollable fury, Titan Bradshaw clubbed the assailant upside his head with a devastating punch, sending him toppling to the floor.

Madelyn gasped and panted, then crawled as far underneath the bed as possible. Both men struggled and traded blows, but Titan's strength was too great. He tossed the assassin across the room with ease, then proceeded to pound his face into pulp. Blood and teeth spilled out onto the floor, and after a few short seconds, the fight appeared to be over.

"Who the fuck are you?" he shouted, slamming the attacker onto his back. Tylar sat mounted on top of him, then smashed his head into the floor several times. "Answer me, you fucking coward! Who are you? Who sent you?"

There was no response, only a gurgling groan. In the chaos, the midwives had come with lanterns in hand, frightened yet curious to see what the disturbance was. Light filled the room, and both Titan and Madelyn were able to see the intruder in full. His skin was a pasty white, his head bald and scarred. He appeared more as a common brigand as opposed to a trained assassin.

"If you don't answer me right fucking now, I'll break every bone in your body!" Tylar wound up a punch and delivered it into the man's side. The thump was so heavy it made Madelyn shiver. But still, the cutthroat said nothing, giving only a few groans of agony in reply.

"Something isn't right," she said, crawling out from under the bed. Jann rushed over and helped her stand.

"Perhaps," Titan acknowledged. "Must be one tough fucker, most men would be spilling their guts after such a beating." He wrapped a hand around the intruder's neck and squeezed.

Madelyn leaned down and wrenched at his mouth, but to no avail. Titan looked at her curiously, but understood well enough what she was attempting to do. There was little difficulty in opening the assassin's mouth, as his jaw was nearly broken off completely. Inside was a collection of blood and shattered teeth, but the most telling thing was the complete absence of a tongue.

"Fucking hell," Titan mumbled. "Looks like he won't be telling us anything after all."

It was a curious yet disappointing revelation. Someone had come in the night to take her life, and there would be no way to find out who the man was or who had sent him. But why would anyone attempt to murder her? She had no enemies inside Bentmont, at least, none she was aware of. Perhaps he was sent by the northmen to finish what they started. It seemed the most logical answer.

"He must be one of Damien Dreadfire's lackeys. Why else would a man with no tongue show up here to kill me?"

Frustration began to boil over into rage. Titan Bradshaw's face began to turn red, his jaw clenched and teeth grinding. "Well, I'll get something out of this piece of shit."

He hoisted the assassin up and shoved him against the wall. What followed was the most barbaric beating Madelyn had ever witnessed. Tylar cursed and roared and rained down a series of blows, each powerful enough to flatten a mountain.

"Nod your fucking head, you coward. Did the northmen send you?"

Again, there was no response of any kind. The man appeared to be barely clinging to life as it was. But even still, he refused to nod yes or no.

"That's how you want to play it? Fine then! Fuck you!"

Again came a torrent of fists, devastating and unmerciful. Each crunch of teeth and bone filled Madelyn with awe and fear. It did little to persuade the assassin to cooperate, however. Enraged, Tylar grabbed hold of him, and with the strength of a bear, threw him clean through a shuttered window. Wood shattered like glass, the assailant falling onto the cobbles below without so much as a scream.

A wet thudding sound sent shivers down her spine. Madelyn knew Titan was an imposing fighter, but had never witnessed such wrath poured out against another human being before. The ordeal was over, this much she knew, but who would send an assassin to her bedchamber in the first place? It was a question nearly as disturbing as the attack itself.

"Are you alright?" Titan asked after poking his head out through the window. He appeared satisfied with his handiwork.

For a moment, she was too frightened of him to answer. "Yes, I think so. But… who was the man? And why did he try to kill me?"

"I don't know." Titan scratched at the back of his neck. "Bold of someone to send a killer here in the dead of night. There's only one person who might know, and he should be here come sunrise."

The thought of staying put was terrifying, but Madelyn was hardly in a position to protest. She was entirely at the mercy of Titan Bradshaw, and had to acquiesce to his judgement for a change. Jann and Wilka set to cleaning puddles of blood off the floor, then assisted Madelyn in dressing. All four of them waited downstairs by the fireplace, the logs inside nearly reduced to ashes. She forced down a plate of bread and eggs, and a small cup of wine to wash it down.

As daylight came, so too did Conrak. He rapped at the door in his customary fashion, signaling it was him. Tylar cracked the door open with steel in hand, reluctant to take any chances.

"What's the matter, Bradshaw? You getting a bit jumpy?" Conrak glanced down at the sword curiously.

"Get in here, and be quick about it." Titan grabbed him by the shoulder and hustled him inside. "We've got a problem. A big fucking problem. Someone sent an assassin to kill the girl. You have any idea who might do such a thing?"

Conrak looked stunned. He stood, silent and wide-eyed for a moment. "An assassin? Here? I..."

"You better come up with some answers real fucking fast. There's a corpse in the street on the other side of the house, and it's only a matter of time before this place is swarming with guards."

"True enough." Conrak gestured toward the door. "I know of a place where we can lay low, at least for a little while. Come with me, and leave your belongings. I'll send for them later."

Madelyn draped a shawl over her head and limped out into the streets. It seemed the pain in her body was a little less, likely from a high of adrenaline, which still had not come down. Being seen outside was the least of her concerns, though it was distressing to see no carriage waiting outside.

"I don't know if I can make it," she complained as the two men hurried outside.

"Unfortunately, time is not on our side," Conrak sighed. "Bradshaw, you're going to have to carry her. We need to get moving, and fast."

Titan was reluctant to take orders, but there were little options otherwise. He scooped her up effortlessly with arms as thick and sturdy as tree trunks. With Conrak in the lead, they traversed down side streets and alleyways, some of which even Madelyn was unaware of. He appeared to be heading toward the manufacturing district, where many of Bentmont's iron foundries and workshops were located.

Were it not for the constant jostling, Madelyn might very well have fallen asleep. Exhaustion had set in, and there was safety to be found in her best friend's arms. Before long, they arrived at what appeared to be a warehouse, its exterior suggesting little else. Conrak produced a key and unlocked a thick, faded wooden door. As they entered, the door was again locked and secured with a large iron bar.

"Now that we have some privacy," Conrak said, "do you care to tell me what exactly happened back there?"

"I was thinking you might have a few answers," Titan replied gruffly. "Who the fuck sends a man with no tongue to kill someone in the night?"

"No tongue, you say? Well then…"

It seemed Conrak was indeed keeping secrets of his own. Were she healthy, Madelyn would have given him a proper thrashing until he was spilling his life's story.

"You better start talking, and fast," Titan demanded. "Every lie you tell is another bone I break."

"Easy there, Bradshaw, I had no hand in this. I am aware of a certain sect of… how shall I say… cutthroats who sell their services to those with ample coin. The name of their organization escapes me, as up until now, I only took it for a rumor. Shadowy assassins lurking about, striking down their targets in the dead of night? Sounds like a bedtime story mothers tell their children to make them behave."

Such a story did indeed sound fantastical, more of an old wives' tale than anything. But a slight bruising on Madelyn's neck was evidence enough, as was the carcass laying splattered on the street.

"So, what do we do about it?" Titan asked.

"It seems recent events are forcing my hand quicker than anticipated." Conrak slung a stachel off his shoulder and set it on the table. "I brought a few texts from the Ivornorium. You're not ready for this, Madelyn, but nevertheless we have to try. Especially after what happened today."

"Not ready?" She cocked her head. "I *am* ready, Conrak. I've done everything you've asked of me and more. I feel stronger by the day. There's nothing I—"

"No," the Sacrithon interrupted. "These are advanced teachings. Even I haven't mastered these techniques. The Sanvalldin were masters of warfare, and the Eveldanyr even more so. Combined with the arcane arts, your ancestors were every bit as deadly as you can imagine. I only pray you can learn a fraction of what they knew. We need every advantage we can get, and time grows shorter by the hour."

Madelyn flipped casually through the pages of one book, then another. It was refreshing to see mostly drawings instead of walls of strange text. But to her disappointment, the images were not moving and swirling as they did in the cave. Still, the depictions were fascinating to behold. Many of the fighting techniques she was familiar with, but most were geared toward fighting multiple opponents simultaneously.

Titan peered over Madelyn's shoulder, his curiosity piqued. "I've seen this before," he grunted, then looked at Conrak. "That night in the Plainhold, when you fought those wildmen. I thought you said only the Eveldanyr could master fighting like this?"

"Anyone can learn the techniques, Bradshaw. But only an Eveldanyr can use them to their fullest. You think fighting four men at once is impressive? If she can master what's in these books, she'll be able to fight legions."

The idea of harnessing such power was exciting, enough to ignite a glimmer of hope in her heart. If such a feat was possible, then revenge against Damien Dreadfire and his horde would soon be at hand. But only if she could manage the near impossible.

How am I going to learn all of this and get my body back into fighting shape in time? The war will be a distant memory before then.

"Come now, Bradshaw." Conrak said, motioning to the door. "Let's leave her be. It takes unbroken concentration to delve into this craft. You and I have some work to do anyway. She'll be safe, nobody knows about this place except for us."

Both men took their leave, though after such a random attack, it was alarming to be left alone. Instead of ruminating on the experience, she decided to dive headfirst into the books, eager to glean as much information as possible. Hour after hour slogged by, and while the depictions were certainly interesting and informative, there was a certain lack of connection to them.

It was difficult for her to explain. After experiencing such indescribable magic in the cave, nothing else could compare. Madelyn felt an overwhelming desire to return to the Ivornorium, her escorts likely hours away from returning. However, Titan and Conrak would likely fight each other to see who would throttle her first if she left unattended.

Let them be mad. I don't need to be supervised like a child. I'm fully capable of making my own decisions, and it's about time I did so again.

Taking up quill and ink, Madelyn penned a brief note, stating she would be at the Ivornorium for the remainder of the day. She folded the note and left it on the floor where it would be noticed, then retrieved a dagger and belt and affixed them to her waist. A hooded cloak would help to obscure both the weapon and her, and keep unfriendly eyes from taking notice. Finally, she placed the books in a worn leather satchel, then slung it over one shoulder. Even inside, the texts radiated an unspeakable energy, their pulsating warmth permeating throughout her body.

Bentmont's markets would be quite busy this time of day, and while risky, there was anonymity to be found in a crowd. Madelyn decided to cut right through the heart of the city, as it was the most direct route to the Ivornorium. Several Droethien merchants she recognized, but thankfully they paid no attention. The markets were too clogged with soldiers for anyone to take notice.

Before she knew it, the Ivornorium came into view. Sunlight caught its polished dome and scattered bright rays in every direction. It was if the heavens themselves were welcoming her back to this place, a place where she might become whole once again. The birds were absent from the fountain today, but evidence of their gluttony lay splattered all around.

Madelyn approached the large doors to the Ivornorium, and rapped several times, then several more as she had been instructed. Minutes passed, with only a soft bubbling of the fountain and distant mumblings from the markets to keep her company. As boredom and anxiety began setting in, the door cracked open ever so slightly, a smell of candles and musty books wafting out.

"Maddie!" Willard seemed more surprised and disturbed than excited. "Em… come in, come in. I wasn't expecting you… especially without your companions."

"I'm feeling better by the day." She removed the satchel and set it as delicately as possible onto the floor, its weight numbing out her shoulder. "Conrak brought me these books to study, but to be honest, something is missing. I was hoping I could take them down into the cave."

There was something unsettling about the old man's face, but he did his best to hide it. "Of course, of course. Please, right this way."

As they walked, a conspicuous silence followed them. Willard Mirren was a man of many words; he had devoted his life to them, after all. But it seemed now, when she was well enough to travel alone, he could find none.

"What a day this has been, Willard. You're never going to believe this, but someone broke into my bedroom in the middle of the night and tried to kill me. If it weren't for Tylar, I wouldn't be here right now. I just can't believe it, who would want to murder me in my sleep?"

"It's… it's difficult to say," the Chronican stammered. "These are strange times indeed."

They arrived in the study room with the secret passage. It was unlikely Willard would have the strength to open the hidden doorway, but Madelyn was feeling capable enough.

"And to make matters even stranger, the assassin had no tongue," she said. "Even when Tylar was beating the daylights out of him, he made no noise at all. Have you ever heard of such a thing? A killer with no tongue?"

"No, no… I've never heard of such a thing."

It was obvious the Chronican knew more than he was letting on. Perhaps it was her growing connection to her ancestors which gave a greater discernment, but everything inside Madelyn's head was screaming. Something was wrong, she knew it in her bones.

"Willard. Look at me."

The old man was slightly hesitant at first, but his eyes met hers with a smile. "What is it, Maddie?"

"You know of what I speak, don't you? You know something you're not telling me."

"That's preposterous, Maddie. I would never lie or keep anything from you. I've known you since you were a child, I—"

Incensed, Madelyn drew her dagger and pressed it to the soft flesh underneath his chin. "You're lying! Tell me what you know, or I'll have your head! Don't think I won't do it, Willard! Don't test me!"

"Alright! Alright!" he gasped and whimpered, tears filling his glassy eyes. "I told the High Marshal you were here, that you came to study the forbidden texts! Now you must understand, Maddie, I'm sworn to protect these secrets! I was entrusted to guard this information, and it is my solemn duty to inform him of—"

"You betrayed me?!"

The air suddenly felt as if it had been sucked out of the room. Madelyn withdrew her blade and stepped back, panting desperately but finding no breath. Willard Mirren, a man who was like a grandfather, had broken every bond, every bit of trust formed over a lifetime.

"I had no idea he would try to harm you," he whimpered. "Please, Maddie, you must believe me! You're very precious to me, you know that."

"Apparently not precious enough to look out for my safety. You're just like the High Marshal and everyone else in the Order; a pack of liars and turncoats. Perhaps I should have accepted Damien Dreadfire's offer and rained death down upon your heads!"

"Please, forgive me! I was only upholding my sacred vow. Forgive a foolish old man, I beg you!"

It would have been satisfying to watch the Chronican's blood leak across the stone floor, but there would be little to gain from it. A man such as Willard was a bastion of secrets, secrets which she might be able to use to her advantage.

"You're going to answer every question of mine, or else there will be consequences. How do you suppose Conrak will react when I tell him you're directly responsible for the attempt on my life? Or even worse… if I tell Tylar? If only you could have seen what he did to that assassin. I've never seen a man beaten so brutally in all my life."

"Yes, yes. I'll tell you whatever you wish to know!" The old man clasped his hands and simpered, a great fear coming over him.

Madelyn saw a dark haze filling the edge of her vision, the same misty murk she had seen before. Each attempt to look directly at it ended in failure, but she supposed it was simply the result of her overwhelming anger.

"Who was that man?" she demanded. "The one with no tongue?"

"He belongs to the Hekalti, the most dangerous organization in Caldakas. They serve at the behest of the King, the High Marshal, or any lord who commands enough influence and coin. Murder is their business, along with espionage, blackmail, sabotage… there is little they cannot do."

Except killing her, she thought. In all of her years of service as a Commander in the Blackthorn Knights, Madelyn had never heard mention of such an organization. It was disturbing to know such a secret could be kept not only from the outside world, but from the highest and most privileged ranks of the Order.

"I see." She placed her dagger back in its scabbard. "So even though you're guilty of betrayal, the High Marshal is the one who ordered my death?"

"Yes… he's the only man I'm aware of who could arrange such a thing. Perhaps Lord Vakaro, but he has little reason to feel threatened by you, if he even knows who you are."

"You must swear to me, right here and right now, Willard. Swear that you will never betray me ever again. Swear it, or I'll have Tylar pull you apart, limb from limb. He isn't called Titan for nothing."

The old Chronican lowered his head and wept, his shame plain for her to see. "Yes, I swear. On my life, I swear it. I have always seen you as a granddaughter, and I should have always treated you as my own, even unto death. I only hope you can forgive me one day."

It was difficult to not rush to Willard's side and comfort him, knowing the loving past they had shared together. But treachery was treachery, and it nearly cost Madelyn her life. Instead, she responded with stony indifference.

"Good. And just remember who I am, and who I know. I'm an Eveldanyr, I've come to accept that now. And the Sacrithon are my champions. You know what Conrak is capable of. And now Tylar is one of them as well."

"If there is anything I can do to make this right, please, tell me at once," he pleaded. "I will make it my mission until my dying day to right this wrong. Please, forgive me."

With as deep of a bow as he could manage, Willard toddled off, a faint whimper and a sniffle echoing behind him. It was one of the most heartbreaking experiences of her life, to have been betrayed by one so close. But there would be little time to dwell on such a thing, as time was growing ever shorter. She picked up her satchel and continued on toward the secret passage.

Madelyn opened the hidden door and took up a lantern, its dancing flame guiding her down into the darkness. Before even reaching the bottom, a bluish-white light reflected off the stone walls, welcoming her with a warm and inviting glow. A sharp, piercing sensation began building in the center of her head, but nearly as quickly as it arrived, it disappeared.

As she entered the heart of the cave, a most unbelievable sight manifested itself. While many texts remained closed and in their containers, colorful, transparent manifestations danced above them. Ghostly scenes played out as they did in the past, each one unique in its own way.

It was easy to forget about all the suffering and betrayals and become lost in the majestic visions. Madelyn smiled, then laughed for the first time in ages. When she reached out to touch a wispy image of a horse and rider, her hand passed clean through with no disturbance.

This is incredible!

Her thoughts were interrupted by the full figure of a man, his short beard colored a deep gray. He wore a shirt of mail over a thick gambeson, his head protected by a nasal helm. The ancient looking man emerged from a large book wrapped in linen, then moved toward the altar. His steps were slow, as if time itself had slowed to a near crawl.

Upon reaching the altar, the warrior drew his sword, cradling it in both hands. He kissed the steel, then placed it down on the stone, as if to seek favor from the gods. Madelyn watched with awe, but to her astonishment, the warrior turned and locked eyes with her. Her heart was racing at lighting speed, but there was a strange calmness to be felt in the apparition's presence.

"H…hello? Who are you?"

There was no response, the warrior instead staring deeply into her steely-blue eyes. There was an unspoken familiarity between them, the sort of bond which she only ever experienced with those not of her blood. But this man seemed to be different, his aura warm and inviting, despite having a fearsome appearance.

"I don't know who you are," she said softly. "But I can feel you. Everything here feels so… so…"

It was difficult to find proper words to articulate what was brewing inside her heart. The ghostly visions felt more like memories as opposed to random manifestations, things her ancestors had experienced once before. Madelyn longed to be among them, but sadly, such a thing was not possible. Or was it?

The warrior took a step forward, then extended a hand. With a single finger, he gently touched the center of her forehead. A sudden jolt of energy nearly made her scream, though it was more alarming than painful. Sensations of extreme cold and warmth coursed through every vein, followed by a surge of emotions. Anger and happiness, serenity and despair, all raced through her heart and soul in a flash.

"You're me, and I'm you!" She smiled, nearly laughing and in tears. "I know what you're trying to tell me!"

Madelyn removed the satchel from around her shoulder and set in on the altar. A shining, golden light emanated from within, dimming the ghostly images around her. The first book was warm to the touch, and had a static tickle which raced down each finger and into her arms.

Cracking open the cover, she saw images of a man clad in boiled leather, wielding a pair of short swords. While unable to comprehend the words scrawled on the page, Madelyn could feel their intention deep within. The warrior gracefully maneuvered both swords in what appeared to be a defensive posture, then completed the motion again and again.

On the opposite page, another image performed a similar routine, but this one appeared more aggressive. Madelyn quickly deduced these to be fighting stances, some which seemed familiar, others completely foreign. It seemed there would be a great deal of studying to be done, and precious little time to do it in.

If I can learn the ways of my ancestors, I'll be unstoppable. She thought with a mischievous grin. *Not even the gods could stand in my path. Damien Dreadfire will be as good as dead.*

From the corner of her eye, she spied a pillar of dark light. It was rising from a book tucked away inside a little alcove, barely visible to the eye. Madelyn could sense a strange, ominous energy radiating from it. Curiously, she moved closer, but was overwhelmed with fear. Something about the text was uninviting, foreboding, even.

But she had to know more. Emboldened by the protective illusions of her ancestors, Madelyn continued on, reaching out with trembling fingers to examine the book. An icy aura pulsated around it, its cover as cold as frost. When she cracked it open, a blackness began manifesting, dimming the ethereal light inside the cave.

At first, its words seemed illegible, little more than the scratchings of a madman. But then, the ancient ink began to morph and melt itself into a ghastly image of a skull, wrapped in withered flesh, with eyes black enough to swallow the sun. A word formed beneath it, first in runes, then in letters more familiar.

"Cthenir…" she muttered. The skull seemed to respond in kind, a grim smile growing wide. Though she had never heard such a name before, a voice inside her head spoke otherwise. In an instant, Madelyn Everly knew what visage she was facing, that of a god most feared. It was the god of death, staring dead into her eyes.

EINARR VI

K NOTS FILLED EINARR'S STOMACH AS HE GAZED ACROSS THE VASTNESS of a grassy field. The lands outside Khorrtal looked much the same as they did the year prior, serene and undisturbed. But the tall grasses held dark secrets of their own, secrets written in an ocean of blood. Alfrid Valens had breathed his last only a short distance ahead, a terrible event which would forever ripple throughout the history of Caldakas.

Einarr paid little attention as he rode into town, stealing his resolve. Not every day at Khorrtal had been grim. In fact, it was also the site of his greatest triumph. Liberating the village was more exhilarating than putting steel through another man's flesh, the love of the Khorrtalli people filling his soul to overflowing.

The village had become a quiet place, a stark contrast to how he remembered it. Einarr's arrival was met by a patrolling pair of spearmen, laden in mail and protected by painted round shields. It was apparent the warband had been absent for some time, as no evidence of their departure was seen on the road. Einarr knew his chances of finding Damien Dreadfire here were slim, but perhaps one of the locals might know where the warband was heading.

"Who are you, and what business do you have here?" one of the spearmen challenged, the grip on his weapon firm.

He remembered the Khorrtalli being a cautious people, though not particularly unreasonable. A tribute to their virtue, no doubt, given a lifetime of subjugation from Betanthia and constant raids from Zylmacia.

"My name is Einarr Rollfson of the Nothanek. I was hoping I might have a word with your chieftain. I've come looking for Damien Dreadfire, but I can see he has moved on."

"Aye," the other man responded. "You'll be disappointed to know that Dhuuld is no longer here. He is marching on Betanthia as we speak, alongside your kinsmen."

Einarr sighed, wondering if it was foolish to ride this far only to come up empty-handed. He looked to the east, then south, trying to decide where best to continue his search.

"You look tired," the first spearman said. "Why don't you rest awhile and help yourself to some meat and ale, eh?"

A deep rumbling erupted inside Einarr's stomach. He was reminded of not eating for two days, and agreed with little protest. He was escorted into the village, where curious locals peeked out from their hovels, some casting a suspicious eye. It was nearly identical to how he was first received a year ago. Eventually, the locals would warm to his arrival and offer their hospitality, or so he thought.

"You can tie your horse up here. There's plenty of warm food inside. Eat and drink your fill. I'll send for Niddeg at once. Dhuuld has placed him in charge, for the time being."

"Your hospitality is most generous," Einarr said. "But the road has made me weary, and I have need of a bed."

"Certainly," the warrior said. "For a coin, the inn has what you seek. Take your leave and rest, son of Rolff. Join us for a feast this evening, Niddeg would be honored to receive you."

Thankfully, the inn was close by, nestled near the village square. A pair of mangy dogs sniffed at the parched earth, snapping at one another before darting off. An elderly woman swept dirt from inside her hovel out into the road, her movements slow and labored. Khorrtal, it seemed, had become dormant, like trees during the chill of winter.

For a single, dingy coin, Einarr found a room suitable enough for a brief rest. For another, he received a pint of mead and a heel of bread, enough to tide him over until the evening's feast. His bed was little more than straw and linen, but a feather pillow proved comfortable. He drifted off to a dreamless slumber, tossing and turning every few minutes. Something about the village seemed to cast an ill will toward him, denying even the comfort of rest.

A low rumbling sound began building in a dark corner of his room, coaxing his eyes open. Staring back were two small orbs of light, motionless and ever watchful. Einarr sat up in bed, back pressed against the wall. He could sense a large presence within the cramped room, and see an outline of the great beast which had stalked his movements since Skaginlef.

"Who are you, and what do you want with me? Are you a servant of Azldyr?"

There was only silence. Like dying candles, the glowing eyes dimmed until they melted into the darkness, their oppressive energy fading in kind. Einarr stood and gathered his effects, content to spend not a moment longer at the inn. He needed another drink, and fast. Thankfully, Khorrtal's mead hall was only a short distance away, given its proximity to the warlord's hold overlooking the village square.

Shambling out into the street, Einarr took notice of how utterly still it had become. Only a faint moaning of the wind in his ears broke an otherwise deathly silence. His horse stood tied to a hitching post outside the inn, drinking from a full trough. Riding to the mead hall seemed unnecessary, as he caught sight of it just ahead.

A plume of smoke drifted up into the sky, carrying with it a scent of roasted meat. Einarr's mouth immediately flooded, his stomach writhing like a ball of snakes. He entered the hall, its interior having changed little over the past year.

Laughter and the plucking of strings filled the air. Two long tables flanked a large pit fire, each fit for a score of men. The hall was mostly vacant, save for a few patrons drinking by the bar. Though Khorrtal had pledged only minor support for Damien's war, the absence of their warriors was enough to make the village feel deserted.

There was roasted meat and ale in plenty, with casks nearly the size of wagons sitting against the far wall. A soft fire was glowing in a stone pit at the room's center, thin wisps of smoke drifting up to an opening in the ceiling.

Einarr moved toward the bar and fetched a mug of ale. He glanced at the other men, the sort of unsavory characters who would content themselves with drinking from sunup to sundown. With each sip, he made certain to keep them within the corner of his eye.

"So, the great Einarr Rolffson has decided to pay us a visit!" A man in a fine blue tunic and tan trousers entered the hall, his arms spread wide in welcome. "My name is Niddeg, I'm a retainer of Dhuud Lurrson. He left me in charge of Khorrtal and its affairs until his return. Consider the hospitality of his house yours!"

Niddeg sat on a nearby bench, tossing his long, fine blonde hair behind both shoulders. He was a soft man, a man of gold and privilege, and certainly not steel. He smiled heartily, but there appeared to be little love in his eyes for a Nothanek man.

"You have my thanks," Einarr said, taking a seat as well.

"I have been told you are here searching for Damien Dreadfire and his host." Niddeg motioned for a mug of mead. "You will be disappointed to know he has not been here for some time."

"Do you know where they set out? I would very much like to find them."

The half dozen men at the bar sauntered over, mugs in hand. They were likely more of Dhuuld's retainers, Einarr supposed, their tunics fresh and finely woven. Around their necks and wrists hung strings of gold, exquisitely designed and some laden with jewels.

"Difficult to say." Niddeg took a long sip of mead. "They left months ago, headed out east, if I recall. From there, only the gods can be certain."

"Surely, you must have some idea of their plans, given you are now the acting chieftain?"

"Tell me, fisherman." Niddeg's smile faded and was replaced with something more grim. "Why are you *really* here? You ran away from the fight. What business does a coward have in our war, hm?"

Were it not for the six men staring a hole clean through him, Einarr might have rearranged Niddeg's face for such an insult. But something was amiss. A foul energy infected the room, something which cared for him not.

"I have seen enough killing to last a dozen lifetimes," Einarr replied, "but I cannot sit idly by while my people fight for a cause I championed. I realize how wrong I was to lose faith."

The petty chieftain emptied his mug, stood, and smiled. "You should have listened to your intuition and stayed home, friend."

Every instinct inside Einarr Rolffson was screaming to flee. Something had gone terribly wrong, but there was little idea as to why. The source for Niddge's sudden hostility mattered little, as it was hostility all the same.

"It would be best if I get back on the road." Einarr stood, eyeing the six men around him. "Give my regards to your chieftain."

In a flash, one of the retainers drew a dagger and lunged, his steel coming perilously close to finding its mark. Einarr shot backward as the other men charged forward, searching for any manner of weapon. He picked up a discarded mug and bashed it over the head of one foe, then shoved another to the floor.

The door was so close, yet making a clean escape was impossible. Einarr ran to the other side of the hall, turning over tables and chairs in a desperate attempt to obstruct his attackers. He was able to find refuge behind a long banquet table, its surface crowded with all manner of plates, mugs, food, and casks.

A knife sat on a dingy metal platter beside a slab of half-eaten meat. Einarr scooped up the blade as a retainer dove over the table, desperate to subdue him. With a swift downward swing, he stabbed the man in the hand, steel biting through flesh and bone and into the wood beneath it. A painful scream rippled throughout the hall, stoking Niddeg's agitation.

"Get him, you fools! Get him!"

Einarr was quickly running out of options. He could stand and fight, but with three men bearing down and Niddeg shadowing their movements, it would only be a matter of time before he was overwhelmed. There seemed to be nothing else of use, unless he resorted to flinging plates and empty casks.

But then, something in the corner of the room caught his eye. Two glowing eyes stared back as before, but now their host stepped forward and revealed itself in full. The giant cat had returned, its orange mane appearing as untamed fire. It stood proud and still, then turned its gaze ever so slightly. Einarr's eyes drifted in kind, until he saw what the beast was staring at.

On the end of the bar sat an oil lantern. Though it was unlit, it could serve as a useful distraction to allow for escape. Einarr waited until the men passed beside the fire pit. Once they were close enough, he hefted the lantern and threw it into the fire, its glass shattering and spraying flaming oil all around.

Dry timbers inside the hall erupted into a raging inferno, engulfing the retainer and his lackeys. Einarr immediately sprinted for the door, throwing it open and tumbling out into the dusty streets. It was only a matter of time before the entire village could see and smell the blaze. He knew he had to flee with all haste, or risk the wrath of hundreds of angry villagers. Luckily, the streets were still vacant. Einarr raced back to the inn, desperate to retrieve his mount and flee from Niddeg's treachery before all of Khorrtal could descend upon him.

With a fierce roar, he snapped the reins and drove his horse as fast as its four legs would allow. A black column of smoke was steadily rising into the sky, and agitated shouts of the villagers rising along with it. Knowing that sentries near the road would present a challenge, Einarr instead decided to cut through its surrounding fields. He prayed the same ground which facilitated Alfrid Valens' downfall would not be his own undoing. Thankfully, the terrain was firm, and his horse galloped through it with little hindrance.

The attack had come so suddenly he was unable to process what Niddeg had said. Why would a man loyal to Dhuuld Lurrson, who in turn was loyal to Damien, attempt to kill him? Had some ill events transpired during the winter? Had the Nothanek stoked the ire of their Khorrtali neighbors?

Many questions raced through Einarr Rolffson's mind, with not an answer to be found. The only thing that mattered was finding Dreadfire, out somewhere in the vastness of Betanthia, and inform him of the treachery at Khorrtal. Einarr prayed that such betrayal was simply the ambition of an embolden retainer, and not the ill will of his master.

I'm coming, Damien! By the gods, let this foul deception harm you not! I'm coming!

LUCETTA VII

THE DAY HAD ARRIVED, DREADED THOUGH IT WAS. SOON, LUCETTA would accompany Charlotte's body to the Westwind Citadel, where she would rest forever. Every dignitary of every stripe would be present for the final procession, from privileged lords to wealthy merchantmen. Attending such an occasion was expected of the royal family, but it was a duty she could have done without.

I suppose I do owe her this last courtesy. She did sacrifice her life to make my dreams a reality, after all. A pity Gareth decided mother wasn't important enough to be here.

While the journey would be short, being amongst the commoners was enough to provoke nausea. Her stomach ached and grumbled, and nearly began thrashing in protest. It was a reminder she had barely eaten these past days, and forced down a helping of bread and cheese, along with a tall glass of wine. Her dresses were fitting much looser as of late, her cheekbones becoming more pronounced.

It was difficult to find an outfit which was not sliding off her shoulders. Thankfully, her wardrobe contained an older dress made of purple silks with a fine golden trim, one which she last wore many years ago. Soon enough, she supposed, a maidservant would have to be dispatched to purchase more appropriately fitting attire.

Pavlos was waiting in the lobby, diligent as always. A royal carriage sat patiently outside, ready to transport them to the Temple of the Dawn. Traveling alongside them would be dozens of Droethien mercenaries, fully armed and armored. Climbing inside proved to be a bit easier, her strength slowly returning thanks to a recovering appetite. Once inside, her carriage rumbled slowly down the avenue, past a burgeoning crowd of mournful onlookers.

A large gathering milled about outside the temple, the city square filled to near capacity. It appeared many had turned out to see Charlotte Bethard one final time, but Lucetta could tell something was amiss. These were not the elite of Cardale, those who came to pay their due respects to the monarchy. Quite the opposite. A horde outside the temple was of unwashed peasants, stinking of fish, refuse, and sweat from an afternoon sun. They stood silent in anticipation of the Queen, their agitation building like a coming storm when her body was not produced.

"Where is she?" a distant voice cried out. "Where is the Mother?"

Hesgrin was standing at the head of the gathering, his eyes wide and wild. Lucetta wondered if the stink of the masses was in fact emanating from his disgusting long beard. Were it a less volatile time in the capital, she might very well have ordered Pavlos to part the wretch's head from his shoulders.

"She is here!" Hesgrin turned and answered, raising both arms into the air. "I can feel her presence, even now!"

As if taken by a spell, the mob of peasants looked on with astonishment. Hesgrin took notice of Lucetta's arrival, and thrust a pointed finger in her direction. He uttered something, his words barely audible over a growing agitation from the commoners.

"She has arrived! The daughter has arrived!" he said, smiling. "She has come to allow the faithful to worship at the Mother's feet!"

Agitation quickly turned to excitement. Peasants began pushing their way closer to the carriage, despite furious commands of her bodyguard. Soon the unwashed sea of masses parted, allowing her free passage to the temple step. Although uncertain of leaving the safety of her carriage, remaining surrounded by a fickle mob was a risk she was unwilling to take.

When she stepped out, the people greeted her with both admiration and awe. Some reached out, desperately trying to touch even the trim of her purple silks. Thankfully, the sharpened tips of Droethien spears were enough to keep them at bay.

"Tell me," Lucetta demanded. "What is the meaning of this? Why have you all gathered here?"

Hesgrin turned, a fierceness building behind his glassy eyes. "We are the Harbingers of the Exalted Mother! We are here to make certain her divine grace, the Queen, is allowed to be worshiped by her obedient servants. She has been touched by the gods, and deserves to be kept and protected, not shuffled off to some dusty tomb."

"I see." Lucetta scratched at the scabs on her wrist. "But I struggle to understand why it matters to you so deeply. When did you take it upon yourself to become my mother's champion?"

"My story is a simple one." Hesgrin drew closer, his stench in tow. "I have spent my life in the lowliest sewers in Cardale. I grew up eating what people like you threw away, things not even dogs would touch. I searched for meaning wherever I could find it, but came up wanting every time."

A hush fell over the square, with all ears listening intently. Lucetta was already growing disinterested, but maintained her faux composure.

"So I embraced the gods," he continued. "I swore that if they rescued me from despair, I would serve them until my final day. For years I begged and pleaded, but no sign of their presence appeared. Until the northmen arrived, and everything suddenly changed."

"And how would that be considered a sign?" Lucetta asked, nearly insulted by what she was hearing. "Those monsters roam the countryside, butchering the innocent and pillaging as they please."

"Because we have become an evil nation!" Hesgrin pointed an accusing finger her way. "Betanthia is rotten to its core, and the gods' righteous people have returned to set things right! Charlotte Bethard's death was at the hands of the divines, and now they preserve her as a testament of their power. So, will you honor her? Will you allow the Mother her rightful place amongst the faithful?"

Despite the reassurance of having Pavlos and his forty men nearby, she was hesitant to say or do much of anything. A single wrong word or action might provoke a violent response from the crowd. But the more Lucetta thought of it, the more her confidence began to return. Who were these people to intimidate her in the first place?

"No," she shouted defiantly. "My mother will be returned to the Westwind Citadel, to rest alongside our ancestors. She is a Bethard! It is her rightful place, not here, in the company of commoners."

"You cannot!" Hesgrin shrieked, spittle flying from his cracked lips. "It is blasphemy! You cannot deny the people this miracle! You cannot deny them the chance to worship at the feet of one whom the gods have personally touched! You must give her to us at once!"

A firm hand wrapped around her bicep. It was Pavlos, who looked far less cocksure than at any point in the past year. "Princess, I think it is wise to get you inside, yes?"

Were it not for a sudden whirlwind of anger rippling through the crowd, she might have disagreed. But Lucetta was not blind to the situation before her. The woman in black was nowhere to be found, and could offer none of its guiding wisdom. Sensing a growing hostility, she nodded in agreement.

The Droethiens formed a protective circle around Lucetta as Pavlos rushed her inside the temple. Their sudden movement incensed the rabble, igniting an explosive fury which swept across the square. Hundreds of commoners surged forward, desperate to make it inside before the doors were clapped shut and sealed.

Pavlos shouted orders to his men, no longer caring to avoid speaking their language. His men hurried inside, several attempting to push the doors closed, but to no avail. With each passing second, the massive weight of peasants began forcing the Droethiens back, until it was clear they could no longer be held at bay.

"Princess!" Pavlos took her by both shoulders. "You must get to safety, yes? Quickly now, you must go!"

She would offer little protest. Lucetta hiked her skirts and ran through the heart of the temple as fast as her slender legs would allow. The sight of Charlotte's body on the altar was enough to give pause, several priests and half a dozen Royal Guardsmen themselves looking to flee. Suddenly, the woman in black made an appearance, standing between two of the purple cloaked men.

The entity's face was deadly serious, though somewhere behind its swirling orange-red eyes was a hint of amusement. "The time has come to show your true strength, Lucetta Bethard."

"What do I do?!" she shrieked, but thankfully the men around believed she was speaking to them.

"We must call for the city watch, immediately!" one of the Guardsmen said, looking at his brethren.

"If we can hold them that long," another purple cloak chimed in. "You men, to the door. I'll ring the bell. Princess, it would be wise to go with the priests and seek shelter. There must be some place in here where you can hide."

With a nod, the men dispersed. Lucetta thought about fleeing to whatever dank tunnel or room the temple housed, but something about the woman in black's gaze told her otherwise. Despite pleading from the priests, she stood firm, transfixed by a swirling hellfire in the entity's eyes.

"What do I do? What should I do?" she whispered.

"You must do what your father has refused to do for years; you must strike fear into the hearts of these savages. Show them your strength.

Show them the price for daring to approach you with hostility. Do not stop until the mere mention of your name is enough to subdue even the boldest among them."

Before she could respond, Lucetta nearly jumped out of her skin as a large brass bell in the tower gonged, its resonance silencing the racket outside. While the noise was nearly enough to shake her to pieces, Lucetta could still hear the woman in black speaking, as if they were alone in a tomb.

"Go now. Do what is necessary. Your actions on this day will be remembered and spoken of for all time. It is your destiny."

It was all the encouragement she needed. With the mob only seconds away from breaking in, Lucetta ran over to Pavlos, clapping the back of his shoulder several times.

"Princess?!" the Droethien said incredulously. "You must get to safety, Pavlos does not know long he can hold on!"

"No, you mustn't hold back!" she said, breathless. "Give them the spear. Teach this rabble what it means to attack a Bethard!"

Knowing what needed to be done, the mercenary nodded, then drew steel. He shouted a command to his men, followed by another. In near perfect unison, they retreated several steps back from the entrance. The doors swung fully open, dozens of commoners spilling onto the floor, one on top of another.

In a tightly packed shield wall, the men lowered their spears and began pushing into the crowd, piercing both man and woman alike with ruthless efficiency. Once blood began to flow, some were eager to retreat, but the mob's momentum had yet to be broken. Hundreds more surged forward, but Pavlos and his gallant men held as firm as a breakwater.

Screams of death and battle were interrupted by a deep gong of the bell, which continued to be sounded. Lucetta prayed the city watch would soon arrive and drive the insurgents away, but it felt as if they never come. She stood trembling, until a cold, leathery hand from the woman in black wrapped around her own.

Together they stood, fingers locked around each other, watching the old home of the gods become a battlefield. The rabble struck back with truncheons and rocks, and any manner of projectile they could find. It had little effect against the sturdy shields of Pavlos and his mercenaries. Bodies were piling up in alarming numbers, nearly choking off the entryway entirely.

"Princess!" Pavlos broke from the action and retreated. His silvery breastplate was splashed with gore, both sword and shield thoroughly soiled. "The city watch has arrived in force! The day is saved, yes?"

Soon enough, the battle would be over. But instead of feeling a sense of relief, Lucetta Eldon became engulfed in a fiery hatred. Who were mindless peasants and an unwashed demagogue to confront her in such a manner? What right did the common man have to challenge House Bethard's rule?

Such disobedience must be met with a swift and terrible response, she decided, one that would never be forgotten. Fear quickly turned into rage, a deep scowl cutting across her face.

"Insolent wretches!" she screamed over the continuing chaos. "Cut them down, Pavlos! Kill anyone who stands in your way! We cannot let ourselves bend to the will of a mob! Teach them the iron resolve of their future queen! Teach them, Pavlos! Teach them!"

If there was a thing Pavlos enjoyed more than gold, it was killing. For the first time that day, his smile returned. As the city watch began to arrive, the tide of battle shifted.

"Push, men!" Pavlos shouted. "Push now!"

His men inched forward, each step followed by a spear thrust. They trudged delicately over dozens of bodies, mindful of a large pool of blood gathering in the entryway. The dead were paid no mind, but those who had not yet expired were given the courtesy of steel.

Foot by foot, they drove the mob out of the temple doorway, but then came to an abrupt halt. Pavlos' men were too few in number to challenge the entirety of the insurgency, opting instead to hold their ground.

Cautiously, Lucetta made her way over to his side. Once, it had been difficult to look upon slain men, even until a short while ago. But this time, she felt a certain satisfaction when staring down on the corpses of those who dared to deny Charlotte Bethard her eternal slumber. Every ruined face, every slashed and perforated torso, and every missing limb filled her heart with a comforting warmth.

She glanced over the Droethien's shoulders and watched as carnage unfolded as far as the eye could see. The city watch made progress of their own, driving into the square as reinforcements from across Cardale rushed to the scene. Blood, steel, and fire were in abundance as the battle raged, losses quickly piling up on both sides. It was only when the rabble caught sight of dozens of purple cloaks that their appetite for combat soured.

The Royal Guardsmen, while sworn to protect the Westwind Citadel with their lives, had sent nearly a third of its strength to assist in the defense of their princess and fallen queen. Lucetta squealed in delight, clapping her hands and grinning like a child on their birthday. In short order, the melee turned into a desperate rout, the mob's resolve collapsing as they scattered like frightened birds.

"Kill them!" she screamed. "Kill them all! Kill them!"

Pavlos and his men loosened their formation and surged forward, eager to quench their bloodthirst. She watched from the top of the temple steps, laughing and cheering, and shouting encouragements to her men. The woman in black came along beside her, looking content as ever.

"You have done well," the entity said, scanning the devastation. "But there is much work to be done. Cardale will not be spared this day, nor the next. You must exert your strength until this fire is snuffed out. Only then will your people come to know and fear you as they have feared your ancestors."

"I must… do more?" she cocked her head. "Hasn't enough blood been spilled? How could anyone possibly—"

The woman in black opened its mouth, revealing rows of large, yellowing teeth. Each one grew sharper and longer until they were nearly daggers in length. "Do not seek to question me further, child. I have given you the keys to your destiny. After all you have seen, after all you have done, you still harbor doubt?"

Glee was quickly replaced by fear, a deep and unsettling fear which burned in her chest like a hot iron. "No, no, I have no desire to question you. I just… I want to make certain everything goes perfectly to plan. I only have one chance to get this right."

The entity halted its grotesque manifestation, its features softening and returning to normal. "Your caution, while expected, will be a hindrance. You must learn to trust in your first instinct, for it is most always correct. And you must learn to trust in my guidance, for it will temper your instincts."

Their conversation was interrupted by what appeared to be an officer of the Royal Guardsmen. The Citadel's protectors were quickly surrounding the temple steps. He thumped a balled fist against his breastplate and bowed.

"My princess, you must come with us. It's no longer safe to remain here."

To that point, she would offer no protest. Although, the notion of returning to the estate and being subjected to Aldred and his inevitable torrent of questions was enough to turn her stomach. Still, there would be safety behind such walls, and the men protecting them. "Very well. Take me home, at once."

"You will be returning to the Citadel, my princess. We cannot guarantee your safety otherwise. Going to your estate is not an option."

Lucetta paused, shocked at being dictated to in such a manner, her eyes and mouth hanging open. "How dare you tell *me* what—"

"With all due respect, princess, these are your father's orders. If I have to carry you out of here over my shoulder, I will."

"My father's orders?" she scoffed. "My father barely knows he's alive. No, I wish to return to my own estate."

The Guardsman stepped forward and took her firmly by the arm. "Your father issued a contingency decree many years ago, in case of invasion or insurrection. Under that authority, I am evacuating you to the Citadel at once."

Pavlos was helpless to do anything, lest his actions destroy all of their carefully laid plans. He gathered his men and prepared to depart from the temple and make their way through a city rapidly descending into anarchy. Priests brought Queen Charlotte's body outside, but the horse and wagon meant to carry her home was nowhere to be found.

"We must get the Queen to safety!" one of the holy men said. "We cannot let this mob desecrate her body!"

Half a dozen Guardsmen were quick to retrieve Charlotte, carrying her high on their shoulders. The order was given to depart, a protective perimeter of purple cloaks leading both mother and daughter home. The city watch marched up front, clearing the streets ahead of any rabble which dared to offer a challenge.

Madness swept through the heart of Cardale like a wildfire. In their rage, Hesgrin and his cultists loosed their wrath in every direction, even against the innocent. Shops and market stalls were ransacked, homes looted, and clouds of gray and black smoke began clogging the avenues. Lucetta coughed and choked, her eyes burning and stinging so painfully she had to keep them shut. Thankfully, the road to the Citadel was short enough, a ripe scent of fish and seawater welcoming her home.

It was surreal to set foot inside the walls of the palace again, at least, this soon. In the grand scheme of things, Lucetta Eldon would have returned to a grateful nation with thunderous fanfare. All of her carefully laid plans were unraveling, despite assurances from the woman in black. It was often difficult to find any solace in the entity's prognostication, especially when her eyes were telling a vastly different story.

Once inside, Lucetta rushed up the grand staircase, anxious to see if the carnage could be witnessed from the palace heights. After only two flights, she began to tire. Sleeplessness and starvation had taken a greater toll on her body than she was aware of. Still, morbid curiosity drove her onward, screams and the indiscernible chaos of battle wafting in through an open window.

It was horror unlike anything the jewel of Betanthia had witnessed in generations. Large black plumes ascended into the heavens, so many they were nearly impossible to count. The temple bell continued crying out, its ring carrying far across a besieged and dying capital.

"Oh no… heavens, no…"

The Royal Guardsmen had secured the front gate, and placed every available man either behind it or on the walls. Thus far, the rabble had not dared to try their hand against the purple cloaks. Instead, they turned their attention to the heart of the city, pillaging and burning the docks and markets until nothing of value remained.

"All of this destruction… all of this death… is all because of me. I did this…"

"Yes, you did," the woman in black said, giving her a startle. The entity moved alongside her, peering outside. "Distressing as it may be, everything is proceeding as planned. There can be no creation without destruction, and for your people to respect and admire your strength, sacrifices will have to be made."

"What good will it be to rule over a kingdom of ashes? I have to put a stop to this, before any more damage is done."

"Of that, Lucetta Bethard, you are correct."

The woman in black motioned back toward the staircase. At first, she was hesitant to trust it any further, but something had to be done before Cardale was lost forever. She hurried downstairs and through the great hall, but was stopped just short of the courtyard, a pair of Guardsmen impeding her path.

"I'm sorry, my princess," one of the purple cloaks said. "It's too dangerous for you out there. Please, remain inside. You'll be safe here."

"I will not sit here and cower while my family's city burns!" She stamped a foot in defiance. "Your captain spoke of contingencies in such an event. I demand an army be brought here at once to restore order!"

Without waiting for an answer, Lucetta pushed past the guards and stepped out into the courtyard. It appeared as if the rioters were ransacking Auburn Row, putting any who resisted to the sword. Some of the Guardsmen loosed arrows from above, content to ward off any who turned their intentions toward the palace.

"You are the most skilled fighters in all of Betanthia! I've seen the way these peasants diminish before you on the streets. Get out there and stamp out this lawlessness, immediately!"

"My princess," the Captain said, wide eyed. "There's not enough of us to take on a horde of this size. Sir Edmund and some of our finest are with Prince Gareth. I know this is distressing, but help is on the way."

Throwing her hands into the air, Lucetta retreated back inside the great hall. There was little more they could do until sufficient force arrived to restore order. She prayed it would not take long, as the southern Commandant and his armies were occupied with the barbarian invasion, and men were in short supply. Still, between the northern Commandant and the garrisons surrounding Cardale, it was unlikely the unrest would last for long. At least, she hoped.

Once safely back inside, she demanded a chalice of wine from a passing servant. The man, near to fifty, disappeared in a flash, returning with a silver tray and a filled vessel atop it. The wine tasted sweeter than she cared for, but was refreshing nonetheless.

"You there," she said sourly. "Tell me where my mother has been taken. I wish to see her."

"The Queen has been taken to the crypt, Your Highness. Shall I accompany you?"

With a scoff and a fiery glare, Lucetta shoved past the servant and set off toward the crypt. The Citadel's dank underbelly was a place Lucetta had feared since childhood. One time, unbeknownst to her mother, she ventured down into the crypt alone. Curiosity soon turned to horror as she became hopelessly lost in its dark, winding corridors, surrounded on either side by stone sarcophagi.

All she remembered of that traumatic event was screaming, screaming until the light in her small lantern dwindled down to nothing. Since that day, returning to the darkness was nearly unthinkable. It even made sleeping without a lit candle or some other light nearby virtually impossible.

Thankfully, Lucetta caught sight of Pavlos as he strode into the great hall. It was a relief to know he was close by once again. "Thank goodness you're here," she sighed. "I was worried the guards would catch on and refuse you entry."

"No, princess," he whispered. "We were able to slip in during the chaos. My men are resting now, yes?" He glanced around the expanse of the great hall, and all of its wondrous paintings and sculptures. "So, this is the palace! Pavlos never would have thought he would set foot in such a place."

Having been born into the splendor of the Citadel, its beauty and awe were wasted on her. The Droethien stole a brief moment to gawk before returning to her side.

"Will you come with me?" she asked sheepishly. "I wish to see my mother one last time, but I…"

It was never easy to admit being afraid, but Lucetta would rather have turned herself over to the mob before venturing down into the crypt alone. Her eyes watered in shame, both hands wringing.

"Why yes, princess. Pavlos will follow wherever you command."

With a nod and an uneasy smile, she led him across the palace, where a stone staircase descended to the lower levels. Here, wine and foodstuffs were stored in great quantities. There were many wooden barrels stacked nearly floor to ceiling, and glass bottles by the thousands, which Lucetta recognized as her favorite vintages of wine.

They continued down to the very bottom, then followed a lengthy corridor dimly lit by lanterns. She recognized this place from her youth, and immediately began to tremble. It seemed unfitting for Charlotte to be left alone in such a place, buried far from the sun's warmth and the cool kiss of rain. But this was their way, the Bethard way, since the earliest days when Cardale was little more than a settlement.

A door stood closed at the end of the hall, its wood aged and discolored from the passing of centuries. Though Pavlos stood between her and the dark beyond, she found herself in tears, and shaking as if taken by a sudden affliction. She clung to the Droethien's cloak like a child seeking protection from their parent.

"Princess." Pavlos paused. "You are certain you wish to do this, yes?"

The answer was most certainly no, but there would never be another opportunity to visit with the Queen, not until returning as a conquering hero. Lucetta nodded and stole her courage, but there was precious little of it in the first place.

Together, they approached the crypt's entrance. Pavlos unlatched the door and was the first to enter, a gust of cool, stale air offending her nostrils. The eldest of House Bethard were deepest inside, while Charlotte would be much closer, to her relief. With closed eyes, she held tight to Pavlos' cloak and traversed the darkness.

A soft scent of burning candles was enough to coax her eyes open. There was a warm glow ahead, undoubtedly the final resting place of her mother. A crushing weight of sorrow came upon her, as if the crypt had caved in on itself. Wiping her tears away, she approached the light and saw Charlotte lying peacefully on a wooden table, a purple cloth draped over its surface.

It was both astonishing and terrifying beyond belief to see how pristine the Queen was, even now. She looked as beautiful and alive as the day Pavlos snuffed out her life, with not a trace of corruption or hint of rotting stench. Lucetta was no expert when it came to death, but she would have at least expected the body to begin decomposition, but not an ounce of it was evident.

"I will leave you for a moment, yes?" Pavlos lifted his lantern and saw distress on Lucetta's face. "Worry not, princess, I will be right here."

Even twenty feet away was too great of a distance, but there was little time to protest or delay. Lucetta mustered her love and courage, and approached the Queen slowly.

"Mother," she sniffled. "I'm so sorry this had to happen. I know what I must do, but the road ahead is invisible to me. I feel like I'm walking through the fog, lost and alone. And now I fear I've only made matters worse."

A dark yet familiar presence began to manifest inside the crypt. Lucetta suspected it was the woman in black, ever watchful and determined to keep her on task. But the entity was content to remain in the darkness, allowing one final moment between mother and daughter.

"This has all gone so horribly wrong," she continued. "The city is burning… the people are revolting… But I couldn't allow them to take you. They have no right! I made certain you were kept safe, and now you're home."

Time was growing short, and Lucetta would need to return to the fray to oversee Cardale's defense. Neither Marcellus nor Aldred would be up to the task, nor anyone on the King's council, for that matter. Someone had to end the madness of Hesgrin and his Harbingers before the city was little more than a smoking ruin.

"I have to go now, mother," she sniffled. "I swear I'll come back and visit you once order has been restored. I hope you're proud of me. I love you, forever."

As Lucetta turned and departed, a soft echo reached her ears. It was faint, nearly as quiet as mice, but she heard it well enough. It was a voice familiar, sad yet comforting, one she had learned first in the womb. It was Charlotte's voice, or perhaps, just a memory of it, calling out in the darkness.

"I love you… daughter…"

TITAN VIII

"**S**HE'S AT THE IVORNORIUM," CONRAK GRUMBLED, STARING AT THE hastily scrawled note in his hand.

Both men shared the same irritation and sudden alarm, as Madelyn had yet to venture anywhere without their protection. With shadowy assassins lurking in the darkness and barbarians descending from the north, the streets of Bentmont were anything but safe.

"Damn it girl," Tylar snarled. "Come on, we need to get over there before someone else takes a stab at her."

Conrak shut the door and locked it, and together they set off toward the Ivornorium as fast as they dared. Traveling inconspicuously might have been simple enough for Conrak, but for a hulking man such as Tylar Bradshaw, it was another matter entirely. Down every avenue and alley, he received stares of curiosity and contempt.

Were discretion not the goal, he might have given each and every one of them a proper thrashing. But now was neither the time nor place. Tylar contented himself with a few sour glares of his own and a shove or two, but nothing that might deter them from reaching the library as quickly as possible.

Before long, the Ivornorium and its glistening dome peeked above the neighboring rooftops, its splendor dominating the skyline all around. He hoped the assassins had not found Madelyn there, as old Willard Mirren would struggle to fend off an angry bee, let alone a trained killer.

They rapped on the door in their customary fashion, signaling the Chronican of their arrival. The door took ages to creep open, and when it did, Tylar burst inside with reckless abandon.

"Where is she?" he demanded.

"She… she's down… there," the old man quaked, pointing a trembling twig of a finger.

Conrak muttered something, but Tylar raced off toward the hidden staircase and flew down it, nearly tripping several times and tumbling to the bottom. Once there, he paused in sudden astonishment at the sight before him.

No… it… can't be possible…

Tylar stood motionless, unable to make sense of what his eyes could plainly see. When last they saw Madelyn, she was a frail and worn shell of a woman, barely clinging to the edge of hope. She had the eyes of an old soldier, weathered beyond her years, with a broken body to match. But now, something about her seemed different, as if an imposter had taken her place.

"What in the hell…"

Standing before them was a woman restored, much the same as he remembered. Madelyn had every bit the physique and demeanor of a proper knight, though she still struggled to maintain solid footing. Still, it was if the torment of the past year had been erased from her flesh entirely.

"Well I'll be damned." Conrak said from behind, a stark contrast to his usual smugness. "So it is true. You *are* an Eveldanyr. My eyes can hardly believe it."

"You look…" Tylar stammered. The words were nearly too fantastical to speak. While Madelyn was a far cry from her former glory, seeing her stand and move about without any assistance was stunning beyond words.

"For what it's worth, the pain is no less. Different, but…" She huffed in frustration. "Do you know the feeling after a day of rigorous training? The soreness, the weakness… my whole body feels like… I don't know. I can feel my bones growing and shifting, if that makes the slightest bit of sense."

Of course, it made no sense at all. Tylar tried his hardest to understand, but was nevertheless disturbed by what he was seeing. It was curious to note the roots of Madelyn's hair. They appeared tinged with black stains, but no more than the thickness of a fingernail.

"It makes perfect sense to me." Conrak lifted his lantern higher to inspect her. "Your connection to this place, to these books, and the people who wrote them is strong. Your ancestors reach out to you through these pages. They speak to you. They imbue you with divine power."

It appeared everything Conrak had blustered about was indeed true. All of the ancient histories, however dull, were right after all. Such a revelation was difficult to swallow, so much so that Tylar began shaking his head incredulously. Surely, such things could only exist in dreams and tall tales.

"I don't believe it," he muttered. "I can't believe it. How is this possible?"

"Is it really so difficult to believe, Bradshaw?" Conrak asked with a hint of annoyance. "There are powers at work here which are beyond you or I. Humble yourself a bit more and you might realize what's happening here."

Such things truly unsettled him, and it was still a struggle to believe any of it, even now. Tylar had seen many things throughout life, things common men would have nightmares over. But every horror he had encountered was mortal and made of flesh, and easily dispatched with sharpened steel. The idea of contending with gods and forces beyond what could plainly be seen shook him to his core.

"Come," Conrak said. "We have much to discuss."

As Madelyn passed by him and up the stairs, a cold presence seemed to follow. Together they returned to ground level and emerged back inside the Ivornorium. Conrak shut the secret entrance, then took a seat at one of the reading tables. A quick glance down the hall satisfied his caution.

"So, what are you cooking up inside that head of yours?" Tylar asked, his chair popping and groaning as he sat.

"Time, unfortunately, is not on our side." Conrak glanced at Madelyn. "But my faith is stronger now than it was this morning. You've shown me wonders, my lady, and I believe your time has come."

"Is there any word on when the army will march?" she asked, looking deadly serious.

"Soon, in all likelihood," Conrak replied. "The last of the southern lordlings arrived just two days ago."

The conversation was quickly making Tylar's blood boil. Conrak's insistence on forcing the girl into battle might very well spell her demise. Despite looking healthier than in months past, she was still in no condition to ride, let alone fight.

"And why are you asking?" Titan lowered his brow. "There's no fucking way you're going with us. I doubt you could even tolerate a saddle for more than a few minutes."

"I have to, Tylar!" she snarled, fists clenched. "You told me to live for vengeance, and that's what I've done. It's the only thing keeping me alive. I'll be damned if I let you or anyone else take that from me. Vengeance is all I have left."

There was a piercing hatred in Madelyn's steely-blue eyes which nearly cut through him. Were this any other time, he might very well have dismissed her with a laugh and a mocking jest, but this time was different. Something about the girl radiated pure dread, an indescribable terror which gripped at the heart of him.

"Alright, alright," he said, raising both hands. "But who are you going to ride with? The Order won't let you anywhere near them, and that's where Conrak will be. I'm sworn to represent the prince in his camp, and—"

"I may have a solution," Conrak interjected, a shit-eating grin crossing his face. "The Order did you a great disservice, but perhaps we can remedy that. The army has been sitting here for quite awhile, and what do soldiers do when they get bored?"

His question brought back humorous memories of times spent sitting in garrison. Tylar remembered many a drunken brawl, and acts of overt stupidity for the sake of a laugh.

"They fight," he snorted. "So what are you saying, Conrak? You want her to go out there and punch the first knight she sees? Amusing as it would be, I don't think she's strong enough for that yet."

"Perhaps not, but I've attended a fair number of jousts in recent weeks. It seems our southern kin are intent on winning bragging rights by unseating a knight. Thus far, no one has claimed the honor." He turned and stared Madelyn down. "Think you can hold a lance?"

There was a brief silence as the girl's hubris faded, reality quickly setting back in. Climbing a flight of stairs was one thing, riding was another. And jousting quite another still.

"I don't know." Her gaze shifted to the floor. "Do you really think this is the way? Do you think the Order will simply allow me back into their ranks if I do this?"

"Difficult to say." Conrak stroked his short, graying beard. "But I suspect it'll create quite a firestorm around here. I know your flesh may not be ready, but what does your heart say? What does your spirit say?"

Everyone knew the answer, or at least, Tylar did. The girl was a fighter and a killer, that much was certain. She looked up slowly, her steely-blue eyes reflecting an ironclad determination. Not even the grave, it seemed, would be enough to stop Madelyn Everly's vengeance.

"Very well," Conrak said. "Gather your strength, my lady. Tonight we show the world what you're made of. I would recommend continuing your studies, and soaking up as much knowledge as you possibly can. Bradshaw, if you would be so kind as to stay with her for the time being. I'll return this evening to our new accommodation, and meet you there."

Throwing Madelyn into a joust against the finest cavalrymen in Caldakas was one of the most reckless ideas Tylar had ever heard, but there was little use in protesting. He grumbled as Conrak took his leave, then searched around for the nearest tankard. Surely there had to be some ale or wine sitting around, he thought. What was a Chronican to do besides reading dusty books all day?

Unfortunately, the only drink to be found was water. On the eve of destiny, it seemed downright unjust to not enjoy the taste of a proper ale. It was, after all, a soldier's drink. Not only was it customary before a fight, but perhaps the drink might bestow some courage upon the girl as well.

"Come on," he said, certain Conrak had departed. "Let's get out of this dusty shithole and fill our bellies. You'll need it."

While uncertain, Madelyn agreed to his offer. She was still hesitant to step out into the streets of Bentmont, but Tylar's presence helped to dispel her fear. There were many common taverns and food stalls all throughout the city, each of them seemingly as good as the last. One could never be certain of what they might find inside a Bentmont tavern, but these days, they were always infested with the King's soldiers.

Together, they entered one of the many nameless shitholes found throughout the city. There was hot food roasting over a fire, and enough ale to drown an army. Unfortunately, an army was already seated inside, the tavern nearly full to capacity.

After flagging down the attention of a barkeep, Tylar ordered two plates of meat and greens, and two pints of ale. A table sat vacant near the center of the room. Not a preferred location to dine and discuss, but it served well enough. Madelyn dug into her food with a vicious appetite, like hyenas to a fresh carcass.

"What do you think about this plan of his?" Tylar asked, sipping at the froth in his mug. "I could tell you my thoughts, but I doubt you would give a shit."

"I'd rather not think about it," she replied. "Can we just enjoy a meal in peace?"

It was clear the eyes inside the tavern were causing her great distress. Dozens of men glanced over casually, some outright gawking, all of them earning Tylar's ire. He cast each of them a searing gaze, though it did little to stifle their curiosity.

"If we had more time, then I might agree," he sighed. "What are you doing, Madelyn? What do you hope to accomplish by getting yourself killed out there?"

Madelyn sat dumbstruck, a piece of bread hanging from her mouth. "Excuse me? Did I hear you correctly?"

"You did. Why are you so hellbent on proving yourself to everyone? You spat in the face of death and made it back home, and now you want to throw yourself headlong into the fire again? Fuck that. You're alive. Keep it that way."

"And what would you have me do, Tylar? Stay behind and live out my days in the Ivornorium, until I become as feeble as Willard?"

Tylar nodded. "Aye, and be glad of it. You're one of the good ones, far too good to lose your soul like I have. Your whole life is ahead of you. Go do something with it that doesn't involve risking your neck over a bunch of bloody savages."

In a flash, she slammed both hands onto the table, then stormed toward the door. Every man within the tavern was watching, their silence absolute. Tylar gulped down the last of his drink, then set off in pursuit.

"I'm a knight, Tylar," she seethed. "I've lived as a knight, and I'll die as a knight. I won't let you or anyone take that away from me."

"Enough of this bullshit," he took hold of her by the arm. "Stop trying to be someone you're not. You weren't meant for this kind of life. It was thrust upon you. The High Marshal was wrong to deny you a proper childhood, the way a girl ought to grow up. But if you don't stop and walk away while you still can, you'll be dead. And for what?"

It was nearly possible to see Madelyn's heart breaking in two, her hope on the brink of dying a second death. As badly as Tylar wanted to reach out, comfort her, and apologize, he knew it had to be this way. Better she lived an uneventful life than not lived at all.

"I died at Morden that day," she whimpered. "All I want is to take that bastard Dreadfire with me. Nothing else matters except that."

"Then let me avenge you. Let Conrak. Hell, let Gareth do it! There's no need for you to be out there. I'll bring you the fucker's head on a plate if I must!"

With fresh tears wetting her cheeks, Madelyn retreated to their safehouse. Tylar nearly slapped himself silly for dashing the one hope she had clung to, the chance for revenge. He lumbered just behind, struggling to keep pace as she muscled through Bentmont's congested streets.

"Slow down," he complained. "What do you want, an apology?"

They arrived outside of the warehouse. Madelyn tried to wrench the door open, but its lock was secured tightly. Tylar produced a key and inserted it into the rusted keyhole, the door groaning as it gave way.

"Just go, please," she pleaded. "Leave me be."

"Not a chance," he shot back. "I'm keeping you in my sight for as long as I can. Wouldn't want you to run off and do something stupid, now."

Madelyn shut herself inside her cramped room, while Tylar contented himself with another drink. He sat on top of a large wooden crate, sipping down ale after ale until the room began tilting ever so slightly. But not even the serenity of intoxication was enough to soothe the sting of Madelyn's anguish. Perhaps it was wrong to dissuade her, after all.

Tylar recalled years past, when he too lusted after vengeance. Campaign after campaign, his brothers in the Order were cut down, until only he remained. Such unrelenting hatred eventually led to despair, which in turn grew into indifference. Cherished memories of good friends and better days became like poison, the only antidote to which was a strong drink.

Don't you see what I'm trying to do, girl? I'm trying to spare you from the life of bullshit I've endured. Nobody deserves to feel this way. Nobody deserves to wish they were dead. Well, maybe Dreadfire. That cunt deserves every bit of suffering he gets.

Hours later, the door cracked open, and in stepped Conrak. It was tempting to throttle him for filling Madelyn's head with absurdities, but ultimately it would accomplish nothing. Nobody seemed to care for the life lessons from an aging soldier, it seemed.

"It's time," Conrak announced, a large sack slung over one shoulder. "The sun is setting, and the men are just getting warmed up. Where's Madelyn? I brought her a little something."

A clatter filled the room as he set the sack down and opened it. Conrak reached inside and produced a helmet, expertly forged and polished to a mirror-like shimmer. Madelyn emerged and stood next to Tylar, gazing incredulously at the sight of it, her lips quivering.

"I do hope it fits you properly," the Sacrithon said. "I scrounged up what I could from around Thorn, and made a few purchases in the markets. Not the prettiest set of armor, but it'll keep you safe all the same."

Madelyn moved apprehensively toward the helmet as Conrak removed a suit of armor and set it on the table. Her fingers ran gracefully across its smooth surface, as if being reunited with a lost family heirloom.

"Thank you for this," she whispered.

"No thanks are necessary," Conrak said. "You go out there and you give it everything you've got. You create such a stir that the High Marshal himself lies awake at night."

Perhaps Conrak was not the insufferable narcissist he appeared to be, Tylar thought. It was a kind gesture, but one which only served to encourage her. But he was beginning to see that keeping Madelyn safe was merely a selfish gesture, one done more for his sake than anyone else's.

It was clear what she wanted, and ultimately, what she needed. Far be it for him to deny anyone the opportunity to avenge themselves. Perhaps it would be better to let the girl have her way, he thought, provided he could succeed in keeping her safe.

"If this is what you truly want, then I'll help you get it," Tylar said. "Just don't go getting yourself killed, or I'll stuff one of those magical books up your ass, bring you back to life, and kill you myself."

Conrak snorted, one of the few times his dry wit went over. Despite being damn near embalmed on ale, Tylar picked up the cuirass and fastened it around Madelyn's torso. Piece by piece she was encased in steel, until only her head remained unprotected.

"Maybe you should lose the hair," he suggested. "Hard to fit all that inside a helmet."

Lightning nearly shot from Madelyn's eyes and struck Tylar down. Despite its incredible length, it was one of the few pieces of her identity which went unmolested by the northmen. Scowling, she began braiding her flowing curtain of blonde hair.

"Alright, alright." He raised up both hands. "Suit yourself. Just don't complain about how hot it gets in there."

"Run it down my back," she said, nodding to the straps on the side of her cuirass.

Tylar loosened the armor and stuffed Madelyn's braid inside it. A gorget helped to mask her tresses, her steel helmet obscuring the rest of it entirely. To the unknowing eye, the girl was little more than a body inside a suit of protective plate, a nameless, faceless soldier of Betanthia.

"Very good," Conrak said, turning for the door. "Are you ready to meet your destiny? Or at least, take your first steps toward it?"

Without hesitation, she followed Conrak out into the streets, though the armor appeared cumbersome. Tylar's uncertainty grew with each of her labored steps, until he began doubting the entire scheme altogether. Rigorous training and light sparring was one thing, fighting Betanthia's most skilled horsemen was damn near suicidal.

The camp was buzzing with activity, the mood jovial. None knew for certain when the army would set out, but many claimed it would be tomorrow, perhaps the day after. There was feasting, drinking, and of course, fighting throughout. Everywhere Titan turned, there was another brawl or test of skill at arms.

A pair of archers competed to see who could command the center of a nearby target with their arrows. Inside the center of a circle of men, two soldiers stood bloodied and bare-chested, hammering one another mercilessly with clenched fists. And of course, a deep pounding of horse hooves and crashing of lance against armor rang out like claps of thunder.

Such a scene was enough to invite old memories from a past life, a time when he was a celebrated hero in the Order. Tylar could still sense ill-favored glances every so often, but the purple fabric hanging down his back commanded silence and respect on its own.

"Easy, girl," he whispered. "I can hear you shaking in there."

Though Madelyn's helmet was on, Tylar could practically see her worry through the steel. From experience, however, he knew strength and composure could reassure even the most skittish soldier. Hopefully, it would rekindle memories of her days in training, and stoke courage in her heart.

A large jousting list stood a short distance ahead. There were many banners planted in the ground, the black and gold of the Blackthorn on one side, and nearly a dozen others opposite them. The King's colors were always most prominent, standing taller and prouder than all others.

"Tonight should be an interesting night!" Conrak grinned. "It seems the southerners aren't yet content in their humiliation."

He motioned over to the knights of the Order who stood in a large group, looking as joyless and professional as possible. Tylar felt both their eyes and hostility as he approached. There was a time when their disdain would have infuriated him, but now it only brought amusement. He made certain to adjust his purple cloak several times, showing off not only its rich fabric, but the status it commanded.

"Finally come to show us what you're made of, eh Conrak?" one of the knights taunted. He was a large, barrel-chested man, bald and bare-faced.

Conrak snatched a freshly poured mug of ale from another knight, bold as you please, and smiled. "No, not tonight. I would hate to embarass you lot in front of these green southern boys. I'm sure my Guardsman friend here would agree with me."

"So then why are you here?" another knight said, low and raspy.

"Well, there's been a lot of talk around camp as of late. Seems I might have found a man who could best any one of you." He gestured to Madelyn, though it brought only hearty laughter.

"Have you gone stupid, Conrak?" the first knight guffawed. "You bring some squire over here and expect us to take you seriously? Does he even have the strength to hold a lance?"

The knights chuckled, some spitting and others turning their backs. Conrak, however, looked completely unphased by their indifference.

"I'll tell you what; if he can unhorse one of Vakaro's best, then he gets a shot at one of you. Anyone man enough to take me up on my challenge?"

"Aye," said Emery, a man who appeared to be the nastiest brute of them all. A spitting image of his younger self, Tylar thought, but with teeth like a wildman's. "But what if your boy loses, eh?"

"Twenty gold pieces to each of you then."

The knights looked at one another, a few exchanging their thoughts in muffled whispers and an occasional ripple of laughter.

"I have a better offer," Emery said. "I say fuck those soft southern twats. Put your boy against me, and if I win, I get *all* the gold."

Such a proposition was intriguing, for Conrak at least. He twisted his face around and nodded. "Very well. I accept your offer. And if my man wins, you owe him something."

"He won't, but go on, tell me what you want. It's gotta be something."

"My demand is simple," the Sacrithon grinned. "No gold. In fact, nothing material at all. If he wins, you owe him your respect."

The knights broke out into laughter, thinking Conrak had gone completely mad. Instead, he stood firm, unmoved by their mockery. Emery nodded in agreement, spitting a foul gobbet onto the ground. "Horse!"

Raucous cheers rang out. A Blackthorn squire darted off to fetch the knight's mount, the camp coming alive in anticipation. Tylar strode over to another squire and snatched the reins of a black destrier from his hands. The smooth-cheeked lad looked as frightened as a deer, and offered no challenge. Neither did the owner of the prized war horse, for that matter.

"Your rules, Conrak," Emery shouted. "Since you'll be the one paying me!"

"Best of five lances. Unhorse is a win."

Emery accepted and trotted off to his end of the jousting list. Tylar had kept his silence thus far, but was ready to strangle Conrak for his hubris. He grabbed the Sacrithon by the shoulder, pulling him in close.

"Have you gone completely fucking mad?" Tylar snarled. "That man is going to skewer her like a pig. She can barely walk straight and you want her to ride? What are you trying to prove?"

Madelyn inched closer. It was easy enough to sense her uncertainty, despite being fully encased in steel.

"Listen to me," Conrak said to her, completely ignoring him." If you want to fight alongside these men again, then this is the only way. They respect strength. They don't care if you were a Commander once, however famous. The only thing that matters is right now."

"I know," she said, voice trembling. "I just… I don't think my body is strong enough. I want to, but—"

"Believe me when I say this." Conrak pointed a stern finger. "You are much more than just this physical form. You may be *in* this world, but you are not *of* it. None of us are, and I have a suspicion you know this better than anyone. So stay calm. Focus. There's great power in you, and it can make your flesh do things you never thought possible."

A boisterous crowd around the lists was steadily building, dozens of men packed in shoulder to shoulder. Word had spread into the camp of Conrak's challenge, with curious onlookers of every stripe and station turning out to see if the rumors were true. It was a rare occasion when a knight of the Order was openly challenged, after all.

A man made his way over to the Blackthorn side, where he was greeted heartily. Tylar recognized his face, or at least, thought as much. There was no doubt, however, that Madelyn knew precisely who the man was. She began clinging to Tylar like a frightened child would to their mother.

"It's Deverell!" she said, panicked. "He's going to recognize me! He's… he's…"

"Don't shit yourself, girl," Tylar grumbled. "You're wearing armor, you look like any other scrawny shit in the King's army. And who the fuck is Deverell anyway?"

"He was with the garrison in Hok. He's the one who ransomed me and brought me back home."

As irritated as Tylar was with her sudden weakness, he was overtaken by an understanding he had not acquired until only recently. He knew now, more than ever, how difficult it was to be seen at your weakest point. Especially by people who only ever knew you to be strong, either directly or by reputation.

Memories of being carted back to Bentmont in chains were still fresh, and stung just as badly. It was perhaps the greatest injustice one could suffer, to be cursed and spat upon by those who swore the same oath of brotherhood. Better to have died clean on the battlefield, as a soldier should, Tylar thought.

"Good," he said. "Then let him see the real Madelyn Everly, not that broken shell of a person he brought down to Bentmont. Let them all see."

While he could only see darkness inside the eye slit of her helmet, Tylar could sense the shifting tide of her emotions. Tough love seemed to have done a bit of good, for once. At first, it appeared Madelyn would not be able to mount such a large destrier. Even in her healthier days, it was a task that would require some degree of assistance. Tylar cupped his hands and awkwardly hoisted her into the saddle. The spectacle prompted chuckles and finger pointing.

Come on girl, you can do this. You have to.

It was one of the most nerve-wracking moments of his life. It seemed like only yesterday when Madelyn was bedridden and near death. And now, Conrak had coaxed her into something she had no business doing. Tylar felt a sudden panic, and made to stop her before the joust even began, but the Sacrithon held out an arm.

"Don't," Conrak said quietly. "She has to do this. Better she should fall in a joust than on the battlefield. This is the only way for her to prove to herself that she's ready. This could be the greatest moment of her life. Don't take it away."

Such sentiment was true enough, but it did little to calm the fluttering in his chest. Within an instant, both horses lunged forward, breaking out into a full gallop. Tylar barely had time to collect his thoughts before Madelyn came racing by, lance in hand, her moment of truth mere seconds away.

He grabbed hold of Conrak's shoulder and squeezed as the joust began. Both riders held their lances true, their armor rattling as their mounts hurdled closer. Astonishingly, the tips of both lances met one another, the wooden shafts exploding into hundreds of small fragments. Such a feat was rare, but not impossible. The knights and southerners looked on, impressed and muttering to themselves.

Fucking hell… Hang in there, girl!

Both riders were rearmed, then sent flying toward one another yet again. Madelyn's form appeared decent enough, but Emery struck a direct blow. She rocked in the saddle, a plume of splinters erupting, and nearly fell backwards onto the dirt. Tylar raced down the list without hesitation, as fast as his legs could manage. It was only by some miracle the girl was able to stay mounted.

"Are you alright? Fucking hell, he could have killed you!"

The hit had certainly shaken her. Madelyn swayed back and forth, groaning and nearly retching from pain. Tylar thought of calling an end to the contest, but was unable to speak the words. Conrak was right; this was the only path forward for her. And now, if she should fail, all of their credibility would inevitably fall by the wayside.

"I'm alright," she whispered. "It hurts so much."

"You've faced worse and survived it," Tylar said. "Remember that. Imagine Damien Dreadfire sitting on that horse, and imagine this is your only shot to take him out. Go on, kill that fucker!"

Madelyn sat up straight in the saddle, staring back at him through a blackened eye slit. While he was no poet as Conrak was, his encouragement seemed to do well enough. She motioned for another lance, a squire trotting over with fresh wood in hand. She took up the weapon and couched it, then drove her foot into the side of her destrier.

In a flash, both riders were racing toward each other once again. Time slowed to a near crawl, moving so slow he could practically count the flecks of dirt kicked up by their horses. He watched with bated breath as they met one another yet again, though this time, the girl's lance found its mark.

By some divine will, Emery was unhorsed and crashed violently onto the ground. A near total silence fell over the list and the field around it, with none so much as moving a muscle. Conrak was the first to roar his approval, clapping and smiling like a drunken fool. Tylar was unaware he had been holding his breath for so long, and exhaled desperately, thankful the girl was unharmed.

"It appears we have ourselves a victor!" Conrak exclaimed, his arms spread wide. "A sad day for the Order, no doubt, as one of our finest and most vocal champions has been bested! Come now, who wishes to see the face of the winner?"

Some of the southerners cheered, but most were too stunned to make sense of what had just transpired. Conrak motioned for Madelyn to come forth, and with the assistance of a squire, she climbed down from the saddle. Tylar trotted over, not knowing whether to offer his congratulations and hug her, or simply let the Sacrithon continue on as only he knew how.

"Go on now," Conrak said to her. "This is your moment."

Madelyn removed her helmet slowly, then jerked her sweaty braid out from underneath her armor. The knights stood dumbfounded, Deverell most of all. Dozens of eyes were upon her, likely hundreds, and not a man made to speak.

"This is Madelyn Everly!" Conrak announced. "Commander of the Blackthorn Knights, and survivor of Castle Morden. By now most of you have heard her story, either around a campfire or whispered somewhere in the streets. She rode into the fires of hell for Betanthia, for each and every one of you here. Try as the northmen did, they couldn't kill her. And now she's back from the abyss, ready to wet her blade and seek revenge."

A hushed silence fell over the soldiers, some struggling to make sense of what they were seeing. Tylar stepped alongside her, chest puffed out, eyeing the awestruck crowd like an attack dog.

"Some of you have heard the rumor that she was given her discharge papers," Conrak continued. "I regret to report the truth of such rumors.

480

For her bravery, for her unselfish service to this nation, she was cast aside. But hear me! She *will* ride again, and rain vengeance down upon the northern hordes! Will you stand alongside her? Will you fight for the one who laid down their life for you? I know I plan on it, as does the great Titan Bradshaw."

Conrak motioned toward him, the eyes of the crowd shifting over accordingly. It was uncomfortable to be at the center of such attention, but a debt was owed. Each man, knight and commoner alike, owed Tylar their gratitude for a lifetime of service and sacrifice.

"This man too is a survivor of Morden. A true hero." Conrak slapped him on the shoulder. "In his shame of defeat, he turned to banditry to survive. I captured him and brought him back to Bentmont to be executed as a traitor. But the fates thought otherwise. Not only is Titan Bradshaw a free man, he is a personal bodyguard to Prince Gareth Bethard. And he too plans to ride into war to seek vengeance."

There was an intensity building within the soldiers and knights, and even the squires and camp followers. They were eating out of the palm of Conrak's hand, enthralled by every word.

"So now, I ask you, will you fight alongside these two heroes?" The Sacrithon threw his hands into the air.

A crashing roar filled the air, echoing far and wide like a clap of thunder. The men looked on with what Tylar could only suppose was hope, likely the first hope they had heard since being mustered for war. Suddenly, the barbarians seemed less frightening to them, though he knew the truth to be otherwise.

"To my brothers in the Order," Conrak shouted, "what will you decide? Will you cast Madelyn Everly aside as the High Marshal did? For me, I will not ride unless she is beside me. Is that not the oath we swore, not only to serve Betanthia, but each other as well? I say Castle Thorn should be pulled down, stone by stone, and the Order torn asunder, should we abandon such an oath of brotherhood!"

While their reception was not as rowdy as the common rabble, they appeared to nevertheless agree. It was one of the more surreal moments of Tylar Bradshaw's life. It was only a short while ago when he was sitting in a dank cell awaiting the end of a Blackthorn rope. But now, together with his best friend, they were being hailed as heroes.

Conrak, you crafty little cunt... I underestimated you.

"I know who I'll be riding alongside." the Sacrithon pointed toward her. "What about you, my brothers? Will you fight alongside Commander Everly, one more time?"

An explosion of approval rippled throughout the camp, enough to rattle the walls of Castle Thorn to their foundation. Betanthia now had its heroes, its standard bearers which would lead the Kingdom into its greatest war in a generation.

"A marvelous speech." Tylar grunted. "All of your book reading appears to be coming in handy."

"Words have a way of stirring greatness within men, Bradshaw," Conrak said, smiling. "They're every bit as deadly as a sword, perhaps even more so. I've done what I can here, we'll see where the men's loyalty lies. Come, I believe a drink is in order."

Together, they flanked Madelyn and started back toward the city. They passed scores of curious onlookers, some offering praise and respect, while some simply marveled in silence. It would have been a lie to say such admiration was unwanted, or uncomfortable. If anything, it felt like an overdue vindication for years of sacrifice and suffering.

While the camp was electric with jubilation, the streets of Bentmont were winding down. It was easy enough to avoid the masses and any unfriendly eyes, with only the main avenues still bustling. They passed through a market street near the Ivornorium, but something was amiss. Madelyn was beginning to sway and stumble, her armor clattering like cooking pots falling to the ground.

"You alright?" Tylar placed an arm around her just as she lost footing.

"Pick her up," Conrak said frantically. "We can't let anyone see her like this."

They had driven the girl too hard. Tylar was caught between anger and worry, though the latter had won out. He scooped Madelyn up effortlessly, then shuffled off into a dark alleyway.

"This is all your fault!" he cursed. "You pushed her too hard and now look at what you've caused!"

Tylar was angry. Furiously angry. He cradled Madelyn's head, her eyes rolling back several times until they drew closed.

"Relax, Bradshaw." Conrak knelt down beside them. "She just needs some rest, is all. As much as you may disagree, this had to be done tonight. Not only for her sake, but for Betanthia. You saw how those men reacted when she unhorsed Emery. We need her on the battlefield. She's become a standard now, someone the men rally behind."

Furious as he was, the idea had its merits. Regardless of whether he was right or wrong, Conrak would certainly be on the receiving end of a tongue lashing, but now was not the time. If anyone saw Madelyn in such a condition, then their efforts would be spoiled.

"Fine," he said. "Now let's get the fuck out of here before anyone sees us."

Together they retreated into the darkness, maneuvering through one alley after another, until their safehouse was in sight. They paused in the doorway of an old building as a patrol marched past, a few of the soldiers speaking of the joust. It was intriguing to hear how quickly word had spread throughout Bentmont, and hearing how they spoke of Madelyn's skills began to blunt Tylar's anger.

"You had better be right about all this, Conrak," he grunted. "Because if she gets herself killed out there, Damien Dreadfire will be the least of your worries."

GARETH VI

A NERVOUS EXCITEMENT WAS IN THE AIR, AN ANTICIPATION BUILDING like the moments before a thunderstorm. Everyone in the encampment could feel it, Gareth especially. He awoke that morning after a sleepless night, hands trembling as he took a sip of whiskey from a small flask. It was all he could do to take the edge off.

Sir Edmund brought with him a rumor from the prior evening. There was talk of the army preparing to march at any moment, and Lord Vakaro would be holding a meeting before midday with his lordlings and senior officers. It was kind of the southern Commandant to extend no invitation, Gareth thought, though unsurprised.

Were it not for my bodyguard, the man might very well strike me down and claim I fell from my horse, or on my sword for that matter. And I'm certain there are enough sycophants in Betanthia who would believe him.

Aldred most certainly would. It was likely he would be waiting at the Westwind Citadel for word of Gareth's untimely demise, but Sir Edmund and his Guardsmen would hopefully frustrate those plans.

Between Damien Dreadfire and Lord Vakaro, Edmund certainly has his work cut out for him. I do hope he's up to the task after all these years.

After dressing in his ornate steel armor, Gareth stepped out into a new morning, rays of sunlight glinting off his polished breastplate. A pair of Guardsmen outside of his tent snapped to attention and saluted, then fell in behind him. Gareth enjoyed being among the soldiers, even though they were under Lord Vakaro's command.

But it was ultimately Betanthia and House Bethard they were loyal to, or so he hoped. Judging from the raucous reception he received while walking through the sprawling encampment, such sentiment seemed to hold water. He saw a familiar face approaching, but this morning, he was without a customary smile.

"Turns out I was right," Sir Edmund Thomas said, brow furrowed. "He's holding a meeting in less than an hour, and afterward the army will march. They're already breaking camp on the other side of Bentmont. Once word makes the rounds, we'll be off."

"Tell me, has he extended any invitation?"

Edmund shook his head. "No, I'm afraid not. And I'm told the High Marshal will be present as well."

"Less than an hour, you say?" Gareth scratched his bearded chin. "Sounds to me like we should arrive early then."

The thought of Jenson Powell made Gareth's jaw tighten. He was unsure who he would like to flog more, the High Marshal or the would-be conspirator lord. Or perhaps he might take a lash to the both of them, before taking their heads.

One punishment for insubordination and another for treason. But no, I mustn't. If we're going to beat this horde back to the forests, we're going to need unity among our ranks. Bide your time, Gareth. It's all you can do.

With Sir Edmund close by, he strode to a hitching post, where his horse was saddled and waiting. A squire assisted him onto his mount, and within moments, Gareth and his entourage of Guardsmen rode at speed toward Castle Thorn. The clacking of hooves on weathered cobbles was the only cue Bentmont's locals needed. They parted with no further persuasion, the center of the road given solely to their monarch.

The looming monstrosity that was Castle Thorn grew larger as Gareth approached. He wished he never had to return to such an accursed place, not after witnessing such heart-wrenching agony Madelyn had to endure there. Its long shadow sent a chill down his spine, the sight of which he would never truly become used to.

Although the massive doors to the bailey were open, its portcullis was lowered, clenched tightly like lion's teeth. Gareth brought his horse to a halt, signaling the Guardsmen to follow his lead with a mere wave of a hand.

"You there," Sir Edmund called out, breaking ranks and trotting forward. "Open this gate at once. Your prince demands an audience with the High Marshal."

A pair of knights on the other side looked at each other in uncertainty, then back at Sir Edmund. "I'm afraid he's not here, Sir."

"Not here?" Gareth blurted. "Where is he then? I demand to know, at once!"

Both knights said nothing, instead trading stupid glances between themselves. Thankfully, Sir Edmund was not in the mood for games. "You had best be quick with an answer. You *do* know who this is, I would hope?"

"I'm sorry, Sir," a knight said, "but we are not at liberty to disclose the whereabouts of the High Marshal, per his orders."

Gareth straightened up in the saddle, staring down his nose at the two knights. "I am Prince Gareth Bethard, and I have suffered enough insolence from the Order. Do you need to be reminded yet again whom you truly serve? The Blackthorn swore an oath of fealty to House Bethard, many centuries ago. You serve at my leisure. If you think for one moment the army which surrounds this city won't tear open these gates and drag you screaming to the gallows at my command, think again. Perhaps your precious charter is in need of reevaluation."

"Very well," the senior of the two knights relented. "He's with Lord Vakaro, at his command tent, just northwest of here. Marshal Powell left not ten minutes before you arrived."

It was an insult beyond comprehension. Gareth had always known the Blackthorn to be a brotherhood of honorable men, defending the borderlands and trade routes of Betanthia. Bards would sing songs of their legendary heroism, though he was beginning to see their embellishments. The Order, like Lord Vakaro and Aldred Eldon, were not what they seemed.

With burning anger, Gareth and Edmund left the gates of Castle Thorn and raced toward the outskirts of Bentmont. The streets were noticeably vacant, at least compared to the last several months. The army was indeed moments away from marching, and there would be precious little time to confront the treacherous Commandant before they set off.

That son of a bitch. He's doing everything under the sun to force me to hang him.

Lord Vakaro's host appeared to have assembled well before dawn. They swarmed about like a hive of bees, so frantic one would have thought the barbarian horde was approaching. Despite a flurry of activity, each man made certain to offer their respects as Gareth trotted by. Sir Edmund's ever-watchful gaze made certain of it.

The command tent was not difficult to find. It was the largest of all other tents, though most had been taken down hours before. Many sentries stood around it, both from Lord Vakaro's bodyguard, as well as scores of Blackthorn Knights, their polished plate armor blinding in the morning sun.

"My prince," one of the guards said, offering a respectful bow. "How may I be of service?"

"I'm here for the meeting." Gareth dismounted. "If you would tie up my horse."

The sentry cocked his head. "I beg your forgiveness, my prince, but there is no meeting today. I've been informed it will be taking place tomorrow."

If there was ever a time when Gareth wanted to scream to the heavens until his throat bled, it was then. Lord Vakaro must have known about his arrival, and saw fit to offer forth yet another insult. Simply holding a meeting without him could have been easily explained away, as Gareth had sent no word of his intended arrival. But now, it was clear that Castle Thorn had thrown their lot in with Ridley Vakaro.

"Very well," he said through clenched teeth. "When you happen to see Lord Vakaro, do inform him I've returned to Bentmont, and am looking forward to this meeting."

Without waiting to hear another word, he climbed back into the saddle and made a hasty departure. Sir Edmund was shouting something from behind, but Gareth's anger drowned out his words. After navigating a labyrinth of tents, he took to the streets of Bentmont at speed, overwhelmed by rage so fiery it could melt stone.

He paused at a crowded intersection near a market, the masses so numerous he could ride no further. Gareth scanned the streets for a tavern or drink peddler, desperate to quench his sudden thirst.

"Just what in the hell do you think you're doing?" Sir Edmund snarled, having come alongside him. "You can't just go riding off like that!"

"I ought to have that man flayed for his insolence!" Tears of fury began clouding his eyes. "All he does is insult me at every turn, and I will not stand for it any longer!"

The commoners were beginning to take notice. Their curious stares quickly grew more numerous, their fingers pointed and voices whispering.

"I know you're upset, and understandably so," Sir Edmund said. "But you have to keep control over yourself. Come, we need to get you off the streets. I think I remember a place around here where we can get a drink. I know we could both use it."

They arrived outside of a shuttered building, itself appearing more as a residence as opposed to a tavern. Edmund and Gareth dismounted, tying their horses off to a hitching post, then made for the door. A doorman impeded their entry, large of chest and likely small of brain. The guard at least knew the sight of royalty, to his credit. Finally, it seemed, there was someone in Bentmont capable of paying their due respect.

"Is it? Are you?" the doorman stammered. "I heard the rumors, but I never thought—"

"Yes, this is Prince Gareth. And I am Sir Edmund Thomas of the Royal Guardsmen. Be so kind as to show us to a private area, and bring a bottle of your finest bourbon."

"It would be my greatest honor, Your Highness! Please, right this way!"

They were taken past a large bar at the center of the room, and down one hallway after another. From there, they ascended a flight of stairs and traversed down another hallway to a private lounging area. A separate bar sat against the near wall, a tall rack of dark glass bottles behind it.

Two large, glass doors stood open on the other side of the room, leading to a small balcony. Below was a courtyard, decorated by expertly pruned shrubs and planters full of colorful flowers. Were it any other occasion, Gareth might have enjoyed a bit of fresh air, but he was in no mood to have other people witness his frustration.

Scurrying behind them was a barkeep, an older gentleman with tan spots on his hairless head. Clutched in his steady hands was a platter with two crystal glasses and an unopened bottle of bourbon. He diligently poured out two generous portions, handed them to each man, then retreated with a bow.

"I'm sorry, Edmund. I… I don't know if I'm strong enough to do this." Each tear felt like a razor falling down his cheek. Neither clenched teeth nor clenched fists were enough to stave off an avalanche of utter despair. "My mother dies, and the men sworn to defend my House are overthrowing it. I never wanted any of this, Edmund. All I wanted was a quiet, uneventful life."

He stared down at his bourbon, the fiery amber liquid which had come to know his sorrows well. Once, the serenity of strong drink was enough to ease his troubles, but it now seemed only to worsen them. Gareth emptied his cup in several desperate gulps, but found no relief from his agony.

"I know, lad," Edmund said softly. "You've always had a good heart, perhaps too good for a world such as this. And your mother's passing could not have come at a more inopportune time. But I want you to remember how proud she was of you, and how far you've come in such a short time. And never forget, *you* were the one that set her free. She left this world a happy woman, all because of you."

Edmund's words were of little consolation. Gareth would have traded all of the pomp and comfort of royal life to have Charlotte back. He might have even put out his own eyes to keep her alive, if given such an option. But the Queen was gone, and the only thing which remained was her legacy. The Bethard legacy. A legacy which was nearing the point of utter collapse.

"I can't believe this is happening to me. The barbarians, the usurpers, and my mother…" He sniffled, then refilled his glass. "What am I to do, Edmund?"

"Keep your head up, and your wits about you." The elder Guardsman nursed his glass of bourbon. "Every king must endure their own hardships, and they rarely come one at a time. There's a reason why a crown ages a man. I know the grief of losing your mother is still fresh, but she needs you now, just as much in death as in life. If you fail, and Betanthia falls to any one of those fiends, then her memory will forever be lost."

While Gareth was in the firm grip of drunkenness, Edmund's words were sobering enough to provide a much needed clarity. The fate of not only his country and people was at stake, but the legacy of every

Bethard since the beginning of time. Every hardship suffered throughout the millennia, every war, famine, and power struggle, was all leading to this one defining moment in time.

"You're right," he whispered. "You're always right."

"Careful now." Edmund smiled. "My ex-wives would beg to differ!"

They shared a hearty laugh over another drink, but their merriment was short lived. Gareth knew that despite all of the encouragement, he still had to face an ugly reality waiting outside. Bentmont was no friend to him, and Ridley Vakaro even less so. Each treachery would have to be dealt with in kind, but by far the most pressing dilemma was Damien Dreadfire and his horde of savages.

"What should I do, Edmund? I want to do nothing more than drag Lord Vakaro and the High Marshal from their beds and… and…"

A thousand bloody thoughts danced through his head, each more grisly than the last. Although he had yet to spill a man's blood, the anger and frustration in his heart could only be quenched by death.

"And in time, you shall." Edmund tipped his glass. "But first thing's first. You need to stick to the plan. Win this war and drive those filthy barbarians from your lands. Do it, and be seen doing it, and you'll gain the loyalty of the army. Soldiers respect a man who leads from the front."

"I'm terrified of it. I'm not a soldier, Edmund. I'm afraid I might panic the second the fighting starts."

Sir Edmund slid his chair a bit closer, his gaze becoming focused and piercing, as if recalling memories from battles long past. "Allow me to tell you a thing or two. In war, all men are afraid. Anyone who says otherwise is a liar. But we do what we have to in order to make it home, despite that fear."

"How do you fight the urge to flee? Especially when the battle turns against you?"

The elder Guardsman took a long drink. "Panic is simply the failure of belief, Gareth. If you truly believe in your cause, and you believe you can make it home, you'll find courage where you once thought there was none. Tell me, do you truly believe we can win this war?"

Gareth paused, but then nodded. Betanthia had been bested twice over the last year, the result of lesser men's failings. Cedric Valens had acted carelessly and marched his men to an early grave, putting the entire Kingdom in jeopardy. But this time, such a mistake would not be repeated, or so he hoped.

Lord Vakaro, while treacherous, was every bit as cunning and ruthless as Damien Dreadfire. That fact alone was enough to find comfort in, at least until the coming battle was won. Confronting him would spark a war of its own, a war no less deadly.

"I do, Edmund," he said. "I have no doubt it will be costly, but it's a price we have to pay. And we must pay it, if we are to survive."

"Then you need to keep appearances up." Edmund slapped him on the shoulder. "You're much more than just Gareth Bethard, you know. You're the face of Betanthia, now that your father has diminished. How would the men react seeing you like this? Would they be inspired, or would they lose heart? As difficult as it is, you need to be strong for your people."

It was a weighty responsibility, to say the least. In fact, responsibility was a concept Gareth had only recently become acquainted with. All of the fame and admiration he enjoyed in recent weeks was merely a debt, a debt which could only be paid in blood. Sending good Betanthian men to their death was a responsibility indeed, the greatest and grimmest of them all.

"I will be strong, Edmund," Gareth said, courage welling up inside him. "I understand what it is I have to do."

"And we'll do it, together." The elder Guardsman smiled. "To whatever end."

MADELYN VI

"The moment you've been waiting for has arrived," Conrak said, leaning against the doorway. "Your old friend, the High Marshal, is holding a meeting with Lord Vakaro shortly. From what I've been told, they intend to march soon after. Are you ready?"

The answer to his question was a resounding no, as Madelyn's strength had not fully recovered. But with enough effort, it might be possible to fool most anyone. She had managed to win a joust against a Blackthorn champion, although her exhaustion had not yet passed. Each day seemed to be better than the one before it, but time was in short supply.

"Good." Madelyn stood and began to gather her weapons, armor, and provisions which were stored in a large wooden trunk. "I plan on being there, whether they like it or not."

"Are you certain that's wise?" Conrak raised an eyebrow.

"I don't see why not. Let them arrest me and haul me out in irons in front of the men. Let the world see how much sway Madelyn Everly still holds in the Order."

It was a risky proposition, even with the most capable men at her side. Fortunately, she *did*, but neither Titan nor Conrak could fight off the entire Order if they decided to remove her from the meeting by force. Still, it was a risk worth taking. No one, not the High Marshal, not Lord Vakaro, and not even King Marcellus Bethard would deny her an opportunity for vengeance.

"Very well," the Sacrithon said reluctantly. "Bradshaw and I will be at your side, but I suspect my privileges in the Order will be diminished as a result. Still, this war is the greatest struggle of our generation, and any sacrifice I can make for the cause, I will."

"Thank you, Conrak. Allow me a moment to gather my things, then we can head over."

With a slow bow, he turned and departed, leaving the door cracked open an inch. Madelyn began laying out her various weapons and provisions on the floor. She had always sworn off the assistance of squires, preferring to handle each piece of equipment personally. Despite rising to the second highest rank in the Order, there was something serene about handling the busywork herself.

In many ways, it allowed her to reflect and weigh the full gravity of whatever deployment she was about to embark on. It was also a reminder of where she came from, and that she was no different than the men fighting on the front line. The idea of being smug, pampered and privileged was revolting.

Even now, that could never be me. No, I'll fight and bleed and die as one of the men.

Anger began to flood her heart. Madelyn was unaware of how forcefully she was packing her bags. With clenched teeth and furrowed brow, she stuffed and crammed her gear into small trunks and canvas sacks, a fire within burning into an indomitable inferno.

It was difficult to fend off memories from the year prior, when she made her fateful ride from Bentmont to Castle Morden. Back then, she was performing the same ritual in the comfort of her quarters at Castle Thorn. Now, she was shuttered away in a dank warehouse.

Perhaps it was for the better, she thought. Reminders of how far one could fall were like therapy for the soul. All of the anger, sadness, and determination she felt helped to sober her mind and make everything so simplistic and clear. There was only one mission; to rain vengeance down on those who had wronged her.

Finally, her belongings were packed and ready for the march ahead. Madelyn took one final look around to make certain nothing had been left behind, which was often the case. There always seemed to be at least one thing she would forget, though thankfully it was never anything vital. Her eyes peered upon an aged trunk containing mostly clothing, many of the articles casual in nature and unsuitable for a deployment. She opened it curiously, sifting through its contents until a particular article revealed itself.

A pair of black riding clothes sat on top, its leather worn and linen slightly wrinkled. While not armor by any stretch of the imagination, there was something about the outfit which piqued her attention. On the corset were various pouches and loops, complimenting a utility belt that went along with it. She packed the clothes into a saddle bag, but something else in the chest caught her eye.

Folded neatly inside was the blue dress she had purchased in Cardale. Madelyn had not seen it in some time, and nearly forgot about its existence entirely. Tears began dripping down her cheeks, first of grief, then of anger. She ran a thumb down the length of silk, its surface smooth and cool to the touch.

The garment brought back painful memories of Corbyn and the time they shared together. Although he deserved to never be forgotten, now was not the time to become consumed with such thoughts.

"I will avenge you, Corbyn. You and Hunter and every man Damien Dreadfire murdered. I swear it."

With a sniffle, she folded the dress and placed it inside a saddle bag. The memory of her knights and lost love would ride with her, to one end or another. Where once the prospect of death seemed so inviting, now, only the desire to kill remained. But even ten thousand dead barbarians would be a mere consolation. Damien Dreadfire had to die, and by her hand.

Outside, Conrak and Titan sat mounted. A black destrier stood beside them, saddled and waiting. The beast was massive compared to her mare, Nora, and looked as if it had stepped out of a night terror. It would be the most fitting companion for the war to come.

Together, they rode through the less frequented streets, hoping to throw off any spies or would-be assassins. Were their location discovered, the High Marshal might very well set the place alight while they slept, for all the love he had in his heart. Fighting the urge to plunge a dagger into Jenson's face would prove most challenging, but for now, there were more pressing matters to attend to.

The tent city surrounding Bentmont came into view, miles of white canvas flapping in a strong western breeze. Madelyn felt a nervous flutter in her chest as they approached, the fighting men of Betanthia giving pause as they gawked and mumbled to one another. It seemed word of the joust had spread quickly, as there were more eyes upon her now than at any point since returning home.

"Your presence here is more powerful than you could ever know," Conrak said, observing a multitude of curious gazes. "This is exactly the motivation the men need."

While touching, such sentiment did little to soothe the grief and rage inside her heart. Madelyn would have thought it to be flattering, if life had not gone so horribly wrong. "Now if only *they* will see it as you do." She pointed to the command tent just ahead.

Titan brought his horse to a halt, then dismounted. His armor rattled and crunched underfoot, his purple cape whipping about in the wind. It seemed he was just as eager to get inside the tent, not only to flaunt his reversal of fortune, but to also take a crack at the High Marshal himself.

He extended a hand and assisted Madelyn down from her large war horse, a slight jolt of pain rattling her joints. Grit teeth and clenched fists were enough to mask the pain, but the frustration of having not fully healed was even more difficult to hide.

"Here lies your date with destiny," Conrak said, bringing his horse about. "But forgive me, there's something I must do first. Bradshaw can see you in, there's no way they'll deny a purple cloak his entry."

Conrak disappeared into the tent city, without so much as an explanation. His sudden departure left Madelyn stunned, though she was no stranger to disappointment. She had come this far through sheer willpower, and could surely suffer a simple meeting. With Titan at her side, they approached the tent flap.

"I'm sorry, Lady Everly," a large knight in plate and ring mail said, a spear clutched in one hand. "This is a privileged meeting, and unfortunately, you are not authorized to attend."

She might very well have cut the man down where he stood, if her strength was recovered.

"If it were up to me, I would allow you past," the guard continued. "The whole camp has been talking about the night you won that joust. If I were a betting man, I would have lost. I never would have imagined someone could come back from what you've been through and win. Not like that. You earned a lot of respect that night."

Respect was well and good, but did nothing to get her into the meeting. Madelyn gave the guard a smile, though it was as empty as a canyon. "You have my thanks, and my understanding."

"Respect?" Titan spat a watery gobbet onto the knight's foot. "If you truly had any, you'd let her pass, seeing as she's here with one of the King's men. And not only that, but Prince Gareth's personal bodyguard." He fingered at the rich purple cloth draped across his mighty shoulders.

"I would see no reason to deny you entry, given your position with the Prince. But unfortunately, she cannot enter. I'm sorry, but I'm under orders."

Another guard made his way over, having overheard the discussion. He lowered the point of his spear ever so slightly, a not so subtle gesture in and of itself. Frustrated, she turned and made her way back into camp, Titan struggling to keep pace.

"I had a feeling this would be a waste of time," Madelyn fumed. "The nerve of these people! I laid my life down and sacrificed everything for the Order, and even now, when my help is needed most, they spit in my face!"

"I don't understand the politics behind it all, if there even are any to begin with," Tylar said. "But this isn't over. You stay put, I'm going to see if I can track down Conrak. If he comes back before I do, by all means, head in there and make your voice heard."

With a nod, Titan started off to the west, muscling past any man who dared to impede his path. Madelyn waited impatiently for a moment, but grew tired of remaining idle. Perhaps retracing their steps would reveal Conrak's location, though truly, she was unsure of where to go. An ale merchant's cart was a short ways ahead. It was hardly the appropriate time for a drink, but then again, there was also no better time. In exchange for a small silver coin, she was given a wooden mug of a fresh, hearty, local brew.

After returning the empty vessel, she walked toward a nearby black-smith. A rhythmic hammering of steel on steel played like sweet music, each clang a soothing metronome. A grinding wheel sat nearby, its stone having sharpened countless hundreds of blades. Madelyn drew one of her short swords and ran a finger down its length. The edge was deadly, but not nearly enough to her liking. She sat and began grinding the steel, up one side and down the other, lost in a near trance.

This good Betanthian blade will be the instrument of my vengeance. Ancestors, hear me. Let me strike down my enemies until none remain. Let me hunt them no matter where they hide.

A group of men came marching over, though at first she paid them no attention. When they began to congregate and mumble among themselves, she could ignore them no longer. They wore the armor of the Order, with black and gold sigils emblazoned on their cuirasses. She recognized none of the men, save for one, but it was difficult to put a finger on his identity.

"And what do you want?" Madelyn then saw one of the men was Emery, from the joust the other evening. She immediately sensed hostility, although it would be foolish for anyone to assault her with so many soldiers around.

"I had to come see it for myself," Emery said, eyeing her suspiciously. "I heard some of the men say they saw you riding into camp. Do you know when we set out? The word is today, I hear."

"To be honest, I haven't the slightest idea. I'm not permitted to attend the meeting with the High Marshal, and now I'm having my doubts as to whether I'll be allowed to join you at all."

Emery scoffed. "Like hell they won't. I have it on good authority that the men won't ride unless you're with them. We've all heard the stories. Nobody could have come back from what those savages did so quickly. And just between the two of us, they're nearly as scared of you as they are the northmen."

"Scared?" Madelyn offered a scoff as well. "Why in the world would they be scared of me?"

The knights glanced uneasily at each other, as if they had come by knowledge they were now afraid to speak. Even Emery appeared hesitant to say anything more, but was clearly the bravest of the lot.

"There's been whispers around camp lately. Now, I don't put much stock in rumors, but what my ears have heard, my eyes can see."

"Stop being coy." She frowned. "Tell me what you've heard."

"Strange things… strange things indeed. Things I can't begin to explain. But it doesn't matter. Either you're with us, or our horses stay stabled. That's all you need to know. And as far as the High Marshal goes… you leave that to us."

Before she could reply, the knights departed, leaving confusion and uncertainty in their wake. Emery was scheming something, though he had little reason to. They had only met once on a jousting list, and had come to know the points of each other's lances better than anything. Madelyn's thoughts turned to Conrak, as he seemed to be an endless pit of secrets.

What in the world could he possibly be telling them? Is he spreading rumors about me?

It was a plausible explanation, especially given Conrak's notion that the war effort needed heroes. Perhaps he was indeed telling stories in the camp and in the taverns, meticulously crafting her a new image. Given the uneasy attention thus far, it appeared most likely. Her thoughts were then interrupted by a horse and rider, which had stopped mere feet away.

"What do you want now?" Madelyn looked up and saw a face most familiar. "Gareth?!" she uttered, dumbstruck at the sight of him. "What are you doing here? I… thought you were in Cardale? I heard about the queen… I'm so… so very sorry."

The prince looked haggard, as if he had not slept in weeks. Still, there was a certain strength and resolve in his hazel eyes.

"I could ask the same of you! When I left, you were still bedridden. I can't believe you're… you're…"

"I know." She gave a sorrowful smile. "I don't even know how to describe what I've had to go through to get here. But enough about me. How are you holding up?"

"As best I can." Gareth's jaw tightened, fighting to hold back his pain. "The ceremony was lovely, but I still can't wrap my head around it all. I thought she had many more years ahead of her. But sadly, I was mistaken."

Hearing the heartbreak in his voice was enough to make her want to cry, but now was a time to be strong. Gareth had done the most unselfish thing possible by riding back west, even though the army would miss his presence little .

"You should have stayed in Cardale and taken time to mourn. You don't have to be here; we have more than enough men to win this war."

"I know," he said, "but this is something I have to do. I cannot let other men fight a war for my family's kingdom while I sit idly by, lost in grief. No, I'm here to fight for my legacy, our people's legacy… and to see your honor restored, my lady."

A sudden tightness in Madelyn's throat choked off her words. All she could manage was a solemn nod, as anything spoken would have broken her down to tears. Here was the crown prince of Betanthia, the heir to the Kingdom, remaining stoic at a time when strength was needed most. And not only for his people, but for her.

He had stayed by her side for as long as time allowed, standing vigil both day and night. It was only when the utmost tragedy befell his family that Gareth left, but now he had returned. Madelyn could have wrapped her arms around him and sobbed. It seemed so few in the world could understand their pain, a common bond which no one would wish to share.

Gareth offered a meager smile. "Lord Kenfield tells me the High Marshal and Lord Vakaro are about to have a meeting. Will you be attending?"

She looked at him helplessly. "No, I was told by one of the guards that I'm not permitted. To be quite honest, I have no idea what to do next."

"Nonsense." The prince dismounted, taking up his horse by the bridle. "You're coming with me. Your voice deserves to be heard. You have firsthand knowledge of what we're up against, and to ignore it is stupidity. Come, we don't want to be late."

With a smile, Madelyn sheathed her short sword and began a short walk to the command tent. She remembered the day they walked the streets of Cardale together, and how Gareth had expressed his affections. He seemed so young and innocent then, almost unrecognizable from the bearded and muscular man he had become. There was something soothing and invigorating about his presence, something which put a slight spring in her step.

They arrived after a brief walk, one of the guards taking Gareth's horse and tying it to a hitching post. This time, not a word was uttered by any of the knights, even the man who dared to deny her entry. She thought of taking the prince's hand as they entered, both for his strength and hers, but thought better of it. Perhaps more surprising than anything was feeling such an impulse in the first place.

All eyes turned toward the tent flap as they entered. Lord Vakaro was the first one she noticed, his height and pitch black hair setting him apart from the others. Renald Fletch stood to his left, staring dumbfoundedly. The High Marshal was to his right, a look of discomfort written plainly across his face. An immediate rush of hatred coursed through Madelyn's veins upon seeing the man she once knew as a father.

Images of murder danced through her head. For a brief moment, Madelyn could see herself drawing a blade and lunging across the table, hacking and slashing until only bloody ruins of the High Marshal remained. He had betrayed every ounce of trust built over a lifetime, and had deserted her at the lowest point a person could fall to.

What a coward. I should have his head right here and now. Not only did he leave me to suffer, but he sends a man into my room in the dead of night to murder me?! Mark my words, Jenson Powell, after I slay Damien Dreadfire and his horde, I'm coming for you next.

"Prince Gareth!" The High Marshal gasped. "We weren't expecting you to be joining us. You have my deepest sympathies for your mother. Betanthia will truly never know another Charlotte Bethard. On behalf of us all, please, accept our condolences."

"Thank you for your kindness," the prince said, measuring each man inside the tent.

"What is she doing here?" Renald Fletch muttered.

The look on Gareth's face very much mirrored her own, although his composure was not as rigid. It was nearly possible to see his hazel eyes turn to molten iron.

"Since we've decided to dispense with the pleasantries, allow me to inform you that Lady Everly has been enlisted into my royal body-guard," Gareth said, raising his chin. "Would you deny your prince his due protection?"

The southern Commandant chewed his tongue, but was mindful enough not to speak his contempt. Instead, Lord Vakaro turned his attention to the other men around him, as well as a large map sprawled out on the table.

"Gentlemen, if I may," Ridley said. "Let us continue with the task at hand. It has come to my attention that as of a week ago, the barbarian army was spotted a mere two weeks from Greenwood Forest." A few audible gasps and murmurs filled the tent, but were silenced by his hand. "As alarming as this sounds, it is not unexpected. We have them right where we want them, between Lake Nisar and the Plainhold."

While the news was distressing, it also had its benefits. With the northmen so close, the Betanthians would be able to fight on familiar ground of their choosing, with supplies and reinforcements close by. More importantly, Damien Dreadfire would have to stand and fight or flee altogether, as there would be no escape to either the east or west.

"Excellent," Gareth chimed in. "If their position is accurate, this leaves us with far more options than they have. We should march at once, and take the fight to them before they can defile any more Betanthian soil."

"We were planning just that, my prince," Jenson Powell said, his eyes locked solely on Gareth. He had resorted to pretending Madelyn was entirely absent, though in all honesty, she preferred it as such.

Better to keep this strictly business, for now…

"And how many men have we mustered?" the prince asked.

"Nearly a hundred thousand." Lord Vakaro pursed his lips. "When the time comes for battle, we will use our superior knowledge of the terrain to our advantage. The bulk of our cavalry will be placed on the right flank, while the Order will take the left. The moment our infantry engage them in the center, I will order our cavalry on the right to engage."

"Would it not be wise to observe their cavalry first before committing our entire right flank?" Madelyn asked, to the surprise and irritation of those around the table.

"Lady Everly, may I remind you—" Ridley began, but was interrupted.

"Excuse me, Lord Vakaro," Gareth said defiantly, though she noticed a slight tremble in his posture. "Lady Everly has fought Damien Dreadfire and has seen his tactics firsthand. Any knowledge she has is worth its weight in gold, and to ignore it would be most unwise."

"If you would allow me to explain, my prince," Ridley continued. "The objective is to force their cavalry to commit to our right, and fix them in place. I have no doubt this Damien Dreadfire is aware of our tactics and traditions, and will expect an exclusive cavalry attack on his left flank. We will suffer losses. But once we have their horsemen tied down, the Blackthorn will strike from his right, and in all likelihood, decide the battle in one swift stroke."

It was a solid plan, and not without its merits, much to her surprise. A delayed pincer attack would be a devastating maneuver, if it could be properly executed.

"Then we will need to fight them on the Plainhold," Madelyn said. "The terrain there is hilly, some steep, though most are rolling. It could provide the cover we need. The further we go east, the more we lose our advantage."

"And what makes you think Damien Dreadfire will fight us there, Lady Everly?" Lord Vakaro snorted.

She paused for a second, replaying the fighting at Castle Morden in her head. "Dreadfire is a cautious man. He'll want to make certain his flanks are as secure as possible. At Morden, he allowed us no escape, and used the same delay tactics as you've proposed here. I suspect he'll want to use the Plainhold to his advantage as well. Can *any* man say they are thrilled to be fighting there? It's an inhospitable place."

"Very well," the southern Commandant conceded. "I shall take your words into consideration."

"Em… do tell me, Lady Everly," Renald Fletch said, his voice as irritating as buzzing flies. "Where exactly do you see yourself on the battlefield? Surely you're in no condition for—"

Gareth was quick to interrupt. "She will be wherever I command her to be. Whether it be by my side, or acting as my liaison with the Order, it makes no difference. The Lady is to be respected at all times. Any disrespect shown to her will be taken as disrespect to not only myself, but House Bethard as a whole. May I count on your fealty, Commander?"

"Absolutely, my prince." Renald bowed his head, snake that he was. Madelyn knew his simpering was a mere act, designed to placate Gareth and lull him a false sense of security.

Lord Vakaro's face was drawn so tightly it looked as if his flesh was about to tear off his skull. He hastily rolled the map up, content to end the meeting as it stood. "In conclusion, gentlemen, we will break camp immediately. Commanders, assemble your men, and have them in formation at once. Within a fortnight, we'll have Damien Dreadfire's head mounted on a spear, on its way to Cardale."

The confrontation could not come soon enough. Madelyn was practically salivating at the idea of finally tasting revenge. She touched Gareth lightly on his arm, offering a hint of smile in gratitude. He appeared nearly as relieved as the other men in the tent to have the meeting adjourned.

"Thank you," she whispered, her words barely audible.

"Come on, let's get out of here." Gareth was the first to depart, although it would have been more amusing to see him stay. As uncomfortable as he appeared, Lord Vakaro and his minions appeared even more unsettled by his presence. She lingered briefly, studying their irritation with sweet satisfaction.

Renald Fletch gathered his assorted papers and stuffed them into a leather satchel. He brushed by her on the way out, eyes to the floor and stinking of shame. It would have been not only easy, but endlessly gratifying to throttle him into a bloody pulp. But at the end of the day, he was a mere minion. The man responsible for supplanting her position of Commander was still in the tent, but Madelyn was loath to remain in his company any longer. She departed the meeting, but was halted almost immediately.

"Allow me to make myself perfectly clear, Lady Everly." Jenson Powell gripped her by the arm. "You are no longer a sworn knight of the Order, and I do not permit you to ride alongside our forces. Gareth Bethard is not the king, Marcellus Bethard is. And according to our charter, we are permitted by the crown to maintain autonomy in our affairs."

She stared into his eyes, but it was difficult to know what to feel. There was once love in Jenson's gaze, but now there was only cold distance. It was obvious by the tone of his voice that he took no pleasure in such a rebuke, but still saw fit to utter the words.

"What I do or don't do is no longer of any concern to you. That little girl you fostered all those years ago died at Castle Morden. You and I have no connection anymore. You're as dead to me as I am to you. And it's for the better." She pulled away from his grasp defiantly, then turned away.

"Be that as it may, I forbid you to ride alongside the Order. I will consider this matter closed." Jenson returned to the tent, his cowardice following closely behind.

A lifetime of devotion to a cause had come to an unceremonious end. A year ago, Madelyn would have thought this day would never arrive. It was inconceivable to think a man such as Jenson Powell would not only abandon her, but send knives in the night to strike her down. The thought of drawing steel of her own and returning such intended treachery in kind was endlessly tempting.

No. Now is neither the time nor place. After I have Damien Dreadfire's head on my wall, I'll settle this score for good.

Without speaking another word, she set off into the tent city. Conrak and Titan were standing close by, though their presence at the meeting would have been beneficial. Neither would have allowed the High Marshal to lay a hand on her in such a manner, regardless of his station. They remained silent as Madelyn stormed past, but immediately fell in behind her.

"And where were you two when I needed you most?" She whirled about, staring daggers at each of them.

Conrak said nothing, instead raising a pointed finger. To her astonishment, Emery and his companions were standing at the head of a growing crowd behind her. These were Blackthorn men, their arms and armor unmistakable.

"We're with you, Commander!" a voice cried out.

The sentiment began to build within the gathering of knights, while Lord Vakaro's men stood dumbfounded. They knew nothing of the life and struggles of Madelyn Everly, but she supposed that soon enough, they would come to learn of it for themselves.

"I told you," Emery said smugly. "We're not riding without you. Some are still following orders like good little sheep, but the bulk of the Order stands behind you."

Their camaraderie was enough to bring a quiver to her lip, despite all of the hatred still smoldering inside. She had garnered respect and admiration from men who knew her little, and some who knew her not. It was a far cry from the love the High Marshal had shown.

Madelyn could find no words to express her appreciation, and instead nodded as the ranks parted before her. It was a small courtesy, but a courtesy nonetheless. One of the knights brought over her horse, and offered a hand into the saddle. Were it not for the anger coursing through her veins, Madelyn might have lacked the strength to mount. She placed one foot in the stirrup and with a grunt, climbed on top of her steed.

Hundreds of eyes looked upon her as she passed through the ranks. Some stared in wonderment, some were ambivalent, but all had come to know her name and the growing legend behind it. It was reassuring to feel respect from those whom she had never met, the respect a proper leader ought to command.

"I need a moment," Madelyn said to Tylar and Conrak as they walked beside her. "I'll come find you."

"Very well, Lady Everly," Conrak said. "Bradshaw and I won't be far."

Both men broke off and began conversing with one another, Tylar glancing several times over one shoulder. Thankfully, a refreshment tent was close by, loaded with casks of ale and wine. Seldom did Madelyn partake in drink, but now was as good of a time as any.

In solitude, she sat and poured out a cup of a fine vintage, processing every detail of the meeting. Personal vengeance would have to wait, that much was certain. Instead, she began pondering Ridley Vakaro's battle tactics which were proposed. They were sound, when taken at face value.

But despite their likely superior numbers and the soundness of Lord Vakaro's strategy, something about the march made her feel uneasy. Although Damien Dreadfire was as vicious as he was cunning, his real power doubtlessly lay with Lazilyth, the old woman. Her ability to peer into the fates was as distressing as it was problematic, as she would be able to foresee every movement of the army.

If she can peer into the future, then surely she has heard every word we spoke today. The gravity of the situation suddenly began crashing down. *Oh heavens… she'll know precisely when and where to strike us!*

Something had to be done, and fast, but Madelyn was unsure of what. While she had learned a great deal in a short time, perhaps more than anyone in centuries, much still remained hidden. Still, if there was anyone who could prevent another catastrophe, one which would spell the end of Betanthia, it was her.

You have to do this. You must, there is no other.

With all haste, Madelyn mounted her horse and set off toward a less populated part of the camp. She found an empty medical tent and began shifting through pilfered scrolls inside a saddle bag, their pages becoming drier by the day. One particular text had an almost oily feel to it, a faint tinge of inky darkness flecking its edges. This was one scroll which she feared to open, given the dark energies radiating from it like rays of black sunlight.

Madelyn picked up the parchment and unrolled it, perhaps for the first time since the text was written. Runes of the corpse god danced across the scroll, surrounding a large, black blotch at its center. While the image appeared to be nothing at first, it soon swirled and morphed into an ominous dark face. Dark, formless eyes stared unblinking, speaking soft words of atrocity deep in her mind. Its gaze was impossible to turn away from, an unfathomable terror causing her eyes to itch and burn.

Every instinct within her soul was screaming to look away, but she could not. Madelyn stared back, uncertain of what to do or say. She would sacrifice anything to see Damien Dreadfire brought to justice, even her own life if necessary.

"Cthenir, god of death and darkness, hear me now. I come to you with great urgency and humility, for you are the only one who can help me now. Grant me the power to defeat my enemies, to blind their eyes to our movements. Do this, and I pledge myself to your service. Let me send unto you an avalanche of dead to feast upon. Let me fill your stomach with the bodies and souls of those who fall to my blade. Hear me, I beg of you."

A trickle of ink began pooling in the corners of her eyes, much as they did before. The murk spread swiftly, jerking Madelyn's head backward and seizing every muscle near to tearing. Through grit teeth she snarled, a vicious, dark energy from the scroll nearly shredding her flesh to ribbons. The pain was unlike anything, even the pain of childbirth, for this she felt deep within her very soul.

A low rumble began at the base of her skull, moving forward into both ears. Through blackened eyes she saw a light, golden at first, but far from welcoming. A bright warmth exploded, though it quickly turned to cold darkness, as if the sun itself had been extinguished. Madelyn dropped to one knee, overwhelmed by an intense surge of black energy, struggling to keep her very soul inside her flesh.

A stagnant breeze kissed the cold skin of her cheek, then faded as quickly as it arrived. She was in a place unfamiliar, one seemingly not of this world. The realm was devoid of light and warmth, no sound nor smell, and no trace of itself left to the senses.

Where... where am I?

The energy was suffocating, nearly strong enough to crush her into oblivion. Madelyn opened her eyes and struggled to stand, as if a great mass were pressing down on her, both knees straining under an unseen weight. When she stood upright, an icy chill turned her flesh to goose pimples. She was no longer in the realm of the living, that much she knew. Truly, this land was home to something else.

A hazy darkness lay draped around her, illuminated by fiery orbs of light floating freely in the air. Thick clouds of mist danced around her ankles, swirling and churning with each labored step. Merely breathing was astoundingly taxing. She scanned the pitch blackness, but found nothing around her, save for what appeared to be a dimly lit pathway leading forward.

I don't have much time, I don't know if I can hold on...

Even thinking was nearly impossible. Madelyn could already feel herself slipping back into the living realm, the forces of this otherworldly place rejecting her like some unwelcome intruder. Slowly, and with every ounce of strength she could muster, she made her way down the spectral pathway, with only a soft glow from the orbs as a guide.

After a short way, she noticed a faint outline of stone slabs on the left side of the path. Upon further inspection, they contained wooden carvings, but most were too difficult to make out. Madelyn trudged onward, determined to see what strange artifacts were housed in the Fate Realm. She saw faces familiar here and there, and locations she knew all too well. One of the carvings was of Castle Morden, its walls appearing to crumble before her very eyes. Though the statues sat idle, they appeared to move ever so slightly.

I know this place! This is the past, and none too distant! I must be close.

Madelyn walked by several more slabs, each adorned by effigies of events she would just assume forget. The path ahead was what she remained focused on. Screams from the night of her tribulation echoed faintly in her ears, bringing back torturous memories. Each step became more labored than the last, every footfall growing heavier and heavier.

A crossroads lay ahead, with half a dozen smaller trails branching off from the main path. They were dimly lit, just barely visible to the naked eye. She suddenly remembered something Lazilyth had said on the night of her tribulation.

"Many paths… many… many…"

And indeed there were. Madelyn could not possibly explore all of them, not before being tossed out of the Fate Realm. Instead, she continued forward down the brightest path, and undoubtedly the one most likely to come to fruition.

There was another stone table ahead, this one more illuminated than the others. The light from a nearby orb pulsated, bathing the effigies in a dull warmth. A large slab of wood served as a backdrop for the scene, an aged and faded piece of oak adorned with the landscape of the Plainhold. Beyond it stood two smaller slabs, each decorated with thousands of small figures, fully armed and armored. Madelyn suspected these were the two armies that were soon to face each other in battle.

Her suspicions were proven correct when she saw a carving of Damien Dreadfire, face frozen in a war cry, his sword arm raised high into the air. The other figure was that of Gareth, mounted and with lance in hand, his horse rearing wildly. Madelyn felt a sudden tightness in her throat as she looked further down the pathway, and to the next slab.

"Please, Gods, tell me this won't come to pass. How can you stomach so much death?"

The next scene was that of a great massacre. Gareth and the Betanthian army lay on the ground, their banners fallen, their life's blood staining the carvings red. She gasped, horror stricken, and ran to the next slab, though uncertain if she wished to see more. There sat an effigy of the savages as they sacked helpless Betanthian villages, spreading their destruction like a great plague, with no army left to stop them.

"No, I cannot let this come to pass!" she said, determined to change the fates.

Truly it must be as simple as moving or rearranging the pieces of wood, and therefore change the course of future events. She ran back to the slab where the battle took place, and tried to knock over the effigy of Damien Dreadfire, but it would not budge in the slightest. In fact, none of the pieces moved even an inch. Even if they could, the last of her strength was fading away, and fast.

No, please Madelyn, you must hold on, just a little while longer! If I cannot change the fates, then maybe I can obscure them from Lazilyth's sight.

Perhaps the crone had already seen the entire course of the future, but Madelyn had her doubts. She was the last of the Eveldanyr, not the old woman, who undoubtedly had acquired her talents through the darkest of practices.

Think, damn you. Think!

Such crushing, spiritual weight was too great to bear. Madelyn felt herself slipping back into the living realm, the otherworldly energy sending her crashing to her knees. Daylight was beginning to build in the distance, like a morning sunrise emerging over a dark horizon. That was when an idea came, though it was doubtful it would even work.

Madelyn clawed at the bottom of her shirt, the fabric hissing as a large section was torn free. No more than a second before the Fate Realm ejected her, she tossed the cloth onto the wooden effigies of the Order and their knights, shrouding them all. There was no way to be certain if her efforts would bear fruit, but it was all that could be done before the light returned.

Within the space of a second, Madelyn was returned to the tent as if nothing had transpired. The scroll was not churning and swirling with blackness as it had before, its page having gone still. It appeared much the same as an old parchment, dry and crumbling, its text faded.

Was it all in my imagination? Have I been lost in a daydream?

Perhaps she had simply gone mad from fantasies of vengeance. It was certainly a possibility, given all that had transpired since the year prior. Madelyn Everly tossed the scroll away, the parchment fluttering to the ground like a feather. It was then she noticed something most disturbing. At the bottom of her shirt was a large tear, and a hole where there was once cloth. The Fate Realm, it seemed, was no dream after all.

LUCETTA VIII

S HE SAT ON THE UPPER BALCONY, WATCHING AS CARDALE GLOWED red. For days, the jewel of Betanthia burned into a smoldering ruin, its populace driven to utter madness. Lucetta Eldon watched the carnage unfold, gently rocking back and forth. A year of sacrifice and careful planning had veered so horribly off course, and now there seemed little chance to salvage what remained.

Wet streaks ran down her cheeks at the sight of Cardale. Thousands were dead, but the number was likely far higher. Judging by reports coming in from the city watch, much of the violence was not from Hesgrin and his cultists running amok. Instead, the disenfranchised poor had taken advantage of the chaos, looting Cardale's wealthier districts and putting what remained to the torch.

It was excruciating to see House Bethard's legacy disappearing before her very eyes. Clouds of smoke blanketed the city, so thick and black they sometimes blotted out the sun. At times, Lucetta could even taste ashes in the air. Perhaps the tiny, black specks were more than just ruined timbers. Perhaps it was bits of charred flesh as well, a terrifying prospect if there ever was one.

And to make matters worse, the woman in black was absent yet again. It was endlessly distressing to be without such a comforting and reassuring presence at a time like this. The entity always had a way of calming her worst fears and putting even the murkiest matters in perspective. But there seemed little sense to be made of such wanton violence.

Please tell me this is still the right path. Tell me I haven't gone astray and ruined everything...

There was no answer. Frustrated, Lucetta wiped her cheeks dry, then retired from the balcony. Perhaps with sleep, clarity might come. Perhaps when she awoke, the riots would simply be a bad dream and nothing more. But there was little reason to suspect the world would be any different, not after everything which had already transpired. The Queen was dead, and the people driven mad, and no amount of slumber and sweet dreams could ever change that.

As she shuffled off to her old bedchamber, a familiar voice echoed up the grand staircase. For a moment, Lucetta was unable to find breath. She stood gasping like a fish out of water, too frightened to blink. It was Aldred Eldon, the last person she wanted to see. With blood running through the streets, it was a wonder what he was even doing in the residential wing in the first place.

"Lucetta?!" Aldred uttered incredulously. "Oh thank goodness you're alright. I was terrified something had happened to you."

In the past, he might very well have delivered a sharp tongue lashing, or even a beating for her absence. But all she saw on his face was relief. Relief she was safe behind tall walls and capable spears.

"I was at the temple to see mother home when they set upon us. Oh Aldred, it was horrible. Were it not for the Guardsmen, I might very well be lying dead out there."

"I'm immensely grateful you're alright. I've been told your personal bodyguard fought gallantly. While I disapprove of you being away from home, I'm thankful you have such capable men alongside you."

His embrace felt as though a leper were wrapping diseased arms around her. Even his scent was enough to trigger her gag reflex, but she did well enough to remain collected. Aldred sighed, his hands running across the bony blades of her shoulders.

"My dear, you've grown so thin. Why have you gone so long without eating?"

"I've been in such anguish as of late, and now with mother passing…" Tears she began to cry were real, both for Queen Charlotte, and for herself.

Aldred's hand moved down the length of her long, auburn hair. "I understand, truly I do. But please, we must do something about this. I cannot afford to have something happen to you, not now… not when the world has gone utterly mad."

While the idea of food was still unappealing, so too was her diminishing frame. Lucetta had little options remaining as far as attire went, her favorite gowns now oversized. She was beginning to feel a slight wiggle to a few of her teeth as well, a distressing development.

"I promise to be more mindful of my eating," she pledged. "I must confess, I hate what I see in the mirror these days."

"Well, you're still every bit as beautiful to me." He smiled. "I'll have the cooks fix you something exquisite."

Despite Aldred's loving intentions, his words felt like more of a chastisement than anything. It would have been endlessly satisfying to lash out at him, but Lucetta instead favored discretion. If he were to ever discover the truth of her life over the past year, it would mean a death sentence for certain.

"How lovely, thank you." She touched him on the arm. "Now if I may… Why are you here? I would have thought the Guardsmen would have the estate locked down at a time like this. I pray it hasn't been ransacked by those animals out there."

"Rest assured, my love, our home is perfectly safe. I've been spending so much of my time here, I've taken up temporary residence." Aldred's face tightened, as if in pain. "And to be completely honest with you, I find it difficult to be at the estate, at least… without you there."

Part of her heart felt as if it was breaking, though most of it had already grown cold. Despite looking as if he had aged a decade in the last year, Aldred was still the man she married, and not every day they spent together was terrible.

"Perhaps once this madness has subsided, we can return home," she lied. "How do you intend on dealing with this uprising?"

"Contingency plans are in motion, and there will be a council meeting shortly. Worry not, this matter will be brought to a swift conclusion. Please, join me for some refreshment. We could both use a proper meal over a proper drink."

At any other time, Lucetta might have contented herself with allowing Aldred to lie and downplay the situation. But she had been in the thick of the chaos already, and knew quelling it would be no simple matter.

A cold breeze swept into the hall, though only Lucetta was able to feel it. The skin on her arms and neck turned immediately to gooseflesh, an all too familiar sensation. Finally, the woman in black had arrived. She stepped out from a nearby room, leaning against the doorway, arms crossed over the front of its black silken dress, smiling and nodding.

"You must tell me everything you know," she demanded. "You mustn't deny me the truth, not when the situation is so dire. I'm not only your wife, but I'm still a princess. I care about what happens to my family's dynasty."

For once, Aldred offered little protest, a surprising development. He motioned down the hall, and together they walked toward the grand staircase.

"The situation is dire, but I believe we have enough men to stamp out this revolt. Lord Vakaro taking all of our most capable lords with him is complicating matters, as neither of us could have foreseen a travesty like this unfolding. I sent dispatches immediately, and received word just this morning that about six thousand men will be arriving from Glimmergulf on ships, another two thousand from Commandant Eldwynn's garrison in Dellhaven."

Such news was both relieving and distressing. While the deployment would likely bring an end to the carnage, the northern Commandant had deprived Dellhaven of much of its defensive force. Lucetta thought for a moment, but decided the more pressing matter was snuffing out the rebellion.

The woman in black began drifting toward them, toying with its collarbone length black hair. The entity's eyes glowed a deep orange-red, but it seemed content thus far to remain silent and observe. After glancing at the woman briefly, an idea suddenly sprouted in Lucetta's head. Perhaps all the death and destruction throughout the capital could be used to her advantage.

"And who will be leading this relief force?" she asked pointedly.

"One of the local lords or lordlings," Aldred replied, "it's difficult to know who will be arriving."

"No, that simply will not do." Lucetta stood defiantly, straightening both her back and skirts. "The people must be reminded of House Bethard's might. They must be reminded that anarchy will not be tolerated, not in Cardale, or anywhere in Betanthia."

Aldred cocked his head. "And what exactly are you proposing, my dear?"

"We must lead the army ourselves. The people need to see us with their own eyes, and know our strength and resolve is unwavering."

At first, Aldred chuckled, thinking she had likely gone mad. But when Lucetta failed to relent, he instead grew disinterested. "My dear, that is absurd. Never in a million years would I risk my safety or yours when we have men capable of—"

Incensed, Lucetta lunged at her husband, pressing him against the wall. For a second, her eyes flared with orange-red fire, much the same as the woman in black. She growled and snarled in rage, the pitch of her voice even lowering briefly.

"Damn you, Aldred!" she screamed. "This is not a polite suggestion, nor a request! Have you not an ounce of manhood left between your legs, or has it all withered into dust? Who are you to act as my father's surrogate? You're a coward, and nothing more."

Swiftly, she departed down the grand staircase, leaving him stunned and in silence. However, Lucetta managed only a few steps before feeling warm fingers wrap around her bicep. "Do you understand what it is you're proposing?" Aldred asked, wide-eyed. "Have you taken leave of your senses? You would risk our lives for what? Glory?"

"I don't expect you to understand," she shot back. "You're not a Bethard, no matter how hard you try to pretend you are. This is my family's city. My city. And our subjects need to know their king and his household have not tucked tail and fled in the face of adversity."

Aldred ran a hand through his thinning hair, aghast at what he was hearing. "This is madness, Lucetta. Pure madness. Grief for your mother has driven you beyond the pale. I cannot, and I will not take part in this!"

"Then stay here and cower, it matters not. When the history of this day is written, let them say Lord Aldred Eldon sat behind safe walls while his wife reclaimed Cardale. And if you even think of trying to stop me, I'll have my bodyguard deal with you. I suspect my men will be here at any moment."

It was nearly possible to see steam venting from her husband's ears, but there was little more he could say. Over the past year, Aldred had learned there were things about Lucetta he could control, and things he could not, and now she had grown bold because of it.

"I'm no coward, Lucetta. I have given my life to the service of your father, and to Betanthia. But this—"

"In my father's youth, he would have put this rebellion down personally, riding at the very head of the army," she interrupted. "But there isn't any life left in him. Who else is going to lead? Gareth is gone, and Trace can barely hold a knife at dinner without quaking. Who then, if not us?"

"We have commanders and lords and men of war to handle such matters, that is why they exist in the first place."

For a man as proud and controlling as Aldred was, she might have thought he would rise to the challenge. But Lucetta was beginning to see just how weak her husband truly was. Diminishing in the face of adversity was not the vocabulary of a Bethard. Although Gareth was a loathsome creature, he at least had enough sense of duty to the family to put his life on the line.

"You would let a lesser man seize the glory for himself?" she taunted. "You wish for the people to call him the savior of Cardale, and not you? I would have thought for all of your ambitions, you would have jumped at the chance to have your name on the tip of every commoner's tongue."

Fame and power were always tempting prizes, even to weak men. Lucetta saw indecision playing out behind his eyes, but thankfully, he appeared to be relenting.

"Are you willing to accept the possibility that either you or I may be injured or killed?" he asked, staring daggers into her eyes. "Are you willing to risk our lives over this?"

"Yes," she answered unflinchingly. "This is our moment to save this city and cement our names in the histories. We may never get this opportunity again. At least, not in our lifetimes."

"Very well." Aldred sighed and started down the grand staircase, Lucetta following closely behind.

Together they passed through the great hall and out into the court-yard, an acrid stench of smoke and death heavy befouling their senses. Near the gatehouse stood a Captain of the Guardsmen, assessing the Citadel's defenses. Aldred snapped his fingers and motioned for the officer to come forth.

"Yes, Lord Aldred? How may I be of service to you?"

"Have your men fetch me some armor and my horse." He looked tensely at Lucetta, chewing his lip. "And find whatever manner of armor will fit my wife, and see to it a suitable horse is prepared. I will return shortly."

The Guardsman raised an eyebrow at his command, but nevertheless executed it faithfully. Only when the men began assembling near the gate did anxiety set in, nearly setting Lucetta's stomach to heaving. She was no warrior, far from it, and had not ridden a horse since her childhood days. Every intuition was screaming to abandon such folly, and leave the killing to men who made killing their business.

From a dark shadow inside the gatehouse emerged the woman in black. The entity floated toward Lucetta, content in her determination. It drifted effortlessly through the body of one Guardsman, then another, as if it were an illusion.

"Will I be safe?" Lucetta asked in a faint whisper.

"For as long as you labor to fulfill your divine quest, no harm shall come to you. I will make certain of it. Go now, and claim your destiny."

Truly, the woman in black was capable of wonders, but stopping spears and arrows was another matter entirely. Still, the entity had remained true to its word thus far, and there seemed little reason to lose heart now.

A pair of Guardsmen emerged from the barracks, each clutching various pieces of armor. Many appeared to be too large for her dainty frame, but after several attempts, they managed to piece together a suitable level of protection. A mail shirt was draped over her gown, the excess slack taken up in the back. They began debating how best to secure a steel cuirass, itself several sizes too large, but Lucetta waved them off.

"No, we mustn't waste another moment on such unnecessary precautions," she said. "I am confident you men will be all the protection I will require."

With a bow, the Guardsmen dismissed themselves. Lucetta thought she looked absolutely absurd in such an oversized shirt, but Aldred would forbid her from leaving the palace grounds without some manner of armor.

I suppose this will do, if my skin isn't torn to shreds by these accursed rings first.

Aldred emerged from the great hall, clutching something with both hands. It was neither a weapon, nor any manner of armor. A trinket, it appeared, something she found most curious.

"I had this brought down for you. I thought it would be best if you wore it." Aldred handed her a silver tiara, intricately crafted and laden with sparkling diamonds.

While not the adornment of a queen, it would be enough to instill awe and fear into those who laid eyes on her. Lucetta found her throat tightening and lips quivering ever so slightly. She was becoming emotional, not from fear or distress, but from love. It was the strangest feeling, one that had nearly become foreign in years past.

"Thank you," she said, smiling. Lucetta placed the tiara on her head, brushing her length of auburn hair aside.

"And also this," he said, motioning to a nearby Guardman.

He produced a purple cloak, not the one worn by royalty, but by men of the sword. It seemed appropriate attire, considering the circumstances. Lucetta would be riding through the streets of Cardale like a warrior princess, not a pampered lady at court. A Guardsman stepped up onto the mounting block and secured the vibrant fabric around her neck.

For the first time in ages, husband and wife stared longingly into each other's eyes, knowing that either of them might be struck down by a rampaging mob. Aldred mounted his horse, then leaned over in the saddle, clasping his hand around hers. It was a touching moment, but one which would be over as quickly as it began.

Crunching steel and synchronized footsteps by the thousands echoed up Auburn Row. The relief army had undoubtedly arrived and made landfall. Lucetta felt her guts begin to churn in excitement as they approached.

"Open the gate!" a man on the wall shouted, much to the satisfaction of his brethren.

With a deep groan, the thick wooden doors crept open. Through a closed portcullis, she spied a thick column of soldiers marching up the avenue, their commander pausing just outside of the palace gates. Before raising the giant steel barricade, an officer of the Guardsmen strode over to Lucetta's side.

"My princess, are you sure this is wise?" He glanced over his shoulder toward the gate. "Once we leave the palace grounds, I cannot guarantee your safety. Anything can happen at any moment."

"Wise? Perhaps not. But nevertheless necessary." Lucetta tapped a heel against the side of her mount. "The people need to be reminded that Cardale is House Bethard's city, and we will not shy away from defending what is ours."

"Very well, my princess. My men will be at your side at all times. Any one of us here would die to protect you."

While reassuring, his words did little to soothe a violent thrashing inside her chest. Lucetta thought she might lose consciousness with as heavy as her heart was thumping, and only a sip of wine would be enough to calm it.

No, I need to keep my wits about me. And there's no time otherwise.

Surrounded by a sea of purple cloaks, Aldred and Lucetta Eldon walked their mounts through the gates and onto Auburn Row. They were greeted by the commanding officer of the army, but Lucetta trotted past him, disinterested. As far as she was concerned, she was the one in charge. With growing confidence, she paused, scanning the faces of the soldiers and shouting her encouragement.

"Men! Brave protectors of Betanthia!" She rode to the head of the column, drawing curious looks. "The hour has come, the hour in which your people and your king look to you. Have courage! House Bethard stands beside you!"

She was met with more disbelief than anything. Lucetta and Aldred assumed their positions, then began to slowly advance through the main avenues of Cardale. It was alarming just how empty the streets had become. Judging from a relative lack of damage, it seemed that perhaps the riots were not as terrible as she suspected.

As they drove further toward the city square, however, the aftermath became disturbingly evident. Dozens of buildings were reduced to smoldering ruins, the streets stained red with blood. Bodies of peasants and noblemen alike lay strewn about, pillaged of effects and butchered like cattle. It was becoming more difficult to breathe, a haze of smoke riding thick on an eastern breeze. The air itself tasted like death.

"Heavens," Lucetta gasped, drawing a hand over her mouth.

"These fanatics are no different than the northmen," Aldred grunted, shaking his head. "Look at what these monsters have done to our city."

Had Lucetta not traversed these very streets mere days ago, she might not have recognized them. It appeared as if a great whirlwind had swept through the heart of Cardale, leaving utter devastation in its wake. Fighting was beginning to break out just ahead, a frantic chorus of screams and battle cries echoing down the broken streets.

"Move forward!" Lucetta commanded. "Kill anyone who stands in our path!"

A unit of spears marched ahead, shields locked and weapons at the ready. In unison, they began drawing closer to the skirmish, ready to confront the Harbingers and their accomplices. Aldred was stirring in his saddle, glancing back over his shoulder several times. An inspiring sight for the men, no doubt.

Just look at my gallant husband. Is he not the pinnacle of bravery? I think I might be sick.

The shutters of a second storey window flew open, drawing her immediate attention. A man stepped forward with a crossbow, snarling his contempt and pointing the weapon directly at her. Lucetta's heart came to an abrupt halt as time itself seemed to slow, her arms raising instinctively to shield from the attack. At his finger pressed down on the lever, a set of pale, leathery arms reached forth from behind, pulling the assailant back and out of sight.

Dumbfounded, Lucetta stared at the now vacant window for a moment, seeing nothing. That was, until the woman in black stepped forth. Its eyes were a fiery orange-red, so hot the air around it seemed to crackle and pop like kindling. The entity disappeared in a flash, appearing further down the street at ground level. A young peasant man held a rock in one hand, his arm winding back and preparing to release. He too was quickly snatched away in an instant, vanishing into the shadows without a trace. As the army marched forward, Lucetta saw the woman in black standing next to a now lifeless corpse.

So it is true… she really is my guardian spirit! Truly, no harm will come to me!

Impetuously, Lucetta drove a heel into her horse and broke from Aldred's side. Ignoring his shouts, she rode past the protective ring of Guardsmen and toward the soldiers just ahead. It was now easy to understand why men of war so loved the thrill of the fight. If not for a lack of weapon and the skill to wield one, Lucetta might well have led from the very front.

"My princess!" an officer shouted incredulously. "I beg of you, it's not safe here! Please, return to the—"

"Nonsense!" she said defiantly. Her eyes caught sight of the woman in black dispatching another would-be attacker. "I will not cower in the face of this rabble! Do your duty, men, and kill them! Kill them all! Kill them now!"

The soldiers paused momentarily, themselves bewildered. But the sight of their princess, riding fearlessly before them, was enough to stoke their courage. With a rippling horn blast, the men surged forward, their battle cries deafening. Lucetta watched gleefully as their spears pierced rioter, cultist, and innocent alike.

Screams and the crashing of steel filled the air like a sweet symphony, turning Cardale's streets into an amphitheater of death. Lucetta imagined dismounting and walking to the city square, splashing in puddles of warm blood like a child in a rainstorm. She remembered the moment when Pavlos informed her of Sir Bryce's assassination, and the sensations she experienced throughout her body.

It was a feeling of pure ecstasy, to feel raw power coursing through her veins. With an utterance of mere words, life was quickly turned into death. All it would require was a simple snap of her fingers and the killing would stop. In fact, the soldiers might very well kill each other, or themselves, if she commanded it.

I've never felt this alive! All of these monsters who would destroy my city and take my mother from me are dying... and all by my doing!

An agonizing groan drew her attention. Lucetta looked down and saw a woman lying bloodied on the streets. She was young, likely only a year removed from womanhood. With blood soaked hands, she clutched at a vicious hip wound, pitifully trying to claw and crawl away to safety. Lucetta dismounted and stepped toward her curiously, eager to see the art of dying with her own eyes.

"You..." she seethed. "You filthy peasants thought you could bring Cardale to its knees. You sought to claim my mother's body for your own. And what did it gain you? Nothing!"

A slain soldier lay nearby, a bloody hand still clutching the shaft of his spear. Lucetta crouched and picked up the weapon, admiring it for a second before pointing the steel head at the rioter.

"No… please! I… I never…" Sobbing, the young woman raised her hands.

"I wonder how it feels to push this into someone's flesh," Lucetta pondered out loud. "Such a simple thing this is, an object of wood and metal. But this simple little thing can bring a kingdom to its knees… which is precisely what you tried to do. And now, you die knowing you failed."

Lucetta stepped forward and drove the spear into the woman's guts, pushing it slowly until it could go no further. She watched as life slowly faded from the eyes of the dissenter, until only a motionless carcass remained. A warm tingle coursed through her body, the ecstasy of her first kill more intense than even the most erotic tryst. She giggled at first, overcome by the sheer thrill of the experience, then erupted into a maniacal fit of laughter.

"Lucetta?" a muffled voice called out. "Lucetta?"

In a near instant, the daydreams faded, and so too had the violence. Lucetta blinked hard, her eyes dry as a rain-parched field. Aldred was sitting next to her on horseback, looking unsettled by her trance-like state.

"Are you alright, my dear?" he asked, hesitant to even touch her.

How long had she sat idle, lost in a fog of visions? Judging by how quiet the streets were, it must have been some length of time. The day itself had grown late, the sun barely keeping itself above the smoldering skyline.

"Please, Lucetta," Aldred pleaded. "Let me take you back to the palace. Come now, it's alright."

She glanced around, confused at first. There was no girl lying dead on the street, no pools of blood where she lay, and not even the slightest indication the kill had transpired at all. It was both shocking and unsettling to have felt something so real, yet see no evidence of it whatsoever.

"Yes…" she muttered. "I've grown tired. I want to go home."

Aldred motioned for a Guardsman to take hold of her horse by the bridle, and turn the beast about. Together, they started back toward the Westwind Citadel. Lucetta felt uneasy stares from the purple cloaks, and hear their faint whispers behind her back. It mattered not, she supposed, though it was still troubling to have experienced so much lost time.

Something caught Lucetta's attention, from the edge of her vision. At first she thought it might be a large fly which had landed on her skirts. As she went to brush the pest away, she realized it was no fly after all, but a large droplet of blood, still wet to the touch.

TITAN VIIII

A chorus of ringing bells rocked the streets of Bentmont, their low tolling enough to rattle the dead awake. Tylar Bradshaw sat mounted, armed and armored, watching as the might of Betanthia assembled into marching columns. Residents of the mighty city turned out in droves, many bringing their children to witness such a historic procession.

One hundred thousand men at arms had gathered here, truly a sight to behold. While he cared little for history, Tylar would have been remiss if he failed to recognize the significance of this day. Such an event had not taken place on Betanthian soil for hundreds of years.

"My fucking luck that I would live to see such times," he grumbled, observing an endless throngs of soldiers.

"Better it should fall to us," Conrak said. "History is unfolding right before our eyes. I fear how this war would play out if the responsibility fell to lesser men."

The Sacrithon was right, though he would never admit to it out loud. Betanthia had already suffered dearly for the incompetence of arrogant men.

"Who's to say it hasn't already?" Tylar quipped. "If old man Valens wouldn't have been so hellbent on vengeance, we'd never be here."

Conrak sighed, knowing he was right. Such an admission was no small feat, especially for men of a nation once so proud. Now, the stink of fear was everywhere. Tylar saw it painted across the faces of commoner and soldier alike.

"Come, Bradshaw," Conrak said, gently nudging his horse. "Our place is at the front."

"If you would have said that a few months ago, I'd call you a fucking liar." Tylar shook his head. "I never would have imagined this."

"Indeed! You've had quite the reversal of fortune, no doubt. The gods have a plan for you, that much is certain."

It would have been a lie to say there were no hard feelings for nearly walking him to the gallows. But Tylar supposed it was all for the better. This path, however bizarre, had led him to many unexpected places. Death was an unrelenting adversary, capable of emerging even in the most unlikely of places. But he had cheated the grave twice in the last year, and became that much stronger in spite of it.

"Piss on the gods," Tylar grumbled. "If they're real, and they sit back and watch as the world goes to shit, then I want no part of them."

"After all you've seen since last year, can you honestly say this is the result of blind luck? I would have thought you'd have a bit more faith than that. You survived Morden. You survived the Plainhold. And you even survived prison. Now look at you. You're gathered here, with all these fine men, to put a stop to the madness."

It was an interesting perspective, but not one Tylar was particularly keen to subscribe to. Such wanton barbarism in a world gone mad seemed like the work of men and not gods. But then again, he had seen Madelyn with his own eyes, and the unexplainable things she could do. If such wonders were not the work of a god or gods, then what could it be?

"If it's all the same in the end, then I guess it doesn't matter," Tylar said. "As long as Damien Dreadfire is dead and his army broken, that's all I care about."

In the distance flew the King's colors, its blue cloth and golden eagle sigil waving proudly in the wind. Alongside it was the black and gold banner of the Blackthorn Knights, a galloping horse surrounded by a ring of thorns. Tylar saw Lord Vakaro and his underlings nearby, though the High Marshal was conspicuously absent.

I always knew Jenson was a coward. Leave it to him to sit comfortably behind high walls, fat and content, while the rest of us do the dirty work.

A sudden flash of purple from the corner of Tylar's eye drew his attention. Riding at the head of a Guardsman bodyguard was Gareth Bethard, armored in polished steel. He looked as a warrior prince ought to, sitting high in his saddle and burning with determination. Beside him was another, a long braid of golden hair unmistakable.

While they were still in friendly lands, seeing Madelyn so far from his side made Tylar's heart pound with sudden fear. Until the last barbarian lay dead, he would be damned if the girl was more than a stone's throw away.

"Follow me," he shouted, cracking the reins and heading at speed toward the royal host.

Conrak and Tylar joined alongside their prince, Sir Edmund, Madelyn, and Lord Kenfield, and proceeded toward the King's banner. Some of the men cheered as they saw Gareth pass by, lifting their spears into the air and saluting. Most of the soldiers were more reserved, their apprehension plain for any man to see.

"My prince!" Conrak smiled and nodded. "And my lady."

As they approached Lord Vakaro, Tylar found himself in a daydream. He stared long and hard at Gareth and Madelyn, riding beside one another. One day, the prince would become a king, and perhaps Madelyn his queen. They certainly looked like a proper fit for one another, each brave and determined, and willing to lay their lives down for the realm.

If the girl was smart, she would go for it. But then again, it's hard to know what goes on inside that head of hers.

"Your Highness," Ridley Vakaro grunted. He was flanked by Commander Renald Fletch, and several of his lordlings.

"Good day, Lord Vakaro," Gareth replied. "I trust everything is in good order?"

At first, Ridley said nothing, his jaw shifting back and forth. "Yes, my prince. All in good order." The reply was as dry as old firewood.

An interesting thought crossed Tylar's mind, one which made him smirk in amusement. *Maybe I should fuck with this arrogant prick. Get under his skin a little. See what kind of man he really is.*

There was a high certainty that doing so would only inflame the situation between the southern Commandant and Gareth. Ridley Vakaro was not the sort of man to be intimidated easily. But perhaps his tune might change, knowing the crown prince had a violent, impulsive man close by.

"Hey you," he said, unable to contain his desire for conflict. "Yeah, you, you grim-faced shitbag. Show a little more appreciation to your future king."

Lord Vakaro's face tightened to the point where his mouth was clamped shut. It was possible to see a vein protruding from his forehead, and growing larger with each thump of his heart. Tylar was having fits of laughter on the inside, but remained as wild-eyed and mad as ever.

It was even more amusing to see the astonished look on Gareth's face. He was a man with the tongue of a commoner, and even he appeared taken back by Tylar's boldness. Someone had to put the upstart lord on notice, and who better to do it than him?

"Was that necessary?" Gareth asked softly, peering over his shoulder.

"Absolutely." He nodded. "Can't go letting a twat like that think he can run roughshod over you. He'll think twice about whatever schemes he's cooking up with me around. Or at least, he better."

Conrak shook his head and grinned, entertained at the exchange. Madelyn, however, appeared as distant as the horizon, silently watching their legions as they marched north. Drummers began beating their rhythmic cadence, accented by a chorus of pipers. The synchronized footfalls of tens of thousands of soldiers rang like claps of thunder, rattling the earth itself.

Despite all the pomp and formality, the citizens of Bentmont seemed anything but jovial. Tylar had been part of many a procession, both departing and arriving, and knew the people to be warm and boisterous, and proud of their fighting men. But now, they remained silent, gripped by an unspoken fear which plagued every man, woman, and child.

Truly, the people must have suspected that if this army was to fail, there would be nothing standing between them and utter annihilation. It was a frightening and sobering reality for a populace so pampered by centuries of peace and prosperity. War must have seemed like such a distant thing, a concern for men of steel, whose lives were forged in the crucible of battle.

"Look at them," Tylar observed. "Now these fat, contented cunts have a taste of what the world is really like. I doubt they've ever felt real fear in all their lives."

"Indeed," Sir Edmund Thomas said. "That's the sacrifice we make when we serve. We get our hands bloody so they can live in peace, and know only the good things in this world. Not every man can dedicate their lives to a cause so others may benefit from it."

A slight trickle of rain pattered onto the parched earth, the first of its kind in months. White clouds overhead quickly turned a misty gray, not enough for a proper storm, but refreshing nevertheless. It was if the heavens themselves were weeping for the men who would not be returning home to their families.

"History is unfolding in front of our eyes, gentlemen," Lord Anderton Kenfield said, smiling. "And, em… my lady. Our names and deeds will be remembered from this day forward, I have no doubt. The people will sing songs of our glorious march to victory!"

While his sentiment was appreciated, those who had feasted on death cared little for its taste.

"If you came for songs, glory, and all that other bullshit, you're in the wrong place," Tylar said. "There's nothing pretty or noble about swimming in another man's guts. You prepared to get that fine armor of yours dirty?"

The joy in Anders' face dissolved, his expression turning sullen. It was easy for men who knew little of war to boast of its virtues. The young and the privileged were often most vocal, though their silence would come in due time. Tylar remembered his own misguided optimism in his first days of service to the Order, and how quickly it faded into disaffection.

"For good or ill, I'm ready to see this through until the end," Gareth Bethard said. "And I thank you all for being here with me. Truly, there's been no finer fellowship in Betanthia, not for many centuries. Come now, who's ready?"

Tylar and the other companions answered in kind, while Lord Vakaro maintained his silence. With Gareth in the lead, they set off toward the head of the army, flags of Betanthia and the Order flying close behind.

Memories of the year prior came drifting back, when he set out after Madelyn on her journey to Castle Morden. If only he knew then what horrors would unfold. If only he had stayed behind during the siege and allowed her to escape. There were many things Tylar would have done differently, but now was not the time for such regrets.

No, now was a time for vengeance. A time for steel. A time to loose a barely contained wrath upon the animals who would seek to devour Betanthia whole. Retribution was coming, and its name was Titan Bradshaw.

EINARR VII

I'VE LOST THEM. THANK THE GODS.

For two days Einarr rode, until neither man nor beast could continue. He was exhausted, without provisions, and without an idea of where to go. But worst of all was the attack itself. How could one of Dhuuld Lurrson's retainers do such a thing? Had the Khorrtalli chieftain proven false, or had his station been usurped?

Either outcome would prove treacherous. The lives of Damien Dreadfire and his closest friends hung in the balance, as well as the free north itself. If Khorrtal had gone rogue, then it could spell any number of disasters. Northern supply lines could be severed. Villages could be sacked. Such uncertainties kept Einarr awake that night, praying to the gods for clarity.

Thankfully, the gods saw fit to provide him with sustenance. A wild pig found itself tangled in a snare trap, one of several Einarr had set. He prepared the meat and roasted it over a small cook fire, and nearly ate the beast in its entirety. Only a few stagnant drops remained in his water skin, an ominous sign to be certain.

In the face of crushing exhaustion, Einarr pushed forward, knowing thirst would come to claim his life in short order. He recognized little of the terrain, despite having traversed it a year prior. It was a near endless ocean of tall grass and weeds, stretching from horizon to horizon.

"Gods, hear me now," he begged. "Guide me, for I am lost and know not where I wander. I am at your mercy. Please, spare my life, and I will do whatever it is you ask of me, from this day until my final day."

Darkness loomed overhead, blanketing the land with shadow. His horse was struggling as well, its pace gradually slowing. It would only be a matter of time before the beast dropped dead, and himself soon after. Einarr stroked his horse's mane and offered encouragement, hoping it would be enough. It was only when death was all but certain that it appeared, a dark mass against a dreary horizon.

An ominous structure stood tall in the distance, its jagged form jutting up from the earth. Einarr found it curious, as there were no mountains to be found for miles. He squinted, struggling to make out its curious shape, but to no avail. Caution gave way to curiosity, and with steel at the ready, he approached.

"No, it cannot be…"

Einarr's mouth hung open as he stared at the broken ruins of Castle Morden, a place he never intended to revisit. For some unknown reason, the gods had decided to return him yet again to another killing ground. Perhaps it was punishment for the atrocities he helped to facilitate, he thought. It would be fitting penance for standing idle while beaten men were cut down like dogs.

Or… what if the gods are trying to tell me something?

Surely, the visions Einarr experienced over the past year were anything but coincidence. There had to be more to the story, he just knew it.

"Alright, Kholdyr, I will not fight you this time. You brought me here for a purpose, and I will stay until I discover what it is."

With no small measure of doubt, he trotted slowly to the ruins of the castle. Its massive keep was still standing, though one side had partially collapsed. Two of its four outer towers were little more than rubble, but several sections of the wall still stood. It was a testament to the quality of Betanthian craftsmanship, he supposed.

Einarr rode around until he came upon the gaping hole in Morden's wall, a hole ripped open by the might of Ruin. The massive trebuchet had performed as expected, and brought the mightiest stronghold ever built to its knees. While it was deserted, something about the fortress felt indescribably frightening.

Even his horse was hesitant to draw closer, but did so at the behest of a heel jab. Gingerly, the beast made its way up a pulverized pile of stone and into the courtyard. Sitting at its center was a collection of fragmented bones, much of it shrouded with debris. The dead Betanthian soldiers were piled high and burnt into ashes, a burial they were fortunate enough to receive.

It was a far cry from how the fortress appeared but a year ago. Once, it was considered the pinnacle of human ability, a monument to the power of House Bethard. But now, it was little more than an open-air crypt. The warband had stripped away anything of use and value, leaving only death and rot in its wake.

There must be some supplies left somewhere. There has to be.

He suddenly remembered that every castle had a cistern or well, which would allow them to weather sieges for years on end. Finding it would be another matter entirely, but the most logical place seemed to be inside the keep. Perhaps he might find a passageway there, or some point of access, if the interior was intact enough.

After tying up his horse, Einarr drew steel and ventured into the keep, mindful to remain as silent as possible. There was no telling what manner of brigand or wild beast had taken up residence since Morden fell. Were it not for a massive hole in the side of the keep, he might have never seen through an endless black void inside.

A pillar of cold moonlight piercing the blackened veil, filling the broken hall with light. Despite being ravaged by fire, some of the mighty wooden beams still stood, but Einarr knew they would not remain intact for long. Hurriedly, he snatched up a discarded lantern, half a candle remaining inside. With the strike of a flint, the candle came alive once again, lighting his path ahead.

There were no provisions to speak of, not in the dining hall, nor the barracks. A few empty waterskins and satchels lay strewn about, but most of what remained was useless. He took the skins back out into the main hall, and searched for the one thing he needed most. After navigating the rubble for what felt like an hour, Einarr was ready to abandon hope.

As the moon drew higher, its light gradually shifted, illuminating a door which he could not see before. Curiously, he opened it, and to his relief found the castle's well just beyond. Desperately, he hauled up a bucket and nearly drank it empty. The gods, it seemed, had led him true. He filled the skins and the bucket for his horse, then made his way back outside.

After a meal of leftover pig, Einarr settled down for a night's rest inside one of the corner towers, or what remained of one. At first, it was difficult to find rest, knowing how many souls had met their demise on this ground. But eventually, exhaustion claimed him, but the respite would end shortly after it began.

He awoke to a sudden commotion, a crashing, crunching, grinding sound shattering the peaceful night. Einarr sprang to his feet, blade in hand, and raced out onto the parapet. A light of greenish-gray pulsated from the pile of ash and bones, the earth beneath it trembling violently. He stared incredulously as a skeletal arm, nearly twice the size of a man, burst forth from the mound, reaching up to the heavens.

"Gods!" he whispered. "What monstrosity is this?"

Panicked, Einarr gathered his supplies and raced down to ground level. He saw another arm burst forth, followed by a pale, spindly body. Its head was dripping rotten flesh, its glazed eyes crawling with tiny worms. Even death itself paled in comparison to the horror Einarr felt at the sight of it.

The creature stood nearly twelve feet tall, growling and shambling like a reanimated corpse. Sharp talons protruded from its bony hands, its teeth like hundreds of jagged daggers. It stared at Einarr through its dead eyes, a low groan building inside its gaping maw.

How such a terror had manifested or what its intentions might be were unknown, and Einarr was not keen to find out. Without a moment's delay, he hopped into the saddle and rushed up the rubble pile, desperate to flee before becoming the creature's next meal, or worse. When he reached the top, Einarr glanced over his shoulder to see how close the abomination had come, but was alarmed to see the courtyard empty, just as it always was.

"Gods, why have you tormented me with these visions?" he cried out, nearly in tears. "By what misfortune have I been cursed?"

He looked up towards the moon, its light so crisp he could make out thousands of blemishes across its face. Since returning to Skaginlef, he had been bombarded with one vision after another, some heartbreaking, others downright terrifying. It was difficult to make sense of any of it.

"Have you been trying to tell me something all along, Kholdyr? Have I been too foolish and too lost in grief to listen?"

But then an understanding came to him. Perhaps the visions were not simply punishment for betraying his oath, but something more. He recalled seeing images of a lion, a snow covered mountain, and now a bone colossus. It had to mean something; such vivid sights simply could not be the result of delusion.

The gods were never one to speak directly, this much he had been taught. Instead, they preferred to speak in riddles, and give only brief glimpses into what might be. Einarr thought long and hard, trying to make sense of everything he had seen throughout the past year.

He was hit with a sudden revelation, one which filled his heart with panic. Perhaps the messages were not meant for him in the first place. Perhaps the gods intended for Einarr to pass these cryptic visions along to the one most capable of making sense of them.

"Kholdyr," he cried out, "forgive me for ever doubting you! Guide my path, and let no harm come to me! Grant me speed!"

With a mighty roar and crack of the reins, Einarr Rolffson set off hurriedly to the south, under the light of a pale moon. Where he would go, and how he would find the warband was a mystery, but now was not a time for doubts. It was a time for faith, a lesson he had resisted since returning to Skaginlef.

But no more, he thought. No longer would he deny the destiny Kholdyr had etched into the fates even before his birth. He only prayed that time had not run out.

"I'm coming, Damien!" Einarr shouted into the stillness of the night. "By the gods, I'm coming!"

GARETH VII

A REPORT ARRIVED EARLY THAT MORNING, THOUGH GARETH WAS already awake. He spent most of the night tossing and turning, his heart and soul wracked with worry. Even exhaustion from riding under the oppressive Plainhold sun was not enough to tire his troubled mind.

Barbarian horde sighted to the north, heading south. Contact within the day. Sixty to seventy thousand strong.

Even after reading the dispatch a dozen times, the words lost none of their terror. It was one thing to speak of war and train against targets of wood and hay, it was quite another to lead men into battle. But Gareth would not be content to remain at a safe distance, which Lord Vakaro and his host were likely to do. No. Come the next dawn, his lance would be piercing flesh, not lifeless training dummies.

There was comfort to be found in a bottle of bourbon, but comfort soon turned to despair. Gareth had tried to remain strong, not only for himself, but for Betanthia, and for his mother. The latter he had failed, and now the fate of the Kingdom was firmly at stake. How could he save millions of people when he was unable to save the person who mattered most?

It was difficult not to retch from the stress of it all. He might very well be one sunrise away from joining Queen Charlotte in the afterlife, if there even was one. Gareth began to pant like a dog, terror-stricken at the idea of what Damien Dreadfire would do if he was captured.

Madelyn got off easy compared to what he would do to me! Oh heavens, I've made a terrible mistake! I never should have come here! I was foolish and headstrong, and now I'm going to get myself killed!

For all of the fear spilling out of him, Gareth might very well have run straight back to Cardale without stopping. The men would undoubtedly think him a coward, but a coward who was alive was better than a brave man who was dead, he thought.

As he babbled and sat curled in a ball, Sir Edmund Thomas stepped inside his tent. The elder Guardsman eyed him curiously, as if an imposter had taken residence inside Gareth's quarters.

"What's the matter, lad?" Edmund secured the tent flap shut, then placed a hand on his shoulder. "Tell me, what's troubling you?"

"I can't do this, Edmund." He sniffled, wiping away drops of tears and bourbon. "I was such a fool, thinking I could become this great warrior king and lead my people to victory. I'm not the man I thought I was."

"What's this nonsense all about? Of course you are!" Edmund tried to pry the bottle away, but Gareth snatched it back.

"A rider came and brought me a message. They're here, Edmund. The barbarians. Within the day, it said… and I'm absolutely terrified. I can't help but think about what they did to Madelyn. They ran through Castle Morden as if it were a shanty with two walls. What happens if we fail and they take me? What then?"

Sir Edmund moved to the bed, grunting as he sat. He gestured for the bottle, which Gareth was still reluctant to relinquish. Bourbon was one of the few things which could soothe his spirits, but today, it only made his panic snowball into an avalanche of despair.

"It's a risk every man takes when they step onto a battlefield." Edmund snatched the bottle and took a long pull, swishing the fiery liquid around a few times. "You think those peasant boys Lord Vakaro rounded up feel any differently than you? Most of them have only the most basic of training. Some have none at all. Do you think they have any less to lose than you? You, who's been drilled relentlessly by Betanthia's best?"

If Edmund was attempting to raise his confidence, it was having the opposite effect. Gareth turned red with shame, tears slowly dripping down both cheeks.

"I've failed at everything else, why wouldn't I fail at this too? Look at what happened to Madelyn, and my mother. When people rely on me to be strong and do the right thing, I always let them down. And look at how they've suffered because of it."

"Lad," the elder Guardsman's patience was being tested, no doubt. "You cannot bear that burden as your own. Do you feel this destroyed every time there's misfortune in the world? There are things we can control in life, but most are beyond our reach. And you have to face that fact with silence, and acceptance. Sobbing like a bloody child is a disservice to you, your family, your friends, your people..."

The sorrow coursing through his veins began to boil away until only anger remained. Hands tightened into fists as Gareth contemplated giving Edmund a swift shot to the mouth. Who was he to speak in such a manner?

"Good," Sir Edmund said. "Be angry. Stay angry. It'll serve you better than, whatever this is. You have to get a hold of yourself. Those men out there are looking to you to be strong. Your ancestors are watching, even now, at this very moment. And you know what, even your mother is here. You think she would be proud, seeing you like this?"

"No..." It was the only reply he could muster.

Charlotte would most certainly be disappointed, but perhaps more sad than anything. He remembered just how distraught she was at the sight of him drunk and lost for hope. It was something he swore to never do again, but like so many promises before, it had ended in failure.

"Remember what I told you back in Bentmont?" Edmund set the bottle down. "Panic is a failure of belief. I'll ask you this question again. Now tell me, with all sincerity, do you believe we can win this battle?"

The question required a fair bit of thought. On one hand, the barbarians were fierce and clever, besting a seasoned Commandant and leveling one of the sturdiest castles ever built. Gareth had strength of numbers, and Lord Vakaro's lethal resourcefulness, even for all his treachery. But there was one asset, likely greater than any, which could turn the tide of even the direst of situations: Madelyn.

He thought about his first day at Castle Thorn, when he learned of her survival. There had been many times when Madelyn was seemingly lost down an endless pit of despair, desperate to end her suffering. But through it all, Gareth had refused to let her quit. If she could claw herself back to life after enduring such horrors, then surely he could find courage.

"Yes," he whispered. "Yes, I do."

"You say that, but do you truly believe it?" Edmund challenged. "If I held a blade to your throat and demanded you say no instead, would you? With your life in the balance, would you still say yes?"

It was perhaps the most pivotal question of Gareth Bethard's life. This was the moment, the truest moment, where he would step fully into the life of a man, and forever shed the worries and fears of boyhood. And he would become not just any man, but a king.

"I would," he answered with waning reluctance.

Sir Edmund drew a knife with lightning speed, pressing the razor sharp edge underneath his chin. The move caught Gareth by surprise, a sudden burst of fear cutting through his drunkenness.

"Would you say it now?" Edmund pressed up on the blade, a stinging warmness of ripping skin causing him to wince.

"Yes!" Gareth said defiantly, jaw clenched like a steel trap.

"Good. And best you remember it. Hopefully that leaves a scar, so every time you look at it, you're reminded."

It was the sort of tough love a father might give, though Marcellus Bethard had abdicated that responsibility years ago. Were it any other man, Gareth would have him clapped in irons and relieved of his head, but Edmund was the only real father he had. It was a harsh lesson, to be certain, but exactly the sort he needed.

"At least it's you giving me my first scar, and not some filthy barbarian." Gareth felt warm blood oozing from the cut. "Perhaps one day, if I have a son, I can show it to him… and give him the same lesson."

There was an unspoken understanding as both men stood, their eyes locked onto one another. War was never an easy thing, but the war inside one's head was often less straightforward. A spear or sword could defeat a foe quickly enough, but vanquishing inner demons required another approach entirely.

"Whatever part I can play in your life, I'm honored to do so." Edmund clapped him on the shoulder. "You're a good lad… no, *man*. You're a good man, and you'll make a fine king one day. Just know this, when the histories speak of you a thousand years from now, they will say that this was the day Gareth Bethard's reign truly began. Make the most of it, what happens tomorrow will last forever. You can do it."

Gareth nodded in agreement, turning to a pitcher of water for relief. A thick film of sweat blanketed his forehead, not from the rising heat, but from Edmund's challenge. Between exhaustion and drunkenness, he might very well have slept the remainder of the day away.

"Now let's get you sorted out. I would suspect Lord Vakaro intends to hold another one of his meetings, and you need to be there."

Every morning began with the same routine. Before even sitting down for breakfast, Ridley Vakaro would summon a meeting of his lords and lordlings to discuss the latest developments. For a week it seemed as if they would never find the northmen, and Gareth secretly began to wish it was still so.

After dressing in his polished steel armor and purple cloak, he stepped out into a new day. With Sir Edmund at his side, they marched over to Lord Vakaro's command tent, which was conspicuously large given his status. Were Gareth a different sort of monarch, he might have taken offense at the sheer size of the Commandant's accommodations.

Lurking closeby was one of Lord Kenfield's men, an anonymous operative Gareth had seen several times already. He was a man well into his thirties, bearded and burly, and dressed in simple armor one might find at any blacksmith. Gareth found it reassuring to know there were men watching those who were watching him.

A pair of guards saluted as both men entered the tent. Surrounding an ornate wooden table was Ridley Vakaro and his usual band of syco-phants, vassals who were more interested in serving their lord than defending the realm.

Among them was Baron Archibald Patton, a weathered southerner who looked to have spent more days on a farm field than a battlefield. He wore an ornate steel breastplate over mail, with a vibrant blue cloak. A short, black beard blanketed his leathery face, a thick curtain of black hair hanging to his shoulders. Perhaps he was Lord Vakaro's illegitimate son, Gareth thought, given their striking similarities.

Another vassal was Baron Richmal Derricks, looking every bit as sunscorched as his counterparts. Gareth had heard his name men-tioned a few times over the years, as he presided over the city of Sothfort. Its trade goods found their way to the docks of Cardale on a near daily basis. He was bald and beardless, barrel-chested and forever scowling.

Something about southern nobility made Gareth feel uneasy. These were not the soft, pampered lords one might find prancing around Cardale, content in their grand banquets and influence peddling. No, these were hard men, forged under a hot southern sun into instruments of war.

"Good morning to you, my prince," Lord Vakaro said dryly. Though every word appeared as irritating as a rash, he said them dutifully enough.

"Good morning, gentlemen." Gareth felt his head still swimming. He threw his shoulders back and stood stoic, despite his lingering drunkenness. "I was made aware of the latest report from our scouts. It appears the hour of battle is close at hand."

"Indeed," Lord Vakaro replied, then turned his attention to a large map on the table. "The barbarian horde was spotted late yesterday. It appears they have brought their full weight to bear, as expected."

"Expected?" Sir Edmund raised an eyebrow. "Bold of you to say anything about this war is expected."

A tense silence filled the tent. Lord Vakaro eyed his lordlings, a grim understanding between them. The southern Commandant appeared hesitant to speak further, his teeth grinding slowly against one another.

"Indeed, Sir Edmund," Ridley answered. "But as a matter of fact, this campaign has unfolded precisely as planned."

There was a fierce arrogance in Lord Vakaro's eyes. A slight hint of a smile formed in the corners of his mouth, but disappeared as quickly as it arrived. Gareth's suspicions, it seemed, were confirmed. He knew something had to be done, and fast.

"And pray tell, Lord Vakaro," he said, alcohol making him bold. "I'm uncertain of your meaning. The crown is most interested in hearing what you know, and how long you've known it."

Sir Edmund's hand drifted to the hilt of his arming sword, but the southern men in the tent were not easily intimidated. Ridley's eyes glanced at the motion briefly, but he appeared unconcerned.

"Privileged information, my prince. I could not risk the security of this campaign, not with so much at stake. But since we find ourselves on the eve of battle, allow me to say that I have been aware of the northmen's movement for some time now. Our late departure from Dellhaven was deliberate, so as to draw them deeper into our territory."

"Deeper?" Gareth recoiled, his face turned sour. "You mean to tell me you've allowed these fiends to rampage across our lands on purpose?"

"A sacrifice worth making," Lord Vakaro replied. "We will crush their army, of that I am certain. And being so deep inside our territory, they will have nowhere to retreat to. No Hinterwood to disappear into. Their only options will be to flee into the Plainhold and die, or retreat across lands they've already ravaged."

A bold plan, to be certain, but one Gareth would have preferred to know beforehand. There was no telling how many Betanthians needlessly died as a result of Ridley Vakaro's gambit.

"I see," Gareth grumbled. "And how were you able to come by this knowledge? The northmen have been rampaging across Betanthia all year. Have you known this entire time?"

"In the interest of time, allow me to say this." Ridley cleared his throat. "Cedric Valens maintained certain… assets in the west, which helped to preserve Betanthia's authority across the frontier. Since his demise, I have taken control of said assets, and they have periodically supplied me with information."

"All for the greater good, my prince," Richmal Derricks said, his voice sounding of stones grinding against each other. "Even speaking of it now carries risk."

Anger was swelling up within Gareth, so fierce he felt the veins in his forehead throbbing. For a moment, he contemplated having the Commandant and his lordlings arrested for treason, consequences be damned. Sir Edmund had been watching carefully, and placed a gentle hand on his back.

"We're grateful for your diligence, gentlemen," the elder Guardsman said. "It appears the matter is well in hand. In the interest of security, as you say, we'll consider this discussion concluded."

Lord Vakaro and his minions gave slight bows of their heads as Gareth and Edmund exited the tent. It was difficult to believe what had just transpired, given how bold his enemies had become. Gareth was seething, and was nearly as likely to turn his rage upon Edmund as well.

"What do you think you're doing, shuffling me out like that?" he asked through clenched teeth. "I ought to have their bloody heads for such treason! They're openly conducting this war behind my back!"

"Now's not the time, Gareth, not the time at all."

Edmund led him behind a blacksmithing tent, and scanned the area carefully. A sharp clanging of hammer against steel made it impossible to think, let alone hear much of anything. Gareth winced slightly with each blow, a shrill ringing sound rattling around in his ears.

"We have to be careful now," Sir Edmund cautioned. "Can't go arresting our best Commandant at a time like this, infuriating as it may be. Believe me, I would have loved nothing more than to part his head from his shoulders, but we have to be smart about this."

"At what point is treason punished?" Gareth crossed his arms. "How am I supposed to rule a kingdom if I let men who openly conspire against me walk free, and continue in their treachery?"

"All in good time," Edmund sighed. "But these are dangerous men, and we find ourselves in dangerous times. I say we stick to our plan. We win this war first, and show the army you're a leader worth following. Then, once Damien Dreadfire is no more, we move quickly while our victory is still fresh. Who's to say Lord Vakaro won't fall from his horse unexpectedly?"

Patience was an insufferable word. It was a wonder Gareth could even stomach such treason, let alone sleep so close to its epicenter. Still, Edmund was right, as he usually was. Tomorrow would be Betanthia's greatest test in centuries, and disunity on the eve of battle could prove deadly. A northman's blade coming from the front was just as deadly as a knife in the back, after all.

"Very well, Edmund, you haven't led me astray yet." Gareth glanced upward, searching the heavens for guidance. "Once Damien Dreadfire is dead, we snuff out this conspiracy, and not a second later. And when I return to Cardale, I'll have more than one head to mount on my wall."

TITAN X

"**T**ODAY," MADELYN SAID, HER VOICE SOFT AND GRIM. EVEN HER HORSE seemed to take heed of the warning, neighing and shaking its head.

Tylar was uncertain what she meant by such a brief and cryptic utterance, her first words spoken that morning. Something was happening to her, something unnatural, it was plain enough to see. The roots of her hair were growing in pitch black, a stark contrast to her golden blonde length.

"Today?" he asked with hesitant curiosity.

"The battle will begin today. In hours, perhaps."

It was tempting to scoff, or even laugh at such prognostication. But Tylar was beginning to understand that something about the girl had indeed changed. Ever since Conrak brought her down into the cave beneath the Ivornorium, the Madelyn of old seemed to be fading away with each passing day.

"How can you be so sure?" Tylar eyed her suspiciously. "We haven't heard anything in days."

Madelyn's gaze drifted off toward the east, as if an unknown voice was calling out to her. "I can't explain how I know, but I just do. I can feel it in my bones. Do you know when you're fighting an unskilled opponent, and you can sense their movements before they make it?"

Tylar nodded, glancing briefly at the corner of a book sticking up from her saddle bag. "Yeah, makes sense, I suppose. It's got something to do with those damn books, doesn't it? You better hope Conrak doesn't see that thing."

Discreetly, she tucked the flap of her saddle bag back into place. "He'll have to accept it, even if he does. These books and I are part of one another now, for better or worse. Every day that goes by, I recognize myself a little less."

It was one of the few times when he hated being right. Hearing it from the girl's mouth was confirmation enough, but now was neither the time nor place to confront her about it. She was meddling in matters that should be left well enough alone.

Around midday, the army came to a halt. Lord Vakaro was likely awaiting a new report as to the movement of the northmen. It felt relieving to be out of the saddle and walking around under his own power for a change. Tylar stretched and groaned, then tugged at his collar to vent the swampy heat building beneath his armor.

He washed down a few bites of meat and bread with an ale, but managed to drink only half of it. The sun was fierce enough to dry out an ocean, and he found himself craving water more than anything. After finding a skin and drinking it down, he set off in search of Madelyn. She proved easy enough to find, as the other knights preferred to keep their distance. Even the bravest in Betanthia appeared uneasy.

Madelyn sat with her back turned, in the shadow of her horse. It was a sad sight, knowing how greatly she cared to be around the men.

"There you are," he said. "Here, I brought you some water. Drink. Fucking sun's hot enough to melt steel."

She neither spoke, nor acknowledged his existence. Tylar looked at her curiously, and noticed a book sitting open, cradled between her legs. A hand was pressed down firmly on one of its pages, the other clenched tightly into a quivering fist. But the most disturbing thing of all was her eyes.

Instead of an ocean of beautiful steely-blue, her eyes had become as black as night. Even the whites of her eyes were as dark as death. For a moment, Tylar found himself unable to breathe, much less move.

"What the fuck?" He recoiled, too horrified to look away.

A faint mist of ash swirled around her, the skies darkening ever so slightly overhead. Even the ground appeared to tremble at the ghastly energy radiating from within her flesh. Tylar lunged forward, grabbing Madelyn by the shoulders and hoisting her to standing.

"What are you doing?" she barked in a rare display of agitation, the black stains in her eyes vanishing.

"What am I doing? What the fuck are you doing? What sort of black magic did Conrak get you mixed up in?"

Madelyn broke from his grasp and closed the book, returning it securely to her saddle bag. She stood, back turned, sighing deeply. "What does it matter, Tylar? If it weren't for these books, I would never be here. I would still be a broken woman, doomed to a broken life. Now, at least, I have a chance to repay what I have suffered."

She turned slowly, sending a cold shiver down his back. Her eyes a ruined mess, her pupils as black as charcoal, the whites around them bloodshot and throbbing with irritation.

"At what cost?" Tylar asked, swallowing hard. "Is it really worth losing the last of who you were for the sake of petty revenge? I made that mistake, and it cost me years of my life. Don't make the same mistake, you're better than that. You're better than I was."

"What was that you told me once?" Madelyn climbed back onto her horse. "Live for vengeance. Live for hate, if you must. Live for everything they've taken from you. Well, what do you think I'm doing?"

With a sharp nudge, Madelyn set off at a gallop toward the head of the Blackthorn cavalry. It was time to ride yet again through the unyielding vastness of the Plainhold. Tylar stood silent for a moment, hating himself for filling her head with such dark notions. It was unfair for someone so pure of heart and principle to suffer his very same fate. But hate was better than despair, he reckoned. At least it forced the girl out of bed and back into the world. At least she was still alive.

Sighing, Tylar set off in pursuit. It was difficult to know what to say, especially when his advice was taken to heart. Perhaps it was better this way after all, having her here and in good health. But the darkness in her eyes was enough to steal the very warmth from his blood. He came up alongside her, hesitant even now to find answers to a single, burning question.

"Not now, Tylar," Madelyn said abruptly. "I've grown weary with talk."

"There's something I need to know," he demanded. "What exactly were you doing back there? You know, with your eyes all fucked up like that."

"I was making certain our movements would be masked from the crone's sight."

Despite all he had seen and heard as of late, it was difficult to acknowledge that such strange forces were at work. But still, Madelyn had proven just how little he truly understood about the world, and the things lurking in dark places. Such thoughts were unsettling, even to a cold-blood killer.

"And how exactly could you know?" Tylar asked, brow furrowed.

"I could describe it for a year and still only scratch the surface." Madelyn's gaze drifted toward the north. "But the fates appear much the same as when we left Bentmont. All I can do is trust that my efforts were enough. Because if not…"

No further explanation was necessary. Every man marching under the King's banner knew what Damien Dreadfire's horde had done to Cedric Valens. Even the slightest miscalculation could spell Betanthia's doom.

"What efforts might those be?" Tylar asked with morbid curiosity.

"Shifting the course of the future is too obvious," she said. "But perhaps minor changes might go unnoticed. Like the weather, perhaps. I only hope it's enough."

Madelyn glanced up at the sky, her eyes swirling with black mist. Tylar was too fixated on her appearance to notice a dimming of the sun's blazing rays behind a thick veil of clouds. It seemed the sudden change in weather was her doing, or at least Tylar thought, but even attempting to make sense of it made him shiver.

"This is where we fight them," she said quietly, yet with commanding confidence.

Far be it from any man to question her judgement. Tylar looked over at Conrak, who had silently observed them for hours. He gave a nod of the head, his face a mixture of insufferable cockiness and absolute awe.

Tylar motioned for the Blackthorn standard and galloped at speed up a rolling hill. On the other side marched the army, the full might of Betanthia's finest Commandant. Carrying the black and gold banner to the top brought with it memories of a life once lived, a time when he was young and idealistic.

Though he had learned to despise the standard and what it stood for, there was a certain comfort in knowing that the time of men like Jenson Powell was coming to an end. Perhaps Conrak, or even Madelyn herself, might hold the title of High Marshal in the near future. That was, as long as Gareth Bethard made it through the battle alive.

Once at the crest, Tylar hefted the flag and waved it furiously, hoping to draw attention. His efforts were quickly acknowledged by a horn blast, faint to his ears, but loud enough to carry wide across the imposing valley. Here, nearly a hundred thousand men would wait, as planned, until their foes presented themselves.

Shockingly, the sky darkened further, and a pale, wispy mist began manifesting across the valley. Could the girl truly be capable of such feats, or had she made a dark deal with whatever entities were inside the sacred texts? It was an answer he cared little to know.

The mist gradually pooled in the valley below, then spilled up and over the hills around it. Tylar recoiled slightly as the haze approached, its touch cold and its scent of rotten vegetation. It was a feeling of pure dread, as disturbing as if a corpse were shambling about at night.

Whatever this is, whatever you've done, girl, I'm thankful to be on your side.

Within minutes, the northmen began appearing in the distance, pausing only to survey the terrain. They were a cautious lot, as he had learned at Castle Morden, but seemed to pay no heed to the weather. The Plainhold was a treacherous place, anyone who had made the journey could attest to such, and conditions could change wildly and without warning.

After a brief pause, the barbarians continued onward, marching nearly half a mile abreast. Tylar felt a knife twisting in his chest, his breath quickening. He exhaled, watching as Damien Dreadfire's horde marched forward, seemingly uninterested in the lake of mist at the valley floor. Perhaps Madelyn had encased the entire Plainhold in a dark shroud, or perhaps the northmen were blind to things he could see. There was no way to know for certain.

Closer the warband marched, until they were nearly upon the army. With each step, Tylar Bradshaw's heart quickened just a bit more, until he could no longer sit idle. With a sharp kick, he galloped back down the hill, the Blackthorn colors racing in tow.

"They're here!" he shouted breathlessly. "I'll be damned, they're actually here."

Despite their skill and ferocity, the Blackthorn appeared unsettled. Many glanced about, desperately drawing strength from those beside them. Tylar took notice as eyes began turning toward him, few at first, until nearly the entire Order was staring.

"This is your moment, Bradshaw," Conrak said, his hands wringing against the shaft of his lance. "Today, your legend will be written anew. Are you sure you're the man for such a task?"

Memories of the past year flashed throughout his head. Castle Morden. Mor Seveht. Bentmont. And now, the Plainhold. Such a strange journey is such a brief amount of time, he thought. But nevertheless, Conrak was right. This was the day he had long awaited, a day of glory and immortality, or an eternal end to decades of suffering.

Either way, he was ready. Tylar Bradshaw tossed the Blackthorn banner to a rider beside him, then drew a mighty length of razor sharp steel. With his blade held high, he loosed a mighty roar.

"Alright, you fucking cowards! Who wants to kill some northmen?"

SYLVIA IV

DEAR GODS… HELP US.

As the thick haze vanished, the might of Betanthia appeared before them. In fathomless numbers they stood across the valley, the sight of it so staggering it shook Sylvia Stormguard to her bones. The enemy line stretched for a mile or more, its ranks so deep they appeared endless. She could nearly feel breath being pulled from the lungs of those next to her, their apprehension more stifling than the sun.

For a moment, the warband stood motionless, unable to make sense of what was unfolding before them. Even Damien Dreadfire seemed taken back, the surprise encounter leaving the confident warlord dumbfounded. It was only when Betanthia's front line presented its arms that he sprang into action, racing down across the line shouting frantic orders.

"Form ranks! Form ranks, I say!"

She watched as Damien drew his bastard sword and hoisted it into the air, a valiant attempt at rousing the warband's resolve. A deafening horn blast pierced the air as Marvath Bonesplitter raced to his designated position on the left flank. Warriors were quickly broken from their trance, and began hastily assembling themselves.

Much of the Rhivothi force was situated on the left, where Dreadfire expected a heavy cavalry strike. Bonesplitter and his nomads would hopefully break whatever charge the enemy could muster, then push the flanks as they had discussed. Sylvia dismounted and took up her position in the center, her warriors looking to the Nothanek for faith, and the Nothanek to the Rhivothi for strength.

"Make ready men, this is the moment we've been waiting for!" she shouted, frantically overseeing the formation.

Her spearmen were well armored, their cuirasses and breastplates lifted from their enemies over the past year. While her men appeared uncertain, Sylvia remained confident they could hold against whatever Betanthia could throw at them.

"There's so many," a Nothanek said in despair, a trembling voice betraying his resolve.

"And when has that ever stopped us from achieving victory?" she answered in growing defiance. "I have seen our people fight and prevail against odds far worse than this. Believe in yourselves, and in the gods, and we will have victory!"

Hastily, the Zylmacians took up their position on the right. They appeared much heartier than their northern brethren, howling and snarling like rabid beasts. Laughter and mocking cries filled the air like arrows, the wildmen at last getting a proper fight. Zander had to restrain several of his kinsmen, who were so impetuous they nearly charged the enemy line single-handedly.

As the warband looked on in uncertainty, Sylvia caught a glimpse of Damien Dreadfire, riding at speed across the breadth of the field. His black armor shone like polished obsidian, his face stern and fearless. As the Betanthians began marching forward, he remained steadfast, unshaken, and as determined as ever.

"Sons of the free north! Of the west! Hear me and bear witness!" Dreadfire wheeled his horse about, the beast rearing and wailing. "Every moment of your lives has led you to this place. Here is where the fate of our peoples will be decided! Here is where we say to King Bethard in one voice that our lands are not his for the taking! Our wives are not their whores, nor our children their slaves! On this day I say to our enemies, to those men who would subjugate us, they shall come no further!"

A raw, desperate anger in Damien's voice was enough to stir the entirety of the warband. Sylvia roared in hatred, hoisting an axe high above her head. Tens of thousands of free northmen and ravenous wildmen stood defiant as the army of Marcellus Bethard drew closer to them, slow and methodical, their armor crunching in unison.

"Give them not your mercy, give them only the mercy of your spear!" Dreadfire shouted, racing to take his position on the left. "Fight now without fear in your hearts! Your ancestors are watching! The gods are with us!"

As he rode by, warriors cheered and saluted their warlord, thumping axe, sword, and spear against shield. Such a frightening display of courage did little to deter their enemy, who continued on without hesitation. To the left emerged a mass of horsemen under the King's colors, their beasts coming to a halt and remaining idle. Sylvia found it curious that the enemy cavalry would present themselves in such a manner, but perhaps it was a testament to Betanthian arrogance. Their riders *wanted* to be seen.

From the center of the Betanthian ranks rose a forest of pikes, some twenty feet in length. Sylvia stood awestruck at the sight, knowing how costly it would be to fight against such an imposing formation. Thankfully, the warband was not without pikes of their own, though they stood closer to the right flank than the center.

"Pikes!" she commanded. "Pikes to the center! Get in position now!"

It was a maneuver worth making, as the cavalry engagement would be taking place on the opposite end of the field. The warband stood firm, positioning their pikemen as the enemy drew ever closer. Sylvia could make out features on their faces, and could see some were equally as afraid. Many of the Betanthians appeared as if they had never seen a northman before, which filled her with a growing confidence.

"Steady, brothers!" she said. "These are no men before us, only frightened children longing for the safety of their mother's skirts!"

A few chuckles broke through a deathly silence, but most of the warriors were so intently focused they likely did not hear. Suddenly, the army came to an immediate halt. The uniformity of their movements and their total silence was enough to send a jolt of fear through even the heartiest northman. To rouse the men's courage once more, she unleashed a blistering war cry, so shrill it could nearly shatter steel.

In an instant, a furious explosion of roars erupted, rippling throughout the entire warband. It was heartening to feel the thunder of their voices pounding against her chest. Sylvia hoped such a visceral display of aggression would be enough to force Betanthia from the field out of sheer terror. Her hopes were quickly shattered as the air itself was torn asunder, a cloud of arrows buzzing by like angry hornets.

The warriors took refuge behind their shields, but dozens were struck and felled where they stood. Sylvia's shield thumped with the impact of an arrow, then another. The wailing of a female suddenly drew her attention. Ingryd Bjornsdottir was crumpled into a ball on the ground, the shaft of an arrow protruding from her right shoulder.

"Ingryd!" Sylvia shouted. "Gods, are you alright!?"

Groaning and clutching at the arrow, Ingryd nodded, her face wracked with pain. "Yes, I'll be alright."

"Go, get out of here! Be quick! Don't worry about us!"

Ingryd was nearly in tears, not from the pain of her injury, but for having to retreat from the field so quickly. With the arrow volley subsiding, the shieldmaiden stood and stumbled to safety, stepping delicately over one corpse after another. It was a relief to know her wound had not been fatal.

"Worry not, Sylvia," Hilde said, her cyan eyes nearly white as hot coals. "She'll live."

"Stay close to me, no matter what happens," Sylvia commanded.

The Betanthians lowered their pikes and drew closer in short, synchronized steps. Her men held firm, lowering their pikes in kind, though fighting in such formations was as foreign as their surroundings. Hundreds of polearms converged on one another like the closing of a fly trap, wood and steel rattling against one another.

Screams pierced the air as spearheads pierced flesh. The exchange was like something out of a nightmare, as if long skeletal claws were reaching out toward her. Sylvia stood braced behind her shield, eyeing the field and plugging any gap in her line with fresh warriors. Some of her men rushed underneath the pikes, eager to slice the legs and bellies of their foes.

As they charged forward, hunched beneath the pikes overhead, the enemy responded in kind. It was the most awkward melee Sylvia had ever witnessed, men stabbing and slashing at one another like beasts tussling in the dirt. But even the heartiest warriors stood little chance against their armored counterparts, and were driven back in short order, leaving behind scores of dead.

With each passing minute, the fight drew closer to catastrophe. Sylvia knew they could not withstand a sustained engagement, and quickly retreated from the front. Desperately, she raced toward a flag bearer, commanding him to wave his banner. A triangular blue cloth snapped fiercely to and fro, frantically trying to signal the archers who were engaging the left flank.

"Come on! Come on!" she said, looking anxiously to the north.

By the grace of the gods, their archers took notice, and within moments they unleashed a torrent of arrows. Sylvia saw dozens of Betanthian pikes fall like dead trees in a windstorm, the barrage having an immediate effect. She raced back toward her position near the front, shouting encouragement along the way.

"Regroup! Regroup, men! The gods fight beside us! Honor them with your spears!"

Thankfully, the enemy had tasted their fill of battle, for the time being. The Betanthian center crept backward, content to disengage for the time being. Merciful as the reprieve was, chaos continued unabated across both flanks. It appeared the Zylmacians on the right were faring better than expected, in spite of their penchant for fighting with little armor, if any.

Sylvia looked to the left, and saw Damien and the cavalry sitting idle far to the rear, eyeing the enemy horsemen from afar. To her relief, Marvath Bonesplitter and his Rhivothi nomads were hammering the Betanthian infantry, their strength and aggression unmatched. Despite having inferior numbers, she felt a glimmer of hope that perhaps the warband might pull off another miraculous victory.

The gods did not forsake us before, not when we faced Cedric Valens, and they have not forsaken us now!

Screams and shouting erupted again from the center, pulling her back into the fray. Again the Betanthians came forward, pikes at the ready, pushing hard into their line. Sylvia prepared to enter the melee once again, but realized she had lost sight of Mikka and Hilde. A sudden rush of panic blurred her vision. Fearing the worst, she muscled through a tightly packed cluster of warriors, screaming their names until her throat burned.

"Mikka! Hilde! Where are you? Mikka! Hilde!"

"I'm here!" a familiar voice called out.

Mikka stood several ranks away from the fighting, splashed with jets of blood. The parched earth was beginning to churn into a reddish-brown stew, a foul smell of death filling the air. There appeared to be no injury to the shieldmaiden, as the blood had likely come from an ever-increasing pile of dead all around. Sylvia raced to her side, giving a brief embrace.

"Gods, I thought I lost you!" she said, sighing. "Where's Hilde?"

A head of pitch black hair caught her eye. Hilde had suffered a gash to her right bicep, but the wound appeared superficial. Thankfully, a Betanthian pike had found her arm and not her chest.

"They keep coming!" Mikka said, distraught. "Can we even hold against this?"

"Yes, we can. And we will!" she answered. "Our line is holding, gods be praised."

"How much fight do you suppose they have in them?" Mikka grunted as a Nothanek tumbled backward into her, his neck opened and gushing blood.

Any answer would be a lie, Sylvia thought. A battle of this magnitude could last hours, or even days, until one side either tasted their fill of death, or made a fatal mistake. While the center appeared to be faring the worst, her warriors remained firm in their resolve. Friendly volleys of arrows did well enough to keep the Betanthians in check, forcing them back every so often.

"When Damien unleashes his masterstroke, these cravens will tuck tail and run," Sylvia said with faux confidence. "We must do our part, whatever the cost!"

The death toll was staggering, and not in the warband's favor. It was becoming difficult to maintain a cohesive formation with such an alarming number of dead and dying littering the field. Each man who stepped forward to fill a void in the line did so with dread written plainly across his face.

Mutilated men lay strewn about like butchered cattle, their bodies trampled underfoot. It was the ultimate injustice for their faithful service, but the gods would see them home sure enough, where glory and life eternal awaited. As the Betanthians advanced once again, Sylvia Stormguard hoisted her axe, stealing every ounce of courage she could muster.

"Stand firm, men, and be proud! Fear not death, for Sjenohor awaits us!"

GARETH VIII

BLOOD AND CARNAGE WAS HEAVY IN THE AIR, SO THICK HE COULD taste it. Gareth sat mounted and armored, Lord Kenfield and Sir Edmund Thomas nearby. He had often imagined what a proper battle would be like, in sight and sound, and feeling. But the chaos transpiring just ahead shattered whatever preconceived notions he once held.

Is this the glory men speak of? Is this the business of my forefathers?

It was cruel and bloody work, to be certain. Gareth felt his hands beginning to tremble as screams of battle met his ears for the first time. Countless days of training could ill prepare him for the reality that was war.

Don't panic. Remember what Edmund told you. Panic is the failure of belief. You have to believe!

"Is it time, Sir Edmund?" Lord Kenfield appeared unsettled by the scale and ferocity of the fighting.

"Soon enough," Edmund Thomas said. "What's the matter, Anders? You look a little green."

Some of the Guardsmen chuckled softly. Gareth was beginning to wonder how his father, drunk and degenerate though he was, managed to survive such affairs. Marcellus Bethard had seen more battles than his own father, King Torbin Bethard, difficult as it was to believe. In old age, the King hardly seemed man enough to handle such a task, a mere shadow of the hero he once was.

Still, Gareth reminded himself that if Marcellus could triumph in battle, then so could he. The same Bethard blood coursed through his veins, the same legacy, and the same destiny. Neither Lord Vakaro, nor Damien Dreadfire and his barbarian horde would put an end to any of it.

"Not quite what you were expecting?" Edmund asked, studying Gareth's face.

"No," he replied. "It's such chaos, how can anyone make sense of it all?"

"I've seen far worse, if you can imagine such a thing," the elder Guardsman said, scanning the battlefield. "All we have to do is keep them in place until the time is right."

It was difficult to tell who was winning and who was losing. All Gareth could see was a frantic melee from flank to flank, one continuous blur of carnage and death. Soon enough, he would be entering the maelstrom against the greatest threat Betanthia had faced in generations. And to make matters worse, he saw the barbarian cavalry awaiting his arrival.

While their center appeared to be holding, the flanks were suffering a much different fate. Both wings began to draw inward as the northmen surged forward, their momentum nearly unchallenged. Gareth felt his gloves moisten with perspiration at the sight of it. He turned in his saddle and squinted, looking toward Lord Vakaro. The Commandant had taken notice in the shift of the battle as well, and was thrusting a pointed finger dead ahead.

A horn blast cut through the screams and clashing of steel. A reserve force, nearly two thousand strong, began marching double-quick to the center, though the left appeared most imperiled. The detachment stopped just short of the action, however, to Gareth's surprise.

"Why is Lord Vakaro sending men to our center when our left is about to collapse?" he asked desperately. "They're not even fighting, they're just standing there! If we lose the left, then we'll lose the entire field!"

"Easy there, lad," Sir Edmund said. "If he's doing what I think he's doing, then the battle should be decided soon enough. He's going to pull our left back and draw the savages deeper in, and make it look like we're losing. That'll leave them vulnerable to the Blackthorn. Once they charge in, we hit those bastards with our reinforcements. At least, that's what I suspect will happen."

"And how many good men will die as a result?" he protested.

"Plenty." Sir Edmund sighed. "Even orderly withdrawals cost lives. But sometimes in war, sacrifices must be made to achieve victory. Let this be a lesson in the nature of warfare. It's far from the glorious, gentlemanly duels that songs speak of. But between those reserves and the Blackthorn, we stand a fair chance of taking the left."

Gareth sat, chewing his tongue. It was difficult to witness men dying in droves and do nothing. Yet, he selfishly began to wish his moment would never come, that the tide would turn and Damien Dreadfire would flee the field in shame.

But alas, his eyes told another story entirely. The battle began to sour with each passing minute. While the initial assault showed promise, the army was ceding more ground than expected. The left appeared imperiled and moments away from collapsing, the men's courage nearly spent. Only the center held true, their pikes inflicting considerable casualties. Edmund was beginning to stir as well, sensing a shift in the momentum.

"My prince," the elder Guardsman said, "I believe the time has come. If we don't move now, our flank will collapse and we will lose the center. These damn northmen are heartier than I remember."

For a moment, Gareth could not process what he was being told. His moment had come, a moment which could potentially decide the fate of Betanthia forever. His stomach heaved suddenly, pushing foul liquid into the back of his throat.

"Does Lord Vakaro—" he began, but was cut off.

"To hell with Lord Vakaro," Edmund said. "It's the right call, and yours to issue. Every second we delay, the greater our losses will be. I'm ready when you are, lad."

With his cavalrymen looking on, Gareth gave a nod, nearly paralyzed by uncertainty. Edmund put his arm high into the air, signaling Ridley Vakaro and his minions that the charge would now be underway. They responded with the wave of a flag, acknowledging his command. It now fell to Gareth to carry out his destiny.

"Very well," he said with uncertain courage. "Prepare to charge."

His command echoed throughout the mass of cavalry. Hundreds of riders began shifting themselves into a large wedge formation. Gareth closed the visor on his helmet, though his stomach was likely to erupt at any moment. A squire sprinted over with lance in hand, and another with a shield. It was a familiar routine, one practiced nearly every morning. Were it not for screams and the chaos of battle, it might very well have been as mundane as any other training session.

Gareth hoisted his lance high, more for his courage than anyone else's. His legs were shaking horribly, so much that it set his horse into motion, the beast breaking into a trot. It was too late for second thoughts now. Edmund and Anders drew up alongside him, the host of cavalry following suit.

Time itself slowed to a near crawl, the chaotic noise of combat becoming little more than a distant hum. All Gareth could hear was the beating of his heart, and low, labored breathing echoing inside his helmet.

Across the field, Dreadfire's cavalry stirred. Content to sit idle no longer, they assembled into a giant mass, then charged forward at speed. It appeared Damien Dreadfire was committing nearly all of his horse, only a small handful remaining behind. The warlord would be taking no chances, considering the progress his warriors had already made.

Witnessing a horde of barbarian riders surging forward was the single most terrifying thing Gareth Bethard had ever witnessed. In a near instant, his bowels quivered and turned to water. But there would be no turning back now, the momentum of his horsemen and their courage propelling him forward.

Believe, Gareth! You have to believe!

Bracing for impact, he lowered his lance and drove it into a barbarian rider, then ducked beneath the thrust of another. Instinctively Gareth drew his silver blade, the steel whistling as it cut first through air, then through flesh. A splash of warm blood sprayed against his steel armor, the savage tumbling from his saddle.

Death was in every direction. Were it not for a sea of purple cloaks around him, Gareth might have been unable to tell friend from foe. The battle was little more than a blur, a frenzied melee of horse and rider, steel and wood, all having at one another in the worst possible way. An incoming lance glanced off his armor, the metal point meeting nothing but air. Gareth answered with a swift downward slash, his blade cleaving the barbarian's neck.

As if guided by an unseen hand, Gareth slashed at anything and everything in his path. Rider after rider fell to his shining silver blade, his sword arm burning with an inner fire. Even his mount fought with the courage of a lion, the beast biting and kicking, and throwing its weight about.

"My prince!" Lord Kenfield said, charging in with sword drawn. He skewered a rider through the back, a reddened steel tip erupting from the savage's chest. "You must pull back! We cannot lose you!"

It was alarming to see how deep into the fight Gareth had wandered. A sudden rush of fear made him forget where he was on the battlefield. Anders shouted once again, nearly grabbing Gareth by the cloak and hauling him away. Thankfully, his trance was short lived, and he retreated back to a protective ring of Guardsmen.

Once at a safer distance, Gareth surveyed the battlefield. His riders were making little progress against the barbarian horsemen, who had proven their lethality in spades. The left flank was near to collapse, men throwing down their weapons and fleeing in terror. Hope was beginning to retreat along with them, and Gareth knew it would only be a matter of minutes before the battle was lost.

But then he saw them, thousands cresting over a rolling hill like a tidal wave. A black and gold banner flew at the head of their formation, the Blackthorn Knights having entered the fray. Beside the bannerman was Madelyn Everly, removed of helmet, her long, blonde braid trailing in the wind. With Titan and Conrak beside her, the heavy shock cavalry plummeted toward the unsuspecting savages with lightning speed.

Madelyn's face was a mess of rage and despair. Tears of pure hatred streamed down her face, her screams of vengeance carrying far across the battlefield. Gareth sat motionless, both in awe but in fear, as she plowed headfirst into the barbarian formation. The resulting crash was so deafening and terrifying it drew the attention of nearly every man in sight.

Their heavy horses had little difficulty trampling their lightly armored foes into the dirt. It was the most shocking display of raw power Gareth had ever seen, the Blackthorn carving through the heart of the left flank with frightening efficiency. Upon witnessing the calamity for themselves, Damien Dreadfire's cavalry promptly disengaged, though many were cut down in their retreat.

Could it be? Have we really won? Has the day been saved?

Sir Edmund trotted over, his armor and sword washed with blood. Behind his lifted visor was a growing smile, but it seemed premature to celebrate much of anything. "Well done, Gareth! Well done indeed!"

"The battle isn't over, Edmund," he sighed. "Madelyn is in the thick of it, I can't let anything happen to her."

"Relax, lad, she's in good hands. I think our northern friends have had enough for one day. Their lines are beginning to break."

From his position, Gareth saw the barbarians fleeing in droves, a horn blast signaling their retreat. Though Betanthian casualties were heavy, it seemed only proper to press the attack, and finish Damien Dreadfire once and for all.

"We should ride them all down!" he said with a confident smile. "Come on, Edmund! Let's settle this right here and right now!"

"Careful now," Sir Edmund cautioned. "There's no telling what they have in reserve. If we go charging headlong after them, it could be us on the losing end. Wars are never won in a single day. In fact, this battle could pick right up again tomorrow, for all we know."

Disregarding such advice seemed foolish, as Edmund Thomas was a man of many battles. Still, it was supremely frustrating to watch as thousands of northmen fled unchallenged across the field. Impetuously, Gareth spurred his mount back into action, cracking the reins and roaring furiously.

Despite Sir Edmund's pleading, he charged toward the barbarian riders, desperate to meet them with steel. However, they were too frantic in their retreat, and were quickly disappearing from sight. Knowing Madelyn was in the thick of battle, he instead turned toward his right flank, which itself was on the verge of faltering.

Somehow, he could sense the weight of his cavalry following close behind. Courageously, Gareth plowed into the fanatical northmen, raining down one sword stroke after another. It was enough to set the savages to fleeing, for they could see the fight had turned against them.

Suddenly, Gareth was struck in the chest with a poleaxe, the sheer force of it knocking him clean from his saddle. He tumbled onto the soggy, red earth in a heap, but managed to keep a grip on his sword. Another northman stood looming overhead, a two-handed axe in hand.

With wild eyes and windblown hair, the savage hefted the axe and prepared to bring it down in a killing blow, but was met with a slash from a mounted Guardsman. The warrior's hands were lopped clean off at the wrist, blood erupting from his ruined stumps. Gareth thrust his sword into the northman's chest, and watched his corpse crumple to the ground.

An armored hand reached down, offering assistance. A familiar purple cloak fluttered around the man's shoulders, much to Gareth's relief.

"You have my thanks," he sighed. "Looks like we have them on the run."

Were it not for the angle of the sun, Gareth might not have seen the glint of steel in the Guardsman's hands as he drew it. They were on a battlefield, after all, but the motion seemed unnatural considering the fight was dwindling down.

Suddenly, the Guardsman pulled him in close, trying to slip a slender blade underneath his cuirass. Instinctively, he grabbed the assailant by the wrist, both men jockeying for supremacy.

"What are you doing?!" he grunted in desperation as the blade inched closer.

There was no reply from the Guardsman, whose gaze was oppressive enough to crumble stone. For what felt like an eternity, Gareth struggled, his foe violently strong. As the steel tip drew perilously close, he spotted another rider charging past, eager to hunt down the fleeing northmen.

With all the strength he could muster, Gareth pushed the rogue Guardsman directly into the path of the horse, trampling him effortlessly. Gareth gasped for breath, desperately feeling around his abdomen to see if it had in fact been pierced.

He retrieved his silver sword, prying it from the chest of the handless northman. Part of him wanted to strike down the treasonous Guardsman, to chop and hack and make butcher's work until only bloody ribbons remained. But there was also a curiosity, to know why and how one so loyal could perpetrate such a crime.

Lord Vakaro finally made his move. I never thought it would come to this, but here I am.

Curiosity quickly won out over rage. Gareth knelt beside the Guardsman, his head gushing blood like a fountain. There would be precious little time to get answers, especially in the midst of such chaos.

"Who are you, and who sent you? Speak, villain!"

There was no answer, only a gurgling groan. Gareth thought the assassin might have been choking on his own tongue and went to offer assistance. A dead man was of no use, after all. But as he pried open the traitor's mouth, he saw there was no tongue to be found. It mattered not, as the false Guardsman gasped one final time, then went limp as death took him.

There was little time to reflect on what had just transpired. Madelyn was still fighting, as were Conrak, Titan, and Sir Edmund. While many of the northmen had taken flight, many more remained, determined to fight to whatever end. Gareth sheathed his silver sword, looking to the men around him.

"Someone fetch my horse, and a fresh lance. I'm not finished with these bastards just yet!"

ZANDER V

IT WAS AS IF THE HEAVENS THEMSELVES CAME CRASHING DOWN, THE calamity so shocking he could hardly believe it. Zander felt his heart sink at the sight of it, the Blackthorn charge slicing through his kinsmen effortlessly. The battle, it seemed, had taken a devastating turn for the worse.

"Damn it! By the gods, damn it all!" He roared in frustration, then turned just in time to parry a sword strike.

Zander planted his axe into the foeman's face and wrenched it free, uncertain of what to do next. Many of the wildmen were breaking ranks and fleeing, though some continued lashing out at anything in their path. For a moment, he thought he spied Jollkud riding hard to the north, as fast as his horse would allow.

"Cowards! Cowards, the whole lot of you!"

His curses did little to motivate his warriors, if they were even heard at all. Zander paused to survey the situation further, a knot tightening in his chest. The damnable Blackthorn were not the incompetent weaklings they appeared to be, given how easily they were defeated at Hok and Castle Morden. He realized if a retreat was not called soon, the Zylmacians would be utterly annihilated.

He slipped a curved war horn from his belt and gave several mighty blasts. At first, the wildmen were in disbelief, many torn between obedience to their warchief, and the thrill of the fight. Casualties were mounting quickly, like heavy snow in a blizzard. Zander again sounded for retreat, agitated at such disorganization.

"Reform the line! Reform, I say!"

Hastily, the Zylmacians attempted to bring a halt to the crushing Blackthorn charge. Lacking in pikes and spears, and experience in fighting proper horsemen, the fight was quickly becoming a massacre. Zander lunged toward a rider, ducking beneath a sword slash and cleaving the horse's front leg in two. The beast toppled immediately, crushing its rider beneath its armored mass. He ripped the knight's helmet free, then sent the axe down across the middle of the man's neck.

Despite their fierceness, the wildmen were becoming consumed by panic. They began routing in droves, nearly trampling one another in a desperate attempt to save their lives. Zander knew there would be no hope in salvaging the fight now. As the battle soured, so did his dreams of glory and legacy. Years of toil and sacrifice to become the most feared warlord in history were quickly melting away. Little more could be done except to flee and fight again another day.

At speed, he began muscling through the ranks, even knocking down his own men at times. If they were too stupid to heed a call to retreat, then they deserved to die, he supposed. The ground was trembling as more knights thundered closer. Zander could nearly feel their horses breathing on his neck.

Nearby was Damien Dreadfire, still mounted and fighting like a man possessed. It was admirable to see him on the battlefield while so many were fleeing. With bastard sword in hand, Dreadfire dispatched every Betanthian in his path, one after another falling to his blade. But there were too many knights and spearmen, all manner of foes drawing in closer by the second.

A well-placed spear struck Damien's horse in the neck, the animal crumpling to the ground in a near instant. The warlord was sent flying, and landed dazed from the impact. As he attempted to stand, a soldier charged in, sword in hand, and slipped the blade in between a gap in his armor, just above the knee. Dreadfire thrashed and roared in agony, clubbing the soldier's face with his gauntleted hand.

Wrenching the sword free, Damien lurched to his feet and removed his skull-shaped helmet. For the first time in years, Zander could see the Borjifan was a mortal man like any other, not a mythical warrior many thought him to be.

But if he dies now, then all my efforts will be for nothing! I need him alive!

Closing the distance to save Dreadfire was as impossible as salvaging the battle. Instead, Zander continued onward, hoping to flee alive and intact. He glanced over his shoulder and saw a rider attempt to strike Damien down with a saber. The warlord ducked awkwardly, then delivered a crushing blow to the side of the horse's head with an armored fist, both man and beast crashing in a heap. Dreadfire jumped into the saddle as the horse found its footing, then promptly set off in retreat.

I wonder if the old witch ever foresaw such a sight! Damien Dreadfire, fleeing with his tail tucked!

Exhausted and gasping for breath, Zander paused and looked out over the battlefield. Pockets of northmen and Zylmacians continued to fight, but their fate was all but guaranteed. It was incomprehensible to know just how close they had come to victory, only to have it snatched away in a heartbeat. Betanthia now dominated the land for as far as the eye could see.

Lurching and stumbling across the field was a face most familiar, though one he loved not. Marvath Bonesplitter had taken flight, his great axe clutched loosely in his left hand. His right arm hung by little more than a tendon and a flap of skin at the elbow, blood pouring out like a waterfall. His mouth was agape and eyes vacant, yet still the Rhivothi continued on.

Would you look at that! I'll give it to him, he's one tough son of a bitch. But I'll be damned before I let the Betanthians claim his head. Oh no, not today!

After a few deep breaths, Zander set off at speed toward Bonesplitter. He sheathed his axe and threw the Rhivothi's good arm over his shoulder, and together they limped onward across the field.

"We've… we've lost…" Marvath panted. "It's over."

"Aye, mate, we're done. Looks like they got you real good."

Looking at the wound was disgusting, but quite pleasing at the same time. It was a small consolation to see such a distasteful man suffer, however short lived it might be. Marvath dropped his axe and clutched Zander's shoulder, desperate to stay upright.

"You were wrong about something, though, mate," Zander said, grinning. "You remember what you said that day in the longhouse? I heard it well enough. I would never stab you in the back. Oh no, that sort of thing is for cowards. With me, you'll always see it coming."

Zander drew a knife and slipped the blade in between Marvath's ribs, pushing it all the way to the hilt. A slight grunt was all that escaped, and he felt the Rhivothi's grip tighten in kind. He pulled the knife out and stabbed several more times, but still Bonesplitter would not go down.

"Just… die!" Zander said, jerking and twisting his blade. "Die! Die!"

Marvath wrapped a hand around his neck and squeezed, a look of fiery hatred seared across his bearded face. The remains of his other arm flopped about like a fish out of water as he attempted to use it, but to no avail.

"You… Bymist… rat!" Bonesplitter croaked, squeezing with every ounce of strength.

Such might from a dying man took Zander by surprise. But the light in Marvath's eyes quickly faded, the force of his grip loosening. Thankfully, none had taken notice of the assassination throughout all the ensuing chaos. Zander could hardly contain his excitement as he left Marvath Bonesplitter's now lifeless corpse behind. Despite losing the battle, being rid of the Rhivothi warchief was every bit the victory he imagined it would be.

It appeared as though the Betanthians would content themselves with slaughtering those who either refused to retreat, or had no opening from which to escape. Small pockets of men continued to stand their ground, but Zander had seen enough. Perhaps Betanthia would attempt to press onward toward their camp and finish what they began. Such a thought made him shiver, as it could mean losing their precious baggage train, and all of its golden contents.

At speed, he trudged across the rolling hills, stopping only briefly to see if hostile cavalry was in pursuit. Thankfully, neither the Betanthians nor the Blackthorn gave chase. At least, for the time being. And with Dreadfire still alive, there was hope that their loss might be avenged.

With Bonesplitter dead, he's the only one left standing in my way. Soon they'll all bow to me, every last one of them. Even those cursed Rhivothi. I might even bed 'ole Stormguard and take her for my queen while I'm at it!

Amusing as his thoughts were, it did nothing to soften the crushing blow of defeat. Would he arrive at the wagon train only to find the warband ruined beyond repair? Would it even be possible to recover from such a devastating upset? Such answers seemed all too clear, judging by the weary and disheveled warriors slogging back to camp beside him.

So few were Zylmacians, perhaps one out of every twenty or so. The Blackthorn charge had been earth shattering, and its result far beyond anything he could have imagined. For the first time in his life, Zander felt panic take root inside his heart. If the wildmen were in fact eradicated, then it would be the end of not only the warband, but the legacy he craved more than life itself.

No, I can't let that happen. I've come too far and sacrificed too much to let my destiny slip away. Azldyr, grant me strength, and vengeance!

TITAN XI

T RIUMPHAL CHEERS RANG OUT AS THE NORTHMEN FLED, THOUGH
Tylar found little to celebrate. From his position, he saw the hulking frame of Damien Dreadfire, his blackened armor standing out like a tree in a desert. The warlord was mounted and taking flight, riding northward with all haste.

"Fucking coward," Tylar grunted, dumbfounded by what he was witnessing.

For all of Madelyn's talk about such a fabled warrior, he had tucked tail and fled like every other barbarian. It was a suspicion Tylar held all along; savages were little more than opportunists and scavengers, who diminish in the face of superior men.

Were it not for tens of thousands of northmen standing between him and Damien, he might have tried to claim the warlord's head and the day's glory along with it. It was a tempting thought, and one which grew more enticing by the second.

He glanced over his shoulder and saw Madelyn, sitting victorious, basking in the adoration of the knights. She had fought well, and with a rage so terrifying she might very well have earned the name of Titan for herself.

The girl's alive, and got her vengeance tenfold. You did good, Tylar, you miserable old prick. You finally did something right for a change.

It was comforting to know he had not failed a second time to keep her safe. However, neither of them achieved their true objective. Damien Dreadfire survived the battle, and had escaped justice. It was both sickening and unacceptable to behold, and began rousing a genocidal madness within him.

"I do believe congratulations are in order!" Conrak said, coming up alongside him. "You just earned yourself a place in the histories, Bradshaw. This day will be one of the Order's finest, no doubt."

Despite inflicting heavy casualties, the barbarian horde still survived. Thousands of them were in flight, and would escape to fight another day. While many of his brethren began to celebrate and be content in their victory, Tylar was loath to let a single northman survive.

"It's not over," he snarled. "Not while Dreadfire still lives. Not while any of these fuckers still live. Keep the girl safe!"

With fury to fight, Tylar pounded an armored foot into his horse, setting off in pursuit of the retreating warband. He cut down one savage after another, leaving a trail of bodies strewn about behind him. The wildmen fell easily enough, many of them poorly armored, if at all. Every slash sent a jolt of satisfaction up through his sword arm, but did nothing to quench his bloodlust.

"Where the fuck do you think you're going?" Tylar roared, planting his sword into the bald head of a Zylmacian. His skull cracked like split wood, a small splash of blood shooting into the air. Savage after savage fell to his blade, but it brought him no closer to the ultimate prize.

"Dreadfire! I'm coming for you, you son of a bitch!"

Tylar knew he was charging alone, yet fear was absent from his heart. Every kill seemed to only worsen his anger, until he no longer had any sense of time or space. His vision had turned a deep shade of crimson, as if the land and sky itself were bleeding.

A pair of retreating spearmen wheeled about as they heard Tylar thundering in. He parried a spear thrust and prepared to answer with a downward slash. But one of the savages struck true, skewering his horse in the neck. He soared through the air for what seemed like an hour before crashing onto the dusty earth.

Groaning and disoriented, Tylar struggled to find solid footing. By some miracle he kept hold of his sword, though his shield was thrown from sight. Thankfully, there was another nearby. It was large and round, made from heavy wood, with banded iron across its face. A cruel spike sat at its center, several arrows driven deep into it.

A score of savages came charging in, baying for more blood. There were too many to fight all at once, this he knew. Tylar Bradshaw stood defiant, and prepared to face his destiny.

Remember what Conrak told you. Breathe. Focus. What do you have to lose?

Time itself slowed as the first barbarian charged in with reckless hate. Tylar sidestepped the attack and followed up with a wicked slash, just as an axe planted deep into his shield. He spun about and parried another strike, raking his blade across a wildman's back. A third man lost heart, retreating nearly as quickly as he charged in.

Despite beating the odds, Tylar's bloodlust was not yet sated. There was an opportunity to retire from the field, to revel in victory and continue the fight another day. But memories of Castle Morden began flashing before his eyes, as did his days spent starving at Mor Seveht. He recalled weeks of rotting in irons, and his fear of the hangman's noose. But worst of all was the sight of Madelyn laid up in bed, her belly large and body broken.

Thinking about the girl and what Dreadfire had done stoked an anger so terrible his flesh could hardly contain it. His body began to tremble, not from fear, but from an anxiety he had never experienced before. This was the time for vengeance. This was the time to take back everything which was taken from him and from those he cared for, and he would be damned if another northman would slink away. With a million bloody thoughts racing through his head, Titan Bradshaw went completely mad.

With the roar of a lion, he raised his steel high into the air as a half dozen barbarians charged in, hoping for an easy kill. He dodged a downward swing from a great axe, then slashed a deep pit into the neck of the man wielding it. One foe down, five to go.

Two swordsmen closed distance from his left. Tylar blocked a wild swing with his shield, thrust steel into a savage's bowels, then spun and hacked the other wildman from shoulder to hip. With half their numbers suddenly destroyed, the remaining three foes turned and fled like the cowards they were.

One savage tripped over the corpse of a fallen knight, his skull thumping awkwardly on the ground. An easy kill, no doubt, but seeing the barbarian panic and scramble away only incensed him even further. Tylar threw down his shield and snatched up a one-handed axe, studying the crude weapon briefly. It seemed poetic that the weapon used to rain terror down upon Betanthia would now be used against one of its former masters.

"Not so tough now, are you?" Tylar snarled, driving the axe head into the small of the barbarian's back.

A pitiful howl rang out, the savage reaching desperately to pry the axe free. Tylar wrenched it out, then rained down one crushing blow after another. Blood and chunks of ruined flesh flew about wildly, until little more than a pile of mash remained. The barbarians looked back in horror at the sight of their kinsman, laying butchered like a pig. It seemed to only aid in their flight from the battlefield.

"Come back, you cowards!" Tylar roared, nearly shaking the earth itself. "Where are your gods now, northmen? Where is your warlord? Why does he cower?"

Enraged, he threw his sword as far as it would fly, the steel sinking into the spongy, red earth. Although the day was won, allowing

Damien Dreadfire to escape judgement was a stinging defeat in its own right. As long as he lived, Betanthia would never be safe. And neither would Madelyn, for that matter.

"Easy there, Bradshaw." Conrak grinned, trotting over to his side. "Can't go killing the whole horde by yourself in an afternoon, now."

A pitiful groan caught their attention. A northman lurched across the ground, one leg missing above the knee. Tylar scowled, watching as a river of blood gushed from his ghastly wound. It would have been easy enough to skewer the man or inflict any number of cruelties upon him. Many knights were gathering around, waiting breathlessly to see what would transpire next.

Tylar snatched a waterskin from a bag on Conrak's mount and knelt beside the wounded savage. He drank long, savoring every drop as the northman looked on in dismay.

"You tree-fuckers thought you could come here and have your way with us, didn't you?" Tylar said, shaking his head. "Bet you never thought you'd be here, bleeding out on this shithole of a plain. Yet here you are, defeated and dying. Serves you fucking right."

He stood, cracking the knuckles on both hands. He felt an uncontrollable rage welling up inside him, a nearly anxious desire to loose his wrath once more. "You damn near killed a good friend of mine. But I'm sure you're already aware. Maybe you were even involved. Doesn't matter now, because you're going to feel exactly what she felt."

A spear lay discarded on the ground, its point nearly black from gore. Tylar clutched the shaft, examining it briefly. He tried placing himself in Madelyn's shoes on that fateful evening, but had not the imagination to do it justice. He spied her golden head close by, standing out among a sea of steel helmets.

This one's for you, my friend.

Tylar roared as he drove the spearpoint in between the dying northman's legs, plunging it deep through his soft flesh. With a single arm,

Tylar pushed and strained until it could go no further. A fair bit of justice, no doubt, but far from adequate. Only when Damien Dreadfire lay dead and put on display would he ever feel satisfied.

As he turned, he spied a host of knights sitting idle, stunned at the cruelty they had witnessed. Among them was Madelyn, her face a mess of rage, exhaustion, and anguish. She offered a wounded smile, a small consolation for the horrors she had endured.

"Thank you," she mouthed, before retiring from the field.

"You're a cruel man, Tylar Bradshaw," Conrak said as he dismounted. "Cruel, but valiant. You're exactly what I hoped you would be. By tomorrow, the entire army will have heard about what you've done here today."

Tylar glanced to the north, watching the last of the savages retreat. With a fresh mount and a pint of ale, he might very well have set off in pursuit of Dreadfire's entire horde.

"It wasn't nearly enough," he muttered.

"It never is." Conrak placed a hand on his mighty shoulder. "But wars are never won in a single day. You've set the tone for the battles to come, and if I were Damien Dreadfire, I would give serious thought to retiring to the forests forever. Come, let's get out of here. The first drink is yours. No one has earned it more. Someone get this man a fresh horse!"

Regrettably, there was no shortage of available mounts. A dismounted knight brought over an armored Strider, its owner felled by a Zylmacian axe. Tylar placed a hand on its neck, knowing the significance of such a gesture. Somberly, he climbed into the saddle as another man brought his sword, having retrieved it from the field.

"I believe this belongs to you, my lord," the knight said, offering it with both hands.

"I'm not a lord," Tylar grunted, sheathing his steel. "I'm just another man."

Conrak scoffed and shook his head. "Nonsense. You're more than just a man. You're the legend I knew you could be. You're a Titan!"

A raucous roar erupted from the nearby knights. They hoisted lance and sword high above their heads, cheering with victorious fury.

"Titan! Titan! Titan!"

Their affection was the same as he experienced after the siege at Brimnora so many years ago. It was as uncomfortable now as it was then, but Tylar embraced it nevertheless. Conrak was right; maintaining the men's spirits and giving them a standard to rally behind was more important than his conflicted feelings.

Thousands of men gathered around to pay their respects, their chants ringing out like claps of thunder. He raised a hand in acknowledgement, however reluctant it may have been.

"The gods spared you for a reason," Conrak said, smiling. "I hope you can see that now. Without you, and without Madelyn, this never would have been possible. Betanthia would likely be a smoking ruin by now, with countless millions dead."

"I've seen a lot of things," he said, "a lot of shit I can't explain. But the past few months have been the most fucking bizarre of my life. Maybe these gods of yours are real after all."

"Come now, Bradshaw. They're your gods too, whether you want to acknowledge them or not. They obviously believe enough in you to spare you from death. How many times has it been now?"

More times than he could remember, to be precise. Perhaps there was some truth to the matter after all, given the impossible situations Tylar routinely found himself in. But if it was all for a greater purpose, all of the death and misery suffered over the years, then so be it, he thought.

"As long as I get to squeeze the life out of Damien Dreadfire while Madelyn watches." Tylar smirked. "Maybe then I'll become a believer. But for now, you best believe I'm going to drink the kingdom dry when we get back to camp."

Conrak chuckled, giving his horse a nudge. "Fair enough, Bradshaw. But not if I outdrink you first!"

LUCETTA VIIII

W HEN THE DUST HAD SETTLED AND THE SMOKE CLEARED, CARDALE was as quiet as a crypt. Lucetta slept not a wink the night before, instead content to watch an orange glow of ravenous flames across Cardale's skyline. The macabre light faded to black in the early morning hours, leaving in its wake a familiar stench, one she had encountered once already.

Death had a peculiar scent, sickly-sweet, and as intoxicating as the finest western perfumes. Lucetta stood on the balcony, smiling, drawing its thick aroma deep into her lungs. While the sight of Cardale's burnt husk was heartbreaking, it was comforting to know those who had been put down were enemies, men who would have counted themselves in opposition to her divine rule.

I did what was necessary, mother. For us, and for our future. If only you could see me now, how proud you would be!

With a new day dawning, she bounded down the grand staircase and set off through the great hall, eager to witness the fruits of her labor. Thankfully, there was no sign of Aldred, as he was either still asleep, or preparing for another damnable council meeting. The familiarity of routine and his lordly privilege seemed more of a spouse than she was.

Meetings and more meetings. And where have they taken him? Nowhere. What a dutiful husband I have…

Not that it mattered. Destiny had other plans for Lucetta Bethard, plans which had already taken her down strange and fantastical roads. But guiding her way was the woman in the black, a spirit which had not led her astray despite doubt and fear, and every other emotion which might seek to cloud her path.

Anxiously, she stepped out into the Citadel's courtyard. Small, dark flecks drifted on the air like black snow. Lucetta stuck out her tongue, much as she did as a child during winter snows. The taste of burning wood made her mouth water, as if biting into a tender steak. She smiled, and nearly began skipping toward the Citadel gatehouse.

When she arrived, the Guardsmen offered a weary salute, their eyes puffy and ringed with dark circles. They looked haggard, having been on watch all throughout the night.

"Good morning to you, princess," one of the Guardsmen said. "You'll be delighted to know the violence has been quelled. Not more than an hour ago we received word."

"Most excellent!" Lucetta said, fingers scratching at one another. "Gather your men, and my horse. I wish to see the condition of my city, and let the people know they have not been forsaken."

Several of the guards looked at each other, each reluctant to speak. "My princess…" another Guardsman said. "Unfortunately, we are under orders from your husband to not allow anyone to enter or leave the palace. There still may be danger out there, and we cannot risk you."

At first, Lucetta stood dumbfounded, unable to process what she was hearing. After everything she had done, after braving the worst of the rioting and leading the relief army personally, she was now being forced to sit idle. No, she thought, it was an injustice that would not be allowed to stand.

"Nonsense," she scoffed. "My husband does not dictate to me when and where I may go. He's an Eldon, not a Bethard. And you men are sworn to obey House Bethard, are you not? Now, open that gate, at once!"

"I thought you might be up early," Aldred said, giving her a startle. He stepped out from one of the gatehouse towers, wearing an ornate breastplate over a dark brown doublet.

"What are you doing out here?" Lucetta cocked her head. "I thought—"

"I would be a poor steward to your father if I slept while his city burned. All night I've stood on these walls, receiving reports and dispatching them. The fighting may be over, but the city is far, far too dangerous to venture out into. I'm sorry, my dear, but I cannot allow it."

Allow? The word sounded nearly as foreign as Droethien. She stood breathless, so incensed she contemplated snatching a Guardsman's sword and parting Aldred's head from his shoulders.

"Well then, allow me to remind you that you have no right to order a Bethard about like some simple handmaid!" she growled through clenched teeth. "The nerve of you, after all this time!"

"May we discuss this matter in private, my dear?" Aldred took her gently by the arm, but Lucetta ripped it away.

"No we may not! I will not be lectured to or scolded like some insolent child! Have you learned nothing about your own wife, Aldred? After everything I have done for this city, and for this kingdom? Is this how you continue to see me?"

From the dark shadows of the guard tower came two orange-red orbs, their glow pulsating ever so slightly. Lucetta swallowed hard, knowing she was on the verge of saying too much and provoking the woman in black. She frantically itched the back of her hand, the skin becoming unbearably dry and irritated. But the warm raking of nails against her flesh helped to soothe her racing pulse.

"I know how much you care, my love," Aldred said softly. "I promise you, I will take you out into the city, but only when the danger has passed. I know how brave you are, and how much you wish to help and set things right. I admire it, truly I do. But please, allow me time. Can you do that for me?"

The answer was most certainly no, but in the interest of keeping peace and avoiding scrutiny, she agreed. Huffing and stamping her feet, Lucetta retreated into the Citadel, a ravenous thirst taking hold. Thankfully, her chamber was stocked with enough wine to fill the hull of a freighter. Each step to the upper floors was as grueling as scaling a mountain, but the thought of sweet wine on her lips was enough to compel her onward.

A passing servant girl averted her eyes and scurried away, like a mouse fleeing a hungry cat. It was an odd occurrence, but not unheard of, as the servants chose to avoid finding themselves on the receiving end of a tongue lashing. Lucetta retired to her chamber and stormed toward the desk where a silver flagon sat, but found it to be bone dry. She hefted the vessel and shook it, baffled at its emptiness.

What trickery is this? Do these damned peasants not know to keep my wine in ample supply?

Lucetta turned and screamed down the hall, commanding the servant girl to return. The young lady responded dutifully, though she shook as if taken by a sudden, violent affliction.

"You there! Get back here, right this instant!" she commanded. "What is the meaning of this? Why is there no wine in my chamber? Have I not told you people a thousand times!"

The servant's eyes drifted up to meet hers, then quickly fell. "I'm… I'm sorry, princess… but… Lord Aldred commanded us not to… to…"

For all of the fiery rage within her, Lucetta might very well have transformed into a dragon. She could nearly feel flames shooting out of her eyes and mouth, hot enough to turn stone into slag. The hall seemed to have turned a deep shade of red, her blood nearly at a boil.

"My husband?!" she shrieked. "Who is he to deny a Bethard what a Bethard wants? And who are you to refuse my orders? I ought to have your head for this, you filthy peasant bitch!"

In a blind fit of emotion, Lucetta swung the empty flagon with all of her might, the metal clanging as it struck the servant's head. She fell backward, a trickle of blood gushing from her scalp and down one cheek.

At first, Lucetta wanted nothing more than to continue bashing until the servant's head was little more than pulp. But seeing the girl sob and clutch her wound made the anger fade away, like fog in a morning sunrise. Such a violent outburst was most uncharacteristic of royalty, and made Lucetta deathly afraid of what had suddenly possessed her. She dropped the flagon and took off down the grand staircase, nearly in tears.

What in the world is happening to me? How could I do such a thing?

Thankfully, Aldred was standing in the great hall, speaking to a Guardsman and the master servant. He looked weary beyond his years, the stress of a violent insurrection exacting a heavy toll. It was sad to see a man of such vigor looking so utterly spent. But Lucetta's sympathy quickly gave way to anger once again, her thirst for wine growing insurmountable.

"Husband," she said, arms crossed and voice echoing throughout the cavernous room. "I must speak with you at once."

Aldred gave a quick glance, then concluded his discussion. His steps appeared labored, as if his feet were blocked in solid lead. "Yes, my dear? Is everything alright?"

"No, everything is most certainly not alright. Is it true you instructed the servants to refrain from serving me wine?"

"Yes, it is true," he answered without hesitation. "You may think I am a negligent husband, Lucetta, but your appearance and your drinking has not gone unnoticed. And not only by me."

If there was anything in the world Lucetta hated more than being dictated to, it was being gossiped about.

"My appearance?" she scoffed. "What about my appearance offends you so?"

"Nothing, but I would be remiss if I said I was not concerned. You've lost so much weight, and the sores on your wrists and elbows are quite alarming to me. I understand the stress of losing your mother, and the unrest, and everything else, but I will not stand idly by while you deteriorate before my eyes. Therefore, I have commanded our wine stores to be kept under lock and key for the time being."

A knot formed in Lucetta's throat, then in her stomach. As a Bethard, she was unaccustomed to being denied anything in life. A king's daughter was a king's daughter, after all, and not to be left wanting for anything.

"How dare you!" she hissed. "Who do you think you are to—"

In a flash, Aldred took hold of her by the arm, pulling her in close. A fiery anger flashed in his eyes, enough to strike fear into her heart. "Now you listen to me. I am your husband! And you have done nothing but embarrass me and dishonor my name for the past year! Your absence, your strange behavior, and your dereliction of your wifely duties has been noticed by many. And I will not stand for it any longer!"

When she made to speak, Aldred pointed a stern finger mere inches from her face. "And furthermore," he continued, "you will not be permitted to leave these grounds without my express permission, do you understand me? That foreign manservant of yours is barred from the palace, and I forbid you to consort with him any longer."

"You!" Lucetta seethed. "You bastard! How dare you command a daughter of House Bethard around like some common serving wench!"

With barely contained anger, Aldred pulled her in closer, their noses nearly touching. His hands were shaking so violently, his grip so tight, Lucetta thought her arm might shatter.

"You are my wife, princess or not. You belong to me, to House Eldon! Your duty is to me! My duty is to the King! Know your place, and act accordingly!"

Stunned and heartbroken, Lucetta pulled away from his grasp and fled up the grand staircase. Were it not for her rage, she might very well have broken down into fits of sobbing. Life never seemed to allow her a moment of joy, it seemed. Every time a bit of it sprung from the earth, it was promptly trampled underfoot.

What have I done wrong? All I have ever tried to do was make this city and this kingdom a better place. Why are my efforts always doomed to failure?

Lucetta arrived at her chamber and slammed the door, a violent crash reverberating throughout. With no wine to ease her sorrows, she instead began pacing back and forth, faster and more frantic with each pass. Perhaps the woman in black had led her astray after all, as the path ahead appeared dark and insurmountable.

An unexpected chill nibbled at her skin, turning it icy to the touch. Each breath grew more visible until she was exhaling misty clouds into the air. From a dark corner emerged the woman in black, her feet drifting above a thick haze. The entity's figure-flattering black silken gown was replaced by a more regal dress of black linen, accented with streaks of blood red. Its short black hair had grown long and layered, falling past its slender waist.

Such a dramatic change in appearance took Lucetta by surprise, though the one constant was its orange-red eyes. Its eyes were always the most terrible thing, and were able to stoke a sense of dread or inspire confidence with a mere glance.

"Be still, my child," the woman said. "Do not despair. All is not lost. Your works have not been in vain."

Lucetta flicked water from her eyes, staring at the entity in wonderment. "You… you look so… different…"

"Indeed. The season of change is upon us, and we all must change with it. Come now, you must not stray from the path you have carved for yourself. You must learn to overcome these obstacles."

"But how?" she pleaded. "Did you know Aldred was going to shut me in like a prisoner?"

The woman in black said nothing at first, the fire in its eyes waning. "Alas, I was uncertain of which path the fates would set you down. But know this; every path will lead to the same destination. Regrettably, the fates have led you down the most difficult one of them all. Worry not, for adversity will only serve to make you stronger."

While her words were encouraging, they did little to change the reality of the situation. Lucetta found herself a prisoner in the one place she never wanted to be. Only an elaborate escape might free her from the palace and Aldred's grasp, but such a feat was likely impossible without Pavlos and his White Spears.

"I swear, I will never doubt you again," Lucetta said, mustering as much confidence as she could. "I just… I feel as if this journey is only becoming more and more difficult, to the point now where I haven't the slightest idea of how to proceed."

Slowly, the woman in black began drifting back toward the dark corner, a black mist around its feet rising. "Be patient, for all shall be made clear to you in time. Look now to your own strengths, and not those of others. Only when you are able to conquer yourself, shall you be able to conquer the world."

Nearly as quickly as she arrived, the woman in black departed, melding into the pitch darkness. Lucetta found the entity's words encouraging, but not in the way she expected. Instead of despair or determination, she felt only rage. Pure, unadulterated rage, the purest kind one could imagine.

She had come too far now to be conquered by lesser men, by those unworthy to stand in her presence. The world had been remade already, changed forever by her actions throughout the past year. Lucetta turned and stared out at a broken city, her hands balling into fists. Despite every obstacle, the kingdom of Betanthia, and then Caldakas after it, would one day be hers.

And if anyone dares to stand in my way, I'll kill them. With my own hands, if I must. I'll kill them all.

MADELYN VII

I T WAS A STUNNING VICTORY, ONE THAT WOULD FOREVER BE ETCHED IN Betanthian history. While the day was won, it felt more like a defeat than anything. Madelyn had killed more barbarians in an afternoon than in her entire life, but the most important one of all had escaped. Damien Dreadfire still lived, and so long as he did, there would never truly be victory.

The knights returned to camp as conquering heroes, Madelyn in the lead, and Titan and Conrak beside her. They rode passed throngs of revelers, so jubilant one might have mistaken it for a royal parade. It was a day that belonged to all of Betanthia, but it was difficult to share in their enthusiasm. Still, Madelyn made certain to wave and represent House Bethard with class and dignity. It was the least she owed Gareth for the opportunity to avenge her tribulation.

This never would have been possible were it not for him. All of the training, all of the struggles… none of it would have mattered had I been kept from the fight.

"Don't look so grim, Lady Everly!" Conrak said, smiling. "This is but one of many victories to come. Fear not, we'll drive those savages back into the Hinterwood, never to return."

"Not if we kill them all first," Titan said, his voice raspy and strained. "They're so fucked up they'll never be able to escape us now."

It was an encouraging notion, though the army had suffered terribly as well. Were it not for the Blackthorn charge going unnoticed, the Plainhold might very well have been a Betanthian mass grave.

"One thing at a time, Bradshaw," Conrak cautioned. "We've got too many wounded. But fear not, we'll meet them again, and soon. Come now, a proper drink is in order!"

"You go on ahead," Madelyn interrupted. "I'm in need of rest."

It was a lie, but one they believed well enough. Madelyn felt stronger than anytime since her tribulation, but was loath to share any company. No, what she desired was solitude and a chance to reflect on the day's work.

"And no one has earned it more," Conrak conceded. "Rest up, my lady. We'll come by to check on you later. Let's go Bradshaw, time for me to teach you a thing or two about drinking."

"Oh fuck right off," Titan snarled as they broke ranks and continued on.

Madelyn tied her horse off to a hitching post beside a smithy's tent, and sat beside a worn grinding wheel. It was hardly the place for one such as herself, a former Commander and now war hero. But there was solace to be found, as celebrations were taking place on the other side of camp.

Few crossed her path, and those who did were racing to join the revelry. There was a certain comfort to be found in her own company, a change which she had not expected. It was difficult to feel a connection with anyone or anything, given the things she had seen and done, in realms which few could fathom existed.

Every time Madelyn summoned the shadows and felt their embrace, another piece of her past life withered and fell away, like petals from a dying rose. What filled the void was not love nor warmth, nor light. Only numbness and scorn. She gazed into a bucket of water beside the grinding wheel, her reflection becoming more and more unfamiliar.

The roots of her hair had turned a stunning pitch black, the darkness itself oozing out from within.

What's happened to me? What am I becoming? I suppose it doesn't matter. The woman who rode out from Bentmont never returned, and I don't know if she ever will.

A sudden commotion drew her attention. She saw Gareth Bethard riding at the head of his bodyguard, a sea of purple cloaks following closely behind. For a moment she felt as if time itself was nonexistent, like being lost inside a dream. Madelyn watched as Gareth brought his steed to a halt, then dismounted to share a moment among the men. He was shaping up to be every bit the warrior king he had always wanted to be.

Smiling, Madelyn set off in pursuit, eager to offer congratulations. It was the first time in months that she felt anything akin to excitement, which provoked all manner of curious thoughts. Perhaps the melancholy which haunted her waking hours was not so insurmountable. Perhaps she could still feel after all.

A large crowd gathered around the prince, each man vying for their chance to shake his hand and offer their respects. Knowing Gareth, he likely found the situation to be equally as incredible. Dozens of camp followers had rolled out casks of ale and beer, and were struggling to fill the mugs of thousands of thirsty soldiers.

Madelyn snatched a tankard off the bed of a wagon, its contents near to overflowing. The hearty aroma of a thick Bentmont ale smelled delectable, and tasted even more so. The brew was a reminder of home and of better times, with people she had both loved and lost. But there was something about the raucousness of her countrymen, something which made the inhospitable Plainhold feel a bit more like home.

It was surreal to see Gareth standing among the men, not as a prince, but as a conquering hero. It seemed like only yesterday when they stood overlooking the Teb River, and outside of the Seascape Inn. He seemed so different then, so timid and unsure of himself. Even when she saw him again at Castle Thorn, and saw the physical changes he underwent, it was difficult to comprehend that Gareth was no longer a boy, but a man.

She studied him with curious eyes, watching as he drank a tall wooden mug of ale with Sir Edmund and his personal bodyguard, pausing only to shake hands with knights and infantrymen as they passed by. It was a bittersweet reminder of times when she was celebrated, like the first day of the siege of Castle Morden. It seemed as if those days were gone forever, though perhaps it was for the better. Even in the wake of Betanthia's most stunning victory in a hundred years or more, many around remained wary of her presence.

I suppose it doesn't matter what they think about me. I did what I had to do, and my only regret is that I didn't kill Damien Dreadfire on the battlefield.

Anger was welling up inside her, which then faded into sadness, and then numbness. Her mind was running away, like it had many times before, to places where a mind ought not to venture. But her downward spiral of darkness was broken by the bright smile of Gareth. Madelyn was startled, somehow blind to his approach.

"Good day to you, my lady," he said. "Is everything alright? Your… your hair…"

Gareth pointed at the black roots along her part line, which were the most visible. While slightly embarrassing, there was little to be done to mask it aside from wearing a helmet or hat at all times.

"Oh, yes. Nevermind that, it's a long story, and I'd rather not discuss it right now. But congratulations to you. You've won a stunning victory," she hoisted her tankard ever so slightly.

"This wasn't my victory," Gareth said, giving a shake of his head. "This was our victory. This was for all of us. Betanthia may not be rid of Damien Dreadfire just yet, but it's all the safer now that he's diminished.

And while they may not speak it aloud, every man here knows what you did for them. Perhaps we might be the ones fleeing and not the northmen, were it not for you."

She scoffed, taking a sip. "It wasn't enough, sadly. There's work left to do. I won't stop until Damien's head is mounted on my wall, and those savages driven back to the forests for all eternity."

"If I have to march to the Forlorn Sea to make it so, rest assured that I will, Madelyn." Gareth pursed his lips and lifted his chin.

It was impossible not to notice a vein running the length of his bicep. She caught herself staring at it intently, as if caught in a trace. She tried to look away, but the thickness of his beard stole her gaze instead. She looked further up his face without even knowing it. There was something in his hazel eyes which felt different. It was curious how she was able to feel anything merely by looking at him, piquing her curiosity even further.

"When did you become so..." she asked, completely unaware she was even speaking.

"So what?"

"So..." she licked her lips. "You know... grown up? No, that's not what I meant, I... I mean... I'm sorry..."

There was an immediate rush of warmth that took her by surprise, building first in her cheeks then filtering down into her chest. Madelyn's breath stood still, each word in her heart a word she dared not speak. But a grin creeping across Gareth's face was telling enough. He understood what she was struggling to articulate. It was not a bashful grin, that of a boy she knew long ago. No, this was the confident grin of a man.

"When I discovered who I really was," he answered, a sudden fierceness building in his gaze.

"I apologize, I shouldn't be saying these things." She turned and made to leave, the burning in her face and chest racing down the rest of her body. Gareth took her gently but firmly by the arm, pulling her closer, ever so slightly.

"No apologies, Madelyn. Life is too short, and it can end at any moment. You know of my affections for you. I said what I said to you that day outside the inn, and I have no regrets, because it's how I felt. I know you and I have different paths to walk in life, and I'm at peace with it. I only hope you can find happiness again, wherever you can find it, and whoever you can find it with."

What? Is he… what is he trying to say?

She should have felt nothing, not for Gareth, at least. He was a friend, or perhaps even like a sibling to her in the past. But now, as he gave a respectful bow of the head and made to leave, she felt an unexpected anxiety which caused her breath to quicken. All the memories of weeks he spent beside her at Castle Thorn came rushing back, as well as the day he joined the army after Queen Charlotte's funeral.

He slept beside my bed every night, looking over me so I would feel safe. He held my hand during childbirth. He came back after laying his mother to rest so he could go to war for my honor. What's going on here? Who is he? Why does my heart feel like I'm making a mistake by letting him walk away?

"Wait," she blurted out, a sudden dryness making her mouth feel like parched earth.

Gareth turned, raised an eyebrow, and cocked his head curiously.

"Aren't you going to have another drink with me?" she asked, a slight tremble in her voice.

"Of course, my lady."

Drinks were never in short supply. Everywhere they turned, there seemed to be another cask of ale and piles of unused vessels to be filled. Were it not for the instruments of war laying all around, one might have thought it was a festival and not a victory celebration. Gareth motioned Madelyn closer, filling his mug to the brim. She took the last sip of her drink, then held it under the spigot.

Gently, he took Madelyn's tankard and filled it. She sighed, watching every movement, studying the lines of his face intently. A slight hint of a grin betrayed his noble disposition, which only added to her increasing frustration. She wished these feelings, whatever they were and wherever they were coming from, would leave.

"Here you are," Gareth said, passing over her tankard.

They walked a short way to a quieter part of the camp, and sat on a wooden bench. Neither spoke a word, their faces buried contently in their drinks. The brew tasted like home, and was refreshing after a long day of sword work. Minutes went by in silence, each one feeling like the passing of hours. Madelyn became overwhelmed with the urge to speak, though she had no idea of what to say.

"I'm glad you're here," she said softly, then cleared her throat.

"As am I." Gareth smiled, his eyes meeting hers.

He loves me, I can see written across his face, as much as he tries to hide it. But why? What is there to love? I'm too damaged to be what he needs in a wife. And besides, I doubt there is any love left in me at all.

They sat, staring into the infinite depths of one another's eyes, content with a peaceful silence between them. There was a deep chasm of conflict within Madelyn that only seemed to grow with each passing moment. In her head, she knew what she had to do; end the war by any means necessary, and bring retribution down upon Damien Dreadfire. And while her heart was in agreement, there was a budding sensation of longing, something which she had not felt for some time. Madelyn took a long drink, swallowing hard as her pulse began to quicken.

Gareth took a drink in kind, but it seemed like little more than an excuse to break their intense staredown. He swallowed and coughed gently, then made to speak, but Madelyn stood and interrupted.

You might as well. There won't be another opportunity. We could all be dead come tomorrow, should the northmen regroup.

"Marry me," she said, a hint of perspiration dampening the under-arms of her blouse. "Tonight."

Had Gareth been in the middle of drinking, he would have spat it onto the ground in surprise. His eyes were as wide as wagon wheels, his mouth lowering like a drawbridge.

"Marry you?" he managed to blurt out.

"Well?" She placed her hands on her hips. "Are you going to or not?"

"Tonight?" Gareth asked, his question as stupid as the look on his face.

"Yes, tonight. There's a little grove just outside of camp. Meet me there after midnight."

Without allowing him a moment to respond, Madelyn started off toward her tent, breathing so heavily she might have fainted. Her clothes had become a swampy mess, her heart stampeding like wild horses. Could this truly be happening, or was it another dream? Was she still holed up in Bentmont, condemned to a bed until the end of her life? No, her proposal was every bit as real as the soreness in her sword arm.

I'm... going to be married. Am I really about to do this? Me, Madelyn Everly. I never would have imagined it.

She raced back to her tent, panic quickly taking hold. It was unlike the terror of battle and the kind suffered in captivity. It was something she had never experienced before. It was the dream of every young girl, to marry a prince and spend the rest of their days in a palace. A future she never wanted, to be certain, but one she could no longer escape from.

What am I doing?!

The question kept rattling around inside her head, each time seemingly more unbelievable than the last. She sat with the tent flap closed, staring at a pattern on the rug for hours until its colors began to bleed together. Night was coming and time was growing short, and soon enough she would have to sneak out from camp and to the grove where Gareth would be waiting.

She glanced over at a wooden trunk, set near a few riding bags which made the journey as well. Hardly anything inside would make for suitable wedding attire, aside from an unsoiled blouse folded inside one of the bags. It would have to do. There were many luxuries one would kill to have in a place like the Plainhold, water being chief among them, and wedding gowns the very least.

It will have to do. I suppose though, he'll be happy regardless of what I wear.

After changing out of her sweaty and bloodstained blouse and into fresh attire, Madelyn gave herself a look in the mirror. It was a far cry from what one would expect a bride to look like. Her hair was a disheveled mess, and would probably be served best in a fresh braid, or piled onto the top of her head in a lazy updo. She examined the roots of her tresses, and how the darkness had begun to bleed further down its length. It was distressing to notice how the discoloration was now nearly two inches long, and seemed to be growing by the hour.

Sighing, Madelyn reached for a wooden comb inside one of her riding bags, when the sight of blue cloth caught her eye. She paused, recognizing the fabric, but wishing it had gone unnoticed at the same time. Madelyn pulled her silk gown from the bag, its gold trim shimmering in the candlelight as if it were the real thing. There were a few wrinkles, but otherwise the gown looked exactly like the day she had bought it.

Painful memories of the afternoon in Cardale came rushing back, the day she looked beautiful and Corbyn loved her with all of the fiery passion that lovers shared. The dress was a reminder of better days, innocent days, when the madness of the world was kept at bay behind the Seascape Inn's walls. However, Madelyn was unsure which was more troubling; the memories themselves, or the fact that she felt absolutely nothing while recalling them.

It doesn't matter anymore. None of it does. Not the Order, not the High Marshal, not even Corbyn. The only thing that matters is today, and what you're about to do. Focus on that.

Knowing the hour was nearly upon her, Madelyn stripped off her clothes and slid into her blue gown, its silken grasp fitting ever so snugly in all the right places. She delicately combed all the knots out of her hair, the length swaying across the back of her thighs like a curtain, then brushed the strands until they shone like gold.

There was no way to dye away the inky discoloration of her roots, so instead she plucked a few small wildflowers from the ground inside her tent. She wove a crown of flowers and adorned herself with it, the small blue and white petals enough to mask the vile black streaks. She took one final look in the mirror and exhaled deeply, feeling an unusual jitter in her belly.

It's time. You deserve at least one good thing in this world, and so does Gareth. At least try to enjoy it, for as long as you can.

Madelyn donned a long hooded cloak and peeked out through the tent flap. Darkness was falling, and the nightly celebrations were beginning to kick off. Music and rowdy laughter made the campsite seem more like a carnival than anything. Thankfully, few paid her any mind as she slipped out into the maze of tents.

As she reached the outer perimeter, a passing patrol offered a curious stare, but no challenge. Her heart was racing faster than a Plainhold Strider, and soon enough a faint outline of the grove appeared in the near distance. The moment had come, the moment when Madelyn Everly would be no more, and Madelyn Bethard would be born anew.

GARETH VIIII

F RANTICALLY HE SEARCHED AROUND THE CAMP, HIS MIND RACING more quickly than his body. Nothing about it seemed real. Gareth had to repeat Madelyn's words over and over again inside his head, but each time it felt even more like a dream.

Could this be real? Is this really happening?

He had to find Sir Edmund, and fast. But locating him among the city of tents would prove difficult. The most obvious place to look would be near his command tent, but with such revelry all around, it was difficult to say where the senior Guardsman might be found. Dozens, nearly hundreds of men offered their praise and congratulations as he searched, and while the sentiment was humbling, it seemed like mere background noise.

"Has anyone seen Sir Edmund?" Gareth shouted.

Some men turned and shrugged, others gave uninformed guesses. Gareth continued on through the maze of tents, shouting for his friend all the way. He passed by a group of two dozen men, each holding a skin of wine or a wooden mug filled to the brim. They were recalling stories from the battlefield, many of them boisterous and likely embellished. As he passed by, they paused and raised their drinks in a toast.

"My prince!" a Betanthian soldier called out, his steel breastplate dulled by a hint of a coppery-red hue.

The soldiers cheered and saluted, and Gareth smiled and nodded in return. It was heartwarming to be revered in such a way by the men of Betanthia's army, true warriors treating him as one of their own. He stole a moment to shake hands with every soldier who approached, but could not get away soon enough. Lord Anderton Kenfield's tent was a short ways ahead, the most likely place to find Edmund. Impatiently, Gareth dismissed himself and continued on.

"Well done, my prince!" another voice called out.

All of the attention was nearly suffocating. It was difficult for a man who felt comforted by anonymity to bask in such revelry and affection. But still, Gareth returned every smile and wave, until arriving at the outside of Anders' tent. Thankfully, he spotted a familiar mop of silvery hair nearby, his friend and mentor conversing with a group of soldiers.

"There you are!" Gareth exhaled and threw up his arms.

Edmund Thomas laughed and embraced him tightly, their hands landing on each other's backs with deep thuds.

"My apologies, I wasn't aware you were looking for me!"

"Can we speak in private?" he asked desperately. "You're never going to believe it."

"Absolutely! Is everything alright?"

Gareth's face was a mishmash of impatience, joy, and even a hint of fear. Edmund cocked his head curiously, then motioned toward Lord Kenfield's tent. When they entered, Anders and three men inside turned and took notice of their prince, and offered their congratulations on such a stunning victory.

"Well done, Your Highness. That was truly a battle to be remembered!" one of the soldiers said, bowing.

"I'd follow you anywhere, my prince," another said, smiling. He thumped a balled fist to his chest.

Though deeply honored, Gareth was anything but interested. He shook hands with the three soldiers, but Sir Edmund was quick to interject.

"If you wouldn't mind giving us the tent, lads. Much appreciated. And excellent work out there today. You've done your country proud."

The soldiers left, and Edmund closed the tent flap. Gareth searched around for something to drink. Water, ale, beer, it mattered little. His mouth was parched and becoming so dry that he was unsure if he could even speak. Thankfully, there was a pitcher of lukewarm water on a crude wooden desk, and he drank nearly all of it down in a few massive swallows.

"So, what's this all about?" Edmund asked, folding his arms.

"Is everything alright, my prince?" Anders asked, but was unheard.

Gareth had to remind himself that this was no daydream. Madelyn was serious, more serious than she had ever been. Even before the war, she was never the sort of person to make light of much of anything.

Just breathe. You have to keep it together now.

"Edmund," Gareth inhaled deeply, his heart nearly exploding. "You're never going to believe this. After we came back to camp, Madelyn and I ran into each other, and we sat down and talked." His armpits were becoming a sweaty mess. "And just before I was about to walk away, she…"

The words were still too incredible to speak, let alone believe. Edmund looked on breathlessly and spread his hands. "And? Well go on, say it!"

"She wants me to marry her. Tonight."

There was the same disbelief in both men's eyes. A silent excitement built within the tent, until Sir Edmund gave a joyous bellow and wrapped his arms around Gareth. Together they laughed, a warm and heartfelt laughter they had rarely been able to share together.

"I don't even know what to say!" Edmund said, nearly shouting. "Gareth, I'm so happy for you! Forgive my saying it, but I never would have thought this would happen, not in a million years! Well, not you getting married, but Madelyn asking you!"

"I know!" he replied. "I still don't believe it myself. But there's only one thing, we have to do it in secret."

Edmund scoffed. "Why? This is something all of Betanthia needs to bear witness to!"

Gareth looked a bit sad, but he was still overjoyed. He thought of his mother, and how much it hurt to know she was not around to share in such a moment. Even though Madelyn was a commoner, he was following his heart, and that was what Charlotte would have wanted.

"Because it wouldn't be proper. The northmen could regroup at any time and strike again, and we can't become distracted with a grand ceremony. And, she's a commoner. She and I would prefer to avoid any unnecessary scandal. And plus, something small and intimate is more our style anyways."

"Fair enough lad, fair enough. Either way, I'm happy for you. If you'd like, I'll see if I can't scrounge up a priest, or at least someone that knows the old rites. I'm assuming you would want them read?"

Gareth nodded. "Yes, I would greatly appreciate it."

While Madelyn despised the barbarians, she would doubtlessly want the wedding rites to be recited. The people of Betanthia put little stock in the gods and archaic rituals, but the loving words of matrimony were still in common usage. Some traditions were simply too important to be forgotten.

With a proud grin, Edmund gave a bow and turned to leave. But before he could, Gareth cleared his throat. The senior Guardsman turned back.

"And I would like for you to be there with me," he said. "My father is dead to me, and you're my oldest and truest friend. It's only right for you to be there."

For only the second time in Gareth's life, he saw Sir Edmund becoming emotional. His jaw tightened, lips pursed, and his eyes grew misty. He nodded, then stepped forward and embraced Gareth once again.

"I would be most honored," the Guardsman said softly. After clearing his throat and sniffling, he turned and started for the tent flap again. "I'll see if I can track down that priest. You need to get yourself cleaned up, you have a little lady to marry!"

Lord Kenfield smiled and spread his arms. "I'm most overjoyed for you, my prince! Allow me to offer you my congratulations. I know you wish to keep this ceremony a secret, so I think it best if I remain here. We can't let Lord Vakaro catch us all so isolated from the army. Who knows what trickery he might try to pull."

"Thank you, Anders," Gareth said, grinning. "We may not know each other as firmly as I would like, but your concern and dedication is most appreciated. Such loyalty will never be forgotten."

"Thank you, my prince!" Anders bowed. "Sir Edmund is right, you can't go marrying the woman of your dreams while still stinking of the battlefield! Go on, we'll keep a close watch over you."

It was true, Gareth was quite filthy, and smelled strongly of sweat and blood. In a near panic, he rushed out of the tent and off towards his own. Around every turn was another soldier, offering drinks and congratulations. It felt wrong to dismiss them, but every interruption only worsened his growing anxiety.

A friendly face stood out from among the revelers, a small group of them gathered near a covered wagon. On it sat a large cask of ale, with piles of wooden mugs beside it. Titan Bradshaw was refreshing his drink, trying to ignore the conversations of those around him. Gareth smiled, but was overcome with a sudden fear. There was no telling how such a protective and violent man would react to the news.

"There you are!" Gareth said, hurrying over. "Come, I need to talk to you."

Titan furrowed his brow, then shrugged his shoulders. Together, they retreated in between a pair of large tents, away from prying eyes and ears. Gareth was half tempted to steal his drink and guzzle down every drop for added courage.

"A fine job out there today. You're just the sort of man this kingdom needs," Titan said, offering a nod of the head. He sensed something was amiss, but not particularly for the ill. "Everything alright?"

"Everything is more than alright." Gareth smiled, but then turned serious. "I have something to tell you. I know how much Madelyn means to you, and how protective you are over her. For that, you will always have my gratitude."

Even mentioning her name seemed to stoke Titan's agitation, a sudden defensiveness stiffening his back. "What did she get herself into now? I swear, if she got herself into another mess, I'll—"

"She asked me to marry her," Gareth blurted out. "Tonight."

Silence came between them both. Titan Bradshaw stared blankly, the wheels in his mind turning over and over again. After a moment, he ran his tongue across his teeth and nodded, seemingly in approval.

"Surprising," Tylar muttered. "I never thought the girl was one for marriage. But if anyone deserves a bit of happiness in this shitty world, it's her. And it's hard to think of a better man for the job."

Gareth exhaled a hurricane of stress. "She never knew her father, and the men closest to her… well, you know as well as I what they've done. I'm certain it would mean the world to her if you were there. I would certainly be honored by your presence."

What swords and spears could not do, words had done instead. The man known as Titan appeared to break ever so slightly, his mouth twisting in every sort of direction. Despite being his future king, Tylar saw Gareth as perhaps a friend as well, one of the few things he yearned for in life.

"The honor would be all mine," Titan gave a bow of his head. "You tell me when and where, and I'll be there."

"Tonight, outside of camp. Make sure no one is following you. We would prefer to remain as discreet as possible."

Tylar nodded. "Well, you might as well invite that cunt Conrak, he probably knew what Madelyn was up to before she even did."

A fair point, and one that made Gareth guffaw. "Rightfully so. It's settled then! You and our closest companions, after dark. Bring wine and gifts, she deserves to feel like the future queen she is."

It was the only time Gareth had ever seen Tylar smile, even if it was only a half smile. For a man so tormented by the past, even he was able to find joy in such wondrous news. It seemed that even on the Plainhold, where life was difficult and short, love blossomed.

Breathlessly, Gareth raced back to his tent, his mind rushing on ahead. With lightning quickness he scrubbed down with clean water and a linen rag, then dressed in his finest purple doublet. A suitable garment, no doubt, with its elegant golden stitching along the trim. Along with black linen pants and black leather boots, he looked every bit as kingly as one would expect.

After an hour or two, Gareth sat watching the sunset, delicately nursing a cup of bourbon. He had to be careful not to drink it down too quickly, an exercise in restraint to be certain. Minute by minute, hour by hour, he waited until the sun made its glorious exit, leaving behind streaks of red against a backdrop of blue and black.

Shrouded by a hooded cloak, he slipped out from his tent, a pair of Guardsmen outside having been briefed. To maintain appearances, they would stand their posts until his return. It was easy enough to navigate throughout the camp as Betanthia's finest celebrated their victory. Music and merriment filled the air, mixing perfectly with roasted meat and the smell of Bentmont ale.

At last, he reached the outer perimeter. A passing sentry paid no mind, himself rewarded handsomely to see Gareth past. There seemed little risk of a barbarian attack this evening, at least according to Lord Vakaro's latest report. Still, one could never be too cautious on the Plainhold. Luckily, the wedding ceremony would be brief, as Gareth and Madelyn preferred it.

Soft torchlight glowed from the heart of the grove, barely visible under the light of a full moon. Each step made Gareth's legs tremble just a little bit more, until they felt like water. He ran both hands through a sweaty mess of brown hair, his heart thundering like horse hooves. This was the moment he had waited countless years for, and yet he found himself apprehensive, even now.

Gareth saw a priest standing in the clearing, surrounded by a dozen or more torches. He was garbed in a simple brown robe, and held a small and aged leather-bound book in one hand. Sir Edmund was close by, his breastplate polished so brightly that it reflected rays of torchlight all throughout the grove. His smile was even brighter.

"Well done lad, well done," Edmund Thomas said, giving a clenched fist a subtle, triumphant shake.

Conrak stood nearby, adorned with a cocky, yet heartwarming grin. He was clad in his finest blue doublet, gold shimmering on his fingers and neck. It made Gareth feel sad to know that none of his family would be present, Charlotte especially. Despite Madelyn being of low birth, he knew his mother would be proud, and would be delighted at his happiness.

It certainly would not be the first time in Betanthia's history that a high-born lord or prince took a wife below his status. King Niklas Bethard was purported to have taken a courtesan as his wife nearly seven centuries prior. A scandalous affair at the time, no doubt. But Queen Sabina would be his strongest champion and most lethal ally. Gareth could easily see his marriage following in such legendary footsteps.

Minutes passed by, each one feeling like hours. There was no conceivable way for him to be any more nervous. He tugged at the collar of his tunic to release a sweltering torrent of heat beneath it, then glanced around the grove. His eyes scanned the breadth of the darkness in search of his bride to be, praying Madelyn's intentions remained true.

You can do this, Gareth. You sat by her side every day. You went to war for her. Surely you can wait a while longer.

Then she appeared. Madelyn's outline was faint at first, but as she stepped closer, the glow of torchlight brought her beauty into full view. She wore a dress of blue silk that hugged her body in all the right places. Her hair was loose and flowing, and brushed so delicately that it appeared like pure gold. On her head sat a crown of wildflowers, meticulously woven together.

His knees felt weak, so weak he nearly collapsed. Never before had he seen her look so stunning, not in all of the years they had known each other. It was a near perfect reflection of the beauty she held inside, as if it was radiating out from within her. As she came closer, each step slow and deliberate, time itself came to a near halt.

There was another figure beside Madelyn as she came into the clearing. Gareth saw the unmistakable, hulking frame of Titan Bradshaw not far from her side, his armor and cloak obscuring him in the darkness.

Together, bride and protector approached the priest. Madelyn turned, looking Tylar dead in the eyes, neither of them speaking a word. After a few moments she embraced him, not as lovers would, but rather as the truest of friends. There was a turbulent sea of emotions swirling about Titan's face as he fought with all his might to remain composed. The gravity of his role in the ceremony was not wasted, apparently. Madelyn had no father to stand beside her, nor brothers of true blood. Tylar Bradshaw was the only family she had.

"I bid you welcome, my prince," the priest said, smiling. "Come, and let us begin."

Gareth extended his hand, trying diligently to remember the ancient marriage rites. He had seen the ceremony performed only twice, first during Trace's wedding, then again at Lucetta's. He remembered them as extravagant affairs, hours long in duration, and attended by the finest families in all of Betanthia.

But on the Plainhold, they would have to make do with far less. Madelyn stepped toward the priest, Tylar standing between her and Gareth. The knight turned Guardsman would have the honor of fulfilling her father's role, and took hold of her hand gently. Sir Edmund could barely contain his excitement, his smile wider than all of Caldakas.

"I am Gareth Bethard, son of King Marcellus Bethard, and heir to the throne of Betanthia," he began, looking upon Madelyn. "I stand here in the sight of the gods, on this good earth, to offer my hand in marriage."

Masking the tremble in his voice and body was nearly as difficult now as it was on the battlefield. It was the day Gareth thought would never come, yet here he stood. He turned his focus toward Tylar. "I pledge my protection, the protection of my House, and my undying affection for all time. This vow I make, from this day until my final breath, until we are reunited once again in death."

"By the sun and the moon," Tylar recited, "and all the stars in all the heavens, I say unto you; on this day, our houses have become one. Our blood has become one, now, until the sun no longer rises, and the moon no shines. Your pledge I have accepted, and this hand I give to you, born from my blood, now bound to yours for all eternity."

Tylar kissed the back of Madelyn's hand, then placed it delicately onto Gareth's before stepping backward. He felt a delicate smoothness to her touch, unusual for a lifelong warrior. Staring into the infinite beauty of her eyes took every ounce of breath from his lungs. Madelyn stared back, a slight, sad loneliness fading into a growing hunger.

Her gaze was intimidating to behold. There was untold strength inside her, a fierceness he had seen in years past, but which had not returned until now. Hours seem to fly past as Gareth stared deeply into her steely-blue eyes, his focus then shifting to her cheekbones, protruding ever so slightly.

Down her face his eyes drifted, until they fell upon her lips. They were as succulent as ripe fruit, the crowning adornment to a near perfect face. Gareth studied them intently, watching as first they drew back into a shy smile, then began to move. She was speaking, that much he knew, but strangely enough he heard no sound.

"Gareth?" Sir Edmund said, though his words seemed muffled. "Gareth?"

Nervously, he broke free from his trance. There was no telling how much time had elapsed. All eyes were upon him, but he had not the slightest idea of where in the ceremony they were.

"Your turn," Madelyn whispered with a soft chuckle.

"I... uh..." Gareth said, fumbling for words. "With all of my heart, yes."

The priest raised his arms in jubilation. "Then let it be witnessed by the gods and all of those in attendance, that this man and this woman are now forever bound to each other. Kiss, and become one!"

It was a moment he had dreamt about for years. In fact, Gareth knew his movements so well, his body began acting all on its own. He placed a gentle hand behind Madelyn's head and stepped forward, just like in his dreams. Together they stared into each other's eyes before closing them, both leaning in slowly.

Their kiss was something out of a storybook; warm and heartfelt, and burning with passion from the very depths of his soul. It was everything Gareth Bethard had imagined it would be, and more. He was now a husband, and married to the woman of his dreams. Except, this was no dream at all. Finally, after a lifetime of loneliness, a dream had come true.

SYLVIA V

Through twilight she stumbled, bloodied and disoriented. A vicious gash from forehead to cheek gushed so profusely, Sylvia nearly collapsed several times. It was enough to blot out the pain from nearly half a dozen cuts across both arms, which felt like little more than mosquito bites in comparison.

Instinct and an iron will to survive propelled her onward. Mile after mile the shieldmaiden trudged, until a flickering warm light appeared up ahead. The warriors around her limped and shambled by, their bodies encumbered by the shame of defeat. It was a sight which seemed nearly as foreign as the rolling fields of the Plainhold.

How could such a thing have happened? Their planning had been meticulous, their execution flawless in every way. Even the crone had seen only victory and good fortune. But now, the remnants of a once invincible warband crawled back to camp, tails tucked and spirits broken.

This cannot be. Azldyr, why have you forsaken us, your most faithful servants? What have we done to offend you so?

In the coming darkness, and with her vision obscured, Sylvia could see only silhouettes of those beside her. Wiping the blood from her eyes was a near futile effort, but as she did, she spied warriors crouched in the knee-high grass, weapons at the ready. Those charged with protecting the baggage train had come forth and lay in waiting, should the Betanthians be bold enough to pursue.

Thankfully, there was no sign of a further attack. It appeared their enemies were content enough in victory, though their cost had been high as well. Sylvia began replaying the battle in her head over and over again, to the point of obsession. While the fighting was fierce and casualties high, momentum had been in their favor the entire time.

We did everything right! We held against their best efforts. The wildmen were winning. Marvath's warriors were winning! How could we have been taken by surprise?

A flurry of activity had turned the hastily constructed camp into a scene of pure chaos. Screams and groans of the wounded were near deafening, the camp followers frantically tending to their wounds. As Sylvia stumbled in through the outer perimeter, she saw dead men littering the ground like fallen leaves. She gave pause, wiped away another stream of blood from her eyes, and stood astonished at the sight of it.

A bloodied Rhivothi bit down on the hilt of his sword as an arrow was pried loose from his shoulder blade. Nearby, a Nothanek was in tears as he clutched the stump of a leg, the limb sawed clean below the knee. A camp follower girl offered a skin of water to a man so ravaged he appeared dead, her face wet with tears.

In the near distance was Damien's command tent. Though wounded, Sylvia knew she had to see if the other warchiefs had made it back alive. As she hobbled on, an elderly blacksmith brought over a fresh linen and skin of water, and began dressing her open gash. The feeling of cloth against broken skin stung like hornets, but it was enough to keep the blood free from her eyes.

Holding the cloth in place, she trudged past a pair of Rhivothi guards outside Damien's tent. They appeared distraught upon seeing their defeated kinsmen, themselves likely craving the glory of Sjenohor. Sylvia passed between the tent flaps, and saw Damien Dreadfire sitting on the far side, panting like a dog. His leg was wrapped in thick linen, the air smelling of burnt flesh. He clutched a large skin of wine in one hand, though it did little to dampen the pain of cauterization.

"Damien!" she croaked. "Thank the gods you're alive! Where is everyone? Did they make it back?"

"Akselson was here," Dreadfire replied, teeth clenched. "I have seen no one else. Have faith, Stormguard, they may yet return."

How any man could have faith at such an hour was beyond comprehension. Fear and despair had broken through the last of her defenses. Sylvia began weeping softly, stoic as she tried to remain. "How could this have happened? Victory was so certain…"

There appeared to be more defeat behind Damien's black eyes than on the battlefield. It was perhaps the most heartbreaking sight she had ever witnessed, seeing a nearly catatonic shell of the mightiest northman since Kuggvord the Grim.

"I have no answers for you," he said, taking a long pull of wine from the skin. "The gods were not with us this day, it seems."

"Has Marvath returned? Where is he?" A sudden panic made Sylvia's throat tighten.

Damien offered no response, his gaze drawn toward a crackling fire inside a nearby brazier, his mind seemingly elsewhere. Frantically, she fled the tent and began wandering about, helplessly crying out for anyone and everyone.

"Mikka! Hilda! Marvath! Where are you?"

Every bloodied face and lifeless body stoked an even greater fear of the worst. Many had returned from the fight intact, by some miracle. But the sheer scale of their dead and wounded was unimaginable. Behind every blade of grass was another corpse, another severed limb, another pile of blood stained rags.

"Sylvia!" a familiar voice called out. "Sylvia, over here!"

To her relief, Ingryd Bjornsdottir was sitting near a cook fire, arm wrapped tightly in a linen sling. Her thick blonde hair was loose and wavy from an unfurled braid.

"Oh thank the gods!" Sylvia said, nearly in tears.

They shared a long, sisterly embrace. Ingryd yelped as Sylvia squeezed too aggressively, but at least she was alive.

"Have you seen anyone else come through?" she asked, desperate.

"No, I've been watching the wounded come in all day. I was hoping you had…"

Time itself came to a crashing halt. Sylvia thought she might throw up from a sudden sinking sensation in her abdomen. Certainly it would have been impossible to notice everyone returning from the fight. There were simply too many warriors to take notice of them all, tens of thousands of them in total. But to have seen none of their other companions? The notion was unthinkable.

"Oh gods!" Sylvia uttered. "Please tell me this is not so!"

Ingryd was nearly in tears from seeing her so distraught. All of the Rhivothi shieldmaidens had looked to her for strength and leadership, and sadly, they earned Betanthian steel for their faith.

"Maybe they are lost or delayed," Ingryd said, "or maybe they already returned."

It was certainly a possibility, given the chaos of not only the battle, but their retreat. To locate but a small few out of seventy thousand would be difficult even under the best of circumstances.

"I've got to find them!" she cried. "Stay here until I return!"

Sylvia raced throughout the camp, desperately searching for those she cared about most. But every face seemed no different from the last. Each was bloodied and battered, some beyond recognition. It was a far cry from the glory days of Castle Morden and Hok, when the northmen were victorious and joyful, and whole.

She spied a faint, golden light emanating from a large, covered wagon. It was a place she feared to enter, even now, knowing who dwelled within it. Hesitantly, Sylvia Stormguard approached the wagon, a faint hint of incense and rot drifting out from within. She entered, nearly more afraid than on the battlefield. The energy inside was dark and oppressive, and powerful enough to force the air from her chest.

Sitting on a high back chair was Lazilyth, the crone who could invite fear into the hearts of even the bravest men. She sat hunched over a flickering lantern, staring deep into its orange flame. Hanging from the walls were various amulets and trinkets, and pelts of woodland animals. The wagon seemed more of a dark shrine than a dwelling, but a fitting accommodation nevertheless.

Every instinct inside Sylvia was screaming to run, to flee the presence of the crone before it was too late. But there were many questions lingering, questions that required answers.

"You…" Sylvia said, her voice tinged with fear. "You promised us good fortune. You promised us victory. And all you have delivered unto us is death! Speak, foul creature, or I'll have your head this night!"

The old woman said nothing, herself unphased by Sylvia's threats. It appeared as if the crone was lost in a trace, her glassy eyes vacuous and vacant. What horrors were transpiring behind them was a mystery, but Sylvia suspected it was anything but the truth. The fates had always proven fickle, this much was known, but now they had proven to be little more than lies.

"You coward!" Sylvia taunted. "You lied to Damien. You lied to us all! And now we have all suffered because of it. Better that you should die, before more die at your hand."

She drew a small knife from her belt, clutching the hilt tightly. Lazilyth's gaze moved slowly from the fire toward the blade, then locked firmly with her eyes. Despite her rage, Sylvia felt only fear, a deep and endless fear that was strong enough to conquer even Dreadfire himself.

"Silence, child," the old woman taunted. "Do not seek to challenge the gods this night. There is foul magic afoot."

In earlier days, she might have taken such threats seriously. But tonight, Sylvia Stormguard was having none of it. She stepped forward, ready to dispatch the old mystic for her treachery.

"You sent us to our deaths," she said, shaking with anger. "How could you not have foreseen such a calamity? You've lied to us since the very beginning!"

Lazilyth shot from her seat, standing taller than the mightiest Rhivothi. A dark shadow lingered behind her, black enough to swallow every trace of light within the wagon. Sylvia found herself frozen in terror, nearly unable to breathe.

"The fates are set in stone, child," Lazilyth croaked. "And I have seen them, as plain as you see me now. I saw only victory in the fires. I saw Dreadfire standing atop a pile of corpses, untouched, and unbroken. Something is amiss. Something has gone terribly wrong."

It was perhaps the only time she had ever seen the old woman so distraught. From the moment of their meeting, Sylvia dreaded being in the presence of the crone. Her origins were uncertain, though many suspected she was a survivor of Borjifa. Few had any knowledge otherwise.

"Then what must we do?" Sylvia pleaded. "Please! Tell me, are Marvath and Hilde still alive? And Mikke? Answer me!"

"Who are you to demand answers from a divine being?" Lazilyth hissed.

Was the old woman in fact a god in the flesh, or a demigod of some sort? Perhaps, but given her lack of foresight, such a thing appeared doubtful. The crone was as fearful as any man throughout the camp, a slight tremble betraying her stony resolve.

"Your threats scare me not," Sylvia said defiantly, clutching her knife. "You have lied and deceived us at every turn. What prize were you promised? What led you to deceive our people and send them to their deaths?"

A guttural groan built in the back of Lazilyth's throat, the flame inside the lantern flickering violently. Sylvia could nearly see the events of what might have happened playing out in her glassy eyes. It was a startling reminder that the crone was anything but a simple old woman. She was indeed every bit the monster men said she was.

"Perhaps you would like to hear your fortune, Sylvia Stormguard?" Lazilyth sneered. "Do you wish to know how the gods have decided your fate?"

Despite her failings, the crone was every bit as terrifying as before. Still, Sylvia remained defiant in her rage.

"Your words have no meaning, witch," she snapped back. "We are broken because of you. Let that be your legacy. Let that be the rotten fruits of Borjifa."

Before the old woman could respond, Sylvia left the wagon. An icy chill seemed to follow from behind, pimpling her skin with its frigid touch. She could hardly believe such an encounter even transpired. Regardless, she was determined to find her friends, or at least learn of their fates.

For the next hour she searched, shuffling through an endless forest of tents. Death and misery was all she found, and in the most heart-wrenching quantity. She even felt pity for the wildmen, with so few having returned. Those who ventured back to camp appeared as little more than remnants of men, their flesh and spirits utterly broken. Still, the ones she valued the most remained lost.

Hopelessly, Sylvia trudged back to the command tent, praying more had returned. She spied another figure inside, but was uncertain who it might be. With bated breath she entered, and saw both Arik Akselson and Valerick the Red inside. Both men appeared unharmed, though their spirits were utterly devastated.

"You made it!" Arik said, mustering a smile.

"Yes, barely," she sighed. "I don't know where it went wrong. We held the center firm! That is, until those damned Blackthorn cut the wildmen to pieces. We were scattered soon after. Have you ever seen such a thing, Arik?"

The Nothanek shook his head. "By the gods, I never would have thought it possible. I have no words."

Valerick sat quietly, staring down at the ground. Had he not made a ritual of bathing in animal blood, Sylvia would have noticed no difference in his appearance. It was clear something had gone terribly wrong. A Rhivothi's spirit was as unbreakable as steel, after all.

"Have either of you seen Marvath?" she asked, though hesitant to truly know.

At first, there was no answer. Valerick reached behind him slowly, producing a bloodied great axe. He tossed the mighty weapon at Sylvia's feet, its handle engraved with markings and the runes of Rej Rhivoth. She stood dumbfounded at first, doubting the very evidence she looked upon.

"He fell," Valerick uttered. "Marvath died with honor, with axe in hand. Truly, he feasts in the halls of Sjenohor this night."

Sylvia slumped to her knees, too grief-stricken to cry. While it was a Rhivothi's greatest honor to die in battle, parting with such beloved company was no less tragic. Marvath Bonesplitter was a man among men, a warrior of violent strength and gentle disposition. Truly, the gods would be blessed by his presence.

"Kholdyr," she whispered, "guide Marvath to the halls of his ancestors. Reward him for a life lived in your honor. And give my dear friend my affections. Perhaps I will be joining him soon enough."

A commotion outside the tent made her heart skip. Perhaps the nightmare had subsided, and her beloved shieldmaidens had returned safely. But something seemed amiss. The Rhivothi guards sounded agitated, their voices growing in hostility. As Sylvia went to investigate, the tent flaps were thrown open, and in strode Zander, the most distasteful man of all.

"Good evening, love." The wildman smiled. "Don't look so excited to see me now!"

Her stomach nearly erupted at the sight of him. Every minute that passed without her shieldmaidens returning was its own separate torture. Desperately she approached Zander, grabbing him by the shoulders.

"Tell me, have you seen the others?"

"Sorry, love." His smile quickly faded. "Can't say I've seen much of anyone I know. I can't tell who's who out there. My people paid a heavy price today."

Zander strode over and gulped down a tall pitcher of water, soaking himself in the process. He cast a distasteful glare at Damien Dreadfire, who sat silently, staring into the brazier fire.

"You realize what happened out there, don't you?" the wildman asked, stepping forward. "That Eveldanyr bitch returned, and she cut down my men. How could this be possible? We broke her! You said she would never raise arms against us ever again!"

Sylvia's blood turned cold in an instant. "That Blackthorn bitch? How?!"

They turned toward Damien, whose face was souring by the second.

"There are forces at work greater than ourselves, it appears," the warlord said somberly.

"But Lazilyth said she saw into the fates!" Sylvia blurted out. "Has she deceived us?"

"No," Dreadfire replied. "We have lost favor with the gods, and they have punished us dearly for it. Our fate was sealed the moment we crossed paths with the Eveldanyr. I was foolish to think the fates could be circumvented."

"And now my people lay dead because of it," Zander growled, looking more agitated than a bull. "I swore myself and all of Zylmacia to you, Dreadfire! I threw myself against Morden for your honor! I kept this alliance together when it was on the verge of tearing itself apart!"

Zander drew a one-handed axe and spiked it onto the ground. It was a challenge recognized well enough in the north, one which left Sylvia lost for words. Damien's black eyes shifted slowly from the brazier to the weapon, then up toward Zander. His face tightened into a frown, the very air itself sizzling with furious energy.

"Damien Dreadfire!" Zander the Zylmacian announced. "I hereby challenge you for leadership of this alliance!"

MADELYN VIII

UNDER COVER OF DARKNESS, THEY RETIRED FROM THE GROVE. IT was a brief ceremony, but more than she could have ever imagined. Madelyn was now a wife, married to the son and heir of King Marcellus Bethard, the most powerful man in Caldakas. She repeated it in her head like a mantra, but still the words seemed as surreal as ever.

Madelyn Bethard. Your name is now Madelyn Bethard.

It was the first bit of joy she had felt since riding to Castle Morden, and enough to make her knees feel weak. A slight tinge of nausea took hold from excitement, and from the unknown. She knew well enough what was to follow the wedding ceremony. Consummating a marriage was to be expected, but suppressing painful memories of her tribulation was a battle greater than what they had just experienced.

How could she give herself to a man after what Damien Dreadfire's savages did to her? Even wild dogs were more noble than the northmen, and especially the Zylmacians. But in order for Madelyn to follow through on her commitment, she would have to conquer old demons and leave them buried on the Plainhold.

That's right, she reminded herself. *The past is dead. You killed it, along with all the men you killed today. Take comfort in that.*

Delicately, she slipped her hand into Gareth's, squeezing ever so slightly. His smile was warm and reassuring, and helped to melt away her troubles.

You have to learn to let go now. It's alright. You don't have to fight alone anymore, or at all, for that matter. He'll keep you from harm, no matter what the cost. He swore a vow to you.

Gareth was a capable protector, however unlikely that notion once seemed. Any doubt was summarily quashed on the battlefield, his fierceness and determination akin to the Bethard kings of old. And one day, Gareth would ascend to the throne, and Madelyn would become queen. Regardless of her common status, Bethard kings could do as they wished, regardless of what anyone thought about it.

Before long, husband and wife arrived back at camp. For the sake of discretion, Gareth let go of Madelyn's hand as they made their way to the royal tent. His accommodation was the largest and most lavish in the army, enough to shelter an entire family with room to spare. A pair of Guardsmen stood alert at its entrance, and snapped to a salute as they entered.

Warm lantern light filled the spacious tent, a haze of incense rushing to meet the outside air. A large table sat at the far end, covered with plates of food and flagons of wine. Beyond a thin curtain was the royal bed, and behind a separate curtain, a small study. While Gareth was a modest man, he was the face of Betanthia, and deserved every bit of opulence.

"Would you care for some wine?" he said, heading over to the table.

Madelyn was nearly shivering, despite the lingering heat. She nodded, eager to nurse away her anxieties and insecurities. Gareth poured out two glasses, and together they shared a toast as husband and wife. As they drank, their eyes never left one another.

"I know what the marriage custom is," he said suddenly, "but I won't make you go through with it if you're not ready."

While the sentiment was touching, it made her feel sad, in a way. A wife was supposed to give herself to her husband on their wedding night, as he was supposed to give himself as well. Were it not for the events she suffered, they might already have found themselves wrapped in the embrace of lovers.

"No, I… I…" she stammered, nearly in tears. "I don't want you to think that I would betray my oath to you…"

"You wouldn't be." Gareth set his wine glass down, and placed both hands gently on her shoulders. "I want you to feel comfortable, and safe. It's my duty now. You're my lady. And one day, my queen."

Sobbing both from sadness and love, Madelyn set her glass down and threw her arms around Gareth, kissing him deeply. It was a desperate, fiery kiss, like the exorcising of demons. Their bodies pressed tightly together, though it seemed like she could not get close enough. His hands danced lightly down her back and sides, flowing across her curves like gentle water.

"It's alright," he said, holding her protectively. "You're safe with me. Nothing can hurt you, ever again."

Madelyn pressed her face against his chest, feeling a heavy pounding within it. With a few deep exhales, her distress began to fade, and was slowly replaced with serenity. Gareth ran his hand through her golden tresses, washing away every worry and care in the world. With peace of mind and love in her heart, she started off toward the royal bed.

"I could put out the lanterns, if you would prefer," Gareth suggested.

Frantically, Madelyn shook her head. "No, please. I have to see you. I need to know it's you, and no other."

"Very well, my lady."

Madelyn removed her crown of flowers and set it gently on a stand beside the bed. With apprehension, she slid out of her blue silken dress, yet immediately covered herself. Scars and pits raked her once perfect skin, reminders of a painful past. Yet Gareth seemed not to care. In fact, his gaze was still firmly fixed on her eyes. His stare had a carnal hunger to it, a fierce yet gentle yearning she had felt once before, but never so intensely. Gareth disrobed in kind and climbed into bed, becoming her forth.

Her moment of truth had arrived. Madelyn could scarcely recall a time when she felt more terrified, but there would be no turning back now. She obliged, lying comfortably on the feather mattress.

"May I have this honor, my lady?" he asked.

With a hint of fear, as well as curiosity, she nodded. Gareth's kisses were as soft as satin, his hands learning her for the first time. Still, their eyes never left one another. Every so often, his touch would invite terror, memories of torture and despair. Yet somehow, he was able to sense her anxiety, and soothed it away as quickly as it arrived

"I'm right here," he said reassuringly. "Just look at me. You're safe."

Gareth stroked her hair lovingly, smiling warmer than summer sun. His embrace was warm and heavenly, their first touch of love more fiery than her first. To be so deeply desired after suffering so brutally was enough to make her want to cry yet again.

But suddenly, panic took hold, images of Damien Dreadfire flashing before her. Madelyn squirmed and threw Gareth off, panting and whimpering helplessly. Her vision had become a spinning blur, a nauseating mess of lights and colors.

"I'm sorry, I'm…" he stammered.

Damien's ghost stood menacingly at the end of the bed, eyes black as pitch, with an insidious grin. She stared in horror, slowly being transported back to that fateful night once again.

"Hey," Gareth said, placing a soft hand on her cheek. "It's alright. We don't have to. I understand, truly I do."

She recoiled at his touch, but found his hazel eyes once again. Fear gave way to sadness, and sadness to regret.

"No, Gareth," she sniffled. "You did nothing wrong. You're so kind and…"

Tears began dripping down her cheeks. Madelyn wanted to give herself to Gareth, truly she did. But the demons lurking in the depths of her mind would not allow it.

"I'm just happy you're mine," he smiled.

Madelyn began sobbing, ashamed at her brokenness. What use would she be as a wife, especially as a wife to a prince? Perhaps death would have been better all along.

"Hold me," Madelyn whispered. "Just hold me."

Gareth rolled onto his back, arms open and welcoming. She laid her weary head down upon his chest, and was wrapped in his gentle embrace. He sighed contently, fingers dancing delicately across her shoulder.

"Get some rest," he said. "We made history today. And I hope every day to come gets better than the one before it."

It was easy enough to forget all they had accomplished on the battlefield. The largest battle in generations had been won, though the day had been costly. And at the end of all the killing was a rare glimmer of peace and love, found in the most unlikely of places. Thinking of all the savages who met their demise at the end of her blade was nearly as comforting as Gareth's touch.

Madelyn lay awake for the next hour, staring at the top of the tent. She was serenaded by Gareth's deep, rhythmic breathing. A million thoughts were rushing through her mind, each one bringing its own uncertainties. It was truly a night to remember, a night any woman would have been fortunate to enjoy.

But something continued to haunt her waking moments; thoughts of fire and death, things she had seen in visions. It was curious as to why she was feeling such things to begin with. Gareth Bethard was now her husband, and she could retire to the Westwind Citadel tomorrow without any incident.

However, such a notion seemed so unimportant. Madelyn rose from the bed gently, so as not to stir Gareth awake, and wrapped a silken sheet around her body. She poured out a cup of wine and drank, and thought. While the inside of the tent was a heavenly oasis, the world outside had changed none. Damien Dreadfire and his marauders were still alive, and out there, somewhere on the Plainhold. Not even the love Gareth poured into her heart was enough to make it whole again.

After finishing the wine, Madelyn made her way into the small study, closing the curtain behind her. On the desk was fresh parchment and ink, and a pile of dispatches and messages which had already been read. Madelyn took up a quill and began scratching her thoughts into the paper, tears slowly moistening her eyes.

It was difficult to express how she truly felt in writing, but Gareth would have to understand. There was no deficiency in his love, which was a drink of cool water in a scorching hot desert. But despite it all, love seemed to do little to take away the numbness inside, the insatiable lust for vengeance which could not be quenched.

After the ink was dry, Madelyn folded the letter and sealed it with a kiss. She glanced over at a tall mirror, studying herself in it briefly. The black streaks in her hair were becoming more pronounced, a ghastly reminder of business yet unfinished.

I know what needs to be done, but I don't know if I'm strong enough to do it…

From a dark corner of the tent, the outline of a figure emerged. It was clothed in black riding leathers, chin-length locks of black hair covering most of its face. A pale blue eye stared back, but this time Madelyn felt no terror. There was a strange and familiar comfort to the entity's smile, which felt warm and hospitable.

It was then she realized what she had known all along. The being was not a ghost sent to torment her, but a glimpse of the future. It was her destiny, manifested in the flesh. It was her.

"Alright," she said. "I understand now."

With tears running down her cheeks, Madelyn gathered her hair around the base of her neck and secured it with a band. While staring into the mirror, she braided her thick blonde tresses, then ran a hand down the length several times. A small knife sat on the table near the dispatches. She picked it up, looked herself over once more in the mirror, then began sawing her hair, just above the band.

Every stroke brought with it more tears, and more painful memories of the year past. It was the last trace of her identity, of the innocence of a life once lived. Madelyn closed her eyes, grimacing at the sound of hair being sawn, until finally, the braid was free in her hand. Short strands of hair fell about her chin, much of it blonde, but the black stains seemed all the more pronounced.

A small wooden chest sat beside the desk, a signet and various other effects inside. Madelyn dumped them onto the floor and coiled her braid inside it delicately. She placed the chest on the desk and set the letter on top of it. The deed was now done. With a smile and a nod, the entity stepped slowly back into the shadows before fading away completely.

Gareth stirred, mumbling something and rolling onto his side. Madelyn knew there was precious little time before the sun would rise. Hastily, she draped a cloak over her body and secured the hood, then stepped outside. The Guardsmen outside thought little of her passing, and continued to stand vigil over their prince.

Fortunately, the camp was still asleep, and venturing back to her tent took no time at all. Once inside, she threw the flap closed and began rustling through bags and chests, searching for the black riding leathers she had packed. Fortunately, they were easy enough to find. After dressing, Madelyn looked herself over for a moment, her reflection foreign yet somehow disturbingly familiar. She had become something else now, an instrument of vengeance and death.

It's time. There's no turning back. You have to go all the way.

With a growing sense of urgency, Madelyn gathered her equipment and provisions, as well as the ancient texts she had smuggled. Before departing, she crept around to one of the blacksmithing tents nearby. A pair of slender short swords caught her eye, as well as a bandolier of knives. She quietly snatched them up, as well as a pair of crossbows and bolts.

A pair of sentries drew near, hastening Madelyn's departure. She quickly loaded her horse with all of the pilfered armaments, then mounted and started off through the camp. Flickering light from torches outside Gareth's tent wrenched at her aching heart. He would doubtlessly be destroyed come morning, an innocent casualty in a war that should have never happened.

I'm so sorry, Gareth. I hope one day you can forgive me.

Madelyn sighed, steeling her rapidly wavering resolve. She approached the northern perimeter of the camp, and spied scores of soldiers on watch. Their torches burned bright, their spears at the ready should any northman attempt to take the army unawares.

Knowing they were likely to offer a challenge, she conjured the darkness from within, her eyes filling with black liquid. Madelyn Bethard faded into the shadows like an apparition, until disappearing entirely from sight. She had become a creature of the night, an avenging wraith, a terror from which no northman was safe.

GARETH X

WARM RAYS OF SUNLIGHT KISSED GARETH'S FACE AS HE STIRRED, exhausted of energy yet feeling so fulfilled. It was the most memorable night of his life. He married the woman of his dreams and shared their first embrace. It was all he ever wanted, to become one with Madelyn in matrimony. And now, at the edge of civilization, with the world burning all around, he found love.

If only Charlotte could have seen the ceremony, he thought. Surely she would be proud, despite Madelyn's common birth. Happiness was the one thing the Queen wanted for him above all else. And here, in a place where death reigned supreme, love blossomed.

Gareth rolled onto his side, throwing an arm around his wife. But there was only emptiness beside him. Madelyn's side of the bed was vacant, and felt cold to the touch. He thought little of it at first, and assumed that perhaps she was having breakfast, or training, or in company with Titan. A fierce heat was building inside his tent, motivation enough to rise and begin his first day as a husband and conquering hero.

"Madelyn?" he groaned, willing himself to stand. "Are you here?"

There was no response. Gareth dressed himself in a blue tunic and black trousers, then made to fix his disheveled hair in a mirror. Upon entering his small study, he noticed a wooden chest with a letter on top of it, sitting on the desk. Perhaps it was a message from Sir Edmund or Lord Kenfield, containing information about Lord Vakaro and his treasonous plot.

Were it not for Madelyn easing his weary mind, Gareth might not have slept until the conclusion of the war. It was endlessly troubling to know a Guardsman, the most loyal guardians of House Bethard, would attempt to claim his life. Nothing about it made sense, but surely Edmund Thomas was off to dredge up answers wherever he could find them.

He took hold of the letter and unfolded it, but was immediately lost for breath. The greeting was not that of a soldier, or a lord for that matter. The letter was written by a delicate hand, female perhaps, its penmanship smooth and like flowing water.

My dearest Gareth,

I haven't the faintest idea of how to begin this letter. So instead, I will let my heart do the talking. You saved me from despair so dark, I could see no light. I gave up and was ready to embrace my death, so I could be rid of the pain forever. But you were there, when so few remained at my side. For that I owe you everything. Even in a thousand lifetimes, I could never repay you for the kindness and loyalty you have shown me. Your love has meant the world to me, when the world made so little sense. But some things that are broken cannot be repaired. The Madelyn you knew never returned home from Morden. You know I could never be the same after what I suffered. I want you to know, whatever little was left of me, I gave to you last night. It was the one right decision I've made throughout this entire war, and I will never regret it. Please don't think I have anything but affection for you in my heart, and it pains me to know this decision will hurt you so deeply. Forgive me. But most importantly, remember me as I was.

With all my love,
Madelyn Bethard

A sudden panic came over Gareth, his eyes pouring frantically over the letter again and again. How could such a thing be true? Had someone played a cruel joke on him somehow? Surely Madelyn would never do such a thing, not after professing her love so strongly.

"No… please…" he begged. "This… cannot be true…"

Gareth gagged, vomit nearly erupting from his mouth. He slumped onto the floor, sobbing so violently his ribs nearly shattered into fragments. It was a blow as devastating as the loss of Queen Charlotte only a short while ago. But there was something more, something which struck him with an indescribable terror.

The chest sat on his desk unopened, its contents unknown. Gareth was hesitant to find out what was inside, but curiosity quickly took hold. He stood on watery legs and toddled to the desk, his trembling hands lifting the wooden lid slowly. A long, golden braid of hair sat coiled inside.

It was enough to shatter his fragile heart into a million pieces. Gareth picked up the braid and kissed it, then pressed it tightly against his cheek. He could smell Madelyn's intoxicating scent, as if she was still there inside the tent.

"No… not your beautiful hair…"

Despite all of the torture and self loathing, Madelyn had refused to cut her beloved tresses. It was a core part of her identity, a reminder of the person she once was and would never be again. To see it now, lopped from her head, was truly a sign that she had no intention of returning.

A fearsome thirst reared its ugly head for the first time in ages. Gareth felt his mouth craving the taste of bourbon, or wine, or whatever drink he could find first. He set Madelyn's braid lovingly back in the chest and closed it, then stumbled backward with a groan. Desperately, he scoured the tent for a bottle or flagon, anything to dampen his pain.

But just as Gareth was about to succumb to despair, a whisper filled his ear. The sound was faint, so quiet in fact that he could barely make it out.

"My… son…"

Suddenly, a swift breeze swept throughout the tent, frigid as a Dellhaven winter. At first, he could scarcely believe what it was he heard. Had Charlotte seen him at such a vulnerable moment, wherever she might be? Had she reached from beyond the grave to offer one final consolation? Even if the opposite were true, Gareth found solace in the phantom voice, regardless of its origin.

"Mother… I'm so lost without you. I need you now, more than ever. I wish you were here so badly…"

Again the breeze blew, softer yet colder than before. Every hair on his arms and neck stood firm, the wind disturbing nothing inside the tent. Sorrow was replaced by fear, but soon enough, fear was replaced by clarity.

You have to be stronger than this, Gareth. This isn't the man she married. You cannot fall into despondency as you did when she first rejected you, or when mother died. You have to fight… fight as hard as you did in battle. Fight for her. Find her, no matter what the cost. Be the man that mother and Madelyn loved. You have no other choice now.

Instead of turning to the bottle and drowning within it, Gareth stood defiant, wiping both eyes dry with the back of his hand. He had suffered far too many tragedies and weathered too many storms to fall back into destructive old habits.

After a few deep breaths, he marched outside, Madelyn's note and chest cradled in his hands. He searched feverishly around the command tent, trying to mask his desperation. The men were still looking to him for leadership, after all. Sir Edmund had to be somewhere nearby, as he made a point to never stray too far.

"Has anyone seen Sir Edmund?" he asked, a slight tremble to his voice.

A few shrugs and shakes of the head was all he received. The elder Guardsman had to be somewhere, and the next best place to look would be Lord Kenfield's tent, sitting nearby. As he approached, a sound of familiar laughter caught his attention. Gareth sighed, struggling to contain the storm of emotions from within. He entered the tent, sullen as the day Charlotte Bethard died. A trio of Guardsmen stood around a table, and immediately snapped to attention. Anders and Edmund turned to greet him, but quickly noticed something was amiss.

"What's wrong?" Edmund's smile suddenly died.

"Out." Gareth motioned toward the tent flap, the Guardsmen exiting with haste. "Edmund… you're never going to believe this. But… Madelyn is gone."

Delicately, he handed over the note, and set the chest down on a table. Edmund's mouth twisted into a frown as he scanned the letter, his head shaking.

"I can't believe this is happening. I'm so sorry, Gareth. One tragedy after another, it seems. I pray you don't blame yourself. Madelyn's decision is not a reflection of you, or anything you did. In fact, you did everything right, and you gave her love when she needed it most."

"It still doesn't take the pain away," he said softly. "And now she's out there, all alone, hunting down Damien Dreadfire. The northmen are not beaten just yet, they could still change the tide of this war at any moment. We have to get her back, Edmund."

Lord Kenfield had been staring at the floor the entire time, uncertain of what to say. He cleared his throat, hesitant to interrupt. "Do pardon my saying so, my prince. I hope you aren't intending to go after her yourself. It's too dangerous, we cannot afford to lose you. Not after all we achieved here."

"Anders is right." Edmund nodded. "I can send my best men after her. But with the barbarians still out there, and Lord Vakaro skulking about, we simply can't take the risk of searching for her ourselves."

It was an endlessly frustrating situation, but ultimately, both men were right. Gareth had become something more now, not merely a member of House Bethard. He was the standard bearer for all Betanthia. His capture or death would send shockwaves throughout the Kingdom, and doubtlessly hasten its demise.

"As much as I hate to admit it, you're both right." Gareth sighed. "Especially after what happened on the battlefield."

Sir Edmund's eyes widened. "I don't know if I get your meaning. What happened on the battlefield?"

"After we broke their cavalry, we charged in and hit their lines, remember? Well, you might not have seen after I was unhorsed, but a Guardsman attempted to kill me. Had I been a second slower, he would have plunged a blade into my guts."

Deathly silence filled the tent, Edmund and Anders staring at each other incredulously. At first, neither seemed to believe him, the accusation beyond fantastical. Even now, Gareth was hesitant to believe it. How could one of Betanthia's most loyal protectors turn on his prince? Such a scenario was nearly unthinkable.

"Are you certain it was a Guardsman?" Edmund asked, disturbed by the allegation.

"I swear to it with my life. When I attempted to discover the man's identity, I noticed he was without a tongue. So, whoever sent him to kill me, knew exactly what they were getting themselves into."

A thick vein began protruding from Sir Edmund's forehead, his face shifting into a faint hue of red. There was fire in the old man's eyes, that much was certain.

"Well then, this complicates matters even further," Edmund Thomas said, running a hand through his silvery hair. "Lord Vakaro is most certainly behind this. He's the only man capable enough of corrupting a Guardsman, or slipping a man into our ranks. We have to make our move, and soon, or else he'll strike again."

"Agreed," Anders chimed in. "The more we delay, the more likely he'll be to succeed. And if he does, all of Betanthia will be in peril."

It was perhaps the most difficult decision of his life. On the one hand, Madelyn was alone and riding towards danger, and on the other, his life hung delicately in the balance. There were precious few resources at hand to tackle both dilemmas, as it was now apparent their circle of trust had grown many times smaller.

"Then I suggest we put our own plans into motion." Gareth said in grim defiance. "Edmund, I don't want you to think this is your failure. Our enemies are of the most cunning variety. I trust you to find Madelyn and bring her back to me. As much as my heart screams out for me to go after her, I know I have to stay here."

"And that, my lad, is why you will make an excellent king," Sir Edmund said, smiling proudly. "Worry not, I'll send my finest trackers after her. She couldn't have gone far, probably a half day or so ahead. We'll find her. I swear it."

It was easy enough to make such a pledge, but following through was another matter entirely. Madelyn was as fierce as a lioness, and not even death itself could impede her path. Even if the hope was faux, Gareth had to trust in it. There was no other option. How could he rightly win the war and guard against assassination with a mind so preoccupied?

"I've lived my entire life without hope, and without faith," he reflected. "But I have faith in you now, Edmund. I remember what you drilled into my head, and I'm not going to panic anymore. I believe."

Gareth took up the chest and stepped outside, desperate for fresh air. For a prince and future king of Betanthia, he felt as powerless as a newborn child. This was not the future he intended, nor one he asked for. All he ever wanted was to be happy and loved, and live a quiet, modest life. But now, it seemed that such a future was permanently beyond reach.

"Dare I ask what's inside that box?" Edmund asked, placing a hand on his shoulder.

As if laying flowers on a funeral altar, Gareth opened the chest slowly. He reached inside and took hold of Madelyn's braid, then dropped the container where he stood. Edmund sighed, himself overcome with emotion. The elder Guardsman remembered the days of her youth fondly, when the world was whole and life made sense.

But there was another who stood dumbstruck, staring at the braid of golden hair in disbelief. Titan Bradshaw looked as if his blood had turned to ice, his eyes wide and reflecting a desperate fear.

"What the fuck is that?" Tylar asked, hoping it was a cruel jape.

There was little Gareth could say. He had not the heart to explain why Madelyn had taken flight, and left behind not only her husband, but her most defining adornment. Even looking at the man was too insurmountable.

"What the fuck has she done?" Tylar stormed over to Sir Edmund, clutching him by the shoulders. "Where the fuck is she?"

"She's gone her own way now," Edmund replied sorrowfully. He stared at the ground, trying to mask his misty eyes.

Tylar looked about frantically, hoping to make sense of a senseless situation. "You better answer me, old man, or I'll—"

"She left me a letter," Gareth explained. "Madelyn… feels the only thing left in her life is vengeance. She's become something else now, something neither her nor I recognize."

"And you're just going to stand there and do nothing?" Tylar asked, incredulous.

"My best trackers are going after her," Sir Edmund interjected. "Wherever she may be, we'll find her."

Such words seemed comforting, but Gareth knew better. Madelyn was strong and determined, capable of overcoming death itself. If she set her mind to a task, nothing would be able to stand in her path, not even the gods themselves, if they were real. But still, something had to be done. Betanthia's future queen had to be found, and brought home intact.

"Your best trackers?" Tylar scoffed. "Fuck that, I'm going out there. And neither of you can stop me."

Stopping Titan Bradshaw was the last thing Gareth wanted to do. Instead, he grabbed the behemoth by his purple cloak, pulling him in close.

"Good," he said sternly. "Now bring my wife back to me. And take Conrak with you. We both know he's going out there once he finds out."

Both men stared at each other, an understanding coming between them. Tylar's face was grim, as if he was expecting to never return. But it was a task he accepted willingly. He set off briskly to fetch horse and provision for the daunting quest ahead.

"Are you certain it's wise to send him out there, given the circumstances?" Edmund leaned in, whispering.

He had a point. Treachery lurked throughout the Betanthian camp, an assassin's blade nearly finding its mark already. It would have been wise to keep a man such as Titan Bradshaw nearby, most certainly. But Gareth was surrounded by the Guardsmen, and Madelyn was alone on the Plainhold. It was a decision that required little thought.

"We're at war, Edmund," Gareth said somberly. "Are any of us truly safe? I can't leave her out there, not with Dreadfire still alive. "

"And now three of our finest are out there, hunting these dogs down. I almost feel pity for Damien Dreadfire. Almost." Edmund Thomas shook his head. "There's nothing more savage and unrelenting than a scorned woman."

True enough, he thought. If there was anyone aside from Titan Bradshaw who could strike fear into the hearts of Damien Dreadfire and his marauders, it was Madelyn. She had started down a dark path since her days in captivity. And now, she would return to the northmen with a terrifying purpose.

"She's not just any woman, she's my lady. My queen." Gareth Bethard stared off into the distance, a faint mist of tears in his eyes. "My queen of scorn."

EPILOGUE

SILENTLY HE STALKED, ARROW NOCKED AND AT THE READY. UDORN studied the buck as it grazed lazily just ahead, unaware it was being watched. A bead of sweat trickled down the shaved sides of his head, but still his gaze remained unbroken. Twelve points he counted, a magnificent beast indeed, and a fine meal no doubt.

Udorn drew back his bow swiftly and silently, releasing the arrow without hesitation. He saw it sail through the air briefly before impacting flesh, the buck jumping and thrashing desperately. It broke into a wild sprint, charging through the tall grass until it fell away from sight.

"You did it, father!" Lidin said, pumping his balled fists into the air. He was the eldest of three, and a month away from his tenth year.

"Silence your tongue," Udorn scolded. "We have spilled blood on this good earth. We must give thanks to the gods for what they have given us."

Together, father and son set off in pursuit of the deer. He spied pointy antlers jutting up from the grass ahead and drew a menacing piece of steel, its blade long and sharp as razors. The Ubneri were a hard people, forged by hard weather in a hard land. Taking life was as simple as breathing, but a somber affair nevertheless.

"He is still alive!" Lidin whispered, cautious not to incite his father's wrath.

Fortunately, the animal would not suffer long. The buck laid its mighty head down, then took its final breath before departing for the next world. Udorn sheathed his blade, content with his kill. Hauling the carcass back to Mot would be simple for a man of his size and strength.

"Come," Udorn said, ripping loose the arrow and hefting the deer. "We must be returning now. The day grows short."

A low rumble carried across the field, emanating from the southern treeline. Udorn nocked an arrow with lightning speed, dropping down onto one knee in a flash. Lidin mirrored his fathers movement and laid flat on the ground, as silent as a shadow. From out of the woods came a horse and wagon, an elderly man and his wife sitting atop it.

An unusual sight, to be certain. Traders were rare at Mot, and for good reason. The fishing village turned stronghold had become a hub for raiders and all manner of scoundrels. Many throughout the deep north knew well enough about the Ubneri and their penchant for violence.

Something stirred on the back of the wagon, drawing his attention. There was another traveler, too large for a child, yet certainly no warrior. Curious, nevertheless. As horse and wagon lurched, closer, Udorn sprung to his feet, drawing his bow back ever so slightly.

"Far enough," he barked, eyes wide and mouth drawn tight.

The old couple nearly sprung from their skin. In panicked desperation, the old man brought his horse to a halt before throwing both hands into the air.

"We mean you no harm, kinsman," he pleaded. "My name is Egar. My wife and I are simple farmers. Please, I beg of you—"

"State your business, or tonight you will be feeding the crows," Udorn demanded.

"I would have word with your chieftain." Egar glanced over his shoulder. "I bring dire news from the south."

In all of his forty years, Udorn had never heard of anything good coming from the south. Those were Betanthian lands, after all, a people they had rarely encountered over the centuries. And for good reason. The Siln River was wide and unpredictable, its mere presence enough to deter even the boldest of invaders. He began to suspect the fear in the old man's eyes was not of his bow, but of things lurking over the horizon.

"Come. I will take you."

Udorn returned his arrow to its quiver, then slung the bow across his back. Father and son hefted the slain buck and laid it onto the wagon's bed. He eyed the strange passenger suspiciously, a mangled woman who appeared to have one foot in the grave. Her other was held firm by a wooden brace wrapped in leather.

It was a disgusting sight, seeing her scarred flesh and awkwardly healed bones. Her face looked as if it was hammered into pulp, and molded back together again. Whether such injuries were from wild beasts or beastly men was a mystery, though Udorn had his suspicions. Seldom would outsiders venture onto Ubneri lands. Those brave enough, or foolish enough to cross their borders did so only with the most necessary purpose.

Slowly, he led the wagon back toward Mot. Silence was their companion, but it was for the better. Any provocation in the slightest, and Udorn would loose a quiver full of arrows faster than a lightning strike. He kept one nocked, fingers running along its feather fletchings. Lidin stayed fixed at his side, ready to flee at the first sign of treachery.

Thankfully, none came. They passed through a shallow creek, its waters nearly evaporated. It was a telltale sign the village was nearby. A withered corpse swung by its neck from a thick oak branch, a scrawled warning over its head nearly faded away. To the uninvited, it was a menacing sign, but to Udorn, it was a warm welcome home.

A faint whimpering came from the wagon bed, a noise he had heard many times before. It was a sound of pure fear, coming from the mangled woman.

"Silence yourself," Udorn said, wheeling about. "Show no weakness in the lands, or the wolves will devour you whole."

Animals were the last thing to be concerned about. Ubneri were as violent as the day was long, and to display anything but strength was to invite an axe to the head. Thankfully, the woman took heed well enough, and silenced her pitiful mewlings.

At last, they arrived outside of Mot, its wooden palisades decorated with weathered skulls and shields of their vanquished rivals. Large doors as thick as tree trunks stood open, though within an hour they would be closed. A pair of archers stood vigil, each perched high in towers on either side of the entrance.

Mot was a lively place this evening, as it typically was. The raiding parties had arrived that afternoon, bringing with them plunder and glory, and tales of fantastical lands. Udorn often resented his life and having to tend to a family while lesser men earned their place in the histories. Still, there was pride to be found in raising a new generation of warriors.

Nearby sat his hovel, a modest accommodation, but more comfortable than most. Udorn had earned his share of glory in years past, raiding more settlements than there were trees in a forest. Inside was his wife, Guri, and their two other children. But there would be no time to see them just yet, not until his business with the chieftain was concluded.

"Tell your mother of our hunt," he said, gesturing toward the door.

Lidin ran inside dutifully, while Udorn removed his kill from the wagon and set it on the ground.

"You may stay and feast this night," Udorn grumbled to his guests. "Come, but remain close. Mot is no place for old men and stray women."

Their arrival had not gone unnoticed. Scores of villagers eyed the wagon curiously as it rumbled down the dirt streets, some whispering to one another and others doubtlessly scheming. Udorn stiffened his back, casting a sharp glare at any man who dared to step forward and offer a challenge.

At the heart of Mot stood the chieftain's hold. It was a massive structure built of stone and wood, covered in a thatched roof. Legend said it was once a ship, the mightiest ship the Ubneri had ever built. During a vicious storm at sea, its hapless crew cried out to the gods for salvation. Their prayers were answered, and Zifnir lifted the ship out of the turbulent waters and carried it to shore, where it would remain for a thousand years or more.

Such tales were for drunkards and little children, Udorn thought. There were certainly plenty of drunkards skulking about the hold, its doors open wide and song and smoke billowing from within. Even on days without a successful raid, there was plenty of revelry to be found. But Ubneri gatherings were anything but brotherly affairs.

Splashes of blood painted the wall beside the door, a small puddle forming on the ground. Likely the work of an axe, and likely the result of a petty squabble. Though, few needed a reason to spill blood in Mot in the first place, as it was as common as rainfall.

"Stay close to me, and speak only when spoken to," Udorn said, pointing a finger. "Look no man in the eye, unless you are prepared to die. Do you understand?"

The old man and woman nodded frantically, their passenger nearly paralyzed with fear. A torrent of shouts and curses spilled from inside the hold, followed by a peal of laughter. After assisting the crippled woman out of the wagon, Udorn led them slowly inside.

He stepped over the corpse of a raider, his face cleaved in two, blood pouring like a river across the stone floor. Hardly an unusual sight, especially after a successful adventure abroad. Spilled across two mighty tables were piles of gold and trinkets, and gemstones of every variety. All of it was Ragruk's tribute, and not a man dared to pocket a single coin. Udorn saw the lumbering chieftain sitting on his massive throne, etched from a boulder of solid granite, and strung with the bones of lesser warlords.

It was easy to see why such a man occupied the throne. Ragruk was a head and a half taller than any man in Mot, with arms strong enough to pulverize stone. His hair and beard were fiery orange, thick and long, and accented with braids. Perhaps the most legendary thing was his temper. Ragruk was not one to be trifled with, and could take a man's head for even the most trivial of slights.

Near the mead casks stood Thaul and Gaxas, shield brothers like none other. Clinging to their arms were pairs of beautiful wenches, natives of the village no doubt. Thaul was spinning yarns about a raid five years ago, the same story he told on a near nightly basis. Udorn had been on many adventures with them both, and found his boasts often rooted in exaggeration.

Across from them was Dulkin One-Eye, a marauder as ugly as sin, and Zeruk, a gangly man with a mouth full of black teeth. They were staring down Udorn's guests suspiciously, nefarious intentions undoubtedly lurking in their minds.

"Avert your eyes," he warned the old man, who was glancing about frantically. "You will not receive another warning."

Not that he would be the one to harm them, certainly not. They were guests under his protection, but Udorn would only defend a stranger's honor so much. A pair of old fools and a crippled woman were hardly worth dying for, not with a wife and a house full of children.

They approached the throne, Udorn dropping to one knee and bowing his head. Ragruk swallowed a large chalice of mead, half of it soaking his long, bushy beard. A mighty belch erupted from the chieftain's gut before he tossed the empty vessel aside.

"Udorn!" Ragruk roared, arms spread wide. "What brings you to my hall this night? Should you not be tending to your household?"

A few muffled chuckles filled the hold, but most paid little attention. Udorn stood, straightening out his tunic. "A good evening to you, chieftain. I have brought with me travelers who come bearing a message for your ears. I have promised them our hospitality."

"Ha!" the chieftain bellowed. "And what message do these old fools bring, eh? What business do outsiders have in Mot?"

Timidly, the elderly man stepped forward, hands wringing. "A thousand apologies for the disturbance, your greatness. My name is Egar, I live on a homestead near the Siln."

Some of the raiders laughed at his uneasiness. Udorn strode to the far side of the hall where giant wooden casks sat, bursting with oceans of mead. He took up a large ox horn and filled it to overflowing.

"Come now," Ragruk grunted, "speak, and be quick about it."

"I beg your mercy, greatness." Egar trembled. "One day when I was out planting the fields, I saw something washed up on the edge of the river bank. It appeared like an animal carcass at first, but I saw it moving. It was a woman, still alive, but barely."

"Many things come down the river," the chieftain said in growing agitation. "And you come to my hall with such a trivial matter?"

Udorn sipped at his mead, slowly moving through the crowd. Ragruk's intensity had drawn curious stares, the music inside the hall dying down to silence.

"N…no, greatness," Egar pleaded, "We took her into our home and brought her back to health. She comes from Pelg, a village along the river. She said men from the south came, bringing steel and fire. They put Pelg to the torch, leaving none alive."

Ragruk leaned forward, placing an elbow on his thigh. He gestured to the broken woman "Come forward."

Delicately, she hobbled forward, assisted by a walking stick. Udorn found himself captivated, too curious to notice just how silent the hold had become. Step by painful step, she made her way toward the throne, stopping at the base of its steep platform.

"Tell me," the chieftain commanded, "who were these men you speak of? What lands do they hail from?"

With water in her eyes, the woman's fractured face twisted, struggling to even utter a word. Udorn was unaware of how deeply his brow had furrowed, his drinking horn cracking from a tightening grip.

"B…Betanthia…" she uttered.

At first, Ragruk seemed confused. He had heard the name once before, but paid it little mind. He sat back, scratching at his beard, deep in thought.

"Udorn!" Ragruk bellowed. "You have raided many lands. Tell me what you know of these people, these… these…"

"Betanthians," he replied, snarling. "Cold men, iron men, men who worship only gold. They are deceivers, destroyers, cruel beasts without honor. Their shadow is long, their hunger endless. And now they bring death to our borders."

"Men who worship gold, you say?" a raider called out, earning an ovation of chuckles and cheers.

It would take little convincing for the Ubneri to set sail once again, to lands yet unspoiled. Even with coffers bursting with gold, their hunger was not sated. Udorn surmised he was the only man who knew Betanthia's might, and what their encroachment would mean for Mot. He had a wife and children to protect, treasures more valuable than gold.

"These are not petty villagers," Udorn cautioned. "None who live have felt their wrath as I have. Fifty oars we were, setting sail to warm waters. Only four of us survived. Two died on the journey back, the other succumbed here at home. Should we do this, we risk Mot and all we hold dear."

His warning did not have the intended consequence. Gold and glory, it was all the Ubneri lived for. The prospect of death seemed enticing, in a way, for many of the untested raiders. They sought adventure, and a name forever etched in the histories.

"Men of gold are fat and soft," another shouted. "Better they should fill our coffers instead!"

"Aye!" a thunderous approval rang out.

Despite his reservations, Udorn could sense the tides of war rolling in yet again. Far be it for an Ubneri to diminish in the face of challenge, he thought. While there would be riches and glory in plenty, so too would be the cost in lives. But it was their way. The Ubneri way.

"What say you, Udorn?" Ragruk rose, the timbers beneath him creaking. "Do the winds of war blow? Do our ships sail to new lands and new glory?"

Udorn nodded, his mouth drawn into a deep scowl. "Aye, let the dogs of Betanthia be drowned by the might of the sea. Let their hovels burn and women shriek."

Ragruk raised his arms high, the raiders whipping themselves into a frenzy. "To war it shall be!"

A WORD FROM THE AUTHOR

THANK YOU SO MUCH FOR TAKING THE TIME TO READ "THE Wrathbringer"! I hope you had as much fun reading it as I did writing it. If you enjoyed the book, please leave a great review (or rating, at least) on Amazon or Barnes & Noble, as well as Goodreads. It only takes a few minutes, and it's the best way for you to support my work and get the word out. Doing so will help ensure that I will be able to continue publishing long into the future.

From the bottom of my heart, thank you for all of your fantastic support!

— *Chris*

v